Books by ROBERT ABEL

SKIN AND BONES
FREEDOM DUES, OR A GENTLEMAN'S PROGRESS
   IN THE NEW WORLD
THE PROGRESS OF A FIRE

THE PROGRESS OF A FIRE

A Novel by

ROBERT ABEL

SIMON AND SCHUSTER   New York

Copyright © 1985 by Robert Abel

All rights reserved
including the right of reproduction
in whole or in part in any form
Published by Simon and Schuster
A Division of Simon & Schuster, Inc.
Simon & Schuster Building
Rockefeller Center
1230 Avenue of the Americas
New York, New York 10020
SIMON AND SCHUSTER and colophon are registered trademarks
of Simon & Schuster, Inc.

Designed by Irving Perkins Associates

Manufactured in the United States of America

1   3   5   7   9   10   8   6   4   2

Library of Congress Cataloging in Publication Data
Abel, Robert H., date.
The progress of a fire.
I. Title.
PS3551.B337P7   1985   813'.54   85-14243

ISBN: 0-671-50931-4

To Hui-ming and Anna Wang;
to those who fought the war;
and to those who fought to bring them home.

CONTENTS

PART I

THE ANIMAL KINGDOM

1

Black
Tortoise
(Chong's First Winter)

S lush pelts the windows. Chong watches it from the porch of his home, shivering. He considers it an early rain, too early, and guesses it will swell the streams, buckle the shells of ice, and send white chunks down to bang the bridge posts. The stream is groaning with unusual ruckus, sonorous and metallic, and Chong dons an extra sweater, then a big plastic bag that he has cut head and arm holes in with scissors. He slaps on a canvas hat and gloves and sloshes down to the stream.

The ruckus crescendos as Chong comes through the snow to the stream's edge. He sees at once the pressure, the immense weight of the ice, which has created a ragged pyramid of blue and white prisms, as if great wedges of glass had been heaped up; and above these, the ice still crawling downstream has been tipped and shattered so that the creek seems to be filled with impatient white sharks, their fins crowding one on another. And they groan and snap as the water boils on underneath them.

Chong walks along this zone of shards and chunks and under the canopy of trees dripping from every branch. The earth, the snow, and stream exude a cold, harsh fog that thickens with distance and erases the woods. When he comes to the bridge across the Lake Ecstasy Road, he can see the ice is under such pressure it sings like rusty wheels on rails, and is heaped up nearly to the road. On the bridge itself in the fog is a strange shadow play of forms, bundled men swinging their arms. Their shouts are half smothered by the mumbling of the stream and the chatter of the ice. Senselessly, it seems, they cross and recross the bridge, first holding their hands high, then dipping below the railing, or leaning over it. In a moment they back away from the bridge with gestures that resemble feeding grain to chickens. Perhaps, Chong thinks, they are measuring something.

He hears a small engine pop to life and, a few seconds later, the harsh blare of a horn, a signal which lasts unusually long.

Then Chong understands.

"Wait! Wait!" he cries, and begins churning through the snow away from the stream and toward the road. He goes down, hands stinging in the slush, recovers himself, and scrambles on. "Wait!"

The horn blares again as Chong pulls himself up the embankment to the road. The cold air rakes his lungs. Clumsily, he lifts himself over the guardrail, and as he does the lights of a large blue blurred pickup go on and off and he hears someone shout, "Hey! Hey, get the hell out of there. Get over here, damn it!"

"You don't have to tell me twice." Chong hurries to the truck.

"Anybody else down there?" A man emerges from the fog, a yellow smear, his face like something seen through waxed paper.

"Just me."

The man swears. "What in hell were you doing?"

"Watching," Chong says.

"You almost watched yourself get an ice bomb in the face, mister." He laughs. "You coulda got hurt down there."

The horn blares again with a force that makes Chong's ears ache.

"OK., Billy, hit it," the man in the slicker says.

Chong sees the cables stretched across the road onto the bridge, and he follows these curving black lines into the fog. He hears an electric crackle and immediately a great percussive *thomp!* fills the air and echoes from the surrounding hills. A ball of steam, intensely white even in the fog, rolls out from under the bridge.

"Try it again, Billy. Make sure you got it all."

"Nothing," Billy says from inside the truck.

"We'll see what we got, then. Let these cars come on through."

The man in the yellow slicker and the man in the dark coat walk out onto the bridge now, kicking the cables out of their way, and search the stream below. They carry on a hushed conference as a few cars hiss past them, and then amble back to the truck.

The man in the slicker puts his head through the pickup window to light a cigarette out of the rain and says, "That didn't do shit, Billy. We got to go again."

"I told you it wasn't enough," Billy says. His grin flashes in the relative darkness of the cab.

"As much ice as there is down there, maybe we don't have enough charge in this whole county."

"I tell you, I can get it broke up," Billy says.

"Yeah, but we want to have a bridge left when you get done, too."

"You want that ice out of there, or don't you?"

"The idea is to *save* the bridge, Billy. Remember?"

"Oh, yeah."

"Go ahead. Give it another shot."

"How about twice as much charge?"

"You're the expert, Billy. But no more. We'll probably have to come back tonight, the way it looks. This stuff is expensive."

Billy climbs out of the cab now, a small man with a face as weather-beaten as a fisherman's, ringed with a graying close-cropped beard. He is dressed in soiled denims, including a blue coat with a collar of fluffy wool on which the rain beads in glistening dots. His baseball cap is pulled to his thick eyebrows, and though he is grinning strangely, he gives Chong a prolonged, almost insulting stare out of the eyes that seem full of grief, and anger.

"You got the key?" Billy says to the man in the slicker.

"No. I gave it to you."

"Nope. You never did. You took it back, like always."

The man in the slicker searches his pockets. "God damn it, we can't have lost the key. Look again there, Billy. You must have it."

"Nope."

"God damn it, Billy, if I have to turn out your pockets, I will."

"You try, and you'll be down there on the ice."

"Will I, now?"

"Nobody's layin' a hand on me. Searchin' me. Like some goddamn crook."

"Well, find that goddamn key, then. It's raining, I want to get this goddamn miserable job over with."

"You're the one who thinks we ought to lock up the charges all the damn time."

"Damn right. It's policy, and a good policy at that. Experience is a good teacher."

Billy turns away now and walks to the rear of the truck. "In the door," he calls. "Left the key in the door."

"Like hell I did," the foreman mumbles.

"What's the sense of lockin' the charges if you leave the key in the lock?" Billy laughs.

"Like hell I did."

Chong endures this bickering and the rain because he wants to see the charges placed in the ice jam, hear the roar of the bomb again. He wants to see the pressure in the stream relaxed, the ice bang down the valley to Lake Ecstasy. Besides, the shadowy, fogged-in dance of the bundled men has a curious calm about it, like something carelessly staged. He watches Billy wrap the black tubes in a band of silver tape and delicately insert what appears to be transistors in the end of each tubular charge, then twist the exposed wires into a single strand. This package he carries out onto the bridge and, in the company of the other man, attaches it to the cables, lowers it hand over hand into the stream.

The traffic is stopped. The horn sounds its irritating warnings. Again the blast, this time an ear-shattering one that also sends a wide canopy of white shrapnel into the sky.

"How the hell much charge was that?" the foreman demands.

"Take a look," Billy says. "Enough to do the job. You can hear it flowing already."

"I'll say enough."

"You still got your bridge, don't you? See any bridges goin' downstream?"

The foreman shakes his head and walks out onto the bridge. He leans over the railing and spits into the sparkling, slithering stream.

Chong, no longer curious, departs for home and a roaring fire. All day he hovers by the wood stove, unable to get dry; and all day he drinks hot tea with ginger and lemon, unable to get warm.

In the evening Chong hears a distant thunder from the lake road and knows the bickering crew is back at work, still trying to save the Reverend James P. Dickey Memorial Bridge.

Chong wakes to a blaze of sushine and hurtles out of bed. It has turned cold again, he can tell from his floors, and from the stinging water when he cleans his teeth. He hurries again to the stream.

The trees seem encased in glass, and when the wind stirs them, they shimmer, and a rainbow of diamonds cascades down. The sun strikes the uprooted shards of ice, a spectrum of colors is cast along the banks. Chong walks through band after band of glorious light, hoping they will stain him indelibly. If there is a path to heaven, he thinks, it shall be illuminated thus.

2
Azure
Dragon
(Spring) [i]

Sunshine smashes into the cold molecules of the earth's upper atmosphere. Chong knows this excites the existence of the subatomic particles and scatters photons, creates phenomena that have the briefest possible life. Wu has told him so. But when his gaze returns to earth, Chong finds a curiosity of a grosser kind: six pigs are gorging on a mound of flowers that have been heaped on a fresh grave.

Chong puts the bottle of wine and the small bag containing birdseed, sausage, maple syrup, duct tape, and a lottery ticket onto the front seat of his station wagon, then slops through the slush at the edge of the road to take in the phenomenon more carefully.

The pigs seem to be enjoying their work, ravaging the flowers, and tossing up clods of freshly spaded earth with their bristly snouts. The six pigs make a noise like children at recess.

What is to be done? Chong looks back across the street to the general store/coffee shop he has just left, sees there a fairly large stake truck with its tailgate askew, and knows where the pigs have come from. He remembers a man at the counter inside in a denim jacket and a green and yellow hat embossed with a flying ear of corn—DEKALB—and supposes he had better tell him what has happened. No doubt the man will find it disagreeable. Meanwhile, the pigs are very happy and excited and Chong thinks they would make a wonderful composition—PIGS AT A GRAVE—and swears, God damn it, he never has his camera when he needs it.

Inside the store, the man, who is eating scrambled eggs, does not at first realize Chong is speaking to him. He has the gray-blue eyes of a wolf, and even when he focuses on Chong and begins, simultaneously chewing the farm-fresh scrambled eggs as slowly and ruminatively as a cow chews a cud, to understand what Chong is trying to tell him, the eyes do not seem to be centered, or connected.

"In the *cemetery?*"

"That's right," Chong says.

The man throws down his fork and jumps up. "I'll be a royal son of a bitch!" As he rushes out, he says something even more violent under his breath.

Chong knows that he is not expected to help, both because he is no youngster and because Americans never seem to expect anything of him at all, as if his Oriental heritage—never mind he has been in the United States since he was sixteen, some forty years—set him outside the normal course of events. In many situations he has discovered himself not so much a person as an artifact. What the hell, he chuckles, and leaves the store, hitching up his pants and watching the burly pig farmer knock soft snow into a little temporary rainbow as he skids over the low stone wall that is the cemetery fence.

The farmer whips off his hat—his baldness surprises Chong—and begins waving it at the pigs. They smugly intensify their gobbling, simultaneously creeping around the pile of flowers away from the man charging upon them. Chong hoists the tipsy half of the truck's tailgate back into place, unties a rope between the two portions, then lifts half of the tailgate down so the pigs can be thrown in. How did they get out? Chong wonders. Pigs do not jump down from these heights any more than cows or rats do.

Very strange!

Chong grabs a length of rope from the side of the truck and crosses the highway into the cemetery. The sky is so blue today! Giotto, Chong thinks. Surely the sun is balanced today on the meridian between winter and spring. The soft snow is everywhere slashed with the crisp shadows of the trees.

Now the farmer seems to be dancing with a pig around the pyre of flowers. He has one rear hoof in his meaty hand and is trying to grab the other hind foot when Chong comes puffing up with the rope.

"You gotta tell me what to do," Chong says.

The pig kicks fiercely; every bit of flab on the farmer's face and body is trembling.

"Grab a leg," the farmer says. "Turn him over."

"O.K."

The pig is braced on his front legs shaking his hips, his whole frame, down to the small points of those cloven front hooves. Chong takes a hoof in each hand and tugs them forward, the pig flops and rolls, bucking, the farmer curses, grabs for the thrashing hind leg of the pig.

"Careful!" the farmer shouts.

Like westling with a demon. Chong's arms are driven like pistons in a lunatic engine. Brueghel, he thinks. Bosch.

"Don't hurt him," the farmer says. "And don't let him bite you. They got a wicked bite." Unaccountably, as far as Chong is concerned, the man laughs like an idiot.

The pig rocks on its spine. He woofs. His teeth snick and snack. Yes, he could eat babies. Chong has heard of such things.

"Can you hand me that rope now?"

"If I let go," Chong says.

"Let go. I've got him."

In a moment, the pig squeals and flops as if it has been shot through the hip; a quick snug knot binds one hind foot to the front foot opposite; the other end of the rope is trussed to a gravestone.

Two of the pigs are still at work on the flowers over the grave, but two more trot away through the cemetery in search of other, at least more unharried, fare. They move gracefully, seem to float over the cloudlike clumps of snow that are zebra-striped with the shadows of the bare trees. How bright the sun! How crisp the wind!

"You head that way, will you? Sort of scare 'em in my direction. When I snatch one, c'mon and give me a hand, hey?"

Chong stealthily circles the mound of fresh flowers and dirt, arms outstretched. He wrinkles his nose and puts on a warrior's scowl, growls.

The pigs do not seem to notice him.

"Hah!"

Chong falls on a pig with a yellow mum hanging from its mouth, girdles its waist with his arms, locks his fingers. The pig slams him with its heavy ass, knocks him into the slush, but tumbles, too, and the farmer quickly has him by the back feet and turned over.

"Hand me that rope," he says. "I've got the bastard."

Chong scrambles to the gravestone and unravels the rope the captured pig has pulled taut. Again, the farmer makes fast work of the tying, and the second pig kicks and bellows.

The farmer is panting now. "We better take it easy," he says. "No sense killing ourselves." He grins his strange grin again. "Though this would be a right enough place for it, hey? Real handy for the undertaker."

Chong studies the word a moment. *Under-taker.* As if he might go along with you, show you the way. . . .

"Hell with this," the farmer continues. "I'm going to call my brother. There's no sense your hangin' around here any more, and I'm sure you didn't plan to spend the day chasin' pigs in a boneyard." He kicks the snow. "Goddamned smart bastards, ain't they?"

"I'm glad to help," Chong says.

"Let me buy you a cup of coffee or something, as long as I'm going over to the store. Piece of pie? You must be bushed. I'll call my brother."

"Cup of coffee sounds good," Chong says. "And a cigar."

"Cigar it is. Not a bad idea." The farmer extends his hand. "I'm Joe Turner, by the way."

"Chong."

"I figured. I see in the paper there you moved into the old Randall place. What? A month ago?"

"That's right."

"Not much goes on around here in the real estate line that doesn't get talked about, you know."

"Of course," Chong says. And even though he has been in Lake Ecstasy so short a time, he has done a little snooping himself, and the name of Turner is not new to him.

The old Lake Ecstasy family owns more land in the county than even the People's Service Utility Company, Chong has heard. They'll sell you anything—wood, pigs, old tractors, loam—but not an inch of ground. They'll do anything you can pay them to do— clean your cesspool, fix your roof, butcher your beef—but "they wouldn't rent an acre to a starving man," according to the bartender at the Lake Ecstasy Village Inn. One of the Turners is a selectman, another owns the local hardware store. How could he not know the Turner name by now?

In the diner, Joe Turner instructs the robust woman behind the counter to "fix up Mr. Chong with a cup of coffee and whatever kind of cigar he wants. He's been a help."

Mrs. O'Day, as she serves the coffee, declares the escape of the pigs has been a topic of interest in the diner all morning. "They just *had* to be let out," she says.

"Yeah?" Joe Turner cradles the phone under his chin.

"And you know who was out there just before, don't you?"

"Yeah," Turner says. "I know." He turns his attention to the telephone.

"Punks," Mrs. O'Day says to Chong. "Every one of them Archer kids."

Chong doesn't understand, but waits. He blows a puff of smoke toward the ceiling and watches it unfold against the fluorescent light, like a wave in a painting by Hiroshige, that clever Jap bastard.

"They don't respect nothin'," Mrs. O'Day rambles on. "That's their father buried over there just this morning, and you see how they act."

3
Azure
Dragon
(Spring) [ii]

On the first warm day of spring, Chong is restless, misses the city life tremendously. On a day like this in New York he would have cruised the fish and vegetable stalls in China-town, poked his nose into a gallery or two, checked in at Browne's to see if any of his paintings had sold. He drives to the "business sec-tion" of Lake Ecstasy, but besides O'Day's diner and general store, there is only Deenah's Pooch Parlor, a gas station, and an apple ware-house and sales office. On the hill above is a truck and tractor repair service, and just beyond that, on the opposite side of the road is the Lake Ecstasy Village Inn, where Chong stayed for a few days while the title to his home was searched and the details of the closing were worked out by lawyers in Royalton, the "big town" in the area, and twenty minutes away.

Chong drives into the parking lot of the Lake Ecstasy Village Inn and considers buying a breakfast, or only a coffee, and talking with Nancy Wallace, the waitress, if she is not too busy. The thought of Nancy warms Chong like toast. He still loves to look at her, and she is the only history he has in Lake Ecstasy. When he looks at the hills surrounding the village or sloping down to the pristine waters of Lake Ecstasy, he sometimes thinks of her, of her generous, sponta-neous decision when she learned he was a painter—thinking at first he meant a house painter—to model for him. He had just moved in, had nothing in the house, and she was taking off her clothes and climbing into the only piece of furniture he then had: a hammock. It was a fine welcome, and how he had painted then!

Nancy had helped him in other ways, introducing him to Rubb's New and Used in Royalton, where he was able to furnish his house well enough; she filled him with neighborhood gossip and introduced him to some of the breakfast regulars. She had insisted her modeling be kept secret, and Chong had no trouble honoring that request, because he knew almost no one else in town.

Chong enters the Inn (under the OPEN DEER SEASON FIVE A.M. sign) and sits at a table by the front window so he can see the sunlight in the trees in the hills. He thinks, I have to have windows, don't I? I have to frame everything. I am such a city boy, I have to see everything through a rectangle. I need to break this down, get out into the world, and see it round and whole.

In a moment, Nancy swings brusquely up to his table. She has styled her hair in a mass of brown curls now, which Chong finds artificial, but he is pleased to observe her and remember the animal ripeness of her body, which he had considered the perfect antidote to the anemic, bony look of women who had posed for him in New York City. Her eyes are the brown of polished walnut, deer eyes, and they take you in with an awful intensity sometimes, an attribute that made Chong think more than once while he was painting Nancy that he was posing for her. Her mouth is lively, her face animated. Chong studies her now to see if she will be friendlier this morning than she has been for a while.

But Nancy is curt and businesslike again today, and Chong finishes his coffee quickly, regards her a little wistfully as she hurries breakfast among the other tables, jokes with the customers. He leaves his money on the table, wondering what has cooled off Nancy's friendship so suddenly. Perhaps he was a novelty who no longer amused her. Too bad! he thinks. He looks out at the hills and laughs, because there it is, the very slope of her!

In the afternoon, as Chong sits on his back steps letting the sunshine warm his face, his meditations are interrupted by the sound of a truck pulling into his driveway, and the slam of a door. Reluctantly, Chong rises and comes around the side of the house to find a sky-blue truck with a squarish red light mounted on the cab, and the pig farmer knocking at his front door, shading his eyes and peering through the screen.

"Here I am."

The farmer comes quickly down the tipsy stairs. "Joe Turner, Mr. Chong. Remember me?"

"Sure." Chong squints, waiting.

"Well, I see you have a little farm here. You got some chickens and stuff."

"Right."

"And I wondered if you wanted a pig."

"A pig?" Chong strokes his chin. The beard stubble rasps on his fingers. "I couldn't afford one."

"I mean, I'd give it to you. Look here." Turner motions Chong to the rear of the truck and points in. "See, this one is perfectly healthy as far as I can make out, but his hind leg is deformed, a birth defect. I can't sell 'im and he's kind of small to butcher just yet. If you want to take him and fatten him up, he's all yours."

Chong laughs merrily. "Really? You mean you want to give me this pig?"

"That's about it."

"I don't know what to say."

"You want 'im, he's all yours. If not, I'll probably kill him."

"I never had a pig."

"They don't take much room. They'll eat anything, just about."

Chong thinks the little pig will make a good model and that he has—so Chong evaluates it—a shrewd look in his eye. There is already a broken-down sty behind the barn where he can run, until he grows old enough to step over the fence planks.

"Will you kill it for me?" Chong asks.

"*Now?*"

"No, no. Later, when it's big enough."

"I guess I could do that," Turner says amiably, "though we usually charge a little for the service. It's not the easiest thing if you're not used to it. Tell you something, too." He climbs onto the bumper and opens the tailgate. "Same as I tell my kids." Now he grabs the pig deftly under the front shoulders and holds it out for Chong.

Chong finds it surprisingly heavy, a furious package, squealing.

"Don't ever name it," Turner says. "That way you won't feel so bad when it's butchered."

Chong considers this a moment, then nods agreement.

By the time he has reached the sty and dropped the energetic, howling creature into the matted wet grass there, Chong has named the pig "Luan," Chinese for "confusion," "disorder," the anarchic state of a people when the government is collapsing, a ruler is weak, an army has invaded, or a revolution has burst into being. The little pig hobbles around the perimeter of the sty, kicking and complaining, and already Chong feels sorry for him, for his strange withered foot and his stupid future.

4
Casco
Bay

The dark cloud rises slowly toward the boat, and as it grows larger, closer, the turmoil at its edges and in its heart is visible. Finally it erupts on the surface with a great hiss, like a sigh, because otherwise the water in Casco Bay is as blue as the sky and seemingly as untroubled. Everywhere the sardines, like fragments of glass, shiver into the air.

Two pencil poppers arc out on fluorescent orange lines.

A dozen gulls sit on the water as the boat drifts in this nearly silent ruckus, the boiling of the little fish, the birds so gorged they can only mimic flight, stretching their wings idly, too dissipated even to do more than make a half-serious threat to terrify the boat.

The poppers dip and bob through the shimmering scales. Now the fishermen can see the bluefish cruising beneath the boat, driving the sardines, lazily consuming, enjoying their orgy, their graceful speed and power. The bluefish are twelve or twenty feet down, appear dark as coal, like torpedoes. They pass under the boat swift as the shadows of birds. Suddenly their backs break water, leaving coiled wakes. And then a head appears, the jawbone white, the big yellow eye, and razor-sharp teeth. It takes the popper in a grip of iron and dips out of sight. All Jim has to do is raise the rod and the fish is on.

"I can't see a goddamned thing," his father complains, pumping the rod slowly. "The glare."

"Keep it moving, Dad," Jim says. "You got one after the bait."

Suddenly the old man's rod dips fiercely, like a diviner over a spring.

"See?" Jim calls.

His father laughs, hanging on. "Whoa!"

Now that the bluefish have ravaged this silver cloud, the sardines have scattered, dispersed, and the boat drifts away from the turmoil, and the two men play their fish, letting them take line when they have strength, reeling in when they falter. The water is so clear today, Jim can see his fish fifty feet from the boat. And down. It seems to him the whole floor of the bay is moving, and then he laughs at himself because it must be another cloud of sardines, more bluefish herding them toward the inescapable margins of their world. His fish comes straight up now, through the wall and into the air, head flailing, scattering diamonds, then sinks in a circle of foam.

"I wish I could see something," Dan says.

"Keep him coming, Dad. I've got plenty of room here."

There are some big fish down there, Jim thinks. They have this whole bay stirred up. Maybe some sharks. In a moment, his bluefish is at the side of the boat, thrashing, his eye already taking on that look of wonder they all have before they die. They shake themselves to come down out of the wonder that consumes them. Jim takes the gaff from its holder, reaches over the side, makes a quick stab into the fish. Blood like burgundy courses down the bright belly. The hooks on the plug rattle. *Sorry*, Jim says to himself.

To his father, he says, "It's a big one. Fifteen at least."

The fish has taken the plug halfway into its mouth, and Jim can see it will take some struggling with the pliers to free it. He unsnaps the plug from the leader and drops the fish into the fish well.

"Ready for the gaff," Dan says.

Jim crosses the boat, gaffs his father's fish cleanly, and swings it aboard. "A beauty!"

"Ayuh." Dan is breathing heavily, but grinning. "Where'd they get to?"

"I don't know yet," Jim says. He scans the water, looking for the wheeling and tumbling of the terns.

Not far from them now, the whole bottom of the bay seems to detach and float up.

"They're right here still. Look at 'em!" Jim shouts.

Some thirty yards away, the water begins to boil as the sardines climb over each other to escape the marauding from below. The surface erupts like a mirror breaking, flutters with panic, and Jim quickly frees his father's fish from the lure, stows it away. He stumbles to the wheel and starts the engine, swings the boat toward the fountain of little fish, heads forward slowly, almost at a drift, certainly no faster than a man would walk. Already the birds come shrieking, keening in.

At the heart of this tumult is something too solid, Jim thinks almost subliminally, and instinctively backs down on the throttle, waiting.

As some great shock wave of force tips up in the melee of little fish and birds. The black snout rises in a rush, spewing silver streamers of water, rainbows, and then the whole great black head rushes out of the water in a clatter of its own being, like a submarine, a whole shiny pockmarked wailing wall of a creature. The eye is open, calm, as the great jaw slams, the tail stirs a wake that tips Jim's boat giddily, like a bottle in a rapids. A jet from the whale's blow hole is sent up with such force the wad of water disintegrates into mist.

Jim is so shocked, so dazzled and surprised, that as he swings the boat around to clear the swell raised by the whale, he shouts with delight. It is a cry he has never heard from himself, that leaves him more awake than he has ever been, the lolling whale and the whole thrashing circus of little fish vivid and perfect in his sight.

His father has cried out, too, but has fallen, perhaps because the deck is slippery with blood. Jim pulls the throttle and whips the boat away from and past the whale, then quickly backs down in water that is not so steeply pitched. He drags his father up from the floor and finds him in a grimace of pain, clutching a big lure tangled in the center of his chest.

"Keep your hands away, you'll make it worse," Jim says, but Dan continues to grab. Jim takes the knife and cuts through the shirt, finds barbs from two hooks have pierced his father's skin. They are not in deep, and quickly Jim nicks the skin above the little punctures, and the plug falls free.

Dan hisses, topples, still gripping his chest. Blood stains his fingers.

"It really hurts, huh?"

His father only rasps, a sound that comes from past the larynx, deeper down.

"Hang on," Jim says. "Can you hang on for twenty minutes?"

Dan's face is pale out of all proportion to the injury. This was the man who calmly walked into the house and called an ambulance when he once cut off a finger with a chain saw. He had picked up the mangled finger and carried it with him to the telephone, presented it to the ambulance driver, then called for whiskey. Now Dan is sweating, his lips seem dry and wrinkled, his eyes are full of terror.

"Twenty minutes," Jim says.

The motor is wide open the whole way back. As the boat cracks and thumps over the swells, Jim is afraid to look at his father, and knows when he bangs too hard into the dock at Mick's Marina and shouts for help, even before he turns to face the fact, that this was his father's last ride on the ocean, that for the last quarter of an hour he has been ferrying the dead.

5
Azure
Dragon
(Spring) [*iii*]

Chong wakes automatically before the sunrise and thinks of the fish. He imagines a fat rainbow trout has slid in under the roots of the tree to spend a cold April night in safety, and the strings of Chong's trap have felt no differently than the root hairs and the thin soft tendrils which have broken through the mossy black soil into the cold heart of the stream. Chong moves slowly because at his age his joints and limbs require it, they set the pace for him, and he does not hurry. He rolls on his side and looks into the bluish darkness of early morning, which is misty and wet—whether from fog and dew or water in his own eyes, Chong is not sure and doesn't care any more—and certainly cold. When he walks down to the stream in his sandals, surely some of the dew will be frosted on the grass, sparkle in the sunshine, and spray onto his toes like jewels. This is how he will come to the stream, festooned in ice and mist, and even the mist of his own breath.

Chong rises and lets the robe he has been sleeping in fall to the floor, pulls on a pair of tattered Bermuda shorts and a blue military shirt. He steps into his sandals and shuffles out onto a screened-in porch where the cold of the morning shocks him into a shiver; bangs open a screen door and walks out into the deep orchard grass; urinates. He returns to the house and from a cabinet under the white enamel sink he takes a brown paper bag from a jumbled hoard of them (and glass jars by the dozens, plastic bag twists, bottle caps, crumpled balls of aluminum foil), stuffs it into the pocket of his shorts, turns on the burner under a silver kettle striped with burn marks, and goes out again toward the stream.

The stream is across an untilled acre overgrown with deep meadow grass and bordered on both sides by trees, on the side away from Chong's house by an extensive woods. The woods creeps up a hill behind Chong's house, too, spills down the slope a little toward his garden space, the old barn, the tilting outhouse, a tiny hotbed, a glorified starter box that Chong has covered with old storm windows now to protect his seedlings from the frost and let in sunlight. That is a color which excites him still: the bright, bright green of the very first shoots from his peas and beans. He wipes the mist from the windows every morning and peers in, hoping to see it. It has never happened while he has watched, but suddenly they will appear, calmly bowed and yet straining to lift their heads, the first pair of tiny leaves opened like the wings of an insect. He has been able to mix a green paint that bright, even vibrant, but never one that is also so fragile somehow, transparent, obviously alive, both cheerful and mysterious.

Chong crosses the stream on the bridge he made by throwing old barn boards across the rusted pipe frames of two discarded beds he discovered in the barn. One of the joys of his new home is that Chong keeps discovering tools, machinery, furniture, dishes—vestiges of the old lives of the place—as if the history of the farm were only too eager to explode up through the soil, like crops, or to be plucked like fruit from the nooks and crannies of his barn and house. Only the day before he had stumbled across what appeared to be a rusty pipe, which, when he tried to pick it up to move it out of the path, proved to be connected to something else. He dug for an hour (which put him to bed with a sore back) and gradually uncovered an iron wheel, half as tall as he was, with a spiked tread. This he had tumbled down the hill and leaned against the side of the barn, amused by the bell-like ringing it made as it socked over the ground, and the jingle of dirt and rust flakes that fell down, and down again with each revolution of the tubular spokes. He loved the useless thing and if he had been younger would have spent the afternoon pushing it around just to hear the music it made.

Now Chong pushes through the bushes by the bank of the stream and reaches into the cold water burbling beneath the roots of the ancient sycamore whose white mottled bark glows in the early-morning light. Chong's fingers sting, and he lifts the trap as swiftly as he can, taking care to unsnag it from the web of roots beneath the tree. The bag buzzes with life: two fish today. Chong laughs as he lays the rope trap on the ground and then soaks his paper bag in the cold water. Yes, there is the rainbow trout he dreamed about, fat, gasping. But there is also a smaller fish, a brook trout, sleek and dark purple, with orange spots. Its belly is creamy white, but also tinged with copper-colored bands. This is a pond fish to be so stained, Chong knows, stained by the tea the leaves have made after falling into the pond and cooking all the previous summer. He wraps the rainbow in the wet paper and scoops the brook trout into the water, where it disappears like the shadow of a bird. Then he lowers his trap again and heads for the bridge.

It occurs to him there is no reason the brook trout should be in the stream. They come down only as far as the dam, the ones stained copper anyway. The brookie, therefore, is definitely a wild trout, unlike the rainbow he was carrying home (a state-stocked fish, surely) and their domain does not usually extend so far. Chong winces. Maybe the dam is leaking. Or falling down. God damn it. He doesn't want to lose his pond. After breakfast he will look into it, even though he is afraid that repairing a dam will be too big a job for him on his own, and too expensive otherwise. Where else could he watch swallows kiss the mirror image of themselves and leave a trail of circles that expanded, collided, disappeared? Where else could he get his ice?

The tiny scales of the rainbow trout glitter on Chong's hands as he prepares his breakfast. Extravagantly, he steams a rice cake in the wok. When he is fortified enough with black tea, he walks out to the dam and finds that, yes, a large stone once in the center of the top course has been dislodged and is lying now in the bed of the stream, a cascade of water tumbling on it, throwing off a beard of foam. Chong's heart sinks. The edges of the pond show mud for about three feet, and clearly the water will fall even farther.

How can he repair this, an old man like himself?

If he uses smaller stones, surely the pressure of the water will push them over.

Son of a bitch.

Maybe wood? Like a gate. Though wood would not last—probably the ice would beat it down come January—it would help for the summer.

Such a big stone down! Chong's fingers rasp in the stubble on his chin as he surveys what could have caused an event of this scale. He notes a scar on the bark of a tree reaching up from the stream below. He supposes a come-along was tied there, and then to a rock.

A mosquito did it, he decides. A Massachusetts mosquito. And lucky the tree didn't break, too, when the rock floated down.

6
The
Sea
and
Its
Bones

T he death of his father was Jim's initiation. Suddenly he was face-to-face with the world, with no mediator, with no one to intercede for him. But he was not afraid, any more than he had been afraid when the whale broke into the air so close to his and his father's boat.

Sometimes Jim dreamed of that whale. But in his dream the whale kept on rising, became an animal of the air as well as the water, the only creature of any kind to have the whole planet for its domain. Passing over towns, the whale would be mistaken for a blimp. It liked most to travel in the rain.

What had taken his father was a heart attack brought on by the day's exertions, the fishing, the fright at the surging of the whale, the blow to his chest when he fell. The barbs were a temporary nuisance and had no measurable effect, the doctors said.

Jim sometimes thought that if he had done the right thing he would have buried his father in the sea, should have given what comfort he could in the last minutes when the whole subtle organization of his father's brain smoldered down to nothing for simple lack of oxygen, weighed him down with something, and fed him over the side.

It would have been better, Jim thought. Anything would have been better. They take all your dignity away. They don't let you die like a creature, a person of the planet, but seal you off from everything and wish you away into the sky. *My father took and ate from the water. He lived on the water. He should have been buried in the sea.*

The bluefish they had caught on that day were very large, and someone at the marina had had the sense to take them home, and the good grace to clean up his boat—his alone now—and tie it up for him. Jim was surprised when he heard how much the fish weighed— sixteen and eighteen pounds—because at the time, in the stretch of sea and sky, and then in the presence of that enormous whale, the bluefish had seemed ordinary and small, like loaves of bread. The sardines, he realized, were probably six and seven inches long and were being consumed like candy. He remembered the first year he and his father went out to the woodlot to cut down a Christmas tree. The snow covered their feet and ankles, sparkled in the sun, crackled underfoot. Though it was bitterly cold, they took their time finding a small hemlock, full, nicely shaped. They cut it, carried it between them down the hill, and fastened it to the racks on the top of the car with some ceremony. They stopped at a tavern, and though Jim was under the legal drinking age, they each had a beer. His father might not have been aware of it, but it was not Jim's first— far from it. And it was a long way from being his last.

When they arrived home, they discovered the tree barely fit through the door, and when they placed it in the corner where it was to stand its Christmas vigil, the branches curled against the wall, and the top bent against the ceiling.

"Do you think we live in a mansion?" his mother teased. "Or was this tree for the town hall?"

In the woods, it had seemed a little bit of a tree. Just right for the living room.

Jim was nineteen when his father died. He had spent a year in college, the University of Maine at Orono, but now he had no money. He didn't know what he was going to do, but thought maybe he could earn a little using his boat and guiding fishermen to striped bass and bluefish on the Kennebec River and out past Popham Beach in Casco Bay, where his father had died. Fifty, sixty dollars a day. He'd have to do something else in the winter, of course. The one drawback to guiding—and Jim considered this significant—was that it might very well ruin his love for fishing in the end. It would become a job. Could that happen?

His mother told him to stay in college, but he didn't, and so he was drafted. Just before he left home, he sold his boat to an old high school friend. He hadn't thought he could ever sell it, especially for such a low price, but it was easy. He felt regret, but also relief. He gave the money to his mother and started on a journey that would take him to Texas, California, Honolulu, Kwajalein, and Viet Nam.

7
*The
Whale's
Progress*

T hey made him a photographer and a film technician. He saw
the war through the lens of a camera, and years later his
dreams would sometimes bring back to him images of events
that he had recorded on film. In other dreams, some of the things he
had photographed could not be developed: the horror trapped in the
emulsion of the film could not be conjured, would not let itself be
seen. In still another dream, the war suddenly twisted as if seen
through the shimmer of heat waves, and the camera melted to his
eyes, cheeks. He woke pulling at the skin of his face, groaning, and
his wife, Anna, would be gripping him fiercely, her face wet with
tears, saying, "It's all right, Jim. You're home."

He took pictures of:

Malaria victims. Children charred by napalm. Trucks loaded with
corpses like logs, the feet toes up. Soldiers, shirts off, sitting on crates
of machine-gun bullets, drinking cans of Budweiser.

Faces. Bodies. Sweat. Machinery. Rice. Water buffalo. Helicopters. A barracks, the remains of a bunk, shards of sheeting, patches
of charred uniform, a finger with a ring on it, bleeding, alone, a mu-
cous spot of something an intelligence officer said was the "rind" of
an eye. Hair? Skin? Blood?

They received word Hue was taking some rocket fire, so Jim's
column was sent up "to check things out." People poured out of the
city down the road toward them, hassling bundles, dragging children.

Refugees. Truck-tire sandals. Dogs. Crates with chickens. A kitchen pan worn on the head.

Tanks, rifle barrels, offices, officers' typewriters. Tiger traps. Munitions. Dead babies.

Dead babies.

Radios. Loaves of bread, stacked.

"A little rocket fire, my ass. This is a shit storm!"

A translucent cubical brown chunk of matter with the exact consistency and density of human flesh is suspended in a thin plastic shell, and then a "projectile" is fired into it. The camera—Jim recommended video tape for the experiments—captured the progress of the bullet through this soft matter as it penetrated the skin, spun, throwing off chunks of the gelatin, making a tunnel to itself, rippling the thick soup with its impact, tearing it open; then the bullet itself changing as it twists into the matter, mushrooming, folding back on itself, ripping a larger and larger hole, then exploding through the other side, hurling in slow motion the fleshlike consommé in sad gobs outward into the air.

One of his pictures that came back to him so often was one he had taken at night when a North Viet Namese soldier had stepped into the beam of an infrared sight and by a miracle of coincidence Jim had taken his picture, silently and in invisible infrared, at the precise instant the bullet passed through the soldier's helmet, his skull, his brain. The soldier's eyes were closed and his mouth was pinched into an "O" which might have been mistaken for a gesture of intense pleasure except for the little spurt of blood, shrapnel, and lead that broke like a star into the upper left-hand corner of the picture. The soldier still holds his rifle, his fingers are tense, he is stepping forward cautiously. Jim was not aware of what he had captured until he had developed the film and a subsequent photograph. The face floated up to him through the developer, red as the whole quiet room in which he worked, and at first he thought the soldier might have been whistling.

It occurred to him long ago that the whole war was on film, it could be called up by computer and studied, and newspapers and television had their own fair share of that mountainous hoard of evidence and imagery, enough to watch the war all over again in real time. No doubt somebody was studying a fragment of that war every day, somebody was handling a photograph Jim had made. If you wanted to look at a detailed rendering of a clip on an M-25, blisters raised on the foot by a certain jungle fungus, the effects of napalm on foliage, on cement bunkers, on radios, on people—it was all there to be sifted through, sorted, catalogued. You could even, if you knew the right code to punch, call up that moment when a bullet collided with a human brain.

To the left, something terribly hot must have been burning, because the figures on the right, the American soldiers falling to the ground in the wake of an orange and yellow and black (the smoke) mortar burst, seem warped and bent as if their images had been fixed on cellophane, wrinkled, thrown to the winds.

You have to know what to look for sometimes. The soldier farthest to the right has a bulge in his shirt. His name was David Hanratty, and he was from Twin Oaks, Minnesota. The little stray piece of shrapnel sliced through his whole abdominal cavity without hitting a thing except his spine.

If you heard the shot, you knew you were all right. The bullets always arrived just before the noise they made.

When he returned home, he didn't stay in Maine long. He couldn't bear the sight of anything that reminded him of his youth and his hopes, and he wanted to travel. He didn't have any money, but didn't much give a damn and went on the road like a beggar, hitchhiking. Later he thought that maybe he had never done anything worse to his mother than leaving so soon. Or to himself. He went in search of the families of the young men he had known who died. He wanted to see if they had lives like his. And he tortured them with pictures he had taken "for himself." This is John about a week before he got it. He was brave. He was a good soldier. He kept to himself. He prayed. He helped morale. He always had a story. He didn't whore and drink and shoot smack or smoke dope (blown through a rifle barrel for a big hit). Everybody liked him. You could get in a file and know that if the air was suddenly saturated with particles, flame, he'd be right where he was supposed to be, doing his job. Here he is on the beach at Cam Ranh Bay, on R and R. That little Viet Namese girl is just a hanger-on, somebody we paid a buck to pose with us. You know how they are. You can't show up anyplace in a uniform and not be pestered to death. John took it all in stride. He was mature, a gentleman, he was just like me.

Crazy!

That's a Huey, a helicopter which took us out to the action; that's a Cobra gunship. You could tell them by their sound a mile away. They said, "Buddha, Buddha, Buddha."

That's Red Barber, a helicopter mechanic. He's still alive, in Massachusetts someplace.

That's a Med-evac. They said, "Crackajacka."

That's John again. You see. He could smile. He knew how to relax.

Now tell me, will you, if John ever thought of college. Did he have a steady girl? Have chores in the barn? If I could, I'd like to see if you have them still, I'd like to see a suit he wore, a bicycle, a baseball mitt . . . anything but a picture, anything but a picture or a letter. Anything, please.

One night Chong pours himself a glass of wine, sits at the kitchen table, and begins to remember New York—always a bad sign. He thinks of Wu, even of his ex-wife, his daughter, of Benny Bergland, and Mrs. Crane, Mrs. Crane, Mrs. Crane. Chong still owes Evelyn Crane, he calculates, $5,500.

She had come to one of his openings in the Village in the 1960s, when Chong was painting huge gaudy canvases, expressionistic nudes, men and women in orgiastic attitudes, in fantasy landscapes with big orange suns hanging over them. One *Voice* critic said they were "either Eden or one second after the Big Bomb hits. You think you know, but on the way out you have to stop and look again. And then you're not sure." At the time Chong thought most reviews were silly (an impression only confirmed with age) but acknowledged the truth that his own lusts were indeed charged by a sense of emergency, of doom knocking at the door—personal, because he was growing older; public, because the world was threatened with thirteen kinds of extinction. Make it fifteen kinds, Chong said to Mrs. Crane. What difference does it make?

She had laughed a kind of throaty cigarette laugh, her breasts quivered in the tight black sweater, and her diamond bracelets glittered. She bought a painting for $300, paid cash for it, came back two days later and bought everything in the place, over $3,000 worth of Chong's paintings and drawings. Chong was shocked. He was flattered, but also a little disturbed that the "success" of his show was due to one woman. To buy it *all* seemed a little ridiculous. He was not solicitous to Mrs. Crane, but he was also curious about her and inclined to be friendly. After all.

A month later, Chong hung another show in a coffeehouse on Sullivan, wood-block prints in four colors, dragons dancing in the sky over houses packed with people busy with all sorts of things, including a lot of lovemaking. Chong was then living in an apartment house on Mott Street with his wife; his daughter was about two, and he worked two part-time jobs. In the mornings he developed black and white photographs for a discount camera shop and at night he waited tables at Coronado's on Wooster Street—where, as it happened, he first heard the music and made the acquaintance of Benny Bergland. In the afternoons he tried to make his art and live some sort of family life.

Chong went to the coffeehouse after a few days and all the prints were gone—all of them. The manager told him that a Mrs. Crane had scooped up everything she could get her hands on—the whole works.

"What's the deal?" Chong asked. "They're just prints. I got a shit-load of them. Forty, each one. My bedroom is jammed with the damn things. She can't think they're worth a whole lot, can she?"

"Don't knock it, milk it," the manager said. "Everybody else I know is looking for an angel."

"This is crazy!" Chong said.

The manager gave a slow philosophical shrug. "Crazy but nice, right? I don't see your problem, Chong."

A few days later, Mrs. Crane showed up at Coronado's, very late, and, yes, Chong remembers, Benny was playing that night, in a mean frame of mind, smashing around on the keyboard, driving the customers out.

"If you can't stand a little dissonance, split." That was how Benny had put it, to anybody who would listen. "A little dissonance wakes you up. If you want lullabies, go across the street to the piano bar. You can get all the Moony-Junie shit you want over there. And the booze is cheaper."

Chong bought Benny a Manhattan. "Man, lighten up. You're going to get fired."

Benny stirred the drink with his finger, gave Chong a big fake smile. "I keep hopin'."

During Benny's break, the owner got pretty rough with him: "I'm paying you for the music, not the mouth. Play, but don't lecture my customers."

In the middle of the argument, Mrs. Crane appeared in the orange glow of the lobby, slim and shapely as a deer or a snake, Chong wasn't sure what he should think. She wore dark blue velvet pants, a tight long-sleeved sweater, and an armload of bracelets. Her dark hair was tied back from her narrow face, and the overhead bar lights made the shadows under her cheekbones deepen. She came directly across the room and laid a hand on Chong's arm.

"I think we should talk," she said. "Bring me a Burgundy, will you, and sit down a minute?" She sat off the main floor in a booth, and when Chong brought the wine she slid across the seat as if she expected him to sit beside her. Chong chose the other side of the table.

"I like your work," Mrs. Crane said.

"Thank you."

"And I'd like to arrange something with you."

Chong nodded, waiting.

"Do you want to talk now, or after closing."

"The manager's on edge tonight."

"I can wait," she said. "I'll drive you home."

Chong slid out of the booth. "O.K. with me," he said.

She walked close to him when they left the bar, brushed against him as she unlocked the door to her orange Porsche. Driving, she rammed through the gears.

"You really have to get home right away?"

"I have a job in the morning, too."

"Christ, when do you paint?"

"Afternoons," Chong said.

"You still have two jobs? You're selling everything you paint, aren't you?"

Chong laughed nervously. "On the other hand, I've only got one customer."

"I told you, I like your work." She turned a corner then swerved to the curb along Washington Square and shut off the lights. The car engine ticked as it cooled.

Mrs. Crane asked Chong to paint her picture, a portrait, however he interpreted that. There were a few conditions, however: She wanted no one else to see it, and for that reason would require him to do all his work in her apartment and leave all sketches, drawings, and preliminary studies in her possession. She spoke in a level, flat voice, as if the speech were a practiced one, as if she had done this sort of thing before. It crossed Chong's mind with a little shock that, yes, she was probably having herself painted by every "promising" artist she could find, and guessing that in time her little collection would be worth a lot and, of course, how flattering to have been "done" by all the New York artists of an age. Chong hated both motives and began not to listen and to watch instead the dark bundles of late New York street life that staggered by the dim edges of the peach-colored lights around the Square.

Chong pursed his lips and scrunched down in the seat, crossing his arms. "I'm not a portrait painter. You know what I do. I mean, I can make a likeness, but anybody else could do it as good. I'm also no good at flattering people. I paint like I have to, and I don't do anything against the grain any more. A portrait, really, doesn't interest me."

Mrs. Crane lit a cigarette and dropped the spent match out the window. The car filled up with the mingled smell of tobacco and her perfume. "I don't want any precise likeness," she said. Smoke curled around her head. "I want your impression, feeling about me, in my house, among my things. That's all. I know you could do that."

"Yes, I could But suppose you don't like it?"

"If I didn't like it, maybe I'd learn something. But I'd pay you. I might destroy the painting, but I'd pay you. In fact, I'll pay you in advance, if you do one other thing."

"More conditions, huh?" Chong tried to suppress the irritation he felt. He was also tired and in no mood for a debate.

"You quit one of those jobs."

"If I could!"

"You can't make much developing pictures," she said. "And it must bore you weary."

Chong figured: eighty-five a week times fifty. "Forty-two fifty is what I make."

"That's what I'll pay you for the painting."

She was right, the machine he ran bored him. Twelve seconds each snapshot, one after another, four hours in the blood-red light of the darkroom. But since when did a job have to interest you? "It wouldn't take me a year," Chong said.

Mrs. Crane laughed. "Then you come out ahead, don't you? You might get some more time to paint? What's the matter? Do you get offers like this every day?"

"No." Chong grinned in spite of himself. "This is crazy. How can I say no?"

"That's what I'd like to know," Mrs. Crane said. "Unless you don't like me or something. Or don't trust me. But if that's your hang-up, I already told you I'd pay in advance."

"If I painted you right now," Chong said, "I'd paint a dragon. I'm a little scared of you, you see. I want to know why you're doing this."

"Then you'll have to get to know me better." Mrs. Crane stubbed out her cigarette. "I'm sure you'll learn very quickly. And I don't think I'm so extraordinarily complicated. And certainly no dragon."

"No?" Chong said.

"I assure you." She opened her purse and fished out a card. "Call me whenever. If you quit that job, you can see me in the mornings. That'd be nice, actually."

She drove him to Mott Street and let him out in front of his apartment. Chong fingered the card as the little orange car slithered away into the maw of New York. What does she want with little China-man like me? Chong wondered. And where's her husband? He must have some interest in where she is at 3 A.M.

When he closed the door to his rooms, the air seemed damp and too warm. His daughter was sleeping soundly, on her belly, her cheek pressed tightly against the mattress in her crib. And when he rolled into bed with his wife, Mai Li woke up enough to slip an arm across his chest, press a warm thigh against him, and murmur, "You're late tonight. I came to bed." Chong felt himself sinking in the jungle heat of his household, but it was all right, he decided, it was where he wanted to be right now.

He quit his morning job and began taking the subway to the upper east side, where Mrs. Evelyn Crane had her apartment, and began to find out a few things. The husband he had wondered about spent most of his time in Washington, where he was a lobbyist for some corporate interest Mrs. Crane did not specify. The Cranes' only child, Richard, was away at a private school in New Hampshire—his first year, but already he had stopped writing letters and Mrs. Crane was "concerned" about him "but not *worried*, you see. He's a capable boy, I assure you. He gets along with everyone."

This was not Chong's first glimpse of such a world, and he was not so naive a student of America that he did not know such lives were possible, if also exceptional. But the kind of freedom Mrs. Crane enjoyed startled him: free to be in San Francisco or the Bahamas tomorrow; to disappear all night in the Village if she chose; to lock her door and be alone and quiet and unpestered for a day, a week, as long as she liked. He was also quite surprised at her fearlessness, at how ready she was to feed an impulse to some adventure or pleasure. It made Chong wonder how he would live if he were free and monied, and therefore he watched and listened to Mrs. Crane with more than usual interest. One day as he sketched her and threw the sketches aside, he thought, *Her fuse is lit.* She could go mad with such freedom, she could turn the wrong corner at the wrong time, could invite the wrong man in, could burn herself down, overdose on something new; but nothing of the sort was happening to her. She handled everything, and nothing went wrong. Chong had to admire her, and her unexplainable good luck, but still felt a vague unease about her, about her overarching confidence, wanted to warn her. But what did he know about these things? What did he know about the laws of the different world she dragged around with her? There was, he realized and accepted, a quantum difference between them. When he returned to his apartment for lunch and his usual work, he felt relieved of some obscure dread. He was an observer of Mrs. Crane only, an adjunct to her life, an artifact in her museum. There was no danger of his being swept away; he knew this as soon as he entered the door to his apartment and was anchored in the pungent smell of diapers awaiting his daily laundry mission, of Mai Li spooning green or orange paste into Susan's mouth, his pushing aside the familiar laundry in the bathroom, or sitting down with tea at the kitchen table to watch the pigeons parade past the speckled, dusty window. Here there was a real floor under his feet, not some spongy pale blue cloud of color.

After two weeks of sketching, Chong wanted to try something larger and brighter, and brought a kit of paints and brushes for watercolors and tempera to Mrs. Crane's apartment. He wanted her to sit on a sofa in front of a large window full of big-leaved plants where a cage with a cockatiel also hung and where it was possible to look out across a series of rooftops that had been beautified and decorated for the benefit of the wealthy tenants in the buildings below. There was not a wooden water tank in view, not even an unpainted ventilation pipe or air-conditioner screen. Chong was, he

believed, thinking in terms of Lin Feng-mien and Matisse and the
Shankhai painters, too, for he meant to paint Mrs. Crane in a quick
flurry of lines and surround her with a spontaneous array of bright
things so as to make the city also seem something that belonged to
her, a part of her home. He meant, in other words, to paint her luck,
and her confidence. She would be something of an odalisque, but
with more individuality than that, just a little crazy and a little too
proud, and like a princess with the Mandate of Heaven overlooking
her Kingdom.

But she kept him waiting, and some of his enthusiasm began to
wane, to change a little to irritation. He did not want, ever, to be
treated like a chauffeur and had insisted always on her punctuality
and strict time limits for their sessions. And when she did come into
the room, the sky in his imagination was already darker, more true
to the leaden gray of New York's atmosphere than the fairy tale he
had been telling himself, to flatter her, and get this job done.

She wore a black robe and fell easily onto the sofa, unbelted and
pulled the robe away in an easy motion, shook her rich brown hair
over her bare shoulders. Chong set his face in order to betray no interest in her nudity.

"Is this all right?" she asked.

"Is it what you want?"

"Yes, it is."

Chong nodded acquiescence, but kept his approval secret. He
could envision how uneasily Mai Li would handle her own bare
body, with awkwardness and shame, squeezing her hands between
her knees, imagining a chill, tipping her head forward in embarrassment. Chong had seen many models, of course, of all colors and ages,
but it always disarmed him a little that Americans could disrobe so
readily and naturally, regard their bodies with such a fatalistic non-
chalance. His Chinese upbringing still exerted itself to this extent,
that if the human body was to him no longer an object of shame, it
nevertheless had the power to excite, and was to remain mysterious
and private, to be offered and bared only in the most intimate of circumstances. A naked body was vulnerable, and to be naked with
someone implied a great trust, or a great carelessness. Mrs. Crane
was without embarrassment, seemed even a little bored with her
body, if not exactly naive about its attractions, since she clearly
knew how to display herself—another intimation, Chong thought,
that she was practiced at this business.

Stretched out on the sofa, she seemed taller than usual. She was spare, streamlined, but with full thighs and breasts as large and firm as oranges. Her skin was the color of sand, her eyes rusty and sparkling, and the hair between her legs was a thick patch of brown tapering to black. When she tilted her head, her long brown hair curled over her shoulders and fell to the cleavage of her breasts. She seemed completely at ease, completely self-possessed. Chong was moved, but he said, he showed nothing. Instead, he adjusted the legs of his easel so that he could sit and paint, and then brought up a chair and began to work.

"We can talk, can't we?" she asked.

"Sure." Chong knocked his brushes against the side of the water jar as he cleaned them, and the notes rang bell-like, loud in the room. "If you get tired, you can get up and move around. Just let me know."

"I did some modeling in college," she said.

Chong mixed his paints carefully. He would be in no hurry. Even now he can remember the colors he mixed on that day, the pale lilac that highlighted her sleek thigh, the shining black robe against the cream-colored sofa, the pomegranate red of the bird's beak, the lemon traces on her shoulders, the bare sky over the city. He thinks he could almost recreate that painting if he wanted to—a violation of contract, though she'd probably never know. He had worked rapidly, letting some half-finished pieces fall to the floor, pinning up another, and another sheet of paper. When he had the form—her thighs realized in a single brush stroke each by a thick, pointed brush—and the face in a good likeness, he dropped the paper down, knowing he could fill in the background and the details at a later time.

Finally, Mrs. Crane rose from the sofa to stretch. "I want to see what you're doing," she said and closed the distance between them in a few steps, leaving the robe on the sofa. Chong remembers that he had just cleaned that special brush, soft-tip camel hair, and had shaken out the water to fluff up the bristles when she stood next to him, so close her thigh brushed his cheek, and touched him then, her fingers curling at his neck, so that he was swept with a wave of confusion and excitement.

Without thinking about it, he accepted the weight of her leaning against him and passed his left hand up the back of her leg, then traced with the brush the veiled blue vein on the inside of her thigh, as if she were his canvas. She chuckled, low, and encouraged him by placing her hand on top of his briefly, and by drawing him closer. Now he ran the tip of that soft brush around the patch of that brown triangle tapering to black, and slowly brushed the crease of her sex. He brushed this groove again, and again, until it parted in a crisp pink line, like a slice from a peach, and she began to knead his shoulders with her strong fingers, to inhale sharply, to lean still more heavily against him. The tip of the brush passed smoothly through the folds, prodded, glided. Chong's ears buzzed; the smell of her perfume mingled suddenly with another smell more animal and demanding. Now he took the brush between his fingers and slowly twirled it, back and forth, as Mrs. Crane went limp, moaned, tangled her fingers in his hair.

"What do you want from me?" Chong's voice strained upward through the cloud of his astonishment. "*Me?*"

She pressed his face to her thigh.

Chong sips his wine and rises from the kitchen table. He remembers that later she had told him he needed to think better of himself, that he had no ego, no dignity. She said she wanted to change that. Certainly that first encounter had left him humiliated, feeling like a whore, and he went home hours later than usual, steamed in shame, unable to look his wife in the eye. He had rushed through dinner and escaped to work as soon as possible. He could not let such a thing happen again. He told himself that it would destroy him, that Evelyn didn't understand how he felt, what adjustments he had to make in his scheme of things to let this go on.

But it did go on, and on, and never, while he lived in New York, ceased to be a part of his life, his new life as he sometimes thought of it. Mai Li must have known, Chong thinks, but Mrs. Crane was not the reason they parted. Mai Li knew and let it be—how odd!

Chong stands in the kitchen doorway now, looks out across the farm toward Sky Pond and Sweat Hill beyond; their shapes merge in the darkness, boundaries collapse. She had loaned him the money to buy this farm, the rich folks' way of getting rid of you, Chong muses, forty acres and a pig. He realizes he is bitter, but that there is no need for rancor toward Mrs. Crane after all these years. When he had inevitably confessed to Benny, on the sidewalk after work, trembling with confusion, nauseated by his own deceit, Benny had said, "Take it easy on yourself, my man. Don't you know? You got a good thing going. Can't you do right both ways? Is anybody suffering besides you?"

It strikes Chong now that he could not honestly answer Benny's question. The moon cracks over the trees suddenly, behind fast-moving clouds, like an eye fluttering in a dream. Chong drinks his wine. If Benny were here, they'd drink and holler to the bottom of the bottle, have pancakes and sausage for breakfast, sleep until noon. But Benny is not here. Chong knows it will be a long night.

9
Home
Front
[i]

Jim met Anna in Boston, where he had managed to get a job in the darkroom of the *Globe*, a fate that he disliked because it had seemed so inevitable: If he survived the war, of course he would work in journalism. At least he was not on the streets (not yet) photographing fires. He developed film and printed pictures for the paper and for a number of business-related public relations tasks and for the "files," that pit of information and images where the work of the researchers, reporters, and photographers was compiled. Jim was always surprised what he could dig up out of those files: The third face from the left in an old YMCA fund-raising campaign photo was a man now charged with embezzling funds from a prominent bank; give us a one-column blowup of that head, Jim. Pronto. Random photos of North End landscapes and buildings turn up the perfect BEFORE picture of a building whose AFTER is a ball of flame rolling skyward in a suspected mob-related arson case. Note the black smoke, the chief said. That means oil. Note the way the fire spread, out from the center, like a star. Somebody laid streamers.

Jim knew what "streamers" were, besides unopened parachutes, for he had photographed them in Viet Nam when the country was at war. They were lines of flammable liquid laid out from a center where a fuse would be lit, kindling and a starter laid down. It was one way to raze a row of huts or bunkers. In Boston it was one of the tools of the arsonist to spread a fire and raise the temperature quickly so that the structure, as the firemen called it, could not be saved.

Anna worked in layout and design, and Jim met her when she asked for occasional special effects work—posterization, high contrast imagery, refining or altering color contrasts, all kinds of decorative screening. She was shy, small, and blond, with jade-green eyes, and for a while Jim thought she was afraid of him. He figured she was married and so he said nothing to her for months. When he did, it was after a long night of drinking and talking on the telephone with Red Barber on the other end of the state, and a short sleep ravaged by dreams of intense heat, as if the city were an oven, bricks ready to explode, girders about to melt, paper ready to flash.

She handed him a sheet of instructions and a dummy of the weekend magazine. In the fluorescent lights in the layout room—much of it coming through the frosted glass on the tables—she seemed pale; an artery that coursed in her cheek and down the length of her neck was visible, a dull green, like a pen mark seen through the wrong side of the paper. She also wore an apricot-colored blouse flecked with pastel flowers; and those green eyes were alive, intense, moist, and curious.

"Jesus, Jim." She laid a hand on his wrist. "Are you O.K.? You look spooked."

"If I could tell you . . ."

"Yes," she said. "Let's talk sometime."

"Now. Tonight."

Her glance hardened momentarily. "No." She studied him almost casually. "Friday? After work?"

"Yes." Why was he whispering? He felt full of steam.

"Hang on," she said, and walked away.

She's so small, Jim thought. If I held her, if I held her as hard as I want to, I could kill her.

By mistake.

10
Repairs

In the morning, Chong rummages in the barn. His wheelbarrow rests in a triangle of sunlight coming through one of the two doors and throws a severe, comically distorted shadow on the floor. When Chong turns toward it with an armload of wood, the shadow of the wheelbarrow looks to him like a long-antlered goat, randy with springtime, one glowing eye narrowed with lust and plotting.

Always difficult in the spring, Chong thinks. I could paint some goats today chasing each other, squaring off.

The load of wood tumbles into the wheelbarrow with a burble of well-seasoned notes. Like a wind chime of wood, a bamboo wind chime maybe. It is easy to see how the Africans discovered the xylophone, the marimba. You work with the wood and it talks to you.

Chong turns back to the woodpile and shakes his head. It is low, and the mornings are still frosty. Two more weeks?

A rat slides over a large gnarled branch Chong had set aside as being too hard, too knotty to split, one he would cut only if he had to, if the winter hung around like a drunk with his eye on your wine, 3:30 A.M. Chong flings a chunk of maple at the rat, misses by a good margin, raises a little cloud of straw dust. The motes sparkle like stars in a knife-edged beam of light invading a crack between boards.

Now Chong takes a closer look at the branch the rat has used as a bridge no doubt all winter long. He stumbles through the loose chunks of wood and hauls the branch out, drags it out of the stall and through the open door and props it against the side of the barn. Now he can see why this log has been waiting around all winter. It is not a log at all but a goat, and the form of the goat is there, rearing, straining to be set free. Chong laughs with surprise. Of course! Here is the day's work. He hustles into the house and down into the cold basement, where he gathers up a fistful of wood chisels and a mallet, stuffs a pair of files into his rear pants pocket, and scrambles back outside.

He contemplates the log only a moment—the goat has not fled— and begins to work furiously.

By noon, the goat is released from the tree. He stands spring-thin, his rib cage showing, rearing, erect with lust, his hooves delicate and fierce, ready to spring; only his rear haunches are entrapped still in the stump from which this creature sprang. This is how he will remain, Chong decides. He has exploded out of the tree. Just far enough.

Chong slips his cold hand into his pants and grabs his cock. *Where is my mare, my bitch, my sow?*

It is time for lunch. He leaves his tools scattered on the ground before the priapic ram, the barn door open, wheelbarrow half filled with melodic wood, and goes inside for cheese, sprouts, rye bread, beer. Sunlight splashes everything! His windows glow!

Chong talks to Turner on the telephone: "I don't know what I can pay you."

Turner is silent a moment. "I'll come and take a look at it," he says.

That evening Chong and Turner stand by the edge of the pond surveying the sad state of its condition. Turner walks out onto the dam and looks down onto the large rock that has been displaced; he hops across the dam and disappears into the woods on the other side, then re-emerges below by the stream, squinting, pulling at the green and yellow baseball cap on his head, spitting. He walks back and forth on the bank of the stream for a while, then climbs out and hops back across the dam.

"No problem," he says.

Chong cannot imagine how such a stone will not be a problem. "Good," he says.

"You're right that sucker didn't just fall off there on its own."

"No?"

"It had some help all right."

"What's happening here?" Chong wonders aloud. "Who cares enough to wreck my dam?"

"I could be wrong," Turner says, "but I suspect it's the same bunch that let my pigs loose that time. Them Archer kids are always raisin' hell of some kind."

"Archer?"

"There's a whole clan of them around here. They got a little motorcycle gang they call The Club, mostly family, but all the other kooks around here, too. You'll hear of 'em."

Turner takes a package of cigars out of his pocket, hands one to Chong, then passes him his lighter after he has fired up. The two men stand on the edge of the dam watching the smoke collect in the still air around them. Usually the fall of the water creates a cool breeze here, Chong knows; the stillness and the drying gobs of water weed and moss on the newly exposed banks of the pond lie about like the pelts of dead green animals, and smell almost as bad.

"How much?" Chong sighs.

"Seven cords of wood," Turner says.

Chong blows smoke through his nose. "Five," he says.

"Ain't one for dickerin'," Turner says. "I meant to cut it myself. I'll have to cut some anyway to get my backhoe in there."

Chong nods agreement. "Seven cords. But no hickory, and no cherry."

"I'll do it careful," Turner says.

The sun is barely visible behind the trees when Chong hears the machine rumbling into his woods along the old fire road and, moments later, the snarling and shrieking of a chain saw. He makes tea, imagining trees cracking and tipping, the pile of sawdust at the stump of each as Turner clears a road to the stream. Chong cannot explain his feelings to himself, how weary he seems, how broken, when, after all, he should be glad his dam will be repaired soon, his pond renewed. The tea cheers him a little; and after a second cup he walks out to watch Turner work.

A tree twists on its stump, collapses slowly, shaking its crown of light green buds as it comes to rest beside the stream. Turner comes out of the woods, chain saw crackling in his hands, cigar traveling across his lips. Chong can see he is sweating profusely. Now the chain saw is silent, and Turner disappears into the woods. In a moment, another engine burbles to life, a baritone, and the sound crescendos until the yellow machine lurches between the trees and onto the bank of the stream, where it stops like an arrogant steed, sturdy as a bull, and roars.

Turner climbs down out of the cab and wades into the stream, water to his knees, inspects the stone that has fallen, and the bed of the stream. Out of the corner of his eye he notices Chong at last and waves perfunctorily, impatiently. Then he slops out of the water and takes command of the tractor again, extends the bucket on the back end, backs carefully down into the water, and turns the machine to face away from the dam. Slowly he inches backwards, water and sand dripping from the deep tread in the tires, until the stream caresses the belly of the engine.

The motor squeals, square metal claws on chrome shafts shoot out from the sides of the tractor and disappear into the stream. The great mandible on the back of the tractor, the bucket, slips gently into the water, and under the edge of the stone. The tractor shakes as if taking a blow and one end of the stone emerges from the gravel of the streambed like a great fish raising its tail before a long dive.

Then how quickly it is over. The claw sinks into the stream again and boosts the rock up into the hole at the top of the ancient wall. The rock falls with a great slap, cockeyed and twisted in its old home, then is prodded and bumped by the fist of the machine, grinds finally into the slot that ancestor Yankees must have made for it and no doubt hoisted into place with block and tackle, oxen, a tripod of sturdy oak logs.

With the settling of the stone into place, something settles in Chong, too. And when Turner has finally coaxed his machine onto the shore and climbed onto the dam to inspect his work and stamp on the stone, Chong walks out and stamps, too, knowing, as perhaps Turner does not, that the two of them are dancing in the morning sun, stamping things into place, celebrating the repair of vandalism, the power of their tools, the return of cover to the starving plants around the edge of the pond.

Turner throws his cigar butt into the stream below him. "You get some mortar and gravel in there before the water comes up too far, and she'll stay right there for another hundred years."

Chong has no reply. In his mind, he is already mixing cement with pond water, shoveling sand and gravel, sealing the gaps. He stamps on the stone, nods in satisfaction.

✱ ✱ ✱

Chong hears it in his sleep when the water spills over the dam again. It begins as one person whispering in his ear, then another and another, until his house is full of whispering people, telling secrets, stifling laughter. He wakes from one level of sleep to another and assures himself it is the water coming over the dam again, water that must have crawled to the brim of the wall in the evening, trembled on the edge of the rock, sent questioning streamers across the stone, which fell like tears, explored the way down . . . then the top of the pond must have slid over in a curtain, surprising the fish which survived the drought, sleepy with oxygen starvation. Suddenly the water is full of bubbles, the stream stirs.

Before breakfast, Chong investigates the dam, the film of water sliding over, the froth in the pool below. He sits on the end of the dam with his feet in the water and whittles fallen branches into miniature fish . . . a mermaid . . . a man with whiskers like a horned pout . . . a sucker . . . a fat frog with knobby knees . . . salamander . . . a water nymph with moonlike breasts . . . a shark, an otter, a trout—and all of these he sets afloat in the pond and watches as they are whisked over the dam in a bright, invisible rush of water and tumbled into a new, a pell-mell life in the stream below. He feels them bang into the rocks, and twirl, and bubble on.

11
Home
Front
[ii]

T he fact that Anna had noticed Jim, had understood at once his
distress, and was willing to talk to him captured Jim's imagination, but also frightened him. He was not sure what people
wanted to hear about the war, were able to hear about it, and normally his anxiety about this, his fear that he would be hated for having served in an unpopular war, left him silent. The people who
worked with him regarded him as unfriendly, or stupid, or very profound, and Jim accepted each of these judgments as being at least
partially true. He was unfriendly, because he was afraid of being
judged recklessly, and because he had learned in Viet Nam that real
friendships could end in terrible hurt; he was stupid, because he
didn't understand The World any more, why people valued what
they valued, worried about what they worried about, loved what
they loved; and yes, he was profound, because he knew now the
absolute fragility of human life, and the great systems that were in
place to wreck it utterly, because he knew and believed that a great
horror was possible at any moment, the ground could open beneath
his feet, that people allowed this to happen and devoted great creative energy to assuring human misery, and slaughter, and terror,
and annihilation. He was a foreigner when he returned from Viet
Nam, an alien. He had been a combat photographer primarily, but
he had still been spat upon in airport lobbies, called "baby killer" by
anonymous passengers on anonymous buses, shunned in bars. He

was happy to remove his uniform at last and disguise himself as a normal human being.

That Anna had seen through this disguise interested Jim, and confused him, too. He recognized that he needed desperately to get outside himself, to get involved in worlds other than the one inside his head, to dilute Viet Nam instead of concentrating on it. He was ready to listen to anyone who would talk to him, to fill him with knowledge and information about other lives; and he was ready to talk, and would have talked if he understood the ground rules of the normals, the people of The World.

Because Anna was perceptive about these needs, she made it easy for him. Neither did she hurry him, and little by little revealed her own history, which let him know that she had lived in The World, knew something about men, and love, and frustration, about what she thought were "the possibilities." She was cautiously optimistic about things, she was patient, and, best of all, did not seem to have overarching expectations about others, or overreaching ambitions for herself. In fact, Jim was a little jealous of her, of her self-control and self-containment, of her self-assurance, and the *safety* she felt. Sometimes he wanted to break through this assurance of hers, to terrorize her into a better understanding of how he saw things, but though he was sometimes tempted, in the end he never saw the point of it. Nobody was going to draft her. Nobody was going to put a grenade under her brandy-colored Rabbit. Nobody was going to slip out of the darkness with a loop of piano wire destined for her pale, her slender, her charming neck. Rockets would not slam into her apartment.

And he just loved the looks of her, meanwhile. How could he explain something that seemed so superficial and silly but was really so special to him, to have this beautiful small, gentle strong woman freely beside him, in time freely undressing with him, lying beside him, and willingly and with pleasure allowing him to be inside her, connected? It seemed like such a stupendous thing to him he could barely contain his alarm that some people in The World, even Anna sometimes, seemed to regard these exchanges as normal and predictable. Anna had had other lovers, and had learned from them, but Jim knew little by comparison. He was still a boy when he left Maine, where sex had meant grotesque struggling in the darkness, and the chill, of cars hidden in stands of spruce; and the women he had encountered in Viet Nam were like dolls to him, alive only in some other world than the one they revealed to him, and their exchanges were cynical and brusque and humorless. He had liked their tea-colored skin, and marveled at their eyes and beautiful little mouths, but they never really appeared to him otherwise, were never *there*. He wondered how some soldiers had fallen in love with Viet Namese women, and had been loved in return, for those he met had left their real lives and their hearts somewhere else. Either that— and this fear stayed with him—or Jim had simply lacked the arts and the knowledge of provoking or waking their humanity, that the fault was in him that he could not inspire a woman to share her reality, that he lacked something essential that made a woman become a woman with him. Had he ever once been loved? he wondered. And then he came home with a curse on him, a stigma, and he had thought that women would always despise him, or would hide their lives from him even while they presented him with their bodies and their sex.

Anna had been to college, and she introduced Jim to phases of Boston that otherwise intimidated him: the museums, the galleries of Newbury Street, the Symphony. Jim found an unexplained enjoyment in these things and discovered that Anna was subtly challenging him to think differently, and more deeply, about his photography, which he had regarded as nothing more than a skill, as a way of making documents. He had never thought much about what a photograph meant, and though he believed he knew a good deal about composition, he had never really studied a photograph as pure design before, as a passage of light and shadow, of shape and color and rhythm. Almost instinctively, he discovered, he was alert to form, had a good eye for detail, and, as the editors told him when he was finally assigned to news events, "a good sense of the story." He took photos that revealed the heart of an issue, event, or tragedy. He knew, though the editors never said so, that disaster was his forte. Somehow he had a knack for the terrible.

He had been of two minds about darkroom work. He hated the routine of it, and the insularity, almost like being in a prison all day. At the same time, since Viet Nam, he would have been glad, he thought, never to touch a camera again for as long as he lived. He didn't have much interest in photographing politicians or rock stars or celebrities, wasn't more than mildly interested in sports photography, and on the rare occasions he was sent out on assignment he found himself absurdly struggling to make three-men-and-a-pencil shots somehow interesting—Lions Club president presents plaque, United Way directors open campaign, Hospital Auxiliary staff prepares for pancake fund-raiser, pastor and elders break ground for new addition . . . On these assignments, it was all he could do to be civil even when he reminded himself that the people involved were doing good things for good causes and that the publicity could help save somebody's life or bring comfort to the afflicted.

"Well, what is it about these assignments you object to?" Anna asked him. "Do you even know?"

"They're so routine," Jim said. "I don't know. Every one's the same."

"Is it the photograph, or is it the people?" Anna continued.

"Why wouldn't I like the people? They're just people."

"I don't know why. But that's the sense I get from you. That you don't like do-gooders."

They were in her car, Jim driving, not long after work one Friday, headed for Maine to enjoy a weekend on Popham Beach, a trip that would include a rare visit to Jim's mother. The traffic was heavy, the air muggy and dense with exhaust fumes. Boston drivers pulled their usual careless, cynical, endangering stunts, and Jim was on edge. He thought about what Anna had just said and it angered him a little, because it was true.

"You're right," he confessed. "It's not just the photographs, the chore of them. It's the attitude of the people or something."

"They think they're special, is that it?"

"Some do, some don't. They're not all self-righteous prigs, I guess."

Anna laughed. "You're so perverse sometimes. Here these people are, trying to better the world, make Boston a happier place, and you hate them for it. What do you think they should do instead?"

"I don't know." Jim spoke with irritation because Anna seemed to be taking him so lightly, and because he was frustrated with himself for his absurd bad feelings. "It doesn't make sense, does it? But when I think of those pictures, and those people, I think of all those smiles and fat and innocence—"

"And you hate it."

"Right," Jim said. "They're such phonies. It's such a lie."

"Phonies?" Anna shot him a grim smile. "How do you know that?"

"Because they're really not any better than anybody else. They just like to think so. And how much difference is it really going to make? What they do? Sometimes I think they do it more for themselves than for the people they're presumably helping out."

"Maybe they do both. What's wrong with that?"

"I don't know," Jim said. "Why do I feel this way? What's wrong with me?"

"A lot of people feel like you do," Anna said. "Just not to the same extreme."

"I see these Shriner guys out there on their motorbikes in one of those parades, hot-doggin' around, you know, and I just want to run out and kick them over."

Anna laughed again, hard. "Jim, that's *terrible*."

"All those potbellied bastards in their funny hats."

"But, Jim—"

"Riding figure eights and circles, burning up perfectly good gasoline."

"Jim, really, you're outrageous."

"I know it. I can't help it."

"They're raising money for a good cause, having a good time doing it," Anna said. "You're such a puritan, you think they should suffer what the victims suffer, that they should rub shoulders with the lepers or something."

"Is that what I think?"

"Isn't it? I'm just guessing. I think, really, you're really more prudish and more idealistic than the people you're criticizing."

"Prudish? Me?"

"You tell me, Jim. Is it true, or not?"

"I'll be damned," he said, a little in wonder. "Nobody ever called me a prude before."

"Well, you are."

"I don't like to see people making light of other people's suffering. And that's what it looks like to me."

"They'd be shocked to hear you say that, I'm sure."

"I'm shocked to hear myself say it!"

"I'm not, Jim. If there's one thing I've learned about you, it's that you always identify with the underdog. Am I right?"

"Do I?"

"Yes."

"I guess I do." He was glad to see the traffic thinning out, pulled into the center lane, and gradually increased speed. "I wonder why, though. And isn't that a good thing?"

"I don't know why," Anna said, serious now. "And I guess it's a good thing as long as you sympathize with the underdog, that you are embarrassed if someone is condescending, or minimizes your pain and hardship, or anger, whatever it is."

"You're too smart for me," Jim said. "I don't know why I put up with you."

"But," Anna went on, "if you take it personally all the time, that means you think of yourself as the victim. And maybe that's not healthy."

"Aha." Jim struggled to understand this. Was it true? Did he think of himself as "The Victim"? There was some truth to that, he had to admit. Did he think he had to be "The Victim," that he was fated to be smashed? Christ, there was some truth to that, too. "I don't know," he said after a long pause, "I really don't know how much control I have over anything in my life. Sometimes I think it's all just a matter of luck, good or bad, and I don't really deserve or earn anything."

"You've got more going for you than you realize," Anna said.

"I got you." Jim reached across the seat and stroked Anna's arm. "You think that's luck? Huh?"

"It's the best thing that ever happened to me," he said.

"But you think it's just luck?"

"Like lightning striking," Jim said.

Anna moved closer to him. "Well, it wasn't luck," she said. "I like you because you're likable, not because I'm crazy. There are things in you to like, Jim."

"Really?"

"Really," she said. "Even if you are a rat sometimes, and kick Shriners off their motorbikes."

Jim put his arm around her, and, belatedly, they laughed together.

Maybe it was the best time they ever had, on the water, prowling around the Kennebec in a boat they borrowed from one of Jim's old high school friends, an eighteen-footer with a thirty-horsepower motor, "a real eggbeater," as Jim described it. Jim had also discovered some fishing tackle in the basement of his mother's house, and even though he knew the line was surely worn and would probably kink mercilessly from being unused for so long, he brought the gear along.

"I mean," he said, "you can't just get in a boat and do nothing, can you?"

"What's 'boating' mean, then?" Anna squinted up at him, hands on her hips. "Don't some people just like to 'boat'?"

"Tourists, maybe." Jim stepped into the boat and stowed the gear. "But I think boating is to boats like, well, like boiling water is to cooking. You get me?"

"I get you," Anna said. "Nobody boils water just to listen to the bubbles."

"Right!"

As it happened, they did not fish. A light breeze and a bright sun made it a perfect day to strip away their outer clothes and drift in some of the river ponds and the wide beautiful marshes that pro- liferated one after another along the shores of the Kennebec. They landed on one of the river's many small islands, picnicked, made love on a deep patch of grass in the shelter of thick shrubbery, Anna's cries of pleasure soft and plaintive as those of the distant gulls, lay naked there a long while, sunning themselves shoulder to shoulder, watching the gulls and the enormous black "shag," the cormorants, careen up and down the river in mysterious pursuits.

Mellowed by the love they had made, by Anna's soft cries, Jim talked a lot, reminisced about his boyhood in Maine and along this river, and of course he thought of his father and talked about him, talked a lot about him, remembering things that took him by sur- prise, that he hadn't thought about for years. Anna listened with interest, her face resting on her folded arms, her green eyes active, seeming to Jim not to take in light but to send it out; and when she looked at him, it was if she were touching him.

He stopped in the middle of a sentence and said, "You've got the most incredible eyes, Anna."

Anna grunted and smiled. "What's that got to do with anything?"

"It's got to do with everything," Jim said.

On the return trip to Boston that Sunday afternoon, they both rode uncomfortably, every inch of their bodies sunburned.

"You think anybody will notice at the office?" Jim asked. "Both of us red as lobsters?"

"They'll notice," Anna said. "I'm sure to get teased."

Jim confessed, finding it difficult to admit: "I never had such a good time, Anna. Never."

"I don't know why we left that little island." Anna touched him briefly. "Half my mind is still on it."

"It's a long winter," Jim said.

Anna scowled. "What's that supposed to mean?"

"That's the Mainer's excuse for all sorts of self-indulgence," Jim said. "It means we're entitled to a little pleasure, since we suffer so much otherwise."

"I'm not suffering much," Anna said. "Not lately."

"I'm glad to hear it," Jim said. "That's a two-way street." He would have said more, said that she had improved his life tremendously, but had a sudden inexplicable loss of nerve. If he had to confess to loving her, that would leave him exposed and vulnerable, and he would have to admit his dependence on her. She was wearing away at the shell he had put around his feelings, but it was still intact, and he preferred it that way. Sometimes, thinking of how much he cared for Anna, he panicked. He dreamed that she reached inside his body and put a hand on his beating heart. The dream terrified him. If he loved her, wouldn't she die? Wasn't that the rule?

When they arrived at Anna's apartment house, they sat in the car a long time, holding hands, kissing.

Anna said, "I've got to spend the night alone, Jim. You've got me all messed up."

"Sure," Jim said. He felt relief, because Anna had let him know what it was she wanted, and because it coincided with his desire, too. He needed a little time to rebuild his shell. He carried her bags inside to the elevator, kissed her good-bye, and then drove to a bar near his own place, feeling free and reckless, love-sated and without desire to do more than observe the life of the bar in silence, and drink. For three days, for Anna's sake, he had held back on alcohol, but now he could make up for lost time. Why shouldn't he? The island in the middle of the Kennebec already seemed far away, and was almost too small to show on anything but a topographical map. He wondered if it even had a name.

But Anna surprised him, and surprised him. He was defenseless against her, and this irritated him; and yet if he showed his resentment, or if he spent a day avoiding her, either to assert his independence a little or to hide a hangover, the all-day illness he felt for drinking most of the night, then he also felt pain. And when she was too busy, too distracted to pay attention to him, did not show him the customary little attentions that assured him he was favored, he felt alarm, a feeling that also humiliated him, it was so undignified. He didn't understand how this had happened to him, that his psyche had been taken captive, that he would feel such torture if she laid a hand on his arm in the midst of a hallway conversation, or did not touch him when he expected or hoped for it.

His deception bothered him, but he believed it was his own business after all, that his drinking existed in a corner of his life that no one could touch. In a way, it allowed him to regard Anna as an innocent, and he told himself he was protecting her from the truths of male life and of what he had learned in Viet Nam. He considered his drinking necessary, medicinal, and he had no intention of giving it up. Far from disrupting his life, drinking made it possible to bear it, to live and work among people whose values often mystified him, and who seemed often to go out of their way to make each other miserable. Unlike Jim, Anna was quite alert to office politics, the interplay and competition between the personalities in each department, and he sometimes listened with a kind of amused consternation to her analysis of the events and maneuverings of a given day, of the "management style" of a certain administrator, of power plays among department heads, of union decisions, of policy, of hirings and firings. She took it for granted he would also be interested in these things, especially since a change of boss could, in her view, enhance or impede his career, but Jim was just not that engaged in his work, and he certainly felt no loyalty to the *Globe*. He had a job. He did it. If the *Globe* didn't like it, to hell with it, he'd go somewhere, do something else.

Anna sensed this, and she told him, "You're making a mistake, Jim. These people are running scared half the time. They don't really know what they think about your work, whether they can really judge good from bad. They're inundated with stuff, they get confused, lose perspective. You've got to boost yourself a little, tell them what to think. Really, if you think they're going to appreciate good work on its merits, you're in for a disappointment. They've got tunnel vision. They're not looking out for other people. You've got to draw a little attention to yourself."

Jim took this in with a little sense of amazement. In the service, remaining anonymous was considered a survival technique, and it never occurred to him otherwise that people would not know how to regard the facts of the case. If he pulled a forty-pound striped bass over the gunwale, then there it was, tail banging against the bottom of the boat, its stripes glowing. No one would have to say, This is a big, this is a beautiful fish. If he presented pictures of children kneeling in the dirt beside the bloody body of what was once their mother, or of an entire acre of houses reduced to a jungle of rumpled steel and splintered beams, no one would have to explain the horror of it, would they? Wouldn't speech of any kind be redundant, even insulting, in these cases? And what could Anna possibly mean that the people they worked with and for were "running scared"?

Scared?

Scared was when the foliage around you was snapping, dropping down, and you did not know where the fire was coming from, or where to take cover. Scared was when the man next to you could not speak because his own entrails had been exploded into his mouth, and you turned from a day of drudgery to this impossible vision: a man's guts in his mouth, the light in his eyes raging. Scared was when you came home to your apartment and reached for the doorknob and couldn't force yourself to make contact, because going in meant trying to sleep, and remembering and dreaming, and so a nightcap or two was the first order of business. It was the damnedest thing when your own hand wouldn't let you in your own door and hung in front of you trembling, and then you were down at Riley's getting drunk and playing pool because nobody there had the least interest in interfering with your search for oblivion. That was scared. Whatever they were worried about in running the newspaper—advertising revenues, say, double-checking reports of a scandal, say—wasn't the same order of scared. Jim found it hard to get worked up over who got what promotions. He wasn't "scared" that he might lose his job. But he was scared. And Anna was beginning to scare him, too.

You know, he found himself thinking, she has this incredible energy. It's subversive. It's infiltrative. She has an incredible knack for waiting. Then she moves when you least expect it. And she always moves with assurance. She's hungry, too, but not selfish. Does she plan this, or is it all a matter of coincidence, or do I give some signal I don't even know I'm giving?

She was not a doll. She was not hiding from him. The next question was whether he could bear the truth of her. Sometimes he thought he might prefer it if she were simpleminded. Where did she get her understanding of people, of their maneuvering and relationships? Yes, but if she was really so smart, he sometimes thought, then why did she want anything to do with him? There were a lot of unattached men at the *Globe*. She could have done better, connected with someone who had good prospects and would advance in the hierarchy. On the other hand, if she was really so smart, then she wouldn't be so readily fooled by him. Right? This thought allowed him to keep Anna at a distance, even hold her in contempt sometimes, as long as she wasn't next to him looking up into his eyes with her curiosity and expectancy. When she was close to him, he always lost the battle not to care about her.

Then one Saturday morning Jim received a telephone call from the City Desk. Through a searing headache he learned that a paint factory in Brighton was ablaze and was told to get there as soon as possible with plenty of film. A writer that he would no doubt meet on the scene had already been dispatched. You could see the pillar of smoke from downtown, they said, twelve miles away, and of course the *Globe* wanted him there.

Jim, barely coherent, swore, launched himself unsteadily into motion, dressed hurriedly, grabbed his kit bag by the door as he lurched out, glad and sure he had taken the time to prepare it with all the film, lenses, filters he would need. Was the camera loaded, though? He checked it in the elevator on the way to the street, found it O.K. When he ran into the parking lot he was afraid for a moment he was going to be sick, and his hand was shaking so badly it took him a while to put the key in the door lock and a moment more to insert the ignition key. Already the car was hot, and it made Jim's head pound. Heat waves wrinkled the hood of the car, and he had a flash of Viet Nam. Once he had humped machine-gun ammo all afternoon. Afterwards, his head hurt all night, and he wondered if he was sweating any less now than on that day. He was barely on the road now and his clothes were soaked already. Even his socks felt damp, and it crossed his mind that the Viet Nam memory had originated there, from the feet up. All night long his head had pounded like this, and he had thought he would go crazy, the pain had been so relentless. And dry feet had been unheard of. It was a miracle they hadn't festered into mush.

Jim had to park about a half-mile from the fire because the roads were barricaded and opened only for emergency vehicles and fire trucks. He ran through a maze of thick hoses to where the black smoke roiled up in violent writhing columns, visible now between close-packed rows of apartment houses. People crowded down to their lawns to observe the fire, anxiety on their faces, as another and another fire truck came screaming down the streets.

Jim was panting when he reached the fire site, sweat stinging his eyes, and here the fire had a voice and stank and the heat of it radiated from everything—the walks, the trucks, the sides of the buildings—and he found himself seeking the heat "shadows," on the side of things away from the blaze. He snapped, moved, snapped, changed lenses to concentrate on the actions of a group of firemen securing a water cannon up close, frighteningly close to the smoldering building side. A dull bass thud rent the air and a ball of neon orange erupted within the structure, followed by what Jim thought an amazing sight. A huge metal drum rocketed into the air, arched over the fire trucks, then tumbled down into the neighborhood beyond. A few minutes later this happened again, and Jim began to understand why the residents nearby had shown such concern. Jim photographed the firemen up close, but kept checking the fire, too, for he wanted to capture the drums of paint exploding, then lifting into the air, plummeting down.

A television truck pulled in beside him, and Jim was instantly furious. He had had to run half a mile through crowds and hoses, but the television photographers were chauffeured right to the fire. And they parked—probably intentionally—so that he had to move now to keep from getting the truck and its lurid call-letter advertisement in his field of vision. The *Globe*, of course, would never run a fire photo with the competition featured so prominently in it. Jim couldn't help it, but the television guys really pissed him off. Prima donna bastards, he'd love to puncture the tires on their truck.

Jim zoomed in on the shield over the face of one of the firemen now. The thick plastic reflected the raging fire, and the fire seemed to be leaping from the man's throat, consuming his head.

A flurry of activity at one of the nearby command centers caught his attention, and Jim moved swiftly to it, hoping in part to catch up with the writer he'd been told would be on the scene. He moved in close to the captain, trying to eavesdrop on the radio talk. He understood enough of the communication to realize a pumper and a ladder truck were being sent into the neighborhood because one of the paint drums had crashed onto the roof of an apartment building and spilled flaming liquid down a ventilation shaft. The captain received this information and gave his orders with an incredible calm, though it was clear at once to Jim that this was, in fact, a terrifying development. The three- and four-story frame buildings of the neighborhood often shared a common side, or had only a driveway separating them; wooden fences snaked from yard to yard; dilapidated garages and sheds lay close behind the main buildings everywhere; rubbish containers and cylinders of propane gas lined every alley. With the resources of the fire department already concentrated on the paint factory, and with the water supply already challenged to meet the demand, an outbreak of fire amidst the nearby residences could all too swiftly lead to disaster. Jim grabbed one of the firemen by the sleeve of his black coat and asked him where the new fire had erupted. The man, otherwise engaged in spinning a chrome wheel to rechannel water flow from a pump, simply extended his arm and pointed off to his left. Jim stood away from the truck, craned his neck, and could see among the rooftops in the nearest block a greasy gray and brown smear of smoke. In the shadow of the truck, he reloaded his camera and took off at a run.

Even just a short distance from holocaust at the paint factory, among the houses of the neighborhood, the air seemed cool, and the world seemed normal—dogs yapped behind picket fences, laundry flapped on elevated lines, cars sat in driveways and along the curb, children played on the porches. But as he charged around the corner, clicking off the first frames of the roll of film, he barged into a line of spectators and saw ahead of him a roof crowned with flames, brown smoke wisping from upper-story windows. The front door to the building was open, and Jim saw a clutch of masked firemen rush in with a hose, yellow tanks swinging on their backs. He pushed through the crowd and started snapping pictures, and on the other side of the building caught a trio of firemen extending a ladder, twisting it into position, hauling on the rope which pulled up the top section by pulleys. Above them, in a window oozing brown smoke, Jim saw a black woman pressed to the glass, and below her own straining face, the faces of two children. Their mouths worked in silent terror as the woman struggled to open the window.

Jim, feeling a sickness that made his head howl, fell to his knees and automatically photographed these frames:

the woman's arm shattering the glass, and the jet of smoke that followed;

the ladder cracking against the side of the building, one fireman on its base already ascending;

the bloody arm outheld, a baby offered as the hands of the second child, brown palms against the remaining glass, clawed;

the baby falling, and the desperate reach of the fireman, his momentum and the weight of his gear causing the ladder to shift against the building;

the baby simply gone in the shrubbery below, the fireman aloft on the ladder agape, one on the ground already slashing into the bushes;

the window smashing open now, the woman leaning over the second child, hanging out into the fog of smoke, blind, shrieking, hysterical;

the embrace of the fireman, another on the ladder behind him not permitting him to fall, the second child passed down;

the mother out onto the ladder, skirt, hair smoldering, suddenly tottering, held, caught, pressed into the ladder;

another ladder banging beside the first, firemen swarming up, assisting;

the woman on her knees, wailing, the baby's face cupped with oxygen mask;

the flight to the ambulance;

the building, capped with flame, sending up a dark blue, black, and brown howl of smoke, the shattered window turning orange, a tumbling vertigo of smoke.

Jim leaned against a car gagging, his camera weighing him down like an anvil. Jesus Christ, he had just seen a baby fall three stories. He staggered into the street and was pushed aside by people loading blankets, boxes, clothing into cars.

"Comin' through here. Get out of the way, folks. Let the firemen through here."

Jim wound the film back into the canister, dropped it in his bag, reloaded. He took a few more photographs, then limped back to his car. If he didn't leave right away, he would surely get caught in this crazy exodus, he thought. Already the intersections were jammed with fleeing people—cars bedecked with mattresses, clothes flapping from open windows. Jim's last photograph: an old man hurrying down a steep flight of stairs, paper bags chock-full under each arm, and on his head three hats. The old man regarded the lens of the camera with a look of cruel wit: Three hats, that's right, and if you don't like it, you can kiss my big black butt!

Jim spent a long afternoon in the darkroom discovering photographs he had forgotten he had taken, the sequence of the falling baby had so jarred his mind, driven everything else out. The desk editor was practically watching over his shoulder as the photographs came out of the solution, and he sent one after another over the wire service.

"Jesus Christ," the editor kept saying. "Jesus Christ, Jim. Let me have that one, too."

"You can't run all of these," Jim said.

"I might try. Jesus."

The sequence of the failed rescue was going on the front page: the baby held through the shattered window, the baby falling, the fireman rushing to the ambulance and administering oxygen to the child in his arms.

He called Anna from the office, and she told him, yes, he should come and see her as soon as possible. He meant, he really meant, to go straight to her, but he had to stop for a drink, and then he had four, and when he arrived at Anna's apartment he felt as if his face were melting.

She let him in, not quite understanding, or misunderstanding his drunkenness for a mix of fatigue and despair.

She sat next to him on the sofa, and Jim collapsed onto her, his mind tumbling like smoke, half of him back in Hue watching the refugees flee rocket fire, half of him in Boston watching a flying baby disappear into green flames.

"I couldn't do anything," Jim said to Anna, his voice strange, strangulated, foreign. "I took pictures. I just took pictures."

"That's your job, Jim. You're not a fireman."

"But is that all I can do? Watch? The baby falling . . ."

"What do you think you could have done?"

"Something. Anything. Why did I come through it all if I can't do anything?"

"It's not your fault, Jim. The baby isn't your fault."

Anna wrapped his head in her arms, and Jim wept, a tremendous guilt soaking him, for his drunkenness, for his witness to death, for his inertia, for his love and terror and disgust, and for having survived a war. He wept the cycle that weeping takes, twenty minutes of weeping, and then Anna took his face in her hands and kissed him, and she said, "I think we should get married, Jim. I don't think we should wait too long to do it."

Jim shook his head, confused, unbelieving.

Anna went on. "I want my kids to have a father who cries about the right things. Do you understand me? I think we should have two kids."

"I'm not crying . . ." Jim tried to say, *About the right things, about what you think I am,* but Anna interrupted him with a laugh, squeezing his face tighter still.

"The hell you aren't," she said. She brushed his tears away with her fingers. "What do you call these? Snowflakes?"

They married in Maine, in a little church outside of Bath where Jim's mother had worshipped for many years. Jim's mother seemed to be the only one a ceremony meant anything to, and so they appeased her and pretended that it was the right, necessary, and desirable thing to do. Anna's parents flew to Portland from Pittsburgh and were more interested in fresh lobster to take back with them for a party than the wedding itself. They were professional people, modern, barely tolerant of the churchy business that meant so much to Jim's mother, and since their own marriage had not been especially happy, they had no illusions that their daughter was about to be launched into eons of bliss. They gave the newlyweds money, Jim found them a bushel of lobsters, and they left.

After the reception dissipated into a few of the *Globe* staffers hanging around to finish the wine, Jim and Anna made their getaway. Anna insisted they take the eggbeater out to the island they had discovered that summer, and though it utterly ruined her ninety-dollar wedding dress when they laid it on the patch of deep moss within the shrubbery, they were really and finally married there. Anna's cries were music to Jim, counterpointed by the rush of the water past their granite bed. They lingered on the island until it was almost too dark to go in, and Jim would remember it as the finest part of that day, the last slow hour of their coming down the river, Anna in the bow, kneeling, pricking the darkness with a bright beam from a flashlight, the water slightly darker than the sky, that wonderful bright beam suddenly lighting up and startling the crowds of ugly cormorants elbowing each other on the slimy rocks.

12
Mountain
Mists

Today Chong takes a little metal box full of brushes and watercolor powders and a pad of paper and sets out for the gazebo. This little half-shelter sits on top of Sweat Hill and is nothing more than six posts sunk into the ground and topped off with a steeply pitched hexagonal Chinese-curved roof. Three beams crisscross like an asterisk beneath this roof and provide support for a plywood sheet on which Chong has left a pot for boiling water, a can with tea bags and some crackers in it, a few extra wooden shingles for the roof, a ceramic pipe, a glass jar with matches in it, and other inconsequential odds and ends. In the gazebo is also a split-log bench and a "fireplace," a hole lined with rocks and covered with a rusting piece of heavy metal screen. It is a fine place to sit and be empty-headed, or to drink, shout poems, and sing foolish songs when his old comrade Wu comes up from New York to air out, to get the stink of exhaust fumes and chalk dust off his hide.

Wu! Chong loves him, the crazy old bastard. Wu, a mathematician, knows more poetry, Chinese and Western, than most poets. Once in a great while he writes Chong long, mind-boggling letters about radio waves, stars, the behavior of sunspots, black holes, genetics, women, contemporary life in China . . . everything! Chong wants so badly to have him come to the country for a visit.

Wu! Chong laughs, thinking of him. Wu certainly would like the gazebo with its hilltop view down into the state forest to the north, up to the fire tower on Mount Greentree in the east, over the Milliken orchards and the town of Lake Ecstasy to the west (the lake itself was too low to see), and, to the south, Chong's pond, the sparkling flow over the dam, and Chong's barn and house.

If only Wu would come in the winter, Chong thought. But he's teaching, he says, doing research, he says, he has tickets to the opera, blah, blah, blah. He needs to see the pond frozen over from up there, a full moon hanging behind it. Then he would understand some of those Manchurian poets better, the northern ones, and some of the Korean poets whom he claims to dislike so much, and those Japanese peasant-poets from Hokkaido, where the monkeys live in the snow of the mountains all year long, fur thick as rugs, and spend so much time in the warm water of the sulphur springs. In Chong's judgment, Wu's mind is still cradled in jungle and city; he needs a little snow and woods for balance.

That would interest Wu, the snow monkeys, the perpetually warm springs in a frozen place, the smell of the springs—monkey and sulphur rank. Earth and animal stink combined. Is that a natural idea? Chong wonders. Bogs stink. The sheep do not smell bad to the shepherd, but certainly they do to everyone else. Chi Pai-shih, who painted ox turds once: "In the morning, the dung on the road smells sweet." Surely the coyotes and the flies do not object to the sheep's aroma. Note how the dogs love to roll in the slime of a rotting pelt! Stir up the bottom of the pond where that gas of decaying leaves and aquatic life has been trapped in the silt; makes you gag, your eyes water. Worse than farts after five bottles of Tsingtao and two bowls of bean soup. Terrible! Rotten potatoes are not so vile.

As he walks along the path beside the barn on the way to the pond, Chong thinks, Suppose a man is born with the nose of dog. Will he be happy or miserable? Ten thousand odors a dog can smell, distinguish, according to Wu. A dog knows every other dog in the neighborhood by its asshole. He can pick out the smell of your tires on the road amidst all the others. He can smell a mouse in the wall, a female in heat, the trail of anything. A whole symphony of smells! Instead of music, the orchestra—no, the olfactestra—would produce smells—burning leaves, a quick shot of swamp gas or gasoline, unfolding of roses, daffodils, lilacs, the smell of fish, of the sea, a rice paddy, fresh parsnips sliced open, the smell of carrots just pulled from the soil, ganja . . . And what of bus exhaust? Cigarettes? The smell of the city, industry?

At the edge of the pond, Chong dips a jar into the water, then holds it up to the sun. The water is still springtime clear with only a few motes swirling in it, tiny particles of dirt, leaves, or grass broken down to dust by tumbling through the rocks upstream, perhaps tiny animals—though the water is still cold. In the summer the water will be green with minuscule plant and animal life, tea-brown with brewing leaves, yellow with bacteria, larvae, eggs, amoebae. If he used pond water in the summer for his watercolors, he would have to know how it would blend with his powders, how it would stain the paper. Perhaps it would also smell. Sure! he thinks. If you used pond water, the painting would smell. A dog would know. If we had noses like dogs, we might have "smellings" on the wall, dabs of peanut butter, a pressed daisy, a drop of camphor.

To cross the dam, Chong takes off his shoes and holds them in one hand, juggling his water jar and the paintbox in the other. The pressure of the flow over the dam is strong, the temperature cold, but not stinging cold now. Enlivening. He leaves his shoes off as he climbs the path which winds up the hill. Here the shrubbery is budding, the red bud casings are bursting, littering the ground, and the tiny green beads of the coming leaves color the air like smoke, a mist. The path is faintly visible, a gentle fold in the wet leaves, like a wrinkle in a carpet. Yes, it is time to write Wu a letter, to plan for a summer visit.

Before he crests the hill, Chong is aware of a faint smell of smoke. It stops him. And branches have been broken off some of the trees and shrubs. A few sheets of newspaper have caught in the underbrush. Is someone there? It has happened before—picnickers, hikers have passed through, leaving little evidence of their stay. But newspapers? Broken branches?

He mounts the top of the hill now and there spread out around the whole circumference of the gazebo is a cruel garden of broken glass—beer bottles—and metal cans, greasy wrapping paper, broken cardboard cartons: BUDWEISER, MILLERS, SCHLITZ. From the rear edge of the gazebo roof hangs a row of odd skinlike decorations. Chong slips on his sandals to navigate the sharp-edged trash. A wet log still smolders in the fire pit, half filled with blackened balls of aluminum foil, more broken glass, charred cans, half a brassiere.

The skinlike decorations prove to be prophylactics, the sperm in them half melting, half frozen in the sun.

The pillars of the gazebo have been slashed with obscenities—

among them, CHONG SUCKS—and the little paraphernalia he had left—the cooking pot, the matches, the extra shingles—has been thrown about like the rest of the litter.

The scene is so wearying, and to think of cleaning up is so wearying, the invasion of his private space is so dispiriting, Chong sinks down on the bench.

His hand slides in some dark filth, causing him to leap up and discover burning like fire on his hand the shit of his trespassers. It had been coiled like a snake there, dark as the wood, waiting for him.

He holds his hand away from him as if it were leprous, wants to amputate it, howls with misery. The graffiti shout at him:

FUCK YOU   EAT IT   SHIT   PISS   SUCK

Chong quickly finds a magazine in the litter and with one hand shakes out a few pages to wipe the shit from his hand and from the bench. On the pages are pictures of women with their legs spread, tongues licking the corners of their mouths, their breasts held as if aimed.

America! Chong thinks, throwing the fouled pages into the fire pit. What a symphony this will make for the dogs when it burns.

He holds his hand away from him as he retreats down the hill and hurries to the pond for a wash, to the barn for a wheelbarrow and a rake.

Matches, too, he reminds himself. I'll need matches for sure.

The next day Chong is in a funk. He feels as bad as if he had been robbed. They could have fouled any place within fifteen miles, so why did they choose his hilltop? Because of the gazebo there? and the fire pit? because it was his? because it belonged to a Chinese man? because it was remote?

During the cleanup, Chong discovered the access of the vandals was by a trail they had cut up from the fire road at the edge of the pond. The road was built ostensibly so trucks could draw water from the pond in the event of a forest fire, but it had been neglected for years and it was doubtful if any heavy equipment could negotiate it. The new trail up from the fire road was a crude rut, apparently torn out by motorcycles, and it was almost certain, Chong supposes, that a washout would be created there, an erosion gash, unless it is covered over and not used again.

He feels as if the motorcyclists have driven up the side of his head, etched a line in his brain. He is too angry to paint, throws his brushes down and stomps out of the house to talk to Luan.

"Tiger traps," Chong says to the pig. "I'll dig a hole, like for an outhouse, see? and I'll plant stakes in the bottom. Then I'll take some of your shit, some of mine, toss it in there. You get the idea?"

The little pig hobbles across the sty, rubs his shoulder on a board.

"Their motorcycles will fall right through the cover, see? You cross a few sticks over the hole, cardboard, cover the whole thing with a layer of dirt, then some leaves. *Brrrrnnnn!* Here they come! *Snap . . . crash!* Yaaaa! Listen to them scream!"

The pig squeals.

"That's right."

Now they have the shit-covered stakes rammed right through them. They are thrashing around in the tiger pit, spouting blood, screaming. The motorcycle is still roaring, thrashing, too.

Chong feels ill now. Suppose you get the wrong one. Suppose you get a hunter. Suppose you get a pretty young woman who rides a horse. You could hear a horse punctured by a stake.

Damn it! These kids—if it is kids, Chong reminds himself—have ruined my thinking today. So much horror. Revenge. Fear. Hate.

"Leave me alone!" Chong shouts, loud enough to startle the pig, who stumbles over himself hurrying into the barn through a square hole cut in the wall. In a moment, the pig sticks his snout into the sunlight and regards Chong with suspicion.

"You'd better be afraid," Chong says. "When Wu comes, we'll put you on a spit. We'll build a fire on the hill, and we'll cook you all night long. That's right. We'll run you through with this long metal stake and turn your body over the flames. Then our teeth will tear you apart."

Chong gnashes his teeth in demonstration for the pig. The pig comes out into the sunshine anyway, roots under a board until he finds grubs or angleworms that he lustily gobbles down.

In his mind, Chong continues building tiger traps, skewering motorcycles. He strips the ozone layer from the sky so the skin of everything turns black as marshmallows held too close to the campfire. He presses the button to initiate World War III, hears the crump of napalm over the nearby trees, the electric crackle of a distant atomic bomb whose hot death rays lash out like a storm on the surface of the sun—the ice caps melt and flood the continents, earthquakes tear huge cities down, the whole damn world convulses, roars, disintegrates to ash.

Chong cowers under a canopy of his own laced fingers. Just a few months ago, he left the city to stop feeling like this, that the drone of idiot bombers was perpetual. *Now what?*

13
Home
Front
[iii]

Boston was manageable, if a little mad, but most of all it was winter. Having grown up in Maine, Jim thought he should have been more patient with this interminable season, but winter was a different species in the city. The few times he had felt the winter was honest was when the weather was described as "terrible," when a blizzard shut down the whole city and you could walk through streets where cars were just clean white quiet shapes, like big sleeping animals under a blanket. Or when it rained so hard he could not see out the windows of his car, or the bar he had holed up in.

He and Anna lived in Cambridge, in an apartment that had a view of the Charles River from the bedroom, if you opened the window and leaned out, so the commute to work was not long, even if lunatic. They rode into work together, but rarely returned at the same time. Anna's hours were more regular, and Jim sometimes had evening assignments, or invented them so he could stay out and drink. Anna did not seem to mind long hours alone. She read, went to an exercise class, she took an occasional adult education course, but mainly she was glad to unwind from the pressures of work and enjoy a quiet evening. They made love mainly on weekends, often in the mornings, for they had few interruptions then and could arrange those days as they pleased.

With two incomes, they were also fairly comfortable. Anna was a little disturbed sometimes that Jim never seemed to have any money, and of course the reason was that he could spend ten, twenty dollars a day on drinks, especially since he tried not to drink too much at home, to keep his habit private.

When Anna questioned him about money, he joked, saying, "You don't understand do you? These days it costs twenty dollars to walk around the block."

She was curious, but she didn't press Jim about his finances. She understood that it cost a fortune to live in the city, and sometimes when they were out on the road, going to dinner, a show, a party, or traveling to Maine, they talked about buying a house in the suburbs, or even further out. They drove through some neighborhoods looking at houses, but in the end they agreed that there was no middle ground for them and they would be happy only in the city or in the country. Suburban life seemed a little too orderly, less open to spontaneous indulgence.

"Maybe when we have kids, though," Anna would say. "It's good for kids to have others to grow up with."

"They learn how to fight," Jim said.

"Sure, but they learn how to get along, too."

Sometimes the news in the papers about Viet Nam, about the protests or "secret" bombings or attempts to find a way out, left Jim smoldering and depressed, unable to talk. Sometimes at parties the war was discussed among his or Anna's friends, and though he was deferred to as a veteran, he found that usually he had nothing to say that would make any sense, the gulf was so great, and not reducible to matters of democracy and communism, political pragmatics, international law, or treaties. Viet Nam was a trick bag, and if Jim thought it had more to do with the many and alien faces of God than the wills of men, this was not the kind of thing he could say to young professionals whose very lives were premised on the ability to manage and control events. In fact, he felt it was not the kind of thing he could say to anyone, not even Anna. He tried to communicate to her how difficult it was, even for someone lying in the dirt of Viet Nam, suffering its heat and rain and bombed-out highways, to know it, its reality, but he never in talking to her blamed it on God. That was something he kept to himself, so she could not see that the war had shaken him free of an ongoing faith in reason, that he was crazy but managing, as he had managed even in Viet Nam, to play the sanity game. *I know what makes sense,* he thought, *only it doesn't.* Anna would not understand what he meant by that, but Red Barber would, Jim believed.

Red Barber had said, "Viet Nam is a reality warp. You step into that place, and you really are somewhere else. Like traveling at the speed of light or something. What you've got to do is leave it there."

Jim thought this was good advice, but sometimes Viet Nam leaked into Boston. He could look at Anna sitting next to him on the sofa and think, My God, who is she? Where did she come from? What are we doing here?

And when Saigon fell at last, and Jim pored through the pictures coming in over the wire of the mobs swarming helicopter doors, the planes loaded with children that went down, the boats so crammed with people their gunwales lapped water, he fell into a silence so deep he was not sure he would ever recover. There was that sense of frustration, that the war had been lost, that the national will had flagged after such prolonged effort, that the sense of mission had changed, a mistake had been made, that old ways of negotiating the world had proved obsolete, that the good will and suffering of the soldier, that the heroism, would be construed as hubris, even mur-derousness. He could have managed this as something horrible and tragic for the moment, a shudder in the evolution of world destiny. But the defeat was not just frustrating; it threatened his grip on things. The reality warp had spilled over into America, into Boston, and blessed be the ignorant, Jim thought, for they can remain sane. They can think of it as just another war and call it history.

Anna, meanwhile, did not become pregnant. She was disturbed about this and sought medical opinion, and the doctors assured her she was healthy and it was only a matter of chance. After a while, Jim went for a checkup, too, and was pronounced potent. One doc-tor asked him about his drinking, but Jim was noncommittal in his reply. He knew he wanted to avoid doctors because of questions like that, but for Anna's sake he had gone, and now they were sure it was only a matter of time.

Two, three years went by, and nothing changed. They had their usual checkups, but the doctors could not explain the failure to con-ceive. Something seemed to go out of Anna in that third year, as if she had become resigned to a childless life, and she became more ag-gressive in her demands for attention, and promotion, on the job. One of her supervisors apparently resented this, and she became in-volved in a wearying, unfruitful battle of personalities. She was also less lively with Jim, and their life together became almost unconscious, a web of habits.

In a way, Jim didn't mind, because he was also more caught up in his work, and his photographs had been noticed and appreciated elsewhere in the country. He had even received telephone calls from editors in Atlanta, Austin, Milwaukee, and elsewhere inquiring whether he was looking for a change. The offers hinted at were attractive, but Anna did not really want to change jobs now, because she had made such an effort and was on the verge of moving up herself. If she had been pregnant, Jim thought, they probably would have left Boston in a minute. He wondered sometimes if she could be made pregnant by another man; and he wondered if in turning aside these job offers, he wasn't making a mistake, for both of them.

When they made love now, Jim thought he could feel Anna grinding her teeth, as if in revulsion, as if he were doing something to her that she didn't like, as if he might even be hurting her. He tried being more attentive, even more affectionate during the days when they were together, but he could not seem to inspire her again and felt himself a failure, and sometimes he blamed this on her and resented her for making him a failure. And sometimes he was too tired or too secretly drunk to make love, and he really didn't care how she felt. That troubled him the most, when he thought of it: His main interest was still in remaining comparatively numb. He even became so unconcerned about Anna's reactions that he became careless and began drinking more at home, more often. In the first years of their marriage, she would have said something about this, but now said nothing when he had another, and another, and did not seem to observe how much he poured into each glass.

At the end of six years, they rarely even saw each other. Anna left for work early now, and Jim started his day at two in the afternoon. They had arranged to have the same days off, but much of his time was spent in doing chores—laundry, groceries, running errands—and they made no real effort to plan for time together, indeed by some tacit agreement even to stay out of each other's way and to cease all inquiries about feelings, desires, hopes, and fears. It was not a great life, but they were comfortable, and there were people a lot worse off. Their work was the main thing; their relationship simply stalled and in some ways atrophied. They weren't warring, and they were too busy to be bored, and time went by.

In the winter of 1978, Jim asked to be promoted to a desk job, a photography editor's post, but a position had not really come open, and he was told his request would have to remain "under consideration" for a while. They gave him a modest raise and encouraged him. They could see that he was getting itchy feet and a little tired of chasing fire engines and photographing wrecks. There was some talk of maybe making him a trainer in photography and darkroom techniques. They valued his expertise and experience, but . . .

Then a series of fires broke out in the city, and if Jim had felt the first one was a routine assignment, the others that followed so quickly were so ruthlessly, so professionally calculated that he became enraged. A crack in his numbness opened, and the heat of these fires seemed to reach into it and germinate a seed long since dormant within him; and he found himself driving through the city, pounding down the hallways at work, elbowing up to the bar in a constant state of rage. He said, and believed, his fury was with the arsonists. He would grab his editor by the shoulder and through teeth clenched so hard his temples throbbed he would describe what he had photographed, the destruction, the terrible efforts of the firemen, the endangered homes, the innocent victims. He raged against the callous disregard of the arsonists, the greed that drove them to such endangering crimes.

"Does this surprise you?" the editor asked. "How long have you been doing this anyway? You didn't know by now?"

"You think that makes it right, because you're used to it?" Jim bellowed.

"Hey, take it easy. I'm not setting the fires, remember?"

"It really pisses me off," Jim said.

"You'll get an ulcer," the editor said.

"Everybody should have an ulcer."

"Why give them the satisfaction?" the editor said.

"I'd love to get one of those guys," Jim said.

"Oh, sure," the editor said. "Then we'd find *you* in the trunk of a car someplace."

Jim seethed. He followed the investigation closely, more closely than the assigned writer, Al Lamont, and this caused friction.

"I'm the writer," Al insisted one afternoon. "Let me ask the questions, O.K.? I can't get the cops to answer if you keep jumping in on me. Believe it or not, there's a technique to this, see? It involves something called tact. Get it?"

"Don't condescend to me," Jim said.

"O.K.," Al said, "let's lighten up, right? We're going to be working on this together for a long time maybe. So let's just be cool."

Over drinks at a bar one afternoon, Jim learned that Al had been a Boston College student who in 1968 had joined a protest against the Viet Nam war which ended in lobbing eggs at Hubert Humphrey, who had come to campus for a campaign speech and who had tried to defend "Johnson's war." Jim had heard talk like this for years, and it always sent him away in a pocket of reserve and numbness, because he knew it was Normal talk, sensible criticism of a politically stupid war, and he had not allowed himself to take it personally. But something about Lamont's smugness made Jim grind his teeth.

He said, "In 1968, you fuckin' cracker, I was taking rocket fire up the ass in Hue. I saw guys get their jaws blown off. Saw kids without feet."

"*What?*" Al threw open his arms in a gesture of outraged innocence. "What did I just say? What did you think, that we wanted you to be there? Why were we protesting but we didn't want you to have to be there?"

"Throwing fucking eggs," Jim spat. He called the bartender down and pointed. "Give me a couple of those pickled eggs. I want to show this guy what to do with an egg."

"Don't give it to him," Al warned the bartender. "This guy's drunk, and he's mad, and if you give him that egg—"

"You're goddamned right," Jim said. "Me and Hubert Humphrey, one of the greatest senators ever, are going to give you an egg suppository."

Al slapped his drink on the bar and with a look of fury hurried outside.

"You still want that egg?" the bartender asked.

"Where were you in 1968?" Jim challenged him.

"None of your fucking business," the bartender said. "But it was a motor pool in Bonn, Germany."

"O.K.," Jim said, feeling a little ill, "it was none of my business. I'm sorry, all right?"

"That's your last drink," the bartender said.

"What?"

"You're eighty-sixed, pal, and I hope you're not driving."

"Christ almighty," Jim said. "What's going on around here?"

"You're scaring the people out of my place, that's what. You're bad for business, pal."

Jim considered hurling his glass into the mirror, but finished his

drink and returned to the office. Lamont clicked away at the typewriter, pretending not to see him, and Jim went down the steps to
the darkroom, where he could be alone for a while. He was surprised at himself. He couldn't believe how angry he felt. It was all
he could do to keep from smashing beakers and lights, throwing
trays around. Cool it, he told himself. Go slow. This is Normal Land.
We don't set up perimeters here.

A few days later Jim apologized to Lamont, took him to lunch,
and picked up the check, something he had grown adept at avoiding
because it cut into his drinking money. It was, in fact, one of the
little strategies of maintaining his habit that he spent as little as possible on anything else. When he pulled up to the gasoline pumps, he
bought only as much as necessary to get him where he was going,
even though this sometimes inconvenienced him greatly, and on
more than a few occasions he had courted running out of gas on his
way to an assignment.

Lamont, habitually nervous, was surprisingly gracious about the
apology.

"It's just real important for us to get along," he said. "I'm not in
love with this job in the first place."

"I just got out of control there," Jim said. "I can handle it now."

"I know you guys went through hell," Lamont said. "Believe it or
not, I know something about it. I have a stack of letters"—he indicated a sizable pile between the sandwich of his hands—"from my
brother. My older brother."

"You didn't tell me," Jim said. "You should have said something.
Where was he?"

"Pleiku," Lamont said.

"Marine?"

"Yeah," Lamont said. "He was real gung ho."

Jim sucked air between his teeth. "Did he make it?"

"No." Lamont eyed Jim, sipped his white wine.

Jim sagged a little in his chair, appetite gone. "You should've said
something."

Lamont shrugged. "I thought I'd write a book, you know, based
on the letters. But other books came out, and this got away from me,
you know. I wanted people to know what he had gone through. And
what the military had done to him."

"It's crazy," Jim said.

"It sure is," Lamont said. "It's like he just wasn't content to live his own life. He had to be a part of something, and was willing to give up his personal freedom for it."

"Yeah, but for what?"

"That's what we say." Lamont twirled the glass in his hands. "That's not what he said. He talked about Marines like gods or something."

"They made a 'man' out of him, just like they used to advertise."

Lamont shook his head. "No. They did more than that. They reconstructed him. This guy had an inferiority complex a yard wide; he was scared of failing, having trouble finding a job. He was ripe for the plucking."

"And they plucked."

"It was his choice," Lamont said. "He could have taken his chances in the Army. But he really got into the Marine myth, you know."

"Like religion."

"Very much like religion," Lamont agreed. "Too damned much like religion."

"I can understand it," Jim said. "We had a lot of respect for the Green Berets, Airborne, you know? They were supposed to know all this mysterious stuff, how to kill with the chop of a hand. Magic. Very powerful."

"I can understand it, too," Lamont said. "I root for Superman in the movies like everybody else. The only thing I don't understand is why a guy volunteers for slavery. And these guys are volunteering for it, they're trusting the people who run the show with their very lives and minds, and they come out of it thinking they're somehow better off as slaves in uniform. I don't get it. They get swallowed up in some Idea, capital I. All over the world this happens, people throwing themselves on the swords of the 'enemy' in the name of something. Take the Middle East. It's a madhouse of Ideas and allegiances. Fanatics galore. What a meat grinder. That's why I hate ideas."

"Yeah, O.K.," Jim said. "You Irish anarchist."

Lamont considered this, a playful smile on his face. "Let's just say I'm not a political fetishist. I don't like ideas, and I don't like flags, because as far as I'm concerned, they're just meat grinders."

Jim laughed, a little embarrassed. The "flag" meant so many different things to him now. He had one, and he flew it from the balcony on veterans' holidays, because he believed he had earned the right to fly it. But when he saw the flag worn like a chip on the shoulders of the city police and firemen, it angered him, and he wasn't sure why. They weren't military personnel. And yet they draped their coffins in the flag, too, like those of his comrades, like that of Lamont's brother. The whole idea made him sick. Was Death, was God, an American?

He asked Lamont, "These arsonists now. What flag are they under? Italian?"

"Not even if they're Mafia." Lamont grinned. "It's the same flag as ours, the true American flag."

"Real patriots, huh?"

"You don't get it," Lamont said. "The real American flag is green." He rubbed thumb and forefinger together. "It has an American president's face in the middle. It has serial numbers on it."

"How did you ever get a job on the *Globe?*" Jim asked.

"I was a Young Republican when they hired me."

"And I was Malcolm X."

"Really. But ten years in this business, and I guess your principles get rusty." He laughed. "I even bought a GM car this year. And I don't see you carrying any banners, wearing any buttons."

Jim winced. "I was in the meat grinder. I guess I should know better."

Lamont raised his hand in mock protest. "I'm not telling you what to think!"

Although he technically had the afternoon off, Jim hung around the file room going over contact sheets he had made of the recent arson fires, running the magnifying glass from frame to frame. Somehow he couldn't let the story rest, and he was a little embarrassed with himself, not knowing what he was doing, really, or why. In part, his anger with the fires drove him to this fruitless business, he supposed. But what the hell was he looking for?

"Hey." Anna startled him, laid a hand on his forearm. "I thought you were off, and working tonight."

"Right."

"And you're still here?"

Jim shrugged. "I guess I am."

"You can't let it rest, can you?"

"It's bugging me, you're right."

"What do you expect to find?"

"I don't know," Jim said. "Something tells me I'll find something."

"What time are you going to be home?"

"Whenever that stupid gala is over."

"Do you have to stay for the whole thing?"

"It really depends on the governor, whether he'll give us a photo opportunity in advance, or whether we'll have to endure the whole show."

"I won't wait up, I guess."

"Don't," Jim said.

"But wake me," Anna said. "I might have something to tell you."

"Might have? What?"

"I'm not telling you here."

"Don't tease me."

Anna kissed him on the cheek and walked off, swinging a little in a way he used to like but hadn't seen or hadn't noticed for years.

He slid the magnifying glass from frame to frame, and he thought, It finally happened. Now. She's pregnant now, and I'm not sure I want to hear that. Now. Do I? You'd think I'd feel good about something, he thought. About that. Something's wrong with me if I can't feel good about that. He saw that his hand was trembling a little and decided he would get out of the office, have a drink someplace, and think this over. Pregnant! Now!

And then a face rose out of the murk, a white-haired man leaning over one of the portable barricades, his mouth open as if shouting, but in what also seemed a kind of ecstasy, his gaze locked on the fire. A kook, maybe. The face, small as it was in the contact print, seemed familiar, and Jim flipped back through the stack of prints to an earlier fire and he concentrated now on the faces of the people in the crowds, an odd, slightly disturbing exercise, face after face caught in an instant of unguarded panic or anger or excitement or wonder. Face after face, and then there he was again. Him!

This time he had caught the face just behind the shoulder of a fireman, thick with eyebrows over harried eyes, a look of swooning, almost of passion, but his body obscured.

I've *seen* that guy, Jim thought. Then he wondered, his excitement ebbing momentarily, Maybe he's a detective. Maybe that's where I've seen him, on the investigating force. The guy had a crease in the middle of his forehead, almost like a scar, a cleft of some kind. That look on his face, though. That was orgasm. Wasn't it?

So now she gets pregnant, Jim thought. Man! Six years ago I was ready for it. He shuffled through the contacts of yet another fire, and again he found the man in the crowd, this time with hands in his pockets, turning his head to spit into a gutter, as usual as close to the fire as anyone could be.

Jim circled the photographs, and though it was against policy he put the contact sheets in a large manila envelope and carried them out of the room. Upstairs, he tried to find Lamont, but the writer was out on an interview, and Jim had no desire to wait until he returned, especially when he wasn't getting paid for it; he grabbed his coat and went out. On the street, he supposed he should have left Lamont a note, but to hell with it; he'd call him later, if necessary. Why get Al all bothered if this was just a wild-goose chase, if the guy in the pictures was a police plainclothes detective, or some well-known fire kook, or something?

The detective Jim knew best was Phil Delancey, a morose older man who moved with all the speed of a drugged moose, and whose haggard face and wrinkled eyes had earned him the nickname "Elephant Man." Delancey bore this insult with the same stoic placidity that he carried with him on every investigation, no matter how sordid the details or how shocking the results. The writers avoided Phil because he never had anything to tell them except the facts, lacked the flair for making dramatic, printable statements that Chief Investigator William Harrow had learned in his years in office.

Delancey would tell you, "The arsonists used a chlorine-based combination retarded fuse to ignite the accelerant, of which they must have used at least six gallons to achieve the temperature increase they did so quickly." But Harrow would say, "These criminals used every nefarious trick in the book to make sure the fire would be out of control before the firemen of this city could battle the blaze."

Delancey was the better cop, Harrow the better talker, and Harrow was the boss.

"I got two minutes for you," Delancey said, throwing open the glass door to the little cubicle he called an office.

"I'm not here for the *Globe*," Jim said. "I'm here as a witness or something."

"Don't tell me that," Delancey said. "I'll have to fill out a form on you. What have you got?"

Jim opened the envelope and showed Delancey the photos he had taken, the face of the man who appeared in the crowds at three separate fires.

"It's the same guy?" Delancey said. "I can't see these tiny goddamn things without my glasses. Shit, this job has ruined my eyes."

"It's the same guy, yeah. I wondered if he's a detective."

"Wait a minute." Delancey lumbered out of the little office and quickly returned with a young black officer in uniform who carried a briefcase under his arm.

"Jim Williams, Officer Green," Delancey said. "Green's going to do a composite from the photos, then we'll run that through the computer, or have somebody check it against the files."

Green went to work, matching features and facial shapes, hair, ears, chin, from those on the transparent plastic sheets to those in photographs. "I don't recognize this guy," Green said. "I don't believe he's on the force."

Delancey eyed Jim a moment. "Your boss know you brought these over?"

"No."

"They never want to give us anything," Delancey said. "They don't want to become an arm of the law. How come?"

"How much credibility would we have—"

"I understand that," Delancey interrupted. "I mean, how come you brought this stuff over?"

"I guess I got mad," Jim said.

"You *guess?*"

"I got mad, yeah," Jim corrected himself.

"I'll do you a favor," Delancey said. "I won't consider this a precedent. This could be a breakthrough for us, but on the other hand, you know what a pain in the ass it is to get evidence from the newspaper? I mean, to use in court?"

"Just let me know if it leads to anything, O.K.? I'd love to see these guys get nailed."

"Yeah, sure."

"Wouldn't you?"

Delancey shrugged. "It's a job. I get pissed, sure, but I can get pissed at the mayor, too. My doctor advises against it. You got one stomach, he says, one ass, one liver, one heart. He advises me that being pissed off is not good for any of these."

Jim scoffed. "How can you not be pissed off?"

"Two ways," Delancey said. "They can give you pills for it, which I got dozens of." He opened and slammed a desk drawer for emphasis. "Or you can take a 'professional' stance, which is called detachment."

"Detachment, huh?"

Delancey tapped his coat pocket. "Screw that Zen stuff. I take the pills."

Jim laughed. "I'll remember that."

"Besides," Delancey said, "in a pinch, you can sell the pills."

Green handed Jim the photographs, and turned the kit around so he and Delancey could see the likeness he had conjured up.

"Jesus, he looks like Einstein," Delancey said, "if Einstein had got his mustache knocked off by Cassius Clay."

"Muhammad Ali," Green said.

"Him, too," Delancey said. "Somebody sure as hell has punched this guy a time or two."

Jim was tired when he came out of the police offices on the lower floor of City Hall, and he considered heading for the apartment and a nap before the "gubernatorial gala" he was supposed to photograph in the evening. But the event was taking place only a few blocks away, and it seemed silly to fight traffic all the way out to Cambridge and back again. He had some dry cleaning to pick up, but that could wait, and he had nothing special he had to do otherwise. With a slice of panic, he thought, Maybe I ought to go look for a crib or something.

Or take some photographs. This thought made him grind his teeth. *Of what?* It had been a long time since Jim had just taken his camera and cruised around the city looking for something to shoot. But he was fatigued already, and in for a long evening of work, and decided he would just hole up in a quiet bar and read the papers and the newsweeklies over a couple of beers. Jim thought he should be freelancing some of his work, and at a tobacco shop he bought a stack of magazines, a little alarmed at the total price, kicked himself for not going to the library for this kind of research. But you couldn't get a beer at the library, and besides, going there meant driving, parking, all that hassle. He took his magazines into a saloon down the street, crashed into a corner booth, and began to read and to drink.

One of the magazines he had purchased was a men's magazine with abundant erotic photographs. The magazine would have made Anna nervous, Jim knew, and though he didn't like them very much himself, he was a little irritated by Anna's prudishness, her insecurity about her sexuality, which Jim thought potentially wonderful. He wondered how much the photographers made and where they found the models—a never-ending stream of them—and what sort of contracts were drawn up with the models and the magazines. The magazine bothered him because it conjured up so many questions. He just couldn't see the stuff as pornography, except the minute quantity of it that hinted of violence, and he thought that if anyone was being exploited by the product it was the men who bought it. Jim understood why men bought the magazine: because they were afraid of real women. In fact, the magazine might help to erase that fear, if maybe not in the best possible way. Jim thought that what the magazine said about men and their fantasy lives or needs was far worse than what they said about women. The magazines weren't even about women, as he saw it, not real women, maybe not even about T. and A., but about the male lack of courage when confronted with the female animal, so mystified by culture and religion. The magazines had helped Jim battle his Congregational upbringing and to accept pleasure as a right instead of a sin, but then he had outgrown them and took little interest.

Still, the magazine made him sad, because it reminded him that sex with Anna had lost luster, that his moves and hers had become mechanical, often abbreviated in concession to their fatigue; it had become almost ritualized. What could he do to reinvigorate it? What could he do to reinvigorate his whole damned life?

The question of whether or not he could make any money on T. and A. photos was settled, for no matter how lucrative it might be, he couldn't do it, constitutionally. And he wondered if he could take photographs of real women, and what a magazine about real women would be like. The idea stayed in his mind like a cloud as he leafed through the other publications and found next to an advertisement for sheer stockings, with shapely legs jutting across the page, a be-shawled Syrian woman clutching a large child with a slash of blood across his head. The Syrian woman howled in anger and sorrow. The woman in the stocking ad smiled a teasing smile. There were pictures of women sorting numbly through the tornado wreckage of their homes in Mississippi, in shock of dispossession, of actresses swinging furs through doors of famous restaurants, of secretaries clicking to work in Chicago, hands gripping the lapels of their coats closed against a chill and grimy wind. How did you break through these surfaces, calculated and uncalculated, to find what Woman was?

Maybe, Jim thought, I should just go up to Maine and take a lot of pictures of my mother. Before she dies. The idea struck him as very painful, looking that closely at his own mother, subjecting her, who would be unwilling in any event, to such scrutiny. Could he take pictures of his mother undressing for the shower, say? "Lady in the Bath," a clichéd T. and A. routine, turned on Mom. Jim shuddered. Jesus, but reality was rugged. Much easier to photograph Anna, though she would object, too. Why these dynamics? Jim laughed at the realization that when it came to people at least there was no such thing as an innocent photograph. Baby falls into shrubbery: Was that pornography? Anna, hiking up a trail in the Maine woods, sunlight caught in her pale hair as if crowned with fire, one eye closed in protest against the camera: Pornography, too? Baby pictures, waiting like a vulture for the smile.

Jim pushed the magazines away and drank his beer in a blank, black mood. Two men came in that he recognized as councilmen, and he quickly stacked the magazines so the erotic one was out of sight. The pols wouldn't bother him, nodded, then sleazed off to a corner of their own. The waiter showed up and Jim ordered another beer, then, as an afterthought, a whiskey on the rocks. Watch it, he told himself. It's a long time until 8 P.M. When the waiter brought the drinks, Jim let the whiskey sit in the center of the table a long time, hoping he would have the simple wisdom and the willpower, to leave it there. Twenty minutes later he failed.

He had never been too drunk to work before, but that night Jim was dangerously smashed. He wasn't quite sure how it had happened, and he was a little panicked as he went into the Hilton that his determination to act soberly was not up to the reality of his physical condition. Lamont was onto him at once, saying, "Can you handle it, Jim? Man, you are really fucked up."

"I gan handul id," Jim said.

"I've still got time to call somebody."

"Id's O.K." Jim's voice rose in irritation.

"Man, I don't know," Lamont said. "Whatever you do, don't talk to anybody. I'll do the name-taking. Hear me?"

"Hear you."

There was no "photo opportunity," and Jim had to take his photographs from the floor, from between rows of tables, anywhere he could, as the dignitaries sat at a long linen-covered table strewn with photographic obstacles—flower arrangements, candleholders, wine baskets. In the best of circumstances, such a sprawling, cluttered setting proved problematic enough, but tonight Jim could not even focus, and he could not really anticipate where the action would flow next. Adding to his difficulties was the presence of television crews, teams from two channels, with their intense garish lighting and the simple menacing bulk of their gear, which they rolled into

place with utter disregard for who might otherwise be in the way.
Jim went through the motions, trying to be as unobtrusive as possible, convinced he was managing, sure he would have something
on film the *Globe* could use. An event this ceremonial was hard for
him to take seriously in any case. All he needed was a good shot of
the governor smiling, close to his wife, that could run on page one,
and everybody would be happy.

Lamont pulled him aside. "What the hell have you got all over
your sleeve, man?"

Jim inspected his coat, discovered from elbow to cuff a thick white
paste. Lamont grabbed his wrist and brushed the mess off with a
napkin. "Potatoes," he hissed. "You stuck your arm in somebody's
potatoes, man!"

"Fuck," Jim said, too loudly.

"You get anything?" Lamont whispered. "Maybe you'd better get
out of here. I hope to hell you've got something printable."

"Sure I do," Jim said. "I'm good."

"Yeah, you're Ansel Adams," Lamont said. "So beat it. I'll see you
later."

Jim lurched between the wall and a long table full of chattering
people, out of the ballroom. As soon as he was in the hallway, his
stomach cramped and he plunged along to a men's room, shoved
into a stall, went down to his knees, camera bag slamming the stool,
and disgorged violently. When the spasm passed, Jim flushed the
mess away and cleaned himself up at the sink. His eyes were red,
his hair matted, and he smelled of sweat and sickness. He washed
his mouth out, spitting into the sink, to the disgust of the others
milling about there. Jim couldn't look at any of them. *Never happened before. Not this!* He sucked in air and fled, feeling ill again in
the lobby and forcing himself to breathe deeply, get control of his
guts. *Glad Lamont didn't see.* He caught a cab, swayed in a vertigo
to the *Globe* offices, and found himself in the darkroom struggling
to stay awake, to wind the film into the developing drum without
twisting or tearing or fouling it against itself. *Set the timer. Right.
Doing everything I should. Right? No sweat. Something will come
out. Now we put the cap on. Now we put the tank on the rollers,
turn on the switch. O.K. No sweat. Now we can turn on the lights.*

Jim had taken about twenty pictures, and he only needed one or
two good shots, and he was not anxious about this, because even a
chimpanzee, he thought, could come up with something usable,
given those odds—one in ten, one in twenty. But when the film came

out of the rinse and he held it up to the light, he was staggered by
the realization that he had made a fundamental, amateurish mistake.
About half of each and every frame was black. Black! He sat down
on a stool with the negatives dripping away between his fingers. He
had not set the camera for use with the flash, and the little mirror
inside the housing did not, therefore, snap out of the way so that the
reflected light could etch the film in a single burst. Twenty times he
had photographed the shadow of the mirror as it followed its normal daylight course, which painted the film in a comparative strip
of time, from one side to the other.

Jim sat in a stupor until he found the courage to review the negatives, hoping to find something salvageable in the half-frames that
were properly exposed. It was all a disaster. The governor's face was
slashed with shadow time and time again. Jim clenched his fists and
groaned aloud. Christ! Would he have to go back to the Hilton?
Would he have time to try again?

Again he perused the frames, slowly now, looking for anything
salvageable. Because the governor's wife had been to his left, her
face emerged from the photographs unclouded, now serious, now
coy, now lit up with laughter. And in one of these half-frames, the
governor was visible behind her, out of focus slightly, his head bent
to the whispering of another tuxedoed politician Lamont would
surely recognize. O.K., Jim thought, that's what I have to do, "reactions of the governor's wife," talk them into running three frames
instead of one. He set up the developer now and in the full red glow
of the safety lights began his attempt to rescue the evening's work,
burning the image of the governor's wife onto paper after paper.

When he came in later, Lamont, tired and irritated, looked the
photographs over in weary disgust. "I don't know if they're going to
buy this, Jim. I don't know how much of the front page is already
made up, you know. I mean, the idea's O.K., but I don't know if they
have the space."

"It's that or nothing," Jim said. "C'mon, Lamont, give me a break."

"Hey! I can't tell them what to run," Lamont said. "You're going
to have to do the talking. Do you have anything at all for backup?"

"No," Jim said. He sat on the edge of the desk, sagging. "I
fucked up."

"Maybe I can work something into the lead to tie in with this,"
Lamont said. "Governor's wife shines at annual gala." He winced,
stuck out his tongue.

"Do it!" Jim said. "I'll owe you one."

"You'll have to do the talking, though," Lamont said. "I've had enough arguments this week with City Desk to last me a lifetime."

"O.K.," Jim said. "I just hope it flies."

"You'd better come in early," Lamont said. "They may not buy this at all."

When Jim arrived home, he was still unsteady, and sleep weighed like a rock on his mind. Anna had asked to be awakened, but he undressed in the dark, ashamed of the mess on his clothes, the potatoes, the traces of vomit and beer. But getting out of his pants, he stumbled, knocked the night table, and rattled the lamp upon it, and then Anna was suddenly awake, and she turned on the light.

"You scared me," she said.

"Sorry. My foot caught in the pantleg." Jim laughed sheepishly. "You got your hair cut, I see."

"It's short, isn't it?" Anna reached from under the covers and smoothed the hair over her ears, a quick self-conscious movement.

"It's fine," Jim said. "It's real nice."

"You were supposed to wake me."

"Didn't I?"

"I mean, like a person, not like a thug."

"I'm still not undressed. I was going to wake you when I was in my pajamas."

"Were you?"

"Sure. What's the news. I'm on pins and needles."

Anna leaned back into the pillows with a shake of her head. She studied Jim for a while, and then her lips began to tremble slightly.

"Come on." Jim pulled off the rest of his clothes.

"When you're next to me, I'll tell you."

"I'll bet I know."

"Don't guess. Let me tell you."

"I'll bet I know," Jim said. "I'll bet I knew the minute you told me you had something to say." He slipped into his pajamas and then under the covers. He turned to Anna and she put her hands on his chest, her fingers curling gently in his hair.

"So I want to know," Anna said, "how you really, really feel about it. Be honest with me. Tell me how you honestly feel about it."

Jim closed his eyes, and sleep tugged at his mind. "About your being pregnant?"

"Yes."

"How do you think I feel?"

"I want you to tell me, Jim, because if it's not the right thing, then it's not too late to do something."

"Oh, baby." Jim struggled away from coma and took Anna in his arms. To himself he said, Six years ago it would have been fine, very fine six years ago. To Anna: "You want it, don't you? Haven't you been hoping?"

"But it's not just me," Anna said. "And it's been so long, I'd almost forgotten what I was hoping for. Don't you understand? I need some encouragement. I need some reminding."

She continued talking, but Jim did not hear what she said, because he spiraled away. He had been on the brink a moment, struggled to find the will to stay attentive, to open his eyes and look into Anna's, but it was as if a huge hand had reached up out of the darkness and grabbed him, a hand that he had leaned into and accepted all too readily, and with it accepted also this fall into oblivion.

"I wanted to slap you," Anna said in the morning. She dressed hurriedly beside the bed as Jim swam out of his hangover, still wrapped in the sheets.

"Why? Didn't I say it? I want this child?" He knew his panic showed.

"No." Anna pulled on slacks with a kind of ferocity. "No, you didn't."

"I was so tired."

"You were drunk. You were stinking drunk."

Jim gripped his head and rolled into the pillows.

"I'm not interested in having a drunk around my kids," Anna went on. "And what are you doing now? Aren't you supposed to be in the office this morning?"

"Yeah, I am," Jim said.

"Well?"

"Well, what? I'll be late. Big deal."

"Jesus, Jim," Anna said. "You're really getting cute. You fall asleep when I want to talk about the most important thing that ever came up in our marriage, you're too hungover to get to work on time, you look like hell . . ."

Jim buried himself in the pillows again. His head felt as if it was burning. *The man with the burning head.* Yet he was sweating profusely, and his feet felt cold. *The man with the burning head is in trouble. With his wife. With his boss. Oh, God, with the cells of his body.*

"You won't even talk to me," Anna wailed. She pulled the covers away from his head. "But you're not getting away with this. You talk to me tonight, or that's it. I'm not shitting you."

This phrase burned into Jim, for it was uncharacteristic of Anna to swear.

"I cut my hair, I put on the nightgown you like. Did you even notice? I waited up for you as long as I could—"

"I noticed your hair," Jim said. "And I was working late. Ask Lamont. He was there, too."

"Was he also drinking with you? Did he pour the whiskey down your throat?"

"Let's talk later," Jim said.

"You can't take it sober?"

"Later!" Jim shouted. He hurled the covers back.

"And I'm not going to live with anybody I have to be afraid of." Anna grabbed up a small purse and a pair of shoes. "So don't threaten me."

"I'm not threatening you," Jim protested. "You've just got me pissed off."

"So get pissed off," Anna said on her way out of the bedroom. "Join the club."

When Jim heard the front door slam, he picked up a shoe and hurled it against the wall. He howled aloud. He was about to indulge in hurling another shoe when the telephone rang. *City Desk,* Jim thought. *Well, fuck 'em. I'm on my way to work. I'm caught in a traffic jam. It's the governor's wife or nothing.* He crashed into the shower, slammed the door on the rest of the world, offered his face to the shock waves of cold water, trying to douse his headache once and for all.

The call had not been from City Desk. They had grumbled about the choice of pictures, but ran them severely cropped and jammed uncomfortably together in just two columns. The hours before deadline were unusually hellish, and nobody had time to bawl him out, and when deadline had passed, everything was fait accompli anyway, and who had the energy for wrangling?

The call had been from Delancey. Jim found a note on his desk that Delancey had been trying to reach him, and when the rush of the morning's details had subsided, Jim returned the call.

"We got a make on your guy," Delancey said. "I guess he's gone nuts or something. The Mob threw him out once, but I guess he's back in business. He's got a lot of names and a lot of addresses, but I just wanted to thank you. You've saved me a lot of legwork. We've got somebody to watch at least."

"Are you staking him out?"

"That's right," Delancey said. "Twenty-four hours."

"Hey," Jim said. "Let me come along."

"Ah, no," Delancey said. "You'd queer it for sure."

"Come on," Jim said. "You owe me one."

"I don't know," Delancey said.

"Think of the publicity if you ever nail this guy."

"I thought of it already," Delancey said. "I don't need publicity, I need a raise."

"Come on," Jim said. "I'll behave."

"I'll check it out with the chief," Delancey said. "But I'm not enthusiastic."

"Well, check it out anyway," Jim said. "Don't you get bored on a street corner all by yourself?"

"Not really," Delancey said. "I take a newspaper along. That's always good for a laugh. And I don't mean the funnies."

Jim talked to Lamont about going on the stakeout with Delancey, possibly getting some pictures of a suspected arsonist.

"Maybe it won't pan out," Lamont said. "That's a lot of wasted time. And do you want to *take* that kind of time?"

"I'm willing to gamble," Jim said. "It sure beats gubernatorial galas."

"Don't mention that," Lamont said. "So O.K., I'll run it by City Desk. Overtime is going to be a problem. Lately they've nixed it all."

"Maybe there's a Pulitzer in it."

Lamont laughed. "Yeah, but what have you done for us lately?"

"Damn it," Jim said. "It's hell working with anarchists."

When Jim came home that night, Anna was waiting for him. He hadn't thought much about her during the day, because he knew he had been outrageous the night before, and remembering his actions stung him with guilt. O.K., he told himself, I got a problem. I guess this thing is getting out of hand. But Anna had been thinking about him, it was clear, and she had apparently also been thinking about what she should say. She was still quite tense when Jim came into the kitchen, settled his kit bag by the door.

"You still sore?" he asked.

"Yes."

"I'm sorry." Jim shrugged. "Things just got away from me last night."

"So they did." Anna pulled a chair away from the kitchen table and sat down slowly, looking past Jim a moment. When she engaged his eyes, her face had fallen, was slack with worry. "But why? Why are you drinking so much? Are you that unhappy?"

"Unhappy?" Jim pulled off his sports coat and sat across from Anna. "Happy, unhappy, just never crossed my mind."

"But something's the matter, isn't it?"

"Really, if there is, I don't know what." Jim locked his fingers before him. "Except that I drink too much."

"People have reasons for drinking too much."

"Yeah."

"And maybe if you don't know why," Anna said, "you should get some help in finding out. Did that occur to you?"

"Yeah," Jim said. "It occurred to me. But that takes time, and costs money."

"Wouldn't it be worth it?"

"I doubt it," Jim said. "I've never seen that it did anybody much good."

"Does this mean you won't do anything about it? Are you afraid of therapy?"

"I'm not afraid of therapy," Jim said. "I just don't think it will help."

"Can anything help, then?"

"I don't know," Jim said.

"You don't know why you drink, and you don't know if you can stop it. That's what we've concluded so far," Anna said.

"Anna," Jim said laconically, "I really don't like being interrogated like a crook or something."

"I don't like it, either," Anna said. "I don't like doing it. What I'm really not sure about, Jim, is whether it's worth it."

"Whether *I'm* worth it?"

Anna looked away.

Jim began getting angry now, and he wanted to strike back. What made Anna think she was so damned perfect? For years she had bored him to death, had lived so privately it was as if he weren't even there. And now she was telling him, in effect, that he was worthless to her. Maybe, he was tempted to say, Maybe that cut both ways. Something had gone out of their marriage, their life together, and she had not done much, if anything, to prevent it or to recharge it. Does it just take one for a relationship to fail, or is some cooperation, tacit or otherwise, the necessary ingredient? Is it neglect or a subtle disguised will that drives people apart? How innocent was she in all of this?

"Whether I'm worth it," Jim repeated.

"We're not kids any more," Anna said. "How much time do I want to spend working on your problems? Especially, you know, if I'm raising a child, if I'm giving up my career, for a while anyway, and everything is going to be so . . . so complex and uncertain?"

"I wish things were simple, too," Jim said. "I'd love to live in Simple-land, wherever that is. I wish people got what they deserved, or thought they deserved, and everything was real sweet and orderly and clean, you know, like a postcard of Holland, and no flyspecks on the windows. That'd be great."

"Is that what you think I'm talking about?"

"No car wrecks, you know. No fires or arsonists. That'd be great."

"Get serious, Jim."

"No wars. Nobody ever shoots your brains out in Simple-land. They don't know what booby traps are. Nobody ever put a grenade inside a corpse, nothin' like that."

"Finally," Anna said. "Finally I get it from you."

"What'd you get?" Jim said. "Simple answers?"

"You're afraid," Anna said. "You're afraid, aren't you, Jim?"

Jim laughed, a little savagely, but with embarrassment, too. "So you think I'm scared?"

"But why?" Anna asked.

"Why aren't you?" Jim shot back. "What right have you got to be unafraid? What makes you so sure you're safe?"

"Sometimes I'm afraid," Anna said quietly. "But I'm not afraid all the time. I couldn't live like that."

"You can't? How do you manage this miracle?"

"The war's over, Jim."

"The hell it is," Jim said.

Anna ignored this remark. "The war's over, so what is it, really, that frightens you so?"

"You think it would help me to know, do you?"

"Yes, I do," Anna said.

"I think it's probably better to drink," Jim said.

Anna sat back when Jim said this. She covered her eyes with a hand, then rubbed her temples with the tips of her fingers.

"I don't know," she said. "Maybe we should get out of Boston. Maybe you should get away from the newspaper and all the crap you see all the time."

"Where is this Simple-land?"

"Jim, I'm just asking you to think about it. Seriously. And soon. There's got to be a place to start, or start over. Maybe if we broke your habits, the everyday routine of drinking and working—"

"How soon?" Jim interrupted, his voice raised.

"Middle of May," Anna said. "I can't wait any longer than that."

"Don't do that," Jim said. "Please don't. I'd understand if you left me, but don't do that. I really don't want you to do it. It wouldn't save the marriage, because it would kill me, too. If you want to know what fear is, you should be inside my head right now. If that's what you wanted, you've got me terrorized. I can't take that, the threat of it."

Anna rose quickly, came around the table, and took Jim's head in her hands. "That's not what I meant to do," she said. "I just wanted you to see . . . I mean it. You've got to save your own life. You've got to do something!"

"But I'm not even worth it . . . am I? Aren't you telling me I'm not even worth it?"

"I'm telling you you've got a chance," Anna said.

Jim gripped his wife around the waist and pulled her body to him. He felt a terrible wave of regret, as if he had lost her already, as if everything was falling away from him. "I don't know. I don't know if I can do it, if I can change."

"You can," Anna said. "I know you can."

But change to what? Jim thought. *To what?*

14
The
Bugger
Machine

Chong stands in front of the Megabucks machine waiting for Mrs. O'Day to take his bet when Joe Turner bangs through the screen door.

"Take it easy," Mrs. O'Day calls to Joe. "That's the only door I got, you know."

"Wouldn't take ten minutes and ten cents to fix it," Joe says. "Then it might keep the flies out, too."

Mrs. O'Day laughs as she makes change from the register for the old man she has been chatting with while selling him pipe tobacco. "Some flies more than others, I guess."

"I see you got the heavy gamblers in here today," Joe says, indicating Chong.

"My last dollar," Chong says. "What the hell."

"Don't waste your money on that game, then." Joe twirls a wire rack full of colored envelopes. "Buy yourself a package of seeds. Says here you can get Swiss chard for thirty-nine cents, peas for thirty, and still have enough for a row of zinnias."

"That's just what I need," Mrs. O'Day says. "A salesman on the floor. A salesman in manure boots. Joe, how many times have I got to tell you not to come in here with those things on?"

"I wouldn't be standing so long, if you'd give me some service."

"Just long enough to drip." Mrs. O'Day wrinkles her nose. "The place smells like a barn after you leave."

"Put a hose out front," Joe says. "Then we could spray off before we came in."

"Use your own damn hose," Mrs. O'Day says.

The old man is standing near the door sorting through his change when Chong sees through the front window—cluttered with hand tools, a display of pipes and sunglasses, a few bedraggled house plants, fishing lures, and other essential country gear—a large green truck pull into the lot and the driver jump out like a sack of grain thrown down. The man, small and bearded, slams into the store, brushes the old man aside—he drops a nickel, which rolls away under a magazine rack—and crowds against Chong.

Chong steps back, regards the man with curious contempt. He seems familiar, but it is a small town after all, and Chong has seen many faces of people he doesn't know by name. Still, the deep-set eyes under heavy brows, the black hair curling at the back of the neck nag his memory.

Mrs. O'Day says to the man, "First it's cowshit come in here, and now you come trompin' tar and oil."

"I don't have time for that crap," the man says.

"Mr. Chong was waitin'."

"I'm on company time. He ain't got nothin' to do. Do you?" The man speaks without really looking at Chong.

"So what do you want, Billy?"

"Six-pack."

"What kind?"

"Any damn kind. The cheapest, whatever it is."

"Narragansett."

"Fine. Hurry up."

Mrs. O'Day puts the six-pack on the counter, and while she makes change the man opens one of the beers and begins to drink. Now he looks at Chong and smiles a broad, fake smile. "Nice day, ain't it, fella?"

Chong smiles and nods.

"You talk English?"

Chong continues smiling, nodding.

The man stuffs his change into his shirt pocket and strides out.

"There goes our taxes." Mrs. O'Day leans her head in the direction of the truck. "You want to give me your last dollar now, Mr. Chong?"

Turner breaks into a laugh. "You do speak English now, don't you?"

"I've seen that guy somewhere," Chong says. "Who the hell is he?"

"Billy Parker," Turner says. "He's one of the Archer clan. You've probably seen him working on the road."

Yes, Chong remembers. On the bridge. He set the charges in the ice that spring morning. His face re-emerges from the mist.

Mrs. O'Day hands him his ticket. "He's one of the town assets. Just check your pocket to be sure he ain't picked it."

They watch the truck swing out of the parking lot onto the road.

"Now there's something for you," Turner says. "You see what's in that truck? Those ropes? That's quite a pulley system. They've been using it up on Deer Lane to winch some logs up out of a drain, where a big oak fell and plugged it up, so the road flooded. Does that interest you?"

"Should it?" Chong folds his lottery ticket carefully, slips it into his empty wallet.

"That's about the only gear in town, you see, that would haul a big stone out of a dam. The only other guy around with a winch like it is Red Barber, who pulls engines with it at his garage."

"And I would bet my life against Red ever messing up a good trout and bass pond like yours!" Mrs. O'Day says.

"Why would he bother me?" Chong waves with frustration in the direction of the departing truck. "Because I'm Chinese?"

"Could be," Turner says. "Though I do also know this, that he wanted pretty badly to buy the old Randall place before you got it."

"Did he?"

"But the bank wouldn't lend him the money, because he couldn't make a down payment."

"He's working," Chong says.

Turner shrugs. "But he's not savin' any, I guess."

"That's when he cut down that tree," Mrs. O'Day says.

"Nobody knows who cut down that tree," Turner replies at once.

"Oh, get out of here," Mrs. O'Day insists. "We all know who did it."

Turner regards Chong with a helpless smile. "See, after he refused Billy the loan, the bank manager went to Boston for a weekend."

"And when he came back," Mrs. O'Day continues the story, "there was a big oak layin' right on top of what used to be a garage, now just wrecked to hell."

"Here again you can't prove it," Turner says. "The bank manager tried like hell to get Parker busted, but nobody saw it happen, and the judge said anybody could've done it, even one of Parker's pals."

"Which God," Mrs. O'Day growls, "has seen fit to give him plenty of, for reasons beyond us mortals."

Chong shakes his head a little in wonder, and anger. "Nice man."

"Some day I'll tell you all about him," Turner says. "Right now I need some of those hose washers hanging beside them fly swatters, and I'd better get back to Ruth with some of that baking powder, too, or she's going to wonder what I'm up to."

"She wouldn't be jealous of me," Mrs. O'Day says.

"She's not jealous of anybody," Joe says. "What she tells 'em is 'Please take 'im off my hands'!" He laughs heartily, but Mrs. O'Day does not join in.

"Now I know you're lyin'," she says seriously.

Chong drives home a little rankled still from his encounter with Parker and what he has learned about him. Maybe he is the very man who ripped the dam open! "Shoving me aside and wishing me a good day," Chong mutters as he pulls up to his mailbox and reaches through the car window for its contents. He is delighted to find a letter from his daugher, delighted and saddened, too, by the familiarity of her thick, determined handwriting. He spins gravel in his hurry to get into the house and read what she has sent to him.

So many letters he should be writing, he thinks. Should write his gallery and let Mrs. Browne know he has work to send along. He could use the money for a trip to New York to visit his daughter. If Mrs. Browne could only arrange a show for him . . . Chong sighs in disgust. Not much demand for his work these days, even before he left the city. Out of fashion!

Inside the house, he rips open the letter from Susan, finds a brief handwritten note, and what appears to be an essay of some kind, neatly typed. Susan writes:

Mother thought you would like to see this. In one of our classes we had to write about our families, and I thought it was the hardest thing I'd ever done, because, although you have told me some stories about your life in China, I don't remember them all, and I get confused. Sometimes I don't feel very Chinese at all. We don't even speak Chinese, except a little. I would love to go to China with you, but it would scare me, too, and I think New York is my home.

But no! Chong thinks. You have a home here, too. I told you. You've never seen it. I even have a bed for you upstairs for when you visit.

And yet he remembers so vividly the last time he saw Susan in New York:

She emerged from the subway, waved, hurried toward him with small steps, on her toes, a happy shuffle, it seemed then, and he took her in his arms with a delight that almost erased his sorrow over the recent divorce. She is getting breasts, Chong thought, as he released her, embarrassed by the public display of affection (which Susan did not apparently feel). Seventeen. He supposed it was time. Her black hair was pulled back, fit closely to her head, flowed away in a long, long ponytail. This amused Chong a little. The Chinese had gone to war to resist wearing their hair in such a style of submission, and his daughter wore it so, unconscious of its historical symbolism, subservience to the Mongolians. She also wore black pants, tightly cuffed at the ankles, shoes with a little heel on them, which made her look older—and stand taller than her father!—a white blouse embroidered on the shoulders. A lady! And, yes, a New Yorker.

They had spent the day together, and Susan talked about the things she was doing, preparing with trepidation for a music recital, receiving outrageously good scores on mathematics tests, worrying about financing college and where she would like to attend, wondering why Mai Li interrogated her so ruthlessly about the boys she dated and insisted she take a self-defense course.

"I could kill you with my little finger," she had teased.

"I'll bet you'd like to sometimes, wouldn't you?"

"Yes," Susan said defiantly. "I wish you were still with Mom."

The telephone calls they had exchanged in the meantime had been almost exclusively on this subject—this wearying subject, as Chong thinks of it. How could he convince her that he and Mai Li were separated for good, that Susan's fantasy of their reunion was futile?

In the letter now, Susan writes that she would like to go to the University of Hawaii, to study mathematics and Chinese language. Jesus! Chong slaps his forehead. Halfway around the world and God knows what it would cost. Goddamn money. It made Chong sick that he never had any, that he couldn't help his daughter more, couldn't take her to China.

For he is feeling that perhaps he is almost ready to return to China now. Not all the wounds have healed, and he has no idea what there would be to return to that he would know and recognize as something related to his childhood. China is imposing, strange, out of scale. He cannot think of it without feeling pain, literally; a headache sweeps over him. Yet he wants to rediscover his origins and it would interest him hugely to see what Susan would think of it, what relation she would make between Chong's scattered tales of his youth and the present state of affairs. He finds already that it is hard to see the words on the pages of Susan's essay, his memory so crowds with images.

"But how did you get here?" Susan had asked him.

"I came from Chicago, with your mother. That's where we met. She was in college, Illinois Institute of Technology. I was at the Chicago Art Institute, preparing to be thrown out."

And even this had been an almost inexcusable oversimplification. Chong had left college because he had to work so many hours to survive, and because already painting had become such an obsession with him that he could not leave it alone without feeling an illness overtake him, a terrible, nauseating hunger. He had taken some courses at the Art Institute, but was not encouraged, his own style had already laid such claims on his imagination. He met Mai Li when he worked part-time at a travel agency where Mai Li had come as a representative of a student organization for information on tours to the Orient. China at that time was closed to Americans, the revolution in progress, an ongoing tumult that both Chong and Mai Li Sung followed with passionate interest.

Mai Li, a Chicago native, daughter of a chemist and his wife, seemed to Chong at first dry and efficient, even a little snobbish; but one day when he had come to his office a little late and found her waiting there a bit impatiently, he offered apology by way of a luncheon, and on that afternoon in the midst of Chong's rambles—he was not used to talking much—she had laughed. And this laugh was so hearty and unrepressed, so free and full of delight, that Chong was awakened to her, pulled out of his self-absorption, and began his pursuit. To his amazement, he discovered that Mai Li was fun, full of ideas and even wicked impulses, and very aware of Chong's own moods, which she weathered easily. He did not frighten her with the intensity of his obsessions.

And even fun in bed, Chong recalls. He had never imagined that anyone could ever laugh in the throes of anything so profoundly serious and solemn as the sexual act. What a balm she had been to his tortured ego. She taught him how to relax a little, that life could be enjoyed after all, and he was happy to slacken his harried pace. Whether it was the time of their meeting, or her own background, Chong could not say, but the way she helped him most was in interpreting American realities. Sometimes he listened to Mai Li with his jaw hanging, and he began to feel less confused about his life in America, more at home at least, or at least able to accept his differences with more pride, as well as a little irony and a little humor. He needed her; he won her; and they wed.

Through the next several years, miscarriages weakened and tortured Mai Li. But even after her most severe disappointments—and there had been several, due to a hereditary "incompetent cervix," as the doctors labeled it—Mai Li had rebounded, more quickly sometimes than Chong himself. Susan did not realize what tender precautions had been taken so that she could be born. It was one excuse they gave themselves for coming to New York, besides Chong's own ambitions as an artist, that the medical care was better, they could find an "Eastern doctor" who would help them achieve parenthood. Meanwhile, except for the term of that pregnancy, Mai Li always worked, once or twice as a hospital receptionist or clerk, but most often in some accounting capacity, owing to her mathematical training and abilities, which Susan had inherited in full measure.

"No, no," Susan had said with impatience. "Even before that."

"Before that? I was raised in San Francisco."

"I mean even before that. What don't you tell me about China? Did you kill somebody or what? You never talk about it much."

"It's just painful, that's all," Chong confessed to her. "It hurts to remember China."

"But I want to know."

"And I'll tell you."

Susan's account passes on these tales, but blinks so much that Chong is sure that Susan has not really grasped the realities of his youth. She was struggling to do that and would in time see the fruit of that struggle. You learn when you're ready to learn, Chong thinks. A trip to China would be good for both of us.

Yes, and frightening. Sometimes good things come out of fright, Chong has told his daughter. You must master it to live at all. The danger is that it will only turn to hatred.

"My father was a runaway," Susan writes, and Chong bursts into laughter at the phrase. "He took a ship from Hong Kong to Hawaii, and another to San Francisco." How simple to say! The truth was that he jumped ship in Hawaii because he was afraid of the captain and of a dangerous task he had been assigned in the engine room. He would have to write to her about this sometime soon. He had run like a rat from a pack of cats, and was confused and desperate. Runaway indeed!

And in San Francisco, though Susan writes that Chong was raised "by a nurse and a seaman," he was really very much on his own, quasi-abandoned to the streets, and certainly did not attend school with any faithfulness. He knew so little English he did poorly and was ashamed of this, and in the meantime San Francisco was a continuous feast for him, so full of riches compared to his native Hunan, so full of American wonders he could not take it all in fast enough.

It was true, one of the engineers on the ship from Hawaii had found him a little job shucking clams in a restaurant and told his wife to care for him. But this was not entirely generous, for the sailor gave Chong instructions to report to him whatever guests his wife might receive while he was away. Oh, and there were guests, Chong remembers, but he never reported them, because his new "mother," Caroline Tracy, treated him well and without grudging, and if some night Chong sat at the table next to a strange man with hairy hands and whiskey on his breath, he did not find this horrifying at all. The men were amused with him but had other things on their minds and left him alone.

The one thing Caroline Tracy did that worried Chong was to make a determined effort to find his parents, something Chong tried obstinately to obstruct, he had hated his father so. He worried Mrs. Tracy would succeed, and wished mightily against it. He was learning to swim and play baseball and he could read the *Chronicle* effortlessly now; his belly was usually full, he could cadge money on the streets from tourists, and what else did he need?

Chong had always made drawings, even as a child, and he continued this, somewhat helplessly, even obsessively, and one of his high school teachers had encouraged and guided him. The man, Oscar Tharp, believed he saw in Chong's drawings the embryonic talents of an engineer—Chong was then drawing meticulously all the objects of his newfound life, all the wonderful *things* of America—and gave him the first notion, ever, of going to college, of leaving San Francisco. Chong received this wisdom with a kind of blinking awe—so much was possible in an American life!—but came gradually to regard it as correct. He could become an engineer!

The year before he graduated from high school, he was given two other incentives to leave the city he loved—the first was a scholarship to that great school in Chicago where the buildings were designed by Mies Van Der Rohe in dark reflective glass, a great black canvas that warped the shapes light threw upon it—an idea that then excited Chong; and Chief Engineer Tracy came home unexpectedly from an aborted trip to Bangkok only to find his wife of a dozen sea-weary years serving a kind of topless tea to a man in underpants. His American home thus rent, and Chong deemed old enough to shift for himself, the San Francisco phase of his life came to a dramatic close, and Chong became a "runaway" again, this time by train, and this time with a destination known.

At the end of Susan's report, the teacher has placed a large red "A" followed by an exclamation point. Some day, Chong thinks, I am going to have to tell her about that trip from Hong Kong to San Francisco. Odd, too, he thinks, not just how things turn out but how people imagine an ongoing story has somehow come to an end.

Lake Ecstasy. Chong shakes his head. What in hell am I ever doing here?

That night Chong lays his brushes down, unsatisfied with the cityscape he has been painting, because it seems artificial to him, and he turns away from it. New York is not yet out of his system, he tells himself with a laugh of disgust. Susan's letter and what it has stirred up in him is still on his mind. Money, for one thing. He tears a few sheets from a drawing pad and sits down at the kitchen table with one of his calligraphy pens.

"I loved your essay," Chong begins. "It reminded me of a few other things you might like to know. But as I think about them, I see that one thing leads to another, or back to another, all the way back to the beginning. I don't like to write so much, but I have all night, and will see how long I last."

Though Susan thinks of herself as American, Chong can see her in the ancestral mirror she has never known. He tells her that of course she looks like her mother and like Chong himself, though less, which he regards as fortunate. Susan looks, he writes, a little like Fai-Shen, her aunt, who looked a little like her grandmother. Fai-Shen died—how can he tell her?—at only nine years, run down by a horse. So much to explain by every simple remark! Few cars in China then, even in the military, and the horse was such a proud possession in China, had always been, celebrated in ceramics as godly power, able to transform fields and carry warriors and goods. The horse was more prized than any daughter—I won't lie to her about that, Chong decides—and so Fai-Shen went down almost without comment, one less mouth to feed. Terrible what starvation does to human love, to human connections! One less mouth to bite at the breast. And her uncle, Kao, ferocious teaser who drank beer from a bowl and who was considered crazy by some, fell in the hills of Hunan as he fought with Mao's army against Chiang Kai-shek. Kao was clever, very good at fixing things, a gambler, and he hated the Japanese. A crude man sometimes, at others almost sentimental, his thick skin pierced by the events of time: the war with Japan; the civil war that sent battles back and forth across the land like vicious weather, and just as unpredictable; the terrible flooding that wrecked farmlands and left the country in a desperate state of scarcity; the exploitation by Europeans and Americans, who literally held the country at gunpoint for so long. Even these things I can bear, Chong writes Susan.

"After all, what did I know! I understood little of this and was enclosed in my family as in a prison. I walked around with a sense of dread for so much of my life that I thought it was normal to feel that way. Sometimes I think it odd and unfair that I would be the survivor among my brothers and sisters. My father hated me so. It was my revenge to live. But I must correct your impression of me as a runaway, too. I know you believe so much in choice and in being responsible for your actions. This is very good! But sometimes we are swept along by events, not to mention the many times the choices we have are obscured by mists, unknown, or simply overrun by change."

A slender green bug with sheer wings flies into the lamp, then falls onto the page, spins in noisy loops until he falls off the table and into the shadow below. Now Chong's thoughts race ahead of his useless pen. Too much to tell! He pushes the paper away and flicks off the light, waits until the purple afterimage fades away from his vision, then goes out to sit on his back porch step. If Susan were here, the things he would tell her!

. . . An American major had come to Hunan to help the Fourth Route Army of the Communists and the Army of Chiang Kai-shek work out their differences and mount a unified campaign against the Japanese, who were not far away, already coursing through Manchuria. The major stayed at the mansion where Chong's father was a tutor and a translator for an English businessman with government connections. In retrospect, Chong could understand what eluded him as a boy: how enormously complex the major's mission must have been. In 1939, China was engaged not only in a war with Japan, but in a civil war. Chiang Kai-shek, as heir to the republican government initiated by Sun Yat-sen, had received the American blessing, but his affection and ties to the Germans were at that point so advanced, and his own manner of governing so imperial, that surely the major had been asked to supply corrective advice, if not more desperate persuasion. As there were only a handful of Americans in uniform in China then, vestigial protectors of American enclaves, the major's presence was more diplomatic than military, possibly unofficial, and indeed he may have functioned most successfully in the long run only as an informant to the U.S. government.

Because of the proximity of the armies—Kuomintang, Communist, and Japanese—the shuffling of forces in the countryside, the town was tense and its people anxious. Chong was afraid, but he had not known what many adults knew, that he had multitudinous reasons for his fear: bombing by the Japanese, attack by the Kuomintang, sortie by the Communists. In spite of all the military personnel present, the staff of the Englishman was strained to the breaking point, and Chong and Kao and others in the nearby villages were called upon to serve in the mansion.

When there are great negotiations going on, Chong thinks, there is always also a great need for servants. The newcomers did everything: peeled vegetables, swept hallways, carried boxes and furniture from one room to another, poured tea, counted chairs at long tables, opened car doors, washed dishes.

During one afternoon more hectic than usual, Chong was racing up a flight of stairs with a bottle of freshly opened wine when he was grabbed by the collar and found himself looking up into the face of an American in military uniform. The man held a disheveled stack of papers in the crook of one arm; a half-smoked unlighted cigarette dangled from his thick lips.

"You speak English, kiddo?"

Chong could not at first reply, unable to switch mental gears.

"Your pop says you can speak English."

Chong didn't understand the word 'pop,' remembering it to be the sound made when a gun fired, but managed, "Yes, sir." It was the first time he had spoken English to anyone but his father.

"O.K., I got a job for you." The soldier steered Chong by the collar to a table at the end of a hallway and plunked the stack of papers down before him.

"But I must deliver a bottle," Chong protested, brandishing the wine.

"Just give it to me," the soldier said. "This is much more important. Listen closely."

Of all the words he had heard so far, these last were the ones most familiar to him, and since they were usually followed by a blow from his father, they made Chong tense and afraid. But the soldier only wanted the forms he had placed in front of Chong arranged in three groups, according to certain key words he would find in the upper right-hand corner of each page. It was a simple problem of sorting and matching, and the only "English" required was the ability to recognize the words to be matched.

It wasn't a staggering task, Chong remembers, but he was terrified of making a mistake, and terrified also that someone would think he absconded with the wine, which had been destined for some general's lunch. When he finished the chore, he checked each stack again and again, trying to muster the courage to carry the papers into the soldier's office and turn them in.

The soldier was surprised and appreciative that Chong had finished the job so quickly. He was himself surrounded by paper and working furiously, obviously a little harassed and impatient. Now he assigned Chong the task of stuffing letters in envelopes, the only difficulty being to make sure the address on the letter matched the address on the envelope it was placed in. After supervising Chong for a while, the soldier let him work on his own. The chore went easily for Chong, but it rapidly became tedious, and although he felt this was important work, he missed the activity in the rest of the house, and especially the giant kitchen, where it was comforting to be in the presence of so much food, and the opportunities for quick surreptitious snacks frequently presented themselves.

And, of course, he recalls, he missed the proximity to the women, to the girls his age, and he had wanted to strut a little before them, to tell them what important chores he had been called upon to perform.

When he reached the end of his stack of letters, Chong had a moment of panic. The addresses on the last letter and the last envelope did not match. This, he thought, could only mean one thing, that at

least one of the envelopes before him had been filled with the wrong
letter and that it would require him to open envelope after envelope
until he found the other mismatched pieces. He studied the anoma-
lous addresses wondering how he could have made such a stupid
error on a task so simple, what he could possibly do to correct it,
whether the soldier, if he knew of Chong's mistake, would beat him
as assuredly as his father would have done. With difficulty, he
opened the top letter on the stack, wrecking the envelope, but found
the addresses correctly matched. He could not go on ruining envelopes forever, could he, because of course they would have to be
rewritten; and now, on top of everything, he had the anxious job of
repairing the envelope he had ruined. He glanced at the soldier, who
was turned away from Chong and furiously hammering away at his
writing machine, then slipped both letters into the good envelope,
and threw the broken envelope away.

"You done already?" the soldier said when he turned around.
"Fantastic." He scooped up the sealed letters and dumped them into
a large canvas bag next to his wooden desk. Now he grabbed a small
red rubber band, wrapped it around his thumb and finger, and fired
it at Chong.

Chong leapt up in fright, and it took him a moment to realize that
the soldier was laughing.

"Hey, kiddo, you don't type, do you?"

Chong was not sure he understood the sentence. "Type?" In
Chong's vocabulary, "type" meant "form," as in "What type of man
is he?" He translated the soldier's question as "Can you make forms?"
Or was the man talking nonsense to tease him?

"Use the typewriter." The soldier tapped the writing machine.

Ah, I see, Chong thought. Make forms, make letters. "No," he said.
"Don't type."

"Nuts," the soldier said, which also confused Chong. "Wonder if
you could learn, though. Come over here and sit down. Sure as hell
you can learn this. You're smart enough."

Shurazell? What did that mean? The English his father had taught
him, even with ruthless dedication, did not quite correspond to the
American version Chong was hearing now. Or had he failed his
father again?

The soldier placed Chong's fingers on the typewriter keyboard,
then pressed his fingers down, one after the other: "I can learn to
type," he wrote.

"See? That's how this little bugger works," the soldier said.

"Bugger?"

"Typewriter."

"O.K.," Chong said. "Bugger, typewriter."

"Oh, boy," the soldier said. "I'd better watch my step around you, I guess."

Chong watched in fascination as the man's fingers plucked the keys, creating words in quick succession: "The quick brown fox jumped over the lazy Chinaman."

"O.K., go ahead and play with this thing a while, until I need it again, and until I find something for you to do."

"Oh, boy," Chong mimicked the soldier. He plunked away, fingers and keys tangling with every other stroke. How had the man made it seem so easy? Why had the makers of the machine scrambled the alphabet so thoroughly? Perhaps it was a code? If the letters were scrambled, why were the numbers in perfect order? He poked away, mangling words and creating chaos.

"You don't have to hit the keys so hard," the soldier said, laughing. "You're not chopping wood or anything."

Chopping wood? The joke struck Chong as incredibly funny, and he laughed heartily. "O.K., not so hard," he said. "Oh, boy."

The soldier allowed Chong to frustrate himself thoroughly at the machine before finding him other clerical chores to perform. Chong was glad to be released from the diabolical instrument, and he hoped the soldier would give up ideas of making him a master of the bugger machine. How could anyone make sense of it when the letters were scrambled so?

That night Chong met his father at home, and as was the custom he reported what had happened during the day. Sometimes when his father was feeling unusually mean he would require Chong to converse with him in English, something Chong dreaded because it inevitably meant blows for his mistakes. This night Chong's father seemed especially tense, nearly hysterical, controlling his inexplicable rage with only the greatest of concentration.

"And how did you conduct yourself with the American sergeant?"

"I don't understand 'sergeant,' sir."

"That's the soldier's rank, Hu Lan! He should be addressed by his rank and his surname. Do you even know his name?"

"No, sir."

"Foolish boy! You must always know the names of the people you work for. How stupid can you be? Suppose someone asks you who you work for and you can't reply? How silly you would seem—if not also a liar. His name is Daniels, his rank is sergeant. Sergeant Daniels. Say it!"

Chong did.

"Say it again. Again!"

"Sergeant Daniels."

"Again! Pronounce the 'el.' "

Chong obeyed.

"And what did Sergeant Daniels require of you today?"

Chong described as well as he could the chores that had been assigned to him, his successful completion of them—of course omitting his cover-up of the mixed addresses—the good nature of Sergeant Daniels, and other things.

"Only by good luck is he good-natured, Hu Lan! If you make serious mistakes, count on it, he will not be so friendly! And he could be replaced at any time." Chong's father sat on a wooden stool in front of a door to the house. Inside, his mother was cooking in the fireplace, and the smell of the food was making Chong's stomach leap. The flickering fire seemed warm and comforting, and Chong longed to be inside, lying down, resting, and eating.

His father continued. "Did Sergeant Daniels require anything special of you? Did he suggest how you could be a greater service? Did he, Hu Lan? Why do you take so long to answer?"

Chong told his father about the typewriter, about Sergeant Daniels' desire that Chong learn how to use the machine.

On hearing this, Chong's father rose from the stool and grabbed Chong firmly by the shoulders with his bony strong hand. Chong cringed with pain.

"Then this is something you must learn at once," Chong's father said. "What can possibly be the difficulty? Come! We shall go to the office and learn the typewriter at once. It will be a great skill to know."

"But I am hungry now, Father."

"Come on! Don't argue!" Chong's father twisted Chong around and began pushing him toward the road and the steep path that wound up through a rocky field toward the mansion, which now seemed far away.

"Can't I eat something first, Father?"

"You! You don't know what hunger is! Quickly! He may close the office."

Chong's next protest was met with a blow to the back of his head that sent him reeling. His father shoved him along the path and across the field to the mansion they had left only a short while before. Guards admitted them, and they climbed the stairs to the soldier's office.

Sergeant Daniels was not in the room, but another man was. Chong's father bowed very deeply to him, requested momentary use of the typewriter, while Chong waited, angry and hungry, in the hallway. He watched as his father took a piece of paper from the desk—so much paper! everyone had thought, valuable as money, and the Americans used it as if it were worthless—and carefully copied the order of the letters on the typewriter keyboard, and their approximate positions. Then, with a pencil, he carefully traced on a second sheet of paper the position and size of the keys, with the symbols they contained, from top to bottom. The soldier in the office regarded this activity with open-eyed curiosity, but Chong's father explained nothing, only bowed and expressed his deep gratitude when he had finished. When he came into the hall, he gripped Chong by the shoulder again and thrust the papers into his hands.

"This," he said, "this is your typewriter."

As they walked briskly back to the family cottage, Chong's father spelled out the new regimen. When he had learned the new alphabet, the typewriter alphabet, he could have his supper. Chong could forget his ABC's; he was now to learn his QWE's.

Chong wailed in dismay and outrage.

"Be quiet" his father commanded. "You must learn to use the typewriter at once. You only have a few days. When you have memorized the alphabet, then you will learn to find each letter instantly on the keyboard. You will make good progress on this tomorrow, or you will not eat. You will know the keyboard perfectly in three days, or you will not eat. As an incentive to rapid progress, I will test you each half-day, and take appropriate action when you do not succeed."

What would Susan think of this? Chong wonders. That he learned to type in three days—not perfectly, but well enough to hack away at the machine.

Now Chong was given more complicated work. He typed up lists of names, organizations, material, addresses, translated brief memoranda from the Chinese and typed these in English once the sergeant had checked his spelling and grammar. Chong typed whole long columns of numbers and abbreviations he could not understand and made copy after copy of other letters and documents that Sergeant Daniels put before him.

And every night his father demanded a progress report.

"Did Sergeant Daniels suggest any way you could become indispensable to him? Any way that your service to him can become necessary?"

"No, sir."

"He did! There is something. You must listen hard! You must find it!"

He looks up into a sliver of moon. These exchanges with his father had tortured him to a kind of rage. Once he had respected his father for his knowledge of English and for his having learned it almost entirely by himself, in China, where there was almost no one to speak English with! For a brief time he had attended a missionary school to refine his pronunciation and experience the use of idioms, but in the main he had educated himself and he spoke with contempt for the missionaries and their doctrines. But his endless badgering and his physical cruelty finally broke Chong's attachment to him, made him yearn to escape his house.

And then the bombing began. The major and his team, including Sergeant Daniels, risked an interlude in the bombardment, clambered aboard an airplane, and fled south. Daniels' legacy was to thrust Chong into the car of a departing Kuomintang official, recommend him with a hasty, "Good man. Use him. He speaks English." Chong was crammed to the floor, traveled the night in a stupefied silence as the car slammed through the countryside. This was Kuomintang style: big black cars, flags, motorcycle escort. Mao, in turn, traveled humbly, in the bed of a truck, his face exposed to the rush of air. Away. Chong, at fourteen, was going away. He was released from his father. He had never been in a car, and through the dread of strange things happening to him, the nausea with the motion of the automobile, he felt an ember of excitement begin to glow within him. *Away!*

The next day (or was it days later? Chong wonders) he was perfunctorily assigned to an "office" in a railroad boxcar. During the following weeks, the car was shunted southward at unpredictable intervals, usually at night. Besides translating a few letters into English, Chong's main task proved to be helping to beat back swarms of people who often tried to board the train. Even so, the train went everywhere festooned with refugees.

Meanwhile, the Japanese moved inexorably down the coastline, taking Tsingtao, Nanking, Shanghai. . . . The cynicism of the older men Chong worked with grew apace as these humiliations mounted and one night Chong was wakened from sleep, urged gently out into the darkness where he and his colleagues began to run. "There is no hope for the Kuomintang!" they agreed. They would lose themselves in the vastness of China, like bubbles in a boiling kettle. It was inconceivable that anyone from the train would come after them.

How insane were we? Chong wonders now. How many accidents shape a life? Why did I survive?

Much later, alone, hungry to the point of fainting, Chong was picked up from the side of the road by an old man and taken to his home, a shack made of scrap lumber, cloth and tin, and fed. The man was awed by how far Chong had come in six months, and when he learned that the young man could speak English (and use the "bugger machine"), he said, "You must go to Hong Kong. You will have some chance there, among the English. Hong Kong is your only hope. If it lasts!"

And already Hong Kong was in chaos when Chong arrived. Chong stumbled about the streets as if drunk, jostled by thousands fleeing the imminent attacks of the Japanese. So hungry he would have done anything—yes, anything, Chong muses, feeling fortunate to have been spared more profound desperation—Chong was helped by sympathetic crewmen to find a berth on an American freighter. The captain, seemingly disinterested in Chong's trials or language skills, seemed unable also to keep his hands from Chong's behind. Chong did not, could not, care. He took the job, then, aided by some of the crew, steered clear of the man who hired him. . . .

When he finally retires, Chong is too restless to sleep well, and he is out of the bed early in the morning. He writes a quick letter to Mrs. Browne, telling her he has new paintings to show and that he needs whatever money she can send along, presuming any sales. He invites her to come visit, to see his new work, not supposing she would actually make the trip. He also writes Evelyn Crane and shamelessly asks for a loan, something to tide him over. And does she know, he asks, any collectors who might be interested in some large-scale erotic nudes? He knows very well this will pique her curiosity.

Then, when it is late enough, he calls Susan, reversing the charges. Mai Li answers, expresses disgust that he can't pay for his own calls, but turns the telephone over at once.

"Your essay was wonderful," Chong says. "It got me thinking of so many things. Also I want to do a painting now, a memory of China."

"That's great, Dad." Susan's voice is thick with sleep still, reso-nates in a way that Chong finds disturbingly mature. He tells what he remembered the evening before, how his father had treated him, drove him from home and into the tumble of history.

"I've been thinking about that, too," Susan says. "About what you've told me about your dad, my grandfather. I can't quite be-lieve it."

"Ho!" Chong says. "How could you? We never even spanked you, but maybe twice. You have no idea."

"I mean," Susan says, "because he was so smart otherwise, teach-ing himself English and math."

"Smart, but not kind."

"But I was thinking," Susan continues, "that maybe, given how ter-rible things were, how easily you could die, maybe he was trying to make you learn English, and then make you want to leave China."

Chong considers this, and the automatic denial he wants to voice is stopped by a chill along his spine.

"I mean," Susan continues before he can gather a reply, "maybe he was deliberately trying to drive you to America or England so that you could survive. Maybe he was being terrible to you because he thought he had to be. He was knocking some sense into you."

"Ho!" Chong says.

"He was smart enough for that, wasn't he?"

"Oh, yes," Chong says.

"Maybe he was being mean to cover up how terrible he felt about what he had to do. I take it you were pretty—"

"Yes," Chong says, "stubborn."

"You see what I mean?"

"Yes!" Chong says. "My God! I have to think about this. It makes me ashamed."

"Ashamed? Why? I thought it would make you happy."

"Maybe," Chong says, "I was too stupid about my father."

"You couldn't know everything," Susan says. "You were just what? Fourteen?"

"Maybe you're right," Chong says. "This is why I miss you so much. I miss talking to you."

"I miss you, too," Susan says. "Why don't you come to New York?"

"Or you could come here," Chong says. "I have a bed."

"I have to work," Susan says.

"I know." Chong is stung with guilt. "But save what you can. Maybe we will go to China together some day."

"Yes!" Susan almost shrieks. "Oh, I want to."

When Chong hangs up—interrupted by Mai Li, who insists the call is getting preposterously expensive—he begins to ruminate on what Susan has suggested about his father. He picks up a pen and begins to draw a little aimlessly the features that would have terrified him before. His father. Through the mists of his memory, the face emerges, not murderous but desperate, driven to cruelties against his oldest son.

Chong thinks with a start, He could be still alive, and Mother could be, too. In their seventies. I could find them in China. Susan and I could.

Has he been wrong all these years? His mind has a ghost in it that still agitates to be set free. His daughter, at only seventeen, has reawakened it. Chong cries out, drops the paper to the floor.

15
Home
Front
[*iv*]

T he *Globe* editors had other things for Jim to do, but the stakeout of the man Delancey called "Tony Bonanza" was Jim's
excuse for avoiding Anna, her inquiries and insistences. He
dropped by Delancey's office every chance he could get, and now
and then would drive with the detective to a street corner near the
stakeout site and observe a change of surveillance teams.

"I really wish we could get inside that guy's place," Delancey had
confessed to Jim. They sat in an unmarked car not far down the
block from the arsonist's building. "But we can't get a warrant. We
don't have anything but your photos, and I don't want to bring them
forward."

"Why not?" Jim said.

"Because you'll get fired," Delancey said.

"Still, the guy must have a yard-long record."

"A football field," Delancey agreed. "But he is presumed to have
paid his debt to society, and also to be on the Mob's shitlist."

"Maybe he's not working for the Mob."

"You're not supposed to think of that," Delancey said.

"Maybe it's some other private organization."

"Just keep it under your hat, all right, Jim?"

"Maybe they just want you to think it's the Mob."

"No comment."

"Or maybe the Mob wants you to think it's some other bunch trying to throw the blame on the Mob."

"Cut it out, Williams. Christ, maybe you're *right*."

"Maybe the Mob wants to get rid of this guy. Maybe they're setting him up for a fall, and meanwhile settling some scores. Two birds with one stone."

"Don't I call him Mr. Bonanza?" Delancey shifted his hands on the steering wheel and glanced at Jim through folds of dark eyebrow.

"No kidding? You think that's it?"

"It's none of your business," Delancey said, "and if you break the word to Lamont, I'll use your photos."

"I'll be damned," Jim said, "It's Viet Nam."

"What is?"

"These Chinese boxes of what could be going on."

"I don't understand a word you're saying," Delancey growled.

Jim smiled. "And you're a damned liar, too."

Delancey nodded, pursed his lips. "Not for publication, any of this."

"Suppose I went into the guy's place," Jim said.

Delancey winced. "Get serious."

"Suppose the guy goes somewhere and I go in and and take some pictures."

"Too much TV," Delancey said. "You wouldn't know what to look for. You wouldn't even know how to get in. But if you did get in and the guy spotted it, he'd know we were on his ass. So don't, just don't, get any heroic notions."

"He pisses me off."

"Or maybe he'd just trot down to the corner for some cigarettes and come right back, and there you are. And then you're dead, and I have to explain this to somebody."

"But he really pisses me off," Jim said.

"We're going to get him," Delancey said. "We're going to be patient, and we'll be right on his case if he makes a move."

"Have you tapped his phones?"

"No comment." Delancey eyed Jim with a hint of menace. "Lamont would never ask a question like that, you know. There's some things you're not supposed to ask. Follow me?"

"I'm not interviewing you," Jim said. "This is personal interest, my own curiosity."

Delancey shook his head slowly. "You newspaper guys!" He rolled down the window and spat onto the street. "When am I ever going to learn my lesson?"

❖   ❖   ❖

One night in April, Anna was waiting for him when he came home.

Jim swayed a little in the doorway when he dropped his kit bag down.

Anna sat in the chair facing him in a pink cotton nightgown that revealed her ankles, and her hands were folded in her lap. She didn't move, but sat as if frozen, and the eyes that fixed on Jim and silently interrogated him became wet.

Jim felt as if she were slapping him. He stood there silently, unsteadily, managed a smile.

Jim rose from bed after Anna left for work the next morning and telephoned the office that he wouldn't be coming in, claiming illness. He told himself he just needed time to think, to prepare himself somehow for changing his life, for curing his addiction. He tried even to be methodical about it, to make a list of the things he should do, something he could even show to Anna as proof of his intent. He could call the Viet Nam Veterans Association or an alcohol counseling center he found in the telephone book; he had the names and numbers of several therapists that friends had passed on to him when the issue had come up in conversation—usually in a bar. Delancey had said that the only program that really worked for drunks and addicts in his experience was Alcoholics Anonymous, but Jim did not see how he could possibly take any interest in such a fundamentally Christian organization. But he added the name to his list and took down the number from the telephone book. Then he left the list on the table, went out to his car, and started to drive.

He went south on Route 128, past all the big steakhouses, the suburban moil of carwashes and truck depots, shopping malls, radio towers, factories, gas stations, chain-link fences, water tanks aloft on legs of webbed steel. He knew he was driving too fast but felt pressed, an intense need to turn this frantic, exhaust-drenched gray civilization to a blur on his consciousness. But the traffic was too dense—trucks snorted shoulder to shoulder ahead of him—to allow him to break into this plane of speed, and he shouted his impatience, cursed and roared, aching for speed and space.

Until finally he could break away and the tires snapped over expansion strips on the road, and the greening roadside shrubbery hissed by in a single band of color. Now he shouted gratuitously, fervently, packed the car with his rage, shouted until he was hoarse, cursing his idiocy, cursing the world, cursing his love for Anna, the city, the armies of the planet, the smoke in the sky, the cycle of life and death, the twists of his life he didn't understand, the future he couldn't know.

At last he slacked off on the speed, settled down to the speed limit, exhausted and frustrated, craving a drink, yes, at least a drunken sleep, and considering whether he wanted to live through, really, the irritations and the struggle his future promised him. Already screwed up, and screwed up good. On the brink of failure. And from there—where? Down. The bottom admittedly held a certain appeal. *Simpleland*. Everything reduced to one obsession: booze. Jim admitted that failure now, sudden, complete, had its allure for him. It was really kind of an amazing speculation that some day he might bump into Anna on Boston Common, cadge money from her for a drink as she walked along with a handsome teen-aged boy, his secret son, and she wouldn't recognize Jim or see that he watched her with relief from the safety of his destitution. Like *The Count of Monte Cristo*. A real blubbery scene: he on the alcohol chain gang, she half deranged by his abandonment and searching the world for news of him. What a tearjerker! One and a half stars. That's what his life was about to come to: one and a half stars on the late show. Fabulous! Jim Williams stars in this chestnut about a Viet Nam veteran who falls prey to booze and prowls Boston Common while his deserted wife searches for him around the globe in the company of their son, a troubled genius. Wonderful. *Cracks me right up*, Jim thought.

And what an ending. He freezes to death on a truck-loading dock, thugs roll him and dump him in the river—no, the sewer—he blunders into a train on the narrow trestle, steps from the curb into the grill of—ironically!—a beer truck. Oh, Jim knows the endings already. He is an expert on endings. Take your pick, he tells himself, endings one through ten. How about number seven: car slams into bridge abutment before movie even starts. There it is, he tells himself, the bridge, the bridge abutment. You could do it now and save yourself a lot of film.

"*Wham!*" Jim said aloud as he drove across the bridge. On the other side he thought, And here is a whole new world, a heaven, with heavenly gas stations and divine diners, and celestial parking lots. A whole new life right here. Cosmic lobster joints. Saintly tire sales. Blissful heaps of rusted cubes—crushed cars—in the salvage yards.

Somewhere else, Jim thought. How the hell do you get to somewhere else?

About an hour later he swung through the rotary in Sandwich, and then arced over the Sagamore Bridge onto Cape Cod. He drove slowly, not much interested in where he was, and only turned off the central artery on impulse, when he saw a sign to Bass River. Bass River! Whatever it was now, with a name like that, it must have been miraculous once, Jim speculated, full of big stripers chasing herring right onto the banks of the stream.

His own "bass river" had been the Kennebec, and Jim thought of it with a deep longing, a tremendous sorrow, as if his father had just died. But it was not his father that Jim mourned now, for he had an image of himself in mind, as a young man on the family boat, bringing the *Sweetheart* up into the current so his father could lob a big plug into the flat V-shaped wake behind a high bulge of black boulders where experience had told them that big bass would shelter and forage, and sometimes come rising through the tea-brown water to smash the bait in a vertiginous swirl of foam. Who was this boy handling the boat so well? What had his potentialities been? How had they been shot to ribbons and his course sent awry?

It was almost noon when Jim found himself in Yarmouth, looking out from the Bass River Bridge toward Nantucket Sound in a severe cold wind that made him tighten his jaw, and after a few moments plunge back to his car. A short while later he leafed through a telephone directory in a desultory cafe where the waitress smoked brown cigarettes and the bald, sullen man behind the counter complained alternately about automobile insurance rates and shellfish regulations. Jim wrote down the names and addresses of the Cape's newspapers, photography stores, and the lone photo-processing laboratory. It was something to do, something that seemed to give this impulsive, even ridiculous jaunt some sense. Jim did not deceive himself on this matter. He had driven simply to escape Boston and vent his rage, and the roads he had taken led here, and he was only trying to excuse himself and to find some way to put a civilized face on his impetuous escape. But Jesus! the thought of going back to Boston, of facing Anna and all the people at the *Globe*, made him physically ill. He had the same old wave of panic as he did when he had not been able to open the door to his apartment and had lurched off to the bar. He doubted he would be able to return soon. His hands were shaking slightly, and he felt rooted to his chair, as if gravity had suddenly trebled in force.

Later, at a church basement rummage sale, Jim bought a hooded sweater and a woolen cap, and then spent the afternoon walking the beach. He did not know where he was, but had been directed to Harding's Beach, where he was told he would have easy access to the water. The high wind drove the breakers far up the beach and left a deep brown-green unbroken mat of eelgrass and rocket weed on the shore. A flounder, tossed from its forage by a powerful wave, lay tangled in the seaweed, and Jim hurried to it, scooped it back into the foam, only to have it wash back onto the sand, so that this time when Jim recovered it he was more deliberate and threw it further out. The fish disappeared with barely a ripple on the gray water. Jim's hands now smelled sweetly of the fish, a raw and live odor that made him almost swoon with the memories it impelled, and he sought a cleavage in the dunes and fell down there in an agony of questioning. When had the break occurred? When had he been separated from the things of the sea that juvenated him? Who was to blame?

He spent the afternoon in this misery and, having no desire to be on the highway, drove farther down the Cape, into Eastham, and took a motel room there, small but clean and brightly lit. After a hot shower, he drove to a restaurant and called Anna from the pay telephone outside.

She was plainly terrorized by this act of his and tried to be understanding, but her every question told him how frightened she was of what he had done.

"It's O.K.," Jim told her. "I'm not drinking, just looking around, trying to sort things out."

"Do you want me to come down there? Are you all right?"

"I'm all right," Jim said. "I'm not going to kill myself or anything."

"Jesus, Jim. Oh, Jesus."

"Isn't that what you're worried about?"

"Jim, I'll come down if you want me to. Tell me what you want me to do."

"I'll be home tomorrow." Jim was amused at his own pretense of calm. "Anna, I want to change. I'm trying to figure out how to do that."

"I'll stay awake," Anna said. "Call me? Please? Whenever you want to."

"Everything's O.K.," Jim insisted. "Go to sleep, go to work. When you come home tomorrow, I'll be there, and I'll tell you what I've been thinking."

"I love you," Anna said.

"O.K." Jim knew he spoke petulantly, and he regretted this.

"Just remember that I do love you."

"O.K., O.K."

When he hung up, a blast of wind rocked the telephone booth, and Jim was annoyed at how cold it was still, almost May, when even New England should have shaken winter out of its hair. He prowled around the little town of Orleans in his car, stopped and bought a bottle of Old Newburyport rum at a package store, because he just needed a shot or two to keep his hands from shaking, and he was going to quit drinking gradually, so that this would be the last bottle he ever bought, and he could husband it a long, long time, perhaps never finishing it, but knowing that he could some day, if he wanted to, just lick away the little corner that he would leave himself, as a test of will.

In the motel room, he gradually quit drinking by consuming half of the bottle of rum in four or five hours, fell into an edgy, hallucinatory sleep in which he shook and trembled, lay with his head against the sweet-sour stink of the rice paddy dike while machine-gun bullets shuddered into the earth around him.

He woke at 3 A.M. in a black sweat, shouting at the television, "Incoming! Incoming!" The face of the television only mirrored back to him a world of gentle curves, gray and dead. Jim wanted to move in. He was on his hands and knees, face pressed to the television screen, wanting only to move into that gray space where no one ever sweated, where the temperature was always seventy degrees, and the eyes he was looking into only looked out, and never back inside, or into the past, never turned their beams back into the brain and lighted up those grotesque islands in the writhing blood-red stream that always flowed there, rank and horrible, sourceless, perpetual.

"Don't you ever do that again," Anna said.

"All I did was drive to the Cape for a two-day vacation. What's the big deal?"

"Don't ever scare me like that again."

"You sound like my mother," Jim said.

"I don't care who I sound like, as long as you hear what I'm saying, and understand that it's coming from *me*."

"I'm writing some letters, looking for jobs down there."

"You are? Why?"

"You said yourself I might be better off out of Boston."

Anna bit her lower lip. "I didn't think I meant you'd get so far away that I'd have to quit, though."

"It's all speculation anyway," Jim said. "Maybe nobody will want me. Jobs are scarce there, and I'm sure they get their pick of applicants."

"You're moving fast," Anna said.

"Am I? It seems to me that every little choice takes forever—every letter, every telephone call. I feel like I use up all my energy even before I start."

"If you need some help, Jim, all you have to do is ask me for it. You know that?"

"I know," Jim said. "Thanks, but I'll do it myself."

The editors raked Jim over the coals, and his protestations about having influenza convinced no one. They had tried calling him at home in hopes of clarifying the mess of his assignment book and turning the jobs over to someone else but had received no answer for two days, and the missed sessions had created havoc and anger.

"Maybe you're out looking for another job," City Desk said. "It's none of my business. But you've got to let me know in advance. It's just simple etiquette."

"I was sick."

"Sure you were. Too sick to answer the telephone. You've been sick a lot lately, haven't you? Even on the job."

"Who says?"

"Never mind. We all like a drink, Jim. But you'd better take a look at yourself. Maybe you need some leave time? Think about it. As far as the higher-ups are concerned, you're on probation."

Jim went down to the darkroom furious and, so he admitted, afraid. Lamont must have screwed him. It was Lamont's fault that he was in trouble about his drinking. Right? Take a leave, huh? Go sweat it out for six weeks in the VA hospital with all the crazies, playing Ping-Pong and talking to college-girl counselors about priorities and choices and budgeting time—making it all orderly.

Jim was mad enough, felt insulted enough to consider quitting outright and at once, when he got a call from Delancey. They were pretty sure that something was going to pop very soon, and did Jim want to come along for the ride?

"Are you going to bust this guy?" Jim asked.

"I can't tell you anything more," Delancey said.

"I'd love to see you nail the bastard."

"Don't jump to any conclusions."

"Did you talk to Lamont? Is it O.K. if he joins the party?"

"Oh, sure," Delancey said. "Bring the wife and kids, too."

"Just Lamont," Jim said. "Will the other papers be there?"

"The other papers will be waiting at the lockup," Delancey said.

"O.K." Jim spoke with enthusiasm.

"We don't care about you," Delancey said, "but if anybody else got shot, we'd feel bad."

"It's great to be loved," Jim said.

"You will wear a vest, or you won't go."

"Those things are heavy. Size forty-two."

Delancey laughed. "We don't have anything that small."

Jim grabbed Lamont from his typewriter and they held a meeting at once with City Desk and the publisher's aide to explain what they wanted to do and to work out the angles, the tack to be taken.

"What's going on here?" City Desk asked. "How come Delancey is suddenly so cozy?"

"I gave him a tip," Jim said. "I spotted a guy in the contact prints. It saved him some legwork."

"Does he have the photos?"

"No," Jim said. "I didn't breach policy."

"You gotta watch that stuff." The editor shook his head. "We've been to court over this already, cops trying to get notebooks and files. You really have to be very careful about that."

"They don't need the photos for evidence," Jim said. "It just saved some legwork, some guessing. That's what Delancey said."

"I hope to hell we're not going to court on this," the editor insisted.

"What's the problem?" Lamont said. "You're not going to back down? Nobody else will have this stuff."

"I know," the editor said. "We want it. But we also don't want to be doing police work."

"We're just going along for the ride," Jim said. "Maybe nothing will happen. Delancey didn't sign a contract."

"Come off it," the editor said. "Something's going to happen, at least within forty-eight hours. I just don't want you getting in debt to Delancey. And you've got to keep eyes clear and noses clean, and don't convict this guy in advance of the trial."

"Right," Jim said. "Objectivity. Accuracy. Fairness."

"We also promise to stay out of the line of fire," Lamont said, "to hold down the cost of our magnanimous health benefits."

"Now we're talking turkey," the editor said. "We don't want to be negotiating burial fees at the next contract talks. It's all we can do to pay your parking fines."

"And we'll be careful where we park," Lamont said.

The editor threw up his hands in disgust. "Get your asses out of here," he said.

Delancey was agitated when Jim and Lamont arrived, confessed to misgivings about having the press along. "So much can go wrong. But the boss thinks we need points with you creeps, I don't understand why."

When they piled into an older blue compact, Lamont said, "I didn't know they still made these things."

"It's somebody's idea of cover." Delancey shoved the seat back for leg room and jammed it against Jim's knees. "They haven't made a decent car since 1959, if you ask me. These damn economy jobs, you have to have a valet waiting to cram you in and haul you out."

Two other detectives preceded them in another car, and uniformed police and fire units were standing by, Delancey explained. They had trailed the arsonist to Newton earlier that afternoon, where he spent a long time in a garage outfitting a van with the chemicals needed for a burn.

"You understand there's nothing illegal about the chemicals?" Delancey asked. "By themselves, the chemicals are innocent enough. But when you combine them—*poof!*"

"Like chlorine and brake fluid," Jim said.

Delancey bit his lip. "The fewer people know that, the easier my job."

A radio transmitter had been slapped onto the van and a helicopter was relaying the van's whereabouts. "Bonanza," meanwhile, had returned to Boston.

"He's been sitting a long time," Delancey said. "I said we should have busted him as soon as he got in that van, but I'm just a sissy around here. Everybody wants to know where he's going. That might explain a few things, too."

"So why did you want to bust him?" Lamont said.

"Because he's driving a bomb around Boston," Delancey said. "I

don't want him lighting up some intersection if some drunken wop
tailgates him."

"Wop?" Lamont said.

Delancey shrugged. "Not for publication."

Jim shifted the two cameras he had strung around his neck to
make himself more comfortable in the narrow back seat. He did not
like the easy camaraderie of Lamont and Delancey, the closeness of
the small car. He hated closed spaces in general, and, he decided, he
hated Delancey's smell. The man worked long hours, and if he
changed clothes now and then he wore the same sports coat forever,
and you knew that as soon as you came within five feet of him. Lamont, for his part, seemed to regard the episode as some kind of
lark, but Jim was anxious and irritated, and he cranked open the
rear window for some air.

"We're going to cruise the neighborhood once or twice to make
sure Mr. Bonanza is not switching vans, or something cagey like
that," Delancey said. "And I hope you guys don't mind waiting. He
got popped at his local pub this afternoon, and he's probably sleeping it off right now."

"You really think somebody who's about to blow up a factory or
something is going to take a nice nap?" Lamont asked.

"You guys don't understand it yet." Delancey sighed. "These are
normal people. They take long vacations. They nap. They even have
girlfriends or boyfriends. They get paid pretty well, and don't have
to go to work every day like us. They make some bucks, buy a bowling alley, retire early."

"You sound like a recruiter," Lamont said.

"With what I know, I oughta be," Delancey said. "I could make
a few bucks on that side of the street."

"So why don't you?" Lamont said.

"Sometimes I wonder." Delancey coughed. "I see a lot of buildings
around this town that ought to be burned down. Only problem is,
they got people in them."

"Delancey," Lamont said, "you need a vacation in some quiet
country town."

"You got that right," Delancey said. "You want to buy me a
ticket?"

They drove through the arsonist's neighborhood, and a few blocks
away the detectives rendezvoused to talk to each other through open
car windows. Jim felt a little sleepy, almost as if he would be too
tired to go through with the night. His mouth felt dry, and he knew

he would like to have a drink, very much would like to have that. It would perk him up.

With a little start, he recognized what he was feeling as a miniature version of pre-patrol jitters. Sometimes he had been so anxious about going into the jungle that he would nod off into a buzzing kind of sleep, shoe half laced or his kit in disarray still. Some of the soldiers had mistaken this for cool: "This cat can nap anywhere, man." But others recognized it for what it was, a built-in kind of drug, an escape. The lieutenant had not been fooled. He stepped on Jim's foot and pressed down, harder and harder, until the pain revived him, and the lieutenant would say, "Prayer time is over. Get ready. Now." Then Jim would slowly grow angry, his hands would be cold, and he would be just a little sick.

After they had driven awhile, Delancey asked Jim if he would like to take some pictures of the arsonist's van. "Can you do it discreetly? From the car?"

"Sure."

"I'll drive by slow."

Jim snapped a few quick frames of the van, black, battered, bearing a front-end bumper sticker that read I'D RATHER BE SKY-DIVING. The back windows were obscured with a decal of geese flying over a mountain lake.

"That thing makes me nervous," Delancey said. "It's a goddamn bomb just sitting there." He spoke into the radio briefly and in code. Then he launched into a dissertation, for Lamont's benefit, on why detectives should have a separate, secret radio band. "Maybe you could mention it in your article," he said.

Lamont asked the routine questions, but Jim tuned him out, curious now about the contents of the van and the kind of man who would use them, assemble them, what kind of people would hire him. Delancey said they were "normal," but Delancey was also a cop and he could be expected to see the world a little off kilter. Hadn't he once remarked, "It's like lifting a rock. You lift a rock and you find all kinds of goodies squirming around. If you don't lift it, you can forget they're even there." They had just lifted a rock, Jim thought, and they had found this black van, and now they were going to lift the rock a little more. The metaphor mildly amused Jim, and he thought of it as city boy's poetry. As a kid, he had lifted a lot of rocks, and most of what he found underneath was harmless, and good bait.

Except that once, he recalled, when he had pulled a rock up on a nest of spiders, and some of the spiders had sped up his hand and into his shirtsleeve, then across his back, and he had run in terror, ripping the shirt off, feeling the spiders racing over him. He flushed with a little tremor of fear now, remembering the episode. The rocks had been in the shade of his neighbor's smokehouse, among bricks and flowers. And after all, the spiders had not bitten him. He had mistaken their own terror and flight for an attack, and he had expected to be bitten, ran screaming through the orchard, trying to tear his shirt off.

Damn it, he thought now. I'm scared of something. I can't be scared of this little detail we're on. What's the deal? Why these jitters?

The spiders had narrow bodies, striped gray and black, tabby-cat colors, and they had legs thick and long and could move with terrible swiftness. He was right to have been terrified, he decided, and lucky not to have been bitten. And it was also the truth that he had returned to the spot where the spiders had emerged and found there a simple hole in the black earth, no wider than a nickel, and the few remaining spiders, circling in slow dismay, would have been at the mercy of the bricks at hand if he had chosen to throw them.

"Any chance we could get a drink someplace?" Jim asked, surprised by the question as if it had come from someone else.

"Forget it," Lamont said.

Delancey chuckled and glanced over his shoulder. "This could be a long night for you, pal."

"I'm bored," Jim said.

"This is the part TV leaves out," Delancey said. "The waiting. And waiting. All the stupid cruising around. Never mind all the stupid paperwork."

"He's not bored," Lamont said. "He just wants a drink."

"This ain't a taxi," Delancey said mildly, regarding passing traffic with an almost belligerent curiosity. After a moment he said, "I could take you past a certain corner, you could photograph whores for a while."

"Thanks, but I'll save my film," Jim said.

"They're dogs anyway," Delancey replied. "Got herpes probably. Some guys I don't understand."

Lamont queried Delancey unsuccessfully about his love life, but Jim tuned out again, more interested in the desultory sidewalk activity of the neighborhood they were in. They were near Chinatown, idling along, all of them in an odd state of mixed boredom and tension.

"Is this car bulletproofed?" Lamont asked.

"The windows, yeah," Delancey said. "But don't count on it. Your best bet would be to hide behind me."

"Don't you guys get a dinner break or something?" Jim asked.

Delancey shook his head. "You need a drink that bad? Hate to tell you, but we'll probably eat in this luxurious car tonight, burgers and fries, you know, some classy drive-through place."

"Great," Jim said.

Delancey spoke to Lamont. "I think your partner really needs a drink."

Lamont turned in the seat and eyed Jim a moment as if he were about to speak, but then must have changed his mind, for he looked away. *Fuck you,* Jim thought. *So I need a drink. So fuck you, Lamont.* Maybe later he could talk them into stopping at a package store and he could run in for a couple of nips. Do you really want to beg for a drink? Jim asked himself. Beg these guys? He settled back with his arms folded. His face felt hot, and he was angry, too, though he didn't know why. Lamont was pissing him off, the self-righteous prick. Writers were such friggin' prima donnas anyhow.

Jim endured his deprivation through the long evening, grew more and more irritated with the repartee between Lamont and Delancey, especially Lamont's barely disguised condescension. Jim thought the effort involved in being so constantly clever should have fatigued Lamont, fatigued his jaw, too. Streetlights winked on. The three of them ate in the parking lot of a drive-in with a golden floating burger enshrined above it in the night sky of the city, tinged pink and purple from the neon lights. The thing about newspaper work, Jim complained to himself, was that you never got to use color. That reminded him to ready his strobe, check the batteries that he would wear on his belt.

About midnight, Jim's head felt as if it were a spring wound tightly as it could be, and he flashed into an argument with Lamont over some petty remark.

Delancey laughed until he choked. "See? This is what drives cops nuts. We even get classes in this stuff—'interpersonal relations.' Which means, how to spend all day in a cruiser with some jerk without murdering each other."

"He just needs a drink," Lamont said, "and he'll be real friendly."

Jim closed his eyes and buried his anger, but as soon as they were through tonight, Lamont was in for a big surprise. A big shiner. A fat lip. Or maybe Jim would break his hand, keep him out of work awhile. Self-righteous prick. The night and the streets rolled around him like a dream. He hated the confines of the car, Delancey's smell, Lamont's cigarettes. Jim nodded with boredom.

Around 1:30 A.M., Bonanza moved. Now everyone woke out of the flat gray space of their waiting into the golden strobing of the car as it passed under streetlights. Delancey seemed to forget his passengers as he narrowed the blocks between himself and the van. The other detectives had occasional visual contact, and the helicopter reported changes of direction.

"He's heading for the airport," Delancey observed. "Want to take bets on where he's going?"

"You know something we don't know?" Lamont said.

"That's right." Delancey pressed his body in a heap over the steering wheel. "You know who the best detectives are? I mean, besides shitwork guys like me who know a little chemistry?"

"I give up," Lamont said.

"Accountants." Delancey managed a grim smile. "Guys who understand budgets. Guys who read bankruptcy claims like poetry."

"I'll remember that," Lamont said.

"Behind every arsonist, there's a fudged budget somewhere," Delancey said. "You can quote me on that."

"Fudged budget," Lamont said. "Say that ten times fast."

The ride lapsed at once into a tense silence interrupted only by crackling radio reports from the helicopter.

"We know where he's going now," Delancey said. "We got his ass now."

The dark ride unfolded, broke down from highway speed into bursts along side streets, crawling past hurricane fences topped with barbed wire, gray truck bodies propped on rusting wheels, black drums stacked tipsily and silhouetted in the blue streetlamp glare. Jim was awed by the bad-movie-set truck-dock warehouse and ruined factory that must have had a whole tumultuous history of ideas and lost jobs, goods, machines made that had no use, the stuff of the earth transformed into junk that a lax economy couldn't save, or just another useless invention, a kind of capitalist art form: the failed product, the failed business.

Somebody has preceded Bonanza, has taken a torch and sparked through the metal web of the fence, rolled it back into a shimmering curl, leaving a van-sized opening. Bonanza stops inside the gash, curls it closed behind him, and is at the door of the van again when the helicopter clatters over the rooftop, a silver wedge of light burning down on him like a visitation, then police cars crunching to halt, blue, quiet strobe, strobe, bullhorn warning echoing from desolate building sides, cement trapping sound in the littered corners of this defeated enterprise.

Delancey is out of the car, Jim close behind him, the camera popping, auto-wind zipping through frames as Jim sequences the closing circle of detectives, the huge swaying light of the chopper above, Bonanza's teeth bared chimpanzee-style, hand dodging inside his black coat as he plunges inside the van, detectives down on the pavement, guns flashing pink and yellow; the van windows are sudden stars, and gunshots echo back from the dark walls, transistors whine as Jim's flash pops and pops.

The van is quiet now, a haze of gunsmoke drifts up into the chopper's silver glare of light, Delancey drags himself up from his crouch like a bear pulling itself up on hind legs, and Jim right beside him when the terrible swat comes, blows Delancey in his great bulk across Jim's body, and they are down together, clawing the asphalt, Delancey's white face skidding on the black pavement, like a mime's white face pushed between black curtains, and already blood from his nose and mouth and the astonishment of his own death rigidifying in Delancey's features.

Incoming! Jim thinks. Behind us. On the roof. Bullets whang from the pavement, sing into the building, hammer the van.

"Sniper!" someone calls. There is a rattle of return fire, and already hands are pawing at Delancey, rolling the bulk of his corpse away, fingering his face; they call for oxygen and EMT, even though Jim knows it is a ritual exercise, a way of paying hopeless respect to the Elephant Man now, and he forces himself into the obscene business of photographing the dead Delancey, the frantic efforts to revive him, the pistols waving vainly over him toward the vacated rooftop; the futile sweep of the chopper's lights over the buildings, the sudden screeling rush of the white van into the parking lot, and the white targetable uniforms of the "emergency technicians" as they bend to their frustrating routine, apply their fruitless instruments, and Delancey is rolled away.

Lamont has Jim by the lapels, his voice slapping, "What about you? So close, man? You nicked? You O.K.?"

Jim thrusts him aside without a word, clicks away, the fire truck in close now, a big nozzle trained on the black van, the van door wrenched open, and out tumbles the white-haired body, face gone into a sleepy mask, hand caught momentarily behind the driver's seat, jerked free by a cop, and then, incredibly to Jim, the cannon on the fire truck erupts a thick gray lather, one prolonged burst, and the black van is filled, dripping with a thick white paste that perfumes the air with the odor of plastic and stale bread.

"Was he dead, Jim? Did you see? Could he say anything?"

Again, Jim thrusts Lamont aside. "Dead!" he says. "Yes, dead."

Lamont staggers back in a fit of coprolalia. He wheels from Jim now, disappears into the uniformed flurry around them. Jim changes film, continues shooting everything, every move.

A detective grabs him by the arm. "Hold it. Let's just check this. You got blood showing, mister."

"I'm not hit," Jim insists.

"Let's just check it out." Gingerly, the man presses on the bloodstains on Jim's shirt.

"It's his," Jim says. "Delancey's."

"Yeah, O.K." The detective releases his grip.

"Oh, God!" Jim shouts. "His blood!" It seems alive on him suddenly, poisonous. Frantically he strips off his cameras, dropping them on the pavement, ripping off his sports coat, the tie, howling as he strips away the shirt, too, feeling blood race like spiders up his arms and across his back, over his entire body, the poisonous blood spreading, burning his flesh.

Pornography. Jim pulled the photographs out of the solution, pitched them into the drier without more than a sidelong glance. Porno. Dead cop. Porno. Dead arsonist. Pornography. Flesh-writing.

When City Desk looked over the pictures a few hours later, he just shook his head, then looked at Jim with a kind of amused disgust. Jim answered with a sick smile.

O Elephant Man.

Jim was lucky he didn't fall asleep at the wheel. Anna had long since left for work, and Jim fell onto the bed without removing his clothes, lay there a long while, panting, his chest heaving, almost strangling, thrashed about in the covers until finally, mercifully, he slept.

Anna brought the papers home with her at noon, but Jim refused to look at them.

"City Desk is thrilled," Anna said.

Jim said nothing, crushed the pillow to his cheek.

"Are you O.K.?" Anna rubbed between his shoulders with one hand.

Jim shook his head no.

"I'm sorry. I'll let you sleep."

Jim shut his eyes again, heard the bedroom door click closed.

Jim cruised through the rest of the week in a haze. He did not drink for several days, and this had two immediate effects: He was short-tempered, impatient with everything and everyone else, quick to snarl if anyone brushed his nerves; and at other times he felt only like weeping. Some simple thing would stand out from its usual context with such force and with such seeming preciousness that it became unbearable in its implications, its beauty, or the terrible tragedy of its impermanence or its astounding absurdity. It seemed to him sometimes that he was examining photographs of the dead, that every instant he perceived was also a dead instant, relegated at once to a mental scrapbook of the past, there to be regarded as fragments of an unfolding fate already known, a history in process, stepping-stones to the inevitable death.

And when the Elephant Man was dropped into the ground on a windy, warm May morning, and the balding obese priest intoned what he must intone, Jim covered his eyes with his hands, and what he remembered made him understand that death was the most common thing of all, nothing at all in the scale of rarities, the coin so current it was all but valueless. Delancey down. Good-bye, Delancey.

Jim walked with Lamont out of the cemetery in silence, Lamont knowing for once to keep his mouth shut, and then they drove to the Regal, and Jim broke his alcohol fast.

"So what?" he said to Lamont.

"What are you talking about?" Lamont said with a tired air.

"So there it is," Jim said. "He dies, she dies, you, we, they die. I—"

"That's right," Lamont said.

"So then what?"

"You mean *after?* Are you getting religious, Jim?"

"No," Jim said. "I mean after you know."

Lamont shrugged. "Life goes on."

"This is it, huh? Making photographs, writing stories, so the *Globe* can run ads that sell panty hose."

"Maybe it's the other way round." Lamont sighed. "I don't feel like a salesman, personally."

"What am I going to do between here and the rattrap that's waiting somewhere? How many days have I even got left?"

"I have some mortality tables you can look at," Lamont said. "Life expectancy is up."

"But is *living* any better?"

Lamont's face was suddenly a study in desolation and anger. He studied Jim a moment, then looked away.

"Sorry," Jim said.

Lamont merely shook his head, sipped his whiskey. Jim felt a sudden impulse to throw his arms across Lamont's shoulders but resisted it. He sipped his whiskey, too, stared into the barroom mirror. I wonder what Red Barber is doing now, he thought.

The letter was apologetic, stating that the management felt that Jim was overqualified and that it would be impossible also for them to meet his current salary. But they also informed him that if he was still interested in the position, the company would be willing to help him find a place to live and to offer as much as possible in the way of fringe benefits, and a thirty-five-and-a-half-hour workweek, to be arranged as he saw fit. Jim was amused at the precision of the figure, thirty-five point five, but the letter itself both attracted and confused him. It was a flag of possible change waving him in the face, and it would require of him as well something he thought unusual in his life—an answer, a choice. He kept the letter in his pocket all day as he worked, and the power of it gave him a new perspective. He did so much by habit, he had been at the *Globe* so long, and so long performed the same duties, that he could carry out his work in a kind of mindless drone. He felt also he could say no to anything he did not want to do, that the power of the job over his life had been broken, and he could go through the day without taking the irritations of the job to heart, because at this particular moment he could be relieved of them, could ignore the difficulties, or leave them to someone else.

The letter disturbed Anna, too, but more profoundly.

"What would I do down there?" she asked at once.

"I thought you wanted to concentrate on the kid," Jim said. "You were going to leave the *Globe* anyway."

"A leave of absence, Jim. We'd only have one salary if I quit work."

"We've only got one now," Jim said. "I spend mine."

"You've been doing better," Anna said. "You've cut down, haven't you?"

"Yes, I have." Jim felt himself drifting away to that habitual place of reserve in his mind, becoming detached. Anna always had an objection. Didn't she?

Anna must have sensed his disappointment, for she quickly continued. "It's just so sudden, I guess." She laughed nervously. "Is it a job you'd like, really? It sounds pretty routine, and it's all darkroom work, isn't it?"

"I don't want to take any more pictures," Jim said.

"Oh, Jim, I don't believe that."

"I don't. It's obscene."

"Maybe you don't want anything at all to do with photography, then. Maybe this film-processing thing is just as bad for you, for now?"

"What else can I do?" Jim said. "Dig ditches?"

"I don't know." Anna fidgeted for a moment, tore to pieces a paper napkin.

"We could go down there," Jim said. "We could look around. Maybe you'd hate it, and then we'd find it easy to decide. Or maybe it's a great place for kids. Can we do that much?"

Anna scooped the shreds of the napkin into a little pile, then swatted them playfully across the tablecloth. "Oh, why not?" she said.

PART II

TRAILS TO THE MOUNTAINTOP

1
Vermilion
Phoenix
(The Summer Now) [i]

Early one morning in June, Chong gets down on his hands and knees and rummages through the bags, cans, and bottles under the kitchen sink until he finds a large aluminum pail—a lard bucket, actually—with a wire handle and a snap-on lid. This is Chong's first-string blueberry bucket, and he has a hunch, given the absence of bluejays in the shrubbery beside the barn, that the blueberries on the shores of Lake Ecstasy are ripe at last. In any case, he intends a reconnaissance.

With his bucket glinting in the morning sun, Chong walks along Lake Ecstasy Road toward the red ABSOLUTELY NO TRESPASSING, NO BATHING, FISHING, OR OTHER NUISANCES signs that border the low-bush blueberry patch and the sandy hill which merges with the pristine sky-reflecting Lake Ecstasy. The water is so clear that on still days it seems to be alternately a great mirror, an opening into the hill where another world begins, blue with fat cottony clouds, or a magnifying lens that makes the lake's dark green bottom seem like a meadow. Chong once spied a hunting knife in the water, and as it was close to shore, he stepped in to salvage it—only to find himself dunked to his nostrils!

Today there is a strong, steady breeze, and Chong knows the lake will be dimpled and opaque, and the hillside will be cool even in the bright sun. As he crosses Old Station Road, he notices a fluttering, a soft dark ruckus in the ditch, and stops to look. There in a tangle

of twigs and pine tufts a little black ball struggles to haul itself out
of the swampy muck.

What the devil? Chong must look more closely still.

There are bits of eggshell clinging to a naked pink chick of rela-
tively large size, big as his fist. The bird is faintly repugnant, a bit
comic in his predicament, but also quite tired and helpless. His sides
heave frantically, and Chong—who hates to interfere; who alters
his stride to miss ants on the road or sidewalk; who leaves a row of
corn outside his fence for the deer, the raccoon, the woodchuck;
who will not save a mouse from a cat or even seal the barn loft (or
the attic of his house) against bats—nevertheless reaches down into
the ditch and takes this throbbing ball into his hand and lifts it up.
The eyes of the bird are like little black mirrors, and the chick seems
oddly calm now, allowing himself to be so plucked up by a human
being and studied.

Broken leg. Broken wing. Apparently the nest blew down. Maybe
a hawk jumped the nest when the chicks were alone, or an owl made
an early-morning raid. As far as Chong can see, this was the lone
survivor, but in his present condition, of course, would not last long
before a 'coon or fox crunched its little bones with needle teeth, or a
snake smothered him in its dark, cold belly. As it should be.

Against his better judgment, however, Chong puts a wad of grass
in his pail, then places the crow chick on top of it. Vigilance will be
required to keep the cats off his neck, Chong muses. Therefore, and
for luck, he names this crow "Awake." After cruising the outer limits
of the blueberry patch and finding the berries still hard and green,
he takes the little crow home. With tape and a wooden stick from a
cotton swab, he straightens its leg, and with a pencil and a thick red
rubber band, sets the wing.

What to feed him? Or her? Chong takes a slice of bread, tears off
a piece, dips it in water, then rolls it into a soft pellet. He pries open
the glistening black beak and pushes the wad down the pink gullet.
Just like a grub. Hey? The beak snaps shut, then opens again, begging. A hit! Chong makes another pellet and stuffs it in, and his finger is pinched with surprising force. The bird makes a little hissing
noise as he vents his demands. More! Chong feeds him half a
dozen more pellets, and still the little bird begs.

Enough, Chong decides. He drops the bird in the pail on its grass
bed and covers the top with a strainer to keep the cats out. Every
time he comes into the kitchen, he wakes the little black thing and

feeds it bread. Later, when he finds harmful bugs in the garden, he drops them in a jar and takes them inside to the voracious little creature. Awake accepts earthworms but rejects tomato worms. He eats grasshoppers, but not Japanese beetles. He eats blueberries, crickets, rice. But he prefers bread, and his favorite dish, bar none, is a chip of soda cracker with a healthy dab of peanut butter and jelly. In a few weeks, Chong cannot open a jar of peanut butter without Awake's raising an uproar of cawing and scratching and hopping, fluttering about the kitchen counter.

I've ruined him, Chong thinks. He'll never survive out there.

When the crow is healed, fat, and flying short distances, Chong takes him outside and sets him loose. But the crow only follows Chong back to the house, waddling and hopping, and waits on the stoop with its head cocked until Chong comes out again. Wherever Chong goes now, the crow follows along, alternately walking and flying, always scolding. But Chong does not let him in the house any more than he would let a chicken in. The bird takes to a tree beside the house at night, and every morning Chong finds him strutting impatiently to and fro by the kitchen door, waiting for bread, or peanut butter when Chong has the heart to prepare such a treat.

The cats are interested, but keep their distance. Now and then the crow opens his wings, hisses, and comes shaking at them like the angel of death—an act of sufficient terror to send the cats slinking back to the porch with their hackles raised.

"A real lion tamer," Chong writes of the crow to Wu. "He follows me everywhere. A damned nuisance!"

The big-shot professor replies: "You describe perfectly the principle of imprinting. Really, you must read Konrad Lorenz, as I've told you so often before. The chick identifies with the first thing it sees, or identifies it with 'mama' at least. Lorenz tells of one poor exhausted duckling whose first glimpse of 'life' was a motorboat. Of course, it was doomed to a miserable, frustrating existence. Imagine yourself falling in love with a diesel train, and you have some idea, I think. We also have here a zoologist who thinks it is an entertaining illustration of the principle to hatch a brood of chickens in the presence of a toy duck on wheels. When she wants to teach imprinting theory to her class, she enters the room pulling her toy duck, and all the chicks come tumbling along pell-mell behind. As you might guess, she is a popular teacher, and a good one, and probably has no hope of getting tenure, therefore. But do not worry about the bird, meanwhile. Puberty will change all. By the end of the summer—or surely by next spring?—he or she will succumb to the stronger instinct of sexual pairing and be gone forever in pursuit of increasing the species. What else could lure the creature away from your gourmet snacks?"

Chong folds the letter, the crow peers in the screen door, his head tilted quizzically. Some farm, Chong thinks. Crippled pig, crow, mice, bats, cats.

"Caw!" the crow says.

Or is it "Ma"?

There comes a night when Chong cannot sleep. Maybe it is the mosquitoes who so often sing their hymns in his ear. Maybe it is the dreams, the sense that someone with ape-broad shoulders has been standing in the doorway of his bedroom, is standing there now. He reaches for his glasses on the night table and stares into the black rectangle of the doorway that seems to breathe, then to swirl and shift like black sand blown down a gray beach.

A thump, and Chong bolts upright, heart hammering. Probably a cat has leapt to the floor from a forbidden survey of a tabletop. Surely it is a cat. Chong strains to listen. Of course, a cat.

All the same, Chong quickly opens the drawer in the night table and picks up two chakras he has made and carefully sharpened. These are round flat pieces of metal with the edges filed razor-keen, meant to be thrown like saucers, and in effect they are throwing knives without handles, with one continuous blade. One of these Chong has made from the main gear of an old bicycle; the other, smaller, is a worn-out blade from a circular saw. He sits on the edge of his bed with a chakra in each hand, remembering their weight, foreseeing their efficient crisp trajectory, their terrible striking force. Such an object hurtling out of the dark, searing the flesh!

A strange grinding noise, then a soft tap. The kitchen door opened and closed? Chong slides out of bed—his back aches—and feels his way to the bedroom door, then, chakras held tightly, arm cocked, jumps softly into the hallway and stares into the kitchen, ready to kill.

The moonlight silhouettes the table, the kitchen fixtures, the blue bottles on a windowsill, the tea can full of flowers. The kitchen door is open.

Open!

Chong crosses the kitchen as quietly as he can and peers out the open door. He sees a shadow dip behind the barn, or he sees nothing. He sees shadows shifting under the trees, or he sees nothing. He tries not to people the darkness, the gray swaths, and patches of moonlight as they shift like oil on water; but someone has been in his house. Someone has just gone out the kitchen door.

The chickens in the night roost burble to each other, but though awake are not excited. Or is it voices on the gentle wind?

Taking a breath to steel his nerves, Chong jumps outside and glides as well as he can in his bare feet and with that annoying backache down the path into the deep shadow beside the barn. He listens intently and hears voices, definitely, coming from the pond.

He moves at once, not down the path, but toward the woods and the creek, which crackles gently and will, Chong hopes, cover his approach to the pond from the side where the dam spills its moon-silver curtain of water beneath the trees.

Chong stalks carefully, feeling the grass, the earth beneath his feet cold and wet, before bearing his weight down. Now he is driven not so much by fear, or by any logic of attacking the demons, but by curiosity. He remembers very well the spoliation of his gazebo on Sweat Hill and the damage done to the dam, and he will not have them—if it is them—taking over his pond, too, littering his swimming spot with broken glass, fouling his soggy little beach.

The water glides in a thin hissing sheen over the dam tonight. Now Chong drops to his hands and knees and crawls through the grass until he tops a small rise and can see the whole near edge of the pond.

Their voices, bell-like, laughing, and sharp, sneering and excited, reach him first in an odd magical blend with the mumbling and whispering of the waterfall. They are out there, but for the moment yet invisible.

Then he sees them. Or their heads. They are in the water to their necks, so that their heads seem to float on the pond's surface, like heads in the sky. Will-o'-the-wisp faces, babbling, an occasional cough or squeal. Two girls, several boys. Probably a carload altogether. Chong wonders how they came here, if they crept past the house and if that is what he heard. Maybe the door had been left open—he couldn't remember closing it—or blew open—he never thought to lock it—and he had merely heard them sneaking by.

There are bottles and cans on the edge of the pond, and a pile of clothes. In spite of the moon, it is dark, and Chong must squint to see anything. He dares to crawl closer in the grass and finds a spot where he can lie comfortably.

In a while they come stumbling out of the water, the two girls first, one fat, the other slender, both white as mushrooms in the moonlight. The large one has a thick, heavy head of hair, which she collects in both hands and wrings forcefully. The thin one pats her face and her body with a sweater, then shakes it out and pulls it over her head in a quick cross-armed motion that makes Chong think of semaphore. In lifting her arms, she has also lifted her small muffin-sized breasts and thrust a hip sideways, showing the sweet, well-developed curve of her thighs, smooth as ivory. Now both girls quickly pull on underwear and jeans.

"O.K.!" one shouts, and the boys emerge.

They are modest, Chong thinks. These are not the ones who fouled the gazebo. This is no devil's orgy.

The boys come out in a rush of foam, laughing and swearing. The tallest, whose hair arcs about his head in springy curls, immediately takes up and lights a cigarette, blows an invisible cloud of smoke. He struts shamelessly, hand on hip, showing himself to the girls. The other boys are already squatting in the grass, pulling on their trousers, reaching for bottles, shaking the water from their long, stringy hair. They are all athletic, muscles deeply grooved and shadowed, arms and stomachs hard.

"I'm goin' back in," the tall one declares. "Come on, Ginny."

"Naw. I'm dressed already."

"You're chicken."

"No. And ain't stupid, either."

"What are you afraid of?"

"You know."

"Snakes, maybe?"

"Yeah. Little white ones!"

Everyone howls, and the tall boy hurls a sheet of water at them as he slides into the water again and drifts to the center of the pond. He tips his head back and continues smoking with an insouciance that almost makes Chong laugh.

"Gin-eee," the boy sings out through clenched teeth.

"No!"

"Gin-eee."

The thin girl stands up now. "Be quiet, Taylor, you stupid jerk. We'll get caught."

"Shheee-it."

Where are the parents of these children? Chong wonders. Did they allow nights like this—cool water, moon, beer, cigarettes, maybe some sex? Unbelievable! Nothing like this was possible in his own youth. Chong's father caged him nightly, ordering him to the attic even before the sun had set. Before he was swept away from home, all the summer nights of his own youth were spent under a roof in the heat, listening to doves scratch along the eaves and coo. Once he had escaped to meet with friends, was caught, beaten by his father. To teach him respect. To teach him hatred.

Now, as the tallest boy returns and pulls on his clothes, the others are scraping a hole on the very edge of the water and piling in paper and twigs. A flame leaps up under an even column of orange smoke, then the fire crackles, and the twigs catch fire. The teens lay back, cradling bottles, shoulder to shoulder.

Chong, himself tired, rises in a crouch and turns to make his way back to bed. There on the dam, water coursing between his feet, is a large ape-shouldered man, half his face and his body brought into relief by the moon and the pale light reflected from the water. At the sight of him, Chong feels he has been hit in the stomach. He sits down at once.

The man has his arms folded across his chest and is watching the teenagers, the little lotus of flame on the shore, and its reflection on the water. He seems stern, yet relaxed. Apparently he has not seen Chong. Surely he has not seen Chong.

Chong raises his arm slowly, cocking it, prepares to throw a chakra. Without acknowledging him, or that he has seen the arm raised, the man crosses the dam, water hissing over his feet, and, once across, disappears in the darkness of the woods.

Chong wakes early, though he has slept fitfully, dreaming that the man had entered his home again, and again. He stands at the kitchen sink stupidly staring out his rear window as the teakettle growls and rattles. The meadow is covered with an impenetrable shifting white haze, as if the northern half of his farm had been erased during the night. It is like smoke.

Chong finds his glasses, cleans and dons them.

It *is* smoke!

Chong is suddenly awake as if slapped. He dashes into the yard and now sees clearly a dragon of orange slithering sideways across the meadow, devouring his grass, smoldering steadily toward the

house. He rushes back inside and calls the FIRE number on a sticker
on his telephone, makes a frantic report to the woman who answers,
then rushes out again with a broom.

The flame of the fire is not much taller than the grass, but
stretches in a long, snaking arc across almost the whole breadth of
Chong's field. The smoke comes toward him in a low curling sheet,
and the air is dry and surprisingly hot. Chong, broom raised, cannot
take himself through the veil of heat to the flame itself and resorts to
swatting sparks that swirl up from and fall ahead of the fire like
snow. The fire crackles like bacon in a pan, and sometimes there is
an eerie high-pitched pinging, almost like whistling. Already the
damned flames have devoured half the distance from the pond to his
house and Chong can see large flakes of ash sailing over his roof.

At last a siren. A pickup truck comes bouncing along the lane
from the barn, then stops and backs away. Another pickup swings
off onto the edge of the road next to Chong's house and two men
pile out and head across the field toward him. In a moment, a yellow tanker, siren wailing, fat as a bumblebee, lumbers into the driveway and whines slowly forward.

One of the men from the pickup hobbles up to Chong, head down
and crouched as if in a bombardment. A thick Mexican mustache
hangs from his lip.

"Holy shit! You got a hot one, mister!" He grins, then lurches
away to wave at the tanker. "Bring it in here, Sweeney. Put 'er
broadside."

Before the truck has stopped, the volunteers are hauling long lines
of red rubber hose from the reels at the tanker's rear.

"Get on that pump, you asshole. It's a hotter!"

The whine of the engine crescendos and the driver stumbles out
throwing open compartment doors, twisting handles. Oddly enough,
to Chong, he clamps a cigar in the center of his mouth; a fluorescent
cap, turned backwards, covers his neck.

Water coughs through the lines.

"Ya-hoo!"

"Get me another nozzle. *Nozzle*, I said. This won't piss a drop!"

Someone shouts in Chong's ear. "Can we draft from the pond?"

"I don't know what you mean!"

"Get water from the pond, savvy?"

"Yes!"

Now Chong realizes that Turner is handling one of the hoses, ambles through the field behind a wide spray of water that throws off little rainbows of mist. Somehow, seeing a man he knows gives Chong more confidence that this rabble can do him some good.

Suddenly the air is still, except for the crackling of the flames.

"Hey!" Turner shouts.

"Choke it, Sweeney! You gotta choke that sucker!"

The engine grinds.

"More! Choke it more!"

And grinds. Then bursts to life.

"Crank it up now!"

For the next two hours, the firefighters chase the curling dragon across Chong's field, stopping once to refill the tank from the pond, and take up the chase again. By noon the flames are down, and Chong's field lies like a wet black steaming carpet by the pond. Chong, still agitated, hustles to his cellar and brings up cold bottles of Tsingtao.

"Chinese beer," he says, handing around bottles to the sooty firemen gathered at the side of the yellow tanker, parked now beside the barn. "Hope you like it. I'm very grateful."

"Won't make you a commie, will it? Drinkin' this stuff?"

"Sure it will," Chong says.

"Tastes O.K. to me."

"Three bottles and you talk Chinese, I'll bet!"

Chong laughs. "Right!"

As Turner accepts a beer from Chong, he asks, "You got any idea how it started?"

Chong shrugs. "Some kids last night, they had a fire going by the pond."

"Skinny-dipping?"

"That ain't it." The man with the fluorescent hat holds out his bottle, points with it toward the pond. "Looks to me like that fire was started in three, four places across there. I'll bet you it was deliberate."

"You know any of those kids?" Turner asks.

"I only heard one name," Chong says. "Taylor. That's all."

The firemen spit and laugh. "That's all, he says."

"Tall kid? Fluffed-up hippie hair?"

"Yes."

"That guy," Turner says, "has been in jail twice already and is only sixteen. First time was car theft. Last time he was in for setting

fire to a tobacco barn. He's out of that Archer family, and I told you
about them."

"He don't give a damn for anything or anybody," the truck driver
declares. "If it was up to me, he'd a been hanged two or three times
already."

"Any idea who was with him?" Turner asks.

"No," Chong says. "Two guys, two girls."

"Real cozy," someone grumbles.

"Bet I know who."

"Don't we?"

The firemen ceremoniously place their empty bottles on Chong's
porch step, then walk back across the blackened field to the edge of
the pond, where for half an hour Chong can see them arguing and
gesticulating.

Gin-eee, Chong remembers. Ginny.

Why am I protecting her?

The summer sun has the perfection of a deep dream, but Chong
is not minding it much. He chews the sour translucent end of a
strand of clover; the purple flower bobs over his belly as he squints,
so that the blue of the sky reflected in the pond fills his whole head,
covers his thoughts like a blanket. The blue has a feeling of ripeness
about it, and yet it is, Chong knows, so insubstantial that he can,
facing a blank page, forget it. He is trying to fill his head now with
an inexhaustible supply of blue sky so that he can tap it on demand,
so that it will leak into the other parts of his thinking and keep him
cool and well-lighted inside. So he can say of himself: today I am
full of blue sky.

> *This blue sky creates the longing*
> *of plants to stretch*
> *like cats;*
> *Can I take it with me, this blue*
> *breath and longing,*
> *a serape,*
> *when I die?*

Then he tapes a piece of paper to the cool enamel top of the
kitchen table and arranges his watercolors and brushes. He paints
a comic gray skeleton beneath the roots of deep green orchard grass

and clover; a tiny blasé cow fills its mouth with purple balls, yellow stars, and green shoots as the bees rocket around. This part of the painting is small, covering the lower third of the page. The rest is a hot wet sky of impeccable blue in which a cloud, a ghost, threatens to materialize. He titles this "Death Has No Sky. (Or Does It?)"

2
Sport
of
Kings

S ometimes the sky over Cape Cod Bay was so profoundly and serenely blue, and the water, striated an ephemeral green and gold and azure, was so gemlike in its perfection, that the mistake of moving from Boston seemed corrected, the promises made to Jim by the company seemed fulfilled, and Anna's misery seemed less than irreparable. He and Anna would walk the beach near their cottage, and their hands might even brush, and fingers lock, and Jim would quell his unending agitation enough to keep the slow, gently swinging pace required by Anna's advancing pregnancy. For ten minutes, they could forget their debts, their arguments, their anxieties, and the irritations of daily life and work.

Jim could almost, at these times, believe that he had fulfilled his promises also to become sober and to wrestle more honestly with the demons that came between him and the light, that urged him to drink, and that gave him such satisfaction in being destitute of memory and thickened in perception.

The company had found them a "house" that was really a vacation cottage that had been casually winterized, not much bigger than an apartment. The location was good, Jim thought, down a sandy lane bordered with red pine and beach plum, in the town of Sandwich, and not far from Sandy Neck barrier beach. He could drive to work in Hyannis in ten minutes, and except for occasional jamups of tourist traffic, the ease of the commute was a welcome change, and a great relief from that part of his Boston life.

He worked his thirty-five point five hours in four days, whenever possible, so that he had three days off in sequence—Sunday, Monday, and Tuesday. He needed this long weekend because he spent his entire working day in the darkroom, and if he and his co-workers were allowed frequent coffee breaks in an elevated lounge with a view of Hyannis harbor in the distance, Jim still felt cloistered, and the comparative absence of daylight in his new life stirred him uncomfortably, in a way he would not have anticipated. Sometimes when he spoke to Anna about his job, he referred to it as "another day in the image mines." He tried to sound as if he were joking when he said this, so she would not have to share in his discontent or feel regret for the change they had made.

In comparison to others at the plant, who tended automated processing machines, Jim had somewhat interesting work, at least. To him fell the tasks of developing the negatives for and then printing the works of the Cape Cod photographers who considered themselves artists, or professionals; and if some were mere hacks, others were quite good, and Jim admired their work and was happy to treat it with special consideration. His craft was appreciated in turn, and within a few months the special orders increased significantly. The business was small enough that Jim met many of the people whose prints he processed, and this provided him with a source of a few new friends, and potential for others. He began to feel a little bit a part of a special network, and that his expertise was valued in that community. Anna, of course, remained at home and did not share in this world of Jim's.

After all the years of black and white newspaper work, Jim found himself excited by color. The dimensions of the world simply expanded before his eyes, and he knew that his own sense of discovery was in large measure what made it possible to search out and emphasize the possibilities of the films that others brought to him.

He had two other assignments that he tried, as much as possible, to reserve for one day of his working week, his longest day. The first was police photography, pictures usually of smashed cars or artifacts to be introduced as evidence in court, and only rarely more troublesome subjects. Sometimes urgency was required in producing these, and Jim resented the intrusion of this work into his thinking about other things. Bringing up the contrast in the black and white feathers on the throat of a loon, brightening the aquamarine blue in the wing

feathers of a wood duck, deepening the shade in that conical swirl
of fern leaves—to turn from this to bullet holes in a car window
jarred him and angered him.

The other special assignment was what the management euphe-
mistically called "art," meaning sometimes photographs of nudes,
sometimes erotic photography of the type ordinarily geared for men's
magazines, and sometimes even cruder, more violent imagery. A
small group of Provincetown photographers were responsible for
most of it, and they produced, Jim thought, a surprising amount of
sexual grotesquerie for markets he could barely imagine. The process
of this business provoked his curiosity, but he did not pursue it any
more than he lavished any great skill on preparing the four-color
screened "separations" needed for magazine reproduction, or took
any pains to improve, in the printing, the quality of the frequently
muddy negatives he had been sent. And after a day of working with
these images, Jim was sick of the body, hated the idea of sex, of all
the grappling and contortions that went into it, of all the sweat and
heavy breathing, hair and skin, orifices. Fish had more streamlined
bodies, monkeys more grace, tigers more dignity. He did not doubt
that beautiful photographs could be made of the human body, or
that sex could be substantially more than animal joining, creative as
the human spirit, but that is not what the Provincetown photographers sent his way, and he left work in a fog of disgust.

It was after his longest day at work that he stopped by the Whale
Inn on his way home. The rest of the week he would do well, drink
only a few beers at home, or not drink at all for one or two days, but
on Wednesday evenings he felt the old compulsion too strongly; the
belief in the beauty of life, even the miracle of Anna's pregnancy,
would be shattered, seem an illusion, and he would not care. And
he would drink. The Whale Inn was not far from his home, and one
Wednesday Anna walked there to meet him, surprise him, and to
discourage him, but he only sat at a small table across from her and
drank anyway, and in silence, defying her and her concern, ignoring
the hand that she laid on his, and her questions to him on why, why
he insisted on doing this when everything else was going well, and
after the promises he had made to her, and to himself. He grew
angry with her nagging, and then he would see her pregnancy, and
the terrible worry in her eyes, and he would pity her and feel contempt for her because she did not hate life enough and had chosen
to cleave to a man who could not do anything right, not even free
himself from misery.

On Thursday, he would repent, would awaken to Anna's lashing, the nausea and pain of his own body, would beg forgiveness, and flee to work, welcoming the darkness, the escape to the dreamlike world he lived in; and when he came home, he would resolve to behave, and he would succeed, at least minimally, and Anna would remind him that if it weren't for these weekly lapses he would be, if not free from it, at least in control of his addiction, and a better and a happier man for it. He agreed. He tried to understand what so easily knocked him off course. He talked to Anna about this, or tried to. He respected her intelligence, but sometimes it threatened and irritated him, or made him jealous, for he wanted to be the one to discover the solutions to his own dilemmas. Sometimes he loved Anna so much he could not bear the sight of her—she seemed illuminated by the life she carried within—or bear the weight of his own guilt; but sometimes, though rarely, she seemed ugly to him, with stringy hair, eyes red-rimmed, her body deformed and even comic, and he could not wait to put distance between them.

The long weekend and Anna's unusual idleness from work changed Jim and Anna's life, too. They were together more now, more married than they had ever been, and Jim found himself a little shy with his usual secrets or to spin his own thoughts for long periods without the intensity of this encounter, and that it was impossible to keep interruption or some response from Anna. She began to occupy a large space in his life and in his thoughts, and this frightened him a little. It was as if she had to be rediscovered and their whole relationship reinvented. The thought of this sometimes made Jim weary, and he fell silent, wondering if he had the energy or the desire to pursue it, as Anna apparently did.

"What if it's a girl, Jim?"

"I'd like to have a daughter. Did you think I wouldn't?"

"We never talked about it, that's all."

"What's to talk about? We don't have any choice about it. I'll take what comes."

"But what would you like your daughter to be like?"

"I don't know," Jim said. "A great shortstop?"

"That's kind of what I thought," Anna said. "See? We do have something to talk about."

Why bother? Jim thought. You can't decide things like that. The kid will be what it's going to be. Grow up to be President, I don't care. Cannon fodder. Drunk. School superintendent. I can't make it happen or not. So what's to talk about? My daughter the orchestra conductor, the astronaut, the B-girl, the bookie. How can I know?

One day Jim took down the screens over the cottage windows, and tried to find the right storm windows to replace them. None of the storm windows seemed to fit properly, as if they had been warped, or more likely, as if the landlord had bought a number of storm windows without concern for proper sizes. The stepladder was wobbly, and Jim had few tools other than dime-store pliers, a hammer, a bargain screwdriver set. He pushed and tugged, trying to hang the storm windows on the hooks above the windows, then force them into a snug fit. Then the ladder buckled, and Jim pitched to the ground; the window he was working with swung from a single hook, threatening to tumble down. Jim dusted off his hands, picked up his hammer, and hurled it with a great *clap* into the side of the house, then retrieved it, and with a mighty heave now, sent it hurtling over the rows of pines in front of the house and out into the street. When he turned around, he found Anna burning a look upon him.

"Don't say anything," Jim said. "Just don't."

But Anna could not desist. "Why," she asked, "are men so damned angry all the time?"

"Men, plural?"

"You and my father. Every time you get like this, I think of my father."

"The asshole who bought these fucking windows could have at least numbered them so I'd fucking know where the fuckers go."

"You don't have to be so . . . so violent about it."

"Just what I need." Jim started toward the road to retrieve his hammer. "A fucking supervisor who is also a fucking psychologist."

"Yes" Anna shouted. "Yes! And also a fucking wife who has to listen to you endlessly bitch about your fucking life!"

Jim stopped in his tracks, astounded that Anna was screaming at him, screaming and crying. "Everything you do, or try to do, just makes you miserable and angry, and I get to listen to it."

"Anna—"

"You hit the house with the hammer, it scared me to death. I thought it was a gunshot."

"Anna—"

"You think you've got it so bad, but you don't even see the good things around you."

"Leave me alone," Jim said. "I'll get the windows up eventually."

"If you don't tear down the house first."

"The house is safe," Jim said.

"I don't see what's so special about a couple of windows to rate all this display of anger."

"No?" Jim said. He turned and faced Anna. "How's this grab you? I was just thinking the job should take about five minutes, and it's going to take all day."

"But you number the windows, and it won't take so long next time."

"And," Jim went on, "it occurred to me my whole life is just like this—five-minute nuisances that last forever, forever I'm trying to fit something where it won't go, trying to work with half-assed tools—"

"I *don't*," Anna shouted, "I don't feel sorry for you. I just don't." She turned at once and marched into the house.

I'll get the hammer, Jim thought, I'll go into the house, and I'll . . .

What? What will you do? he asked himself. Waste the bitch? Bash her brains out, huh? He felt sick at the thought, and trudged after his hammer, head down like a shamed dog.

With the change of season came a change of light, and with fewer hours of daytime Jim sometimes emerged from the darkroom into an amber sunset under deep purple clouds, or into darkness outright. Anna reported to him her delight in the fall, the lingering warmth provided by the ocean waters, slow to cool, so that she could spend pleasant hours outdoors still. She was content now, too, to make what preparations were necessary, and what their small house would permit, for the baby's arrival. Jim encouraged anything that interested her and would keep her occupied and free from brooding, and when a photographer came to him asking for help and consultation on putting together a book, Jim recommended Anna, practically forced the union of their talents, and celebrated their informal contract.

Anna liked the work and the photographs she was arranging and editing, and because she was so hungry for something to do, she also undercharged the photographer and did not report all the hours she spent on the project, trying to gauge what would be reasonable for the man and undervaluing herself in the process. Jim warned her about this, but did not insist, for he was happy to see Anna's mind engaged, her talents exercised. The job did not last very long, but

Anna and the photographer had become friends, and when the book appeared—a pretty, slender volume—the man gave Anna a copy and inscribed it with a warm, appreciative note. Anna was pleased with the result, and began to study book production, reading about it, and creating "dummy" layouts from sheets of scrap paper, locating handmade books and borrowing them for a while because she could not afford their purchase.

One night as Jim and Anna slipped into bed, Anna said she would like to make a book, a handmade book, a single copy. She would like, she said, to use Jim's photographs, and practice making a book so that when the baby came she could make another one, a record of the childhood, and some day make a gift of it.

"I like the idea," Jim said, "but I haven't done anything with the camera lately."

"You'd better get in shape," Anna said. "You're going to want baby pictures."

"I don't know what I can do with the camera any more," Jim insisted. "And it's not a good time of year for it, dark so early."

"You have all the weekend," Anna said.

"And film's expensive."

"You can get a discount, and do your own processing," Anna said. "It won't cost you an arm and a leg."

"I don't know."

"And I really want to make this book," Anna said.

"There's better photographers than me."

"But I want to make this book with you, not somebody else."

"I'll think about it," Jim said. "About what I can photograph. Everything seems used up."

"Used up?"

"Everything has been photographed already."

"So? It hasn't been photographed by you."

"Yeah," Jim said, "but I just mean it doesn't interest me much to do what's been done over and over. It embarrasses me, frankly. I see so much of the same stuff over and over."

"Well, think about it, will you? I really want to do a book with you." She shifted uncomfortably in the bed, laughed. "God, it's hard to sleep with this belly. It gets in the way."

"Damn it," Jim said. "I should have started nine months ago. I should have made a record of your belly."

Anna laughed, touched his face. "Well, do it now. Take a picture of this heap. In the covers. I feel like a whale."

"You mean now?"

"Yes, now. Why not now?"

"Well, sure." Jim threw back the covers and rolled out of bed. "Why not now?" He pulled his camera case down from a closet shelf, and opened it on the foot of the bed. Anna had the covers pulled to her chin, peered over the mound of blankets and baby, a wrinkled smile on her face. Jim felt a little nervous and self-conscious, a little embarrassed.

"This is loony," he said.

"So what?" Anna replied.

"Right." Jim set up his tripod with a photo light, watching Anna watch his preparations with amusement, and he thought that she was right, that belly of hers was really a marvelous and solemn thing, and it deserved a photograph or two.

The darkness came down, and every day Jim went to work in the dark, and every day returned home in the dark. During the day, too, the sky was often a mass of leaden clouds packed tightly together, black-bellied and turbulent, gushing rain. On his weekends, Jim could not bear to remain inside, and as long as the season permitted, he grabbed the gear he kept ready on their tiny screened-in porch and went fishing from the nearby jetties and the beaches. He knew he was abandoning Anna, that he was not facing the reality of her pregnancy, and should have been doing more to prepare, and to prepare himself, for the birth, the changes in their lives this would bring about. But he could not bear to be indoors, he said, and Anna said she understood this, and patiently she went about making the house ready, installing shelves in the bathroom, buying clothes and sterilizers, setting up a little crib that crammed their bedroom and that Jim collided with in the darkness of his morning preparations for work. I can't bear it, he thought. The house is too small, too occupied, and there is no room for me here. All week I am in this dark little cell with these images like dreams hurrying past my eye; and when I come home, am I to be smothered, too?

The ocean satisfied him in a way that he did not understand. He wanted a boat to be even farther out into it, to be lost in it, surrounded by it, with the land invisible to him, disappeared. The scale of the ocean, its inhuman vastness, matched the size of his hunger, his sense of the void in his own life, a kind of perpetual void that never filled with anything. Maybe the child would fill it, would consume that terrible emptiness he felt, and which the ocean reflected.

Drinking helped. He knew that drinking helped a lot to reduce this sense of the unending void, and when it would be too obvious to Anna that he was failing their agreements, he would take a bottle, or beers, and he would sit on the beach in the darkness watching the tip of his fishing rod, drinking and calling this fishing. The night would crowd in over the ocean, and these two vast darknesses would combine, and the rod tip would slash forward suddenly, felt more than seen, and Jim would become engaged in some dark struggle with some invisible creature until, exhausted, the dogfish or the bluefish would thrash into the foam at his feet and be gaffed. He would slap the body of the fish onto the sand with a grunt of satisfaction, inspect it in the dim beam of his flashlight, rebait, and return himself to the dark business of being alone, and free from the abrasions of the world.

But already in mid-November the fish had left the beaches, the striped bass and bluefish anyway, and since it was unforgivingly cold, he could no longer make this a convenient excuse for avoiding himself, his wife, and the future careening toward them. Jim was scared now. He found less occasion and less excuse to drink, and this made him irritable. Sobriety was nothing if not just aggravating, time crept along so slowly, so full of tiring and demeaning little efforts, arguments, decisions. He spent time with Anna, trying not to begrudge it, trying to remember and rediscover how he had been in love, how to give Anna some ease from his own impatience and irritability. When he drove into the driveway, saw the storm door opaque with condensed steam from Anna's cooking, he sometimes sat for a moment in the car, listening to the wind rock the pines, or just sat in silence until it was too cold to bear, and if Anna asked him why he had stayed in the car so long, he would say there was something on the radio he wanted to hear, some news item or some song he liked.

Anna talked to him at suppertime, and they made plans and decisions that Jim did not really remember, and were for him just a way of passing the time, of seeming to be present in his marriage. Half his mind was on the beach, or elsewhere, in the past, thinking of a red dusty road into the jungle, with corpses on either side of it. Whenever Anna mentioned his camera, the book they would be making together of their child's life, he thought of Viet Nam in a vague, cloudy sort of way, like the murky algaed water of the ponds there, the muddy flecked water of the streams.

The baby came in January, during a sleeting snowstorm that made the roads to the hospital treacherous, that made the trip slow going, and Jim terrified of his own impatience. When the pains stunned Anna, he pulled to a halt on the roadside to give her some small relief, then drove again, enraged that he could not stop the car without the car fishtailing in the slush on the road. Anna was frightened, too, but happy, and she bore her pains with some shock at their intensity, but also, Jim thought, with a kind of brave detachment. He had seen worse behavior from men with insignificant wounds.

When he pulled into the emergency ward entrance, Anna's contractions were only minutes apart. She was wheeled inside, and Jim forgot everything, the doctor's name, the name of the insurance company, his telephone number. There were forms to fill out—the child was not even born yet, and already the bureaucracy closed around it. Jim dashed upstairs as soon as he could and was allowed to sit beside Anna, dressed now in a simple pale green smock; her hair tied back, and in the fluorescent light her skin took on a purple tone, and her lips seemed unnaturally red.

"You forgot your camera," she said, a wan smile on her lips.

The nurses came by at intervals and sent Jim outside the curtain while they checked the dilation of the cervix. He listened in anger to Anna's whelp of pain, her protest at the intrusion; and then, in spite of the breathing exercises she had learned, in spite of Jim's efforts to coach her in controlling the intervals of pain and release, they drugged Anna, and she rolled on the cot, and the little smock twisted up her body, and Jim tried to keep her from rolling off the cot and to pull her smock down over the scarlet gash that formed between her legs, the sight of which—the blood, matted hair, pulsing skin—made him dizzy with animal fact. Anna, dozing between the pains, drug-dozing and fighting for consciousness, babbled, dreaming aloud—she mentioned shipwrecks, the leaking toilet Jim had long ago repaired, a one-eyed Teddy bear she used to have, and would he please take the lilacs from her ears?

Then she was wheeled into the delivery room, a smear of blood on the inside of her thigh, and she went out of the room with her arm collapsed over her forehead, moaning softly, almost the moan of sexual pleasure, but too suddenly sharp and outraged that it all could be so fierce and continue so long.

Six hours later he was led through a maze of dimly lit corridors to greet Anna as she was carted from the delivery room, too exhausted to smile, mouth slack, her skin wan; and they held up for his quick inspection a scarlet shriveled imp, eyes closed like a kitten's, fists clenched, a bandage dangling from her belly, and for the last moment nameless—and so small! How could she have raised such a mound on Anna and emerged so small, as if she had left behind in entering this world, another, at least a castle, with a view of the sea?

Anna managed to grasp, so lightly, Jim's arm, and out of her haze of fatigue, to say, "Theresa, right?"

"Yes," Jim said. "Theresa Anna Williams." Welcome, he thought, to the computer age, the thermonuclear age, the age of gene splicing, space shuttles, crowds, and wars. We don't know what's in store for you, but welcome, welcome, my daughter!

And he was filled with a happy rage, like a warrior who has caught the enemy bathing in a quiet pool.

So the winter passed in the pungent, cloistered reality of Theresa's presence. The grandmothers came in turn, staying a week apiece at a nearby motel, since the cottage was too small for them, and they each refused as outrageous Jim's offer to turn himself out for them. They gave Anna company and bad advice, cooked meals of pedestrian quality designed to promote heart attacks and cancer, but Jim's own excitement was so overflowing that the peccadilloes and complications of his own mother and mother-in-law were easily ignored. Even the usual cynicism of Anna's mother seemed tempered, and the usual advice she had for Jim on improving his career (by courses in motel management, computer programming, or mail order catering) were absent from dinner-table conversation.

"Maybe she's just given up on you," Anna teased, whispering to him in bed.

"She did manage to make some remarks about the house."

"She just said it's small for three. She's right."

"What she means is 'You can't even provide my daughter and granddaughter with a decent house.'"

"Don't take her so seriously," Anna said. "She's behaving pretty well overall."

"I won't go on the attack, don't worry." But Jim was not sure he believed this. He felt vulnerable, that he was not doing enough, that he was, in fact, flirting with serious failure. He could not bear criticism now, for he was doing enough of that on his own. He was scared. And if pressed he knew he would retaliate. He was ready for it, jumpy in his excitement and the rediscovery of his love. One thing at a time, he thought. Test each step before you put your weight down. That's how we'll do it. One thing at a time.

Now Jim came home on Wednesdays as on other nights, and he endured his craving to be drunk as much as possible by distracting himself with Theresa and Anna. For a while, whenever Jim walked into the house, nothing seemed real, he seemed to float about a foot from the floor, felt claustrophobic, choked by the presence of the baby, and one night when the baby had howled so insistently, so unrelievedly, that Anna was at wit's end, nearly hysterical, Jim called an old friend at the *Globe* for advice and was told with a laugh, "Buy the kid a pacifier."

"Pacifier, sure," Jim said. He fled the house to a drugstore not far away and found, to his amazement, one whole section bedecked with pacifiers and infant toys, bought several of each. The rest of the world seemed so calm, meanwhile, in no emergency state, going about its simple routines, that when Jim returned to the steamy cottage, pungent with diapers, the baby still shrieking in Anna's harried arms, Jim took Theresa, applied the pacifier with instant success, and told Anna to get out of the house.

"Go on," he insisted. "Go see a movie. Anything. Have a frappe."

"I can't go out," Anna said. "I look like hell. I feel like hell."

"I'll throw you out," Jim said.

Anna washed her face, threw on a jacket, and in a moment was gone. Jim carried the little bundle of Theresa from room to room, just walking, thinking about little. One of Theresa's hands tangled in the hair over his ear, and it amused him to think of the child's curiosity about an ear that was almost the size of her whole face, a nameless object, huge, floating in a consciousness that did not separate ear from hair, from drifting along in the expanded world she had suddenly been propelled into. If I could photograph what the baby sees! Jim thought. A shoe you could put your arm into. But how destroy the reference points we've learned?

The kid sure likes motion, he thought. Like the Viet Namese children, the ones he had seen, always in motion, too. Hurrying, hustling, pulling your coat, five-year-olds smoking cigarettes, teenagers selling their bodies, and that woman he had seen carrying the dead baby in her arms—and photographed her, yes—unable to accept the death, the loss, hoping for some American miracle to animate the still, unblinking eyes. The woman was deaf, and the child was scarless—this wreckage the result of concussion, the shock wave from an explosion. Jim pressed Theresa to his chest, remembering this, awash in anger and sorrow for a moment. Not too hard, he told himself. Don't squeeze the kid too hard.

And he thought of Anna entering a drugstore alone, sitting at the clean marble counter, free now from the intensity of the child's demands, the cloistering of the cottage, the tension diminishing. How many hours had the little brat been howling in her ear? Playfully, affectionately, he spanked Theresa's butt and voiced his complaints.

"You think you're the goddamned center of the universe, don't you?"

The pacifier fell out of Theresa's mouth and bounced on the floor, and Jim now felt his daughter's little mouth gnawing on his ear. He had to laugh. So this was fatherhood: Piss on your lap, barf on your arm, spit in your ear. And it was also suddenly obvious, eye-wateringly so, that still another little animal fact was coming to his attention. Theresa was already grumbling and fidgeting with the twin discomforts of an empty mouth and a full diaper.

"Theresa," Jim said, "I want you to grow up tomorrow, O.K.?" How long before she was out of diapers? he wondered. Two years? Three? Christ, he might change her a thousand times before this was over.

In two hours, Anna still had not returned. Good, Jim thought. She went to a movie. A cold wind from the bay shook the doors on the house, but it was otherwise incredibly quiet now, except for Theresa's breathing, which notified Jim somehow of its every little catch or change of rhythm.

The problem is, Jim thought suddenly, I never learned to do nothing at all. I'm waiting is all I'm doing. For the next shot. And I don't know where it's coming from.

When Anna came home, Jim was ready for bed, in his pajamas, and Theresa was sleeping soundly. Anna, her face cold from the weather, still in her coat, took him in a prolonged embrace.

"God, thanks," she said.

"You'll have to do that more often, I guess."

"I sure will." Anna released him slowly. "Especially when I get such an appreciative homecoming."

For in spite of himself, because of the close contact with Anna, the warmth of her thigh against him, Jim was aroused.

"It's been a long time," he said, even blushing a little.

"I'm sure we can do something about that." Anna tore off her coat. "Not everything yet, but *something* nice."

By springtime they had been through half a dozen childhood miseries, all of which had made the winter seem long indeed, and Jim greeted the encroaching sunlight hours with relief and expectation, almost as if he had been released from prison. And meanwhile, he had not stopped drinking entirely, but he thought he was managing pretty well, with lapses that he hated and could not explain, and more powerful in his own affairs. He wanted to be a good father. He did not want Theresa to grow up in the shadow of a drunk, so when he did drink, his guilt was more terrible than ever, because he was not just failing himself or Anna, but Theresa, too. The guilt was crushing, and became a deterrent in itself.

A few times during the winter, too, Jim had called Red Barber at his home in Lake Ecstasy, and they had talked for hours, confiding in each other, checking on each other.

After bouncing around the country for a number of years, Red had landed in this rural town and liked it enough to start his own garage. The ex-helicopter mechanic now worked on tractors and trucks, a business he complained about as being too successful, as leaving him too little time to enjoy the hunting and the fishing he loved.

"This year," Red had reminded Jim, "this is number fifteen. Can you believe it? Fifteen fuckin' years ago, we were there. It doesn't seem that long."

"No," Jim had agreed. "Part of me is still there."

"I can dig it," Red said. "You'd think in fifteen years, a guy could bleed it out of his system. Jesus, man, that's about a fourth of your life! We're almost twice as old now."

"I don't feel that old," Jim had said. "I feel like I'm just getting my feet wet."

Red laughed quietly. "I sure can dig it, Jim."

They exchanged invitations to visit every time they talked, but working life interfered, and Jim did not feel it fair to leave Anna alone for a long weekend, and for some reason also Red never found the time to make the five-hour trip east.

"I gotta make hay while the sun shines," he would say.

Jim understood. But he really wanted to see Red and find out more about his life in Lake Ecstasy. Red seemed happy. In spite of the dearth of women his age, there was apparently plenty of other mischief, and life was not frantic. Red described the winter as a "ball-buster," but said it brought out the best and worst of people in the village, their cooperativeness and ingenuity, their parochialism and stinginess, their desire to reach out and celebrate, their habits of caution and reticence. "You just kind of have to make your own world." He laughed. "And like it or lump it!"

One night when he had been out shopping, Jim returned to learn that Rosey Hunter had called him and left a message.

"Oh, yeah? What'd he say?"

"You'll love it." Anna read from a scrap of paper. "'Don't gyrate. Rotate!'"

"For Christ's sake. Did he leave a number?"

Anna handed him the paper. "Some of your old buddies are a little strange."

"Rosey and I weren't exactly friends," Jim said. "But we're not exactly enemies, either. I can't imagine what he wanted."

Jim tried the number again and again, even days later, and at unusual times, but never with any success. Obviously Rosey used the telephone to call out but not to receive calls. That was very like Rosey, to be in control of everything, not to allow himself any surprises.

Rosey, huh? What the hell could he have wanted?

He had shared an intimate moment with Rosey. They had been walking beside a dike through a rice paddy when a spot appeared above them near some shrubbery, and instantly, as if they had both preknown the event and understood what it was, so perfect was their understanding of the peril that spot represented that they reacted thoughtlessly, instantly, like animals, traveled through a wedge of gray water and fell behind the dike, Roosevelt tumbling so that he and Jim lay in the water face to face, when the grenade struck the top of the dike and rolled slowly down, retarded a little by mud, between their eyes. And this, too, was done without thought, Jim's hand over his shoulder, scooping the grenade up, its weight reduced only to heat in his hand, lobbed it over the dike, where it immediately detonated, moved the entire dike over a foot, and buried Jim's and Rosey's faces.

"I could've had it," Rosey said later, "but my hand was trapped under my piece, which was trapped under me."

"Oh, bullshit," Jim bragged. "Man, I'm always saving your ass."

"Him with no weapon, and savin' my ass," Rosey replied. "Some day I'll take a minute's vacation, and we'll see about that."

One of the men who had witnessed the incident, who had dropped to one knee and chopped the shrubbery to confetti with M-16 bursts, told them, "You dudes didn't even splash water. Just flat walked right over it. Never saw such hustle in my life, two dudes bookin' over water like Jesus in a hurry, grenade on your ass looked like it was floatin' up there. Some serious truckin', chum."

They had come that close to buying it, both of them: two seconds? A yard of mud between them and that ear-splitting *krang!* The earth had pulsed as if it had a big heart. And this was the question he had never dared ask the man who shared that instant with him, whose fates were tied to the absurd chance of a few thoughtless animal seconds: Is it O.K., Rosey, if we fuck up? Is anything more expected of us because we survived? Do we have a right to fail?

Spring had never been more welcome than it was in 1982, and people born and raised in Maine, Jim knew, had a special regard for the season, no matter where they might move. It was also a tantalizing spring, wet and cold, but there was daylight in Jim's evening at last, and already his daughter had taken on a little personality, alternately severely studious, in the grip of her curiosity, and full of kicks and grins and wild delight. Of course she could fuss and cry, but she had Jim and Anna well trained by now in her requirements, and they frequently anticipated her discontent and relieved it. Anna was a good, devoted mother, but she also claimed time for herself, which Jim thought necessary and healthy. Although he sometimes craved the beach, Jim did less fishing that spring, too busy with work and the baby. He felt he was changing. He allowed himself, as he held Theresa over his head and shook her into giggles, a shred of hope.

And then it was as if they had set a trap for him, a tiger trap, and he plunged from the trail into the pit.

The landlord, a busy man in his fifties, who had otherwise paid no attention to Jim and Anna, decided their summer rent should be raised, to compensate himself for the revenue he was losing by not taking in tourists. Jim listened in a numb silence as the man explained the economic realities of Cape Cod summers and outlined why he thought he deserved more for making the great sacrifice of allowing Jim and Anna to stay in the cottage. Jim stood on the front steps swaying in mounting disbelief and anger, unable to find words to express his shock, and contempt.

"We've kept right up, haven't we? We've been good tenants, right?"

"No question about that," the landlord said. "No, I'm just talking about the market, you know. I mean, in a few weeks I could be making a few hundred a week on this cottage, see?"

"Yes, but you rented it to us," Jim said. "So you couldn't be making hundreds a week. So you're off base there."

"I mean, I've got to get more out of this property, or I'm going to have to ask you to leave."

"So that's the program." Jim rocked on his heels. "So why don't you get it all down in black and white so I know what you're talking about."

"I didn't want to involve lawyers and all that," the landlord said.

"I know it costs money," Jim said, "but why don't you do it anyway?"

"I thought we could settle this more like man to man," the landlord said.

Jim turned and went inside the cottage. He shut the door softly behind him, sat on the sofa and tried to find reasons why he should not just rush outside and throttle the landlord next to death. Because, Jim told himself. He said he had a bad heart, and a bad back. He's a walking invalid. He couldn't fix the flashing around the chimney or carry in the new water tank because he had a bad back and a weak heart. If I grabbed him, he'd die. If I punched him in the face, he'd die of fright or he'd call in the police, and then I'd be fixed. So I guess I have to get a lawyer. I guess this is not the wild west where we can just shoot it out or duke it out. It's not man to man. He'd better watch that man-to-man shit or he'll get his ass knocked down the cellar stairs. And where are we going to go at this time of year? Maybe the fucker has just got me where I can't kick.

But if they throw us out of here, Jim thought, this place will not be livable. Bad back, bad heart, he'll have to hire fifty guys to put this place together again. Maybe I should tell him that.

The landlord came to the screen door and peered in, shielding his eyes with a hand. "Jim?"

"Put it in writing, Mr. Martin, and then we'll have something to talk about."

"I'm sorry you feel that way, Jim. Listen—"

"You know how it is when you're getting screwed, Mr. Martin. You're not inclined to be friendly. Why don't you go away now and send me a letter?"

"See, Jim, my daughter is interested in this place. I mean, it's her idea, you know. I mean, I've got to think about my kids, don't I?"

Now Jim rose and shut the inside door very quietly, too. He sat down again and Anna came out of the bedroom. "What's going on, Jim? What's wrong, honey?"

"Leave me alone for ten minutes and I'll tell you. And don't answer the door."

"Who's there?"

"Martin. And don't open the door, because if you do I will commit murder on the man."

"For Christ's sake," Anna said.

Jim pounded his clenched fists onto his thighs. "I'm serious. Leave me alone."

Anna retreated to the bedroom. The landlord did not knock.

During the week, Jim waited impatiently for a letter from the landlord, and asked around on the job about possible new places to move to. Everyone was skeptical, since the tourist season was at hand, and the only possibilities that anyone could think of were apartments in Hyannis, Yarmouth, or Falmouth. Jim mentioned his plight to some of the clients, too, and they expressed the same fatalistic disgust and the same lack of hope as his colleagues. One of the photographers Jim worked with, Roy Simpson, said, "The guy's timing is pretty diabolical. I'd take him to court."

"I guess I'll have to."

"I'll ask around," Roy said. "But tourist lucre is pretty forceful around here." He talked sympathetically for a while, his shrewd leathery face animated as an Eskimo storyteller's, already tanned, his hair gray-streaked and seemingly windblown, his voice almost irritatingly practiced, the kind Jim might have expected some women to like for its precision and self-assurance. But he was also a good photographer, and Jim respected him. Jim had just printed a series of Roy's pictures of killer whales, photos taken from a dory in Nova Scotia, some remarkably daring, and almost all of them technically perfect and quite moving. And when Roy invited Jim to a Memorial Day cookout, Jim was happy to accept.

"Maybe you'll meet somebody there who isn't on the greed train,"

Roy said. "They'll all be from the Wellfleet area, though."

"I just want a place to live," Jim said. "I sort of figured Wellfleet was out of my class."

"Come anyway," Roy said. "Meet my wife. All that jazz. I'll show you some of my stuff."

"I'll try not to be too jealous."

Roy laughed.

"Really," Jim said. "These whale pictures are sensational."

He went from developing the whale pictures to some T. and A. from the Provincetown group—only it wasn't just T. and A. this time, but juvenile T. and A., and some of it implying violence. Jim had thought he had seen everything and could accept it, that he could detach himself from the subject and do his work, but the material of today's assignment disgusted him. A large male hand gripped the thigh of an adolescent girl; a pubescent black child with her legs spread was tied by the wrists to a bedboard; one girl pressed into a crouch looked over her shoulder with almost animal terror; a young black male was back to back with a white girl, their arms lashed together. Adults, he thought, can do anything they agree upon. But this is criminal. I should do something about this. He left in a fit and took an early lunch break, and a long one. He couldn't eat anything on his plate, and he couldn't go back to that stuff, so he ordered another beer and sat looking out of the restaurant window, and a small cluster of Canadian geese paddled down the narrow tea-brown Swan River toward Nantucket Sound. He had a terrible impulse just to go home, to grab some fishing gear and head for the outside beaches, wash his mind in the white noise of the big Atlantic surf. But Christ! he thought. He was just about out of a house, and didn't need to be risking a job, too. The real precariousness of his situation struck him with unexpected force, and it was true, really and frighteningly true, that he could lose everything really quickly now if he wasn't careful, if he wasn't smart. But how the hell can you be smart when you don't have a choice? Tell me, Jim said to the ducks, to the sky. What the hell choice have I even got?

He returned to work a little drunk, and he worked fast and sloppily, not caring to dignify the pornography with any effort of his own.   .

When he came home that evening, his head pounding, Anna told him the letter from the landlord had arrived, and she had taken it, and their lease, to a lawyer in the neighborhood. She was quite astounded to discover that not only did the landlord want to raise their summer rent by a hundred dollars a week, but the lease they had signed provided for this seasonal "adjustment." The lawyer could not say at the moment whether the clause which allowed for the increase was legal within the state's code for leases, and that the research to find out would cost three hundred.

"The landlord wants another thousand, and the lawyer wants three hundred," Jim said. "Great. This is a wonderful town."

"If we win, we can save seven hundred, but we'll have to move in the fall anyway," Anna said. "If we lose, it will cost us thirteen hundred, and we'll still have to move."

"I think we're fucked," Jim said. He thought, Maybe I'll burn this box to the ground. Sorry, boss. I lit a candle to the Virgin, and it caught the drapes. Sorry about that, motherfucker.

"So what are we going to do?" Anna asked.

"We've got to find another place," Jim said. "What a hassle."

"I've got all day to make calls," Anna said.

"You'll have to get the paper as soon as it's out. You'll have to go right to the news office for it."

"We'll do it," Anna said. "T'isa likes a ride."

"Sure." In Jim's imagination, the cottage seethed with flame. He felt hot, too, and he needed a drink to cool his mind.

For the rest of the week, Jim came home to the same news: Anna had looked at a place or two that would have been very nice to live in, but they were only being offered for summer rates.

" 'Come back in the fall,' they say. And then what?" Anna shifted Theresa on her hip. "Move out next summer?"

"If we can even find one, maybe we'll have to take an apartment."

"Give me a little more time. I called today about a duplex. In Harwich. The lady seemed very nice."

"They're all nice when they've got your money."

But on Friday, Anna did have news.

"I didn't find a house, but I think I've got a job."

"How did that happen?"

"Bill recommended me. He thought I did a nice job on his book. I'd be working with him."

"I didn't know you were in touch."

"We weren't," Anna said. "He's just got this boring job taking photos for a catalog for Thorndike's in Hyannis."

"Sure. The big department store. So?"

"So, he remembered me for the design and layout part of it."

"What about T'isa?"

"That's the best part. I can do it mostly here, except for a trip to the printer now and then, or to have the department-store people look it over."

"It won't last, though, will it?"

"No," Anna said. "Maybe for the summer. It will make us enough to keep Martin off our necks."

"Shithead, you mean?"

"Yeah, Shithead. We wouldn't have to move, and then in the fall it would be easier."

"I'd rather not give him the satisfaction."

"I know, Jim."

"But I'm glad you got the job. Is Bill going to send his photos through me? Did he say?"

"He didn't. I'll ask him."

"We might be doing a book together after all." Jim laughed.

"Oh, sure," Anna said. "A thriller. Girdles from Thorndike's."

"Do people still wear girdles? Bras? That kind of stuff?"

"Yes, dear. Even makeup has made a comeback."

On Memorial Day, Jim and Anna drove to Wellfleet to meet the Simpsons and their friends. There had been a Memorial Day parade in Hyannis that morning, but Jim did not participate in it, or even observe it.

"Why don't you go?" Anna asked on that morning.

Jim shrugged. "I stored my uniform way back under the house. I'd have to crawl in there to get it, and it probably wouldn't even fit now."

"I don't think this will be like the last few years," Anna said. "I think the public is finally accepting the Viet Nam veteran."

"I already accepted them," Jim said. "I know what was asked of them."

"So? Don't you want a little recognition?" Anna went on. "Don't you want to meet the other vets from around here?"

"I'd like to meet the guys, yeah," Jim said. "It's just so confused now. Viet Nam is mixed up with everything else. I don't know what it means to parade any more."

"Isn't it obvious?" Anna said. "Memorial Day means a day to remember."

"Then that's not what I need." Jim found himself smiling, but it was the kind of smile he might give to a salesman as he closed the door on his foot. "What I need is a Day of Forgetting. I've had enough of the dead."

Later as they drove to Wellfleet, Anna cautioned Jim about his drinking, asked him not to overindulge.

"I'm not planning on it," he said. "But I don't know what kind of party it is. I have an idea it's some high-class hippies, but I could be wrong." He told Anna then about Roy's work, his admiration for it. Then he changed the subject, told her how good she was looking, and meant it, in her new dark green slacks. She had been exercising to regain muscle tone lost in pregnancy, and the results were good, very good, he said, and ran a hand over her thigh.

"You should do a little running yourself," Anna said. "You're showing a little flab there." She pinched him at the waist for emphasis.

"I really ought to get in shape," Jim said. "You're shaming me, looking so fit."

The people at the Simpsons' party were also looking fit, Jim thought, downright sleek, as if they had nothing more to do than jog the beaches and enjoy the sun. Although Roy had said the dress would be casual, many who came were, in fact, in clothes more formal and expensive than Jim had imagined would be the case, and he felt a little out of place. People were friendly enough, they talked to him and to Anna, but they seemed also to be standing a little aloof, posturing a little, expecting to be admired. Jim drank only beer, paced himself with caution.

Jim conversed with Roy as the host built a pyramid of charcoal briquettes, doused it with fire starter, lit it with a match. A whiff of black smoke curled up before the fire began to burn with greater and greater authority, and the smell staggered Jim with a memory he tried at once to put aside, but then succumbed to in midsentence, losing his train of thought, and not really hearing the introductions Roy was trying to make.

The very shape of the flame, and the pyramid of black carbon, and the smell of it, was so like the Buddhist monk who had sat cross-legged at the American Embassy in Saigon, flashed into fire, endured that terrible moment without screaming, without flinching from his meditative posture, who seemed to take his pain, and the death in it, like simply another thought, that Jim had to close his eyes a moment. Even then, the purple afterimage forced the memory upon him, the monk in flames, his skin crackling like bacon, like a victim of napalm. Jim turned away from the grill a moment, then back to Roy and the woman he was with.

"I'm sorry," Jim said to the woman. "I didn't get your name. I just got a little dizzy."

"Are you O.K.?" she asked. "Can I get you something?"

"I'm fine," Jim said.

"Does this happen often?" the woman asked.

"No," Jim protested. "It's not serious, I'm sure." He smiled and took a deep breath.

"Jean," the woman said. "Jean Anderson. I'm Dr. Anderson's wife." She pointed to a man in a black suit and with a bushy head of hot-combed curls who was helping himself to a plateful of hors d'oeuvres. She was quite tall and slender, with brown hair cut boyishly close to the ears. She had a pleasant but empty face that Jim distrusted.

"Jean's also a psychiatrist," Roy said, squirting more fuel into the fire and creating a little inferno of flame. "She's got some interesting ideas about the red meat and fire rituals we supposedly civilized people call cookouts. Right, Jean?"

"I'm sure Jim wants to hear my social theories," she said. "And I do like the way you play with fire, Roy. Keep it up, and we'll be rushing you to the clinic. That way you'll get a lot of attention."

Roy laughed, shrugged in embarrassment. "It must be nice to be a shrink. Nobody can ever say you're wrong."

"Oh, that's just a game we play," Jean said. "But if we really want to scare people, we just clam up and look wise." She turned to Jim. "What about you? Are you a photographer?"

"No," Jim said. "I'm nothing, just a technician at a photo lab where Roy brings his work."

"Nobody's nothing," Jean said. She shifted her weight just a little provocatively. "And anybody can see you're not 'nothing.'"

"I mean, nothing special."

"Your wife would disagree, wouldn't she?"

Jim involuntarily searched the lawn for Anna. "You'll have to ask her."

"She's pretty."

"Thanks."

"You didn't get a pretty wife by being nothing."

"I'm sorry," Jim said, "but I'm kind of a lousy talker."

"Shy?"

"Yes."

"Roy told me you were once a combat photographer. Why didn't you mention that?"

"Why didn't you say you were a psychiatrist?"

"That's fair," Jean sucked an ice cube as she eyed Jim. "People don't like to talk to psychiatrists. It's an unfortunate occupational hazard. I didn't want to scare you off, I guess. How do you feel now, by the way?"

"I was remembering something unpleasant, that's all." Jim regretted saying this at once. "Something from Viet Nam."

Jean's face was less empty now, was crossed by a shadow she could not control, that made her seem harsher. "I see. Were you in combat?"

"Yes. As a photographer. But I carried a weapon when it was necessary. When I told you I wasn't a photographer, I mean I'm not a photographer any more."

"I see."

"Do you?" Jim spoke a little aggressively, not knowing why. Perhaps he had enjoyed catching her a little off guard.

Jean shrugged, as if suddenly uninterested. "Well, I suppose you saw some barbarous things—what?—a dozen years ago?"

"Right. Closer to fifteen."

"Have you had problems?" she asked. "It's none of my business."

Jim raised the beer. "I drink too much."

"Oh, well." Jean raised her glass. "Don't we all?" She took Jim unexpectedly by the elbow. "Come over here and meet my husband. Murray has done some work with veterans. And I already know he likes your wife."

"Why not? She's beautiful."

"Murray's a sucker for green eyes and a nice tush."

"Your eyes are brown," Jim said.

"Go on," Jean teased him, bumped against him with her hip. "That's half the list."

"Careful, Jim," Roy called. "Two drinks and she loses all inhibitions."

"He's lying," Jean said. "I'm quite disgustingly under control at all times." They approached Murray now, who was spooning beans into his mouth, nodding with animated agreement to something being said by an older woman next to him.

"Look what I found," Jean said to him.

Murray looked up suddenly, an impish smile on his face. "He's gorgeous, but does he know he's in danger? Hi!" Murray laughed and took Jim's hand. "Just kidding."

"Murray likes to pretend I'm a man-eater." Jean clutched Jim's arm even more firmly now, pulling him close. "That seems to turn him on." She introduced the two men, telling Murray, "Jim was a combat photographer in Viet Nam, is now a photo technician in Hyannis, he drinks too much, and is married to that woman you've been ogling since we got here."

"I don't think I've ever been so neatly summed up," Jim said.

"Me neither," Murray said.

"It's kind of shocking to be so simplified."

"You said it," Murray agreed.

Jean laughed nervously, her body trembling. "I never unintentionally crushed two egos at once before."

" 'Unintentionally' is the operative word, yes," Murray said, winking at Jim. "And I don't think either of us is standing here in tatters. Are we, Jim?"

This sort of game did not amuse Jim, but he answered quickly, "Are we, Murray?"

"So tell me about your wife." Murray laughed.

Jean crossed her arms on her chest and looked away, apparently searching the crowd for an escape.

"First tell me about yours," Jim said evenly.

Jean shot him a quick glance and a little smile, but she said nothing, then shifted her gaze to Murray, waiting.

"The resume, or the intimate details?" Murray said.

"I think I'm getting over my head," Jim said.

"Oh, don't chicken out now," Murray replied. "Jean and I are a bit infamous for verbal swordplay. A bit like mom and pop at the deli, only a little more Freudian."

"I don't know a damned thing about Freud," Jim said.

Murray scowled. "I don't know a damned thing about combat, I suppose."

"Jean said you've done some work with veterans."

"Some work, some veterans," Murray said. "I've never been under fire."

"No," Jim said quietly. "I don't think even Russian roulette would give you that same feeling."

"Oh, Murray's tried that," Jean said.

Murray closed one eye and pointed his fork at Jean. Whatever he was going to say, he decided against it. Instead he simply said, "We could be having fun, you know."

"Russian roulette?" Jim asked Murray.

Murray snickered, returned to his beans. "The sport of kings."

Jim felt a little staggered, sipped his beer. He was glad when the conversation was interrupted by people who knew the Andersons, and he slipped away in search of Anna. She was sitting under a tree on a little bench talking to a younger woman in a billowing yellow smock. Jim sat on the lawn close by and listened as the women talked in a relaxed, intimate way that he envied, about children, about growing up, about reinventing, rediscovering childhood. Their talk was serious, but they laughed, too, in the way of women, as Jim saw it. Strange to think that a man who had played Russian roulette had his eye on Anna. Jim was not surprised by male attention being directed toward his wife; he considered it healthy. What struck him odd was the juxtaposition of Anna and Murray, incongruous, impossible. Anna would hate him, of course. Jim watched Murray and his wife seem to peck at each other, but the question of why Murray would have taken the chance of blowing his brains out stirred Jim uncomfortably. Revenge? Despair? Some warped streak of macho in his educated head?

Jim left the women, bided his time in conversation with Roy, and as soon as he had another chance he spoke to Murray. "I'm interested in the Russian roulette business."

"I know you are." Murray wore a look of near despair. "I wish Jean hadn't mentioned it."

"It just doesn't seem like something a psychiatrist would do."

"On the contrary," Murray said, engaging Jim's eyes. "I consider it wonderful therapy. It clears out the bullshit. I'd recommend it in special cases if it wouldn't get me tossed out of the profession." He smiled. "Doctors have a thing against cures that are presumably worse than the disease."

"Could you say why?"

Murray sighed, surveyed the lawn. "Do you play pool?"

"A little."

"I'll bet. Look, Roy's got a table in the basement. Suppose we pretend we're having a game."

"You're on," Jim said.

"Just let me freshen my drink. You sticking with beer? I'll get you one."

"Thanks."

Murray moved quickly, with a kind of bullish agility, a New Yorker's expertise in getting through crowds to the head of a line, a kind of assumed authority that amused and irritated Jim at once. Drinks in hand, Murray directed Jim with a nod to follow him to the house. Before he obeyed, Jim finished his beer and found a carton to put the bottle in. Since the game might last a while, he took another bottle with him.

Murray apparently knew the Simpsons pretty well, because he was waiting in the doorway to the cellar when Jim came in. "Hit that light switch," he said, indicating that his hands were full with bottles and glass.

Downstairs, they stripped the canvas cover from a fine pool table covered by a felt that was usually described by the manufacturer as "goldenrod" in color. Jim preferred the classic green, but the table was in excellent condition.

"So you play a little." Murray selected a cue from the rack on the wall, then spilled the balls onto the table. "You were probably one of those guys who spent six hours every day in the day room making a fortune at nine ball."

"I didn't make any fortunes in the service," Jim said.

"Neither did I." Murray told Jim he had been drafted into the Army in 1957 and served three years before he went on to college, graduate school, internship. "I hated the Army. With a passion. But I couldn't even get thrown out. I kept getting away with stuff."

"Really?"

"Really. It screwed up my life. It gave me a little power complex, you know. I thought I could get away with anything."

"Everybody's young once."

"I even played with immortality, you're right." Murray racked the balls. "That's where the Russian roulette came in."

"You got away with it," Jim said. "Here you are, almost twenty-five years later, all set to play straight."

"O.K.?"

"Yeah, sure. I love straight pool."

"So I got away with it, true. Unfortunately"—Murray looked at Jim—"one of the guys I played with did not survive."

"No shit?"

"It was fairly persuasive," Murray said. "Go ahead, break."

"Maybe you do know something about combat," Jim said.

Murray shrugged. "I know something about guilt anyway. Guilt and foolishness."

Jim shot lightly, trying to leave the rack as settled as possible and to bring the cue ball back to the bottom rail.

"You owe me one," Murray said. "You didn't take a ball to the rail."

"I'll break again."

"That's all right." Murray bent to the table with obvious expertise. "I like that five ball up there."

"How old were you?"

Murray laughed, made the shot. "Nineteen."

"Jean made it sound more recent."

"I know," Murray said. "Some things stay recent, though. There are some things we choose not to forget."

"Choose?" Jim said.

Murray regarded Jim with such directness that it was almost insulting. "Yeah, choose."

Jim scoffed. "I didn't even choose what happened to me, much less whether I could remember it or not."

"That's a lie." Murray's shot came off the rail and cracked open the rack. "A convenient lie."

Jim felt stung, and a little angry. He wasn't sure he understood what Murray was saying, but if he did, he thought it was horseshit. "I don't choose my nightmares, either. I didn't choose to survive. I just lucked out."

"Don't be a coward," Murray said. "Change channels."

"I'm not a coward."

"Sure you are," Murray said. "That's why you drink. That's why I drink, and why Jean drinks."

"I'm not a coward," Jim insisted.

"You're a fucking coward." Murray moved around the table and lined up another shot. "Everybody's a fucking coward."

"With all due respect," Jim said, "I mean, I'm aware you're a psychiatrist and all, but I think that's crap."

"That's what makes being a shrink so interesting and challenging," Murray said. "Everybody thinks they're exempt."

"Exempt?"

"From death." Murray missed a shot now, and stood away from the table.

"I don't think I'm exempt," Jim said. "I think I've got one short life, and it's going fast."

"And yet," Murray said, "you allow yourself to screw it up."

"You got a funny way of making people responsible for being hit by lightning."

Murray laughed. "You're old enough to know you shouldn't run around in the rain with a lightning rod attached to your head."

Jim saw that he was shaking as he lined up to shoot. "I am not a coward," he said.

"No need to be nervous," Murray said. "It's just a friendly game."

"You seem to think you know a lot about me on short notice." He backed away from the shot and stood up.

"Why not?" Murray said. "Experience tells me that people aren't all that different. You want to believe you're not a fucking coward like everybody else, O.K."

"What possible good does it do to believe otherwise? I mean, suppose I say to myself, 'I'm a coward.' So then what?"

"Good question," Murray said. "My answer would be another question. So then what do you want to do?"

"Jesus Christ," Jim said.

"Hey." Murray shrugged. "Come on and shoot."

"You kind of got me pissed off, Murray."

"Don't blame it on me," Murray said. "You've been pissed off."

"I mean, really pissed off, Murray."

"Take your shot. You'll feel better. Maybe you should have a little more to drink, too. Then we could really get serious."

"Goddamned right I will." Jim swilled his beer, wondering why he was allowing Murray to bozo him. "Then maybe we should go upstairs. I've got an idea."

"Why? Don't you like this friendly game. You scared of it?"

"I want to give you some combat experience," Jim said.

Murray laughed. "I'm not fighting you."

"I'm not talking about a fight," Jim said. "But a contest. You're not scared of a different game, are you?"

"I don't know," Murray said.

"Come on." Jim slapped the empty bottle on an end table and loped up the cellar stairs. Fuckin' coward, huh? Murray was a shrink, huh? Well, if a shrink put you in a certain place, then he ought to be able to take the consequences, shouldn't he? He wants to play with fire. He looked back when he reached the lawn and saw that Murray had emerged form the cellar, pale, blinking like a mole.

"Roy," Jim said to Simpson, "I don't want any spectators, but would you help me out here with a little contest between Murray and me?"

"I thought you were playing pool."

Jim picked up the can of charcoal starter fluid and a box of matches. "It's not quite real enough."

"You guys are pretty drunk, aren't you? Maybe you'd better wait for another occasion."

"Ah, no," Jim said. "Really, I may not see Murray again. I may not get another chance."

"Chance for what?"

"Come on, Roy," Jim said. "It's just a game."

Reluctantly, Roy followed Jim around the front of the house. Jean, her curiosity piqued by the activity, followed along, too, keeping a discreet distance, fondling her drink as she walked. Jim stopped, waited for her, and said, "We don't want any spectators, thanks."

"Now there's no way you can keep me from watching this. Don't tell me Murray got himself into a fight?"

"O.K.," Jim said. "Call everybody if you want to. I don't give a shit." He took Murray by the elbow now and sat him down on the brick steps. Then Jim squirted the starter fluid, laying a streamer. After about twenty feet, he turned around and came back up the other side of the sidewalk, and when he reached Murray, sat down beside him, drenched their feet with the fuel, and put the can on the sidewalk between them.

"You know," Murray said, "this is certifiably loony behavior."

"You can quit any time," Jim said. "But you might be interested to know this smells a little like Viet Nam. Roy? You want to get down to the end of that streamer and light it for us?"

"Me?" Roy almost shouted. "You guys are nuts."

"I don't know," Jean said. "I think it's kind of interesting. I think everybody should see this."

"Why don't you take my place?" Murray said to her.

"I don't want to mess up my shoes," Jean said.

"You can wear mine." Murray laughed. He turned to Jim. "O.K., war hero, what's this supposed to prove?"

"Will somebody please light the starter?" Jim said. "The smell is gagging me. Jean? Will you?"

"Sure," Jean said.

"Get me a drink first, will you?" Murray said to her.

"Quit stalling," Jean said.

"Oh, come on," Murray said. "If we're going to do this, let's do it with a little panache, anyway."

"Forget it," Roy said. "You guys aren't doing this. Not here. Not at my house. No way. I won't allow it." He took off at a run.

"See?" Jim said. "Now he's going for a hose or some damned thing."

Murray reached into his jacket pocket and fished out a lighter, which he tossed to Jean. "Darling? I guess we'll have to forgo the amenities."

"It's a shame." Jean flicked the lighter and adjusted the wick so that the flame curled up in a large hook. "You really should have a drink to toast each other. And with all the photographers around, you'd think we could get a shot or two for the scrapbooks." She ambled down the sidewalk and with little difficulty lighted the streamers. She stood back with arms folded on her chest, eyes blazing, flickering with delight.

The flame wavered slowly, pale blue, licked ahead curiously, then leapt up in an orange crown and spurted ahead. Anna came charging around the corner of the house, leading a small group. With a cry of pain, she ran directly to Jim, grabbed him by the arm and tried frantically to pull him from the steps. Jim simply grabbed the railing and held on.

"How touching," Murray said.

Jim watched the flames lick up the sidewalk as he held on to the railing against Anna's struggling. She cried for help, but the flame rushed silently ahead now, like a snake striking. Murray pumped Jim's hand quickly. "Congratulations! See you at the hospital!" Then he leapt from the stoop.

Jim watched the flame devour the puddle at the bottom of the stairs, then felt a shock of water so cold it made his legs dance, and he cried out involuntarily, "Ah!"

Anna pulled him up from the step now, and Roy doused him with spray from the garden hose, cursing, shouting. Murray and Jean applauded vigorously. Jim said nothing. He kept his eyes almost closed and allowed Anna to lead him to the car and stuff him in. He was not a coward, right? But if he was not a coward, he asked himself, then why did Anna's sobbing as she drove him home, why did Anna's sobbing vibrate like a cold bell, like the legs of a thousand spiders all along his spine?

3
Vermilion
Phoenix
(*The Summer Now*) [*ii*]

One day Chong sits for two hours in front of a blank canvas unable to make a mark. Finally, he throws the brush against the wall and walks outside, hatless, hands jammed in the back pockets of his shorts. He wanders aimlessly past the barn and petulantly swipes at Awake when the bird drifts down from his perch in the maple toward him.

"Leave me alone," he shouts. The bird veers off with a shriek.

Luan squeals in his pen.

"Shut up," Chong tells him. "You make too damn much noise."

He heads out across the field, crosses the bed-frame bridge, and enters the woods, which is cool, flickering with sunlight and shadow, moist. Mosquitoes whine past his ears and Chong swipes at them.

"What the goddamn hell good are goddamned mosquitoes anyway?" he mutters. "Goddamn bastard black flies, too. Get the goddamn hell out of here. Fuckers! Go harrow somebody else."

Just ahead, a deer breaks through the bushes, dips his head, bounds into the thickets. Chong crouches to see the deer, white tail flagging, drift and dance into a grove of hemlocks where it is as dark as a tunnel. The sight of the deer relaxes Chong a little, as if he has been handed a gift. Yes, relax, he tells himself. You get so uptight you don't see anything. He stops a moment to polish his glasses and realizes he is, stupidly, close to tears. What the hell is wrong now? Slow down, he thinks. Slow down, slow down, and look.

Chong walks toward the boundaries of his property, flailing gnats. In this section of his land he has taken down a few old trees for his winter firewood, because, for one thing, the old fire road cuts through the woods here, makes it possible to load the wood into a wheelbarrow and move it out.

A redstart flits through the mountain laurel beside him. The black and orange bird seems almost too delicate to fly, almost to be blown about like a leaf. The markings on the wings trace orange circles in the air. Then gone. So ephemeral, and yet it has happened millions of times, Chong supposes. Ephemeral and eternal. How can a thing so delicate survive? Obviously it was not a matter of strength. More like the reed that will bend with the wind and not break, its power in being supple and passive. Or like the water strider, riding the current, bobbing like a cork.

Along the edge of the old fire road Chong finds something he thinks defies imagination: The webs of the ground spiders, which he has seen studded and glistening with dew, are today misted green. They are chartreuse! They lie about beneath the trees like green silken handkerchiefs. At first he cannot understand this phenomenon, but as he surveys the roads he finds the scrub pines are pollinating, putting up little spires from the tips of their branches that resemble something fried, or scorched paper, and which give off an almost invisible green dust. Of course! Chong has seen this dust collect in swirls on the surface of his pond and thought it ugly, like scum. Probably the spiders are green today, too, and their prey will taste of pine. Is this a treat or a great seasonal annoyance, a green summer snowstorm or a thing of indifference to them? Chong wonders. He peers carefully into a tunnel in one of the webs but can see only two slender black and yellow striped legs on the edge of the darkness. He is tempted to tap the web with his finger, but is afraid the spider may be too fast for him, and he doesn't want to be stung.

Farther along the road and closer to the base of Sweat Hill, which his gazebo tops, Chong finds the traces of a trail that one of the volunteer firemen had told him was cut by members of the Lake Ecstasy snowmobile club. The man had come to Chong for permission to retain a camp which they said would be used for winter picnics and a point of rendezvous on some of their winter outings. He promised the area would be free of litter, and since Chong was grateful to the volunteers anyway, he saw no harm in allowing it. He wanted to get along with the people of Lake Ecstasy, and he presumed the camp would be small, discreet, and probably temporary. To his surprise, he found that, in fact, the snowmobilers had driven an old school bus down the fire road and along the trail they cut, then built a foundation of stone and wood beneath it. The inside of the bus had been stripped of its seats, except for a few, which were arranged parallel to the side walls now, a sizable tin stove had been erected inside—its black chimney cover like a Chinese peasant's hat—and a supply of folding tables and chairs had been stashed under a metal plate in the floor. The volunteers warned Chong that late in the fall deer hunters would take the bus over for a few days, litter the grounds, and "do their damnedest to burn up all of our wood."

Chong, swatting gnats vigorously, presses through the shrubbery into the clearing where the yellow bus lies like a grinning, somnolent tiger. He knows at once the place is inhabited. An assortment of old pans, including a skillet, is propped against a log to dry. There is a pile of cans in a shallow hole. And leaning against the front fender is a battered dark red ten-speed bicycle.

Chong waits a moment, and when he is certain no one is in the camp makes a quick inspection of the grounds. Two of the little pans have come from his kitchen. Some of the cans in the trash pile could only have come from his cupboard. Who else in Lake Ecstasy would have water chestnuts and straw mushrooms, black tea and dried tangerine skins? In any case, it is not the fare of campers, nor even that of a food thief who can see in the dark, unless he has a taste for Chinese cooking. From the rear bumper of the bus, a double strand of garden twine—Chong thought the birds carried it off—stretches upward into the slender branches of a sycamore. And on this line hangs a small pair of denim trousers, a brown and white striped sweater, and, like perky little sailing flags, three pieces of apricot-colored women's underwear.

As he retreats to the house, Chong muses that almost inevitably a vacuum will be filled, if only by human particles. Jamaican Rastafarians take over the toolsheds of the rich; dispossessed Dutch youth fill abandoned warehouses; a cardboard box in any city will become the temporary bedroom of some aging urban waif. Calcutta: Chong shivers. Every cranny filled. He remembers an old bomb shelter hidden in the shrubbery of a New York garden that the street children made their midnight home, the apoplectic response of the landlord when he made the discovery through their sexual detritus. Outrageous, the idea of making love in a bomb shelter.

And yet, inevitable as it seems to him that human driftwood

would settle in the eddy of the bus, Chong is anxious about his neighbor, or neighbors, whether they are of the numberless shadow trespassers of the world, or invaders. Is there only a girl, or are there others? Would she be allowed to be alone?

There is nothing to do but wait, Chong thinks, wait and spy. And so during the rest of the day Chong keeps the camp on the periphery of his attention, looks for any wisp of smoke a wood fire might betray, and in the evening he makes another trek to the clearing and settles quietly into some shrubbery near the edge of the pond. The frogs, now momentarily quiet, reinvent their incredible din.

Chong is not good at waiting, and he understands this about himself. If he could only idle his brain and make it quiet! But even asleep it stirs up a brew of images, rhythms, vague rumblings, crisp speeches of startling insight, photographs of his desires and fears. He lies down and listens to the chirruping of the crickets, the honking and haranguing of the frogs, the sustained razor-edge buzz of some huge insect Chong cannot name. This juxtaposition of dreams and the wild abundance of natural life interests Chong. The mind was a blank slate, yet contained its own menagerie. But it was formed by nature, too. Nature created dragons of sorts, but not those triumphs of the imagination; on the other hand, who could have invented the grasshopper, the clam, something as incredible as the crayfish, or even the delicate mosquito?

Through these speculations, Chong hears the mundane sound of a can falling on a rock, and he sits up. In the gray light of the evening woods, a girl squats in the even darker shadow of the lurid bus, trying to light a piece of paper with a cigarette lighter. The lighter sparks and sparks and does not flame, and finally the girl, with an angry snort, hurls it into the bushes. She shakes her head in frustration and throws her hair over her shoulder with a quick swipe. Now Chong remembers he has seen her before, her hair floating on the black surface of his pond, her pale body splashing out in a momentary ruckus on the night before the fire that consumed his field. Chong rises and comes through the shrubbery with a little warning whistle.

The girl bolts up in terror.

"Don't be afraid, Ginny," Chong says. "You are Ginny, aren't you?"

"Who wants to know?" the girl replies.

"I do." Chong searches in his pocket for a packet of matches, then stoops and ignites the paper from the little flame. "I like to know the names of my guests."

"Yeah, I'm Ginny."

"What are you cooking tonight?"

"Nothin'. I'm just cold."

"Bring some wood from under the bus, something dry. These twigs are all green."

"Look. I'm not staying long."

"You can stay as long as you like. Don't worry about it."

The girl hesitates, then turns and rummages under the bus for firewood. She brings forth a chunk in each hand, but tosses them toward Chong so that she does not have to come close to him. Chong places a small log on the crackling twigs, makes a fan of a pine branch, and swings this gently back and forth until the coals are bright and crackling. Chong holds out the branch to Ginny. "Here. Fan your own fire."

"Look, it's just temporary," Ginny says. "A couple more days." She does not come closer.

"I'm not here to throw you out," Chong says. "But I want you to know something. If you want anything from me"—he reaches out with his fan and ticks two empty cans on the ground—"you only have to ask and I'll give it to you gladly. You understand? But if you steal from me, I get angry."

Ginny is quiet. She puts her hands in the hip pockets of her jeans and rests her weight on one foot—an almost insolent, denying slouch.

"I'm not taking charity," she says.

"You're taking it now," Chong says. "The only difference is you're not asking for it."

"I'm not a beggar, either. I can go somewhere else. I'm goin', in fact."

"Or," Chong says, "you could do some work, and I'd give you food. Don't tell me you're not hungry."

"Would you pay me?"

"I don't have much money," Chong says.

"What would you want me to do?"

"You can't get warm over there," Chong says. "Come over here where I can see you."

"I'm not cold now." Ginny leans against the bus.

"Well, my garden needs weeding—"

"I could do that."

"My barn needs cleaning."

"That sounds too hard."

"You could take your time at it. No hurry."

"Yeah?"

"I want to plant some grass seed and cut some brush. I have plenty for you to do."

"And you'll give me food. If I do."

"Yes. I'll give you food. Or you can have your meals with me, and I'll cook."

Ginny does not respond for a while. "But I want to stay out here in the bus."

"Are you alone?"

She hesitates. "Mostly."

"I don't want a big crowd of people out here. I'm not running a park."

"Yeah. O.K. So?"

"So? You want something to eat now? Or do you want to wait for breakfast?"

"What? You mean have supper now?"

"If you want. Or just some hot chocolate or something."

"Mr. Chong?"

"Yes."

"I'm afraid of you."

He pokes the fire and sparks scatter into the air. "I can see that. I think it's kind of funny somebody would find me ferocious." He chuckles. "A fire like this lights your face from below, makes you look like a demon. Upside down. But I'm not a demon."

"What do you *do* around here anyway? Nobody knows what you do."

"I just make things," Chong says.

"Like what things?"

"Like paintings and sculptures. What about you? Are you in school?"

"I don't do anything," Ginny says. "Except get in trouble."

"It's not hard to do, is it?"

"No." Ginny's voice falls as she speaks, and Chong respects this by remaining silent for a while.

"I guess you won't want to leave this nice fire now," Chong says finally. "But you come by in the morning and we'll have breakfast. Then you can pull some weeds. In the morning"—Chong draws his hand over his face—"these demon shadows will be gone. I won't seem quite so terrible." He laughs, amused at the idea of his demon self. Halloween man, an Eskimo storyteller in a mask. It would be nice to do some firelight paintings, he thinks, the range of colors is so extreme. You know, he wants to say to Ginny, but reserves the speech because he realizes it will seem like madman talk, the incredible heat of the sun has nothing to do with burning oxygen. It is self-generated, the thing invents its own heat and light, and in consequence the world is possible, food is possible, vision is possible. Chong stirs the flames a last time, then pulls himself out of his crouch, mindful of his back, and heads off through the woods to his house. This time as he crosses the dam the frogs ignore him completely. Their cacophony goes unabated. He is razzed all the way to the door.

His head is still full of the firelight and the glow of embers, and Chong sits at his kitchen table with some pastel chalks, drawing lines of color next to each other, trying to rediscover the harmony of the fire. He thinks also of skin tones in firelight, the flickering of the cream-colored light on her cheek and forehead as Ginny leaned against the bus in the periphery of the glow, of the darkness of his own skin in firelight, like an Indian's. It amuses him to think of himself squatting by the fire with the demon-mask of the shadows on his face and in the presence of this young white woman. But it does not amuse him that she is there and alone, and his enjoyment is gradually canceled by his increasing worry. Something could happen to her out there. Perhaps he shouldn't allow it, her staying in the bus. He steps to his sink to wet a piece of paper, thinking the paints would better give the liquid sense of firelight if moistened, and looks out of his window for some sign of fire in the woods. But he can only see his own face reflected in the glass, and it startles him a little because he looks old indeed, as if the demon mask had not left his face but had somehow been indelibly transferred there. He thinks he should at least be able to see some trace of the distant fire, unless she has let it die out and is asleep. Chong passes through the kitchen door and stands for a moment in the cool air looking toward the pond and his woods, able to see now without the interference of his own reflection, before he realizes that someone is standing there, not fifteen feet away.

"What are you drawing?" Ginny asks.

Chong laughs with relief, recognizing her voice. "Nothing much," he says. "Just colors. Fire colors. Your campfire."

"It's out now," Ginny says.

"Do you drink tea?" Chong asks.

"You said hot chocolate."

"Yes. Sure. Come in." Chong turns and enters the house, and in a moment Ginny squeezes through the door, almost as if the screen were too heavy to pull open. Her face is smudged with dirt and ashes, and her hair, long and brown, is flecked with small bits of leaves and dry pine needles, sure signs she has been lying on the ground. She wears blue jeans, and a simple flannel shirt that is buttoned closed at the throat and which is too large for her. With a start, Chong realizes that the shirt she is wearing is his!

"It will take a minute to fix things," Chong says. "Meanwhile, if you want a hot shower, you go right through there. You can lock the door."

"I'd like to." Ginny's face falls.

"Sit down at that table for a minute and don't cry," Chong says. "I'm not going to hurt you, Ginny."

"I'm not cryin'. I'm just tired as hell."

"Right. I know what I have. How about some toast with peanut butter and raisins with that hot chocolate?"

Ginny has her elbows on the table, her hands over her eyes, as if shielding them from the light. "Yes, please."

"It won't take long," Chong says. He wants so badly to embrace her, but doesn't dare. She would bolt if I did, he thinks. She sits at the table trying to press her tears back into her eyes.

Chong rummages in the closet in the hallway between the kitchen and his "living room" where he paints, and finds a towel and washcloth. He places these on the table at Ginny's elbow. "Go ahead," he says. "When you come out, we'll have a snack."

"I'm not scared," Ginny says. "I been livin' out there a week already, and it doesn't scare me."

"Good," Chong says.

"As long as they don't find me, it's just fine," the girl says.

"Yes," Chong says. "It's a good hideout."

"I'm going to shower now." Ginny bolts from the table, grabbing the towels.

"The light is overhead," Chong calls. "Swing your hand around and you'll find the cord."

The light comes on; Ginny shuts the door; and in a moment Chong hears the shower running. Chong laughs at how quickly she must have undressed, and he takes his time warming the milk and making toast because he knows very well Ginny will be in the shower a long time—probably, he supposes, until his hot water is all gone.

I wish my daughter were here, Chong thinks. Susan's older, but she would know what to do, what to say. She would be able to make the bridge.

Chong shaves the wedge of chocolate into a saucepan, adds sugar, and stirs. He warms the milk, too, so that the chocolate will not congeal into knots when he mixes the two, and he turns on the broiler in anticipation of making toast. When he and Mai Li separated a year ago, Chong left with nothing, would not argue over the household goods, could not bear any debate over who should have the desk, the easy chair, the teakettle. Mai Li was not greedy and would have negotiated fairly, but Chong could not then stand the idea of making an inventory of each item in their marriage, most of which he considered junk, somehow tainted with his failure to be endurable as a husband—to keep his vile depressions to himself. But this was not the first occasion on which he remembered, and desired, the kitchen toaster Mai Li had kept. It was odd, and stupid, to be remembering and regretting the loss of such a simple common appliance, one so easily replaced for a few dollars, but Chong wishes he had the toaster now, or at least had thought to replace it sometime before this. He wants to make excellent toast now. He wants Ginny to be pleased and feel at home, and if he burns the toast in his oven she will have all the more reason to find him odd and frightening. Mai Li kept everything because it gave her some comfort and was the practical thing to do. Chong had been stupid, he supposes. He didn't really know what his life was going to be like, suddenly bereft of family. But he should have at least imagined the need for a toaster.

Oh, the truth was he couldn't fight with Mai Li for anything, because he felt he was wrong, that he was the criminal, that she was right to be tired of him, that he was not fit for organized family, social, and working life. He didn't deserve a damned thing, and could not perform the charade of taking things away from their marriage trove as if he had such a right, as if he had any moral foundation to support his arguments for a toaster or a . . . what else? There was nothing besides the toaster that he had ever wanted. Except Susan, of course, to whom he had no right, and who in any case was not to be included among these *things*. Adultery? Yes, guilty. Mental anguish? Oh yes, definitely, since he never thought to hide frustrations when he couldn't work, or when his work was bad, never disguised his anger and sorrow when the world seemed to him full of horrors. Incompatibility? Yes, Chong thinks, but I don't know what it was exactly that finally broke Mai Li from her habitual tolerance.

She said, "We always arranged our whole lives for your benefit. So you could do your damned painting. I lived my whole life with you in a panic the bottom would fall out."

Chong had sensed this fear in his wife from time to time, but was unaware of its proportions. Eventually, added to the weight of his other crimes, it smashed their union. He spun away into a few weeks of disorientation, sleeping on sofas in the apartments of Benny Bergland, then Wu, then Benny again, a few nights in a hotel room, sponsored by Mrs. Crane, until she recommended the expedient of Lake Ecstasy. Why not? Chong thought. He had driven through the village with Mrs. Crane one fall on a lovers' lark and had thought the place was wonderful. They often talked of it, fantasying it the corrective to New York. So Mrs. Crane had rescued him, and he had come in the late winter to Lake Ecstasy to live, and to mend his wounds.

"So nice to have a whore to look after you," Mai Li had said.

A peasant again! Chong had laughed when he moved into the cold house that first day of March just four months ago. The snow drove across the fields and his windows frosted even on the inside, so that everything around him seemed dead and white and cold. He had nothing. Nothing but blue sky.

And yet he came by things, people gave him furniture, utensils, loans of money they probably didn't expect to see repaid, they gave him pigs and kindnesses he didn't deserve and rarely was able to repay, and tools, and they left him alone. He was like an ancient puppy. He could live on leftovers. Or like a troll. He could also live by his wits.

When Ginny came out of the shower, her hair was wrapped in a yellow towel, like a turban. The absence of hair around her face showed off her ears, which seemed large to Chong, though not quite comically so, and it showed how thin she was, too, cheekbones visible, her neck gaunt, swimming in the collar of his flannel shirt.

"You want a clean shirt?" Chong asks her.

"No."

"Why not? You seem to like my shirts well enough."

She shrugs a little helplessly, attends to drying the ends of her hair that have crept from under her yellow turban.

"It's O.K.," Chong says. "I'm not angry. But I would like to know when you 'borrowed' my things."

"You'd be gone," she says. "I don't know. You'd drive away, and I'd come in. You don't lock anything."

"Did you ever come in at night?"

"No."

"No? Really?"

"I swear."

"Somebody's been in at night," Chong says. "I was hoping it was you."

"I don't know," Ginny says.

"Don't know what?"

"Who it was."

"Your hot chocolate's ready. Come sit at the table here, in the kitchen. I'll fix some toast. I hope I don't burn it."

"My mom makes toast in the oven, too," Ginny says. She sits at the kitchen table with some attempt at formality while holding the turban together with one hand.

"Can I ask why you're not staying with your mother?" Chong says.

"Because of Parker," Ginny says. "He's supposed to be my step-dad, but he isn't really. I don't want to talk about it now, O.K.?"

"Sure," Chong says. "It's none of my business." He crouches down to place the bread into the broiler, burns his fingers on the hot tray, swears involuntarily. He stands and searches for a potholder. "But can I also ask how you've been getting along out there? Surely you didn't survive on water chestnuts and mushrooms?"

"The kids bring me stuff," Ginny says. She holds the mug of hot chocolate in both hands, the turban sags, and she briefly presses each cheek to the cup to warm herself.

"The kids?"

"My friends. They bring me stuff from the gardens around. We cook it over the fire. It's good."

"What do you do for water?"

"The pond."

"I guess you're pretty well set, then? Right?"

"Yeah." Ginny greedily slurps the hot chocolate now. "I'm set."

"You still think you want to work for me?"

"I can do it," Ginny says.

Chong lowers himself to the broiler again, pulls out the rack, and gingerly flips the slices of bread. The aroma fills the kitchen, makes his mouth water. When he stands again, Ginny is not at the table, and Chong sees she has left her towel on the back of the chair and is sitting with her legs pulled up on his sofa in the living room. She hangs her wet hair over the arm and runs her fingers through it idly, drying it in the air. The hot chocolate sits precariously in her lap. Chong finishes the toast, butters it, spreads on peanut butter and dots the slices with raisins. He puts these on a plate and carries them in to Ginny, but her cup is now on the floor, her cheek resting on the sofa arm, and she is quite asleep. Chong turns out the stand-up lamp beside her and sits across from her in his wooden rocking chair. He waits for a while, but when he sees she is not going to awaken, he eats the toast slowly, licks the peanut butter from his fingers, and wonders what he will do with this new addition to his farm.

Chong is dreaming of being caught in a flood, waters are pouring over him, but he wakes to the sounds of the toilet singing and apparent physical distress. Is Ginny sick? He is out of practice with these things, and lies perplexed and still very drowsy until Ginny pads back to the sofa. Chong waits for a while in his limbo between sleep and wakefulness, but when Ginny seems to be breathing slowly and deeply he drifts off again, too.

Ginny sleeps late, and wakes only when Chong puts his hand on her forehead.

She bolts up, brushes his hand away. "What are you doing?"

"I was checking your temperature," Chong says mildly. "Are you feeling all right?"

"I'm feeling fine," Ginny says. Then she winces and falls back on the sofa.

"Or maybe not so fine," Chong says. "You'd better stay right there. Do you want a blanket? Some tea?"

"Hot chocolate?" Ginny asks.

"Please."

"Please. Yes, please."

"Are you a little delirious?" Chong asks.

"I don't know where I am. I can't stay here," she adds with a cry.

"You can stay here until you're better," Chong says. "I don't think it will take so long to cure you."

"I feel dizzy," Ginny says.

"When did you eat last?"

"I don't know."

"You get some hot chocolate, then a poached egg," Chong says. "I should have made you eat last night."

"I don't want to eat."

"You will."

"Just some hot chocolate, please."

"Sure." Chong thinks she seems tense, ramrod stiff. Her eyelids flutter and she grips her shirttails fiercely. Before he starts the hot chocolate, he brings her a pillow and pulls a blanket around her small maturing body, attentions she receives nervously. "I wish you'd stop being afraid of me," he says.

He makes plenty of hot chocolate, and it is good that he does, for throughout the course of the morning and early afternoon Ginny drinks four or five cups of it. She also eats three poached eggs, four or five slices of toast with peanut butter, raisins, and honey on them, an orange and a banana, half a dozen crackers with cheese, a bowl of pork and chicken soup (she carefully picks out all the mushrooms), and half a jar of cashew nuts. Chong is sorry he has no cookies, because he is sure she would have eaten a bushel. At about four in the afternoon Ginny says, "I think I'm feeling better."

"I got that impression," Chong replies. "Do you think you'd like some supper?"

"In a while, yes," she says. "I think I'll be ready to eat by suppertime."

"I'm sure you will," Chong says. "Do you have any requests?"

"No, not really," Ginny says. "Unless you might have some spaghetti."

"That's easy to do," Chong says. "Spaghetti it is."

"I really am beginning to feel better." Ginny twists out of the covers and sits up, stretches, and runs her hands through her rust-red hair. She looks a little pale but is otherwise healthy as far as Chong can tell. Her green eyes are preternaturally alert, in a way Chong associates with intelligence, perhaps superstitiously.

"Kids always recover fast," Chong says. "My daughter's the same—you can't keep her down."

"I didn't know you had a daughter. Where is she?"

"She's in New York with her mother."

"Are you divorced?"

"Yes."

"Oh," Ginny says. "My mother's divorced. Almost."

"Where's your father?"

"I don't know," Ginny says laconically. "Does your daughter know where you are?"

"Sure," Chong says. "I visit her now and then." He realizes, three, four months ago. How could so much time have passed?

"That's nice," Ginny says.

This simple, sincere remark, and the almost whispered tone of voice gives Chong a sudden glimpse of Ginny's world of feelings.

"When did you see your father last?" he asks.

"I don't know. I don't remember." She crosses her legs and leans back with a yawn. "My mom says she'll kill him if he ever comes around. She says he hasn't done nothing for us."

"Would you like to meet him, though?"

"I don't know. Maybe," she says. "But not if he's such a jerk. He may be dead anyway. Sometimes my mother says he's dead."

"You don't believe her?"

"No. I just think my father doesn't want anything to do with us. He just don't care about us."

"Why wouldn't he care?" Chong says. "I don't understand."

"Me neither," Ginny says. "Whenever I think about my dad, I get sick."

Chong nods, a little surprised at her remark. In a way, it is a fairly mature statement of an understandable neurosis; and in a way, too, it suggests that her present discomfort is really psychosomatic—with Chong standing in for Dad as the object of fear, or disgust, or taboo. Chong sighs in misery. Why is everything so complicated? Because of his age, there is no escaping a "fatherliness" in his relation to Ginny, and that prejudices the situation at once, in ways that neither of them can fully understand. Father: the word makes Chong wince. Father means the stinging lash of things, Chong on his knees, book open in front of him for the hated English lesson, his father towering above, needling him.

"And why have you failed to learn this simple lesson, Hu Lan?" Chong remained silent.

"Perhaps because you lack discipline, lack focus. You must concentrate."

Now the blow would come, sharp and stinging, on the neck, and as a child Chong did not see any irony in the delivery of such pain, swallowed a cry. It was hard to change this view of his father even now, to see him as Susan did.

As he chats with Ginny now, watches her gather the covers about herself, hears her examine him like a detective, he also thinks this: That while his own youth had been marred by the overbearing attentions of his father, a man trying to beat Chong into perfection, establishing impossible and frustrating standards, Ginny's childhood has suffered the complete opposite relation, an absence of father, whatever a father could be both in the best and worst sense of his roles. She has been deprived, but she has also been spared, and Chong wonders now if some of her young agony is not the agony of ignorance—Who is she? What is expected of her?—and freedom—What can I become? What should I become? Chong shaped himself in part by reaction, by demolishing the models of his father, by rebellion and escape. At least he survived, unlike his brother, Kao, who threw their father's elitist principles down, joined Mao's army, and died in a battle with Chiang Kai-shek. For his own part, Chong flowed with history in another direction, to America, not to war—his father might have respected that—or to science—which his father loved—but to art. But which is the worst thing? Chong wonders now. To attempt to mold a child with total will and force, as his own father had done, or to leave a child, as Ginny's father did, in an utter vacuum of discovery and self-invention? These speculations sadden him a little, for they also give him no clue as to how he should regard and treat Ginny. He is not her father, and cannot be. Right now, he muses, he is little more to her than a restaurant.

I don't think she will mind, Chong thinks, if I use Chinese noodles instead of Italian. I don't think she will know the difference. He descends the cellar stairs and collects some tomatoes he had stored in there, finding several that are ripe to softness, perfect for a sauce. In the kitchen again, he is dicing onions and garlic when Ginny appears in the doorway.

"What's all that stuff for?" she asks.

"Spaghetti sauce."

"Don't you have a jar of it?"

"No. I make my own sauce."

"I just like the stuff from the jar," Ginny says. "I didn't want you to have much work."

"You'll like my sauce," Chong says. "I always make it this way."

"You must spend a lot of time cooking," Ginny says.

Chong smiles and nods agreement, turns his eyes away from an especially pungent onion. "I like to cook. I have lots of time every day." He pauses, wiping tears. "It may surprise you to know I am a very good cook, too."

"The best spaghetti comes from a can," Ginny insists.

"Bah!" Chong growls. "Wait till you taste this."

"How can a Chinese man make spaghetti? You don't even have the right noodles."

"You're such an expert, maybe I'll make you do the cooking."

"I'm not an expert," Ginny says.

"What's your background? Are you Italian to be the spaghetti expert?"

"My mother's family is French. My dad's was Irish."

"What is your last name, by the way?"

"It's Cahill. But I could change it to Parker if Mom marries him. Or I could change it back to Mom's maiden name, Thiebault. I don't know. Which do you like best?"

"Oh, no," Chong says. "I wouldn't make that decision for you. Or you could make up your own name."

"How could I do that?"

"Pick out a name you really like. Something that goes with 'Ginny.'"

"How about 'Skinny Ginny'?" She laughs.

"I didn't say it had to rhyme. Here, wash these peppers."

"You can't put peppers in spaghetti!"

"Of course you do."

"I can't stand cooked peppers." She bobbles the peppers into the sink.

"They won't be cooked much. You're such a spaghetti expert, maybe I'll call you Ginny Spaghetti."

"Ugh! I'll kill you."

"How about Ginny Killer, then?"

"Ugh! Ugh! You make lousy names."

"You'd better make your own, then, quick."

"How about Ginny Lovely?" She mocks a model's pose, throwing an arm behind her head, placing a hand on one hip.

"It's possible," Chong says, believing also that her satire of herself is not as successful as she imagines, since she really is attractive, physically more adult than she knows. "But is that how you really want to be known?"

"Sure. What's wrong with that?"

"Nothing. It's just sort of . . . *blah.*"

"Don't you think I'm 'lovely'?"

"Sure, but so what?"

"*So what?*"

"You heard me. I don't think there's anything special about being 'Ms. Lovely.' Now, take this stuff on the counter and put it in a bowl and feed it to the chickens."

"You feed garbage to the chickens?"

"They don't think it's garbage," Chong says. "It's not rotten, it's fresh."

"It's still garbage."

"You must be feeling better, all right. You've got some sort of bee in your bonnet."

"It's fun to argue with you." Ginny scrapes the peelings and scraps into a bowl and pushes out the door. Chong watches as she crosses the yard toward the barn, then returns to his sauce making. He begins browning the onions when he hears Ginny scream.

Chong races outside, vegetable chopper in hand. "What's the matter?"

Ginny is standing beside the barn with her hands over her face. "This stupid *bird!*" she cries. "He tried to land on me."

Chong laughs. Awake is fluttering on the ground beside Ginny in a dance of impatience. "He just wants his supper," Chong calls. "He won't hurt you."

"He attacked me!" she shouts angrily.

"He doesn't know any better," Chong says. "He just wants to be your friend."

"Stupid bird!"

"Pick up your bowl and come back in."

Scowling, Ginny returns to the kitchen. "I thought he was going to kill me," she says. "I never saw a bird that big."

"He can be a nuisance," Chong says. "But until he grows up, I'm afraid we're stuck with him. He tries to be friendly, but he just doesn't know how, you see. He's a bird, but he doesn't know it yet. He thinks he's a people or something."

"People can't fly."

"He's not too smart, you're right."

"What's his name? 'Stupid'?"

"No." Chong laughs. "Maybe it should be. Actually his name is 'Awake.'"

"How'd he get that name?"

"I named him that for luck. So the cats wouldn't get him."

"I didn't know you could name things like that."

"Why not? The bird doesn't know its name anyway. At least I don't think it does."

"What else do you want me to do?"

"Nothing right now," Chong says. "Just wait for the sauce to cook."

"Don't you have a TV?"

"No," Chong says.

"How do you wait without a TV?" Ginny asks. She wanders into the living room and begins an inspection of Chong's brushes, jars of paints, tools. She kneels on the sofa and stares out the front window toward the main road. One of Chong's cats leaps up beside her and Ginny begins to stroke it, roughly at first, then with more consideration. Chong turns the flame down under his sauce and tries to think about what he should do with Ginny. In a moment, she comes back into the kitchen and straddles a chair.

"After dinner, I'm going back out to the bus," she says.

"You feel good enough, do you?"

"Yeah," Ginny says. "I can't stay here."

"You keep saying that," Chong says, "but you seem to have made yourself at home. I even have a real bed you could sleep on upstairs."

"It's because if they found me here, you'd be in real trouble." Ginny rubs her eyes. "Otherwise I'd stay."

"Who'd cause us trouble?"

"Parker."

"I'm not worried about Parker, Ginny."

"He'd kill you," Ginny says. "He'd beat you."

"That's against the law," Chong says. "I'd call the police."

"You've got to be joking," Ginny says. "Parker don't care about that."

"Are you afraid that Parker will beat you if you stay here?"

"Yes."

"But he won't if you stay in the bus? Why wouldn't he?"

"At least I'm not with anybody."

Chong shakes his head, then turns to stir his sauce. "You're welcome to stay here and I think you should stay here. If you do go out to the bus, after all, I want you to know you can come here any time, for any reason."

"I'll still work for you," Ginny says. "And you can feed me."

"I'm really worried about you staying out there alone," Chong says. "I don't know if I should allow it."

"Well *don't* worry," Ginny says. "Don't you know my name? From now on I'm Ginny Strong."

Chong winces. "I can't make you do anything you don't want to, Ms. Strong. But just remember what I said. The invitation is open. You can move in any time, at any hour, whenever you need anything."

"Like spaghetti," Ginny says.

"Seriously."

"I know."

"Tomorrow we're having chicken and peas," Chong says. "Your job will be to weed the garden. And pick some peas. I'll show you where the tools are after supper, and you can get busy as soon as you wake up."

"O.K.," Ginny says.

"I sure hope I'm doing the right thing," Chong mumbles. "I hope you know a weed when you see one!"

After dinner—Ginny ate the spaghetti though she claimed it was horrible—Chong shows Ginny his stash of garden tools in the barn and walks with her out to the garden. He explains what he wants her to do, and as he talks with her, his suspicions about her ignorance concerning garden plants is confirmed. He points out to her his spices—thyme, parsley, sage, basil—because these would most easily be mistaken for weeds. She recognizes corn, onions (Chong's scallions), and tomatoes, but not the other vegetables—cabbage, zucchini, bok choy (which she might have been forgiven), peppers, radishes, beans. Chong demands that she pay attention, since his garden is so important to him, and Ginny chafes a little under his vigorous tutelage.

"I don't see what the big deal is," Ginny says. "You can buy any of this stuff at the grocery store."

"Ho!" Chong says. "You don't see a big deal, huh? This garden is a living thing. This is *food*. It's fresh—much fresher than any store—more nutritious, cheaper. It's not crapped up with bug poison, all that junk, either."

"It takes so much work," Ginny says.

"So it does," Chong says. "Like all good things. You sound pretty lazy to me." He tells her how his family in China had used every available space to grow vegetables and spices, rice in a window box, turnips beside the house, bamboo shoots in a wooden planter beside the door. Ginny seems impatient with this lecture and soon breaks away for the bus.

"Hey!" Chong calls after her. "If Susan comes here, will you stay in the house, then?"

"Who's Susan?" Ginny turns, backing away as she continues toward the woods.

"My daughter! You remember?"

"No. I don't know. I don't think so." She hurries away.

Chong breaks off the tip of a piece of wild mint, and takes it into his mouth. The idea of bringing Susan to live with him for a while for the summer had popped into his head quite spontaneously, and he chuckles with pleasure at the idea of having his daughter in the house. At the same time, he knows that Mai Li would be incredibly suspicious of his motives and drag him into explanations and negotiations of the strictest kind. The mint fills his nostrils and stings his tongue. Mai Li should have been a lawyer, he thinks as he returns to the house, a contract lawyer. The idea of reading a contract gives Chong a headache, and he turns his mind to other things.

Or tries to. He sits at the kitchen table doodling, but still puzzling about what he should do with, to, for, about Ginny. On an impulse, he calls New York.

"I need a toaster," Chong says when Mai Li answers.

Mai Li laughs. "What the hell are you talking about? Can't you buy a toaster in Massachusetts?"

"What are you doing?"

"You didn't call to find out what I'm doing."

"Sure I did."

"I'm auditing financial statements for two small businesses. You remember Fred Soo?"

"Yes, I remember that thief."

"I *am* busy, Hu Lan. What do you want?"

"I have this idea I would like Susan to stay with me a few months. Maybe until school starts again."

There was a long silence, and Chong says, "Hello?"

"You want Susan to come. O.K., why?"

"Maybe she would like to get out of the city. Maybe just because I'm her father."

"You never do anything 'just because.' But I'll ask her. You know she has a summer job."

"Don't tell me, with Mr. Soo."

"Why, yes. She waits tables and buys vegetables. He's being very nice to her."

"Mr. Nice Guy, Mr. Soo."

Mai Li laughs again, dryly. "You sound jealous, old man."

"How old is Mr. Soo?"

"Older than you."

"Well, it doesn't matter now."

"Why do you want Susan to come, really?"

"It's strange, but I have a young woman here."

"Ah?"

"About Susan's age. She has no home. She's almost an orphan. It's very complicated."

"A stray cat."

"Yes, something like that, but a real person. I don't quite know what to do."

"And you think Susan would know?" Mai Li sounds frightened.

"At least maybe she could get her to talk, so I would know what to do."

"I think you'd better call the authorities, at once," Mai Li says. "I think you're asking for trouble. You could be jailed for kidnapping. How old is she?"

"Well, I can't let her starve. She's fifteen or sixteen, maybe. And anyway, who are her authorities?"

"Hu Lan, you are so helpless. Massachusetts must have a foster parents program, or a state division of youth of some kind. How old are you? Look in the telephone book."

"I suppose that's sensible."

"You can't keep a young girl, Hu Lan. Every kind of trouble will come down on you."

"You're probably right."

"I'm not sending Susan into a mess like that."

"It's not a mess."

"Not yet."

Chong sighs in exasperation. "But couldn't Susan come anyway, just for a few days?"

"I'll ask her," Mai Li says. "But she's not coming until that girl is taken care of."

"Sure, sure," Chong says. Unaccountably, he is angry, he is not sure with whom—himself, Mai Li's common sense, the world. "Tell her I called."

"I always do, don't worry."

"Does she miss me?"

"It's possible," Mai Li says. "But she's busy working and seeing friends. She's at a movie now."

Chong reflects that there are no movies in Lake Ecstasy, except for one drive-in which shows soft porn; the theater in Royalton is the other extreme, concentrating on Clint Eastwood, Cheech 'n' Chong—the name rankles—and other mindless family fare. The idea gives him a momentary craving for New York. Susan cannot be enticed by the region's cultural life, certainly. The annual arts fair consists of dolls made from recycled soap bottles, crocheting, collages of pine cones and birds' feathers.

After he finishes talking to Mai Li, Chong looks through the telephone book for the "authorities" she suggested he call. Of course, he will only have to stop by the county courthouse in the morning to get the advice he needs. Maybe he will do that. Meanwhile, another idea occurs to him, the best he'd had in a long time.

He washes himself and changes clothes, adopting a pair of long pants and a sturdy blue shirt. Then he climbs in his battered station wagon and drives a short distance through a din of crickets and katydids in the simmering fields to the Lake Ecstasy Village Inn. A fluorescent sign in the curtained window says OPEN, but Chong knows from experience that this is no guarantee. Mr. and Mrs. Verano who operate the inn whenever they feel like it are also quite capable of forgetting the sign in the window. The best clue whether the inn is doing business is the number of pickups parked outside—the clients apparently rouse each other with telephone or CB calls—and this evening a considerable constellation of these are gathered around the doorway of the ancient hotel. The battered sign hanging over the spongy porch is almost invisible in the evening darkness, and only a single bare bulb over the entranceway and a pulsing neon beer sign indicate the place is inhabited.

Except for the Veranos, Chong would not often have visited the inn, for while the neighbors and friends who gather there are quite boisterous and familiar with each other, they have been consistently reticent with Chong. After three months, he is still a stranger there, and made to feel like one by the customers. The Veranos are different. They talk to him. On occasion, in fact, they have talked his ear off.

Jukebox music slaps him as he opens the door, and Chong has to hunt along the bar to find a seat that is not occupied. He can hear and smell a hamburger sizzling on the grill, and in the "back room," a large open space surrounded by wooden chairs, a small crowd is lounging around the pool table, where a quartet of men hold cues and concentrate with amazing seriousness on their game. The crowd responds with whistles, grunts, or laughter after each shot, and Chong presumes that quite a bit of money is at stake to cause such abnormal concentration.

One of the players is black, which is for Chong an extraordinary fact. For Lake Ecstasy itself has few black families, let alone Orientals, and the only other people of color Chong has ever seen in the Village Inn are Indians, who, in every other respect, except their walnut skins, exactly resemble, in dress, speech, political opinions (as expressed in the bar, at any rate) and choice of drinks, music, and food, the other patrons of the bar. Certainly the black man is a stranger in town, which would have made him a curiosity even if white, and the interest in the game behind him at least partly a result.

Mr. Verano, whose gray hair is in the usual disarray, as if he has just waked up, hobbles down the bar to Chong, smiles, and nods.

"What kind of crazy business are you drinking tonight?" he asks. "You always go for those crazy drinks, don't you?"

"I don't see what's crazy about them," Chong says.

"Go on. Try me."

"A stinger," Chong says.

"No problem." Mr. Verano reaches behind him for the bottles of brandy and crème de menthe. "You're the only guy who ever came in here asking for Drambuie or Cointreau. I bought that damned expensive stuff after you asked for it, and what the hell, haven't sold a drop since. My missus tried some and she said 'Now what could that do for you that blackberry brandy couldn't?' You see? Here comes a cultured man in here, and nobody appreciates it. So how the hell are you, Mr. Chong?"

"Pretty good." Chong motions toward the back room. "What's going on?"

"Hot game, I guess," Verano says. He mixes Chong's drink and then hobbles the length of the bar pouring beers and trading jokes and comments. When he returns, he asks, "When are you going to do my portrait?"

"I told you I don't do portraits."

"Never heard of an artist that wouldn't do portraits. Did you, Sam?" He pokes an older man sitting next to Chong.

"Whatever you say, Cal," Sam says. "What are you talking about anyway?" He gives Chong a curt nod and turns his back.

"Mr. Verano," Chong says, "you know a man named Parker?"

Verano looks around the bar. "He ain't here now, but he probably will be. Why?"

"I need to know about him."

"No you don't," Verano says. He puts his elbows on the bar and leans close. "He's a wild son of a bitch. I'd like to keep him out of here, if I could. When he gets to drinkin', you don't know what he'll do."

"Is he married?"

"I don't know what the story is." Verano looks down the bar. "He was. But I hear he's living with Carey Thiebault, what's her name, Cahill now. I can't keep up with all the changes. These people hop around like fleas in a hot skillet."

"What do you know about her kid?"

"Carey's? Jesus, I don't know. She's in school, I guess. She ran away pretty regular for a while, but they threatened her with the state school, and she stayed home."

"What's the state school?"

"Industrial school, they call it. That's where they send all those punks who shave their heads Mohegan. The kids who steal get sent there. You know. It's a school for punks." He stands up, grimaces as he straightens his back. "Stick around. Parker will be here eventually."

"Don't tell him I asked, O.K.?"

Verano shrugs. "Why would I do that?"

Chong swings around on his stool and watches the pool game in the back room, tries also to assess who these people are he finds himself with tonight. This does not seem like big adventure—beer, a pool table, television—and yet Chong is certain it has provided the arena for numerous authentic dramas, replicas of others taking place across the county in places like this one. A whole big slice of America is on a drunk. What does anyone come looking for who comes to a place like this? The Village Inn is not known for its fights, though a few had occurred within its walls, and a few more in the parking lot. The only music comes from the jukebox. The decor is ordinary—different colors of crepe paper signal a change in seasons (though the Veranos are not too particular about this, except at Christmastime, and one can drink a Thanksgiving beer while staring at a Halloween pumpkin)—the food is ordinary, the clientele is working class and apparently ordinary, and even the mischief seems ordinary. And yet, with no overwhelming incentive of any kind to bring them, the Village Inn is always crowded with customers when it is open.

Chong looks up and down the bar for an incentive. Perhaps it is only to get out of the house. Or to get away from the self. Chong knows many people who cannot stand to be alone. But if he were thrown into solitary confinement, Chong knows how he would spend the time: painting in his mind. He could be trussed and thrown on a cold pallet, and he would still paint, and the painting would give him some hope.

The man beside him, "Sam," Verano had called him, was clearly a farmer, and he had been all day among his animals and in the expanse of his garden and fields, alone, but too busy to notice it much, and he was too tired, or it was impractical because of darkness to do any more. Chong overhears him talking to the next man down about machinery of some kind, the tools of their trade.

"Is that four block or six?" the man asks Sam as Chong listens. "If it's a four, I'll take it off your hands. You can get one of those kits, you know, and fix it yourself pretty cheap."

"Needs rings, too," Sam says.

"Well, what would you want in trade?" the other man says. "I mean, just for the sake of talkin'."

"What about that buzz saw of yours?"

"Oh, no," the man says to Sam. "Couldn't part with that."

Chong recognizes also an older man named Sweeney, a fireman who has been to his home, and who nods to Chong when they meet but has little to say otherwise. He sits at the end of the bar alternately watching the baseball game and picking cards from a deck for his cribbage hand, bangs the cards down with a boisterous thump when he plays them.

He doesn't recognize anyone else, but is amused by the coming and going of all the baseball caps on the men—jaunty and businesslike at once. The younger crowd, Verano has told him, hangs out at the Mountaintop Lounge after nine o'clock. That's where the young women were, mostly, the music there was loud, the lights dim. Chong had only visited the "competition" once, and found it glum and sweaty, too charged with sexual posturing. The Village Inn was more like home.

One of the men, long hair curling on his shoulders, wears a small gold ring in one ear, but he converses easily, laughing, with a stocky fellow whose black hair was cut in close-cropped military fashion once popular among the sons of the men returned from World War II. One of the women, slender, chain-smoking, wears tight jeans and pink slippers, topped off with a checkered flannel shirt that parts to reveal a green T-shirt beneath emblazoned with the message GET IT WHILE IT'S HOT—ADAM'S SAUSAGES. Her companion is heavy, wears a simple sack dress tied with a red sash, and Chong has been in the bar when this woman broke into song, something she did, Verano told him, whenever she achieved the proper state of drunkenness.

"Might take sixteen beers," Verano had said. "But some thinks it's worth waiting for. I'm a country music fan myself."

Chong thinks now of Nancy Wallace, licks his lips. She was so bright and worldly, Chong cannot believe she has not found something more lucrative to do than wait on tables at the Village Inn.

"Are you kidding?" she had said when they had a chance to talk. "Tell me what there is to do around here, and I'll do it. I've been looking for months, since my divorce. This is it, Chong."

"So why don't you move? You could go to Boston, New York."

"What the hell would I do there?" she asked. "Hey. I'm a country girl. I don't make much here, but I can ski to work, right?"

"I guess. I just thought you'd feel pretty limited by this place."

"Yes and no," Nancy said. "Work's not the main thing in my life, you know. Mainly I think of work as just something to get me by, so I can get to the good stuff."

Chong laughed. "As long as you're happy."

"Yeah, well." Nancy pulled her red-brown hair over one shoulder. "You've been divorced. You know it mucks up your mind for a while."

"Don't worry about it," Chong said. "You're a beautiful woman." He had been perfectly sincere in his remark, but Nancy wrinkled her nose in disbelief, even annoyance.

"Hot stuff, I know."

"Really," Chong said. "You can model for me any time."

"Will you pay, though?"

"Sure!" Chong said, surprised at the question.

"You're on," Nancy said. "You let me know when you get moved into that place and I'll come model for you."

The memory is interrupted now as Verano places his elbows on the bar in front of Chong and imitates firing a pistol in the direction of a man who had just come in the door.

"There's your pal," Verano says. "The one customer I could do without."

Chong tries to be unobtrusive in his inspection, which Parker abets inadvertently by heading straight for the back room as soon as he orders a beer and shouldering his way among the spectators there.

Although he has seen Parker before, Chong has never had a chance or a reason to look at him closely. He is comparatively short, with a sparse, well-kept beard, and though broad across the shoulders, seems almost frail through the hips and legs. He is in his late thirties or early forties, Chong supposes, and thinks Parker's face is prematurely old and weather-beaten. Parker wears army fatigue pants, workboots, and a camouflage T-shirt, holds the beer bottle firmly in one hand, drinks with quick snaps of his head, his eyes flashing. But he also seems relaxed, not at all a creature of menace, just a little swaggerish, a little aggressive. Now and then he stares at the black man playing pool, but his look is not so much insolent as one of delighted, perverse surprise: *Look what we have here!*

The black man seems to notice Parker at once, to single him out for a prolonged visual appraisal, and to habitually recheck his whereabouts. Parker is not otherwise remarkable, but he obviously has some presence of interest to the pool players. He finishes his beer quickly, comes to the bar for another, and returns to the pool table. Chong gets a pretty close look at the man, sees the graying heavy eyebrows, salt-and-pepper sideburns, the hint of a scar at the base of his neck, hears the surprisingly soft voice. "How about another one here, Cal?"

"Sure, Billy. But go easy tonight, will you?"

"Don't worry about it."

Parker gives Chong a swift hard glance out of pale blue eyes, returning Chong's scrutiny, a look that turns Chong away from his observation almost in shame.

"That's him," Verano says when Parker moves off. "I hope you're edified."

"Was he in the war?"

"I think so, Viet Nam, of course. But I don't think he was in combat."

"He has a scar."

"Oh, yeah," Verano says. "He tells more stories about that than I have fingers and toes to count. But I knew his dad, and I know how he got it. When he was a kid, see, he was climbing up on the gas stove to reach something, like kids do. He had on a bathrobe or something. And his sister turned on a burner, set his clothes on fire. Old Bill, his dad, came out of the bedroom, saw Billy there running around in circles, screaming, covered with flames. He was in and out of Boston for years after that, getting grafts and what all. You'll see him out working on the road with his shirt off, and it ain't pretty. He's a foreman for the county. He drives trucks, I guess. They all sit around a lot, I think, all them highway guys. If they put down as much tar as they drink coffee, we'd be an end-to-end parking lot, believe me."

"You have any idea what sort of father he is?" Chong asks.

"Christ, no," Verano says. "He's awful when he's drinking heavy. Still, he holds a job. He seems normal otherwise. But it's tough, you know, when your kids aren't *really* your own, if you see what I mean. They might not accept your discipline so easy. And I'm sure Billy can be pretty goddamn rough. His first wife gave up on him, got beat one too many times. What does that tell you?"

"Thanks," Chong says.

"For what it's worth," Verano says.

Chong pays for his drinks and leaves, feeling a little tired, and confused. Mai Li is probably right, he decides. He should go to the Town Hall and find out what to do. He is sorry it is so late, because he wonders most of all how to face Ginny, to see what else he can find out that would help him decide what is best for her. He drives home slowly, pondering, savoring the clear night. Fireflies wink their moonglow in the woods; a big bat cruises through a mist of bugs around a rare streetlamp; some ragged small animal scoots across the road.

When he shuts off the ignition, the engine continues to run, whang, and bang for a while. Chong listens to it helplessly, cringing at the possibility of car trouble, or car loss. He certainly is in no position to buy another car, and it makes him wish he could be doing more to make money, make a trip to New York, visit his gallery, make the rounds. He has some new things to show. Why hasn't Mrs. Browne answered his letter? It means he has to take some slides, prepare a portfolio, travel, wine and dine, hustle—all the things he hates. It will take weeks just to get ready to be in a position to try to make money—all very dispiriting. With a last violent bang, the engine finally quits.

"Hog farts," he says to himself. "Why didn't I go into computers or something? Chemistry? Even groceries." He laughs at himself, but with a trace of bitterness. Susan certainly has the right idea, specializing in numbers. "Maybe," he thinks, "I could make some money if I died." But the thought panics him: Would anybody really notice?

He looks toward the woods but can see nothing in the darkness, hears nothing but the frogs and insects. He decides to stroll out to the camp, grabs a flashlight from the porch. If Ginny is awake, he will ask her about the authorities, about other relations who can help her. She is a chronic runaway, Verano says. Maybe she needs some kind of counseling.

Not much water was spilling over the dam at this time of year, and so it is comparatively quiet by the pond. A mockingbird is raising havoc, but as Chong makes his way across the dam, he can hear unmistakable sounds of quarreling—Ginny's voice and another's, a young male's. Chong does not use the flashlight but picks his way through the brush toward the camp. The fire near the bus is all coals now, glimmering, shooting out an occasional lone spark. Chong can only see a dull phosphorescent outline of a person leaning with one hand against the side of the bus. Ginny presumably is inside.

He hears, "Get out of here, Taylor. I don't want you here."

"You can't stay here by yourself."

"Why the hell not?"

"I'm stayin', that's all."

"Taylor, I don't want you here. Get it straight, can't you? Can't you see I don't want you around?"

"You need protection."

"I don't need protection. If you'd get out of here, nobody would know where I am."

"Everybody knows anyway."

"Well, thanks a shitload, then."

"I didn't tell 'em."

"Who else knows?"

"You can't do somethin' like this secret, Ginny. Don't kid yourself."

"Do Mom and Parker know? Shit, if they do—"

"Who do you think sent me? Parker told me to look out for you."

"*Shit!*"

"That's why I'm stayin'."

"Oh, Taylor, God damn you. I'm almost as afraid of you as him. Why doesn't everybody just leave me the hell alone? You're always trying to screw me, and I hate it."

"I won't try it."

"You will. I know you will. I won't be able to sleep around you. *Please* go away, Taylor."

"Billy told me to stay here, and that's what I'm going to do."

"Taylor, you're not staying here, and I don't care what Billy thinks. I'm not goin' back there."

"It's going to get cold out here, Ginny."

"So? I won't be here when it's cold. I'll have some money, and I'll be gone by then."

"Where are you going? And how are you going to get any money?"

"None of your business."

"You don't even know, do you? You're jivin'."

"Taylor, get lost. I'm not tellin' you anything."

"That's right you ain't. So just shut up. I'm here, and that's a fact. You know you can't stop me if I want to come in there."

"I can and I will. This door is locked."

"You can't lock a bus door."

"Go away, Taylor. *Go away.*"

Chong rustles the bushes on either side of him and begins to swear in Chinese. He places his flashlight under his chin and flashes it on and off, on and off, and continues his growling epithets.

He cannot really see Taylor now, sees only his leap from the firelight into the darkness. Chong now puts the flashlight behind him and flashes it on for a long moment, hoping his shadow would leap huge across the small campground. He shouts like a dragon, like the Wizard of Oz, "*A yuh maka maja fu chien ho! Ayaa.*" His cry echoes through the woods, and is answered by Taylor's thrashing away. Chong carefully picks his way through the bush into the clearing, but then, waving his flashlight, he leaps over the fire and begins to careen around the campsite, shouting, kicking dirt into the fire. "*Myung lao fi ya nang sun wajo! Ho! Ha! Ho! Ha!*" He hides behind the bus a moment, and then dashes into the clearing again with another string of epithets, warbles, cries, hullos, screams.

The woods are completely still now. The mockingbird, the crickets, the frogs have all lapsed into silence. Chong chuckles, and says, "Ginny, come on. We go to the house."

There is no answer from the bus.

"Ginny? Come on." He taps on the door now. "You must come with me now."

Finally the door of the bus creaks open.

"Chong?"

"Yes, come on, Ginny. We're going to the house."

"Chong, you scared the shit out of me. I'm still shaking, you bastard. I can't even walk."

"Taylor didn't have any trouble." Chong giggles. "He moved right along."

"My heart's poundin' like a drum."

"Come on. One more night at my place."

"We'd better hurry. He'll be back."

"That's right. Bring your toothbrush."

She rummages in the bus and suddenly bursts from the door with an armload of clothes and a large object Chong cannot identify until he briefly flashes the light over it; a teddy bear stares back. He silently follows Ginny down the trail to the dam. As they cross quickly over the parapet—dry except for a narrow sluiceway in the center— Chong thinks he hears a *plonk!* close by in the water, turns quickly and slashes the borders of the pond with a beam of light.

The noise makes him think that Taylor has circled back, is following them, and has hurled a stone.

The beam shows only the brush and the trees.

"I can't stay in your house," Ginny says.

"I don't see why not." Chong puts his flashlight on the table. He has not turned on any lights.

"Because people will think things."

"Think things?"

"They'll think we're screwing."

"Ho!" Chong laughs in amazement, but he admits a pang of guilt, too, for he is not innocent of such a thought himself. "An old man like me?"

"They think I screw everybody," Ginny says. "Even my mother does."

Chong rests his chin on his hand and looks through the darkness toward Ginny. "Tell me honestly," he says, "are you pregnant?"

"No," Ginny says. "I don't know. I mean, I don't think so."

"You didn't leave home because you thought you might be, though?" Chong turns on a night light over the stove and the kitchen is bathed in dim blue light.

Ginny sighs in exasperation and looks away. "Chonger, I left home because Parker tried it with me." Her eyes rim with tears and her voice rises. "You *see* now? It's impossible. He makes me want to die. He won't leave me alone."

"Oh, my God," Chong says. "How impossible that is. And your mother doesn't know, does she?"

"I tried to tell her. She doesn't believe it. She pretends she didn't even hear it."

"You have to find another place to live," Chong says. "You can't stay out there this winter. You won't be able to stay out much longer at all. And clearly you need protection of some kind."

"You can't protect me. Not from Parker, and those assholes. All those guys he knows. The Club."

"Like Taylor?"

"Yeah, like Taylor."

"Did Parker send Taylor around to watch you?"

"That's what he did, I guess. He won't leave me alone. He thinks he can run my life, but he can't. He thinks he can keep me from doing things, but he won't. I'm not his goddamned prisoner."

"Ginny, I think we'd better get some help."

"You won't go to the police."

"I think we'd better."

"It won't do no good."

"Why not?"

"You know how many police there are?"

"Well, no."

"There's two. The chief and one part-time guy. And they both know Parker, because Parker works for the town. He drives the town's trucks, snowplows, and stuff, and he does road work."

"We can call the state police."

"Don't!" Ginny shouts. "You're trying to get me killed. They'll say I'm a runaway, and they'll put me in that girls' training school. They already told me that."

"You have to live someplace," Chong says. "You have to get out of this mess."

"That's why I'm leavin' here," Ginny says. "I'm going away."

"But where?"

"I don't know. I'll find someplace."

He doesn't quite understand why, but Chong begins to get angry now. He grumbles and swears, jerks his chair back from the table, and paces the room. "Oh, for Jesus Christ's sake," he says. "This is ridiculous. There's got to be something. Some agency or something. You can't live like a dog out there."

"It's not like a dog. It's better than that girls' school. The beds are iron with flat mattresses. The girls fight all the time. They're bitches. Everywhere you look is a big wire fence. There's not much grass. Everybody treats you like dirt."

"You don't have to pull weeds, though?"

"I'm not joking," Ginny says. "You don't think it's bad, because you've never been there."

"But you have?"

"They showed it to me."

"Who's 'they'?"

"A social worker."

"When was this?"

"When I ran away before."

"You ran away from Parker before?"

"No. Parker wasn't there then."

"So why did you run away?"

"I don't know. Who cares?"

"Ah," Chong says. "So now you think they won't believe you ran away because of Parker."

"I don't care what they think."

"So now you really have to run away, and they won't believe it."

"Yeah. They don't believe anything I say."

"And why should I?"

Ginny regards Chong angrily, with almost the look of a cat stalking prey. "Because you're the only one I ain't lied to," Ginny says. "I thought I could talk to you. To *somebody*."

"Of course you can," Chong says.

"If I can't talk to you, I can't talk, period."

"You keep talking to me," Chong says. "I can keep secrets. You couldn't break me with torture even. I am a vault."

"A vault!" Ginny snickers. "You don't look like a vault."

"No?"

"You look like a jug!"

"Ow! That hurts!"

"But a nice jug."

"Well, O.K.," Chong says. "There are nice jugs in the world. They hold nice things."

"That's what I meant," Ginny says.

Maybe we can be friends after all, Chong thinks. She can sting you. She can still laugh. He wonders if he should tell her that he has seen her almost-stepfather less than an hour ago, but cannot see what possible good it will do. This is such a small town, Chong thinks, he will be here soon. What will I do then? Taylor will surely have something to tell him, when he finally gets home, probably drunk. But he won't come tonight. He won't have that kind of energy.

"Ginny, I really don't know what we're going to do with you," Chong says. "But maybe we should sleep now and see what we can figure out in the morning. I have a real bed for you upstairs. Your very own." He snaps off the night light.

Almost as soon as he does this, Ginny rises from her chair and crashes against him in a death grip, sobbing into his shirt.

"I never did anything," she says. "All I did was just get born."

"I don't know what to do right now," Chong says. "I've got to think."

"You could adopt me," Ginny says. "You could visit me once a month. That'd be great."

Chong is almost afraid to put his arm around her. He listens hard, and the air seems to hiss. "Let me show you your bed," he says.

Chong does not sleep in his bed, but in the overstuffed chair in his studio. He wakes at every unusual sound, and when a car pulls into the driveway at 3:30 A.M., he is up immediately, prowling his windows. The car turns around, lights wash across the porch, perhaps it is Parker or Taylor, perhaps it is only innocent business. At four, when the first predawn light emerges, Chong rubs the tension out of the back of his neck and falls sound asleep for the first time that night.

By seven-thirty, light is pouring in the studio windows. Chong rises and goes about his ablutions and makes his morning rounds through a haze of sleep, guided by routine. Awake hops after him as he opens the chicken coop and throws out canisters of corn. He leaves the gate open today so the chickens can wander around the farm—Ginny can help him with the evening roundup.

Luan is getting fat already and his deformed leg has almost disappeared into the haunch above it. He is fairly agile, definitely intelligent, and continuously hungry. Feeding him is getting to be expensive, since Chong does not generate many scraps for him to enjoy. Ginny can help him make another batch of mush, too. She can tend the fire as he stirs in the grain and silage. Awake teeters on the wire fence around Luan's pen, fixing Chong with his shiny black marble of an eye.

"All right, come on," Chong says. "Graham crackers today."

He is feeding the bird, tossing chips of graham cracker onto the backdoor stoop, when Ginny comes down.

"How's the bed? You sleep all right?"

"The bed's O.K. But I didn't sleep much."

"Because of Taylor?"

"Yeah. I'm sure Parker knows where I am now."

"What are you going to do if he comes here, Ginny? We'd better decide."

"I can't go back there."

"I believe you," Chong says. "You shouldn't have to go back there. You do need some protection."

"But he'll try to take me. I know it."

"He's not coming in my house."

"Says you."

"He's not," Chong says. "That's all there is to it. And if he comes, I guess you had better just stay away from him, and let me do the talking. You can hide in your room or in the barn. What sort of car does he drive?"

"He drives a pickup, four-wheel drive. It's built up, yellow, with a green band around it. My mom has an old blue Valiant."

"What's Taylor drive?"

"Any old thing. I don't know where he gets all his cars. They're just beaters."

"Sit down." Chong motions to the kitchen table, pulls out a chair, and sits down, too. Ginny's hair is rumpled and her face imprinted with creases from her pillow. She looks a little wild and very young this morning. "What do you want to eat?"

Ginny shrugs. "I'm not hungry."

"Scrambled eggs and toast it is," he says. "You'd better wash up."

"Yeah, sure." Ginny does not move.

"How would you like to take a trip to New York, to see Susan, my

daughter?" The idea has just that instant occurred to him. "You'd
be safe there."

"You'd better not take me across state lines," Ginny says.

"Would your mother give you permission? Could you call her and
find out?"

Ginny shrugs, already despondent. "You don't understand, Chong.
She might say it over the phone, but you can't trust her. We'd get
to Connecticut, and the cops would grab us."

"I didn't know there were so many laws about all this," Chong
says. "I suppose we could just go, and take our chances."

"I'll think about it," Ginny says, "Maybe I could go by myself.
But I don't know if I want to go to New York."

"Well, think about it then." Chong rises and goes about making
breakfast. Ginny scrapes the chair back from the table and goes into
the bathroom.

The more Chong thinks about Ginny, the more afraid he becomes.
He decides he will use the morning to snap photographs of his recent paintings and watercolors, and then take the film to be developed in Royalton later on. While he is there, he will stop at the
county courthouse and ask some questions about child protection
and foster homes, try to get some advice and information about how
to deal with Ginny and her parents before things get really messy.
She has given him fair warning about how much trouble he can be
in, harboring her, leaving himself open to certainly disagreeable
visits from Parker if not legal charges from her mother. And what if,
after all, things are not really as terrible as Ginny has described
them? He has seen Billy Parker and it is plain that he has to put his
pants on one leg at a time like anyone else.

And yet Chong knows some things about living with a brutal parent very well. His own daughter had called him "runaway," and he
grew up through his teens in what amounted to foster care, though
far less formal than that, without the guidance of a real father, or
even the frequent presence of a substitute one. Maybe this is part
of the attraction he feels for Ginny and her tangled fate: She has
been saved from chaos.

If he knew the truth of Ginny's situation, his decision would be
easier in many respects. But there is a complicating fact, and Chong
does not dodge it: He likes having the girl in his house, and he likes
the girl. His motives for protecting her are far from pure, and this
also nags him with guilt, for he is not entirely playing fair, and if
he is earning Ginny's trust after all, it is not on completely honest

grounds. Chong thinks it absurd to imagine himself as Ginny's lover, but the simple fact of her presence is undeniably a paradox to him, frightening and welcome, maddeningly gnarled with the complexities of her life and yet simply wonderful, too. Well, he will try to do right, to go to Royalton to see what the technicalities are, the legalities. But he also knows he feels like a betrayer and will not release her with any joy. She will hate him for it, no doubt, even if it is the best thing.

Ginny eats her breakfast and goes to work in the garden. Chong can't stand to watch how she handles the hoe, for she is awkward and attacks the weeds with far more than sufficient vigor. He concentrates on arranging his paintings against the side of the house just out of the direct sunlight. He hangs a bedsheet on the clotheslines behind him to throw reflected light into the shade where his paintings are lined up, and snaps away. Some of the watercolors have to be repinned so the corners will not catch the light breeze and the paper flap or tremble just as he pushes the trigger.

Such a review of his efforts for the past year—more than a year, he groans—is always painful, if also surprising. It is irritating to imagine what a viewer, the gallery owners, critics, will say of a particular piece, or of his efforts in general. He has more pieces than he had remembered making, which is gratifying, but once again he is struck at how many times he completely reverses his first impression of a work he has finished. Many things he had finished with a spark of joy seem slight to him now; some things that seemed too easy, almost hack work, now stand up with deeper resonances and even just better craft than he recalled. One truth remains through all this analysis: Those paintings are best that he has not worked to death, that he has not pestered to extremes, even though he had been struck with the impulse—perhaps the compulsion—to carry them further. His greatest struggle with himself is knowing when to quit. Not so easy to do as to say, Chong knows. Without some discipline, he crowds a canvas into chaos. Several of the paintings he decides not to photograph at all. He yearns for simplicity, for understanding it. His camera is telling him how cluttered his imagination has been.

He rises to find Ginny standing behind him, her forehead beaded with sweat, face smudged, holding the hoe like a spear. Quickly he takes her picture. She threatens him with the hoe, and he snaps this, too.

"So what's the matter? Too much for you?" Chong asks.

"Bugs!" Ginny says. "They're driving me nuts."

"I'll get some bug dope," Chong says. "I should have thought of it. Take a coffee break."

"I don't drink coffee."

"You didn't stay out there long."

"Long enough," Ginny says. "Look at my hands. Blisters. They hurt." She opens her hands in an appeal for sympathy, then closes them into fists. She drops the hoe and sits down on the grass. "Besides, I wanted to see your stuff. I always wondered."

"You did?"

"Lots of people wonder," Ginny says.

"So what do you think? Crazy?"

"Yeah. Real crazy." She laughs. "But I like those." She points to some recent watercolors, abstract, fairly busy, trying to capture that wonderful purple glow of that soft grass which dominates nearby fields. The sense also of how sunlight quickens everything. "And those. But aren't you ashamed?" She indicates now two large paintings of doll-like nudes, cartoonish figures he hopes were burning with mischief and energy—no somnolent passive beauties for him, no corpses floating in dream rivers.

"Why should I be ashamed?"

"Because they're naked."

"Oh, come off it. That's not pornography."

"Some people think so."

"I can't worry about them," Chong says.

"I don't like that one." Ginny points to *Death Has No Sky (Or Does It?)*

"Why not?"

"I don't like the skeleton. I don't . . . it makes me feel sort of dizzy."

"Yes, it's not pleasant thinking about death."

"So why did you paint it?"

"Because death is a fact, and at my age I have to think about it. I know better than you I won't live forever."

"Maybe that's my father," Ginny says.

Chong kneels and pulls up some strands of grass which he tosses into the breeze. "Actually, it's everybody," he says.

"My father's dead, just like that," Ginny says. "I'll bet he died in a field, just like that one, and was covered up by the grass and the flowers, just like that."

Chong shrugs. He looks at the painting a moment, and then at

Ginny, who is squinting in the sunlight, shielding her eyes with a hand.

"I'm sorry it made you sad," he says. "I guess I'll have to do some happy paintings now that you're around."

"You could do one of me," she says.

Chong laughs. "I might."

She points to a watercolor of Luan, a fat pink blob with smart little eyes. "I could be a better model than that stupid pig of yours."

"O.K., O.K." Chong says. "We'll see about that. Help me put these inside, and I'll run to town. On second thought, don't help me. Your hands are dirty."

"Where's the bug dope?" Ginny says.

"Hold your horses." Quickly Chong snaps another picture.

"Cut that out!"

"I thought you wanted to be a model."

"Not in dirt and jeans."

"I've got to finish the roll somehow," Chong says.

"Well, take a picture of your pig if you like him so much."

"O.K., forget it." Chong laughs. "You can wash up at that hose there. But don't turn it on until I get these paintings inside." He knows at once what he wants to do: a painting of Ginny in firelight, beside the bus. Let them try to make sense of that! he thinks.

In town late that morning, Chong asks at the county clerk's office if there is a county juvenile officer and is directed to the police station to meet with Sergeant Chomski. The officer is muscular, blond, and young; the blue shirt he wears threatens to burst at the seams, and he wears a now-what's-the-matter look on his face. Chomski is pecking away at a typewriter, shouts to the policeman at the counter, "How do you spell 'Prevaricate'?"

"L-i-e," the desk officer says. "Look it up."

Chomski keeps Chong waiting while he labors through the form, and then waves him through the swinging door to a chair beside his desk.

Chomski looks uneasy in the chair, too big for it, unused to sitting down. Chong himself is uneasy about their lack of privacy.

"You want to fill out a complaint?" Chomski asks.

"No," Chong says. Momentarily he is at a loss for words and Chomski regards him impatiently.

"You got a problem with some kid? Where're you from anyway? Over in the lake?"

"Yes, I'm from the lake area," Chong says. "But I need some information. I mean, what should be done if a kid needs protection from his parents?"

"You have a specific case, a specific family in mind?"

"Not necessarily," Chong says.

"Is the kid still at home?"

"No."

"O.K. That makes a difference. In the area? Or long gone?"

"In the area, I believe."

"Kids who are really in trouble usually don't hang around," Chomski says. "Anything's better than home, so they go, and they keep going. Is this a question of parental assault? Has the kid been physically hurt?"

"I think so," Chong says.

"If the kid really needs protection," Chomski says, "we can find a foster home. The parents won't know where the child is until the courts decide. But getting the kid away from the parents is not easy. Kids say a lot of things that aren't true sometimes. You need proof. A doctor's statement, a police report, a social worker's investigation. Hearsay won't fly."

"I see," Chong says. "How do you choose the foster parents?"

"We have a file." Chomski opens and closes a drawer beside him. "The parents volunteer, they also take courses on how to deal with these kids, they're checked out by the state. They get a little support money from the state, but nobody's in it for the bucks, believe me."

"Suppose the kid ran away to a friend's house and wants to stay there, and the friend or the parents of the friend say, O.K., you can stay with us."

"There's not a judge in the county that would support that," Chomski says. "The parents could sue you to hell and back."

"Suppose the kid has no father. The mother has a friend, a man, and she sends the man after the kid, who is staying with a friend. Does the mother's friend have any more rights than the friend of the kid?"

"Jesus." Chomski runs a hand through his hair. "I'd tell the mother that if the kid wouldn't come back, she'd better call the police. You're talking about a fiancé or something, right?"

"Yes."

"Actually, the mother should go on her own, first. If the kid won't leave, or if the friend prevents the mother from seeing the kid, that's when the law can step in."

"Thanks a lot," Chong says.

"No problem." Chomski stands up and stretches, straightens the creases in his pants. "I'd advise these people to get lawyers, by the way. I'm not a lawyer. It's all I can do any more to figure out what I'm allowed to do in this job. I have to check with the judge on every damn thing anyway."

Chong leaves, a cloud gathering behind his eyes, a headache coming on. He feels vulnerable and a little ashamed, because it is clear he has no legal right to offer Ginny protection, and has now made himself known to the law. Maybe better to have stayed away? he wonders. But at least he is assured that Parker, until he marries Carey Cahill, also has no legal prerogatives toward Ginny. It is Ginny's mother who must act and who alone has the legal right to make decisions for her daughter. Frustrating not to know what she's like, Chong thinks. Frightening not to know what she will do when she learns Ginny has been staying with him. A hornets' nest, Chong ruminates. How far has my hand been thrust inside?

Chong knows he is going to have to be cagey with Ginny now. He doesn't want to let her know too much about his research and what might be in store for her, because it might drive her away again, into even worse trouble. For the moment, he is going to have to bide his time.

4
The
Mechanics
of
Paradise

The dusty blue pickup went past the driveway through the
pines, stopped in the road and backed up, then swung
sharply between the pillars of the trees and came to rest in
front of the cottage. A stranger emerged, and as Jim went down the
steps to greet him he peeled away the layers that time had painted
over the Red Barber he once knew and found in this new person in
this new place the man he had known in Viet Nam. Once clean-
shaven, Barber now sported an unruly red beard, coarse and short,
and the nest of violent red hair he had once carried like a torch had
thinned out, exposed a broad suntanned, freckled forehead. Barber
also wore a pair of thick "Hollywood" shades that seemed almost
comical, complete with little chrome stripes on the ear bars—no,
Jim realized, they're fishing glasses, polarized and tinted for seeing
into the water. Barber's shirt was open to the waist, indicating the
ride had been hot in the early autumn sun, and as Jim advanced on
his old friend, Red seemed a little dazed. He whooped when he saw
Jim and they were both locked in a bear hug and swinging each
other all over the yard, pounding each other on the back and hollering like idiots.

"Look at you!" Barber cried. "What a fat son of a bitch you turned
out to be."

"You're bald as an egg, man. I don't believe it."

"I can still whip your ass, boy!"

"You never could!"

"Jim-bo, Jim-bo, here we are, by God, here we are."

"I'm fuckin' glad to see you, Red. I'm fuckin' glad you're here, bald head and all."

"Will you cut that out? Or I'll wear my hat at the dinner table."

"I'll bet you scratch a lot of faces with that burr you got hanging on your kisser."

"Faces and places!"

They laughed and swung around the yard, punching each other, babbling.

"Come on, Red. Time to meet my very own."

"That's your ladies on the steps, right? I've wanted to meet them. And ain't your wife a fox!"

"Keep your distance, boy!"

Anna stood in the doorway holding Theresa on her hip. In the bright sun, their mutually blond heads of hair seemed unusually ephemeral and light, as if haloed, and Jim was glad to see that Red's good cheer had, momentarily at least, erased the worry that Anna had brooding on her face all morning. Red was such an imp, so full of bounding life and so obviously enthusiastic about his reunion with Jim, meeting Anna and Theresa, that he sparked everyone, including the kid. Theresa was trying to hide her head in her arms, sucking her thumb in a coy way, but Red already had her grinning.

He gave Anna a smooch that sent her tottering and looked her over with unabashed lust. "Yeah," Red said. "No wonder."

"Run for cover, Anna," Jim shouted. "The man's an animal."

"Well, bring the animal in, then," Anna said. "He may need to be fed and watered."

"So how can you stand living with this guy?" Red teased as Jim came up the stairs and followed the others into the cottage.

"It's not a subject we discuss in public," Anna said half seriously, glancing at Jim, "but he must have some redeeming qualities."

Jim had winced at Red's question, and he knew the time would come, when they were alone, when he would have to tell his old friend what the situation was with him and Anna, describe the struggle to keep the marriage afloat, Jim's struggle to really once and for all put his wife and daughter at the center of his life and "cut out the shit," the booze, the wandering, the angry outbursts. Had Red known, of course, his jovial remark would have been tactless. But he was still innocent. Obviously Anna was going to play it straight, too—good PR for now. The sight of Red charged Jim with a cornucopia of questions, emotions; and his happiness at seeing him bumped against his worry about what they would finally say to each other, about having to confess—or could he?—that he just wasn't handling things that well, things were too slippery for him, he was having trouble making sense of anything, of not dissipating his care, of getting the right focus.

Red could hardly be contained in his chair. Anna pressed a beer upon him, and he was on his feet in a moment, gesticulating wildly, explaining how he had stayed up for two nights finishing off some tractor and truck repairs so he could make this visit and this fishing trip.

"I busted my fanny," Red said. "I had a wrench in each hand. I tore that John Deere apart in about twenty minutes. The ball joints on that truck thought they weren't going to give. 'No way,' I said. 'I'm going to see my buddy Jim.' I got a refund coming from Griprite because, mister, they said their tools don't bend, ever. I got a surprise for 'em."

Anna slipped into the kitchen after a while and Jim could hear the clatter of pans and tableware.

"Hey! You're not fixing anything to eat, are you?" Red shouted. "Forget it. Tonight's on me. Let's go out. On me, I mean it. I've been thinking about clams all the way down here. I'm celebrating. I'm so happy I finally got out of that shop. We've got to go out."

Anna appeared in the doorway. "I'll just fix something for T'isa then." She looked at Jim. "Maybe I can get Dana to look after her awhile tonight."

"Give her a call."

"Bring the kid," Red said.

"She'll fuss or fall asleep," Anna said.

"However you do it is fine with me," Red said. "I hate to tell you, I'm a little wacky without much sleep. I might just do like a kid myself."

"You want a nap?" Jim asked.

"Are you kiddin'? You think I came down here to fall asleep?" Red threw an arm over Jim's shoulder and gave him a crushing hug. "Here's my first confession," he went on. "I can't believe I'm here, because . . . You ready for this, Anna? It's a little spooky."

"How spooky? I don't know what I'm ready for until I hear it sometimes, Red."

Red acknowledged the remark with a nod, studied Anna intently, then plunged on. "For years, you know, I haven't been able to go near the ocean." He laughed. "I don't know why I'm laughing, because it's not funny. It's one of the things I came back with. The ocean scares the shit out of me. But maybe I got it beat. I got this far. I could never even get this far before. You couldn't get me to go to Boston. And that's why. Because of the damned ocean!"

"We've got a lot of ocean around here," Anna said. "It's permanent."

"I don't want to bum you out," Red said. "I don't go crazy or anything, I just get sick. It's just a little weirdness. I'm not dangerous or anything."

Anna spoke to Jim. "He looks dangerous to me. I don't care what he says."

Red laughed.

"We don't have to go fishing," Jim said. He looked at Red through a wave of something akin to grief. He could understand, or thought he could, how the ocean could reek of evil, how the water could threaten to bear him away again to hell, to kidnap him. Dear God, don't send us back, don't ever send us back. And Red was not making excuses, Jim knew. There wasn't any need for excuses. You did what you could to survive or succeed in the world, and when the time was right you reconnected. A certain healing was required first, a settling into place. Even now, the sight of Red jarred Jim almost into tears of rage and regret and frustration, but he swallowed them down now, and they didn't seem necessary.

"Of course I want to go fishing," Red said simply. "I want to beat this thing. Jesus, I go fishing all the time in the country."

"Just keep me posted," Jim said. "Otherwise, I'm not going to worry about it."

"Right. Good. That's the way I want it," Red said. "Christ, Jim, it's good seeing you! I'm a damn prisoner of my own business, you know? Beautiful little town, lots of fat trout, I'm all the time in the garage banging knuckles. Cabin fever is my middle name."

"You must like it," Anna said, "or you wouldn't hang around there. You ought to be able to go where you want to, doing what you do."

"I looked around some. Sure, I could go other places, but I do like the lake. And where else could I go and be my own boss?"

"You never did like taking orders," Jim said.

"It's constitutional, from birth," Red said. "My whole family's that way."

"What's this Lake Ecstasy like, anyway?" Anna wobbled as

Theresa banged into her, demanding attention. "I can't believe the name."

Red described the village, the nearby towns, the countryside. He named some of the people he knew and described a typical day for him.

"I can't say I'm exactly *ecstatic* about living there," he said. "We've got poverty, we've got crime, we've got assholes and greedy bastards and stupid politics—dogs and zoning are the big issues. People nose around your private life a little too much sometimes. But, Jesus, it's a beautiful place. I've got a lot of space. And most people will do anything for you, if you ask. If I didn't allow myself to get so damned busy, the pace of things is pretty easygoing. There's no real pressure. Nobody's breathing down my neck, except maybe the bank, and even then, you know, what I paid for my place wouldn't buy you a bedroom down here. I'm one of the lucky ones, I'm making good money, comparatively. The folks without money aren't quite so impressed with scenery, I guess—though everybody and his brother considers himself a sportsman. I don't know if they'd give up their woods for a few factories, or not. I almost doubt it. In some ways, it's the wild west. I wonder if there's anybody without a rifle, a shotgun, bow and arrow, some damn weapon of some kind. Guns and motorcycles. You should hear it during pheasant season—the place crackles. Deer season—stay out of the woods."

Over more beer, Red told Jim and Anna what he knew about the history of the place he lived in. The town was settled in the late eighteenth century by an ex-British ex-Army officer who had somehow become the leader of a mystical religious cult. The major brought his followers with him to the shores of Lake Ecstasy, where he baptized and bathed with his followers in the buff and generally behaved in a way that was completely outrageous to their sterner and more puritanical religious neighbors, Shakers and Dunkers among them. Though the major's cult eventually dissipated through intermarriage and the harassment of more conservative newcomers to the area, Lake Ecstasy's reputation as a source of religious inspiration and healing power lived on.

"They made a big deal out of it in the nineteenth century," Red said. "We've still got the old railroad inn in the town. It's boarded up and people want it torn down, but it's still there. People came from all over the east coast for baths and canoeing under parasols and séances, inspiring lectures, all that jazz. But I guess that faded out, too. People blame it on the automobile, I don't know why. It seems to me you could have motored out to Lake Ecstasy if you wanted to."

Red laughed in embarrassment. "I'll tell you what my thing is. I'd like to see that old inn turned into restaurant and dance hall and town meeting place. People keep worrying that somebody's going to torch it, and it's close to a lot of homes. Kids are always screwing around in there, you know. I don't blame 'em. I love to go in there myself. Sometimes I'll get a little stoned and sneak inside—I've got a key because I'm on the volunteer fire department and I'm supposed to 'inspect' it now and then—and just sit there in the dark in this big creaky place. You know what a guitar would sound like in there? You'd feel like you were right inside a guitar, I'll bet. I'd like to take somebody in there who could really play the guitar and listen to it resonate. The place was built of chestnut, can you imagine that? It won't come down too easily, believe me."

"Doesn't anybody else want to save the place?" Anna asked. "It sounds beautiful."

"They don't speak up if they do," Red said. "The place gets a lot of bad publicity. Vandals love it. Somebody painted a great big FUCK YOU on one of the gables last year, intelligent stuff like that, and that riled some people up. They got tired of looking at it, and finally I got the fire ladder out and painted it over. Otherwise, I think the neighbors would have torn it down themselves."

"So what's it like when you're in there stoned?" Anna prodded. "Any ghosts?"

"You people are going to think I'm completely nuts," Red said. "It just smells good. I don't know what to say. I'm embarrassed. The mice will run right across your shoes, like I'm not even there. I like to imagine dancing in there—I do!—you know, in the old suits and big full gowns of the nineties. Nostalgia, maybe. I love it."

"What would you do if you didn't have to make a living, Red?" Anna grabbed Theresa off the floor and swung the child onto her lap. Theresa writhed and whined in protest.

"Christ, what a question. I don't know. I'd catch a lot more trout. I'd travel. I'd probably try to go back to Viet Nam. Just to look around."

"Yeah," Jim said. "Me, too."

"I mean," Red said, "I'd *fly*. Unless I got this thing beat, about the ocean."

"I'll bet you do," Jim said. "You made it this far."

"Now, Anna, you've got me thinking, damn it," Red said, pointing

at her with his beer bottle. "If I didn't have to work. By God, I think
I'd like to fix up that old inn, too. And I'd hire a guitarist to play in
there. Maybe I'd learn to play myself. I wouldn't be one of those
guys who wouldn't know what to do without a job. I got some ideas.
Once I thought I should build my own boat. Maybe I could get over
this thing if I built my own boat. But I never did. I don't think it
would be impossible, and I think I'd feel safe in a boat I built. I've
already given it some thought, believe it or not."

"I believe it," Jim said.

"Man, listen to me talk," Red said. "I haven't talked so much in
three years as I have in the last hour. I'm boring you to death."

"Tell me about this boat," Anna said.

"You and your questions," Red said. "You're the one who's got me
flapping my jaw. Jim keeps feeding me beer, getting me looped. And
you haven't had a beer yet, you bastard. What's the story?"

"I'll have one in a while," Jim said. I don't want to get started, he
thought. I promised Anna. I promised.

"I never knew you to turn down a beer," Red said.

"I've had more than my share," Jim said. "I'm trying to quit drinking so much."

"I see." Red glanced at the bottle in his hand a little guiltily. "But
drinking beer's not drinking, is it?"

"It sure is," Jim said. "In my case it is."

"You smoke, though? I've got some good smoke in the pickup.
Home grown."

"Sure," Jim said, nodding toward Theresa, who was now pulling
Anna's hair unmercifully. "But later, O.K.?"

"It's been a long time since we smoked any grass," Anna said.

"You miss it?" Red asked.

"I don't think about it much," Anna said. "It seems we really don't
have the *time* any more, you know, with T'isa, and both of us
working."

They talked some then about their jobs. Anna was laying out and
designing a catalogue for a department store chain, an assignment
she expected to last the year. Jim described his darkroom work.

"I just can't get used to not having any daylight," he said. "Especially at this time of year. I go to work in the dark, I come home in
the dark. Sometimes that bugs the hell out of me."

"I can dig it," Red said.

"The only thing that makes the job interesting is that I get all the
wacky assignments, the stuff that nobody else wants to do."

"Like what?"

"Like what they call 'art' photography, which is pin-up stuff, 'T. and A.'"

"Or worse," Anna said. "Some of the stuff is pretty bizarre, pretty disgusting, I should say."

"And I get some police lab work," Jim said. "All the savory stuff."

"I don't know." Red sucked his beer and looked away a moment. "I say this as a friend, right? But you could be doing better, Jim. You should be."

"I *was* doing better. I blew it."

"That was yesterday."

"Let's not go into this right now, Red, all right?"

"Right," Red said. "I just wondered why you weren't in business on your own, why you didn't have your own studio."

"That's what I want to know," Anna said. "Thanks, Red."

Jim gave a little cry of distress. "You know how many cameras there are on Cape Cod? You know how many people consider themselves photographers? Do you have any idea how professionals around here make a living with their cameras? They take school pictures. Tons of kids. Line 'em up, snap away. It's a factory job, and it's all on bid. You don't make much. And weddings. Line 'em up, snap away. Brides and school kids, wedding cakes and football teams. Or catalogues. You photograph food processors, sweaters and pajamas and girdles."

"It could be true," Red said. "I don't know the photography business."

"And after a while, you take so many pictures," Jim went on, "it's like everything and anything is a photograph. All those images. You get so you can't tell the ordinary from the extraordinary any more. Man, I have developed so many sea-gull pictures, so many girl-friends in bathing suits, so many silhouetted ships at sunset. Sometimes when I pick up my camera now and I think maybe I'll go out and take a few pictures, a few dozen pictures, I get embarrassed with myself. What am I going to make a picture of that isn't corny as hell, that hasn't already been trampled on a thousand times? Ice on parking meters—corny. Smashed cars—corny. Dew on compass grass, fern buds unscrolling like the necks of violins—corny. I don't know if there's a photograph left."

"I see what you're saying," Red said. "I think I see here a little burnout on photography."

"You could call it that," Jim said.

"I think maybe you're on a plateau. You're resting up, and then you're going to go on to something new."

"Is that the way it works?" Jim said almost savagely.

"That's the way it works," Red said. "It says you're thinking. It says you're not a machine."

"Listen to him," Anna said. "You've got a friend sitting there, Jim."

"Red," Jim said, "I know this guy from Provincetown who takes pictures of junk cars. He has been taking pictures of junk cars for years. The guy is completely tuned in to junk cars; he finds them everywhere, back of tumble-down garages, half buried in sand, forgotten in some briar patch. He has photographed thousands of junk cars."

"So?"

"So? Don't give me that," Jim said.

"Is this guy a photographer or just a nut?" Red said.

"When he's a photographer, it's by accident," Jim said.

"Anything wrong with that?"

"What's wrong is that the guy is so obsessed with junk cars. He thinks it's the only subject there is. And *I* think maybe that's what you have to do to become a good photographer."

"And you don't want to be like that?"

"No," Jim said. "I don't want to be like that. When I drink, I drink like that."

"So you're afraid you'll become like Mr. Junk Car?" Red said. "You'll just get kind of compulsively involved with one thing over and over again."

"Not just that," Jim said. "Suppose it's the wrong thing?"

Red shook his head. He started to say something but changed his mind and ended with a shrug.

Anna broke the silence. "But what would be 'the wrong thing'? That's what I don't understand."

"But if you think that," Jim said, "then anything at all is a good subject, then everything remains the same. A coconut is as good as, as a baby, or a dead raccoon by the road. A can of soup is the equivalent of a heron or something. In which case, it's impossible to make choices, and everything is a photograph. You might as well be a machine."

"Some things mean more than others," Anna said. "But what is meaningless? Anything you photograph is going to say something, Jim."

"So it's a question of what you want to say, isn't it?" Red asked. "You've got to find the things that say what you want to say."

"It's not that simple," Jim said. "It's not even a matter of using the camera to search for those things, which I would say was a worthy enterprise for anybody. Kind of a photographic trial and error."

"I'm getting lost," Red said.

"Suppose I already found the subject," Jim said. "Suppose I already photographed it, photographed it too much. Suppose I hate it. Or am afraid of it."

"Ah, shit," Red said.

"You're afraid of the ocean, aren't you?" Jim said.

"I was," Red said. "I'll let you know pretty soon." He pressed the cold bottle to his forehead a moment. "But me and you are different, Jim. If I'm scared, that doesn't mean you have to be. If I haven't quite beat it, or don't, that doesn't mean you can't. Don't lay that on me, man. That makes everything just too crazy—I'm scared I'm going to be scared, because if I am, you'll think you'll have to be scared too. I can't deal with things on that level—too dizzy for me. Way too dizzy."

"But you got something there," Jim said. "Maybe I'm staying away from the camera like you're staying away from the ocean. Maybe we're in this together more than we'd like to think. Is that possible?"

"Yeah." Red nodded his head slowly, looking down at the floor. "It's fuckin' possible." He glanced up quickly at Anna and apologized for his profanity.

"Don't worry about it," Anna said. "You can't talk about Nam and not use profanity." Under her breath she added, nuzzling her daughter, "No fuckin' way. Right T'isa? No fuckin' way."

The departure for dinner did not go smoothly. Theresa did not want to be left with the baby-sitter and made her feelings known with a vigorous tantrum. The teenager who had come to care for the child was obviously a little confused about what to do, but finally Anna calmed Theresa down enough to make a getaway.

"I always feel so guilty when I leave her," Anna said in the car. She was crammed between Jim, who was driving, and Red, who had surprised her by not climbing in the back. His thigh pressed against hers. "It really makes it hard for me to enjoy myself."

"There's some powerful ties there," Red said. "But you've got a right to enjoy yourself, too. It's not going to kill your kid to be without Mom for a while."

"Keep reminding me of that, will you?" She told Red that this
was the first time in quite a while that she and Jim had done anything together, since normally they traded off the baby-sitting
chores. "I see the early show and he sees that late one." She laughed.

"You let this foxy lady out on her own?" Red said. He howled like
a wolf. "I'm moving down to the Cape, man. I'm going to prowl this
neighborhood every night."

Anna pulled away from Red in mock horror. "Why doesn't some
crazy woman marry you and put you out of your misery?"

"Because she'd have to be crazy, that's why." Red ran his hand
through his hair. His tone of voice changed. "Actually, I'd love to
have kids."

"So?"

Red put his hand on his heart. "So, the woman I love has other
ideas. She's independent and wants to stay that way. She works. She
dates other men. I've tried every trick in the book."

"But have you tried finding somebody else?" Anna asked.

"I'm pretty stuck on Nancy," Red said. "I often wish I weren't, believe me."

"It sounds like you're going to have to look around," Anna said,
"if you're really, truly serious about getting married."

"I've been too busy to look around," Red said. "I mean, Lake Ecstasy's a small place. You can 'look around' there in five minutes. I'd
have to do some traveling to look around, and I kinda think I'm too
old for that kinda stuff sometimes."

"Old and gray," Jim teased. "Old Red will henceforth be known
as Old Gray." He wished he and Red were alone. He'd have something to say about marriage and fatherhood and guilt. Maybe he
should have been able to speak his mind with Anna present, but if
he did, he knew also the conversation would peel off into struggle,
possibly acrimonious. It was not the time to be speaking his mind,
and in any case Jim believed it was secrets, if not hypocrisy outright,
which made most marriages possible at all—little white lies. You
sacrificed the truth about ephemeral irritations for the sake of the
longer-lasting harmony. And you ignored also the truth about desire, possibly even love, that it was general—cupid firing with a
mini-gun, 2,000 rounds a minute—not so specific as the pragmatic
institution of wedlock required. Jim had been faithful because he
had wanted to be, and also because, he had to admit, there was little
opportunity to be otherwise. Marriage was about responsibility as
well as intimacy. When you married, and especially if you had chil-

dren, that gave a lot of people rights to peek through the blinds. You were making some pretty incredible agreements to live a married life, Jim thought. You let the preacher, the teacher, the insurance agent, the judge, the doctor, and relations galore come into your bedroom and sit at your dinner table. What your marriage was supposed to mean became a lot of people's business, and if you didn't believe that, all you had to do was to try for a divorce. One of the little white lies you told yourself in marriage was that it was private and special, not an institution at all, but a special event in the history of the world—like the birth of a particular child with a particular set of genes. We are not statistics.

"Keep it up," Red said, "and I'll leave you with the check tonight. Hear me?"

"If I take this next right," Jim said, "I could show you a nice little stretch of beach and a good fishing jetty."

"Let's take a look," Red said.

Jim ignored a glance from Anna and turned right, breezed down a narrow road arched with trees sending down a thin snow of yellow and brown leaves. Suddenly the sky opened, and the road turned sharply through a dune crowned with sparse grass and dark green beach plum shrubbery. Jim drove slowly along the narrow parking lot, and watched Red as he also gazed out across the water, which was dark under a canopy of clouds stained purple and pink by the sun setting somewhere behind them. On the horizon, the shadow of the earth sat waiting to engulf them in night.

"What are we looking at?" Red asked. "What direction is that?"

"Nantucket Sound," Jim said. "You're looking south. Nantucket's out there, George's Banks."

"If I put my boat in here and took off, where would I end up?"

"Long Island," Anna said.

"No shit? How would I get to England?"

"See your travel agent," Jim said. He laughed, not because he thought himself amusing, but because he recognized Red's confusion with his whereabouts on Cape Cod. Newcomers were easily disoriented, because the Atlantic Ocean, Cape Cod Bay, and Nantucket Sound surrounded it—everywhere you turned there was water—and because the Cape's sudden hook, an "L" on its back, changed the direction of the roads and made many of the roadside markers ridiculous. On Route 6 East, you might actually be traveling north, or on Route 28 South you might actually be traveling west. The side roads could be even more confusing, since few of them were straight, probably following old Indian trails or cowpaths. He and Anna had a joke about taking "shortcuts." Whenever Jim made a "shortcut" to save them time, he was sure to get lost, stray wildly from his intended course. This was almost the nature of the Cape to him, the antithesis of the city block, or the mile square of farming lands.

"I mean by sailing," Red said.

Jim pointed to the east, where night was waiting. "Right down this coast, past Monomoy Island there, whose lights you can see now, and out into the Atlantic."

"Fantastic!" Red said.

"Everything O.K.?" Anna asked.

"It's beautiful," Red said. "But I am awfully hungry."

Jim turned the car around and headed for the restaurant.

As they lingered over the remains of their dinners, Jim found himself becoming terribly impatient. His head felt hot, and the jingle of glass and ice at the bar made him almost salivate for a drink. He sucked his gums and drew in a deep breath, and he thought, *It's like I'm afraid, almost like being afraid.* He could feel sweat beading on his temples, and he looked at Anna to remind himself of his promise, for some support, and realized with wonder that he was close to panic. Red was here, Anna was here, sitting at their table, alternately teasing each other and then dipping into serious conversation. Things were good, and he was safe, and yet this terror had just swept over him. He looked around the restaurant and saw only the most ordinary of activities in progress, and still there was sweat on his temple and his right hand was gripping the seat of his chair. He endured, then relaxed again.

They returned to the cottage to find Theresa sleeping soundly, the baby-sitter listlessly sprawled in front of the television. Jim walked the girl down the hard packed and sandy lane and across the main road to her house, enjoying the clear night, and when he came into the cottage again he found Red sitting on the folding bed that Anna had made up.

"Bedtime already?" Jim asked.

"I just go with the flow around here," Red said. "Anna thought maybe we'd be getting up early to fish."

"We could do that," Jim said. "Or—"

"Let's 'or,'" Red said. "I'm kind of charged up as a matter of fact."

Jim slipped into the bedroom and closed the door. Anna was in bed reading a book in a little circle of dim orange light.

"I thought Red and I would have a little ramble," Jim said.
"Where?"
"Just out and around. We'd like to talk."
"Sure," Anna said. "But be careful, will you?"
"What's to be careful about?"
"Red scares me a little, Jim."
"Really?" Jim shrugged. "I don't see why."
"The way he talks about using drugs. He's pretty casual about it.
He seems a little reckless."
"I don't know," Jim said. "If he is, he's only dangerous to himself."
"Nobody is ever dangerous to himself," Anna said. "Somebody always gets taken along."
"He won't hurt you," Jim said. "You're not exactly in his line of fire."
"I am if you are," Anna said. "So be careful, will you? The two of you together is a dangerous combination."
"I'll be careful," Jim said. "And stop using the word 'dangerous,' O.K.? It makes me feel like a crook." He lowered himself to the edge of the bed, trapped Anna in the blanket and gave her a kiss. "I am not a crook," he said, imitating ex-President Nixon.
Anna did not smile. As Jim shut the door, she was still looking at him, and she seemed very tired.
They walked, then, under the stars, to the Whale Inn, where they sat at a table in the small dining room under a neon bar sign. With a pang of dread, but with more than a little desire as well, Jim ordered a beer, and he and Red talked and talked about men they had known in Viet Nam.
"Remember Morris? 'Buzz-head'? Divorced and remarried. He's happy as hell, I hear, a realtor down in Arkansas. Making good dough."
"What about Warner?" Jim asked. "You ever hear about him? I heard he was farming in Montana."
"Oh, shit, you didn't know about that, huh? Jim-bo, he is fuckin' dead, man. I hate to tell you."
"How in hell—"
"Stupid. Stupidest thing I ever heard. He was hauling some chain back to a neighbor. Carrying it across a lawn. He borrowed this chain for some damn thing on the farm. Let's see, I heard this from Griswold."
"Tell me about him, too."
"Wait a minute now. Griz told me that Warner was carrying this

chain, and he fell into the neighbor's leachfield. He broke right
through the damned lawn, you know, and went down and was
buried in sludge."

Jim rocked, hearing this. "He died—"

"Stupid!" Red slammed his fist on the table.

The stories wrapped in and out of each other. Griswold ("Griz")
had visited Teter in Vermont, Teter had visited Red, Red was visit-
ing Jim.

"You know who I hear from now and then?" Jim said.

"Rosey?"

"Right. I played pool with him a few times in Boston. Or tried to.
He called me once or twice."

"How's he doing?"

"Hangin' in there. You know what he does?"

"Probably everything and anything."

"Right. Mainly he gambles. He had some jive job loading mail
trucks or something, but mainly he's playing poker and shooting pool
and messing around and messing up."

"He'll never change," Red said. "Christ, we ought to visit him up
there."

"I don't know about *that*," Jim said. "The dude's into too much
mischief for me. He's into some pretty heavy stuff, I think."

"Dealing?"

"I don't know about that," Jim said. "It wouldn't surprise me. He
knows a lot of those guys who went to South America, you know,
hired by the political pricks down there."

"I've got to check him out," Red said. "I'll bet he's got a line on
a lot of stuff. How come he phones you anyway? I heard he was not
real friendly with white folks."

Jim shrugged helplessly and drank his beer. "I guess I did him a
favor once. He just checks up on me. I can't really say we're buddies,
but we're not enemies."

"Interesting guy," Red said with a hint of amusement. "One minute he's cold as ice, the next he's positively what-do-you-call-it?
More than friendly. Generous."

"Lately he seems pretty wired. That's the impression I got from
his phone call."

"He never was the most *relaxed* guy."

"You can say that again. It's like he's still in combat. He seeks it
out."

"That's Rosey all right," Red said. "Well, I wish the fucker luck. He's one of those guys that stays in your mind for some reason. All the nobodies and forgetables, even the guys who bought it, you meet some that just stay in your mind like permanent fixtures. Rosey would be surprised how much I think about him."

"I learned a lot from him," Jim said. "About staying awake. But I could never decide if he knew how to handle fear, or if he was just a little crazy."

"He used to sit around with his eyes closed an hour before night patrol, or going on guard duty. He said it built up his night vision. Remember that?"

"Hell, yes," Jim said. "But that wasn't crazy."

"He was always coming up with stuff like that." Red shook his head. "We lucked out, Jim-bo. Just don't go walking into anybody's leachfield."

Jim and Red stumbled into the cottage at 3 A.M. Jim was drunk, but not spinning, bearing a kind of drunkenness that made him glad there was nothing left to drink in the house, because he would have finished it. His talk with Red had left him with the same sensation, a paradox of being sated, or not wanting to hear another word, and a sense, too, that nothing much had been said after all, that there was everything left to understand, and know.

Partly out of guilt, he roused himself from bed shortly after Anna was up, dressed, and went into the kitchen for coffee.

Anna said, "You don't look too bad this morning."

"I behaved," Jim said. "I was careful."

"Did Red have a lot to say?"

"He sure did. So did I."

"I wanted to be a fly on the wall," Anna said. "I really wish I could hear what you say to each other when I'm not around."

"We're not keeping secrets," Jim said. "It's just that it's simpler, not to explain who everybody was. Or what happened. Red can say one name, you know. He can say 'McAllister.' And that's all he needs to say to me. But with somebody else, we'd have to fill in all the details. And when you do that, sometimes the story gets weird, gets twisted. It's hard to explain."

"I feel left out, though."

"Well, don't," Jim said.

Red was snoring grandly in the other room. He was wrapped in the sheets like a mummy, and an amazing event for Theresa, who kept toddling into the living room to regard Red with a thumb-sucking awe.

"She doesn't know what to make of him"—Anna laughed—"she's just fascinated." She poured Jim more coffee. "Guess you guys have canceled the fishing, huh?"

"We'll go this afternoon," Jim said. "The tides are late, and we can fish right up through sunset."

"Will you have supper here?"

Jim nodded toward Red. "From the looks of it, it's going to be a two o'clock breakfast. And I don't know when we'll get back. We might get into some fish and be real late. Then again, I don't know about him, how he's going to take it."

"I'm betting he'll be all right," Anna said. "I don't think he would have come down here if he wasn't ready for it."

That afternoon, Jim took Red to a nearby beach with a long jetty at one extreme that also enclosed the mouth of a river. He chose the location because it was accessible and they could be away from the water quickly if Red was uncomfortable. They fished there, casting plugs, for half an hour, and when Jim saw that Red was enjoying himself and eager to catch fish, he decided to move on.

"We'll see if we can do any better on the Bay side," Jim said. "We'll put on our waders and hike down Sandy Neck, see if we can stir up something there."

"Lead me to 'em," Red said.

It was an afternoon of intermittent dense clouds that broke apart to permit big wedges of misted sunlight to beam down onto the water. A light breeze blew over Cape Cod Bay but the water was only moderately choppy.

"I can't get over the color of the water here," Red said. "It's gorgeous—blue as the sky. I thought it would be gray, you know." He waded in from the beach to his waist, and made a long cast. Jim walked a little farther down the beach and cast, too.

Almost at once there was an explosion behind his lure. Jim saw it from the corner of his eye and missed the strike because he had been watching Red. He kept the lure popping on the surface of the water and in a moment he saw the head and back of a bluefish arc out of the water, and he had another powerful strike. This time Jim did not miss, and he leaned back on the rod listening to the drag whine as the bluefish tore away line.

"Hey!" Jim called, pointing to his rod. The bluefish surged out of the water, shook its head, then walloped down.

Red stumbled in surprise, and made a hasty cast that sent his line skipping over the water. He howled in misery, but a bluefish oblivious to the fine points of casting technique obliged him by smacking the bait anyway.

"Hotcha mama!" Red hollered. "Yi!"

Red was enough of a fisherman to keep his cool, and he played the bluefish patiently. His eyes were aflame with excitement when he finally dragged it onto the beach.

"What a fish!" he kept saying. "What goddamned spirited fish."

Jim shook his own fish free from the lure. "Get him off there and get back at it. They may not hang around long."

A dozen sea gulls were swirling close to the surface of the water, then plunging down for scraps of the bait being chopped up by the bluefish below. The school had moved only a short way down the beach and was still in casting range. Jim cast again into the boiling water and again the water shattered into spray. Jim was delighted that this should be happening now, with Red on hand. He was glad Red would get a chance to experience the excitement and the abundance of the sea, its generous phase. It would help to cure him, Jim thought. As he played his second fish, he watched Red cast, and cast again, and finally tie into another fish.

The blitz ended a short while later. Jim and Red could not keep up with the bluefish as they pressed their hunt down the beach. They watched as the entourage of gulls spiraled farther and farther out of reach, and then walked back the way they had come, collecting their fish—eight in total, ten to twelve pounds each.

"They're a mighty fish," Red said. "I lost as many as I caught."

"You're a good fisherman," Jim said. "You didn't let them bully you. You used the drag like a pro."

"It's not so different from any other fishing, just on a bigger scale."

"You ready to try these on a fly rod?"

"Hah!" Red said. "With those teeth, that would really be an exercise in futility."

Jim left the fish on the beach and walked to the car for his filleting knife. He brought a thermos of coffee with him, too, and he poured Red a cup as he set to work gutting the fish and removing their heads. Some of the fish were still alive, and Jim stunned them by picking up a rock and tapping them between the eyes until they were still. Though he had seen it done on some fishing boats he had been on, he could not himself clean a living fish.

The knife carved the underbelly open, Jim pulled out the entrails and then chopped through the spine, tore off the head. The detritus he flung toward the water, and washed his fish in the curl of the wave, a red cloud spewing from the silvery cold envelope in his hands. He had almost finished the chore when he looked up to find Red in obvious distress, the thermos hanging from his hand at his side, coffee spilling into the sand.

"How you doing, Red? Are you all right, buddy?"

Red shrugged helplessly. "I was doing great. I was having a ball."

"I'm almost done. We'll get out of here."

"All those heads, man. It's a little eerie, you know. They got eyes like coyotes, yellow, what can I say?"

"Two more minutes."

"I'd really like to bury those heads," Red said. "You know?"

"They're just fish, man."

"Maybe not just. Not just fish."

Jim washed the last fish in the surf as quickly as he could. "You want to call it a day?"

"I want to bury those heads is what I really want."

"They'll be taken care of, Red. They'll be used. There are so many things here that will bury them for you."

"Yeah, well, maybe if we just got out of here."

"That's what I'm saying. You think you can help me with the fish?"

Red fell to his hands and knees on the beach and began to retch. The coffee emerged in a brown stream, and Red convulsed again.

Jim could only take four of the fish at a time, and made one trip to the car, and on his return for the second batch, he found Red burying his own vomit a little frantically.

"Well it snuck up on me there," Red said. "I'm O.K. now. I'll help you with those fish."

"I got it now."

"O.K., hero. You hassle it. I'll grab the rods and the sand spikes, all that jazz." Red was sweating so hard the perspiration dripped from his nose.

"You were doing great," Jim said. "You were catching blues like a champ."

Red laughed in embarrassment. "I got my share, I guess. But man, those heads did it to me. I took the liberty, I tossed them all in the water."

"Good," Jim said. "That's where they belong."

"I could use a couple of snappers to clean the old mouth out,

Jim-bo. Can I buy you a beer? Or a Coke or something?"

They would have made a savage little photograph, Jim thought suddenly: those heads in a ragged line at the water's edge, foam curling around that yellow stare, blood bubbling, the soft white entrails on the sand. "I might have a couple of shots myself," Jim said. "We've got a nice mess of fish to celebrate."

5

Vermilion Phoenix
(*The Summer Now*) [*iii*]

G inny is so tired from her labors in the garden that morning
that she falls asleep on the sofa late in the afternoon while
Chong is preparing dinner. He trims pink wedges of chicken
from the bones and watches Ginny toss and turn, her eyelids fluttering as she dreams. She has shown him the blisters on her hands, and
Chong understands he will have to find some other excuse to keep
her busy, invent some lighter work for her. He decides he will have
to see or somehow talk to Ginny's mother, but how he will do this
without either Ginny or Parker interfering he does not know. The
idea of meeting Carey Cahill also frightens him a little. I'll visit
Turner when I get a chance, he thinks. Turner has kids Ginny's age.
He knows the town. Maybe Turner can help me. I would rather talk
to Turner first. Chong is not sure whether this is cowardly, or wise,
or both, but he feels relief having thought of it. He can put off dealing with Ginny's mother a little while longer.

In a while, Ginny comes into the kitchen, shoulders drooping, her
eyes puffy.

"You look like you've done some work," Chong says.

"Everything hurts," Ginny says.

"You'll get used to it."

"Get *used* to it. No way. I quit."

"No work, no eat."

"Chonger! I can't do it. It's too hard."

"We'll find something else for you to do," Chong says. "I mean, until your hands are O.K."

"Yeah, but look at them, will you?"

"I already looked. You think I never saw a blister before?"

"You're mean," Ginny says. She stands next to him and peers into the wok as he tosses the chicken in ginger and garlic slices. The meat crackles. "That smells good. Hurry up. I'm starving."

"I got a lot of junk on the porch I need to sort out and haul to the barn or someplace. Tomorrow you can help me with that."

"I don't even want to think about work right now."

"I know. You want to think about eating."

"Right!" Ginny says. "Now you're talking sense."

Chong dumps the snow peas into the wok and continues stirring. A haze seems to be removed from the peas as they cook, and they become a bright, a fundamental green—a wonderful intense peak color that always tells Chong when they are done. He ladles the food into a bowl.

"You're not planning to stay out in the bus tonight are you, Ginny?"

Ginny shrugs in exasperation. "Taylor's a creep. If he'd just go away like I asked I could stay out there."

"Well, what can I do?" Chong asks. "I can't tell the police to keep him away from here, can I?"

"It wouldn't do any good," Ginny agrees. "There's too many ways to get here through the woods. You can come from the orchard, the cemetery, the state park . . . lots of ways."

"How long has it been"—Chong hesitates a moment before continuing—"since you've spoken to your mother? Do you think she has reported us to the police? When I asked about calling the police, I was partially thinking about that."

"She knows where I am," Ginny says.

"How does she know?"

"I called her," Ginny says. "This morning, when you went to Royalton."

"What did she say?"

"Oh, I don't *know*." Ginny slams herself into a chair at the kitchen table.

"She must have said something."

"She's so mixed up," Ginny says. "She tells me one thing, then another. First she says come home or else, then she says, *No* don't, stay where you are."

"I guess she's not too helpful?"

"She doesn't know what Parker's going to do. She can't do anything until she figures out what he's going to do, or what to do about him."

Chong shakes his head, contemplates the incredible knottiness of some people's lives, all the wrangling and indecisiveness, the broken relations, like a rock tearing through a spider web. "It seems your mother is not too lucky with men."

"My mother is stupid," Ginny says, but recants at once. "No, she's not stupid. I don't know. She's confused. She never knows what to do."

"Do you think I should talk to your mother?"

"No!" Ginny shrieks.

"Why not?"

"Because I don't want you to!"

"But that's not a very good reason, Ginny."

"It is, Chong. I can't stand to think about it. She'll trick you. She'll make it sound like everything is fine, and you'll believe her. When it's not true. If you see her, she'll say, 'Oh, thank you, Mr. Chong, for being so kind to Ginny, but you see she is just a runaway and she should come home now where everything is fine, and we all love her.' And it's a lie! Parker just wants to fuck me and mess me around, and my mother doesn't want to believe it, because she thinks Parker has a good job and will keep her safe."

"Do you think maybe she loves him? Loves Parker?"

"I think my mother is too afraid to be in love."

Chong reels with this announcement. He looks hard at Ginny, and she seems older to him now than he had believed. He puts the dinner on the table, and sits down brooding. "So you think your mother is that desperate?"

"*Desperate?*" Ginny wrinkles her nose, as if the word disgusts her. "I don't know what that means. But maybe, yeah. I never thought of it that way." She quickly wipes her eyes, using both hands, shakes her head. "Chong, it's scary to think that. To think my mother is so afraid. Desperate, for God's sake."

Chong does not apologize. "Let's eat now," he says. "We can be miserable later."

"Shit," Ginny says, spooning the chicken and peas onto her pale blue plate, "shit, shit, shit."

* * *

That evening Ginny is restless.

"There's nothing to do around here," she says with a vengeance.

Consequently, Chong tries to instruct her in stretching canvas. As he expects, she does an amateurish job and is indignant when Chong pulls the staples out of the small frame he has given her to work on and tells her to start again.

"You want everything to be so perfect all the time," Ginny complains.

"No one can paint on a floppy canvas. Besides, some things have to be done right or they might as well not even be done. You can't build the foundation for a house of of . . . out of . . . bubble gum, say."

"Bubble gum! You think some funny things."

"You see what I mean, though? If the canvas is not tight, then the primer will crack, and if the primer cracks, then the whole painting is ruined."

"What's primer?"

"The first coat of white paint. You'll see. As soon as you can stretch a canvas, then I'll show you how to apply the primer."

"Yeah. Really?"

"Yeah, really." Chong's back is killing him, and he tosses the canvas pliers on the floor and eases into a chair. Sometimes he just has to get off his feet for a while. "You work on that now, see how tight you can get it. I'm going out for a minute."

"Where are you going?"

"I'm going to get some beer for me, and something for you for breakfast."

"I want to go out, too."

"Where are you going to go and not get into trouble?"

"I don't know. I want to see my friends. If I was in the bus, I could see my friends."

"Another problem," Chong says wearily. He understands that at her age, friends are of paramount importance, that it will be futile to argue with her about it or try to keep her isolated. "Make some calls while I'm out. Maybe we can arrange something. I don't want a houseful of people, though."

"I don't have a houseful of friends anyway," Ginny says.

Chong grimaces. "I'll bet."

He goes out into a russet evening, and the pond, already in shadow, seems made of wax. The plants in the garden are starkly silhouetted,

the corn appearing oddly tropical, the long leaves folding in their
centers like the wings of bats. He drives to O'Day's general store and
buys beer, milk, and eggs, as he had said he would, then continues
down Royalton Road toward Lake Ecstasy village until he comes to
Turner's farm, and turns into the driveway. A pair of large dogs
howls around the car as he pulls up to the porch, and because it is
already dark Chong cannot see them well and is afraid to open the
car door. Then the porch light flashes on, and a woman comes out
to scold the dogs and quiet them down.

"I'm looking for Joe Turner."

"Is it something I can help you with?"

"I just wanted to talk to him."

"Well, he's down in the barn. You can find him down there. Or
you can wait. He should be done soon. At least I hope so."

"I'll come back if he's busy."

"I'm sure he wouldn't mind." She looks toward the barn, and
Chong can hear the sound of a circular saw blade whining and ringing. "Don't worry about the dogs," the woman says. "They're all
bluff."

Chong takes a deep breath and opens the car door, which, as he
has feared, sets the dogs howling again. The woman calls and scolds
them, and when Chong finally steps out of the car, the dogs circle,
and nose him, finally seem to relax, follow him to the barn. The saw
shrieks and whines again, and Chong sees a wedge of light falling
onto the ground where the barn door is open. He pokes his head in
and calls.

Joe Turner looks up from a sawhorse where he is marking a board
with a fat yellow pencil. "Hey," he says.

Behind him, in the deep shadows of the barn, there is a sudden
turbulence, almost like a wave breaking along a beach, and the
squealing of pigs. As his eyes adjust to the dim light, Chong recognizes the backs and ears of swine crowded together in a pen, their
restless shifting. "Don't let me interrupt anything," he says.

"What can I do for you?" Turner says.

"You're going to think I'm crazy," Chong says. "I came to gossip."

Turner laughs. "If it's anything I can't handle, I'll send you up to
the house. Ruth's more up to date than me. What's buggin' you?
Somebody botherin' you lately? Somebody givin' you a hard time
down there?"

"Well, I'll tell you," Chong begins. He isn't sure what he should
say, but he tells Turner that he has found Ginny in the bus behind

his pond and doesn't exactly know what to do. He wants to know what he can find out about her home life.

"Oh, I don't think you want to get mixed up in that." Turner shakes his head for emphasis. "Maybe it's not for me to say, but that's what you might call a rats' nest, Chong."

Well, Chong confesses, the girl has had some problems with an unwanted visitor, and he has taken her into his house for her own protection.

Turner carefully saws off the end of a board, stands thinking a minute as the blade hums into silence. "If it was me," he says, "I'd just take her right on home."

"She says she's got problems there."

"I don't doubt it," Turner says. "What else did she tell you?"

"She said her father left the family some time ago."

"You see," Turner says, "that's problematical. Some say Ted Cahill left because he *wasn't* Ginny's father. That's gossip pure and simple, you understand. But that's what you came for, and that's what some people say. He's down in Florida now, I hear."

"Ah." Chong rocks on his heels, hands in his pockets. "You think Ginny's wrong about being in danger at home?"

"I'm just saying I wouldn't make it my business, you see." Turner picks the board up from the sawhorse and taps it on the barn floor. The pigs behind him jostle again. "I'm trying to think what I could tell you that would help you," he continues. "There's been a lot of stuff over the years, but I never saw any need to piece it together before. This is such a small town, Chong. Such a small town. I hate to say it, but I even used to date Carey Thiebault in high school. I did. She's always been good-lookin', and kind of . . . I don't know what to say. It's like she's not there, really, like she really needs somebody to tell her what to do and what to think and who she is."

"No personality."

"That's right," Turner says. "Only it's not just that, either." He pauses. "You take my wife. She knows what she likes and doesn't like, she can make up her own mind about things—and how—and I don't worry about her if, say, I got laid up or killed. She knows what to do. Christ, she knows more than me about most things. But you take Carey there. If you told her that bears make good pets and put a bear in her house, she'd say it was a good pet even if the bear was eating her foot off."

Chong nods his approval of Turner's metaphor, hides a smile. "I see."

"Well, I wonder if you do," Turner says. "I'm not saying that to be smart, but because I think right now that's maybe what Carey has got in her house, a damn wild bear that tells her he's just a good old guy come round to put thinks in order over there."

"Parker."

"Yeah, Billy Parker."

"Who's this guy Taylor?"

"That's Parker's cousin, Taylor Archer. See, this is how tricky it all is, Chong. The Archers have a reputation around here that goes way back. If I had six hours, I couldn't tell it all. They've stolen cars. One of 'em burned down the church once—just last year, not that we could prove it. Another has been smashed up in a motorcycle accident, and there was a cute little girl with him, too, who is now pretty scarred up. The rumor goes around that they're involved in drugs—using and dealing. They all stick together like flies on shit, too, because nobody else will have anything to do with them. Now you see what you're getting into? It's not a healthy situation."

"I appreciate this," Chong says.

"Normally I wouldn't talk like this about anybody," Turner says, "because I believe people have a right to live the way they want, even if I don't think it's pretty. I also don't believe in cleaning up after people. We all got our own problems, right?"

"I guess you're right."

"Well, if you don't have problems of your own, that's good and you're lucky," Turner says. "But I only told you these things because you're kinda new around here, and I'd hate to see you get trapped into something."

"I made the right choice coming here," Chong says. "Thanks again."

"No problem," Turner says. "So how's that dam holding up? I meant to ask you if I could do a little fishing up there, but I've been so busy I never got around to it."

"You still have some wood coming," Chong says.

"Oh, I know, but that's fall work," Turner says. "Once it frosts, I'll be up there, don't worry."

When Chong returns home, Ginny is not in sight. He checks her bed upstairs, but it is empty. He finds the canvas she has stretched, drums his fingers on it, and knows she has taken some time and pains to make it so tight. He walks out past the garden, across the dam, and to the bus; but it is quiet there, too, and the fire pit is cold, damp-smelling. God damn it, he thinks, she could have left a note. He wonders if she has left for good, and given what Turner has told him, maybe that would be the best thing. On the other hand, maybe she has only arranged to be picked up by some friends and intends to come back later. He knows he doesn't want her going out at night. Who would be responsible for her? Too much could go wrong. Suddenly, he is frightened, hurries back to the house, looks up Carey Cahill's number in the telephone directory, dials, endures his panic that he won't know what to say. This is none of his business, as Turner has said, and making it his business is asking for trouble, as Mai Li and the policeman had warned him. So why does he persist?

"Carey Cahill, please," he says when a woman answers.

"Yes?"

"Mrs. Cahill, this is Mr. Chong."

"Can I call you back?" Carey's voice seems tired.

"I'll be here," Chong says.

"Thank you," Carey says, and cradles the telephone.

Chong sits down at the kitchen table with the feeling that he has been hit in the stomach, and realizes his heart is racing. Is this fear? He looks at his hands, and they are shaking and tingling. Parker must be in the house for Ginny's mother to be so circumspect, Chong guesses, and the need for circumspection itself signals trouble. What would he do now if Parker showed up at his door? Chong's fright bubbles over into anger for a moment, then into frustration, then into a kind of melancholy which makes him feel absurd. Events seem to be taking charge of him. He has taken the bait, and now there is a hook in his lip. If he were more like Turner, he reasons, this would not be happening. Of course, this would mean also that he was less like Chong, more detached, and more rational. What would I have done, he wonders, if the stray cat in the bus had been a young man? And he knows at once the answer: sent him away, told the police to come after him, agreed with him to find another place to stay. In part this would have been true because the boy probably could not suffer the same kind of abuse as Ginny claimed was inflicted upon her, but also because in Chong's kindness to Ginny there was an undeniable note of hypocrisy, an attraction, and an attraction probably not vastly different from that of Parker's. Chong faces this. In all honesty, it gives him pleasure to have Ginny in his home, and he enjoys taking care of her. In all honesty, he knows also that he would

never force himself upon her, that he is not afraid of behaving brut-
ishly toward her, of preying upon her. He cannot do this, and if this
is the only danger their being together presents, then she is safe
from him.

In part, it is not even her sex that attracts him—though he has certainly been lonely enough, and has felt deprived enough sometimes—but her youth. How flattering it would be to have someone
that young and pretty take an interest in him. He could all the more
easily numb the fact of his true age, the stray progress of his fate,
the time spent, gone, unrecoverable, the inevitable approach of the
endless night. He could lie to himself that he was still young, too,
that his hard-ons were infinite. Given the chance, he could love such
a young woman with the word he had used to describe Ginny's own
mother—desperation. He would turn himself into the tantra master,
endlessly spewing and reclaiming his sperm, endlessly united with
the child symbol of endless creation. Or that would be the lie he
would try to tell himself, that he was a god and not subject to the
laws of mortality. Like Tseng Tsung, the emperor who declared
himself holy and therefore immortal, and who nonetheless suffered
the inevitable frustration. Not so easy, Chong thinks, giving up this
desire to stay in the fray, to recycle oneself through the troubles and
miseries, to keep breathing down the blue sky, the smell of decay,
the smoke of fireplace and battle. Ginny is innocent of what she
means to Chong, and of course she doesn't deserve such celebration,
or such cherishing.

"Too many strings attached," Chong reminds himself. "Clear your
sights. Take her home. Be objective. Quit your desiring." All of this
he knows to be good classical Chinese advice, which he has absolutely no hope of taking. For Chong also knows he has a streak of
larceny in him, that he is a gambler, endlessly also on the lookout
for loopholes in the laws and taxes of human misery. Tseng Tsung
was a royal fool, of course, a royal desperado, and Chong does not
really believe he is going to get out of life alive. But doesn't everyone
hate the barren life, the dreams of deserts, isn't even the Gobi occasionally festooned with shimmering tents and scarlet flags?

What nonsense, he thinks, waiting for the telephone to ring.

About eleven-thirty, Chong is stretched out on the sofa, arms
folded on his chest, when he hears tires squeal on the road in front
of the house. In a moment, he hears a car pull into his driveway, and
then a sharp banging on the front door. Startled and a little dis-

ordered, Chong slips out the kitchen door and around the side of the house, into the blaze of headlights from the car, and finds Taylor striking the front door impatiently.

"What do you want?" Chong demands.

Taylor spins, lopes down the stairs. "Where's Ginny? I've got to talk to her."

"Not here."

"Well, where is she?"

Chong says nothing, angered by Taylor's assumptions that his questions should be answered. He folds his arms across his chest, and stares at the boy.

Taylor grips his black leather jacket on either side of the zipper. "You're telling me you don't know where she is?"

Chong only smiles, nods.

"You gotta know," Taylor says. "So where is she?"

Chong continues smiling, shaking his head.

"Taylor, let's go," the driver calls.

Chong cannot see who is behind the wheel because of the blazing lights, but the voice sounds young, certainly not Parker's. Taylor swears, flings himself into the car, which lurches backward onto the highway, surges off with a whimper of tires.

Chong stands a little stunned in the sudden silence, the smell of exhaust surrounding him, Taylor's aura, as he thinks of it now. Something is going on. Something has panicked Taylor. If he weren't still anxious to receive Carey Cahill's phone call, Chong thinks it would be wise to place himself in the barn and watch what other visitors might come calling tonight. His adrenaline is flowing, and he is wide awake, buzzing, and very worried. What does Taylor want with Ginny? What has he heard? What has happened to send him on the highway searching?

Inside again, Chong turns off the lights and sits by the telephone. He stands up every time he hears a car pass the house. Infrequent as traffic is in Lake Ecstasy, Chong realizes he has learned to ignore it in the same way that he blots out the noise of the train that rattles and blares through the valley at 2 A.M. every night. When he closes his eyes, the room seems to hiss. He is hearing everything now, the refrigerator ticking, a mouse gnawing in a kitchen cupboard, the very molecules of the air knocking together.

At one-thirty, the telephone rings.

"Mr. Chong, this is Carey Cahill."

"Hello, Mrs. Cahill. I called because—"

"I talked to Ginny. I want to say thanks, but . . ." To Chong she sounds breathless.

"Yes?"

"I want to ask you a favor."

"If I can do something, I will," Chong says.

"I don't know why, though," Mrs. Cahill says. "Why should you?"

"Sometimes I wish I didn't care," Chong says. "It would make my life a lot simpler."

"Oh." Mrs. Cahill speaks with an irritated lilt to her voice, as if she has been hurt by his remark, taken it personally. After a moment, she continues: "Can you look after Ginny a few more days? No one else in town will do it, you probably know. I want to make some calls and things, and then we're going away from here."

"It's all right," Chong says.

"You don't know anything about me," Mrs. Cahill says.

"No. Only what Ginny tells me. And you don't know me."

"That's true," Mrs. Cahill says. "Only what Ginny tells me. But I don't know if I have any choice."

"About what?"

"About trusting you."

Chong considers this with unease. He wants to believe what Mrs. Cahill is saying, but before he can voice a clear objection, the woman adds, "I'm so alone in this, Mr. Chong. Everyone has left me. Except Bill. I'm trying to find out what the truth is. But which way to jump, I don't know."

"I understand," Chong says.

Mrs. Cahill is silent a moment, and then says wearily, "Well, maybe you do."

"Ginny can stay here, but I can't really make her do anything, you understand," Chong says. "She has to want to stay."

"I can't make her do anything either," Mrs. Cahill says. "I don't know what to do with her."

"She was here earlier, but she left."

"I know. She came home for a while. I was out and she had a row with Bill. It was terrible. It was worse than ever. It was too much. That's why I want to go away."

"Do you have a place to go?"

"I have to make some calls first. It might take a couple of days. I can't call while Bill is here, I mean I could, but—"

"I understand," Chong says.

"You must think my life is a mess." Mrs. Cahill laughs uneasily. "Well, it is."

"It's none of my business," Chong says, "but maybe it would be easier if you got away from Parker."

"That's what I want to do, yes," Mrs. Cahill says. "It's just not so easy. Everybody's got problems. Everybody else does. You can't just walk away from a house and show up at someone else's." She is silent, and Chong listens to her breathe into the telephone. "It's just so goddamned complicated." Immediately she adds, "I shouldn't be telling you this."

"I'll be patient. I'll take good care of Ginny," Chong says. "If she lets me."

"That's good to know," Mrs. Cahill says. "Ginny should be there soon. Tell her I love her. We'll go away as soon as I can get it worked out."

Chong sits in the dark after Carey Cahill hangs up, listening for Ginny's return. There is a ruckus that startles him for a moment, but which he identifies finally as a cat rummaging in a kitchen cabinet, probably with its claws in a mouse—a soft, thudding struggle. He decides to turn on a light in the kitchen to let Ginny know he is home, but when he comes past the window over the sink, he can see the flicker of a campfire reflected in the pond. Of course, he thinks. She has gone to the bus. She might even have some friends with her. He will just take a look to make sure, and if she is there, he will return to the house and sleep. He is very weary. He wants things to settle down, and to close his eyes and sleep.

Though he is at ease, certain he will find Ginny and some friends at the campsite, Chong stays close to the trees along the riverbank so that his approach to the bus will remain unobserved. He picks his way slowly through the meadow grass and the occasional downed branches until he comes close to the dam, where, with an instinct he would not have credited himself with, he drops into a crouch in a patch of mint and big-headed daisies. He feels even before he sees a presence on the dam itself, what resolves out of the darkness and the light cast by the campfire into the outline of a man in the apparent attitude of pissing into the stream below. A red dot of cigarette glow lights up for an instant a bearded face. Chong can see now, too, the outline of the man's body on the side where the fire blazes, his open jacket a polished reflective leather.

And the fire itself is not just a campfire, but roaring and crackling, a bonfire, and out of its self-generated noise there comes also the sound of shouting, crude laughter, curses. Chong's skin crawls as if he has been stung by a spider. He dares not move while the man on the dam remains so close.

Someone near the bus shouts, "Hey, Dawg, quit playin' with yourself and put it away. You think we ain't seen it enough?"

The man staggers as he laughs, perilously close to stumbling into the water. Something sparks past the man's head—he belatedly throws up an arm to protect himself—which, when it hits the pond behind him, Chong recognizes as a beer can. He can see it spark as it bobs, then hears it clink against the stones as it tumbles over the dam and down the stream.

The man staggers across the dam into the glare of the firelight, and Chong moves now, closer to the edge of the pond so that he can see a larger portion of the camp and the clearing. Past the bus, on the far side of the open area Chong can see, and merged into the darkness of the woods is a row of motorcycles, the chrome sparkling. On the ground in front of these lounges a pair of women, their leather jackets open to bare skin, their hands cradling cans of beer. They smoke aimlessly.

Now a man strides up to the fire and throws a cupful of liquid toward it—a tremendous dragon of flame snarls into the air and vanishes with a roar.

"Yeah, all right," one of the women cheers.

"You like that, don't ya?" the man bellows and exchanges remarks with the women that Chong cannot hear. He hears other voices, too, from a man he can see from his limited vantage point, but thinks there are at least two others, possibly a fourth. He counts three motorcycles, their front wheels slanted at identical angles, their spokes shimmering as the fire twists and grabs at the space around it.

Another man appears by the fire, this one short and broad-shouldered, with a protruding stomach. He holds a branch in the flame for a few moments, and when the tip is ignited, brandishes it in the air, making the flame snarl, and then in a move that sends Chong to his belly, charges to the edge of the pond and hurls the flaming spear end over end into the pond.

Chong's heart races now. He had thought he was being attacked. Warily, he begins to back away from the dam into deeper cover.

Another of the men takes up a spear and the game of hurling it into the pond. He holds his spear like a lance and throws it so that the missile does not tumble until it has reached the peak of its arc, where it seems to hang for a few seconds before plunging with a hiss into the dark water. A third, then a fourth man joins in the contest, and the women rouse themselves and come forward, too, so that they are assembled between the fire and the pond, raucously cheering, booing, and applauding when each of the men throws the flaming stick out into the night and the black water.

Just before it strikes, a phantom flame seems to spurt up from the depths of the pond and collide with the one tumbling down from the sky.

Chong continues his slow retreat. A motorcycle crackles, then comes growling toward the pond. The driver brakes and spins the bike sideways, the woman riding behind him hurls a flaming stick into the air that falls quickly at the water's edge.

"Booo! You can do betta! C'mon! What the fuck kinda trow wazzat?"

"We'll show you how t'do it. Mandy, saddle up."

Chong takes to the cover of the trees now and hurries back to the house. He wants these people gone from his camp, from his land, and he fears a fire. He is going to call the police at once and comes into his dark kitchen with a whimper of worry, reaches for a light, when he feels himself taken around the waist, howls low in his throat, strikes out in terror, hard, feels the dull slap of his fist against something hot and soft.

"Ow! Chonger! Chong, it's me," Ginny cries.

"Ah, Christ, I'm sorry," Chong says. "Are you hurt? You scared me."

"Yes I hurt," Ginny wails.

"I'm so sorry, I didn't mean it." He clicks on a light and finds Ginny sitting spread-eagled on the floor, a hand pressed to her shoulder.

Chong falls beside her at once, embraces her awkwardly. "Let me see."

"You hit hard," Ginny says. "I didn't think you could hit so hard."

"Move your shoulder. Can you?"

"Yes. It just hurts like hell."

"Nice greeting I gave you, huh?"

"Where *were* you?"

"By the pond. There's some gang at the bus. I've got to call the police."

Ginny laughs now. "They won't come."

"Who won't?"

"The police."

"Why not?"

"That's The Club. By the bus? There's only one cop. He won't go in the woods after The Club."

"I'm calling anyway. They're going to start a fire. I don't want them out there."

"You're asking for trouble," Ginny says. "Was Taylor with them?"

"He was by here earlier, but he wasn't with the bunch out there."

"That's his cousins. They're Parker's friends."

"What a nice family!" Chong says. He pulls himself up and heads for the telephone. "You've been home, right? I've talked to your mother."

"She sent them after me."

"What are you talking about?" Chong picks up the telephone receiver but keeps his finger on the switch while he waits for Ginny to answer.

"My mother, Chong. She sent The Club to get me. She had to. I told her I was going back to the bus. That's where I wanted to go."

"Ginny, your mother asked me to keep you a couple of days. She said she was making arrangements to take you away."

"She lies! She always says that. She hasn't got any money. She hasn't got anyplace to go."

"She sounded very concerned about you."

"Yeah, I'll bet. She's so concerned she left me with Parker."

"But she wouldn't send The Club," Chong says. "Parker, maybe, but not The Club."

"Suddenly you're a big expert on my mother. You believe her more'n you believe me."

"Oh, boy," Chong says as he dials the police. In a moment he receives a recording asking him to leave a message, his name and number. He is given another number to dial in case of an emergency. Flustered, Chong starts to explain why he wants the police to come, that there is a gang in his woods hurling flaming spears into the pond, but the message seems so complicated and strange that he is suddenly stymied with embarrassment. Imagine some person trying to make sense of it! He leaves his telephone number and paces to the kitchen window, where he is relieved to see only the bonfire still ablaze. Maybe they have found something other to do than play with fire, he hopes.

"You had a fight with Parker?" he asks Ginny.

"Worse." Ginny sits at the kitchen table and lays her head down. "I'm so tired."

"We can talk in the morning if you want to sleep."

"I can't sleep now. I'm scared. My feet won't even stop shaking."

"What happened?"

"He tried it again, but I cut him."

"You cut him? How?"

"I grabbed a meat fork in the kitchen sink. I got him right in the side, and I felt it go in, and something made an awful noise. A grating noise."

Chong feels his voice evaporating. "Where was your mother, girl?"

"Bowling," Ginny says. "She's on a team."

Now Chong sits down. He stares at Ginny and is about to speak when the telephone rings. Chong stumbles into the living room and answers.

"Chief Dawson returning your call."

"Yes." Chong tries to sketch clearly the situation in the woods.

"Did you talk to them?" the chief asks.

"No. I was afraid to."

"Is the area posted?"

"No," Chong says.

"So what's your objection? To the fire?"

"Yes."

"Is it still going?"

"Last time I looked, yes. A minute ago."

"Any property damage?"

"No, but I'm worried about it."

"Are they close to any buildings?"

"Just the bus."

"You got a permit for the camp? Zoning?"

"The bus is the snowmobile club's."

"Oh, yeah," the chief says. He coughs. "I'll look into it."

When the chief is off the line, Chong slams down the receiver.

"I told you," Ginny says.

Chong swears. "He doesn't want to do anything."

"Who cares if they raise hell in the woods?" Ginny asks. "That keeps them from being someplace else. You think the chief wants to go after some trespassers at three A.M.?"

"I've already had one fire," Chong says. "As a matter of fact, the firemen thought maybe Taylor did it. You were there that night. I saw you."

"You must've got an eyeful."

"It was an interesting party. It was also dark." He waits a moment. "So?"

"So."

"Don't play dumb. Did Taylor do it?"

"Yeah," Ginny says. "Me and Taylor."

"You too? *Why?*"

"Taylor was my friend."

"Now wait a minute." Chong has a surge of panic. "You were such friends before, why not now?"

"Because," Ginny wails, "he started running with The Club, after Parker came around. And I don't like them. I hate them."

"What does Taylor need The Club for?"

"I don't know." Ginny shakes her head. "He's scared. They make him feel safe. Nobody messes with The Club."

"Do they really want him hanging around?"

"Not really," Ginny says. "But he just tries all the harder to get over. And The Club uses him, and laughs behind his back."

"Is this why he set fire to my field?"

"Oh, Chong, it's so complicated."

"Tell me."

Ginny groans. "Well, one thing, his brother was killed in Viet Nam."

Chong feels a wave of disgust. "I see. He thinks I'm Viet Namese? He doesn't know I have been in this country more years than he has been alive? To him, all 'yellow' people are the same?"

"Don't get mad at me," Ginny says.

"You helped him."

"His other reason was that Parker wanted to buy this place before you did."

"So I have heard," Chong says.

"See, and Parker couldn't, because his credit was no good. It's kind of complicated. He had some money, but nobody would take it. The bankers wouldn't say why, and Parker got mad. So he got in trouble with one of them."

"What kind of trouble?"

"I don't know. He threatened the guy, then did something to his house or garage or something."

"So he and Taylor got really mad when a yellow man bought the farm, right? My God, and now you come and live here."

"But it's more than just you, too. See, Chong, The Club hates everything about snowmobilers. The Club thinks they're all the town's goody-goodies. They think the farm should be theirs."

"Let me ask you something, and let me beg you to be perfectly honest with me. It's very important."

"I won't lie," Ginny says.

"So, this business with Parker. Did he try it with you before you came here, before the bus? Or only after? Or really never?"

"He beat me, Chong. First he beat me. Then I came here to the bus. Since then he tried it twice. Tonight was the second time."

"So why did you come here, really?"

"I didn't think anybody would find me. Where else could I go?"

"You didn't choose it because you knew it would really make Parker mad? Because you knew it would hurt him?"

"Yeah, maybe," Ginny says softly. "I hate his guts."

"Oh, boy," Chong says. "Now you know what else, don't you? What else has happened?"

"No." Ginny is next to tears. "Except I got you in trouble, too."

"That's right," Chong says. "They couldn't have a better excuse for coming after me."

Ginny bolts from the table, but Chong grabs her by the wrist.

"I've got to get out of here," Ginny says.

"You have no place to go."

"Taylor will take me. Someplace."

"You hate Taylor, too. Forget it. Sit down and let's think."

"I'm too tired to think, Chong."

"Me, too, but we have to." He tugs gently at Ginny's arm and she sits down again. "I don't believe you did it on purpose anyway," Chong says.

Ginny speaks matter-of-factly. "My mother hates me."

"I don't think so."

"I told you she sent them after me."

"I can't believe she'd use you that way. Use you to scare me, to get me in trouble."

"She wants what Parker wants. She hates me because I hate Parker."

Chong shakes his head, a little dizzy. "She said she wanted time to arrange going away with you, away from Parker."

"I wish she would," Ginny says. "She knows we should go. But I don't think she really wants to. She's more afraid of that than she is of Parker."

"Parker seems like such a demon. Why does she want anything to do with him?"

"I don't know," Ginny says in exasperation, slumps in the chair. "She thinks she's got to have somebody, and it's Parker or nothing."

"Isn't she attractive? That's what I've heard."

"She don't think so," Ginny says. "She worries about it."

Chong recognizes the problem, feels a twinge of familiarity, even of complicity. Vanity, thy name is middle age. "I don't know, Ginny. For the time being, I think we have to give her the benefit of the doubt."

"What does that mean?"

"We'll wait for a couple of days and see if your mother doesn't do what she says."

"She won't," Ginny insists.

"There's only one way to prove it," Chong persists, "and that is to wait."

Too tired to argue more, Ginny goes upstairs to bed, and Chong looks again out the kitchen window toward the bus. He can see no sign of the fire and in a moment motorcycles snarl past the house, horns screeching. Seconds later, lights flash across the barn and Chong steps outside the kitchen door, finds the police cruiser in the driveway. Chief Dawson slouches behind the wheel writing on a pad as Chong approaches the car window.

"I got 'em to put the fire out," Dawson says.

"I appreciate it," Chong says. "I already had one fire here."

Dawson is unshaven and his hat rests on the car seat. He looks tousled, sleepy, and very irritated. "Do us a favor and post that camp," he says. "Either that or just tear it down. It's bound to attract trouble."

"I really didn't think you'd come," Chong says. "I'm very grateful."

"Sometimes all you have to do is flash your lights," Dawson says. "Tonight they weren't in a fighting mood." He hands Chong the pad he has been writing on. "You want to sign a complaint, or just forget it?"

"What do you think?" Chong asks.

"I can't advise you on that."

"Off the record, though?"

"Don't," Dawson says.

"O.K.," Chong says. "I don't want tons of trouble."

"What about the vandalism?"

"I didn't know there was any vandalism," Chong says.

"I mean, to your car there. Did that happen tonight?"

Chong turns and walks to his station wagon. It has been spray-painted in fluorescent orange scroll—on one side, CHINK, on the other SUCKS, and on the hood, FUCK GOOKS. All four tires are flat. Chong regards his car in a state of sad wonder, returns to the cruiser embarrassed, angry, confused.

"I didn't even see that," he says to Dawson almost in a whisper, laboring so to contain his fury. "I don't have any idea who did it or when it happened. Between nine and now, that's all. It wasn't the bikers. I don't see how it could have been them. And I didn't hear anything."

Dawson heaves himself out of the cruiser and, pad in hand, inspects the tires, touches the paint with a finger, smells it, scribbles a few more notes, regards Chong coldly and without speaking as he slides back into the cruiser, jams it into gear, and swings onto the road, heading, perhaps coincidentally, in the direction the bikers have taken moments before.

Late in the morning when Ginny joins him on the back steps, he shows her what has been done to his car.

"That's Taylor," she says. "That's the kind of stuff he does. The Club doesn't do that, except for Taylor. They call that chickenshit. If The Club wants you, they don't do chickenshit. They play for real."

6
Breakers

"**Y**ou never go anywhere in a straight line," Anna had said. She made the observation as a description of Jim's way of doing things, but Jim took it as a statement of principle, Anna's Law of How Things Work. And, facing another winter without daylight, Jim sensed very strongly that he was not settled, that his and Anna's sojourn on the Cape was likely to be brief after all. The fall had seemed one long sunset of Alaskan duration, and now that the evening sunlight had also disappeared, he found himself locked in a struggle to keep his spirits up, not just to be overwhelmed by darkness.

In some ways, the new apartment in Brewster was an improvement on the cottage they had surrendered to the landlord's greed, but it was no bargain, and so far the neighbors had not proved especially friendly, or interesting. One had a huge dog which tore up the hallway carpet and frightened the children, including T'isa, with its barking. Jim had asked the people to please control the dog better, and was astounded by the hostility of their reaction. They said the kids provoked the dog, complained that dogs had no rights, and said the neighbors were out to get them. They passed Jim in the hallway or parking lot without looking him in the eye or acknowledging his wave of greeting. Another neighbor felt free to drop in on Anna at any time and give her a minute-by-minute account of her bowling games or detailed descriptions of her problem laundry. And even as devoted as she was to T'isa, Anna was not truly happy, Jim could see.

"Sometimes I think we made a mistake," Jim said.

Anna looked past him. "Sometimes I think you're right."

"So what do you think we should do?"

"I don't know," Anna said. "Do you want to quit?"

"Then what would I do?"

"I don't know," Anna said again.

In this spirit they sidled into the winter, and the winter enclosed them. When Jim came home from work, he and Anna exchanged a few comments, he was told what T'isa had done during the day, and he spent some time with his daughter, feeding her before he and Anna sat down to eat, spooning peas and carrots into her mouth, encouraging her to gnaw a green bean, picking her bottle up from the floor where she threw it often and with gusto. He went through the motions of fatherhood, not feeling much, and he wondered sometimes what it was he was supposed to feel. He was continually distracted, unable to focus much on anything, and really only clear about things after an hour at the Ship Ahoy or the Whale Inn, or the Salty Dog, where he stopped after work for the "Happy Hour." He drank shots and beers and drove home in the dark, and once inside, things became muddy again in his mind.

Then one evening in late November, when Jim came home a little later than usual, and a little drunker than usual, and T'isa had already been fed and was pulling pans from a kitchen cabinet, Anna said, "I think I'm going back to the *Globe*, Jim."

For a moment, he wasn't sure he had heard Anna right, and let the information settle. "You *think?*"

"I've written some letters and talked to Josie on the telephone— my old friend who's now the supervisor. She said she'd take me back. I could start in January."

"January," Jim said.

"We're not doing much here," Anna said. "We're sinking. I want to wake up a little."

"Yeah?" Jim rubbed his temples. "I don't think they'd rehire me, though."

"Jim, it's hard for me to say—"

"So don't say it yet. Give it some thought."

"Jim, you haven't really come through, you know."

"So is this going to be it? You're going back to Boston with our kid, and leave me here?"

"You don't have to stay here."

"Of course not. But you don't intend to take Dad with you?"

"No," Anna said.

"You want a divorce."

"Of course."

Jim felt a rush of heat along his neck, and his head wobbled. "Well, ain't this a bitch."

"You're not getting any better," Anna said. "Our money's going down the drain, to landlords, and to drink. For months I've been watching you sit there after work, and you don't even look back sometimes, like some kind of cipher."

"A cipher." Jim nodded, leaned down to pinch T'isa's cheek. "Ain't this a bitch, sugar? Your pop's a fuckin' cipher? How's that for news?" He looked at Anna coldly, feeling almost a lust to beat her with his fists. "So what are you going to do? Are you going to hang around until January? I'm sure you've got it all planned out."

"I'd hang around if you wanted to talk about it."

"About what?"

"Us. What we can do. The divorce."

"I don't want to talk about it," Jim said.

"The alternative is to hire lawyers, I guess."

"So hire. So when are you leaving?"

"This weekend, I guess. I can stay with Josie until I find a place."

"I don't believe this," Jim said. "And I appreciate the straightforward way you went about it all, letting me know your thoughts."

"I've tried to let you know . . ."

"Like hell."

". . . for two years, Jim. But if you do want to talk about it now, and to listen, I will stay. There are some things you should know. About me. About yourself.'

"Maybe you should just write me a letter," Jim said.

"I want to be fair to you."

"Fair!"

"And I hate to see you just stagnating and wasting your life."

Jim put his hat and coat on and went out into the darkness and a cold fog. He slammed into the car and headed for the Whale Inn at a reckless speed, and when he pulled into the parking lot under the LOUNGE sign that seemed to fill the air with dull orange dots, almost like the colored smoke flares dropped in the helicopter landing zones, he said into his own cupped hands, "Just like that, she's leaving me just like that."

He stayed the rest of the week at a room in the Whale Inn, and ignored the messages Anna sent to him at work. When he finally returned to the apartment, he was surprised to see how much Anna had left behind for him—but the bed was gone, and the bedroom itself was a real ghost town, or like the cellar hole of a burned-down house. Anna had also left a note on the kitchen counter, but Jim crumpled it up and threw it away without reading it. He had bought two fifths of rum, and he placed these on the kitchen counter, not bothering even to put them away. He didn't need to hide them. Hell, he could sleep with one—Anna had left him the sofa at least—if he felt like it. The road was clear now. If he wanted to, he really could just drink himself to death.

Out of the aching of his head, the fog and muddle of the week, Jim had somehow managed to call his boss and explain his troubles.

"Well, do what you can as soon as you can," Mr. Garson said. "The work's piling up already. Don't let it get you down, Jim. I need you around here."

Oh, he didn't let it get him down! He just drank until he couldn't think, and that was the end of that. The binge lasted a week, but Jim could not remember much of what had happened during that time. He had spent part of one evening crawling around a parking lot looking for the keys to his car, which remained lost for two more days, and it had taken him all night to walk home, since no one would pick him up hitchhiking, and a portion of his drunken ramble had been down a beach, crunching over clam and periwinkle shells in the darkness, a cold wind stunning him, and the tide, running in unusually high, swamping his shoes. Almost everything else was lost to memory. He had played a lot of pool, hadn't he? Didn't he win a lot of drinks at an Irish place in Harwich where a fisherman wanted to take him outside and "clean his clock"? Oh, yes, and hadn't he stared into the mirror at the toney place down the road where the lights were piss-colored and the waitress had let him slip his hand into the side pocket of her black satin pants?

Three days passed before he recovered enough to start piecing things together, to call Josie Connors through information and locate his wife and daughter in Boston, and start a slightly more civilized way of bringing things to an end. Not that it mattered all that much to Jim now. As he had told anyone who would listen for a whole week, he figured his life was just plain fucked now, fucked for fair and forever. Fucked. It had taken him fifteen years, but he had finally done it, and didn't he therefore have a right to celebrate his own wake? Sure as hell he wouldn't get another chance. Right, soldier?

Fuckin' A right.

Oh, yes, Jim remembered later. I spent two days in Viet Nam, remembering Viet Nam. That happened after I walked into the VFW in Hyannis, and those three guys were standing there sullenly drinking, Viet Nam written all over them—long hair still, one with a wild beard, but their age, their slightly slack-kneed, stoop-shouldered, open-eyed bearing said "Nam." They were talking about Agent Orange, and Jim wondered aloud if Agent Orange was the reason his wife did not become pregnant for so long.

"Well, if it was," the bearded veteran growled, "be glad she didn't have no kid, because if she did, it might of been screwed up."

"The kid she has was O.K.," Jim said.

The long-haired veteran wondered, "You know, I'm just sayin' this, but are you sure it was yours?"

In his drunkenness, Jim had agreed. "Maybe you're right," he had said. "Maybe it's not even mine. Probably couldn't be mine, in fact. There's nothing wrong with her."

The darkness of the winter was relieved only by the stream of images that passed before Jim's eyes in the glow of developer light. Some days he felt as if he were intercepting dreams, or as if he were trapped in a long sleep from which he might never awaken. When he walked the beach at night, the very foam of the breakers seemed to bubble with faces. But the lengthening days at last began to relieve the intensity of his introspection, and he knew he must come to some resolve, to break his inertia. Therefore, late in the spring, on the fifteenth anniversary of his release from the Army, and the finish of his combat tour in Viet Nam, Jim drove to Boston to find Anna and T'isa, to see what amends could be made, to learn what was expected of him. He had left work early and had a long weekend, and he thought maybe if he had any remaining sense he could understand better what had driven them apart. He wanted only to listen. He wanted not to be spared any longer what Anna's true feelings had been, and he wanted, with a degree of desperation and desire that surprised him, to see and hold his daughter. Jesus! he wondered. Would they even recognize each other? Maybe his daughter would forget him. He hoped the occasion might provide him with the excuse he needed to renovate his life, possibly even to recreate the marriage he had once enjoyed.

But Anna would not see him on that day. She said it was not convenient, that he should have given her more notice, that she did not care to indulge his spontaneous whims. She had made other plans. It was not just Anna's refusal that triggered it, but the profound iciness of that refusal as well, hope-shattering, and Jim's own guilt that his worst fears were being realized, that she was retaliating for the years he had imprisoned her in his own aura of misery and ineptitude.

Jim had an attack of vertigo, of nausea, of a great seasickness that tumbled him from bar to bar. There was haze of smoke in the air, like the haze over the trees in Viet Nam through which the helicopters passed like dreams of fish; and the litter in the streets, endless islands of broken glass and crumpled cans, reminded him of the dump at Saigon, the world's largest and ever-burning heap of military refuse—a solid mile of garbage that burned and smoldered as the women and children combed through the detritus of American life in Saigon. Even occasional booby-trapping couldn't keep the people away from the dump, Jim remembered being told. Women would come up screaming with a hand gone, and still the people came and prowled and scavenged. They salvaged everything. Old tires were made into shoes. Cans were flattened into construction materials so that whole roofs bore in endlessly repeated units the insignia of a U.S. brewer. Shell casings, the brass valuable in itself, found their way to the Viet Cong.

There was even, Jim remembered, a Chinaman—Ho? Was that his name?—who made a fortune scrapping U.S. military goods, the downed Saber jets, the wrecked tanks, the shattered field artillery. All around the world were crappy little armies needing parts for the antique Yankee weaponry that gave them power. Ho salvaged and sold any and all metal detritus of the war. He had a Swiss bank account, private planes, and the Saigon politicians bowed and scraped when he was around. Of course Mr. Ho sold to the Viet Cong. Mr. Ho—was that really his name?—was not notoriously scrupulous. Heroin probably traveled with the other goods that passed through his hands. You never leave any empty cargo space on a ship. He was living in Arlington, Virginia, now, Jim had heard. When Giap's troops came storming into Saigon, Mr. Ho was already airborne, somewhere near the coast of Java, maybe, or nestling down in Bangkok, where the news of the American defeat was stirring like a cold wind, making skins crawl with mixed delight and sickness and fear.

At ten cents a pound, scrap value, a single five-ton truck would be worth a thousand bucks, Jim figured, though the parts would be worth considerably more. Jim wondered what had happened to all that stuff when Ho didn't get it. The proceeds should have gone to the vets, he reasoned. They said Mr. Ho never stopped talking, never slept, speedy with greed and wheeler-dealing, perhaps realizing his time was now and soon enough gone, with wild swings between the laughter of a man who has hit the jackpot and a murderous cursing anger laden with threats that he could and did keep. He had two favorite English phrases, Jim was told: "Yeah, yeah, yeah," spoken as if he had heard it all, seen it all before, that nothing surprised or scared him; and "You better get with the program, mister," a bit of a threat, a way also of letting you know—or of making you feel— reality was on his side, or that he could make reality mean what he wanted it to mean. If you had something he wanted, he could make you squirm. It's just power, Jim thought now. All the same. Fuckin' crooks rule the world.

So *what?* So why was he thinking of this now? Jim drank, trying to clear his mind of the war, and of Anna. Maybe it had to do with wreckage. And what some people made of it. Perverse as it may be, Jim told himself, some people thrive on a war. Some people survive on detritus. Like the crabs feeding on the head of a dead fish. Like ants ringing the ice cream cone spilled on the sidewalk. Maybe he could take a lesson from Ho after all.

Ten hours later, Jim woke in his car feeling sick and angry and lost. He was cramped from having been curled up on the front seat, and he pushed himself outside to let the night air cool his head, and maybe stop the world from swaying like the deck of a ship. He couldn't stay parked where he was, because the police would find him, but he had pulled over in the first place because he had been too drunk to drive, and he was still . . . *gone,* as he thought of it.

A tractor-trailer smashed past him, then growled up an entrance ramp to Route 2, heading west.

Two in the morning and nothing on the road, Jim thought. Lake Ecstasy is three and a half, four hours away. I'll follow the truck, his lights will give me bearings, and Red will put me up for a couple of days. He wouldn't begrudge it. Fifteen fucking years ago, and I was in California, free from the Army. He'll want to celebrate that with me. I know he will.

A nd what was Red Barber doing on the fifteenth anniversary of Jim's discharge from the Army? Red Barber, who in 1968 was helicopter mechanic, poker player, savant of Saigon's brothels, opium smoker, taker of chances, teller of stories, a man whose heart was permanently lifted by a five-day love feast with a Hong Kong woman whose full name he would never know, and a man whose ambitions and feelings had been permanently fractured by what he saw in Viet Nam? Red Barber, woodcutter and fisherman, frantic woman chaser of Lake Ecstasy, fierce lover whom women never trusted, a fact he could never understand but came to accept as part of his fate, a sad part, which would dog him to death? What was Red Barber doing on that day?

Ten years earlier, after five peripatetic years of moving around the country from one unfulfilling job to another, he had come to Lake Ecstasy. He had intended to fish for trout, but his jeep broke down on the trail behind Sweat Hill and he had to wait three days for parts before he could fix it; realized there was not a good mechanic in the area for heavy machinery, trucks, and tractors; and while mulling this proposition caught six beautiful fat and scrappy brook trout in Clear Brook, now Chong's brook, so-called; met Nancy Wallace at the Lake Ecstasy Village Inn, who cohabited fiercely with him for a solid week; and with his senses so rattled by the good things of country life, settled in. He was no stranger to loneliness, could pass days working without company, like the hermit he often was in spirit, still in retreat from a world in which Viet Nams were possible, and Barber's Big Machine Service was thereby quietly born in the hills of western Massachusetts, Quineckticut County, the little rag of a village, Lake Ecstasy.

He repaired tractors and manure spreaders, bought five acres of woodland bordering an unpopular state park with a pine-covered mountain and a dank swamp at either extreme of its borders; and he built a cabin back from the road, a garage, and a small barn to work in and to store parts. None of the structures were ever finished, and probably never would be, but after Viet Nam Red had lost a great deal of fussiness about what one needed to live and how one could live, and he put certain pleasures crucial to his sanity and ability to continue to care about other people above finished floors and staircases, matching furniture, precious patterned silverware, or paneled playrooms.

Red had an idea that of all the terrible emergencies in a person's life, most of which a person did not even recognize, indeed could not recognize at all moments and remain sane, the least of these had to do with how things looked—appearances. He had the best socket wrenches money could buy, a kind that would bear up under the full force of his considerable strength, but his "silverware" came from Rubb's New and Used. Red believed in keeping the house warm enough to prevent the pipes from freezing, and he thought the answer to a wood stove dying out at 4 A.M. was another blanket; more heat than that was a luxury that you saved for a rare winter party, the once-in-a-while you actually lucked into persuading a woman to come home with you. Nancy say. Who still kept crossing Red Barber's mind. And who insisted, on a rare winter night visit, that he warm up the bed before she would go near it, she didn't care how.

"Just do it, Barber. I can't stand those damned icy sheets."

On the day Jim sought out Anna and T'isa in Boston, Red Barber woke early and alone. He had deliberately refused to take any repair appointments for this day, because he was determined to go fishing and to make the day last. By 6 A.M. he had parked his truck in the bushes on Royalton Road and was wading Chong's stream toward the dam. He had smoked a joint with his coffee in order to slow things down, and the tumble of the cool water between and around his legs now was healing and cleansing, a pleasant ruckus of bubbles and splashes, and the endless motion put a lie to the illusion of things being fixed in place. He wanted to break the spell of machines, and the tumble of water was helping to do that. He made slow progress toward Chong's dam, where he knew there would be some fat rainbows basking in the superoxygenated pool below. They'd be taking perch bugs, he figured, dragonfly nymphs, or stone fly, or caddis. It didn't matter. He had tied a few of each the night before.

Red waded, enjoyed the sensation, caused by the tumble of water and light, that the earth would sometimes suddenly tilt, that he was losing balance, like a bait fish caught in a rip. He made a series of casts to a deep green pool beneath a black broken trunk—its roots hanging like coarse hair into the water—before he realized the tree was staring at him. There was a face in the tree. When Red saw it, his hair crawled, and then he felt a momentary flash of anger as if someone had played a practical joke on him.

For the face in the tree was not an accident of natural forms combining to create a resemblance that Red's drug-enhanced perceptions would piece together—though it was nearly that—but deliberately carved. The face in the trunk was old, with a great beard that disappeared seamlessly into the bark of the stump. The exaggerated eyes were a disturbing combination—one open almost in terror, the other half closed in a state of dreaming. The sight of it irritated Red Barber on that morning. He felt it was an imposition, something artificial shoved into the life of the stream, and he resented it as much as he would resent the presence of a billboard or litter. He did not like to feel he was being watched, and he did not like to feel the woods was so well or so thoroughly used.

Then his line snagged under the stump and Red walked into the deep colder water to retrieve his nymph. He knew this would disturb the pool and end his fishing there, but the presence of the face on the stump really did bother him, however foolishly. He followed the line under the stump in the tangle of roots—his white arm seemed to bend in a gentle curve, and when he reached the nymph he tugged gently on it. And pulled up a little tangle of string, a sack with a lively sparkling trout in it—*a goddamn net.*

Whatever opinions he might have had about this Chong, who supposedly owned this land which no one should own and which he was fishing on, they were now stirred and muddied by the presence of that damned face, which the Chinaman had certainly carved, and the net, which was illegal, unsporting, and somehow primitive in the directness of its purpose and its obvious efficiency. At least Chong knew where to put the damned thing. Red debated with himself whether he should slash the net apart or take the fish within it or both, but let it settle back into place and moved up the stream toward the dam. Then his back-cast caught in the branches of tree, and again and again he thought he had a strike and reeled in a sleepy log of a sucker, which he tossed into the bushes, and when he was bending over to unwrap a coil of line from around his knees, his new polarized sun glasses fell out of his shirt pocket and washed quickly down the stream. Red searched for the glasses for twenty minutes and became so irritated he decided to pack it up and head for home. He wasn't having any fun, he was just getting pissed off, so why push it. He didn't get that much time off.

He drove to the Lake Ecstasy Village Inn and went inside for breakfast. Nancy was waiting tables and brought him a menu on the run.

"Catch any?" she asked.

"How'd you know I was fishing?"

"I also know your waders leak."

Yes, Red knew his pantlegs were wet from the knees down, where the boots were seamed in to the trousers. He had tried a dozen times to patch the leaks without success. Waders leaked. They always leaked. He accepted this. Anything he could not fix in a dozen tries could not be fixed, that's all there was to it.

So why wear them? he wondered. Because it was part of the ritual. Because you'd like to be able to go to the Village Inn afterwards and have breakfast without changing clothes or sitting around with a wet ass and paying the bill with soggy money. Because some of the guys who showed up here would have to say something about your wet pants and what happened? Couldn't you hold it? Red hated that kind of stuff, wore waders.

Nancy returned looking so wide awake she jangled. Her motions were magician-quick as she wiped the table and picked up the debris. Her hair was tied back in a bun today, and her brown eyes flashed.

"Now I'll tell you something," Red said. "You're beautiful, but you've had too much coffee."

"Since when did you become a health food nut?"

Stop it. I just want to put my arms around your hips.

"I'll have a number three, but a large glass of orange juice."

"You smell good," Nancy said. "You smell cold."

"I'm not cold," Red said. "Not around you."

"Thanks. I needed that."

"Lots more where that came from."

"You're incorrigible," Nancy said. "But it's O.K. today."

"I've got the day off," Red said.

"Jesus Christ." Nancy snapped her washcloth at him. "What makes you think I care? Besides, I'm going to Royalton to see about a typesetting job."

"You don't want to set type," Red said. "It's tedious as hell."

"It's tedious as hell being poor," Nancy said.

"Well I hope you don't get it."

"*Thanks,*" Nancy said.

"It'll keep you away from me."

"Maybe it would do me good."

"I'm being selfish," Red said. "I'll miss you."

"Royalton's only twenty minutes away."

"But I mean in the A.M., like now."

"They'll find some other luscious fanny to take my place. Good looks are cheap around here."

Stop it, please. Red reached out for Nancy, but she dodged away, scribbling on her pad. I'll miss seeing you in the morning. I'll hate knowing I'll have to call you and make arrangements. That it just can't happen. Any time. That it will deprive me of an important fantasy. A possibility.

So he ate his breakfast and came back to the cabin and it was only 9:30 A.M. He was already feeling burned out, as if it were already too hot. He had a silly craving for ice cream and put a record on the stereo, played it loud, loud, and flopped on the sofa trying to decide whether he should try to finish off the floor in the upstairs bedroom or cover the insulation on the back wall of the garage area, patch the leak around the chimney or repair the broken window in the bathroom, or maybe even hook up the jeep to a dredge he could borrow from Harley Wilson and dig out some more of his basement. He had plenty to do. If it wasn't so hot, he could even split some wood, and of course it probably would be cool under the trees.

A mountain of love, a mountain of love.

You should be ashamed.

A steady banging made its way through the roar of the stereo, and

Red swung off the sofa to find Dave Cassidy peering in the door window. Dave's blond beard had a halo of reflected sunlight on its fringes.

"Yeah, yeah." Red opened the door. "Come on in. Nothin's happening."

"You been fishing?"

"Yeah."

"How'd you do?"

"Let's talk about the weather or something."

"Too bad."

"You want some coffee?" Red said. "You want to put any of that in your system? Speed kills."

"A little speed won't hurt you," Dave said. "As long as you mix it with heroin."

They laughed, sharing an old joke. They had once tried this chemical concoction, allowing themselves to be injected by a Boston bizarro they found hitchhiking through the town with an anemic underage girlfriend, a very funny messed-up guy, and they spent the night tearing down the side of an old barn in the woods, possessed by an awful contradiction and the need to tear something apart. Red's brain felt in tatters, his consciousness like clouds ripped up by storm winds. Dave had said, "It was like somebody made a pincushion of your brain." They never tried it again. Red remembered the bizarro and his girl stole a pair of long johns and a six-pack of beer, which they could have had for the asking.

Red made the coffee as they talked. Dave's four-wheel-drive truck was having problems and Dave was hoping to make a trip to the Cape for surf casting. Dave had planned to leave the next day, but he couldn't make the trip now because the truck was in such bad shape. Dave was going to make the trip with Sally Wollner, a camping trip, and it was a terrible blow not to be able to—

"All right, all right," Red said. "Jesus Christ. We can get the damn truck fixed. Just don't give me any crap about surf fishing. You probably won't get out of the tent."

"No, really. Sally wants to learn surf casting."

"Sure. I want to be an astronaut."

"We can do both. Why not?"

"More power to you. Just don't complain about not catching any fish. So let's have a look at this truck."

"Hey, thanks," Dave said. "I thought it might go easier . . ."

"You had me figured right out, didn't you?"

". . . so I bought a tab of acid."

"Ah, hum," Red said.

"I thought half a tab each would be an aid to conceptualizing this whole problem."

"I agree," Red said. "You just pull your old truck right into the garage there, and we shall study and await inspiration. Allow me to make some lemonade, meanwhile, electric lemonade."

Dave reached into his coveralls and pulled out a small ball of aluminum foil which he carefully unwrapped to reveal a clear ovoid tablet. Red took it and in a moment dissolved it in the pale yellow swirl of the lemonade. Back to machines. He had the usual butterflies of anticipation, but another, stronger part of him was already arranging the tools he would need and making hunches about what he would find wrong with Dave's engine. Surely it would not be difficult to cure.

They drank the lemonade, listened to the engine of Dave's machine, debated the meaning of every ping, rattle, chug.

"Carburetor," Red said. "Must be cleaned."

They took the carburetor apart, spread it in perfect layers on newsprint, senseless headlines leering out of the shadows the metal shapes threw around themselves, one very dark, a second lighter, grayer, because of the cross-play of the lights.

"Now that we got that out, I think we might as well pull the fuel lines and clean them, and the fuel pump," Red said. He wiped the grease from his hands, and the smell and haze of gasoline rose around him like heat waves on a Viet Nam highway. "Then we'll move right into the valves, because I can see you're leaking oil there, and we'll probably need some gaskets."

"Oh, oh," Dave said.

"We've got to do it," Red said.

"I can see where this is going right now," Dave said.

"There's no other way," Red shrugged.

In three hours, the engine was completely apart, laid schematically across the floor of Red's garage. Beautiful polished pistons with their egg-shaped shadows and planetary rings, gleaming towers, the crumpled camshaft a dull red in a thin iridescent streak of murky oil, the push rods and tappets in an orderly squadron of pieces, tappet springs lined up like barrels on a wharf, each rod lying on a smear of oil, a petroleum shadow of itself, the whole carburetor with its tiny brass floats and valves like residents of a futuristic motel.

"Wouldn't it be great to have an accordion car?" Dave asked.

"A what?" Red scooted across the floor on his creeper admiring the whole intricate web of the engine he had stripped to its skeleton and laid out on the clean sheets of newspaper.

"Man, you know. An accordion car."

"Oh, sure, an accordion car. What? Does it make music when you drive? What?"

Dave laughed. "Sure. It could do that. But I mean a car that has a section in the middle like an accordion, so you could go right around the corner, and the whole car would bend."

"Yeah, but, when you took off, the ass end would just sit there for a while."

"Right!" Dave said. "And then *zingo!* The thing would come ripping up to the front part."

"You want a car like that?"

"Wouldn't it be great?"

"It sounds like an amusement park ride or something."

"Right," Dave said.

"We could make a car like that," Red said. "Let me think about that." A memory banged into him. "There's something else I've wanted to do."

"Yeah?"

"Yeah," Red said. It was incredibly complicated to tell, because Red had to start way back in time when he was on the road at night driving a truck full of helicopter parts to a base near Danang where he was going to work on some Hueys. The truck was equipped with dim "cat's-eye" headlights to avoid detection by snipers and he was traveling along at night on a torn-up road with few markers. The markers that he did pass were glass reflectors on a fluorescent background, and in the fields where no public lights broke the darkness the markers stood out with a surreal intensity, as if they were illuminated planets or stars glittering in a void.

"So I got this idea," Red said, "that I wanted to build a tunnel and fill it with reflectors. Then you'd drive a car or just roller-coaster through this tunnel. And a bright beam off your vehicle would light up these reflectors, and a beautiful flashing pattern would unroll as you smoked along the tube. You see what I mean?"

"Oh, man," Dave said. "You're blowing my mind. A whole *tunnel* full of reflectors."

"Yeah. In patterns. Like animation in a cartoon."

"And we're barreling along in there in our accordion car?"

"Yeah, right."

"Man, oh man, oh man," Dave said. "Let's build the fucker."

"I want to," Red said.

"I know where we can get some giant drainpipe."

"No shit?"

"When they widened the Royalton Road, they tore out all the old drain pipe, and it's just laying back in the woods. Really, miles of it."

"Jesus. How wide?"

"You can stand up in it."

"Jesus. And it's just laying there?"

"Yeah. Some of it's bent and torn a little."

"No problem."

"*Miles* of it, Red."

"We should build a model of it first," Red said. "Then we get the bugs out of that. Then we build the real tunnel."

"People would come from all over," Dave said.

"Yeah, well, I don't know if it should be a tourist thing."

"Red, a thing like that—*wow*. You could use mirrors, too."

Red allowed himself to imagine what it would be like to roller-coaster through a tunnel filled entirely with brilliant glass reflectors, spirals and explosions and stars and zigzags of light, the quiet hum of the wheels as the intense beam picked out the glittering tornado of shapes.

"So. You want to get this engine back together?" Dave said.

Red scooted around the floor on his creeper. "Dave, we could just use reflector tape or something for now."

"Yeah, but the engine's apart."

"Yeah, so it is."

"And I really want to go on this camping trip with Sally."

"A shack-up trip, you mean. That's going to be one funky tent afterwards. Jesus, she's got great legs."

"Yeah. Everybody notices that. So let's not get off the track too far."

"You'll be swimming in come."

"Cut it out, Red."

"I'd sure like to build that tunnel, though," Red said.

"I'll help you," Dave said, "as soon as I get back."

"After we put the engine together, let's go look at those drain-pipes. O.K.?"

And this is what Red Barber did on the anniversary of Jim's re-

lease from the Army: He fished; he lusted after Nancy Wallace; he
took apart and reassembled an engine; and at 2:30 A.M. he stood
with David Cassidy inside a battered drainpipe in the woods of
Lake Ecstasy and inspected the walls with the dim beam from an
old flashlight. He went to sleep at 4 A.M. and dreamed sheets and
streams, a whole tumbling river of light, like a ride through the
heavens. The dream was so beautiful he woke to the emptiness beside him, the unfinished floors and cracked windows of his cabin,
with a pang of sadness that did not leave him for a couple of days.
And when he saw Jim Williams stroll into his garage with a big grin
and flapping jaw, he felt a rush of resentment and worry, then
cooled off in the salvaging thought that just maybe he was being
rescued after all, brought back to earth.

"Hello, motherfucker," he said.

Jim just stood there grinning and looking as if at any moment he
might be sick.

To keep her occupied, and to keep himself from worrying, Chong sets Ginny to work sorting out the junk he has stored in boxes on his porch, and then carrying what does not get thrown away into his attic. The attic is hot and dusty, and after only a few trips up the wobbly accordion ladder Ginny is bathed in sweat, and rebelling.

"Besides, I can't see what you want with half of this crap, anyway," she says. "Why don't you just throw it all out?"

"You never know when you are going to need another teapot," Chong says. "If you throw it away, it's gone forever."

"But who needs all those books? They're heavy. How many can you read at once anyway?"

"A good book is something that lives with you for a long time," Chong says. "I like to read books again and again."

"You know what a library is?"

"Sure. Do you know what Lake Ecstasy's library is like? Or even Royalton's? They don't have very many books I need."

"Nobody needs books."

"You wouldn't know, so don't talk. Besides, maybe I want to read a certain book at three A.M. when the library is closed."

Ginny picks a book from a battered box, blows off the dust, and reads the title aloud. *"Materials and Methods in Modern Printmaking."*

"Fancy stuff," Chong says. "Too technical. Too many chemicals."

Ginny reads another. *"Common Poultry Diseases."*

"Very good book!" Chong says.

"Just what you want to read at three A.M."

"Yes, if your chickens are sick."

"But why do you keep them in boxes if they're so important?"

"You're right. I should build some shelves. I just haven't taken the time."

"Tales of the—How do you pronounce this—Gun-ji?"

"You better not read that book," Chong says. "Very spicy."

"Spicy?"

"Never mind. You just put that one away."

"It must be pretty good if you don't want me to read it."

"Common Poultry Diseases is good, too."

"You know what I mean."

"Don't let me catch you reading that book."

Ginny slips the book back into the box, hefts the load to her waist, and clunks up the stairs. She is absent an unusually long time, but Chong has other things to worry about and goes outside to inspect the damage done to his car. He will have to take all the tires off and have them fixed or replaced, a stinging extra expense that will also jeopardize his plans for a New York trip. He will need some advice on how to remove the insulting graffiti, and wonders if there is a solvent that will do the job without spoiling the finish underneath. Chong debates whether he should attempt removing the tires himself, but decides to call a local mechanic and have it all done quickly, whatever the expense. He knows he does not have the tools for the job, and he can all too easily imagine the car falling off the jack onto the ground, or onto him.

Inside, he calls the two local garages and is told the mechanics are too busy to come to his rescue now. He calls a third number, Barber's Big Machine Service, and is about to hang up—the phone rings such a long time—when a man finally answers. Unable to disguise the irritation he feels, Chong explains what has happened, that he is having trouble finding anyone to do the work for him.

"It's not really my line," the man says. "But I could come over this evening, I guess. Those other guys won't do it, huh?"

"No," Chong says wearily.

"You got any other transportation?"

"No."

"You need to get anyplace today?"

"No."

"I'm kind of stuck here until after dinner," the man says.

"I'll appreciate it whenever you can come," Chong says.

"You're the sculptor, aren't you? Who bought the old Randall place?"

"I do some carving," Chong says.

"You know anything about glass, and how maybe you can fix it to metal?"

"A little," Chong says. "I have some books you could look at."

"Great," the man says. "I'll get there as soon as I can."

When Chong hangs up, Ginny is still in the attic. She must be getting pretty uncomfortable, Chong supposes, all that heat and dust, and all those spices. He is relieved that he will have some help with his car, and curious, too, why the man would ask about glass and metal. The name Barber is one Chong has heard from Turner and from Nancy Wallace, but he has never met the man and knows little about him. Such a small town, Turner had said, and yet new dimensions to it kept unfolding before him. How well, Chong thinks, how well I am beginning to understand this!

A long time passes before Ginny comes downstairs again. Her hair is limp and the T-shirt she is wearing is damp with sweat. She does not look at Chong as she goes out to the porch again, but when she returns, she asks him, "When did you do those paintings up there?"

"You're supposed to be working, not snooping."

"I can't help it," Ginny says. "You have so much to snoop through."

"Which paintings?"

"The biggest ones. The naked ones."

"Those are called nudes," Chong says. "I did those just after I first got here, a year ago."

"Do I know that woman?"

"Impossible," Chong says. "They're just paintings."

"She didn't pose for you?"

"Who didn't?"

"I don't know her name. She lives near the orchards, by the old railroad depot."

"They're just paintings," Chong insists.

"Do you think I could be a model?" Ginny asks.

"You could be a very nice model," Chong says. "You could also be a painter. Anything can be a model—a jar of flowers, even a bug."

"So why do people like these nudes so much?"

"Oh, boy." Chong ponders Ginny's question, a little unsuccessfully, because he is thinking simultaneously of the slashed tires on his car and of Nancy Wallace, who modeled for the paintings Ginny had discovered, and indeed the very woman Ginny had identified. It is impossible for him to answer Ginny's questions about nudes in general without thinking of the model, Nancy, in particular, whom he met shortly after moving to Lake Ecstasy, in one of the oddest, most spontaneous, and throughout its brief span also the most trancelike encounter of his life. This was not an overtly sexual encounter—no such luck! Chong thinks—but he had painted Nancy with intense sexual interest, and she had responded to his appreciation—should he call it that only?—as if he had been an incubus in her very bed. Chong had slept in a hammock on the porch for a while until his back paid the price, and it was in this hammock that Nancy had chosen to pose. Chong's patient, caring, excited attempt to portray her somehow excited her as well.

Crazy! he thinks with a laugh. Lucky! Some women want to climb around on the humps of hunchbacks, so who could tell what was possible in the lunatic world of desire? Chong laughs. Life is too crazy, or life is not crazy enough.

Chong tries to answer Ginny's question. "Because the human body is the most difficult thing to portray, because it is exciting, because it always suggests a living person, a life. Don't you think it amazing that dead, lifeless paint can be made to seem alive, and sometimes even sexual?"

"You never see any naked men, though," Ginny says.

"Fewer in this day and age," Chong says. "But I think that's changing."

"So would you model for me?"

"Ho!" Chong laughs. "I would, but first I don't think you are a practiced enough artist to draw the human figure, you see. Second, I am shy about these things."

"Even around me?"

"Especially around you."

"How come?"

"I'm not sure why," Chong says. "I'm self-conscious. You would make me feel old."

"You're not that old."

"Thank you, but I also know I will never make a living modeling men's briefs."

Ginny laughs, hard.

"I guess I shouldn't have said that. You are amused?"

Ginny laughs so hard now, she staggers out to the screened-in porch. "I'm sorry," she calls, still shaking and laughing. "I can't help it."

Chong raises his arms and flexes his muscles. "I'm Mr. Muscles," he says seriously. "Buy my shorts."

Ginny slams out the screen door now and disappears around the side of the house. Chong imagines himself the model in an advertisement for men's clothes, patch over his eye, and has to laugh, too. No, such an image would not sell underwear or shoes or ties. Still, Ginny's reaction has embarrassed him a little, and when she returns to her chores, he gathers a sketchbook, some pens, and a folding chair and heads for the little swamp of cattails and sawgrass at the end of the pond where Little Brook enters. After all these years, he thinks, he is still not rid of his ego, and he hopes to lose it, at least diminish it, in looking out at the summer-lush fecund swamp. In this light, the blank page is so bright he must avert his eyes.

The cattails seem to him specious, an impossible invention. Chong sits in the heat watching the bumblebees nod the purple heads of clover with their weight, rifle the tiger lilies, totally immerse themselves in the light of the flowers. Imagine being able to crawl into the bowl of a flower. Nothing seems real, seems possible today, the fat purple clovers, or the little yellow flowers, stars on long thin stalks that crowd through and tower over the grass on every inch of his farm at this time of the year. All so translucent, so perfect, they mock him. There are so many shades of green between his sandaled feet and the edge of the swamp that he grows disgusted with himself, with his vanity for ever attempting to recreate it on canvas or paper, to create anything beautiful . . . all illusion anyway. Those copulating pigs he had finished painting not long ago, down there in the corner of the bristling cornfield, a little bit of a parody on poor Rousseau, would never reproduce themselves. What an odd business! To make things that are not real.

How did I get stuck with this? Chong wonders. Damn bees! Damn flowers! Damn planet!

He turns his attention to a cluster of milkweeds where a squadron of red black-spotted bugs with the shapes of kites are silently siphoning the plants' life into their own. He pays attention to these creatures. In spite of his mood, he still wants to get them right. He had once thought and had once hoped that there would be a time before he died when he was through practicing once and for all. But the mind—at least his mind—was too rebellious and too forgetful to be trusted on a free course. He had seen himself in the mirror a million times, but did he still know, really, what he looked like? The only apparent thing now is that he is no longer a demon to a certain young woman, but a clown. Chong scoffs at himself, and since when did he expect to be taken so seriously by anyone?

After an hour or so of drawing, Chong is hungry and returns to the house with his gear. He does not inspect the camp, because he is certain he will find it littered, scarred with tire tracks, branded by The Club. He would like to forget that Ginny's presence implies The Club in the same way that the painting of a nude implies sex. For now he is happy to bowdlerize and not worry in too focused a way when the telephone will ring, and what Mrs. Cahill will say. As soon as he opens the refrigerator, Ginny comes into the kitchen.

"I'm hot," she says.

"Take a shower. Even better, take a swim."

"I don't have a suit."

"Wear a T-shirt and some shorts. Look in the second drawer in the dresser on the landing and you'll find something."

"I'm too tired to go swimming."

"You've been working hard. How about some lunch?"

"Yeah."

"Yes, please."

"Yeah, yeah."

"Take a shower and I'll fix something."

When Ginny emerges from the shower, Chong has a lunch waiting for her—sandwiches and a glass of milk that a ray of sunlight through the kitchen window has caused to glow. The aura of the room, and the young woman sitting at the table, is one of intense nostalgia, of déjà vu, something that has happened before in his life and which now seems familiar to Chong. Time seems to have been caught in a pool, the flow compressed and slowed, and ages accumulate before Ginny pulls her straight damp hair over a shoulder, lifts a sandwich from the plate, and demands, "Why are you staring at me like that?"

Reluctantly, Chong feels the spell broken, the pool of time rush along its inevitable stream again. "I'm sorry. I was just daydreaming."

"About what?"

"Oh, I don't know. Whatever you daydream about."

"What's the matter? Are you all right?"

"Sure. Why?"

"You sound sad."

"Well, I am, a little."

"I'm sorry if I teased you," Ginny says.

"It's not that."

"Are you thinking about last night?"

"Yes, and about where you might be going."

"I'll bet Parker's hurting today," Ginny says. "I got him good. I'll bet he's mad as hell."

"I imagine he is."

"I wish I knew what my mother was doing."

"Yes," Chong says. "I keep hoping the telephone will ring."

"I hope it won't," Ginny says.

"Why not?"

"I know I'm not going anywhere. My mother's just talking. She's probably calling the cops on me for stabbing Parker."

"I don't think Parker wants anybody calling the police."

"Besides," Ginny adds, "I want to stay here awhile."

"For God's sake, why?"

"It's better than home. I'm not scared all the time."

"And I'm such a great cook, right?"

"Wrong," Ginny says.

Chong grunts, "You don't leave much on your plate, I notice."

"I guess you're not in a mood to kid around."

"Not really," Chong says. "Sorry."

"That's O.K.," Ginny says. "I know I'm a pain in the ass."

"You are not," Chong says firmly. "I'm just trying to sort things out. When you're a pain in the ass, I'll let you know."

Ginny is silent a moment. "It's a great sandwich," she says with a little smile. "You make the best peanut butter and jelly in the world."

Unamused, Chong says only, "You can do the dishes when you're done." He takes his sketchbook into the living room and lays it open on a footstool. He doesn't know why, but the sketches of the milkweed pods interest him more than usual—they are, for him, so carefully detailed that they seem almost grotesque, superreal, and strangely menacing, as if he had regarded the plants as poisonous. This is a new, inhuman note in his work, work which is ordinarily playful, even satiric, and it worries him a little. Oh, yes, there have been many bitter painters in the world, usually old men, but Chong did not think until now that he would ever be counted among them. Or was this a phase? He couldn't allow himself to think the world was a poisonous place just because his thoughts have taken a rancid turn for one day.

Chong becomes aware after a moment that Ginny is standing in the doorway to the kitchen, and when he glances in her direction is startled to see that she is naked. Her clothes are partially draped over the chair she has been sitting on and partially on the floor. She stands with her feet together, one knee a little ahead of the other, and leans against the doorjamb with her hands clasped in front of her.

"What do you think you're doing?" Chong asks.

"I want to model for you," Ginny says. "I want to make you feel better."

Chong nods, a little confused and disturbed. "It is a very nice thought, but you really don't owe me anything."

"Maybe I won't be here much longer." Ginny gives her head a nervous shake. "You don't have much time to get a picture of me."

"I took photographs, remember?"

"I mean a real picture."

"A real picture?" Chong laughs quietly. "There are photographers who would resent that."

"So is it O.K.?" She opens her hands and looks over her own body as if to appeal his forgiveness for being unclothed.

"You have persuaded me," Chong says. "But now you must sit over there on the window seat." This is impossible, Chong thinks, an impossible situation. The girl hops to the window seat without any trace of shyness, assembles herself in the sunlight, a velvet-blue sky behind her. This could never happen in China, Chong thinks. It would be impossible in China.

Maybe once, Chong supposes. In Shanghai, maybe, where the children were sold, where some of them begging in the street were rounded up for the pleasures of the decadent. Young boys with Englishmen, girls younger than this for the wealthy American, the rich Frenchman. Opium and young girls like this, flocks of children, thin, easily spent, half numbed in spirit, enduring all conceivable depravities. Somewhere it still goes on, Chong knows. Child pornography rings in Boston, chicken hawks in New York—a yang to the yin of Christmas trees and the sweet warmth of a mother's breast.

But this one has a little tan on her shoulders that ends almost

comically around her muffin-sized breasts, and another that circum-
scribes her muscular haunches. Is this depravity? Chong wonders.
He could have said no to her, but this is not China, and she is not
starving, not even very innocent, like so many of her American con-
temporaries. There is no blackmail in this, no desperation, only a
tang of depravity to it, Chong decides, since I am regarding her at
such a distance, since the kisses I would trail along her thigh are
mere abstractions, mere fantasies. How irritating that fantasies are
defined by that, by smoldering away into futility, into nothingness.
Chong is not a madman; something reins him in. Something always
reins him in.

And is it the generosity of her gesture that encourages him to
leave this on a level that is chaste? Chong understands that she is
sincere about wanting to please, but also a little hypocritical, a little
vain, happy and excited to be confirmed in "art"—not understanding
really that she will be confirmed only in the eye of a certain artist
who does not do portraits, who will have little regard for her expectations.

"What would your mother say if she could see you now? Did you
think of that?"

"Don't worry about it. She doesn't care what I do."

"I'm sure she does."

"You're wrong. She doesn't. Parker would care more. He'd be
jealous. He'd be real pissed."

"That doesn't exactly relieve my worries."

"Forget Parker. He works all day, he drinks all night. He's just
stupid." She pulls her knees under her and looks out into the yard.
"He's just a pig who cares about nobody but himself."

"You think everyone is like that, do you?"

"Yeah."

"Suppose I said I care about you, about what happens to you?"

"I wouldn't believe you either."

"Why would I say it if I didn't mean it?"

"I don't know. People do it all the time, though."

"Put your legs down and sit closer to the window, please." Chong
picks up the drawing pad and places it on the easel. Before he looks
at Ginny again, he regards the sketches of the milkweed pods that
had troubled him, pods packed full of white silken fiber that will
carry the seeds away on the autumn winds. The pods are full of that
hidden luxurious substance, ready to burst, knobby as pickles, sea-

green. He is almost as interested in continuing to advance this drawing as to begin with this impromptu figure study Ginny has thrust upon him. When he looks up again, Ginny is kneeling on the window seat and has unceremoniously presented Chong with her behind, a "moon," as the Americans say, and to the Chinese the supreme insult. This is what the Chinese soldiers do to their Russian counterparts across the demilitarized zone: drop their pants and bend over. But of course she has no intention of insulting him.

"Please turn around."

"What?" she says. "Oh, sure. I was just lookin' at that stupid pig." She shifts into a position that Chong likes very much: her arm on the window ledge, left calf crossed almost boyishly over her right thigh, her long brown hair is lit up in a little halo of reflected sunlight. But no angel! Chong knows. The most touching thing to him is a slash of yellow light over the curve of her shoulder.

"That pig is a big nuisance," Chong says. He wants to talk a little, to make Ginny less self-conscious. "Tip your head a bit, and don't look at me. And don't *smile*."

"What's his name?"

"Tip it the other way. If I tell you, you'll feel bad when we have to do him in."

"What difference does it make which way I tip my damn head?"

"It's the light. How the light falls."

"Oh, yeah?"

"Yeah."

"I wish I could see what you mean."

"You can't see yourself now, can you?"

"No." She pouts. "So what's his name? I don't care if you kill him. That's what he's for."

"Luan."

"Does that mean something?"

"Yes. Now don't move for a minute. I'm looking at the way some strands of your hair catch the sunlight, little ropes of light, like silk cords, you know, the way milkweed silk looks in the sun."

"You think of some funny things."

"Don't you think of things like that?"

"No."

"Sure you do. You just don't pay attention to them."

"What do you mean? Of course I pay attention to my thoughts. How could I not pay attention to them?"

"You don't," Chong insists. "You focus on different thoughts. Just like looking into water. You also have to be ready and waiting to have certain thoughts."

"I don't see how you can do that."

"Try it. You'll see. It's easy."

"I don't think it will be easy."

"You just like to argue with everything I say. I do care about you, too."

"Cut it out."

Chong drops his pen and feels a foolish wave of anger and impatience. "The more I see the sunlight in your hair, the more I care. But probably not for the right reasons. You see, I know you are going to grow old. You're going to get hungry and want to move from there. You're going to change, and I don't know what's going to become of you."

"I don't either." Ginny shakes her hair, then roughly grabs it in both hands and pulls it behind her head as if to hide it from him. "What's stupid hair got to do with anything anyway?" she shouts. Then quietly, "So I'm scared. Big deal, huh?"

"Yes, it's a big deal," Chong says. "I won't say you're wrong to be scared, either. But there are other things. Life is sometimes very, very good. You'll have lots of fun."

"Yeah?"

"Yeah. Don't use that smart tone. It's not classy."

"Fuck 'classy.' Besides, what is it?"

"Good for you," Chong says. "Classy is one less foolishness to worry about."

"So what do you want me to do now?"

"Tip your head."

Perversely, she tips it the wrong way.

"That's good." Chong sighs. "Now hold still for a minute."

"You never told me his name, by the way."

"Yes I did. Luan."

"Does that mean something?"

"Mixed up."

Before the word is even out of Chong's mouth, Ginny bursts into a laugh. "Mixed up!" she howls, then her pose is fractured completely as she collapses in laughter on the window seat, kicking her legs into the bars of sunshine coming through the window—like stalks of rice in the wind.

Chong hates himself. He is so in love, he closes his eyes. Surely someone will murder him for this impossible love.

Barber arrives in a yellow jeep with a trailer in tow, snakes into the drive, and is out of the car almost before it has come to a halt. He is tall, wears a full red beard, a bright blue baseball cap turned backwards, mechanics' coveralls, gray with white widely spaced stripes. The patch over his pocket reads "Red."

"I didn't have any trouble finding your place." Barber indicates the station wagon. "Not with your neon sign there." He has small even teeth, and what Chong regards as a fierce mouth. His smile seems bitter, forced.

"Can that be taken off?"

"Yeah, sure," Barber says. "I'll put the tires on and you can drive it down to the shop."

"You can do it tonight?"

"Unless you want it repainted."

"Not necessary."

"It'll take a couple of hours. Can you wait?"

"Yes!" Chong says.

"You gotta be pretty burned up about this."

"I am, yes."

"Wouldn't you just like to get your hands on 'em, though?" Barber drops the gate on his trailer and rolls out a long-handled orange hydraulic jack. He hands Chong the plug end of a bright orange extension cord attached to a power socket wrench. "Can you run this into the house and plug it in? I don't think it'll reach the barn there."

Chong trails the cord into the kitchen and inserts the plug in the socket. Ginny is watching Barber from the living-room window with obvious fascination.

"You know this guy?" Chong asks her.

"Sure," she says. "Everybody knows Red."

"How come everybody knows Red?"

Ginny shrugs. "He's on the fire department. He's got his own business. He's popular."

"I see." Chong feels an absurd flash of jealousy, goes out to the stoop to watch Barber work.

And Barber works quickly, wasting no motion. He jacks the car up part way, pops the hubcaps off, buzzes the nuts free, then raises the rear of the car high, and pulls off the wheels. He slides what appears to be a short piece of railroad tie from the trailer, pushes it beneath the rear axle, then drops the car onto it and moves his jack to the front end. He repeats the moves, unceremoniously heaves all four tires into the trailer.

"I'll run these down to the shop and bust them on my machine," he says. "But what do you want me to put on? You got snow tires? If you do, I can put on some cheap retreads until you switch over."

"That sounds good," Chong says.

Barber backs the trailer out onto the road with clear expertise, and Chong goes inside for some tea.

"You know he's doing you a favor," Ginny says.

"Why? I'm paying him, aren't I?"

"He doesn't usually do this kind of stuff."

"No?"

"He just works with tractors, trucks, big stuff like that."

"Maybe he needs the money."

"I doubt it. He's usually got a whole parking lot full of stuff to work on. People are always trying to get him to work on their cars, but he won't."

"He sounds like an enterprising man." Chong realizes there is a trace of irony in his voice. He knows Ginny's high regard for Barber should not pique him, but it does. And Chong knows also he is stupid about engines, has never had the patience to understand them. Expertise like Barber's makes him feel useless. He has trouble fixing the toilet if it doesn't flush right.

"What they say about Red is 'He's a pro.' That's what everybody says."

"You like him, don't you?"

"Yeah, sure," Ginny says. "All the girls do."

"How does he accomplish this enviable feat?"

"He's just a good guy."

"He's handsome."

"Yeah, really, but that's not it."

"What does it mean, 'He's a good guy'?"

"You're awfully curious about him."

"True. I'm also curious about what 'all the girls' like. I've always wondered. So he's handsome, and he's got a going business, and he's his own boss. Is that all it takes?"

"What else do you want?" Ginny says, her tone incredulous.

"I don't know. I'm asking you."

"I guess it's just because he does things without making a big deal out of it. He knows what to do, and he does it, and no jive. When he fixes something, it stays fixed. It's not pretend-fixed."

"If that's true," Chong says, "I like him, too."

"It's true," Ginny says.

Barber returns in about an hour, bounces tires from the trailer to the station wagon, buzzes them into place.

"O.K., Mr. Chong, bring the car on down, and I'll get that paint off."

"You wanted to borrow some books?"

"Oh, yeah. Could I?"

"What are you making?"

Barber laughs in embarrassment. "I'll tell you at the shop, O.K.?"

Chong rounds up some books on mixed-media sculpture and a magazine with an article on epoxy resins and their applications. The station wagon starts reluctantly, and for a moment Chong fears the vandals have done something to his engine or to his gasoline, too. But then he is on the road and driving too fast because his "new" tires are so quiet in comparison to his old ones. Chong passes Turner's farm at sixty miles an hour, a fact that shocks him when he realizes it, eases up on the gas as he continues into Lake Ecstasy village, and on the other side of town, up a steep drive and almost hidden in a stand of pines, to Barber's Big Machine Service.

Red is waiting for Chong in one of the two bays of his little shop, overhead doors open, holds a Styrofoam cup of coffee. He signals Chong into the bay and when Chong roars in pulls the doors down behind him.

"This is going to take a while, if you want to get a cup of coffee or something," Barber says. "I think the Inn's open tonight. At least I heard it was."

"I brought the books," Chong says.

"I won't look at 'em now." Barber says, holding up his blackened hands. "Thanks, though."

"So what are you making?"

"Yeah, well, I'm not sure I'll do it." Barber rummages among his tools, selecting round brushes made of fine wire, attaches these to a common power drill. "But I'd kind of like to make a kind of light sculpture, using reflectors, you know, like highway reflectors."

"They make reflective tape," Chong says. "You just slap it on."

"Yeah, right. But I want a lot of variety. And intensity."

"I think some of those reflectors on cars and signs are bolted down, aren't they?"

"That's right." Barber begins to buff the obscene fluorescent paint with the brush, raises his voice to be heard over the whirring and grinding. "But I think I want to do something really large, and I was hoping to find a faster way."

Chong is very curious about this enterprise now. He shouts a little information about epoxy, about its versatility, its expense, its dangers.

"That might be the route, though," Barber shouts back. "I can get an air mask from the fire department. The fumes won't be a problem."

Now Chong and Barber shout back and forth over the din of the electric-powered brush, discussing reflectors and plastic and glue and what happens to plastic, glass, metal when they are heated.

"You know about reticulation?" Chong shouts.

"About what?"

"Re-tic-yu-lay-shun."

"What's that?"

"You heat up glass just right, then douse it in water, cold water. It cracks all over, but not enough to break."

"Oh, wow," Barber says, obviously excited. "Think what that would do to a beam of light. Man! That gives me a hundred ideas!" He shuts down the drill for a moment, raises his goggles. "You can see what's happening here." He runs his fingers over the area he had buffed. "It's not perfect, but I can't do much better unless I take the body paint off, too."

"You're doing fine," Chong says. "I don't mind a few pink spots."

Barber laughs. "I kind of like it myself. You'll have the only car in the lake with a blush on it."

Chong is hoarse from shouting, and he tells Red he will sit for a while in the Village Inn, since there seems to be nothing he can do to help.

"I'll come and get you when I'm done," Barber says. "I'll be ready for a beer myself about then."

"Good." Chong rubs his throat. "Maybe we can talk some more at lower volume."

Chong surveys the cars and pickups in the Village Inn parking lot because he does not want to encounter Billy Parker. The Inn is not usually as crowded as it is tonight, nor as apparently festive. The back room is thronged, and a thick cloud of smoke curls lazily in the lights over the pool table, which is entirely hidden by the jam of bodies around it. Chong squeezes through the crowd to the far end of the bar, partially because he is curious about what is going on and can see better from that vantage point, and partially because he will be closer to an exit if Parker should appear. If this happens, Chong has already decided he will slip out past the EMPLOYEES AND GUESTS ONLY sign that marks the way to the Inn's inner quarters and a fire escape door to the outside. Chong knows these rooms and the exit well, from the days he stayed here waiting for his title to be cleared.

That had been a strange, lonely time, Chong remembers, not long after his divorce became official, and when he was bored and frustrated by his own work, feeling like a hack and a failure. His paintings and prints were also not selling well, and he would have given up altogether the attempt to start a new life away from the city, to re-energize himself, if Evelyn Crane had not come through with a substantial loan.

"Take it," she insisted. "I can always get my money back from real estate."

Verano hobbles down the length of the bar to serve Chong.

"Just a beer tonight, Cal. What's the matter with your leg?"

"Ankles." Verano reaches beneath the bar, uncaps a beer. "Gout's acting up."

"Another hot game back there?"

"You said it. Eight-Ball Championship. Best of seven games. And we got Tank Younger against Lily Walker, both undefeated."

"Lily?"

"Yeah. That's what's got everybody so excited." Verano leans close. "They call her 'Crazy Lily.' She's a deer hunter, too. Bow hunter. Always gets one. Tank's vowed he will never be beaten by a woman. He's takin' it real serious, and I'd say there's some bettin' goin' on."

"What's the score?"

"I'm not sure. Can you see the blackboard?"

Chong turns on his stool, uses one rung to elevate himself. The blackboard reads, LILY W. 11, TANK Y. 1, and Chong reports this to Verano.

"Tank's takin' it so serious, he's psychin' himself out," Verano says.

"Lily's got a way of throwing you off your game, too, pretends she doesn't know what she's doin'. And notice the blouse. She ain't hidin' nothin'."

A groan and some laughter draw Chong's attention to the table. Lily, tall with curly reddish-brown hair and large emerald-sparkling eyes, pounds the butt of her cue on the bar floor angrily and swears. She has apparently missed an important shot. As she moves away from the table, Chong notes the sleek, green slacks she is wearing, the scoop-necked pale yellow blouse. She shakes her hair out of her eyes and leans against the wall, one foot on a chair rung, hands folded over her cue.

Tank surveys the table. He is in his mid-twenties, a sturdy, well-built young man in bib overalls and a black and red checkered shirt. He has no mustache, but a thin, neatly trimmed beard outlines his square jaw. As Verano has said, he concentrates with such determination on his game that when he bends to the table to shoot he seems almost in pain. One after another, the balls drop into the pockets. Tank takes his time, sizing up each shot, until there is a burst of applause and whistling that signals his apparent victory.

"They take it pretty seriously," Chong says to a man next to him, a man about Tank's age, very slim, with deep-set eyes and a drooping mustache.

"They sure do," the man says amiably. He relates to Chong a story he had heard fragments of already, from Verano himself: how the fire department volunteers and others had found the antique pool table in the Inn's bowels, and resuscitated it over the course of a year. The job required not only replacing felt and leather—the walnut frame and slate bed were monumentally sound—but some serious carpentry work on the floor and the foundation of the bar so that the table would remain truly steady and level and bear up to its weight and the combined weight of the players and spectators around it. Chong remembers now that Verano had once shown him a set of hand-painted ivory billiard balls—which were not used except for solemn occasions and otherwise kept in a safe—that had been made in India. The table's provenance apparently began in England; and it was an unusual size for American games, but it was such a spectacular find that the players themselves had put a great deal of energy into its rebirth, and it became legendary, practically a local shrine, and to criticize it for its dimensional quirk might even get you a quick invitation to the parking lot.

"It hasn't hurt Cal's business any, either," the young man confides, poker-faced.

"You betting on Mr. Younger?"

"*Mister* Younger." The man laughs. "Oh, I don't care who wins, really, except Tank is such a good-hearted guy I'd hate to see him lose."

"Lily's pretty good?"

"Damn straight she is. She beat me five games to two. Two games I didn't even get a shot. She ran the damn table." When Chong asks, the man explains the game quickly. The object is to sink the eight ball, which is black, before your opponent. To do this, you must first sink either the seven solid-colored or the seven striped balls. "What Lily's really good at," the man says, "is keeping herself from getting snookered or, if she misses, leaving you with nothin' to shoot at."

Chong studies her as she leans against the wall sipping from a paper cup as Tank breaks the rack in the fifth game. He shoots with such power that Chong does not even see the cue move, and the white cue ball itself leaps into the air as the triangle of balls bursts into chaos. Lily has an animated face and responds to jibes from the spectators with mugging, winks, even sticking out her tongue. Without such childishness, she would be quite attractive, Chong thinks, certainly robust and angular, with beautiful breasts that she is obviously aware of and willing to exploit. Chong is impressed, if also a little intimidated by her prepossessing size.

When she finally gets a chance to come to the table again after the break, Tank has sunk all but two of the striped balls. Lily mugs, wrinkling her nose as she lines up her opening shot, declares, "It's impossible. No way I can make this." The ball drops, and Lily laughs, as if surprised. "I'll be damned. And good position, too."

Chong is amused at how rock solid she is before she shoots, how smooth her stroke is, how fixed and clear her eyes are just as the balls roll away from her cue. Most of her shots are made with an uncanny lack of force, Chong thinks, the balls barely making it to the rim of the pocket before they fall—every shot she makes has this built-in drama, one that has an obvious effect on Tank, who chews gum fiercely and tugs at his hat brim as he sits and waits for Lily to miss.

"Well, you did all the work for me, Tank," she taunts. "You cleared 'em out really good." She continues around the table, delicately putting the balls away. When she gets to the eight ball, she stops and regards Tank playfully. "Ta-daaa!" In a mock announcer's voice she says, "Theee eight ball. Will Walker make it one rail cross-side for victory number three, or will she blow it?"

"Ah, shut up and shoot," Tank says.

Lily knocks the black eight ball into the rail and it meanders back across the table and tumbles into the pocket. Cheers and catcalls rock the Inn, men and women stamp on the floor, hats fly.

The young man next to Chong says, "It's do or die for Tank. Lily needs one more, and he needs three. It looks real bad for my man."

Chong has another beer as Lily and Tank duel under the yellow green-shaded lights. There is all at once a strange beeping sound that Chong cannot locate until the man next to him says, "Oh, shit, here we go," slaps a small black box attached to his belt, and along with two or three other men scurries out of the Inn.

The next game takes a long time to complete, both players being extra cautious with each shot. Verano explains, as Chong has another beer—and begins to feel the effects—that it is a very defensive game being played now, neither player finding it easy to make shots. But then Tank catches fire, makes five balls in a row, and leaves Lily an impossible play.

"Snookered! You bastard!" she sings out. "That's downright ungentlemanly."

This charge is followed by booing and laughter, and when Lily misses her declared shot, Tank returns to the table at once and wins his second game.

"Never known you to hang around so long," Verano says over the hubbub. "Didn't know you were a pool fan."

"Ping-Pong," Chong says. "Actually I'm waiting for Red Barber. He's working on my car."

"Well, he won't be working on it right now," Verano says. "It might be a while."

"What makes you say that?"

"You heard them beepers, didn't you? That's the firemen going out. Barber's a fireman, I'm sure of it."

The news sinks Chong into a funk. "Maybe I'd better check. I'll be too looped to drive if I stay here any longer."

"What the hell," Verano says. "Enjoy the game. I'll fix you some coffee before you light out. What've you got to lose but a little time, right?"

"I guess so," Chong says laconically. "What's time?" He curses under his breath, turns on the barstool, sips his beer as Tank wins another game, tying the overall score at three games each and creating pandemonium in the Inn.

Chong slips off the stool and tries to telephone Ginny to let her know he is going to be late, but the telephone rings and rings without an answer. At least it's not my house that's burning, Chong thinks, if the telephone works. Ginny may be swimming, she may not be answering because she is afraid it will be her mother or Parker, and Chong chastises himself for not having worked out a signal with her before he left.

Irritated and a little gloomy, he returns to his spot at the bar, half watches the final game in the eight-ball match, worries about Ginny. He'll wait a minute and call again. Maybe she is swimming, maybe she is just out for a while. He feels a headache coming on and rubs his forehead with the cool, damp bottle of beer.

Meanwhile, Lily seems to be making short work of the game. After Tank's break and a few shots, she has come to the table and steadily, flawlessly, carefully put away all her balls.

"Shit!" Lily raises a clenched fist to the ceiling.

Chong cannot understand what is wrong. She has only the eight ball left to make. But through the chuckling and groaning of the crowd, and Lily's careful, prolonged study of the table, he understands that she has blocked her own last shot, and what should have been easy has been made difficult by an unlucky roll. Finally she comes to the table, drives the eight ball into the top rail, and watches and jumps as it rolls the length of the table toward a corner pocket, boggles there, but does not fall, trickles a few feet away.

Lily wails and spins from the table.

Methodically, mercilessly, Tank sinks the remaining balls on the table. Sweat beads on his forehead as he lines up for the tournament-winning shot, and his jaw tightens visibly.

"Lots of green there, Tank," Lily says. "You should've had better position."

"No sweat," Tank says, positioning himself with special care. A little smirk crosses his lips.

In one swift motion now, Lily has her blouse off, tosses it carelessly over the back of the chair beside her, and leans over the edge of the table. She speaks to Tank, but her words are inaudible in the whooping, cackling, complaining, and whistling that follow at once the baring of her breasts.

Chong stands, using the stool rung to raise himself, trying to see over a bobbing head before him. But it is a strange, somehow sad thing that he sees amidst the hilarity around him: part Lily, part Ginny, the adolescent in the woman, like a sad ghost inside this brazen joke.

"Lily, put it back on," Verano pleads. "You'll get me shut down."

Lily only smiles now as Tank pulls his cap to his eyebrows and readjusts his cue. She raises her chin a little and stares at Tank, her firm, full breasts yellow as grapefruits in the bar light, her hair falling in precise ringlets over her cream-colored shoulders.

"Why don't I have a camera right now?" Verano complains to Chong. "Jesus, these people are nuts."

"You want a picture of this?" Chong laughs.

"You bet I do."

"I'll give it a try."

"That's a deal," Verano says.

Tank shoots. The eight ball tumbles cleanly into the pocket. Lily steps up to Tank and shakes his hand vigorously, shouting, her breasts bouncing. Chong covers his ears and sidles out of the bar through the dark lobby of the Inn, leaving behind him the banshee howling of Tank's victory celebration, banging of bottles and glasses on tables and bar, Lake Ecstasy's victory hoopla over the summer eight-ball tournament and a pair of bared breasts. Well, there are ways and there are ways to make history, Chong supposes. Lily has made it her way—inconceivable, Chong feels, that Lily's grandchildren will not hear of this event—and whether she knows it or not, Chong intends to commemorate it for her, for Verano, and for the people of Lake Ecstasy. Haven't painters done as much for the Empress Dowager, the very Buddha, for Montcalm and Wolfe, for even the five-o'clock-shadowed lowly Nixon? Who more worthy of celebration than Lily Walker, who bared her breasts in a futile attempt to become the local pocket billiards champion? He has the scene fixed clearly in his mind, and it warms him as he stumbles out of the ruckus into a cool, clear, and serenely silent night. Chong, he tells himself, somehow you're looped. His feet, as he heads up the hill toward Barber's, feel made of lead. He thinks of Szu K'ung Shu, who liked his drink, his harmless mountain revelry:

> *What does it matter*
> *If I am too drunk*

> *To tie the boat tonight?*
> *We shall drift beneath stars*
> *And in the morning wake*
> *Among the reeds and rushes*
> *Of the shore.*

Ho! Chong thinks. But for Ginny, I could fall asleep in my car. I could redo Szu K'ung Shu. He stops beneath one of Lake Ecstasy's two streetlamps, and composes:

> *What does it matter if I sleep*
> *In my graffitied car tonight?*
> *The morning will find us*
> *Traveled round the globe and back,*
> *Mosquito-bit, but safe*
> *In a fart-filled metal coffin on wheels*
> *With pinkish sunrise blush.*

Chong nods his head. Sometimes his own life amuses him, it is so mad. So mad!

Chong is sitting under a tree watching storm clouds nibble away at the outer rim of a moon that is nearly full when Red Barber's jeep bounces up the driveway and skids to a stop beside the garage. Barber is still wearing his fireman's coat, and the white fluorescent stripes on the cuffs and across the shoulders, and the letters across his back, LAKE ECSTASY F.D., seem to float free in the darkness, moonglow, too. Chong pulls himself to his feet, a little headachy now that the first enjoyable flush of his drunk has dissipated, and drags himself down the hill to the garage.

To Chong's surprise, Barber takes him by the shoulders.

"Do you know where we've been?"

"No," Chong says. "What's the matter?" He knows already from the look in Barber's eyes that the fire has been at his own home.

"I didn't want to waste a minute, and this is the first break I've had to tell you," Barber says. "But somebody torched your barn."

"Yeah?" Chong says. The news makes him ill. "House O.K.?"

"The house is fine. We contained the fire to the rear section of the barn." Barber releases his hold on Chong's shoulders. "I'm sorry. I know it will sound stupid of me to say it, but it could have been worse."

"Yes, sure," Chong says. A wave of confusion sweeps him. Half a barn gone? He imagines blackened beams jutting into the sky, steaming. "Did you see a girl? Was anyone at the house?"

"I didn't see anyone but other firemen," Barber says. "And a pig."

Now Chong grips his head in a wave of panic and nausea. "Oh, boy," he says.

"I think it's repairable," Barber says. "I don't think you'll need to pull the barn down or anything like that."

"Why are they doing this to me?" Chong wails. "Why don't they leave me the hell alone?"

"Get in the jeep," Barber says. "We'll take a look. I'm sure it's not as bad as you think."

"I'm worried about Ginny," Chong says.

"Ginny who?"

"Ginny . . . " Chong almost says "Strong,"—"Cahill. She was staying at my house."

"I didn't see anyone there," Barber says. "I'm sure she's all right. Nobody was hurt. The house is fine, so don't worry about that."

On the road, as Barber hurtles through the darkness, the jeep bouncing almost comically at every depression, Chong feels woozy, very drunk indeed. He listens with only half his attention as Barber describes how the fire was fought, details the reasons for believing the fire was started and not otherwise an accident of electricity or some machinery in the barn itself. Chong is stupefied with the fact that Ginny was not at the house when the fire occurred, apparently is not there now, and he finds his hands shaking with terror and uncertainty.

"We called the state police, and they're sending a fire marshal down," Barber says. "This is your second fire, and the first was as suspicious as this one. I guess you know Joe Turner."

"What? Oh, yes, I know Turner."

"He said you talked to him a while ago, maybe you have some idea how this could happen."

"Who can be sure? How do you prove something like this?"

"You're right, in a way. But some of this is kind of familiar," Barber says. "Too damned familiar, I'll tell you. We've had some reason to think some of our local boys have pulled this kind of crap before. And I have to tell you something else, maybe you'll think it's weird. But I look around, Chong, and the last fire you had and this one— I don't know how to explain it, but it bugs the hell out of me. It's buggin' me right now, in fact. And that is that after both these fires we're picking up our hoses and stuff, and I get this tremendous rush of remembering Viet Nam. It's like I drop right down a hole and am back fifteen years in time. I'm not a kook, and this doesn't happen to me a lot. But both times at your place something triggered that memory, that feeling."

"You think it's something connected with the fires?"

"Positively. Maybe it's the way they were set. You get some training in that. I told you you were going to think I'm nuts, but tonight I think it was the smell that did it. I can't put my finger on it."

"How soon will the state fire marshal arrive?" Chong would like, he knows, to find Ginny and talk to her before he has to talk to an officer from the police.

"He may come right over tonight. If not, tomorrow. It looks like it's going to rain, and he'd probably want to see the place before that happens."

Chong thinks he can smell the traces of the fire even before he can see the farm. It is acrid, and yet sweet, too, a mixture of wood smoke and manure and gasoline. A fire truck remains at the edge of the road, red lights winking, an island of glare, and Chong can see as Barber pulls into his driveway firemen hoisting coils of hose into the truck, pools of standing water reflecting the red light—the windows of his house flash to the tempo of the fire lights, too—a pile of blackened boards. He jumps down from the jeep and looks the barn over at once. From the side facing the road there does not seem to be much damage, except for a charred rectangle around an upper window. But as he passes its length, the damage seems more and more serious, and the rear wall is completely gone, charred beams extend into the air without connection, the flooring for the loft is blackened, standing precariously. In the beam from Barber's flashlight, Chong can see that the grass behind the barn, in the area where Luan had run, is gone, the earth baked brown, testifying to the intensity of the heat.

Chong is a little staggered by the reality of this event, cannot really see what is before him, since the memory of the barn in its aging wholeness tries to superimpose itself over what is actually before his eyes now.

Joe Turner steps out of the darkness, grabs Chong by the elbow. "I'm sorry as hell this had to happen to you," he says at once. "We've got to put a stop to it." His black fire helmet is topped by a sooty shield that has been pushed up from Turner's face. In the uniform,

Turner seems shorter than he is, amazingly broad. His face is creased with fatigue.

"I don't know what's going on," Chong says.

"I'm glad we got here when we did," Barber says.

"That's for sure," Turner agrees. "You had a real hot one here for about ten minutes. It almost drove us out. And if that had happened, I wouldn't have given much hope for the house, either."

"Joe, when's that fire marshal supposed to get here?" Red asks.

"They had him on the radio a while ago," Turner says. "They had a big lumberyard fire up there yesterday, so he's not real interested in hurrying down here to check out a barn fire."

"He knows there's suspicion of arson?"

"Sure he knows." Turner pulls off his helmet and wipes his brow with a blackened handkerchief. The hair around his temples stands out like thorns or wet feathers matted with sweat. "But you know the story. Anything forty miles outside of Boston is on its own, except for paying taxes."

Barber lays a hand briefly on Chong's shoulder. "You've still got your house." After a pause, he adds, "And your car. It was probably lucky we had it in the shop when we did."

"Yes, real lucky," Chong says with a note of irritation he can't fully disguise.

"I'll get your car back early in the morning," Barber says.

"Please, don't worry about it," Chong says. "You need your rest. I'm not going to be in a big hurry for my damned car."

"You want to spend the night at my place?" Turner asks Chong.

"I can't see why."

"O.K.," Turner says. "Just asking."

"Unless you think they're going to come back."

"I don't really know what they're going to do, or even, for a fact, who the who is we're talking about," Turner says. "Although we have theories by the yard, right, Red?"

"Theories up the ass," Red says. "Until we catch somebody. Until we get something really concrete."

"I think I'd better stay here." Chong wants to be home in case Ginny returns. It is possible she does not even know the barn has been burned, he supposes, but then puts that thought aside almost in embarrassment. How in Lake Ecstasy could she not know by now that such a colossal event had occurred? Chong considers affirming the firemen's suspicions, and the names of Parker and Taylor are on his lips when it also crosses his mind that there are good reasons to refrain. If Ginny is with them—his breath catches when he thinks this—he could bring harm to her by making such a charge. And even though he has already talked to Turner about Ginny's presence, Chong is vulnerable, too, surely to be asked why such a young woman was living in his home. He hedges, says only, "I want to hear what the fire marshal thinks about this. I want to call my insurance man— so many things."

"Then that's where she sits," Turner says. He and Red Barber wander to the open end of the barn, where they stand discussing the remains, the damage to the structure, whether the interior flooring ought to be pulled down. Chong is too distracted to follow the details of their conversation, goes into the house, and makes a quick inspection of all the rooms. He hears an ungodly thudding as he comes downstairs, flings open the cellar door, and finds Luan twisting, shaking, ramming into the posts under the stairs, a cardboard box stuck on his head. Chong laughs with relief, hurries down the stairs, and pulls the box off. Luan squeals in fury, kicks his hind foot, retreats to a dark corner of the cellar. Outside again, Chong encounters Turner coming past the kitchen door.

"Oh, Jesus," Turner says. "I forgot to tell you about your pig."

"I found him," Chong says.

"Scared the hell out of you, I'll bet?"

"He sure did."

"I didn't think you wanted him cooked just yet"—Turner laughs— "so I grabbed him when I got a chance and tossed him in the cellar. Hope he hasn't wrecked the place."

"I appreciate it."

"No problem."

"The pig appreciates it, too."

Turner laughs again and moves off to the truck.

Chong's head is aching fiercely now, and he enters the house almost blinded by the pain. He finds aspirin in the bathroom cabinet and shakes out a couple of pills, drinks them down with water that seems too warm, then falls into a chair in the living room, exhausted, his head pounding. On the easel in front of him is his sketchbook, open to his morning's drawing of milkweed pods. He sits up suddenly, grabs the book, leafs through the pages. The drawings of Ginny are all gone. Nothing remains but the ragged strips of paper on the edge of the pages that had been held by the spiral spring binding. These sawtoothed pieces fall into his lap as he fruitlessly leafs through the sketchbook again and again. The drawings of Ginny are gone. No matter how many times he turns the pages, they do not reappear.

Perhaps it is a week before Chong can walk out of his kitchen door and not feel humiliated and incensed by the sight of his blackened, broken barn. He has not painted since the fire, but has busied himself with chores, cleaning up the camp by the bus, manicuring his garden, attempting to build bookshelves with old crooked barn boards. He has written letter after letter to New York, in a sort of nostalgic fit, and even suggests he might like to return, at least for a visit, even though he also knows, given his finances, this is unlikely at best. He writes these letters in the gazebo on the hill, because from that distance the predicament of his barn is so less immediate and can even, by the end of the week, seem a little comical. He writes a curt letter to Browne's Gallery complaining about lack of communication, and income. Because he has left the city, does this mean he became an artistic orphan, too? He is circumspect with Mai Li, telling her he is doing well enough when he is not irritated by the vandalism of the locals. He is a little more honest with Evelyn Crane, admitting his fright at the torching of his barn; writes Wu a letter of bravado and rancor; and to Benny, Chong writes a letter of woe and tears.

With his daughter, however, he inevitably becomes philosophical:

> I don't know if this is bad luck or fate from which I am expected to learn something. Is it punishment for my self-indulgence? So you see, besides my outrage I also feel some guilt, as if they are right to attack me and drive me out. Isn't this foolish? But I think you will see the influence of my father here, because he made me ashamed of everything except hard work. This is why I do not believe, ultimately, in individualism, though I do believe that individual effort can change things at least a little. Touch one person, and you touch a network. Wu tells me, "There is a psychological ecology as well as an environmental one." I believe him. Even the dead influence us. I mean practically, not just spiritually. My father's memory, the sun setting, these are not isolated things. Tell me, young scientist, what you think of these ideas? I miss talking to you.

All the same, Chong is happy to be where he is, to sit on the hilltop and do nothing. The trees are sometimes alive with little birds, delicate, wild song; and when there are no birds, still the trees glow in the sunlight, shimmer, seeming almost to breathe. The air is so rich with oxygen beneath these incandescent branches, Chong feels a little giddy.

The new contradiction in his life is evident at nightfall. Before the fire, he had always been happy to explore his land, the pond, the stream, in the dark or the moonlight, and relish the night breeze, the mist, even the night rain. At night, his gazebo was to him a kind of peasant's Moon Pagoda. But now the night worries him, a fact that makes him doubly angry when he admits it, that he is staying inside his doors because he has been intimidated, that he has lost a freedom and a great pleasure has disappeared from his life. This angers him, and he is more than ever aware of the sounds of the night, attentive to any interruption in the natural, expected flow of sounds and alert to any possible flicker of fire at the camp. In rebellion against this state of mind—for intellectually he is not persuaded it coincides with a living, real threat—he grinds the station wagon to life, and drives to the Village Inn.

"You're getting to be a regular," Verano says when Chong takes up his seat by the door to the kitchen.

"You're getting to be pretty predictable yourself," Chong says.

Verano shrugs. "Bills. What can you do? You'd think they'd let an old man retire in peace, but oh, no."

It is here that Chong discovers the things he has not been able to learn by telephone.

"I see your pal Parker is in jail for a while," Verano says.

"I didn't hear about that."

"I guess he beat that Cahill woman pretty bad, and she or somebody called the cops."

Chong shakes his head. "That's a real rat's nest over there." He knows he echoes Turner in making this remark, supposing it is common fare and safe. "What about the kid?"

"The runaway there, she's been sent to Florida to be with her dad."

"Florida!"

"That's what I hear. I guess Ted Cahill's working as a janitor someplace, and sometimes picks oranges. I guess he's going to try to get his kid a job in the groves."

"What town is that?"

"Oh, hell, I don't know," Verano says. "I went to Florida once, and that was enough. I spent all my time in traffic jams on Route

One down there. I said to hell with it, didn't even stay the week. You ever been?"

"No," Chong says. "California, but not Florida."

"Don't bother," Verano says. "Cockroaches big as squirrels. Mosquitoes? Christ, you have to tie yourself down to keep from being carried off by the damned things."

"You don't know how she got down there, do you?"

"Who?"

"The runaway." The word feels strange, dishonest, in Chong's mouth.

"That cousin of Parker's took her, I guess. The car-thief kid, the one who was in the state school for a while, Mr. Big Shot Taylor Archer. Those Florida folks won't stand his shit, by God, they'll coldcock him every time he opens his mouth. Just what he deserves."

"Why didn't they just put her on a bus?" Chong wonders aloud.

"Are you kiddin'?" Verano laughs. "You put that kid on a bus, and you wouldn't know where she'd end up. Besides"—Verano lowers his voice—"that Club outfit keeps pretty tight reins on anybody close to them. They got some serious secrets to keep, I think. Drug business, so I hear. Maybe that's another reason they sent Archer down there. You know?"

"Well, it's a real rat's nest," Chong observes again. He imagines Ginny on the highway with Taylor, arms crossed, sullen, pressed against the door to stay as far away from him as possible. The tension would be palpable. Maybe she has his drawings in her suitcase. It will be a miserable, hot trip at this time of year, and precarious, considering the beaters that Taylor drives.

Verano asks Chong about the fire, about what has been discovered, and Chong waves the question away in disgust. "I don't even want to talk about it."

"Can't say I blame you." Verano wipes the bar in a cursory way and limps down to his other customers, who are engaged in a discussion of a recent deep-sea fishing trip they have made.

"Ain't as good as it used to be," one says, to general agreement.

Chong drifts back into his fantasy about what Ginny's trip must have been like, tries to imagine her father. He will be tall and thin, have sandy hair, deep-socketed eyes, a sharp, narrow, feminine chin. Chong is guessing, of course, based on what Ginny looks like, assuming as the neighborhood does not that Ted Cahill is her true father after all.

In only an hour or so, Chong returns home drunk enough to be sleepy, but still too jittery to sleep well, his night crammed with busy dreams of travel by water, a canoe shooting through rapids, a rubber raft on a turbulent sea surrounded by sinister toothed creatures he cannot see beneath the foam. He wakes once to see silver ropes of water coursing across the bedroom window, accepts the rain with pleasure, although the drumming on the roof and the occasional acceleration of the wind intensify the uneasiness of his sleep. He studies the pat-pat-pat of large droplets to be sure it is not footsteps, rehearses the whine of wind in the screens to reassure himself it is not the creaking of a door spring.

In the hills, a muffled peal of thunder. The sound reaches Chong like the friendly growl of a large predator. He dozes, wakes, dozes again.

9
Gang
Wars

Red put Jim in a little room he intended someday to turn into a guest room and study. For now it held a bed and a mirrored dresser, but was still unfinished, the floor made of plywood sheets, the walls still showing the brown paper backing of the insulation. Though Jim had not asked to be hired, Red had made it clear that while Jim was welcome to stay as long as he wanted to, there was no work for him in the garage. Red said he could not make any money if he hired anyone else, and while this was probably true, Jim thought it more likely that Red just liked to work alone at his own pace and without having to give orders to explain how a job should be done. Red was also something of a perfectionist. Working for him would have been difficult in any case, since his standards were so high.

After getting Jim settled, Red took him outside and pointed to the pickup truck parked beside his garage. "Don't ever park in front of this truck," he told Jim. "I roll this when we get a fire call. You may not realize it," he said with ministerial seriousness, "but you are looking at the Lake Ecstasy Volunteer Fire Department assistant chief and head mechanic."

"Sounds mighty."

"I answer only to God," Red said.

"But what's it mean, really?" They entered the garage and Red resumed work in the engine of a tractor.

"It used to mean a good excuse to drive down to Lake Ecstasy and spray water all over each other," Red said. "We called it training. But lately we've had some problems. We've had to learn a lot, fast. Brush fires. We've got a lot of big empty tobacco barns around, too, since the cigar company moved out of here. Somebody gets a kick out of torching these. Pain-in-the-ass stuff. Wintertime it's chimney fires."

"Maybe I'll ride with you next time," Jim said.

"As long as you're staying with me," Red said, "you are a member of the fire department, will report for all calls, and attend all training sessions. You read me?"

"What's the proper form of salute?"

"Well, let's see," Red said. "Mainly the guys just raise a beer, and fart."

For the first few days after he arrived, Jim did little but sleep late, lie around the house brooding about himself, write letters to Anna, and worry about being broke. Technically he had a paycheck coming, but since he had left his job without notice, indeed had realized he had in fact left his job when he arrived in Lake Ecstasy, he did not want to endure the aggravation required to get it. It would take a while to transfer funds from Hyannis, and he didn't have much in his checking account anyway. But he was going to need something to get along on. He questioned Red about what jobs might be available in the area, but Red was not optimistic.

"First," he said, "don't sweat it too much. I'll loan you some money until you can get on your feet. Secondly, get on your feet."

"I really appreciate it, Red."

"Don't think about it. Just pitch in. I ain't about to police your area."

"It won't be a problem."

"Good," Red said. "Now let's get down to something really important."

"Yeah?" Red's tone worried Jim. Was he going to start lecturing him? About drinking? That Jim couldn't take.

"Women," Red said. "Now I know you are going to be interested in this subject."

"I don't know if I am," Jim said. "I'm out of practice."

"That won't last long," Red assured him. "I want you to appreciate the situation, the opportunities, and the limitations of life in the sticks vis-à-vis women. You with me?"

"I raise my beer, I fart."

"Good." Now Red launched into a semi-solemn, semi-comic description of Lake Ecstasy bachelorhood. He wanted Jim to appreciate that he was seriously in love with one Nancy Wallace, and would not expect him to hinder his sincere, sometimes diabolical, sometimes desperate attempts to woo and win her. He named other women Jim might find entertaining, but was not to take a deep interest in. Lake Ecstasy also had some special rules about these tedious games, Red explained. One was that you could still get yourself beaten to a pulp by overbearing conduct in the wrong place at the wrong time, by some cracker who thought he had rights in the case. Rule number two was that in spite of rule number one and its primitive cast, many, many of Lake Ecstasy's females, married or otherwise, were truly liberated, as Red put it, "kind of second-generation hippies, out of that mold. In the sixties, this place was home to a couple of communes, back-to-basics people, that sort of evolved into a less visible alternative community. Their kids go to Sunday School, and they know about Buddha and meditation. Some guys on the fire department drink beer and wear baseball caps, but they'll skinny-dip in the lake and trip twice a year. Middle America's here in force, don't get me wrong. Republicans are always getting elected to office. But so is the Shit Man."

"Who?"

"The Shit Man."

"All right, so who the hell is the Shit Man?"

"Weren't we talking about women?"

"I guess I can wait to hear about the Shit Man."

"Well, all I was going to say about women in Lake Ecstasy is that you've got your basic mountain hillbilly code and your hippie code and about sixty combinations of each."

"Oh, yeah? How about a free-love Christer?"

Red raised a wrench. "I know of one. Who knows? Maybe there's another. A redhead, kind of chubby. Lila Crowe. Really, she'll tumble you and try to convert you at the same time. Kind of an evangelical lay."

"Sounds interesting."

"It is, once. But then it gets boring. It's her way of dealing with guilt. Besides, one of the guys who works at the state park is currently on her case. In the summertime if you drive by her shack you can hear them singing hymns."

"Jesus, Red. Is that what you do for fun in Lake Ecstasy?"

"Why not? We'll sneak over there some night through the woods. You'll get a kick out of it."

"I don't think so," Jim said. "I think I'm more interested in the Shit Man."

"You'll meet him some night," Red said. "He comes into the Village Inn or the Mountaintop sometimes, blabbing away on the latest theories of how to use shit. He's got a little farm, and he's experimenting with all the things you can do with methane, and if you want to know the differences in methane potential in chicken, pig, cow, horse, human, or maybe even elephant dung, all you have to do is make the mistake of asking him, and he will bore you stuporous with his experiments and findings and readings."

"You laugh now," Jim said, "but when the Persian Gulf is sealed off—"

"You want a two-hour talk, you just say that to the Shit Man, and see what happens. In fact, I'll make you a bet right now, that if you mention the Persian Gulf to the Shit Man when we meet him, God help us, he will talk for, let's see, forty-five minutes nonstop. I mean, he will not even drink from his beer for that period of time."

"You're on," Jim said. "Forty-five minutes."

"Sucker." Red disappeared under a truck, creeper wheels squeaking. "When you meet the Shit Man, you'll learn the meaning of fanatic."

He banged away for a while beneath the truck and then squeaked out again, biting his knuckles and wincing in pain. "Another kinda strange person you're going to meet is this guy Chong, a neighbor down the road. He's a painter. I hope you get a chance to walk into his place, because it's *full* of drawings and paintings and stuff all over. The guy must eat, sleep, and drink painting, and yet he doesn't even seem really conscious of all the work he has, and all the work he does."

"Is he good, though?"

"*I* think so, what I've seen," Red said. "Of course I also cherish a 1950 Mercury, which some would tell you is bad taste. Christ, my hand hurts."

"You want to do something for it?"

"Just wait," Red said. "It always goes away. Anyway, this guy is a little on the primitive side, not razzle-dazzle. Some of it's even funny."

"I didn't think art was supposed to be funny."

"Oh, it isn't," Red said. "It's supposed to be like sex, you know, serious, capital 'S.'"

"I take it he's Chinese."

"Which is true. Also American." Red searched among the wrenches beside him on the floor until he found a suitable one. "I don't know if that's the reason, being Chinese, but he's had some trouble with some of the locals. Pretty serious trouble. I'll fill you in on that because I kinda think we ought to watch out for old Chong. I'm under the impression that some folks don't want him around here."

"What folks is that?"

"I'll fill you in on that, too," Red said. "But let me see about this drive shaft a minute." He squeaked back under the truck until only his feet showed, one foot scratching the other as he grunted and banged away. When he rested, he shouted, and Jim knelt down, then finally lay down on the cool floor to listen to Red and watch him work. In this attitude he learned the dynamics of Lake Ecstasy, according to Red Barber, ex-comrade-in-arms. Jim began to feel a bit more at home. It was apparent he was going to stay awhile after all.

For a few more days Jim could not seem to stay awake, rose in the afternoon, and did little more than endure the hours until he began in the evening to drink. He felt as if he had no energy, and the simplest decision taxed him so much that he simply returned to his bed or fell asleep on the living-room sofa. It occurred to Jim that he was behaving as if in mourning, grief-stricken, but he had no confidence that a healing process was taking place. And then, witnessing Red's daily bustle and unflagging energy, Jim began to feel guilty, and as much to disguise his self-disgust and the guilt he felt about Red's comparative industry, he began to explore Lake Ecstasy, driving the roads into the hills, stopping at roadhouses when he emerged from the canopy of trees, discovering the region's highway map, the points where streams crossed roads, where hills permitted long views down into the valley, where dappled roads were crowded with trees, hedges, fences.

Red advised Jim on where to fish, and in time Jim prowled the streams and lakes, learned a different geography, could talk now with Red about the deep pool beyond the toppled oak in Chong's brook, as they called it, or the shale ledges on the North River that oozed cold spring water in a turbulent, nearly musical rut formed

by ledges and huge boulders. Jim also walked the rim of Lake Ecstasy, then prowled the trails through the scrub oak, red pine, and
blueberry meadows that surrounded it. Here, it occurred to him,
would be an excellent private place to run, a combination of long
slopes and flat sandy stretches, all well shaded and rarely visible
from the roads. Jim had never been so out of condition, and it made
him feel old, and it made him think, too, though he only wanted to
be with Anna, that if he met a woman now, he would be ashamed
of his looks, of the fat he could squeeze around his midsection, of
the softness of his arms, and he would have no confidence. Damn it!
Why was it so hard to break the inertia of bad habits? Jim squeezed
the fat on his belly until it hurt. Look at Red, he said to himself. His
gut's as hard as a rock. He looks good, he looks ten years younger
than I do.

And so Jim began to run, clumsily, stupidly at first, and the pain
of it seemed absurd, and scared him sometimes when his chest
ached. Sweat stung his eyes, and bugs harassed him, and he couldn't
see that it was doing any good. Red gave him a few chores, and Jim
found that when it was not too hot he enjoyed splitting wood, the
rhythm of it, the sense of accomplishment it provided, and even
looked forward to slinging the maul in the cool of a morning for an
hour. Sometimes the maul would lodge in a curly piece of oak or
elm, and he would have to wrestle it free or lift the whole stump on
the maul's end to smash it down into the chopping block again, and
the strain of this, and the pleasure of it, went through his whole
body, made him gasp with strain, and when the stubborn log finally
broke, he would stand back bathed in sweat, heaving, nearly sick
with the work, and beginning to feel very good. He knew a physical
strength was returning to him, a sense of balance, of speed and alert-
ness that made him feel younger and reminded him of what he had
been like in the days of his soldiering.

Some of the trails through the hills around Lake Ecstasy were
serene—cool, dappled, private, padded with rust-red pine needles,
clean; but some had been discovered and were well used—for ro-
mance, for parties, for dirt-biking, and in some sad cases for dumping
trash. Jim was always a little shocked when he would come over a
sandy rise or around a sharp turn in a trail to discover the blueberries strewn with broken boards, chunks of plaster, broken glass,
paper, crumpled toys, oil cans, sometimes the sudden, almost comic
appearance of a smashed television or a disemboweled washing ma-

chine or finger-smudged refrigerator. The village dump was only a few miles away, and it made little sense to Jim that anyone could even find it convenient to use the otherwise appealing trails near the lake for their garbage. Either it was an act of contempt for the utility company which owned the land, or it was simple piggishness. Even in the few weeks that Jim had frequented the trails, the amount of trash seemed to grow. Occasionally Jim stopped and sorted through the detritus, hoping to find a letter or an address label, as well as to see any pattern in, make any sense of, the dumpings. But whoever was doing it was conscious enough about it to remove labels from magazine covers and envelopes, and they also apparently knew the trails very well. From what Jim could tell, most of the trash was probably dumped by someone paid to clean houses and yards, perhaps to prepare the house for rental, for the trash also contained paint-spattered plastic sheets on occasion, old lath, broken ceiling tile. Jim was a little embarrassed by his interest in and his anger with the dumping, since it was hardly an earthshaking crime. He just felt insulted by it, as if someone had trespassed on his privacy.

Red put it more bluntly. "It's like somebody shitting on your table. That's how I feel about it."

It amused Jim to keep an eye out while he jogged for the traffic on the lake trails, to try, when he heard the soft putter of an engine or saw the glint of a windshield through the trees, to catch up with the vehicle and note its license plate. Once he heard the growl of an engine down the hill, along a trail under high-tension power lines, and he sped down through the brush, attempting silence and speed, whacked branches out of his way, stung his legs in low briars, then plunged onto a sandy trail where he was confounded to find a scene ripped out of his past, a shock of déjà vu: A jeep was pulled off the trail into the brush, and a 105-millimeter howitzer sat solidly in the middle of the trail, its muzzle elevated under camouflage netting, and a half-dozen men in military uniform idling beside it. Jim whooped in surprise, and the soldiers regarded him with bored, dull eyes for a moment, before returning to their instruction.

"Oh, yeah," Red said later. "The National Guard does some weekend Mickey Mouse out there."

"They had a 105 in there," Jim said. "I kept waiting for it to go off."

"They don't shoot any live rounds. They just practice the drill, you know."

"Lucky for you. They were zeroed in on your garage."

"That'd be my luck," Red said. "Come out of Nam in one piece, then shot to hell in my own home by some summer-soldier fuck-up. That'd cap it."

"I kept waiting for it to fire," Jim said again. "Damnedest feeling. I'm still flinching."

"Those babies could howl," Red said.

"Outgoing sounded fine. You could sleep through it."

Red laughed quietly. "Sometimes the power company will send a chopper out to inspect the power lines. One day I was in the stream that comes out of the lake, which is technically posted, and *wap!* this chopper comes cracking over the trees real low. That brought it back in a rush, Jim, very vivid, very scary. My knees were knocking, and I'm holding this fishing rod like a weapon, feeling like an idiot. But that chopper just tripped me right back in time. Then it drifted over, and I saw the blue and white colors, and the feelings gradually went away. Of course, I was stoned. That helped."

One weekend, Jim managed to go two days without drinking and woke early Monday morning agitated and angry, and his head pounded savagely. Don't even fucking drink and I still get a fucking hangover, he thought. What's the fucking use? Red's truck was gone, and Jim assumed he had risen early to fish before starting the day's work. Jim milled around the house awhile, then decided to hell with it, he'd run the pain out of his system, either that or kill himself. He stretched out quickly, then took off down the road toward Lake Ecstasy at a merciless clip, a section he usually walked because the pavement pounded his ankles and knees. But today he didn't care. If he had a heart attack today or his knee cracked, he would welcome it, and he just didn't care.

He slashed into the woods along a narrow trail, and the sun, when not screened by leaves, was directly in his eyes. You never hunted, never fished into the sun, used it to confound, and blind the prey, rarely photographed into the sun unless you wanted silhouettes or a halo of sunbursts around the image, and Jim had observed the principle in Viet Nam whenever he could. Except that the sun had been everywhere. The sun had pounded them relentlessly.

He clawed his way along the trail, broke onto a sandy fire road, where now he almost collided with a wall of pale blue, swung away, still running, and over his shoulder saw the two cars nose to nose, a bearded man in a white T-shirt and dark glasses leaning into the window, ducking, it seemed; and when Jim was a little farther down the trail, he turned and took in the scene a bit more carefully, the blue and white cars nose to nose, the bearded man still leaning in the window of the white car, where Jim could now see the silhouette of another head, long-haired, and he thought, Monday morning rendezvous. Lovers. Maybe a little dope transaction. He slackened his pace a little now, feeling hot, too hot to continue his murderous pace, but glad now he had put himself into motion and had pushed himself so hard. He plunged down a steep trail to the edge of the lake and without hesitation smashed into the ball of sun on the water's surface, saw the light shatter around him like a cool explosion as he dived, kicked, spun in the water. He burst up, shaking his head, the pain much diminished, his body in a state of excited pleasure that was nearly sexual. He frolicked a moment in the illegal waters, then slopped in his soggy sneakers along the shore until he found another trail that led up through blueberries and scrub oak to the road. Just ahead of him a huge hawk fell from the top of a pine tree, snapped open its wings, and cruised the surface of the water, a twin rising out of the lake, almost touching him, talon to talon, until the great bird flapped up into the shadowed woods on the other side.

When Jim returned to the house, Red was hard at work on the engine of one of the town's trucks. The repair must have been something of an emergency, for all signs indicated Red had been interrupted—his fly rod lay across the kitchen table, his waders, which he usually hung up at once, were heaped by the open back door, and three beautiful brook trout lay ungutted in the kitchen sink. Jim hung the waders and was walking down to the garage to ask if Red wanted him to clean the fish when he heard the howl of the town's fire alarm.

Red charged out of the garage at once, waved Jim to join him. *But I'm not ready,* Jim thought, even as he began to move on Red's command. *And I don't know what to do.* He heaved himself into the truck as Red started the engine and switched on his CB radio.

"Charlie, what have we got?"

The radio crackled a message that Jim found difficult to decipher, but Red seemed calm, even a little amused as the truck banged down the road and into the gravel driveway of the town garage.

"Grab some boots and a helmet from the wall there, and let's take a ride in the fire truck," Red said. He scrambled out of the pickup, unlocked the station door, pointed to a row of helmets and jackets near the door.

"Should I put them on now?"

"Of course, turkey!" The overhead doors went up with a clatter, and Red heaved himself into the cab of the smaller of the two engines in the station, an army truck that had been modified with iron piping around the front end. It carried only a small water tank, a pair of portable pumps, and a large coil of red rubber hose. Jim threw on the gear and stumbled to the truck. The high boots slapped against his bare skin.

"Let's go beat some brush," Red said. "Hope you're not too tired."

"What's happening?"

"A brush fire by the power lines. Right by the lake, Charlie said."

"I just came from there."

"See anything?"

"Yeah. A couple of cars. People talking."

"Probably dropped a cigarette. It won't be much."

As they came whining up the hill, they could see a thick column of gray smoke that threw itself upwards, then curled away with the wind over the lake.

"That's not brush," Red said. He stopped at the entrance to a sandy trail, shifted into a lower range, and then they jounced and slammed through scrub oak until they came upon the power line trail and saw only a short distance ahead a car engulfed in flames so hot that they were nearly invisible.

"Charlie," Red said into the radio, "see if you can find somebody to bring the tanker up, and notify the troopers, will you? What we have is a car fire."

"That's one of the cars I saw this morning," Jim said. "It used to be baby blue, but look at it now."

The paint had already burned away, leaving a black shell. The interior tumbled orange and black.

"Probably stolen," Red said. "Hope nobody was in there. But it had to be torched to burn like that."

"So what do we do?" Jim asked.

"Watch it burn," Red said. "If any of the brush catches, we'll soak it down. Right now it's too hot to get close to anyway. Cars burn so goddamn hot. If it was next to a house, we'd have to get on it, of course."

In a short while, some of the brush did begin to smolder, and Red gave Jim a patient lesson in handling the hose, starting the pump, getting water into the lines, controlling the pressure.

"Throw some water in there now," Red said. "Soak the brush good. Just don't get too close to that car in case something blows."

Jim opened the nozzle and sent an arc of water into the brush beside the trail and the burning car, was surprised at how alive the hose became in his hand. It was an easy, even a pleasant chore, though he kept a wary eye on the car, which continued to roar. Parts of the frame were glowing cherry red, and Jim could see into the interior, where springs in the seat cushions were white-hot spirals in almost comically neat rows. He could see all the way through the car into the trunk. Red had pointed out to him that the headlights and plastic gasoline tank had already melted or exploded. Jim could feel the heat of the car now, too, surprisingly fierce. He heard the tanker growling down the trail, and when he looked back he saw also a police car, door open, the officer in earnest conversation with Red.

In a moment, Red jogged up to Jim. "We're going to tie into the tanker, since you've about used up the water here. And I'll take the hose awhile. The chief wants to talk to you about this morning, what you saw."

"You're spoiling my fun," Jim said.

"Don't worry." Red patted Jim paternally on the shoulder. "There'll be more. No shortage of fires lately."

Jim talked to the officer, a baby-faced man in his fifties who asked his questions while looking away, as if distracted by the fire. He wrote on a pad and once in a while told Jim to "slow up a second. I want to get this down. O.K. So what else can you tell me about these guys?"

"Well, I thought one was a woman. The profile suggested long hair to me."

"But you're not sure."

"No. Now that I think about it."

Later the officer explained to him it was the practice of some thieves to steal cars, drive them lakeside, as he referred to the shores of Lake Ecstasy, strip them of all salable gear and parts, then burn them to destroy fingerprints or other evidence.

"It's been going on for years," he said.

"Too bad I didn't have my camera," Jim said.

The officer looked at Jim, his eyes bright with the blue of sky and lake, and his blue shirt. "Yeah, too bad." He looked away again, and Jim sensed a weariness in the man, not exactly a sadness but a fatigue with the endless mischief men could invent and carry out. "I wonder why Monday morning, though. They usually operate at night."

"Maybe they work nights now. I mean, at a job."

"It's possible," the officer said. "And there's only one place around here with a night shift."

"You think they're from around here?"

"That's problematical," the officer said. "Royalton, maybe even farther off. We've had guys from New York up here, hunting, fishing. You wouldn't *have* to be from around here to know these trails." He smiled professionally and politely. "Well, thanks."

"Nothing to it," Jim said.

Red, apparently bored by his duty, was tossing esses and spirals of water into the sunlight, changing the spray from the nozzle to a hissing fog that threw off a rainbow of invisible droplets to a thick slopping burst that he would sometimes turn on the car with snap-crackling, hissing results.

The officer shook his head and pointed. "For a grown man, he's worse than a kid sometimes."

"I try," Jim said. "But he's hard to keep in line."

The officer nodded in agreement. "He's a hot ticket all right. But for a guy like him, you know, we can overlook a few things. We like him around here, which is more than I can say for some that have moved in."

"He's a good man," Jim said. "But don't tell him I said so."

The officer laughed, then took shelter from the heat inside the cruiser, one leg protruding from the open door. The car burned with less ferocity now, like a jeep that had hit a mine, or a four-by-four stunned by VC rocket fire. Viet Nam. Even in Lake Ecstasy. Let's get this over with, Jim thought. I want to take another swim.

One crystalline Sunday morning Jim sat on the porch of Red's cottage drinking beer and feeling stymied. The day was beautiful and yet Jim could think of nothing he wanted to do. When he arrived home late last night, Red told him that he had met a pair of the local Wild Women in a bar and had talked about Jim to them. They were eager to meet him, Red said, and promised to be swimming in Lake Ecstasy in the early afternoon. But even this prospect did not inspire Jim. He had seen the Wild Women one evening when he jogged on one of the high trails past the lake where they were swimming. They were big-boned and vigorous. One had Indian-black hair that she wore to the waist, was thought to be of Portuguese origin and called Mary of the Trees by the villagers who knew of her love of forest and lake; the other had faded blond hair so fine it seemed almost invisible, like mist, was very tall and almost ungainly, except when she was in the water, where she swam like a dancer. Red said she was called Cougar Sal, after the automobile she drove like a wizard. The two were inseparable, lived in a cabin in the hills, where they kept a summertime garden they didn't pay much attention to, chickens, and a huge old Collie notorious for the bounty of its affection, and which was said—untruthfully, Red reported—to be trained to grab men by the seat of their pants and drag them to the women's cabin, where they were demolished by orgiastic rigors.

"The dog's toothless," Red affirmed.

So Jim sat in the sun swatting flies and brooding. Where was he going to find the handle on things? He considered returning to Boston, where he could at least see his daughter now and then and keep better tabs on what Anna was doing, whether she was, in fact, pursuing the divorce as she had threatened. The thought drove him to the refrigerator for another bottle of beer, and as he pried the top off he could hear Red's feet banging on the upstairs floor—a welcome sound. In a moment Red was careening around the kitchen in his bare feet, hair uncombed, eyes matted with sleep.

"Fresh coffee," Jim said.

Red grunted approval, but stumbled past into the bathroom, then showered and prepared himself for the day as Jim finished the beer and began to feel a little buzz. Why, he wondered, am I throwing the day away? What the hell am I doing? He continued his meditations on the porch as Red banged through breakfast preparations, filled the air with the smell of sausage. In a few minutes, Red was seated beside Jim, a beer in one hand, a plateful of sausage and biscuits in the other.

"You had any breakfast?" Red asked.

"No."

"Why not? You'd better quit sulking and start eating a little. You'll make yourself sick."

"Really, I'm not hungry, Mom."

Red laughed. "Suit yourself."

"I guess I'd feel a little freer if I were earning my keep," Jim said.

"I told you not to worry about it."

"I know, but I'm not exactly setting the world on fire out here."

"So? Take a break. Now's your chance to think things over. Which, from the hangdog look of you this morning, you have been doing."

"Am I as fucked up as I think I am?"

"I doubt it," Red said. "You just need to get some confidence back."

Jim nodded agreement, although he didn't know that Red was right or that his "problems" could so easily be summed up. "So how do you do it, Red? How do you keep your spirits up?"

Red munched his sausage, looked away down the hill. "I don't have your entanglements," he said. "Sometimes I think I came here to hide out. It's easier here. If I get angry, I can go out hunting or something. I don't feel I have to take it out on people."

"But I thought you wanted to get married and have kids."

"Sure," Red said. "Now I think I'm ready, but I'm afraid I waited too long. Maybe I'm just on a wild-goose chase."

"But you've made a life here. A pretty good one. People know you, you make some money. I swear to God, you sometimes even seem happy."

"Is that a crime?"

"Sure it is."

Red laughed, ate in silence awhile. "There's really nothing to it, Jim. I try to do what feels good and not get caught at it. I like to work, and I got work to do. Otherwise, I don't want anything special except to have no bills and be left alone."

"Can you really be left alone?"

"I've had to work at it. Sometimes you've got to defend your turf."

"But how come you don't have the bug? How come you don't want a yacht and servants like everybody else?"

"How come everybody else wants that?"

"That's no answer."

"So what's the answer?" Red speared his last sausage and studied it intently. "Because we saw how the Viet Namese did it," Red said. "What do you need? Jesus, they didn't even have crappers, fed their shit to the fish in the pond."

"Not much."

"Not much is right. I don't quite relate to eating fish fed on shit, but the point is how little you can make do with, right? The less you got, the less you got to worry about."

"That's a way of looking at it."

"Hey! What's eatin' you, Jim? You got ambition all of a sudden? You want to get rich, drive a Cadillac?"

"I'd like a hot shower, though."

"I can dig that." Barber twisted open another bottle of beer and flung the top over the porch railing into the bushes. "But I figure a couple of solar panels will take care of that."

"You got it all figured out."

Barber sucked down half a beer, eyeing Jim. A trickle of foam soaked into his beard. "You miss the city, or what? You want some action? What's the problem, buddy?"

Jim slapped a mosquito on his elbow. "I don't know." He was surprised at how difficult it was to say even this simple thing. He didn't even want to talk.

Barber looked at his watch, then planted his beer on the porch railing, stood, hitched his pants. "Well, I know what I want to do, and that's, one, try that hole below Chong's dam one more time, and, two, slide on over to the lake for a quick dip. Or maybe not so quick, depending on who's there. Why don't I meet you there in a hour, if you feel like it?"

"Right."

"If I *ain't* there, you know I'm stacking up some rainbows."

"Good luck."

"And if I'm not there and those two fine young things are sunning on the grassy knoll, well, old buddy—"

"I'll put in a good word for you."

"Excellent."

"I'll tell them your lust is great."

"Wonderful. Just like that."

"But first you want to catch some trout."

"No. Tell 'em I'm scraping the bark off trees, something like that. Like a horny elephant. The need is on me."

"O.K., the need is on you."

"But don't, for Christ's sake, scare them off."

"I don't think they'll be scared by a little lust," Jim said.

"Not those two."

"I'll just keep 'em interested. You're so horny, sperm is running out of your eyes."

"Hey, what the hell. It's always spring around here, right?"

"Right."

Barber clattered down the stairs to the pickup and in a moment was gone in a roar of dust. Jim was glad to be alone. He leaned back in his chair and put his feet on the railing. Anyone coming down the road might have supposed him at ease, peaceful, enjoying the beautiful day. But he was thinking of Anna. For some reason he remembered a yellow shirt she wore on a day like this, daffodil-yellow, with a scoop neck that showed off her shoulders. A cardinal fluttered by into the shrubbery beyond the brief yard, but Jim hardly noticed. He was remembering the line where her jaw met her neck, how she would swallow hard when he put his lips there, how still she would lie if he took the skin ever so gently between his teeth.

A trio of hornets had crawled in Red's abandoned bottle, buzzed against the green glass, then floundered into the stale beer, where they writhed like poisoned tigers, but in silence.

Jim thought he might just get in the car and drive to Boston.

But of course not. Maybe, though, it would be all right with Anna after the shock of his appearance.

No.

No, it wouldn't be all right.

Jim jogged the trails now almost daily, and he punished himself. Red did not approve of the severity of Jim's exercises but confined his criticism to some occasional teasing. But the running not only hurt Jim in ways that felt good to him, felt just; the routine of it and the discipline of it forced his mind or led his mind into new channels, and Jim was surprised to find in the midst of laboring up a sandy hill how clear and single the thoughts would be that entered his otherwise empty head. The running was like some sort of meditation, an Indian way, as Jim thought of it, to batter down the preoccupations of his body and its habits and addictions, and greet himself on a less humbling and freer plane. Running, in a curious way, was like chanting, and Jim found that while he ran his thoughts took on an almost musical quality, sometimes comical and balladlike, but sometimes almost poetic, as if he could discover meaning in his wayward existence. What opened up to him was the fact of his persistent anger, steeped for fifteen years now, and that at the core of his being was a terrible sadness that he could not rinse away. What a stupid war it had been. What a folly it had made of his life and those of the men who died.

One day Jim crossed the road from Lake Ecstasy and jogged the trail along Chong's brook and along the border of Chong's farm. Jim had once seen Chong rummaging in the blueberry bushes on the shores of the lake, a T-shirt draped over his head against the sun, one hand flailing flies with a pine branch. It was hard to imagine anyone hating this man, who just seemed eccentric to Jim and harmless after all. The farm seemed almost abandoned, with scant evidence (except for a random chicken and a cat or two) that anyone tended it at all.

Now there was no sign of Chong in the garden or yard, and Jim pushed himself up Sweat Hill on a trail that passed a school-bus camp and, farther along, a hilltop gazebo where Jim might rest if running the hill was too punishing in the heat. As he neared the bus, he was startled to hear the growl of a motorcycle, and he glanced over his shoulder to see one, then two slithering along the trail behind him. He was annoyed by their presence in this otherwise peaceful stretch of woods, and moved to the side of the trail to allow plenty of passing room. He supposed the riders were following the same trail he meant to take over Sweat Hill, down along the brook, then up again into the state park and the trails there, where, technically, motorcycles were not allowed. Another glance over his shoulder and he saw they were quite close now, engines crackling, both in black helmets with polarized bug-eye plastic shields that made it impossible to see their faces.

What instinct or what training was it that caused Jim then when the motorcycles were upon him to cut sideways into the shrubbery, the handlebars of the bike swiping beneath his arm, the wheels gouging the earth where he had just been, engine screaming, and the second bike also slashing into the shrubbery, branches crackling inches between rider and Jim, who went down, slashed by the branches, his ankle singing with pain. He rolled into the brush as the bikes slipped and twisted up the trail and turned back on him in the same black file, one after the other, wheels gouging into the mossy, pine-needled turf near his head and legs. Jim shoved himself up, clawed deeper into the laurel and brambles, as the bikes turned to make another pass, the lead biker stopping this time to shout something at Jim that over the roar of the engines and muffled by the dark shield, sounded like ". . . your own business." Jim shrieked curses back and searched the ground for stones to hurl, disappointed and frustrated at the absence of suitable retaliatory weapons. Then the bikes whined away.

Jim was left with a burning anger and in utter confusion. Had he

been mistaken for someone? What in hell's name could have provoked the attack, the seemingly senseless warning? His heart ham-
mered in anger and in fear, and he wondered if they would be lying
in wait for him if he continued on the trail, or if they would attack
again sometime in the future. By God, he would get a gun, and
bring it with him. . . . Jim seethed now, and he imagined the course
of the bikes along the trail through the woods and wondered if he
would have time enough to return to Red's and grab his car and
race to the state park in time to see them emerge. The one serious
problem was that the state park had more than one trail leading out
of it, and Jim now, as he struggled to recreate what had happened
to him, had to confess he was not that certain of what he had seen.
And if he told the police, what could he say? Two apes on bikes had
run him off the trail near Chong's pond, Sky Pond, as the official
maps would name it. What kind of bikes? What age men? Any dis-
tinguishing marks? Apes? That's all. In black helmets with dark-
brown shields. Fucking coward apes!

Some day I'll find them, Jim thought. I won't need the cops. I'll
fucking fix them and their bikes, too. He took a long look at the
slashes and welts on his arms and legs and decided to return home.

Home! Jim laughed, sweat stinging his cuts. I've thought of Red's
place as home.

Red mentioned the attack on Jim to Joe Turner after one of the
weekly fire department training sessions as the volunteers lingered
at the station house drinking beer. Of the volunteers he had met,
Jim liked Turner the most; he seemed to him the most straightforward and agreeable, not entirely lacking in Yankee reserve but having much less of it than others in the department, who seemed so
cool to Jim as to be rude. Turner presumed, confirming Red's theory,
that the attack had been made by the men Jim had implicated on
the morning that car had burned.

"Probably some of those guys in The Club," Turner said. "Everybody knows what they're up to, but nobody can ever catch 'em to
prove it. We got about two and a half cops for this whole area, and
they aren't the bravest men in the world, if I can speak frankly."

"Go ahead," Red said. "Speak frankly."

"Now don't get me in trouble." Turner told Jim that one of the
policemen was his brother-in-law, "and he's not gettin' chubby because he loses too much sleep over his work." He went on to say

that "probably what you saw there was a couple of the Archer family boys, maybe even this guy Billy Parker, who works for the town, believe it or not, but one of the chief hell-raisers around. Billy loves trouble," Turner said. "He eats it for breakfast, lunch, dinner. He can't wait to get in a fight with somebody, no matter how feeble the excuse."

"And he gets away with it," Red said.

"Has for years," Turner agreed. "Oh, he's done his thirty days' work release now and then, assault and battery, that kind of thing. But they don't nail him with the good stuff."

"They're afraid to," Red said to Jim. "You see what they did to you."

"If it was them," Turner interjected.

"Well, I won't stand for it," Jim said. "If that's who it was, they can't threaten me."

"They told the cops, somebody told the cops," Turner said, "they'd get their house torched. Some people think these barn fires we're having are just to emphasize the point. These boys have guns, too, you know. Rifles. They're not playing."

"I don't care," Jim said. "I won't be intimidated."

"I'm just saying," Turner continued, "that you'd better not be underestimating these boys. They earned their reputations. And they stick together."

"I hear you," Jim said.

By the end of Jim's first summer in Lake Ecstasy, he'd been to several fires. Another car was abandoned and torched, at the Milliken orchards this time, and there were brush fires; but there were two that Jim would remember for a long time. The first was at Chong's barn, a fire that was well under way when Jim happened on it, returning in the evening from a trip he made to the Mountaintop Lounge to give Red a little time alone with Nancy Wallace. Red had planned the date for days, caught some rainbow trout which he was going to cook with almonds and wine. What Jim learned later was that these plans had already been scrapped because Red had found it urgent to work on Chong's vandalized car. Red and most of the rest of the volunteers were already on the scene, but because the shaft in the hydrant across from Chong's house had jammed, they had difficulty getting water, and the interior of the barn began to roar.

"If that fucker goes, the house will go, too!" Red had said. He worked like a demon possessed, trying to free the jam in the hydrant, and while the other firemen made do with water supplied by a tanker, he and Jim finally pulled the whole inside of the hydrant apart and reassembled it. The main screw had been jammed with rocks the size of tennis balls and Red was furious about it: "They didn't just jump in here!" he raged.

When the water spurted through the hydrant at last, the volunteers could double their attack on the flames, and quickly knocked them down, working from inside.

"You wonder if it's just this hydrant they jammed," Sweeney said, "or if they have screwed around with all the hydrants in town?"

"We'll have to check them all, but something tells me it's just this one," Red said. "And the bastards should hang for it."

"Sure they should," Sweeney said. "Which bastards?"

Jim was awed by Red's fury, but he recognized it, too, as kindred to what he had felt in Boston. He could also see that Red was right—somebody wanted Chong out, and they were playing rough. Too rough, Jim thought. More like, insane.

The other fire he remembered broke out at the log cabin home of an elderly couple who lived in the village section of Lake Ecstasy. Pilot lights had apparently gone out on a propane stove for some reason—perhaps due to water seeping into the lines—and when the old man came down in the morning and lit his customary pipe, he set off an explosion that ripped out the kitchen wall and left the propane tank itself blazing from the nozzle, shooting out a blue and orange jet of flame that terrified Jim when he leapt down from the truck and saw what the situation was. Rescue first was the rule, and Red and Turner strapped on air packs and plunged into the smoldering house while Jim and two others were ordered by Chief Suski to set up a "triple Y" of three hoses, charge the lines, and advance on the hissing propane bomb. The men on either side of Jim set up a screen, an "umbrella" of fog that burst and shimmered from their nozzles, protecting them from the heat as Jim moved forward between them with the third nozzle ready to smother the serpentine snarling flame.

Later, Jim had to admit that something about the fire had been therapeutic for him. For days afterwards, he felt exhilarated, almost gay. His hands hurt when he flexed them—the result of gripping the hose so hard—as if he had been in a firefight. More important, he felt as if he had been jarred awake, as if the risk had slapped something vital in him, opened his ears, improved his vision, cleaned his tongue. The worst moment had been the best for him, when he had slapped the spray from the hose into the billowing flame, coming between the protective "fog" of the other two hoses, and the fire had demonically overarched the three firemen and reached around their spray like the arms of a lover and touched their heads, their backs with a hot kiss. It had been hot enough to blister the shoulders of their coats. They stank like burning tires. Their shoulders steamed. The fire roared at them: "You!"

Jim nestled in the circular rainbow sheen of the fog and pressed the stiff column of water on the root of the blaze. The fire did not lash out again. It had tasted their helmets and their shoulders, and then collapsed under the pressure of the cold stream from the nozzle between his hands. Jim did not think they had vanquished the fire, beaten it down; instead, he felt they had enticed it away from them, to a nervous, then a deep sleep. Trickery, not power, made the difference. The three of them on the hoses had been lashed, and knew it, and went to bed that night with the tang of fire on their hair and their skin.

Like napalm, Jim thought as he fell asleep. And what, what was there about a fire that had made them all so jubilant as they flicked their lighters open and burned down the grass huts of the Viet Namese? There was that moment in any fire, in any structure, when the shape of it, the skeleton, was revealed like a red idea, then dripped and tottered, exploded or metamorphosed into ash and drifted up into the sky. God! It made him sick and happy to see a thing stripped to its core and then evaporated as if it never did exist.

He fell asleep warm, glad for his burns.

Norman Morrison. A monk in flames. *I understand*, Jim dreamed. And for the next few days he went about as if the edges of his brain were on fire. He was happy.

The old man died of his burns; the woman, carried from a bedroom closet by Red and Turner, survived, then moved away to live with relatives. The property went up for sale, and Joe Turner bought it before it was advertised.

ontrary to his expectations, Chong's garden is flourishing,
and he enjoys the first cupfuls of cherry tomatoes and a harvest of broccoli that is almost too abundant for his simple
needs. Squash are beginning to form now, too.

The shock of seeing his blackened barn has not completely diminished, and though it still saddens him to regard it, he can now at
least stand to make plans for cleaning it up and renovating it, if the
miracle should ever occur that he would have money to do the job.
He needs a good place to store his paintings and prints, and the barn
loft might provide that, properly fashioned.

As he has asked him to, Turner has made a new pen for Luan,
closer to the stream. The pig seems utterly unconcerned about
Chong now, and insolently turns his backside to Chong's greetings.
I know, Chong thinks. What have I done for you lately?

The sky is so blue!

The pond now, at the end near the swamp, is teeming with frogs
of all sizes. They have a stripe of gold dust behind each eye and are
as green as jade. Now and then there is a boil on the surface of the
water that tells Chong a bass has found a meal. He scratches his
chin. Bass fried in cornmeal with cherry tomatoes and broccoli. Excellent. He will even have some corn soon. The garden is extremely
important to him now that he will have no extra money at all, not
for anything. He wishes he were younger. He could begin cutting

some firewood, and tells himself to ask Turner if anyone would be willing to cut wood for sale and pay him a percentage.

He is teeming with ideas for paintings and drawings now, and switches from one project to another as spirit dictates. He makes a cartoon, a large sketch of the painting he intends to do of Crazy Lily Walker's bid for the Lake Ecstasy Eight-Ball Championship, amuses himself by drawing the faces of everyone he knows in the village and arranging them in a little parody of those medieval paintings crammed with the haloed faces of church dignitaries and biblical luminaries both. He discards one with persons floating above the bar like the floating Buddhas of Tibetan art, Buddha in all his manifestations being too arcane for Lake Ecstasy. Besides, he has always loved American saloon art—the beautiful backs of chubby women emerging from cloaks of buffalo skin. Since those days, Chong has thought, the back has been very much underappreciated. And who in their right minds would ever compliment a woman on her shoulders and a straight spine?

He works, and the days pass full of sunlight. He worries about money, about making money to help Mai Li and Susan, calls Joe Turner, who tells him he will be too busy in the fall to cut any more wood than what he has coming for repairs to the dam and remaking the pigpen. Chong calls Barber also, who is not interested in cutting wood for himself, since he has a supply close at hand, but who has a friend living with him for the time being who might be willing to take the work on if he can't find another job in the meantime. When he is in the woods, Chong regards the trees with new eyes, feels like a rapist, and though he understands that trees with split bark and dying limbs, and also trees with tall slender trunks and a small crown of leaves, are overabundant and should be harvested, it is these trees that he finds beautiful and interesting. A tree takes so long to grow—forty years—and comes down so quickly when the chain saw bites through it that Chong finds this work a little unnatural and obscene. In the past, when the tools were not quite so finely honed, the men who harvested the trees must have had a better sense of the trees' slow, difficult, tenacious, enduring lives, Chong believes. Did they, therefore, respect the tree and cherish their work and the resulting wood more? Chong has put an ear to the smooth bark of the white and black birch trees, and he knows that sometimes they hum, transmitting the vibrations of the earth, that they have a secret, audible life.

This won't be a "harvest" but a slaughter, Chong tells himself, and is immediately irritated by his sentimentality. Damn it! Cutting will improve the forest, prevent disease, let in sunlight (so the poison ivy can grow?), provide fuel and work. And money, he reminds himself. Money.

One day Chong receives (among the sweepstakes promotions and newsprint fliers from grocery stores) a cornucopia of mail from New York. Two letters! He opens the one from Browne's Gallery at once, and saves the other from "E. Crane" as one might set aside dessert. The letter from his gallery is not signed by the owner, Chong's friend and admirer, but by a new manager, a man unknown to Chong, who informs him that Mrs. Browne has been in Europe since the spring, and the enclosed check will bring Chong up to date on the sales, two watercolors and a painting. Chong collapses in a funk. He squints at the check, afraid to acknowledge the disaster it will surely represent.

Six hundred dollars. He checks again to make sure a zero hasn't been dropped from the figure, but no, it is not $6,000 but $600.

Thanks! Chong says, to Mr. Whoever-you-are. Thanks a load, you scum. This is what Mrs. Browne would sell of mine in a month! Chong fans himself with the check, feels a little sick and quite disheartened. The manager said nothing at all about looking at Chong's new work, as if he had seen enough of the "old" to satisfy him. He crams the letter and the check into his shirt pocket and carefully peels open the letter from Mrs. Crane.

Ah! A check. A loan! The blue slip falls into his lap. Fifteen hundred! New life! Riches! Eagerly, he dives into Evelyn's letter.

The occasion of its arrival alongside the accounting from Browne's turns out to be not at all coincidental. Mrs. Crane reports she made a trip to the gallery to investigate Chong's complaints and encountered an incredibly rude young fellow who had mounted a show of graffiti and punk artists entitled "Close Ups and Cut Ups," and who didn't even recognize Chong's name.

"The gallery resembled a butcher shop," Mrs. Crane tells him, "and there was talk of 'human carnality' and the world coming to an end so that ethics is obsolete, and other nauseating topics."

Inasmuch as she had found the gallery so changed and so unresponsive to Chong's work and interests, she had taken it upon herself to notify one Todd Oslip of Oslip Galleries, "a collector of what he calls 'primal works' and erotica, among other things," and to introduce him to the paintings Chong had made of her so many years ago.

"Do you know," she writes, "this is the first time anyone has seen them other than my husband, and some of the help?"

Oslip, she says, wanted to buy the nudes of young Evelyn Crane right off the wall, and was "crushed" that she wouldn't part with them. "He has some business in Boston," she adds, "and should be contacting you about a visit. I understand your loyalty to and affection for Mrs. Browne, but she is readying to retire and I think you have to look out for your own interests a little better than you have."

But how do I do that? Chong wonders. Away in Lake Ecstasy? He looks at his two checks. Now! Now he can fix his barn.

After dinner that evening, Chong finds himself uninterested in his work and a little bored. Too uninspired to write any letters, too broke to make telephone calls until he deposits his checks in Royalton, he decides he will drive to the Village Inn and kill some time there. When he starts his car, he notices the gas gauge is close to empty, although it seems to him that it was only a short while ago that he filled the tank. It makes him a little angry, and it makes him wonder whether his gas is being siphoned. He has been sleeping very soundly lately, perhaps a little too soundly, thanks to his increasing habit of drinking wine all evening. He knows it is not a good idea to drink alone, and yet it seems a harmless enough thing to do. He reminds himself to begin harvesting the wild blueberries from the shores of Lake Ecstasy, for they make a wonderful wine, and good commercial wine is expensive. Yes, and the raspberries should be coming in soon, too, on those high sandy plateaus where Small Stream emerges from the state park. Ho! The sweet, sweet brandy one can make from those blood-red berries!

There are only a few people in the bar when Chong comes in, and Verano complains he will close early if business does not improve.

"Ah, what else have you got to do?" one of the barflies says. "You'd go home and watch the ball game on TV, same as you're doing now."

"Damned if I would," Verano says. "I only got this on to please you guys. The Red Sox don't want to win the pennant anyway. Management won't let 'em."

"*What?*"

Chong drinks a beer quickly and is about to leave when Verano brings him another before he can refuse it, and inquires about his progress on the Crazy Lily painting. "You are going to do that for me, aren't you?"

"Sure," Chong says. "I'm working on it now."

"Am I going to be in it?" Verano grins and blushes a little.

"The price goes up for that," Chong says. "But sure, why not?"

"Don't let me put ideas in your head. You just do it your way. When do you think it will be done?"

Chong shrugs. "A couple of months maybe."

Verano is clearly surprised. "I didn't think it would be that hard to do."

Chong is about to explain the process when he feels a hand on his shoulder and turns to find Nancy Wallace facing him. He cannot help blushing with pleasure as she sits down on the next barstool.

"Never saw you here at night before," he says.

"Don't you think I see enough of this place in the morning?" Nancy's brown eyes flash in anger, and she crosses her legs in irritation, jiggling her foot. "Actually, I was waiting for Red Barber, who said he'd meet me here"—she inspects her watch—"ten minutes ago."

"He's a busy man?" Chong is always a little distracted by his memory of Nancy in the hammock at his home. Tonight she wears blue jeans and a checkered shirt open at the throat. Her good looks are not fashionable, but, Chong thinks, she looks strong and agile both, like one of Degas's dancers who would make the stage floor boom when she came down on a foot, yes, one of Degas's dancers who could also split wood.

"He works too damn hard, if you ask me." Nancy smiles sheepishly. "What brings you to town?"

"Just wanted to get out for a while." Chong pauses. "I'm glad you sat down. I thought you were mad at me."

"Mad at you?" Nancy laughs quietly, pays for the drink Verano brings her. "Not really. I just have my moods, you know, like everybody else. If I'm mad at you, I'll let you know. Don't worry about that." She sips, draws her hair away from her eyes. "I've just been finding it a little rough sometimes since my divorce. Phil, my ex-husband, is taking it hard, and I hear about it from his friends."

"You feel guilty?"

"Yes and no," Nancy says. "You've been through it. How do you feel?"

"It's the worst experience in the world," Chong says. "And yes, I feel guilty. But then, I feel guilty about everything. About sitting here, not working, about spending money for drinks—"

"You have a daughter, too, right?"

"Yes," Chong says. "I miss her all to hell."

"At least I don't have kids. Then again, if I had kids maybe I wouldn't be divorced. Seems like we broke up over nothing."

Chong is curious about this, but believes he also should not pry into it. Nancy says nothing for a while, and Chong, to keep the conversation alive, asks her if she is native to Lake Ecstasy.

"Seems like it," Nancy says. "But by Yankee standards I guess I'm a newcomer. I followed my husband here about ten years ago." Though Phil had a Ph.D. in zoology and Nancy had a master's in history—they had met at the University of Wisconsin—they found it impossible to land jobs, were always considered "overeducated," and it was one of the strains on their marriage that Phil was working as a foreman at the Milliken apple orchards rather than in some university or commercial laboratory. Coming from the Midwest, they had found the region of Lake Ecstasy beautiful, so beautiful that it almost compensated them for the sparsity of their income, the meagerness of their home, the waste, as Phil saw it, of their educations.

"But I guess I endured that a little better than Phil," Nancy says. "Anyway, that's water over the dam. I promised myself I wouldn't rehash all that in public."

"I don't mind listening," Chong says.

"I know you don't," Nancy says. "You're a sweetheart."

"Ho!" Chong laughs. "Not likely."

"A real bastard, I know."

"Well, it's true. I am. A stubborn bastard."

"I can see that in you," Nancy says. "That's O.K. I'm kind of stubborn myself sometimes."

"You can endure a lot of pain?"

"You bet I can," Nancy says. "When I was a kid, we used to have a contest, to see who could keep their bare feet against the electric fence the longest. I always won." She grins. "And once, I remember, I was riding a horse in the woods too fast, of course, and I caught a branch right here, under the ear, in the side of the throat. See the scar?" She lifts her hair so Chong can inspect the smooth creamy-white neck.

The sight of it makes Chong's heart beat fast. There is just a dimple of a scar, and he longs to touch it. "I thought I looked you over pretty good," he says. "I didn't notice any scars."

"I kept my hair down so you wouldn't." Nancy laughs. "Anyway, the damned branch went right through, like an arrow. I stayed on the horse, broke the branch, rode three miles back home like that. My father was feeding the pigs when I came up to him smeared with blood, and I said, 'Dad, I think I cut myself.' My dad said he got weak in the knees when he saw me. He drove to the hospital like a drunk."

"Did you cry?"

"I cried because I was scared to be left alone in the hospital, yeah. But not because of the pain."

"I hate pain," Chong says. "I hate gouging my hands when I carve, or banging my knuckles on a pipe, all that stuff."

"Me, too," Nancy says.

"But I'm like you," Chong says. "Sometimes I have a headache so bad it blinds me, but I don't stop for it. I feel worse if I let it get the better of me."

Nancy nods in agreement, regards Chong with an intensity that makes him nervous. "Sometimes I think I'd have been better off if I'd have had less tolerance for pain. It's amazing how I let myself be so unhappy for so long. Why did I do that? I wasted a lot of good years allowing myself to be so miserable."

"Now I'll tell you a story." Chong looks away a moment to get some relief from Nancy's gaze. "About being miserable for a long time. But in this case I couldn't get away from it."

"That's what we all think."

"No, really. I was trapped. This was when I came from Hong Kong to Hawaii, on my way to America. How I got to Hong Kong is too long a story, but I lucked into a job on a freighter there. O.K.?"

"Right." Nancy smiles, settles back with her drink.

"I was put in the engine room. I did whatever I was told to, mainly pulling levers on steam valves, and endlessly oiling shafts and checking hydraulic levels. Everything hot, always hot. There was one job I hated, that gave me nightmares."

Nancy waits. Chong continues.

"There was a bearing connected to the drive shaft that turned the propeller outside, which drove the ship. On the trip to Hong Kong, the bearing overheated and cracked, and the result was that the whole ship vibrated so terribly they had to take the bearing out. But the bearing also supplied tension to the drive shaft, so that you couldn't put any great pressure on it, any great speed or power, until it was replaced."

"They did this in Hong Kong, obviously," Nancy says.

"Yes and no," Chong says. "You forget that in 1938 and '39, China was nowhere near being an industrial nation. There was no store you could run to and buy a ball bearing, chromed steel, almost three feet in diameter. You might have been able to order one from England, but then you would have to wait three months for it."

"So what did they do?"

"They had a bearing made. In fact they had three or four bearings made. But they were made of wood."

"Wood! How long could *they* last?"

"That's why they had so many made. Meanwhile, down in the engine room we had this one huge wooden bearing taking up the space where the broken metal one once was. As you, my educated friend, will know, such a bearing very quickly becomes hot and threatens to catch fire. In fact, when it started to smoke my job was to cool it down. This was the job I hated." Chong pauses, sips his beer.

"Go on! Don't stop now."

"What I had to do was crawl down a catwalk into the area above the bearing, and I opened a portal there and a whole big jet of water came blasting in. We'd flood the compartment, close the portal, and then pump the water out."

"But nobody could close the portal!" Nancy says. "The pressure would be tremendous."

"You bet I closed it. If I didn't, we'd get too much water down there and have hell to pay. It would slosh up against the hot pipes and against the boiler, and we'd all come out of there red as cooked crabs."

"How often did you have to do this?"

"Once every two hours."

"But wasn't it dangerous?"

"When I opened the portal, there was a tremendous rush of water, and it could have knocked me off the catwalk onto the bearings and the drive shaft, and that would have turned me to paste."

"And you did this from Hong Kong to Hawaii?"

"And now you see," Chong says, "why I jumped ship in lovely Kalihi. No, before you ask, we didn't dock in Pearl Harbor or Honolulu, because the fees there were too high for our low-budget ass-grabbing captain."

"Were you the only one who opened the portal?"

"On my shifts, yes. Because I was the only Chink. On the other shifts they drew lots."

Chong made his way to Honolulu by foot and used the seaman's papers he had been given in Hong Kong to talk his way into a berth on a steamer that shipped mahogany, teak, and fabrics to San Francisco. There, Chong was taken under the wing of the ship's chief engineer, who admired his spunk and took pity on Chong, mistakenly believing him to be an orphan.

"Maybe I missed my big chance in San Francisco," Chong says. "The guys on the ship kind of wanted me to be on call when the ship came into port, and make some deliveries. Since I had no identity in America and a ship's records were easily disposed of, they seemed to think I'd be perfect for the job."

"Smuggling what?"

"Yes. I never knew. Opium, I suppose. What else?"

"It had to be opium," Nancy says.

"And one of the reasons I said no, you know, was that now I was in America and I thought I don't need to risk that. I can do anything and get rich. Wasn't I in for a surprise!"

"When did you start painting, anyway?" Nancy asks. "I never heard you say, not that we've talked all that much."

"Christ, I don't know," Chong says. "I must have been interested in it when I was very young, because I remember one of the pleasures of a typing job I had was that I could steal paper—two or three sheets at a time, in my shirt. I kept it neatly stacked under a cot. It was terrible pulpy paper, so rough that sometimes the unprocessed wood chips, very small, would fall right out, leaving little holes in the page. The paper was like thin newsprint, gray and flimsy. But I treasured it. I remember it was too absorbent for ink, but very nice for charcoal."

"Do you have any drawings from those days?" Nancy uncrosses her legs, relaxing, leans against the bar.

"No. I left everything behind. I traveled with almost nothing."

Oddly enough, Chong can remember some of the drawings he made as a child. Some were quite crude, even violent, perhaps expressing the anger he could not otherwise display toward his father—a horse down with a broken leg, a runaway cart smashing into a stone wall, a pig hanging by its feet, a house in flames. But also small things rendered with affection—a cat sleeping in the sun, his sister's wooden shoes in a stand of flowers, mists capping the strange phallic hills so typical of the region. And military things galore—weapons, soldiers, the machines of combat, cannons coughing a black smudge of smoke, bombs and shells bursting in sharp thick slashes of black and red. What a world! Chong thinks now. Unending wars, endless terror.

"I was thinking as you were talking," Nancy says. "About Red, who is apparently standing me up, the bastard. He must have been through some hell in Viet Nam, but he doesn't *seem* like a scared person, you know what I mean? He can be downright jolly, to use an abused word."

"You like him."

Nancy smiles, then purses her lips in reflection. "Between you and me, yes. A lot. I just don't trust him."

"No?"

"Maybe it's my problem, not his."

"Maybe you don't trust anybody now. Any man."

The little muscles around Nancy's mouth flicker, and she sips her drink quickly, finishing it off. The mouth tells the truth sometimes, Chong thinks, it will give you away. Nancy's mouth is not relaxed, the corners of it are always jumping, showing nervous dimples. Otherwise she seems possessed of an animal calm, like a fox with its chin on crossed paws, both quiet and ready to sprint at once.

"I don't even trust you." Nancy pokes Chong in the ribs. "Not even you, you mean, stubborn bastard. You old fart. You old turn-on."

Chong laughs, enjoying the teasing, embarrassed. He cannot help desiring her. How futile!

"I guess I'm just not ready to remarry," Nancy says. "You know? Nobody can be everything to another person. It's impossible. I'll tell you the truth, Chong. I'm a different person with every man I'm with. I find myself actually changed, find new people inside me. Some I like, some I don't. Do you understand?"

"I think so," Chong says. "But I don't think you're schizophrenic. You have a center."

"You think so? I don't know. All I know is I don't like repeating myself too much." She turns on the barstool and hooks a thumb toward the door. "That bastard Barber hasn't shown up *yet.*"

"I'm glad," Chong says. "I get you for a while. Maybe he's at a fire."

"He isn't at a fire. He's fixing a damn, what do you call them, road grader. He thinks the damn road grader's more important than I am."

"Probably not," Chong says. "Maybe he thinks you understand better than the highway department."

"Just like a man. Defending each other. Why should you care if I get mad at Barber?"

"He could at least give you a call," Chong admits.

"At least!" Nancy says. She laughs in exasperation. "Maybe I'll just haul my ass across the street there and see how he's coming along."

"Couldn't hurt," Chong says.

"Except it's not real dignified." Nancy spins away and knocks open the door with a sharp thrust of her arm. A blow like that, Chong thinks, and you'd feel it. He can see Nancy through the screen, pausing, sweeping her hair over her shoulders, and the look on her face for an instant is one of anxiety; or is it, Chong wonders, just the light on the porch that has given her such a cast? He finishes his drink, his mind pleased to cling to the image of Nancy, but disturbed a little, too, by the glimpse he has had of a private place in her world where she is not happy. I'm getting too plastered, he thinks, and imagining things. Time to go home.

Not long after, Chong feels his way to the bedroom, strips, and falls on the bed. A breeze from the window caresses him like the fingers of a woman, and he is quite content, imagines that if he was not quite so tired this would be a grand night for a swim in the pond. Sometime tomorrow, when he has tired of painting, he will pick blueberries. The shores of Lake Ecstasy should be laden with them now, awaiting trespassers. He knows he will find a ruckus of birds there, and maybe also a clutch of skinny-dippers, who like the thin stretch of sandy beach hidden by ancient overarching pines.

Perhaps because he is so tired, so out of rhythm with himself, Chong does not sleep well, and after a few hours of tossing is suddenly wide awake and sitting on the edge of the bed in a sweat. He has heard a terrible noise, like a spoon falling on the kitchen floor, and he feels absolutely defenseless without clothes on, and absurdly unable to decide whether he should grab his trousers or a chakra from the dresser drawer. Then he hears footsteps outside the door to his room, catapults himself across the bed, hides behind it, telling himself that he will leave by the window.

"Stop right there," he cries. "I'll shoot you dead."

"Chong don't."

The voice comes to him in an almost strangled gasp, and Chong cannot believe he recognizes it.

"Don't Chong. It's me, Ginny."

"One minute." He snaps on a light, grabs his trousers. As he is pulling them on, Ginny steps into the bedroom, a hand shielding her eyes, her hair matted and wild, jeans and shirt muddied, a smear of caked blood under her nose. With a little cry, she falls onto the bed. Chong pulls her hands away from her face, sees that from her temple to her jaw her face is purple, and swollen.

"What happened?"

"I fell," Ginny says. "Let me sleep here, please."

"Don't even think of going to sleep," Chong warns her. "You look like you may have a concussion. Get up!"

"I'm so *tired.*"

"I'll get you some tea, and then you're going to Royalton."

"Royalton? Why?"

"That's where the hospital is."

"I just fell," Ginny says. "I'll be all right."

"Bullshit." Chong pulls her by the hands from the bed, unnerved by Ginny's cry of protest. She's so thin, she can't have had a thing to eat for weeks!

God damn it to hell, Chong thinks as he slams the kettle on the stove. No goddamn gas in my car, and everything is closed. He shakes Ginny as she begins to nod at the kitchen table.

"Listen. Don't sleep. You could go into a coma. Do you have a headache?"

"Yes . . . no . . . I don't know."

"Who did this to you?"

"*Nobody.*"

"My ass." Chong heads for the telephone, dials Barber's number. The telephone buzzes a long time, but Red finally answers. Chong explains that he needs a car or some gasoline, he has to drive to Royalton, an emergency, and he's out of gas. Barber seems only minimally coherent.

"I'm pretty screwed up," he tells Chong. "You get here, and you can take my pickup. I'll come along."

"I can drive, I just need gas," Chong says.

"See you in five," Barber says.

Chong switches off the gas on the stove and hustles Ginny out to his car. He swears as the old Ford growls, reluctant to turn over. When it starts at last, the engine ticks and rattles like an antique sewing machine.

"Who did this to you?" Chong demands as they drive to Barber's. "Come on. Talk. You've got to stay awake."

"I don't want to talk about what happened."

"Talk about anything. How did you get here? Where have you been? I thought you were with your father in Florida."

"My father's dead," Ginny says.

"Don't screw around with me," Chong says. "What's the story?"

"Taylor took me to Florida," Ginny says.

"I heard that much."

"I got there, and I stayed with my so-called father, who just left me at home all day, and at night he'd just sit in a chair and stare at me."

"Didn't he find you a job or something?"

"He barely even spoke to me," Ginny wails. "Once in a while he would say, 'You look like your mother.' But not much else. It was creepy. I couldn't understand it. He just sat there with his hands folded between his knees staring at me."

Chong doesn't know what to say. "What did you do? How did you get back?"

"My head hurts," Ginny says. "I don't want to talk."

When Chong swings into Barber's driveway, he sees lights on in the garage, a pickup in one of the bays, already running.

"What are we doing here?" Ginny's tone is one of alarm.

"Changing cars. Come on."

Barber is at the window as soon as Chong stops the car. "Can you handle it? I'm a little . . . um . . . unconnected."

"No sweat," Chong says.

"You know the way and all?"

"Yeah."

"Jesus," Barber says, nodding toward Ginny. "What happened? That's quite a bruise."

"She fell," Chong says. "I want to make sure she doesn't have a concussion."

"Wait one minute. I'll get some ice."

"Will that help?"

Barber shrugs. "It'll help keep her awake."

"O.K.," Chong says.

They change cars, and in a moment Barber hands Ginny a plastic bag filled with ice. Then they are on the highway to Royalton, and Chong realizes he is without a shirt.

"Keep talking," he commands Ginny.

"Where was I?"

"Your father was staring at you."

She yawns. "Yeah. So some kids I met took me to Orlando. There's a place there, it's supposed to help runaway kids. A lot of kids run away to Florida."

"I've heard that," Chong says.

"So they called my mother, and a whole lot of crap, and they get my father to come there. And you know what he tells them?" Ginny's voice rises in disbelief, and agony.

"Ah, shit," Chong says.

"He says he's not my dad. He says I'm not his daughter! He asks them, he says, 'Look at us. You think she looks a bit like me?' "

Chong swears, glances at Ginny, who leans against the door, eyes closed.

"Don't close your eyes," Chong says. Louder, "*Hear me?*"

"Yes." Ginny sits up.

"So how'd you get back?"

Ginny shivers. "Parker and Taylor came and got me."

"Oh, boy," Chong says.

"You know what they did?"

"No." Keep talking, Chong thinks. Talk.

"They made a vacation of it. They came down on their motor-cycles. The whole Club came down, six or seven of 'em."

"And you came back on a motorcycle?"

"The whole damn way. My back's screwed up. I saw nothing but the back of Parker's black jacket for two whole days and nights."

"What happened when you got back?"

"Chong, this is tiring me out. Can't we talk later?"

"I can't have you falling asleep," Chong says. "How's that ice feel?"

"Cold! What'd you think?"

"Your headache gone?"

"No."

"So keep talking. Then what? How long have you been home?"

"About a week."

"How's your mother?" Chong slows down to take a series of sharp curves.

"She can't decide what to do."

"How'd you get beat up?"

"I fell."

"O.K., you fell. That's what I told Barber, and that's what I'll tell the doctors. But you'd better tell me the truth. Was it Parker?"

"Yeah," Ginny says. "Who else?"

"For the usual reasons?"

"Yeah."

"Don't you think this has got to stop? Don't you think we'd better go to the police?"

"No," Ginny says at once, with vehemence.

"Why not?"

"*Because,*" she wails. "I'll die if I go to that goddamned state school."

"But where can you go? Where can you be safe from that man? He should be locked up."

"I can't prove anything," Ginny says. "There's never been a witness."

"I'll testify," Chong says.

Ginny laughs. "I don't think so."

"Of course I will."

"If you say anything," Ginny says, "Parker will show the pictures you made of me."

"God damn it," Chong says.

"That's one of the reasons I got beat."

"What are you talking about? Parker beat you for posing for me?"

"Not for posing."

"What'd he say?"

" 'You're fucking that old Chink, aren't you?' That's what he said. He doesn't see how I could 'fuck that old Chink' and not him."

"This has got to stop," Chong says. "This is insane." A thought strikes him with thunderous force: "And what did you tell him, Ginny? Did you tell Parker that it was true, to hurt him?"

Ginny is silent.

"Well?"

Still Ginny says nothing.

"Ginny, I've got a right to know. I could be in very big trouble."

"My head hurts," Ginny says.

"*Tell me.*"

"That's what I told him," Ginny says.

Chong reels, almost gags. The tires whimper on the dark road. "Thanks a lot," he says.

"I'd never say that in court," Ginny says.

"You wanted your revenge on Parker," Chong says. "And you used me."

"That's not the only reason," Ginny says.

"No?"

"No. He's done something to my mother, Chong. I don't know what it is. She isn't the same as when I left. She's sick or something. But she can't let go of him, and she doesn't want me around."

"Jesus, now what?" Chong feels cold and rolls up the window quickly. "Is it drugs, Ginny?"

Ginny's face is in her hands, and her body trembles.

"Jesus Christ." Chong reaches across the seat and places his hand on Ginny's shoulder a moment, but she flinches from the touch. "You'd better come to stay with me. At least for now. Hear me?"

"Yes," Ginny says, sobering herself slowly. "I want to."

"Because it's better than home," Chong says. "And you could still be with your friends. And . . . because I'm such a good cook."

"And because you have cats," Ginny says. "And a pig, and a crow."

"That makes a lot of sense," Chong says.

"And a room just for me, where I don't have to worry about someone coming after me."

Chong permits himself a wail of grief and confusion. "O.K. Let's get our story straight for the doctors. They're not going to believe it, so we'd better have it pretty well rehearsed."

She was picking blueberries, they decided, on the shores of Lake Ecstasy, fell down a slope coming home after dark. Chong found her stumbling along the highway.

"What about the ice?" Ginny says. "Won't we have to tell them about the ice?"

"Maybe we will," Chong says. "Just say I had it in the truck. In a cooler, O.K.?"

"O.K.," Ginny says. "But I think this is stupid. I don't think we should even go to the hospital."

Chong takes the corner into the hospital emergency entrance a little wide, and one tire bangs over the curb. He parks in front of the EMERGENCY VEHICLES ONLY door, helps Ginny down, and takes her inside. A nurse hurries down the hallway toward them with a wheelchair, and before Chong can launch into an explanation the nurse says, "Mr. Chong? I understand we have a possible concussion here."

"I'm not sure," Chong says. "Better safe than sorry. Mr. Barber must have called?"

"That's right." The nurse asks Ginny her name, has her quickly seated in the wheelchair. "I'm Betty. I'm a friend of Red's, a friend of a friend anyway. If you've parked by the doors, you'd better move your car. Then you can meet us down in Room Three."

Chong nods, hurries back to the truck. He parks across the street from the hospital, sits a moment in the truck trying to calm down. He is afraid of the questions that will be asked, that calls will be made to Ginny's mother, maybe even the police. He is not sure what could happen now; and if he is relieved that Ginny will soon be treated and is surely safe now, he spins with confusion and anger when he thinks of Parker. Is it really Ginny's decision to make on what should be said and done? He groans and returns to the emergency ward.

Betty has Ginny seated on a high cot covered with a stiff white paper. Ginny's legs dangle, swing idly, and she looks very sleepy. In the bright light of the ward, the bruise looks huge, ugly, swollen.

"I've got to ask you for a lot of information which you might not be able to supply." Betty smiles stiffly, apologetically. She has a broad forehead that reflects the glare from the lights, as if her skin is covered with a lotion of some kind; her eyes are a rusty brown; her lips, full. "Red suggests the family might be indigent?"

"I guess he knows the family, too," Chong says. "He's probably right. Her mother's unemployed."

"And no father?"

"No."

"He's dead," Ginny says. "I don't have a father."

"I'm sorry, honey," Betty says. "How're you feeling now? Your head still ache?"

"Yes!" Ginny tries to hold back tears.

In a moment, a young bearded man with round sparkling glasses strides into the room, stethoscope dangling from his neck. He nods perfunctorily to Chong, introduces himself as Dr. Miranda, and tenderly takes Ginny's face in his hands.

"No need to cry," the doctor tells Ginny. "You're going to be O.K. Just tell me if it hurts when I touch you."

Chong sighs with relief.

Ginny, they decide, will spend the night at the hospital under observation. The idea is quite frightening to her at first, and she begs them to allow Chong to stay, too—an impossible demand.

After Ginny has been taken upstairs, washed, and bandaged, the doctor inquires whether Chong is very close to the family.

"I think it's more a matter of there being no one else close by," Chong says.

"It's an unusual bruise for a fall," the doctor says. "No scraped or broken skin."

Chong says nothing to this. "What's a concussion anyway?"

"Actually, it's a bruise on the brain," the doctor tells him. "Right now I don't think she has a concussion."

"What time should I come tomorrow?"

"I'll make my morning rounds before ten," Dr. Miranda says. "Why don't you call us then?"

"Yes." Chong closes his eyes and shakes off a wave of fatigue. When he climbs into the truck again, he is too tired to drive, lies down on the seat, and falls into a tremulous sleep.

When he wakes it is only 4:30 A.M. Chong sees little sense in driving to his home and back again, sits up and dozes for another hour, feeling chilly without a shirt. Then he drives into Royalton, hoping to find a drive-in fast-food restaurant, cuts sharply into a grocery-store parking lot when he spies a Red Shield drop-off bin. He pulls up to the container and without getting out of the truck looks it over. A box of old clothes has been stuffed into the gate, and Chong rolls down the window and begins to sort through them, finds shirts and blouses, leotards, warped shoes, and finally a black and red striped sweater with an ugly green stain along one sleeve. He pulls this on quickly, and though it is a boy's size and a little small—it will ride up over his belt line—Chong supposes it will give him enough dignity to enter a restaurant and later pick up Ginny at the hospital. The box also contains a black and red checkered golfing hat which Chong finds irresistible it is so comic. He adjusts the band on the back, dons it, and admires the demented look it gives him in the rearview mirror. A short distance down the street Chong finds the inevitable Coffee Cup Diner and adds Red's pickup to the collection already bunched around the door.

Chong lingers as long as he can stand it over breakfast, and then at eight o'clock, goes into the streets to wander around Royalton— one of the most boring towns he has ever been in, an unsalted soda cracker, a biscuit without gravy, lumpy mashed potatoes. The only places of interest to him are the Red Shield and Army-Navy surplus stores, neither of which are open at this hour. When the town-hall clock finally peals nine, Chong wanders to the Royalton Library, housed in a renovated church, and reads newspapers under the suspicious eyes of two gray-haired women until it is ten o'clock and he can call the hospital on the library's pay telephone. Ginny, he is told, can be taken home, but is going to require some care and medication, and will not be allowed to engage in any strenuous activities for several days. Dr. Miranda also wants to see her again at the end of the week, and would like Mr. Chong to call him at his earliest convenience.

"He wants me to call him? Why?"

"I don't know," the secretary says. "I'm just reading his note here. I believe he has some questions about the family situation."

"Oh, yeah," Chong says. He obtains the doctor's phone number and office hours, then cradles the receiver. Maybe Miranda would know what to do about Parker, Chong thinks. The policeman he consulted before said the testimony of a doctor could be crucial— and if Miranda could not testify on sexual abuse, since he had no proof of it, he could certainly testify on physical violence, couldn't he? The next question is what would happen to Ginny then? Whatever it was, it could not be as terrible as what was happening to her now. All right, Chong decides. I've got to do something. Maybe Miranda is the place to start. Maybe Miranda will know what to do.

Ginny is brought into the lobby in a wheelchair, and her head is wrapped in a loose towel.

"They cut my hair off," she says in indignation. "Can you believe it?"

The nurse who is wheeling her, says, "It's not all of it off, dear. Just a patch. In three weeks you won't even notice."

"Three weeks!" Ginny says in disgust. "Do you believe it?"

"You seem to be feeling better," Chong says. "At least you seem to have some spunk today."

"Get me out of here." Ginny looks at him closely now and rolls her eyes. "That hat. That sweater."

"Your chapeau isn't the most elegant I've ever seen, either." Chong helps Ginny out of the chair.

The nurse hands Chong a clipboard. "Sign this, won't you? And that green slip is for you, a prescription you should fill right away."

As they leave the hospital, Chong hesitates a moment to regard the reflection of himself and Ginny in the smoky-dark glass door. The dim light of the portico beyond and the amber haze of the glass give Chong the impression of looking at a snapshot of himself through the eyes of his grandchildren. Imagine being remembered like this, in his too-tight striped sweater and checkered hat, his rounded belly and grizzled face; and on his arm this waif, bruised, turbaned, wearing crumpled clothes, hanging her head in embarrassment.

"Christ, we'd turn heads in New York City," he teases.

"Just get me out of here," Ginny says. "Take me home."

"That's the next question. Where's 'home'?"

She grips his arm fiercely. "Aren't I staying with you? *Please?*"

"Yes," Chong says, dreading the decision already. "I can't send you back to Parker, that's for sure."

11
Bad
Girls

J im bit back on the craving the first two beers had awakened in
him. No, he didn't want to be a drunk again. Or did he? He
thrashed around the bar talking, trying to stay busy, sidled up
to Red, who was right now trying hard, and in vain, to persuade
Nancy Wallace that she and her sidekick, Betty, would be vastly
improved by accompanying the two men to their cabin home for
some popcorn and music and . . . whatever.

Frustration was meanwhile written all over Red's face. His baseball cap was pulled to his eyebrows and his lips were pursed in a
serious way, a way that gave his thick mustache a walruslike bristle.

Nancy and Betty had stumbled into the Mountaintop Lounge a
few minutes before. Red was under the impression they had showed
up because he had invited them, at least because he had alerted
them that he and Jim would be there. Since Red knew the women
well, Jim felt a little like a third wheel on a bicycle. They had tried
to clarify it all for him, but Jim was not paying good attention. Betty
had first met Red when he was taken to Royalton Hospital for
smoke inhalation after a forest fire. Was that it? Betty was a nurse;
Nancy, as Jim knew well, was Red's cause in life. It was Red's belief,
he had confided earlier, that Betty was ripe for the plucking, just the
right kind of woman for Jim in his present straits—"Quiet. Discreet.
Lovely. Not looking for a home." But both women were demurring
now. They said they had been on their way to a movie in Royalton

and had stopped at the Mountaintop for one drink. But Betty's Datsun pickup couldn't be started again and was sitting useless in the parking lot outside. They really had not planned to meet Red and Jim, and it was just a very awkward coincidence.

"After all, Red," Nancy said, "what do you think we are? Call girls or something?"

Not in the mood for any games, Jim had taken the women at their word and moved off to play some pool with a group of volunteer firemen from Lake Ecstasy village. They talked about what jobs might be coming open in the area—an oil deliveryman was retiring, the Early brothers were looking for guys to cut cordwood—and encouraged Jim to make inquiries, gave him names to contact, phone numbers to call. When the volunteers left, Jim moved back to his space at the bar beside Red and tried to lift himself out of his malaise, the awful sense he had of just wanting to drink himself numb, as he knew it would be easy to do, to slip back into the old self-destructive habits that had plagued him for years. He was also embarrassed by the courting Red had taken on for both of them. Anna was probably . . . Jim couldn't complete the thought.

Nancy was the livelier and the more talkative of the two women. Jim liked her but thought she was a little too quick and defensive sometimes, maybe because she was so used to parrying propositions in her waitressing job and didn't take many, if any, of them seriously. She was also more attractive than Betty, Jim thought, Betty the silent brown-haired one with the sometimes annoying tic of squeezing her eyes shut tight for a moment. Maybe it was just new contact lenses. Maybe she was nuts. Jim wasn't sure he cared. He glanced at her, thought her a little overweight but not undesirable. Jim did not think of himself as God's gift to women, but he resented a little the idea that he would be considered, and paired with, the "second best," as that was apparently determined in this unspoken system. It wasn't exactly a great boost to his ego to think he was picking up the slack in this situation, and Betty must have felt something similar, which would account for her reticence and little flashes of defensiveness, and her hanging back. She was not really impolite, but neither did she show more than an occasional spark of interest— not that Jim fanned even those brief flames. God damn it, he wanted to be distracted from the desire to be drunk, to drink past memory, and he could not seem to manage the distraction himself, and it was a good bet the women—they were evaporating before his eyes—were not going to provide it either. Would Anna be in a bar like this? Listening to some slick bastards in computers . . .

"The only reason you want us to come over there," Nancy said, "is that you probably have a pile of dishes in the sink and a heap of laundry lying on the bedroom floor."

"That's utterly outrageous," Red said. "Jim and I keep immaculate quarters, and we don't expect maid service from our women. That's a slanderous accusation."

"You know what they say." Nancy spoke to Red, but she eyed Jim now with frank curiosity. Her brown hair fell in a disarray of thick ringlets around her face, which was full and pleasant. "It begins when you sink in his arms, and ends with your arms in the sink."

"Nancy here"—Red indicated her with a nod of his head—"she's got this criminal notion that men in this neck of the woods are not in tune with the twentieth century. She thinks we're the barbarian horde or something."

"It's a deliberate lie," Jim said, trying to engage in the banter. "She's seen me in the Royalton Laundromat."

"I thought you were stealing underwear." She laughed.

She drinks margaritas, Jim realized. A few of those should put her on her fanny. Unless.

"Stealing underwear, huh?" Red nodded his head gravely. "I never thought of it before, but bad as our luck's been, it may come to that."

"Why blame it on bad luck?" Nancy teased.

"Watch out now," Red said. "I know what you're going to say, and it's going to be nasty."

"There are lots of things you could blame it on."

"You're going too far now," Red said.

"Like unfinished floors, and windows that aren't sashed."

"Well, O.K." Red shrugged. "I stand accused. There is a lot of work to be done at my place. On the other hand, none of the *women* ever volunteer to lift a hammer. Oh, no."

"Or you could blame it on your ugly face."

"Unfair!" Red howled. "Jim's not ugly. Why do you think I let him hang around? Christ, I figured there'd be a line at the cabin door with him around."

"Could be," Nancy said. "I take it back on Jim's half of it."

"This woman knows how to grind a man down." Red sighed. He

stood up and ordered drinks for everyone from the bartender with a wave of his hand.

Jim sipped his beer and stared into the banks of bottles across from him. He wondered how many he could drink before the alcohol killed him, if it was really possible to commit suicide by booze. He guessed he could do six margaritas with no trouble, and he was tempted to play the "what's-that-you're-drinking—maybe-I'll-try-one-of-those" routine. Christ, what a feeling, as if he had landed on a planet with three times the gravity of earth.

Red elbowed him. "Hey. Nancy's wondering if we know anything about fixing Datsuns. Her friend Betty there—remember Betty?—has got a Datsun that won't even start. That's why they're even here in the first place, if memory serves correct."

"I think I forgot how to fix Datsuns," Jim said. "I'm afraid these nice girls are going to have to stay here and drink with us all night."

Red turned back to the women. "It wasn't what we planned on doing tonight, you know? I mean, we've been workin' all day, and fixing cars—it's dark out there, and hot, for Christ's sake—that just wasn't top priority."

"Aw, come on," Nancy said. "Aren't we friends?"

"Talk about exploitation," Red said.

Jim fell away from the talk again. He didn't have the energy to keep up the games. What the hell would it amount to even if the women did come back to the cabin? Squeaky bedspring blues, Red had called it. You try to outsqueak the other guy, louder and longer, because it's such a drag lying there with your woman listening to the other guy's bedsprings squeak on and on after you're spent. Or the other woman keeps hollering, or laughing, or something. You keep thinking about the other bed. About Anna in bed. There, thought it, God damn it. Wonder who she's with, what he's like. What they do.

Jim regarded himself and Red and the two women in the mirror. What was the special, the unique reason for any of them to sleep together—for fucking, let's call it by its right name, Jim thought—except selfishness? The illusion of special interest was pleasant, and the lovemaking—fucking, come on—was sometimes exciting and fun and sometimes melodramatic, and sometimes even a little serious, a little engaging and corrupting and captivating. But the mornings rubbed all that out. He had seen women literally panic—What the hell am I doing here?—and he had felt the panic and the disgust himself. How did I get into this? Who is this woman? What have I done? He hadn't even had a real good look at this Betty, and she didn't seem any more inclined to talk than he was. Suppose they ended up together as part of the Friendly Foursome?

"Hey, space cadet." Red elbowed him again. "You're not paying much attention here, but I believe these beautiful young women are offering us a deal we can't refuse."

"A deal?"

"We fix their Datsun, they fix us breakfast."

"Well, just what is the problem with this Datsun anyway?"

"It won't start," Betty said. It was the first time she had spoken, as far as Jim could remember.

"Well, what does it sound like?"

"Dead, completely. Or maybe just a little click, or a buzz."

"Oh, oh," Red said.

"Yeah," Jim said. "We could be letting ourselves in for a big project here. Are you sure we want to go through with this?"

Red grimaced. "I gave my word."

"Then we have no choice." Jim finished his beer. "Excuse me a minute," he said and headed for the men's room. As he stood up to the urinal, Red came in.

"Well, pardner, what do you think?"

"I think you're a bandit," Jim said. "A sleaze even."

"You still have those battery terminal brushes in the glove compartment?"

"Yeah," Jim said. "But don't you think we ought to make it look a little more complicated? *Mystify* it a little?"

"On the other hand, we could dazzle them with the power of our magic. They'll be grateful, so grateful if we fix it fast and let them know it was no problem."

"Look," Jim said. "I'll go out there right now and clean those terminals. Then when we leave, you just sort of pull some mumbo-jumbo and tell Betty to start it."

"Beautiful," Red said. "We'll blow their minds. I'll do my Viet Namese fix-engine dance, some shit like that."

"Right."

"It's that blue Datsun out there, with the white cap on the bed. And while you're at it, see if you can find out if there is a mattress in the back of that thing. I always wondered."

"Any bets?"

"She wouldn't dare," Red said. "This is too small a town."

"Bullshit," Jim said. "I say there's a mattress in there. She doesn't seem the type, but that type never seems the type, and is. You follow me?"

"You're on. Two bucks?"

"I mean, why does she have a little camping-type pickup in the first place? Two bucks says it's not because she loves the field and stream."

"And I say she's a regular schoolmarm, easiest two bucks I ever made."

Jim slipped out the back door of the bar to the parking lot, and his first thought was just to run, to run out, break away from the joint, the beer, the game with the women. The night was clear and warm, the stars were vivid, and the nearby stream tumbled down the slope past the mock waterwheel with a summery tintinnabulation. The alcohol haze and craving flooded him, but he shook it off and crossed the short distance to his truck, where he found the battery terminal brushes and a screwdriver in the glove compartment. In a moment, he opened the hood on the Datsun, twisted the connecting cables off the battery—white-crusted with deposits as he suspected—and with his brushes scrubbed the terminals and the contacts, then replaced them and tightened them down. The job took about three minutes, but Jim stayed out a while more, breathing the warm air down, the night, resigning himself to the nonsense. Under the stars, nonsense. O.K., so that's the program. Before he went in, he cupped his hands around his eyes and leaned against the rear window on the cap of Betty's pickup. He could make out very little—there seemed to be a garbage pail in one corner and a box of books or thick magazines in the other—but there was certainly no mattress on the floor. Maybe she wasn't the type she didn't seem to be after all.

He was a little disappointed actually, not because he might lose two dollars to Red—he could always lie about it, after all—but because it deflated his fantasy of Betty's potential, what went on inside the camper on that blue and white Datsun.

Inside the bar again, Jim found a beer waiting for him at a table that Red and the women had moved to.

"Now we can see you at least," Nancy said. "We thought you were Red's shadow."

"That's what I thought," Jim said. He took Betty's hand as playfully as he could manage it. "Nice to meet you," he said, and was surprised when she gave his fingers an eager squeeze.

"I was just telling these ladies about the kind of respect the Viet Namese showed for American machines, and the kind of almost like a voodoo power they had over our engines, I mean, once they got to know them."

"He's so full of bullshit," Nancy said.

"I wouldn't knock it," Jim said seriously. "Those people know a lot of things we have yet to discover. After all, that is an ancient civilization."

"My brother was in Viet Nam," Betty said.

Jim looked at her now with more interest. He was a little in suspense about what she would say, because it could be very stupid, very insensitive; it could end with just that remark, or she might know something about what had gone on there, and how some of the veterans felt about it. She was a nurse, true, but in a way the remark was out of bounds, not part of this game they were playing, because it opened up new, possibly scary territory—whether she was aware of it or not, that was the question.

"He told me a different story," Betty went on. "He said that he once gave a small group of people in a village a pump to help them irrigate their fields. They had been carrying the water in leaky little buckets or something, and he went through a lot of red tape and got this little gasoline-engine pump, which did all the work they were doing in a tenth of the time, something like that."

"I think I know this story," Red said, "but go on. I'm curious."

"He showed them how to use it and everything. But when he came back after a week or so, the thing wasn't running, and the people were carrying the water in buckets again."

"Yeah, right. Exactly," Red said.

"So my brother tries to fix this engine. But when he starts it up, it starts, and when he pumps water with it, it pumps fine. So he's puzzled, right? He wants to know how come they're not using the pump."

Red cackled and slapped himself on the knee. "I love it, I love it."

"Of course, he didn't get a real good answer. People are trying to be nice. After all, he's got a machine gun hanging from his shoulder— No, he didn't say that part."

"Don't editorialize," Red said. "You'll get in trouble. Me and Jim carried those weapons, too, you know. At least for a while."

"You told me you were a mechanic," Nancy said.

"I was. I am. Over there I fixed helicopters."

"Anyway, let Betty tell her story," Jim said.

"Well, that's about it," Betty said. "I mean, they were very embarrassed about not using a perfectly good pump. Then one of the people allowed as how it might be a little too loud and might be offensive to their ancestors, who were buried in the fields. And another said, you know, the ancestors expect you to work in a way that shows reverence for the land where they are buried. And anyway, the pump pumped too much water, and there was a certain number of turns each family member was supposed to take each day, and if they didn't do it, they felt cursed or something."

"Your brother," Jim said, "how did he feel about that?"

"He was kind of miffed. He felt they were being kind of ignorant."

"Does he still feel that way?"

"Far as I know," Betty said. "I don't think he has any good feelings about those people. It's just not possible for him."

I don't want to know any more about him, Jim thought. Don't say anything else. This could mean anything, this could get us way off the track, could take us to hell.

"He was wounded." Red made it a statement, as if he knew.

"Right." Betty paused, and said simply, "He lost a leg."

Red nodded. "Yeah. A lot of anger there. A lot of hate." He looked around and waved to the waitress and quickly changed the subject. "So you're saying you don't think the Viet Namese have the engine voodoo I'm talking about?"

"Hell, no," Nancy said.

"Well, I'm going to prove it to you, because it was taught to me, and I use it all the time," Red said. "I'm going to fix that truck of Betty's, and I'm not going to lay a hand on it."

"Horseshit."

"Well, O.K., I guess there's no use talking any more about it, but I mean to give it a try when we get out of here. One thing you have to understand, though, is that too much doubt will scotch the whole thing."

"You're doomed, then," Nancy said, "because I doubt it all the way."

"All I'm asking is for a temporary suspension of your disbelief," Red said. "That's all."

"Oh, brother," Nancy said. "Maybe it'd just be easier to have the thing towed to a nice safe American garage."

"Well, you can disabuse yourself of the idea anyway," Red said. "There is no such thing."

"As a safe garage?"

"I'm not kidding." Red moved his chair closer to Nancy.

"You wouldn't want to play some pool, would you?" Jim asked Betty.

"I'd be embarrassed. I'm no good at it."

"I guess you don't shoot much at the hospital, do you?"

"No." Belatedly, Betty laughed.

"I'm not good at pool, either, but tonight what I'm really lousy at is sitting still. I'm not trying to be rude, I'm just antsy, you know."

"You're not being rude. This isn't a date." She looked him over in a kind of sidelong way, and Jim pretended not to notice. "Well, I'll give it a try," she said. "Promise not to laugh."

"No way." They rose and moved to the pool table, chalked their cues, put the quarter in the machine, and listened to the rumble of the balls as they dropped into the bay where Jim could reach them. They were cool in his hands, delightful in their weight and smooth perfection. Once he had thrown a cue ball at a man who had pulled a pistol on him, a one-legged man, an ex-sailor, and the ball sailed the length of the bar and through a window. They were perfect, very satisfying to throw, and they were always cool to the touch. Suppose he told Betty this story, and how the man lost his nerve and didn't, couldn't pull the trigger after all? Would she think that he was violent and be afraid, or forgive him for his wilder youth? Women could be amazingly forgiving, after all. Sometimes they even seemed to be attracted to the cruel and the reckless. Ah, Christ, who knows what people want? Jim thought. The cue ball is perfect, you can't ask for anything better, anything trickier to control, anything nicer to touch.

They played a slow game, a game of "slop." The mild concentration required helped Jim's state of mind; even the deep green of the felt on the table helped to relax him.

"I hope Red didn't make you feel like this was supposed to be a blind date or anything," Jim said. "Really, I had no expectations."

"He's always got something to say, doesn't he?"

"Do you really blame him, though?"

"Blame him? For what?"

"For what do you think? Trying to get us together."

"Everybody likes to get laid." Betty was looking down the cue stick at her target and did not see Jim blanch at the frankness of her remark. "It's just that he's got a lot of . . . of choice, doesn't he? What does he think of us, Nancy and me?"

Jim took a shot, which he made difficult in order to make it interesting, and narrowly missed. "I hadn't noticed the lineup at the cabin door," he said, "not that I'm a great observer, either. From what he's told me about you and Nancy, he thinks you're good people."

"Good people, huh?"

"Yeah."

"Not just body heat."

"Not just. But hope springs eternal, I guess. I'm not sorry I met you. I hope I'll see you again. Can I?"

"Sure you can. But I'm going on nights in a while."

"Any time you say."

"Well, let me think about it. It's just the job makes things complicated. I'll see what my days off are going to be. I'll call you."

"Fine," Jim said.

"I will call you."

"Sure." Who gave us these lines? Jim wondered. The exchange rolled out of them almost automatically, without thought. Even the whores in Saigon had had their little patter down, practiced, the only English they knew or had to know, enough to answer the usual, almost inevitable questions. Where you from, GI? What your outfit? How like Nam, sodja? You buy me a drink? You like fucky-sucky me, my man?

About midnight they all left the bar together. Red had his arm around Nancy's waist, but Betty and Jim walked side by side without touching. Jim was a little irritated, not only because there was no promise for him in the rest of the night but because he wanted more to drink and battled this craving. His hand brushed against Betty's, but she pulled it away and put it in her jeans pocket.

"All right now," Red said, spreading his arms and stopping the procession. "I want you, Betty, to hold your ignition key right out in front of you, and use it like a sight to stare at the engine of that little Jap *maicar*. Did you know that's what they call automobiles in Japan? *Maicars*. Really."

Betty held up her key as instructed, but her mouth was twisted in a way that said she felt like a fool.

"O.K., now you two fold your hands, like in prayer, that's right, and say *Om*."

"You're nuts, Red," Nancy said, but she began to hum as commanded, and Jim joined in.

Red hopped to the front of the Datsun and, after bowing before it, shot his hands toward the pickup, gobbled like a turkey, and stamped his feet.

"Cawa dawa maga wobelo be go go go," he chanted, and then repeated this strange cry as he hopped around the car. Then he bowed again. "It's all yours, Betty, if you'd be so kind."

Betty shook her head in mock disgust, slipped into the driver's seat, and put the key into the ignition.

"Never," Nancy said.

The Datsun growled and popped to life.

Red shrugged. "I don't know why, but it works every time."

"Hey, wait a minute," Nancy said. "What is this? What did you do?"

"You saw what I did," Red protested. "Now let's get some breakfast. You made a deal."

"But you didn't *do* anything. That's no fair."

"I just laid out some of the most powerful magic on earth, and you tell me I didn't *do* anything. God!" Red slapped his forehead. "Women are weird."

"What did you do? You must have fixed it before."

"Not me," Red said. "I never touched it."

"Then Jim fixed it."

"But when?" Jim asked. "When did I have a minute?"

Betty revved the engine of the Datsun.

"Jim, you go with Betty there, huh? Nancy and I will meet you at the cabin." Red urged Jim gently in the direction of the Datsun.

"What's the story?" Betty said when Jim slid into the seat beside her.

"They want us to follow them to Red's cabin."

Betty jammed the Datsun into gear and pulled up behind the pickup Red was driving. "Really, what did you guys do to my truck?"

"I cleaned the battery contacts," Jim said. "It took about a minute."

"Is that all?"

"That's all that was required," Jim said.

"I *was* surprised when it started," Betty said. "I couldn't believe it."

"Red puts on quite a show, doesn't he?"

"That's Red," Betty agreed.

They drove in silence for a while, and then Betty asked, "Is Nancy planning to stay, do you know? I mean, stay the night?"

"I don't know," Jim said. "You'll have to ask Nancy."

"I've got to get up early tomorrow for work," Betty said.

"Hey, no problem. I'll even take a rain check for breakfast."

"You're a nice guy, Jim."

"Uh huh."

In the cabin, Red set to work building a good fire in the fireplace, crushing paper and breaking twigs. Jim supposed this was Red's idea of romantic atmosphere.

"I don't know how they did it, but I guess we owe these bastards a breakfast," Nancy said.

"Eggs and sausage in the fridge," Red called. Fire lapped up the chimney and sent a curl of fragrant smoke to the ceiling.

"Jim cleaned the battery contacts," Betty said.

"Traitor!" Red said. "You squealed."

"She weaseled it out of me."

"Women can do that to a guy," Red said. "I won't hold it against you. But after all, ladies, give us some credit for a quick diagnosis of the problem, and a very, very swift solution. I mean, we could have made a big deal out of it. I mean, you could have been towed to a garage and given some mechanical jive and a bill for sixty dollars, you know."

"We're grateful, Red," Nancy said. "We're so grateful we just might pee our pants. And drink your booze. What have you got in *that* line, by the way?"

"There's some Molson's in the fridge."

"Ugh."

"And some apple wine in the cellar. Homemade."

"That sounds interesting."

"Jim? Will you do the honors?"

"You really want some apple wine with breakfast?" Betty asked.

"Christ, yes," Red said. "The latest medical findings approve of it one hundred percent."

Jim pulled open the door to the cellar and went down the narrow steps into the darkness and the cool dampness. He swung his arm in front of him in the basement searching for the light cord, and finally brushed it and turned on the light. A long black snake was draped over the wooden cartons that held Red's supply of wine bottles, and it raised its head and flicked its tongue as Jim moved toward it. Jim waved his hand, and the snake ducked its head and glided off the boxes into a dark corner, where only the little points of reflected light could be seen on its eyes.

"Getting any?" Jim asked the snake. "Rats, I mean. And don't be coming up the stairs to sleep by the fire tonight, either. We got company." He gently pulled a bottle out of the carton, blew the dust off, and returned to the warmth of the living room.

"How many of those have we got left?" Red asked.

"A dozen, I'd say."

"Did you see Jack?"

"Oh, yeah."

"Jack who?" Betty pulled off her jacket and threw it across the back of the sofa.

"Jack Daniels," Red said. "The black label. A friend of ours."

"What kind of friend? A pet?"

"Just a tiny little spider," Jim said. "The kind you find in any basement. This one likes to hang around the wine bottles."

Red laughed and called into the kitchen. "How them eggs coming?"

"Hold your damn horses," Nancy shouted back. "I can't find a damn thing to cook with out here."

"I'd better help her out," Red said, "before she sticks her hand in a mousetrap."

The fire roared and pinged now, and Jim pulled a chair up close to it. "Sit here, why don't you?" he said to Betty.

"Go ahead," she said. "I'm O.K. here."

"Suit yourself." Jim sat by the fire, and in a moment when he glanced over his shoulder he saw that Betty had stepped into the kitchen. He could hear Red and Betty and Nancy, fragments of their conversation.

"Why? What's the matter?" he heard Red say. "Oh, come on." A little disgusted, Jim rose and went out the front door onto the porch. He leaned on the railing and watched his shadow lurch away in the dim light from the window. Beyond the road, where the woods started, the world seemed to drop off into a black abyss. It was the kind of dark he wanted to fire a flare into, to make sure it was empty of enemy troops. He heard them assembling their machine guns, snapping open the ammunition cans, threading the bullet belt into the magazine. Any minute now they would open fire, the tracers would scratch lines on the surface of the night, the house would rattle with the impact of the hurtling lead.

Tired and aggravated, he sat on the steps with his head in his hands. *Go ahead. Open fire.*

"Jim? Hey, Jim." Betty looked out of the door. "They asked me to ask you if you wanted some of this apple wine?"

"Yeah, sure. I'll be right in."

Betty stepped onto the porch, and immediately wrapped her arms around herself as if cold. "What are you you doing out here?"

"Nothing." Jim stood up and stretched, and when he turned around he was almost face to face with Betty. She put a hand on his elbow, sat down on the step, and tugged him down next to her.

"I've got a problem," she said. "Nancy wants to stay the night."

Jim said nothing.

"And if I don't stay, it's going to be a big logistical hassle in the morning, you know, because I have to leave so early for work."

"You can sleep in my bed," Jim said, "and I'll sleep on the couch."

"Jim, it's not because I don't like you."

"Look, I told you, it's O.K."

"I'm afraid." She waited a moment, and said it again. "I'm afraid."

"Well, for Christ's sake."

"I can't help it."

"I'd be interested to know what makes me so scary, that's all."

"It's not just you, see. It's because . . . because you're a veteran."

"Yeah?"

"Don't be like that. Help me a little."

"I'm sorry," Jim said. "I'm a veteran—no choice of my own, by the way, except I'd rather be a vet than a calamity."

"Of course. But I told you about my brother."

"Yes. He lost a leg. I hate to hear that stuff, and I really am sorry about it."

"When he came home, he told me a lot. I mean, he told me what he was thinking and feeling, and it scared me."

"I can believe it," Jim said.

"I don't mean what happened. I mean, what he said about himself. I mean, for example, being with whores, and what that was like. See, I wouldn't want to be compared or expected to be like that, to do those kinds of things."

"Some brother you got."

"What do you mean?"

"Telling you stuff like that."

"I know, but he just wanted to tell somebody the truth."

"Well, I don't think of you as a whore, and you don't have to sleep with me, and if you did—"

"Don't, Jim. Don't say it."

"O.K. I won't."

"Because that's not the only thing. Not even the big thing. That's not what hangs me up the most."

"It'd be enough." *I can understand your disgust.*

"I'm even scared to say it."

"I think I'm scared to hear it," Jim said. "But I want to hear it."

"Well, it's that, my brother anyway, he killed people."

"Yes, that's what we did all right. All kinds of ways. That's why people fight wars."

"I mean, my brother said he learned how to do that, and now when he's really angry—and that's often—he thinks how easy it would be. He learned how to kill, and he thinks how easy it would be to solve some of his problems that way."

"So? Has he? Has he ever tried to kill you?"

"No," Betty said. "No, he hasn't."

"Well, I think your brother has done some advanced thinking on this," Jim said. "When you see him, you tell him I learned something from him."

"I'd never tell him I told anyone what he said. I mean, that wasn't a story about what happened, like the story about the pump. But what did you learn?"

"What I'm afraid of, too."

"Of killing someone?"

"Sure. The closest target. That's who always gets it."

"See? That's what makes me afraid, so damned afraid. You guys are like loaded pistols. It scares me to death."

"You're not the closest target," Jim said. "And nobody's angry with you. You're the safest thing going."

"I don't understand."

"Well, think about it a minute. Among Buddhists, you know, suicide is an honorable tradition."

"I don't understand any of this!" Betty almost shouted.

"Yes, you do."

"Is it that bad? Do you think he wants to kill himself?"

"I hope not," Jim said. "He lost a leg, though, and that must make it tougher. I hope he's got some compensations."

"Like what? Like what can compensate for that?"

"Somebody who loves him. Somebody who will teach him how to love again. Somebody with that kind of patience."

"He's the one who's impatient. He tried so hard, he can't get anything. He drives me crazy."

"I'd like to meet this guy," Jim said. "He sounds like me. We'd argue, I'm sure. I think those Viet Namese were right about that goddamn pump, for example. But I understand his impatience. And look at me. I've got it soft. I came back physically intact. In fact, I came back with a hell of a nice tan, and I was in great shape, and such a *bastard*, I had a lot of friends, a lot of young women who were curious. I've had it made pretty much, and I'm still impatient, and man, have I fucked up! It's unbelievable how much fucking-up one person can do in fifteen years. Unbelievable."

Betty leaned against him. "It's buggy. Can't we go in?"

"Sure, let's go in," Jim said. "Just don't think I feel sorry for myself, because I don't. O.K.? I've fucked up, but I'm not completely gone. I can handle it."

"I understand," Betty said.

After they finished their midnight breakfast, Jim slipped into his room both to rummage in his closet for a sleeping bag and to give Nancy and Red a chance to climb discreetly into the loft. He heard the bumping of their stockinged feet on the floor and their quiet, playful laughter. He presumed Betty was still in the kitchen, but when he turned around with his sleeping bag she was standing in the doorway with her arms folded across her chest.

"I don't want to chase you out of your own bed," she said.

"It's no trouble, really."

"Won't you be cramped?"

"The sofa's comfy enough. I've slept on it numerous times."

Betty dropped her arms and looked away for a moment. "I guess I'm trying to ask something awkward."

Jim waited.

"I guess I'd like to sleep with you, Jim, beside you, but I don't want to . . . to—"

"To make love?" *To get laid. To fuck.*

"No, I don't want to do that."

"You think you could trust me?"

"What do you think?"

"I wouldn't mind. It's body heat, right?"

"I really don't want to make love."

"You've made that clear."

"Am I being silly?"

"Of course. What's wrong with that?"

"I suppose I'm asking for trouble."

"I haven't killed anybody lately. I don't pillage or rape."

Betty covered her face with her hands for a moment. "Please, Jim. Enough."

Jim sat on the edge of the bed and undressed quickly, then pulled on a pair of pajamas and swung into bed. "I'll even warm it up for you."

Betty turned off the light and undressed in the dark. The dim light coming through the door outlined the T-shirt she left on and just the crown of her hair, and Jim thought for the first time she was quite shapely and beautiful. She hesitated for a moment, then lifted the covers and slid into bed. Jim held out his arm, and she nestled her head against his shoulder, but held her body away from him.

"This is nice," she said. "We'll be warm."

Upstairs the bedsprings crunched, and Nancy gave a soft cry.

Betty, still holding her body away, curled her fingers on Jim's chest. Now there was a loud thump and Nancy laughed wildly; in a moment, Red laughed, too. Then it was quiet for a long time, and Jim was almost asleep when the bedsprings began to clang in a forceful, earnest rhythm. Betty turned away with a nervous cough, and Jim cupped his body around hers, the curve of her buttocks in his lap, and he couldn't help it but came erect.

He remembered a whore he had been with in Viet Nam that he had taken, as they called it, "dog-style." She was small and apparently quite young, and not at all interested in what was happening to her, as if she were in a constant state of shock. Her encouragement had been a mockery, a cartoon, somehow incredibly objective and self-contained. It took him a long time to climax, and the girl was angry with him as a result. She had reached back between her legs and stroked his balls as he thrust himself into her again and again with increasing fury and violence. And the girl began to swear at him and demand that he take it easy, crazy bastard, what are you doing? He flailed against her and finally climaxed, then threw her limp body off in anger and disgust.

Wasn't there one thing in life he could really, mindlessly enjoy? Did everything have to be botched?

He pulled himself away from Betty now, and wrapped the pillow around his ears so that he could blot out the sounds of Red's and Nancy's merry copulations.

When he woke in the morning, Betty was gone, the Datsun was gone, and presumably Nancy was gone, too, off to work at the Lake Ecstasy Village Inn. Red had either gone along with them or had returned to bed and was sleeping soundly. Red's cap was not hanging on its peg by the back door, and Jim heard no heavy breathing or snoring from the loft, so he presumed the house was empty. He went back into the bedroom to dress and found a note stuck in the corner of the mirror on his dresser.

"Don't think badly of me," Betty wrote. "It will seem silly to you, but I did very well to stay the night. I was afraid at first, but it went away. If you were awake this morning, things might have been different. I mean, you looked good to me. I promise I'll call you."

Jim folded the note carefully and replaced it on the mirror. He appreciated it but was aware, too, he wasn't satisfied. It was funny! He couldn't even get laid when he had a woman in his bed. She was afraid of him, because he had fucked whores and knew how to kill people with the weapons supplied by his government. What was he supposed to do? Cut off his hands? Castrate himself? Put out his eyes?

He knew he shouldn't take it personally. The note intended to make him feel good, and for a moment he allowed it to do that; for a moment he felt lifted half a notch up on that, and when he thought of Nancy upstairs, too, enjoying herself with Red, he had to admit that even if Betty wasn't really one of them, there were probably— or so he believed for now—some good girls in the world after all. He rolled back into bed and took his cock in his hand and tried to imagine what a really good girl would be like in bed. She'd be on top of him and keep her eyes open, she'd spread her legs wide, and as they made love she'd say nice things to him and allow him to do the same, she'd come powerfully, her whole body atremble, and she wouldn't be afraid, she wouldn't be afraid of him, she wouldn't be afraid of holocaust, or brutality, she wouldn't be afraid of having children, she wouldn't be afraid, she wouldn't be afraid of a god-damned thing.

12
Double
Rainbows
[*ii*]

A day of rain follows their return from the hospital, and Ginny lounges in the darkened house resting, saying little, eating almost nothing. At the table over untouched lunch she says two things that interest Chong, that hurt him in ways he prefers to keep secret from her.

"If I got those drawings from Parker, you wouldn't have to worry so much, would you? You wouldn't worry about going to court."

"I'm not even worried about it now," Chong says. But he is. He is not sure that a jury of Mrs. Veranos and Mrs. O'Days and Turners would regard the drawings as innocent. Later Ginny remarks, touching her face, "I guess you wouldn't want to draw me now, looking like this."

"You're not going to have a scar or anything," Chong says. "You'll be your old self in no time."

"I don't want to be my old self," Ginny says.

Chong listens to the rain. It is such a perfect rain, so gentle and steady, that he finds a yellow plastic slicker and goes out into it with his blueberry pail. The rain crackles on the plastic slicker like fire in brush, and a little halo of steam rises around his body, and the hood of the slicker causes the world to seem to be bathed in a soft yellow light. Chong crosses the road and follows the stream to the shores of Lake Ecstasy and then wades into the blueberry bushes, which are laden and so ripe that even in the rain they give off a smell like wine. The bushes, though low, and the leaves, though small, remind Chong of tea bushes in China, and he wonders if blueberry leaves would make a blueberry tea. Down the hill, the surface of Lake Ecstasy dances under the pelting of the rain. Above, the bellies of the clouds are as dark as the blueberries themselves. The rain is cool, and slackens gently as Chong continues picking. He feels the rain is washing his mind. It is just what he needs.

At home again, he places the full bucket on the kitchen table. Ginny rises from the sofa and comes in.

"You've been eating blueberries," she says.

"Sure. Why not?"

"Your lips are blue."

"Maybe I would taste like blueberries if you kissed me."

Ginny wrinkles her nose. "Maybe."

"You think I should make a pie with these?"

"Yeah." Ginny is enthusiastic. "I could go for that."

"It's the best medicine," Chong says. "When you get better, you'll have to pick some blueberries, too. We can make a whole lot of pies, and I want to make some brandy, too."

"I didn't know you could make brandy out of these."

"Sure. Why not?"

"You're always saying that." Ginny mimics him. " 'Sure. Why not?' "

"It's nice to have a critic in the house." Chong pours the blueberries into a strainer in the sink, begins to sort through them, picking out the leaves and bits of branch that have fallen into his pail. As he works, his hands become spotted with purple, a little like bruises, but redder. He can see why the Indians, say, would stain their bodies, because it is an attractive color, somehow quite summery. Better yet, he thinks, glancing at Ginny, then repenting the thought at once, painting the other's body, rubbing the breasts, the thighs, with blueberry blue, using the skin for a canvas, the hands for a brush. Chong sighs, exasperated with himself.

The afternoon passes quietly. Ginny naps and even reads, and the house fills with the smell of blueberries cooking. When the rain stops, Ginny puts down her book and goes out behind the house to walk barefooted in the grass.

"Chong!" she calls. "Come here, quick!"

Alarmed, he hauls himself from his chair, struggles out of the nap that was threatening to overtake him, and bangs out of doors.

"Look," Ginny says. "Look at that! I've never seen that." She points above the trees across the pond, in the direction of the receding rain. The arc of a rainbow disappears into a silver haze over the trees and into light gray clouds above; and above this is another arc of colors, paler, more iridescent, but seemingly substantial as a bridge, too.

"Two at once!" Ginny marvels. "Have you ever seen that?"

"A long time ago," Chong says. As the sun drops a little toward evening, its rays penetrate the clouds in palpable shafts and the highest rainbow flickers in and out of visibility. Then the lower one pales, too, and the sky goes orange.

When he goes in to rescue his pie from the oven, the house seems small and silly, even a little ugly. But it sure smells good! Chong thinks. It smells like heaven.

The next morning, while Ginny sleeps late upstairs, Chong calls Dr. Miranda.

"I was hoping you'd get back to me," the doctor says. "I'm pretty concerned about Ginny. About her home life."

"She's staying with me right now," Chong says.

"Do you think that's the best thing?"

"I don't know," Chong says. "She can't go home. Suppose she gets beaten again."

"So you believe she was hit?"

"Don't you?"

"Yes," the doctor says. "But I didn't have a complaint from Ginny, and you seemed to, ah—"

"Yes, I lied, too," Chong says. "She's afraid that if she isn't at home or with me she'll have to go to a state school. She hates the idea. I think she'd run away first."

Now Miranda tells Chong he doesn't think that should be a worry, and that what he would like to do is find a foster parent family for her, a situation in which she could be protected for a while, where the people in her present household would not know where she was, "until the situation improves." Miranda is silent a moment. "You understand?"

"Yes," Chong says. "What do I have to do?"

"You may have to tell a judge what you know about the situation, how you came to be involved."

"I'll do that," Chong says.

"I think it's the best thing."

"I feel like a traitor, though," Chong says.

"When you bring her in for the checkup on Friday, I'll talk to you both then. All right? You're doing the best thing."

"O.K."

"I'll make some calls today," Miranda says. "Do you feel you're in any danger there?"

"I don't know," Chong says. "It wouldn't be very difficult for them to guess where Ginny is."

"If you think you are, you should obviously take her somewhere else. You understand that?"

"Yes." Chong speaks with irritation. Where? Where, for God's sake?

Moments after he hangs up, Ginny tumbles down the stairs, tears streaking her face, and slams into the bathroom. Chong can hear that she is sick, and tries to open the door, but it is locked.

"Ginny? What's the matter?"

"I heard you," Ginny says. "Who were you talking to?"

"I was talking to the doctor."

"You're sending me away, right? *Why?*"

"You're not going to that school, Ginny. The doctor wants to find you a family to stay with."

"I don't want to stay with a family."

"It's not safe here. You know that."

"I can't believe you're handing me over."

"It's a family, Ginny. I can't protect you, and Parker won't know where the family is."

"Well, when am I going?"

"Come out of there, Ginny. I can't hear you. We've got some things to talk about."

"You promised me you wouldn't tell."

"I know," Chong says. "I feel like hell. But what if Parker comes after you here?"

"You could shoot him," Ginny says.

"I couldn't, Ginny. I don't even have a gun. And it wouldn't be right."

"Yes, it would!"

"Come out now. Let's talk this over."

Ginny opens the door slowly, collapses against the jamb, her robe askew so that one of her breasts is visible. She looks hopeless and beaten, the side of her face is a darker blue than ever before, and her face is wet. Chong cannot help himself, cradles her in his arms.

"Ginny, the doctor wants to put you in a family, a family that

Parker won't know about. You won't go to that school, and you'll be safe."

"What about my mother?"

"They won't do it unless your mother agrees."

"Parker won't let her."

"The doctor will convince her. He'll take her to court if he has to, and Parker, too."

"But what about you?"

"You're the one we're worried about. Parker is ruining your life. It's not right, and it's not fair."

"I know, but I got you in trouble, too."

"I'm not in trouble the way you are."

"You don't understand. You didn't see how they treated my father in Florida. They humiliated him. They drove their bikes right across his porch. They spit on him, and made him kneel. They made him cry."

Ginny pushes him away now, and stumbles into the kitchen, collecting her robe about her, drying her eyes with the lapels. "So when will I be going?"

"In a day or two."

"What do I do if Parker comes?"

"I don't know," Chong says. "I think you should stay inside, don't let him see you here."

"That won't stop him."

"Maybe, maybe not. If he comes in, you'll have to hide somewhere."

"Oh, Christ, this is stupid," Ginny says. "This is a small house."

"We'll do it like this," Chong says. "I'll pull down the stairs to the attic. If Parker comes, you'll hide up there, behind the paintings against the wall. First, you pull the stairs up after you."

"How do you do that?"

"There's a rope. I'll show you how."

"It's hot up there. I'll suffocate."

"I'm going up there, and I'll pull one of the windows out."

"That'll be a giveaway."

"You got any better ideas?"

"No."

"If you get any better ideas, let me know. Maybe he won't come for you. But he must know where you are. Where else would you have gone?"

"I don't know," Ginny shouts. "I'm confused. Why is all this happening to me?"

"That's something I can't answer," Chong says. "Come on. I'll show you how to work those stairs, and then I'll fix you some breakfast."

That afternoon, Chong pins his cartoons of Tank Younger and Lily Walker at the pool table to the wall of his living room beside the sketches of faces he has made during the past week—face after face of people he knows, remembers seeing at the Village Inn—Turner, Barber, Verano, and Mrs. Verano, and other townspeople—but cannot resist adding sketches of other people, too—Benny, and Mai Li, and Susan. As he blocks it in, deciding where each figure will stand, and in what attitude, Wu's face peers over the face of one of the volunteer firemen—Chong finds himself involved in this painting, which he had thought light, a pastime, something to play with while more "serious" ideas percolated, and involved with an intensity he cannot understand. It is as if he felt the urgency to record his Lake Ecstasy life, his Lake Ecstasy mind, almost as if he were afraid it was coming to an end, presaging a calamity of some sort, or if he did not, that he would forget everything about his life. The painting will have to be larger, he sees at once. The scene in the Inn will have to be a cutaway, and everyone—Parker, too, Taylor, even Mrs. Cahill, whom he has never seen—will have to be in the room, and the view will have to be from Barber's hill, and the beautiful hills will ring the Inn, and the perfect blue sky with a double rainbow will light it, and a corner of Lake Ecstasy with skinny-dippers and teeming blueberry bushes will float in the upper left quadrant, and Nancy Wallace will be in it, swinging in a hammock, and Betty the nurse and Dr. Miranda—*all the saints*, Chong thinks, *what a silly idea*. But the painting explodes, grows before his eyes—deer, frogs, cats, dogs, Luan, Awake, a motorcycle gang—*the whole graveyard*—apple trees, fat trout sleeping in the roots of trees—*the whole world*.

Now, Chong growls, I have made myself a miserable, complicated project. It could have been so simple. I could have cranked it out in a few days. But now I want to make something beautiful. Yes, and I want Ginny in it, and while everyone goes about his and her business, unknown, almost unseen, down in this little section of this little corner, like the way Brueghel minimized that fool Icarus, my barn will be smoking. And should I put the faces of Taylor and Parker there? Would I dare?

The painting won't fit behind the bar now, Chong thinks. It's going to be too big. I'm going to have to stretch another canvas. But I don't have a canvas big enough! A bedsheet, then.

Chong scurries upstairs and sorts through his tiny trove of linens until he finds a new, stiff, crisp bedsheet, Christmas present from Susan last year which he never used. Yes! This is the size.

Then he is outside, laying out boards in the sunlight, marking them for cutting, getting ready to make a frame. This takes a while, since he wants to do this carefully, and since such a large canvas will need a substantial frame.

Ginny watches him from the kitchen window. "Bring it in here," she says. "I can help you. I can hold corners or something."

"I will when I get the frame ready, O.K.?"

"Make sure it will fit through the door."

Chong laughs. "Right! Thanks!"

They work even through the hour they usually eat, and on into the evening, stretching the canvas, stapling it, Ginny and Chong on hands and knees tugging at the cloth, pulling it taut, working out wrinkles.

"You're not painting this whole thing?" Ginny says. "It's huge."

"Too small," Chong says. "But I don't want it to take forever."

After a quick meal, an omelette and toast, Chong primes the canvas, not with white as he normally would, but with a bright cerulean blue. This is a labor that takes him hours, and when he is nearly finished he says to Ginny, "You see, the sky and the lake are already painted."

"How will you know which is which?" Ginny laughs.

"See?" Chong says. "Already you are becoming a painter. Water is almost always the color of the sky. And what do you care if I put some birds in the sky of the lake?"

"What are you talking about?"

"You know how birds fly into windows?"

"Yeah."

"The reflection of the sky in the lake will be so perfect, the birds will fly into it!"

"And drown!" Ginny protests.

"No," Chong says. "And fly!"

"But that impossible."

"It's magic," Chong says. "In a painting, anything is possible."

"You're crazy," Ginny says.

"I don't want to be so tired," Chong says. "I want to keep going."

"Just take a nap. Then get up and work all night."

"See?" Chong points at her with his brush. "You *are* a painter. Unfortunately, that is easy for a young woman to say, not so easy for an old Chong to do!" He collapses in the chair, regards the huge rectangle of blue before him, the faces and sketches pinned to the wall. He glances at Ginny and laughs. "I got an idea. You're going to help me."

"Cut it out. How can I help?"

"You're going to paint clouds, and trees, and roads."

"I can't draw anything."

"I'll show you. I'll do the drawings, but you can lay down some colors."

"Me?"

"Yes, you. You can take your time, be careful. And I'll show you a few tricks. There's enough room, see?" He jumps from the chair. "You paint clouds up here while I paint down here. Then you paint roads down here while I work over there. Very good idea!"

"Just great," Ginny says. "Maybe I'll screw it up. Did you think of that?"

"I can fix anything," Chong says. "No sweat." Almost anything, he corrects himself. "Anyway, I won't give you anything you can screw up too much."

"I'm not ready for this," Ginny warns him.

"Tomorrow," Chong says. "You'll dream about it, and you'll be ready. Now tell the truth. Don't you love that blue?"

"Yeah," Ginny says. "It's a nice blue. I just hope it *stays* a nice blue."

In the morning, Chong sketches on the blue field of the canvas, mixes paints in jars—fast-drying acrylics mixed with water and gesso. Ginny comes down early, too, surprised to find Chong already at work, and that he has prepared paints for her to use, is already bursting with instructions.

"Let me get something to eat," she protests.

"Oh, right," Chong says. "Stomach first."

"Yeah, stomach first."

"Your face looks better this morning," Chong observes. "The bruise is smaller."

"It still looks like hell," Ginny insists. "And it itches."

"Tomorrow we'll see the doctor again. Did you take your medicine?"

"Yes, I took my damn medicine," Ginny says. "I hate it. The stuff makes me fart." She disappears into the kitchen.

Chong chuckles, begins blocking in areas of the canvas, feels so free in the big space, works for a sense of rhythm across the whole span, staggers areas of action and inaction, sharp focus and repose, has already decided to follow the wisdom of the medieval painters and children and proportion things according to their importance, not their objective scale. From Chong's pond, which is eye-sized, to Lake Ecstasy, a heaven, and to the sky, there are rivers of blue, the veins and arteries of this world—for he will paint them (if he can!) as living things, as live as the animals that live within them, the fishermen and swimmers enjoying them.

Ginny comes into the room hesitantly, hands in the hip pockets of her jeans, but Chong does not give her a chance to be sulky, pulls her to the canvas, takes a brush and shows her what he wants done.

"This brush makes a fan-shaped mark. Tree! See? You make trees all along this line, close together, like so. And then you stagger them behind, right? Until this area is filled."

"That's a lot of trees!"

"Yeah," Chong says. "After that you can pave some roads, then make some clouds."

Tentatively, Ginny makes her first mark. "Ugh!" she says. "It's too thick. Look."

"So? One thick tree," Chong says. "You can work a little faster, and not so much paint will come off."

Ginny pats the canvas now, leaves a green smudge.

"Just do it easy," Chong says, "with a little rhythm." He takes her hand in his, marks the canvas. "Ba-bum, ba-bum. See? So easy. Painting is musical, too."

Ginny laughs quietly. "Ba-bum."

"That's it. Very nice tree."

"Some tree, with no trunk, and no branches."

"I'll do that later."

"This should be autumn," Ginny says. "That's when trees are nicest."

"God damn it, that's right!" Chong stops painting for a moment, regards the canvas. "So what we'll do is make this woods over here the fall woods, which you can paint when I mix some more colors.

That way, we can have the water reflect those colors, too, and we can have rainbow-colored streams in there. Very nice!"

"You can't have summer and autumn in the same picture," Ginny scoffs.

"Why not? This isn't a photograph."

"What is it, then?"

Chong shrugs. "What do you think? A dream? A fantasy? A state of mind? Something to make you happy when you look at it. Who cares?"

"Yeah," Ginny says. "Who cares? Can I make a different kind of tree?"

"Not right there," Chong says. "Right there we want a pattern, a nice rhythm."

"Yeah, I know. Ba-bum, ba-bum." She marks the canvas as she talks.

"Now we're cooking with hot bean paste."

And so the morning passes, Ginny filling in the areas of repetition, and crude colors, and taking on also a few more difficult tasks requiring patience and delicacy, a branch dotted with tiny white blossoms, little new moons of black, suggesting the shadows on rivets in a bridge, tiny rectangles of purple and stripes of white on the wings of a duck. Chong, meanwhile, composes face after face, constructs houses, sends a flock of pigeons in the air over the stone castle in the state park, fills the Village Inn with cheering souls, paints the yellow bus in the woods, campfire blazing. He begins to ache with the bending, his eyes water from the concentration.

"Don't you think we should eat?" Ginny says. "It's almost two."

"Stomach again," Chong snorts. "Just like a clock."

"I missed my medicine, too." Ginny wipes her brow with the back of her hand, leaves a wide, gray smudge of paint.

"Well, take it now."

"I don't like to take my medicine on an empty stomach."

"I hear you." Chong tries to steady himself, to put a little dot of yellow window-light in a small green eye. This is always difficult, because if the dot is the least bit askew, the eyes seem crossed, and not lively and intelligent, but unfocused, distracted somehow. And correcting a thing so small in another thing so small can lead to disaster. He takes his time, each dot very slowly aimed and quickly placed.

"Chong!"

"Yeah, yeah. Two more eyes. Slice some cheese, why don't you?"

Then Ginny is going past him at a run, bounding up the stairs even before Chong hears the low growl of the motorcycles, and the click of the engines shutting down, one, two. Without dropping his brush or the pan lid he is holding as a pallet, Chong goes at once to the kitchen door, and out.

Parker and Taylor sit on their motorcycles in leather jackets open to bare skin, Parker with a half-smile that is also a sneer, Taylor with his mouth open, eyes blanked by dark shades. The two men sit in silence a moment, and then Parker says, "What're you painting, Mr. Chong? Naked kids?"

"What do you want, Parker?"

"Hey, he really acts tough, don't he?" Parker says to Taylor as he swings off the bike. "What do you think I want? I want to take Ginny home."

"You're too late," Chong says.

"Now." Parker advances rapidly. "Carey ain't signed nothin'."

Chong swings inside the screen door, but before he can slam the inner door, Parker has already thrust himself into the kitchen. He smiles cruelly, then opens the door wide so Taylor can follow him in.

"You round her up, Taylor. Mr. Chong and I are going to have a talk."

"Get out of my house," Chong says.

"Take care of the phone there, Taylor." Parker points to it, and Taylor snaps open a switchblade knife, loops the cord, and slices off the receiver. Then he glides into the living room, calls Ginny's name.

"I'm going to send you to jail," Chong says. "I don't care what you think you can get away with."

"You know," Parker says coolly, "I've been here before. I know this house. I watched you flop around in your blankets. I don't know why I didn't fuckin' kill you then."

"They'll have to pipe sunlight to you, Parker. I'm going to have you put under the jail."

"Shut up." Parker slaps Chong idly, sends him flailing into the counter. His ears ring, and he cannot see well when he pulls himself up.

Taylor calls Ginny's name again.

"Now that I got your attention," Parker says, "I think you ought to understand what's going on here. This is a rescue operation. You're keeping this little girl here, and abusing her, and all like that. I got pictures you made of her naked, and I wouldn't be surprised if she didn't have a bruise on her face right now, where you forced her to do something nasty. Lucky for Ginny, Taylor and I showed up."

"Lucky for Ginny, she's not here." Chong can barely control his voice, his chest heaves so.

"Ah, fuck that," Parker says.

"I took her last night to the doctor."

"You didn't go anywhere last night," Parker says. "But you will go to jail. It's just so lucky we decided to stop by here. They won't believe what we seen you doin'."

In the drawer behind him, Chong knows, there is a butcher knife, there is a rolling pin, there are skewers and forks—Parker has already tasted the tines of a fork! He waits, hoping Parker will be distracted, breathing deeply, deeply, trying to calm himself.

Momentarily, Taylor is in the doorway to the kitchen. He shrugs. "I see all her stuff up there." He indicates the upstairs with his thumb. "But she's not there."

"Check the basement." Parker points to the door.

"Why don't you just get out of here?" Chong says.

"Why don't you shut the fuck up, like I said?" Parker steps swiftly forward, kicks Chong, hard, in the ankle.

A flash of pain shoots up his leg, and Chong crumples to one knee, choking back a cry, afraid that if he makes noise, Ginny will hear and reveal herself to end his torture.

"Save some for me." Taylor laughs. He opens the cellar door and clicks down the stairs. "Ginny," he calls. "Let's go home."

"This is getting ridiculous," Parker says. "You better let us have the kid, or this is going to turn into a really difficult rescue operation. I mean, difficult for you. You don't want this to be any more difficult, do you?" He grabs Chong by the hair and pulls his head up to face him. "Huh? Can you hear me?"

He knows it will cost him a blow, but Chong forces himself to smile. He wants to forget his body, to become nothing. And then Parker surprises him, and hurts him, with a thrust of knee to Chong's chest, and Chong feels a terrible cracking inside, and the hurt goes deep, into his kidney, into his leg. He is in San Francisco suddenly, a child again, under water, swimming, looking up at the shark, and its grin, struggling to breathe.

Then there is another fish in the water, bellowing *What the hell are you doing, Parker,* a fat green fish, behatted, and Chong swims up out of the ooze of his fright, coughing, feeling a wetness on his lips that makes him sweat and tremble.

"Mind your own fuckin' business, Turner," Parker spits. "Get out if you got any sense."

"The hell I will, mister."

Parker lunges for Turner, and they lock into a grasping reptilian struggle, Chong awake enough now through a pounding headache, sees the black leather back of Parker, the odd dinosaurian rubber waders of Turner, clunking of leather boots, rubber boots, Chong pulls himself up by the counter, hurls open the drawer, hand stutters among the knives until he has the fat handle of the cleaver, cocks his arm, and out of the cellar door, the doglike black braying form rips into him, and he is down, under hot leather, feeling the rasp of Taylor's zippers and the stink of him! Gasoline and sweat!

There is a thunderous crash, the edge of his very kitchen table bounces absurdly by his head. A table! Like a blunt guillotine missing its mark, and the little tea tin once full of flowers rolls absurdly back and forth, back and forth in the strange silence.

Again Chong pulls himself up, sees Turner in his fishing waders, hat gone, hands over his eyes, and a red stain over his fingers. Motorcycles snarl, roar away.

"Chong?"

"Yeah, Turner. I'm O.K."

"Tell me, when I take my hands away. I'm afraid to look."

"Oh, God," Chong wails. "All right."

Turner drops his hands and a red arc opens on his forehead.

"It's not your eye," Chong says. "It's higher."

"Call somebody, will you?"

"They cut the telephone."

"Can you drive?"

"Yeah."

"Can you drive to Royalton?"

"I'll drive to Barber's if I can't drive farther."

"Let's go."

"One minute. Ginny comes too."

But she is already in the kitchen, shrieking, staggering at the sight before her.

"Stop it, Ginny!" Chong commands her. "Grab some towels. Help us. Get some towels for Turner. Quick!"

"Your lips are bloody," Ginny says.

"Towels! Come on."

Turner is outside, throws himself in the back seat of Chong's car.

Chong cannot straighten up completely, the pain in his chest is too severe, and he slides behind the wheel with difficulty. Now Ginny, towels flying, tumbles into the car, too, as the car grinds and then pops to life.

"Here, Mr. Turner, here's a towel."

"What the hell's going on here?" Turner rasps. "One hell of a fishing trip."

"They're after me," Ginny says. "Parker wants to take me home."

"I thought you were in Florida," Turner says.

Chong wails, "God damn it! I'm almost out of gas."

"My pickup's just down the road," Turner says. "Take us there. Can you drive a pickup?"

"I'm getting lots of practice." Chong swings out of the driveway, chugs over the culvert, and wheels toward the fire road.

"Stay on the highway," Turner instructs him, "or you'll just block me in." He sits up now, his head visible in the rearview mirror, turbaned, a red spot showing in a blur through the pink cloth.

They pile out of the car.

"Goddamn waders," Turner says. "Help me get these off, will you?" Carefully he sits down, extends his feet, and Chong and Ginny pull on the boots. "Ridiculous goddamn situation!" Turner shouts. "I'll kill that asshole if I get my hands on him again."

The waders come off with a rush.

"Take it easy." Chong finds it hard to speak, breath short, holds his hand to his chest.

"I think I can drive," Turner says.

"You sure?"

"Yes!" Turner speaks angrily, waves toward the truck. "Let's move!"

As soon as they are on the highway, Turner grabs the CB microphone from his dashboard. "Break eight. Come on, Big Shoulders. Gimme that Big Shoulders. This is Butcher Boy." He repeats this.

The radio crackles finally. "Bring it to me, Butcher Boy."

"Listen, Red. Chong and I have some serious injuries. Can you drive us to Royalton?"

"Come on back, Butcher Boy. I copy that you are injured?"

"Yeah, me and Chong."

"Swing by here if you're mobile. We'll ferry you, no sweat."

"Butcher Boy clear."

"Barber!" Chong says.

"You got it."

"Can you tell him to have a Dr. Miranda meet us?"

"Come on back, Big Shoulders." Barber is on the air at once, and Turner conveys Chong's message. Turner has trouble with the towel coming loose, and Ginny climbs higher on the seat, on her knees for a moment, helping to resecure it. They snap past Turner's farm now, and Joe coughs out a laugh. "Suppose my wife sees us. Won't she be shaking her head?"

"Barber could call her, too," Chong says.

"She'd just worry," Turner answers him.

Barber and another man are waiting at the roadside when Turner barrels into town. Red is at the window as soon as the truck rams to a halt.

"Jesus Christ, what happened? You're covered with blood."

"Parker cut me. Hit Chong pretty hard, too."

"Jim here"—Barber points to the man next to him—"will stick tight to the CB. There's not room for all of us anyway. You want him to call the cops?"

"Damn right I do," Turner says. He pushes over on the seat so that Chong and Ginny are crushed against each other and the door. Turner straddles one of the two gearshifts on the floor.

"So what do I tell the cops now?" To Chong, Jim seems gaunt, with deep-socketed eyes, as if dissipated, as if he hasn't slept or eaten. It is a frighteningly hungry look, but the man's eyes are alert and they regard the strange trio in the truck with genuine concern.

Barber is already rolling, shouts out the window, "Parker attacked Turner and Chong. Tell 'em we're headin' for the hospital. CB channel eight." The tires whine as Barber accelerates, rams through the gears.

"You look like hell, Joe," Barber says. "How do you feel?"

"Dizzy," Turner says. "I'm glad you're driving. How about you, Chong?"

Chong coughs. "I can't seem to catch my breath."

"I know you, don't I?" Barber says to Ginny. "Aren't you a Cahill?"

"Yeah, Red. I'm Ginny. You saw me before."

"You O.K.?"

"Scared, that's all. They didn't touch me."

"You got a bruise there."

Ginny blushes. "That's from before."

"One messed-up bunch," Red says. "What the hell happened?"

"You'd better ask Chong," Turner says. "I was fishing in the pond when I heard the motorcycles pull up, thought I'd look in. Christ, there's Parker scratching his crotch, and then I see Chong on the floor, squirming around. I'm in my damned waders."

"What's Parker's beef with you?" Red says. "Or do I know?"

"I can't talk now," Chong says. "It hurts."

"Speak of the devil." Red points to the rearview mirror.

At once Chong snaps around in the seat. Side by side, cruising at the same speed as the truck, about one hundred yards back, are Parker and Taylor.

"Shit!" Chong shouts.

Ginny slumps down in the seat.

"What's the story here?" Barber says. "Are they armed? I mean, what the fuck's going on here?"

"They want me," Ginny says. "They want to take me home, and I don't want to go."

Turner is on the CB again. "Come on, Jim. Come on, buddy, this is Butcher Boy." He tries again and again. "God damn these hills!" He slams the microphone into its holder.

The radio crackles, but the message is garbled, static chaos.

"You think they'll move on us?" Red asks. "I don't want to push it in these hills." Already the greenery passes in a silver blur. "We're not about to outrun those bikes anyway."

"You and I both know those bastards are capable of anything," Turner says.

"I think they're just following," Ginny says. "I think they just want to know where you're taking me."

"Couldn't they guess?" Red says.

"I hope Jim called the cops," Turner says. "And I hope you're right, kid." He pats Ginny on the knee. "I want a piece of Parker's fanny real bad, but right now I'm a little too dizzy to fight."

"If they come around me and block the road, hey? What do you want me to do?"

"Don't stop under any circumstances," Turner advises. "Run 'em over, but don't stop."

"Suppose they've got a gun," Red says.

"If they got guns," Turner says, "they won't come around us, don't worry. They'll shoot us in the back."

"Now what the hell have you got me into, Joe?" Red shouts. "Look. They're movin' up now. Movin' up fast."

They crest a hill and the motorcycles are right behind them, about fifteen feet in back of the truck. Taylor, his shades glistening, and Parker, hair sprayed around his head like tentacles, ride impassively there, the rumble of their engines steady.

"All I have to do is touch the brakes," Red says, "and we'll have motorcycle all over us."

Turner, holding the towel with one hand, rummages under the seat.

"What the hell are you looking for?"

"A chain," Turner grunts. "We toss a chain out the window, and that could raise a little hell."

"I really wish I knew what the fuck was going on here," Red says. "Do we really want to be killing these people? Do we, Joe? I mean, that's big trouble. The biggest."

"No problem," Turner says. "The chain's gone anyway. I let my goddamned brother-in-law use it and he never brings anything back until I scream for it."

"Can't say as I'm sorry," Red says. "I'm not really hot to kill anybody, even those peckerheads."

"I got it," Turner says. "Snake Hollow Road? What do you think, Red?"

"How would I get there?"

"Through my father-in-law's old farm."

"Sure!" Barber says with enthusiasm. "If we can shake them a minute at Schuylerkil, we can go four-wheel up that logging trail."

"Where I got my deer last year."

"And right up the river."

"You got it!" Turner says.

"Get ready for some sharp turns ahead," Red says. "We'll do a little bouncing, too, so hang on."

"Here comes Schuylerkil."

Red takes the angled right turn at the last possible second, with a howl of rubber, without touching the brake, then accelerates up the hill.

"All right!" Turner shouts. Parker and Taylor have swung out around the back to avoid collision, and are still on the main road, braking, slowing down, seemingly small now in the view down the hill.

Now Barber cuts sharply left onto a narrow dirt road that winds into the woods.

"Stop now and I'll jam it into four-wheel drive," Turner says.

The truck slams and skids on the dry gravel, stops, and Turner drives the lever between his legs all the way forward. "Run it!"

Stones bang the underside of the truck, and with each bounce and jar, Chong feels a pain in his chest. Ginny clutches him as they careen down a steep, ragged hill.

"Them bikers," Turner says between jolts, "will have . . . hell . . . getting down here . . . without spilling."

"See 'em yet?"

"No," Chong says.

Turner shouts directions to Red. Soon they are barreling down a pasture lane, raising a plume of yellow dust.

"They won't have any trouble seein' that!" Red waves to the smokelike column behind them.

"Doesn't matter," Turner says. "When you get to the river, gear down and take us across."

"It's our ass if we get stuck, Joe."

"Not here," Turner says. "Unless you take it too fast. Here's where old Alphonse used to take his tractor across."

At the riverside, Red brakes, pulls into first gear, crawls through the rocky, warbling stream. The engine whines as he creeps out the other side and up the bank.

"Get on it now!" Turner cries.

They race across a field of hay stubble, encounter another stream. Red gears down again and the truck wades and walks through fast-coursing water that reaches the rocker panels.

"Should've brought a picnic lunch," Turner says.

"I know I'm stirring up some trout in there." Red laughs.

Chong feels quite sick, closes his eyes, chokes back on what is in his throat, afraid to imagine it.

"That's Snake Hollow there." Turner points ahead to a row of white cement posts strung together with a stout silver cable. "Any way you can, get up there now. Then it's straight to the hospital."

Chong is bathed in sweat. Ginny clutches him still.

Chong wears the bandage around his chest like chain mail, feels armored, and the drugs he has been given induce a feeling of careless unhappiness, a mild irritation.

"Dr. Doran says you'll be fine in a couple of weeks," Miranda says. "Some torn ligaments, bruises. Very painful, of course. You won't be eating anything too salty with those lips."

"No," Chong says.

"The painkiller works all right?"

"I don't like it," Chong says, "but it kills the pain."

"You can reduce the dose in a couple of days if you don't like the side effects."

"I sure don't."

"I'm glad to hear it," Miranda says. "A lot of people would just as soon be numb. You could sell those pills for a nice price on the street."

"I might have to," Chong says, "to pay my medical bills."

Miranda acknowledges this with a wry smile. "I was afraid something like this might happen," he says, "but the situation is this. We have a home for Ginny, but not until Saturday. We don't have enough foster parents, and you can't overburden these families. Saturday's the first opening we'll have."

"Two days," Chong says. "What are we supposed to do until then?"

"There are legal problems, too." Miranda wads a small piece of paper and tosses it into a wastebasket. "Ginny's mother is really upset. We sent a counselor around, and I'm afraid that may have also contributed to Parker's sense of mission."

"If you want to dignify it."

"I don't," Miranda says. "We also don't have the judge's consent yet, although we think she'll rule tomorrow. For what it's worth, today's events are being passed on to her, and that should be helpful."

Chong laughs, then winces as pain bites him in the chest. "We all do what we can."

"So that leaves us in the awkward situation of having no place to put Ginny for two days and two nights." He regards Chong critically a moment. "Under the circumstances, it would be very unwise to take her to your house, ever."

"I don't know what to do," Chong says.

"Why don't you stay in town?" Miranda says. "Off the record. Take two rooms at the City Hotel. It's safe. You can get everything you need there. It's only for two days."

"I'm broke." Chong shakes his head in disgust. "But maybe my friends can loan me something."

"You won't need anything," Miranda says. "We'll bill it to protective services."

"There is such a thing? Maybe they could stay with Ginny, too."

"We really are shorthanded," Miranda says. "And in fact it's not what Ginny wants. I already talked to her. Would it inconvenience you a lot?"

"I don't know," Chong says. "I don't know how I got into this. I don't know what I should do."

Miranda nods, then looks away out the window. The blue light from the sky flashes from the little circles of his glasses. "It's incredible what some kids have to put up with, isn't it?"

"Yeah." Chong wraps himself in his arms, feeling a chill. "So if you'll call the hotel, then I'll take her over."

"And you'll stay?"

Chong nods assent, wearily. "Protective service is going to buy me a steak, though," he says.

Their rooms are not adjacent, but on the fifth, the top floor of the tallest building in Royalton. From his window, Chong can look down into the main street and onto the roofs of the Royalton "downtown" stores—the hardware, the James Bros. Heating and Cooling Center (wood stoves and air conditioners in the window), Vin's Pool Hall, The Royalton Tap (Happy Time 4–6), The Better Place Ladies' and Children's Fashions, Rubb's New and Used Furniture, Ryan's Drugs and Fountain . . . Ginny's room, down and across the hall, has a view more sylvan and ecclesiastical over a few rows of carpenter gothic gingerbread homes to the rolling hills beyond that separate Royalton from Lake Ecstasy, and between the spires of the Saint John's Catholic Church and the Royalton First Congregational.

Chong visits Ginny in her room and finds her quite excited by and pleased with her quarters, a real color television and a huge bed—so much space to herself! And yet also nervous to the point of nausea about what will be happening to her.

"It'd be great," she says, "if I could just stay here. It'd be great to live right here in town, with a room like this."

"You couldn't afford it," Chong tells her.

"But maybe if I got a job."

"I don't think there's much going on here that would pay you very well."

"So? I don't need much." Ginny pouts. "Why do I have to go and live with somebody I don't even know."

"Well? And why not? I'll bet they're very nice. They must care a lot about kids, to take them into their home."

"That's what Miranda said." Ginny flops on the bed, kicking her legs. "Something about this room makes me feel better." She rubs her hands and arms over the covers, as if making an "angel" in the snow. "Everything's so clean. And there's a shower."

Chong laughs to himself, tries to remember the first time he ever stayed in a hotel, wonders when it was that he lost Ginny's sense of the marvel of it and began to notice the frayed rugs, fingerprinted window shades, the smell of the mattress under the too-bleached sheets, the jumble of plugs overburdening a single socket. The City Hotel was not exactly a hospitality utopia, either. The clerks downstairs and the help in the "lounge" and restaurant were dim-witted, lugubrious, and needed to be prodded to perform the simplest duty or respond to the most routine question. But for Ginny it was an adventure, and Chong was amused by her pleasure.

Late in the morning, Dr. Miranda calls Chong and tells him that the judge wants to talk to Ginny that afternoon. "She'll want to talk to you, too, I think."

"All right," Chong says wearily. "I guess I'm involved."

"I guess you are," Miranda says. "Ginny can be thankful for that, if you aren't. By the way," he adds, "we haven't been able to get hold of Mrs. Cahill, and we think she may be in Royalton looking for you. It's only a short walk to the courthouse, but if you could do whatever is necessary to make it quick and discreet—"

"Oh, sure," Chong says. "Old Chinaman, young girl. I'm sure nobody notices. How do you want us to disguise ourselves?"

"Look, I'm sorry," Miranda says. "I'll see what I can do about getting an escort for you."

"A cop, you mean."

"Yes, an officer."

"Good!" Chong says. "Please do that."

When he hangs up, he feels sleepy to the point of fainting, perhaps because of the drugs, and finds himself irritated that he can't just lie down and nap but must trudge down the hall and report to Ginny what Miranda has arranged. As he walks the hall, even the dark red carpet with its splotches of black fleur-de-lis irritates him— the splotches seem to crawl, like bugs. Goddamn firetrap! he tells himself, and the thought makes him shiver. *Jesus, these pills could knock me out, and I wouldn't even know I was cooking.*

He finds Ginny watching a soap opera on the television, lowers himself onto her bed, and conveys Miranda's message. Then he can't help himself, but slides into a nap, glad he is not alone, vaguely aware of Ginny beside him, kicking her feet and rocking the bed gently as she watches the television; and vaguely aware, too, of the garish colors and the narcotic babble that the television emanates, and mixes with his own drugged dreams: a beautiful woman brushing her teeth with a motorcycle is being calmly, rhythmically taken from behind by a doctor, and the floor, the tabletop, the desk, the chairs, are inundated with crisp pieces of fried chicken and panty hose more sheer and with more stretch than ever before.

"You should've waked me sooner," Chong cries. "I don't even have time to wash up! And, Jesus, I don't know if Miranda ever called back."

"I tried to wake you," Ginny says. "I've been trying for half an hour. I thought you were dead."

"I hope the judge understands." Chong rubs his hand over the stubble on his chin. "I don't even have a razor."

"Miranda could have called here if he didn't get you," Ginny says. "He didn't."

Chong steps into the bathroom, washes quickly, aware that he has been sweating feverishly in his sleep. The porcelain feels quite cold to him. He curses, trying to wake himself fully. The judge is going to ask questions, and it would be difficult enough to answer coherently without also being half out of his mind.

Downstairs in the lobby, Chong recognizes the policeman he spoke to almost a month ago, the truant officer.

"You looking for us?"

"Right." A bulky, muscled man, the officer introduces himself as Sergeant Chomski. If he remembers Chong, he shows no sign of it. "Judge Carson asked me to bring you over."

"So what does she want?" Ginny asks.

"I don't know," Chomski says. "I don't know the details of your case. Nothing." He leads them out of the hotel and down the block at a leisurely pace.

Ginny walks close to Chong, rubbing shoulders. "I'm scared," she whispers.

"I understand," Chong says.

"It's a trick and she's going to send me to that school."

"No, Ginny," Chong insists. "You're not at fault for anything. They want to protect you, not punish you."

When they reach the courthouse, a squat, crumbling building of sandstone and a red tile roof, Chomski takes them in a side door at the basement level. The sudden darkness causes Chong a moment of blindness; huge purple dots swim away from his eyes into the corridor, and a wild disconcerting shriek fills the air, echoes crazily from the linoleum, enamel, cement surface of the hallway.

"You can't take her from me! I won't have it."

Into his confusion now, hands are slapping against his face, and instinctively he covers his eyes, an action that sends a sharp pain across his chest, makes him cough, wince, sink down against the wall.

Clouded, imprecise as his vision remains, Chong sees only a strange silhouette thrashing before him, humped, squirming, though it also seems slowly to be brought under control, and he can decode the tumult as Sergeant Chomski containing a furious woman.

"Take it easy, lady," Chomski growls. "Take it easy or I'll put the cuffs on you. I mean it."

"That's my daughter. He's trying to take my daughter from me."

"Let's relax," Chomski says. "Relax. Maybe you'd better have a talk with Judge Carson, too. But I'll lock you up if you don't settle down."

Ginny has crouched beside Chong, helps him to his feet. She bites her lip, holding back tears.

"He's not taking me away," she says. "He's trying to help me. More than you ever did."

"God damn it," Mrs. Cahill's disembodied voice begins, but Chomski interrupts her at once.

"Let's take this upstairs," he says. "That's what the court's for, that's what the judge is for. You're not going to settle anything down here."

"I'd like to kill you," Mrs. Cahill barks at Chong.

Chomski warns her: "Anything you say now, I'm listening to, and I'll report it. You understand?"

"Yes." Her teeth flash as she speaks.

Mrs. Cahill comes into focus now as Chong's vision clears, bright purple spots still at the periphery of what he can see in the dim light. Chong wants to scream back at her, Why don't you people leave me alone? But he is too tired and does not want to provoke another outburst. So she is short, shorter even than Ginny, with wide hips and graceful shoulders. To pursue her daughter in Royalton she has dressed not unconsciously in pale blue slacks with a matching nylon jacket, has even tied a sheer white scarf around her neck, the bow coquettishly to one side. So civilized, Chong thinks, compared to me. . . . In the dim light, Carey Cahill's eyes appear black, and they peer from a secret depth, as if she sees from somewhere behind the surface, as inside a mask. Her high cheekbones seem almost Indian, curve down to a pointed chin, and even in her fury her pursed lips, large and full, seem oddly sensual. No wonder she was famous in Lake Ecstasy, and even Turner once pursued her. Her beauty has not faded much. As they move down the hallway into better light, and Carey Cahill eyes Chong angrily, he can see that her eyes are green, too, like Ginny's, and her hair, though it has lost brilliance with age, must once have been the rich brown-red that Ginny's is. Certainly there is no doubt of their relation! And it is so odd to see them together, Ginny stumbling ahead, bent over in shame, her mother, elbow in the hand of the policeman who seems so huge beside her, marching with anger, the short heels of her pointed shoes smacking, smacking on the tile; and they are both beautiful, and absurd, and sad, Chong thinks.

In the elevator going up, Mrs. Cahill's lips curl in anger and she starts to say something to Chong, but stops when he holds up his hand and shakes his head. Whatever it is she wants to say, he does not want to hear it. He tries with this gesture to let her know that he has reached a limit, that if she goes beyond this he will retaliate. She seems to understand, or she cannot decide what she wants to say, and Chong does not care. But when Ginny leans her head into Chong's shoulder, her mother grabs her by the arm and wrenches her away.

"Mom! Cut it out!"

"O.K.," Chomski says. "Hands off. Everybody."

"I'll touch my daughter if I want."

"No." Ginny tugs her arm free. She points to the bruise on her face. "This is what happens when people touch me."

Mrs. Cahill covers her face with her hands for a moment. Mercifully, then, the elevator doors open, and Chomski ushers them all down a bright, polished wooden hallway, their reflections and those of the lights and the high windows in gleaming smudges in the varnish, into the quiet lobby of a large office. An older woman looks up from a desk piled high with papers and smiles at Chomski.

"Is this the Cahill case?" she asks him.

"Yes it is."

"I'll let the judge know you're here."

The judge sees them one at a time, Ginny first, then Mrs. Cahill, and finally Chong. Chomski has remained in the office, sometimes chatting amiably with the secretary, something that helps to relieve Chong's worry, since it is so clear that his problems, Ginny's, Mrs. Cahill's, are ordinary, nothing to distract the rest of the world from going about its business, complaining about friends and relatives, electric bills, and political decisions, planning for vacations, weddings, funerals . . . The interviews with Ginny and her mother have lasted over an hour, and Chong is in a mild stupor when he is at last called in, passes Mrs. Cahill whose red-rimmed eyes nevertheless do not prevent her from slashing him with a sneer of hatred and defiance.

"Sit down, Mr. Chong." Judge Carson folds her hands on her stomach, swivels in her chair behind a large oak desk. She is middle-aged, her graying hair pulled back in a tight bun, so that her forehead seems high and blank. She tilts her head and looks Chong over without saying anything for some time.

"Why," she says finally, "did you allow Ginny, or ask Ginny to come live in your house?"

Chong opens his hands in a gesture of helplessness. "Because she was living in a bus, a camp, on my land. She was stealing my food and clothes. She had no water, except from the pond."

"How long did she live with you?"

Chong knows now it will be a long session, that Judge Carson will want to know everything about him. Already he is weary with explaining, and he hasn't even started. One after another, perfunctorily, the questions come. And inevitably:

"Tell me about the drawings you made of Ginny."

"She posed for me."

"Did you discourage this?"

"It was a fait accompli."

"How so?"

"I was drawing. She came into the room without clothes on."

"You didn't tell her to get dressed?"

"No."

"Did you touch her?"

"No."

"Why didn't you tell her to get dressed?"

"She said she wanted to model."

"Did she ask permission?"

"Yes. But after she was undressed."

"And you gave it."

"Yes." Chong looks at the judge. "But I didn't think it was my permission to give or not. And she said she was doing it to repay me, to thank me."

"Did this seem reasonable compensation to you?"

"It seemed harmless. I didn't expect and never asked for any compensation. I didn't take her in for pay."

"She said you asked her to work for you."

"Why not? I thought it would do her good. She doesn't know how to work. It's a good thing to learn, isn't it?"

"So you did all of these things in the pure spirit of helping a homeless child, and not because she is quite an attractive young woman you could have at your mercy?"

"Jesus," Chong says. "She is never at my mercy. The kid is not helpless. She has a mind of her own, you know. She's tough."

"I don't know that," the judge says. After a pause: "Did you ever have sex with her?"

"Never."

"Ever kiss her?"

"No."

"Did she ever sit on your lap?"

"No!"

"Did you ever fondle her or pet her?"

"Absolutely not."

"Did you ever spy on her?"

"Spy on her? What do you mean?"

"Watch her when she was showering or getting ready for bed?"

"No," Chong says wearily. "You know I have a daughter Ginny's age? Why would I want to spy on anybody? These questions make me—"

"These are questions I have to ask," Judge Carson says. "I ask them because experience has taught us that they need to be asked. Please be patient. I'm trying not to jump to any conclusions, and the decision I have to make regarding Ginny is very important to her, and to her mother. Wouldn't you say?"

"Yes, I don't envy you. I'm sorry. I'm not feeling so well."

"Tell me about that. Why do you think Mr. Parker attacked you?"

The afternoon wears on. Chong has been so long in the chair answering questions that his hips begin to ache. "Do you mind if I stand a minute? My leg is falling asleep."

"Go right ahead." Judge Carson looks at a clock on her desk. "I didn't realize I was keeping you so long."

Chong stands and stretches. "I never sit so much. I paint standing up, then I work in the garden."

"Where can I see some of your paintings?" the judge asks.

Chong outlines his gallery problems for her. "But at my house I have many things you could see. Many, many things."

"Can you tell me what your painting is like? What subjects you paint, that sort of thing."

Chong smiles, recognizes the question as an attempt to understand him, to make a judgment about his character.

"Maybe," he says, "what I would tell a judge about my painting is not what the judge would see. It's not an answerable question, because I could also make observations about you, on how you react to what I do. This is not a question of what is right and wrong in painting."

"It's possible you might find me stupid and insensitive about your work," Judge Carson says.

"I never said that."

"But, it's possible, isn't it?"

"Yes, Your Honor," Chong says, "but generally I see that people who admit the possibility are either completely uninterested in art and do not consider their ignorance of it as anything the least bit important, or they have a tolerance of artistic ideas bred of their own curiosity."

"One hour with me and you're beginning to sound like a lawyer already." Judge Carson betrays the hint of a smile. "One last question, Mr. Chong. Do you think it would be outrageous to ask you to look after Ginny one more night at the hotel, until she can be taken to her foster home?"

"I want to get free of this," Chong says, "but one more night is O.K."

"Our only alternative is the jail, and I don't think she'd understand that."

"She would take it personally," Chong says. "You agree she can't go home?"

"I do," the judge says.

"Maybe if someone else could do it tonight," Chong says. "I'm taking medicine that makes me sleepy. If someone came to take her, I couldn't stop them."

"We're asking our night patrol to look into the hotel every hour," Judge Carson says. "It's all we can do."

"O.K.," Chong says. "I thank you."

"I hope I haven't tired you too much."

Chong merely smiles and nods.

"I didn't think she would care if I went away." Ginny sits Indian-style on the bed beside Chong. "She was even crying. When I saw, I wanted to go with her."

"Yes, but you said she refused to stay away from Parker. She wants it both ways, and she can't have it both ways." Chong leans back on the bed, tries to adjust himself so he can sit up and watch the television without the tape across his chest pinching him. "This could be temporary. Some day you'll be with your mother again. I'm not surprised she was crying. She's having her daughter taken away. She has to admit, that in the eyes of the state, anyway, she has not been a good mother."

"But she has sometimes, Chong. She just doesn't know how to do things. She can't make up her mind."

"Evidently she decided that Parker is more important to her than you are." Chong regrets saying this at once. "I mean, for now."

"But he's in trouble and probably will go to jail. Maybe she'd feel bad about dumping him. And she still doesn't understand about you. She's treated you like dirt."

"She believes Parker. He obviously showed her the pictures, and told her what to think of them. And even if she doesn't think we were lovers, she's bound to be upset that you took your clothes off in front of me."

"If I went back with Mom," Ginny says, "maybe I could steal the pictures back. Then you wouldn't have to worry so much."

A little amused by Ginny's bravado, Chong asks, "What makes you think I'm worried?"

"You're worried. I'm worried about it, too. Because it's not fair." Ginny grabs Chong's ankle, grits her teeth. "Besides, those are *my* drawings."

"Actually, they're mine," Chong says.

"But weren't you going to give them to me?"

"No," Chong says. "Honestly, I don't think I meant for anyone to ever see them."

"But that's not why you do drawings, is it? Don't you want people to see them? And buy them?"

"Sometimes you do things for yourself and your friends," Chong says. "When you posed for me, I thought it was a secret, between you and me. See?"

"I thought maybe people would see them," Ginny says. "Maybe people in New York."

"Hand me my pills, will you?" Chong stretches, trying to rid himself of a cramp. "I wasn't going to take one, but my chest hurts."

"Is it bad?"

"Bad enough."

"So why wouldn't you want to take a pill?"

"Because it will make me sleepy, and then you'll have to go off to bed too."

"Oh, no." Ginny hands him the brown bottle, stretches for the water pitcher and the glass.

"Oh, no, what?"

"I'm not sleeping in there by myself. Suppose Parker comes after me."

"They won't let him in downstairs."

"There's all kinds of ways to get in here."

"He doesn't even know where you are!"

"Want to bet?"

Chong takes his pill, mutters. He has to admit he is not convinced Parker is not stalking them, and that Parker also has good reason to continue his pursuit of Ginny. He would be a hero to Carey if he brought her back, and he could play out his wicked game of rescuing Ginny from Chong's depraved attentions. Chong can see already that he will be on the hot seat, that Parker will fight for his freedom with that lie. With half his mind, Chong almost thinks he deserves it. He looks at Ginny with remorse, feeling old. He knows he has desired her. He has even told himself that he loves her, as if that would excuse any carnal exchange between them. She surprises him by straightening one of her legs, then half standing by the bed to return the glass and the pill jar to the stand.

"Couldn't we watch something else?" Ginny says.

"Sure. I don't care. Whatever you want."

"Don't you think you should get a TV now?"

"No." Chong laughs. "All I see on that damned thing is advertise-
ments. More ads than anything!"

"You're weird," Ginny says.

"I know it." Chong smiles wanly, feeling alien indeed, as if encased in a bubble, the Good Witch of the North, or something like
that. On the television, a woman puckers her mouth obscenely as
her hair swirls in slow motion about her face. Chong has seen the
advertisement three times in the last hour and can almost recite it.
More bounce in your curls. Tell me, he thinks, that this is not more
obscene than my drawings!

Ginny settles back on the bed, reclining close to him now, her
head propped on her hand, a seemingly awkward position, the kind
that only teenagers can hold for long. A drawing of that pose would
make the viewer tense, create its own tension, desire for change to
a more restful stance. Then she turns on her stomach, her side brushing his, and asks, "Are you going to finish the painting?"

"The painting?"

"The one I was helping you with."

"Jesus, I don't know," Chong says. "I was in a good mood doing
that. Now I'm not in such a good mood."

"I liked helping," Ginny says. "I wish I could stay with you until
it was finished. I even told the judge that."

"Maybe you could come and visit and we could finish it then,"
Chong says. "But I don't know what your foster parents will say
about that."

"I don't want any foster parents," Ginny says. "I want to do what
I want to do!"

"Maybe they're terrific."

"Yeah?" Ginny grips her head. "Oh, Christ, I don't know!"

"You'll just have to wait and see." Chong yawns now. He feels a
kind of helpless fatigue, allows himself to reach out and touch Ginny
on the shoulder, trying to offer comfort. She covers his hand with
one of her own, and Chong can feel that her cheeks are wet.

"Hey, what's this?" he says. "You're not crying?"

"Never," she says, her voice, high, squeezed. "Never, never."

"You're going to be O.K.," Chong assures her. "But you can cry,
too. You've had a rough time. Things are pretty uncertain."

"Ha!" Ginny swings off the bed and bounces into the bathroom,
spools paper off the roll, daubs her eyes and blows her nose. She
shuts and locks the door, which disturbs Chong a moment, until she

emerges again, her hair brushed out over her shoulders. She flops on the bed and takes Chong's hand again. "I just wish I knew what's going to happen. There's so many things I'm thinking about. I want to know, like, will I go to school in a new place, or will I be back here with my mother. If I have to go to a new school . . . God! I won't know anybody. They'll ask questions."

"You'll find friends," Chong says. "You'll be popular. It'll be a chance to start all over. You can be the kind of girl you want to be."

"I'll be too scared," Ginny says. "I want to see my old friends."

Chong has nothing to say to this, understanding her anxiety. Finally, he tells her, "I did it, you know. I came alone to a whole new country, new language, everything. You won't have it that hard."

"Still," Ginny says.

"I know you can do it," Chong says. "Look at me. I didn't know you before, and now I do, and I like you."

"I know," Ginny says. "I can tell. And that bothers me. Because, will I see you again? And I don't know why you like me, because I got you in trouble. And it's my fault. Sometimes I think anybody who likes me is stupid."

"It's not your fault," Chong says. "It's mine. Parker's. Taylor's. Your mother's, too."

"I don't understand it," Ginny says.

"Who does?" Chong groans.

"You were just trying to help me."

"Ginny, listen," Chong says. "I think I'd better be honest with you about that. I'm no saint, right? Yes, I was worried about you. Yes, I wanted to help you. But I also felt attraction, not so innocent."

"Yeah?"

"Yeah. Just another dirty old man. Just like Parker."

"Uh uh." Ginny shakes her head. "Not like Parker."

"No?"

"Because Parker forced me. You never forced me. You never even said anything. Until now. And you wouldn't force me. I know that."

"No," Chong says. "I would kill myself first."

"So you're not like Parker," Ginny says. "Don't say that, because you're not. There's a big difference."

Chong laughs quietly. "I wish I really thought so, kiddo."

"Well, I think so." Ginny buries her head in his chest.

"Ouch!" Chong says. "Ow, be careful."

Ginny laughs now, rolling onto her back. "Me, too, Chong. I hurt my face when I squeezed you. That's what Parker did to us. We hurt if we hug."

"Thanks to good old Parker." Chong listens to his heart beat in his ears, slowly and powerfully, knows that in spite of the pain the contact with Ginny has pleased him. He relaxes, allows her to nestle against him. The effect of the pill comes on now, and Chong feels drowsy and warm, even a little amused at how the garish colors of the television light up the room, a jazzed electronic palette that makes everything seem superreal and synthetic. He glances into Ginny's face and finds her studying him seriously. She seems pale, as if afraid, and Chong wonders if this is only an effect of the contrast between Ginny, her proximity in the darkness, and the lurid colors flashing at him from across the room.

Ginny kisses his neck now, and Chong knows he should protest, but the gesture he makes to push her face away translates so easily into a kind of caress, stroking the cheeks of her face, his fingers combing through her hair.

"You're crying again," he says.

"I'm not crying," she says softly. "I'm just . . . leaking. I mean, it's not like crying, really."

Chong laughs at this. "I never heard that before."

"It's stupid, I know. I'm stupid, I can't help it."

"Cut that out." Chong shakes his head vigorously.

"I'm going to make love to you," Ginny says.

"No. You're not. Forget it."

"I want to give you something."

"Oh, you have," Chong says.

"I don't want you to forget me, ever."

"I won't. How could I?"

"It's my decision. You're not forcing me."

"I don't think it's a good idea," Chong says.

"Maybe we'll never see each other again."

"I'll bet we will," Chong says.

"I'm going to." Ginny begins unbuttoning his shirt.

Chong puts his hand on top of hers, and this protest, too, proves feeble, metamorphoses into tender touching, guiding her hand. She opens his shirt, kisses him across his shoulder, but Chong finds somehow the will to stop her, holds her hands tightly as a lyric from an advertisement booms into the room, and Ginny's cheeks flush with reflected television light.

"Turn down the television," Chong says. "I want to tell you something."

"If we leave it on," Ginny says, "nobody will hear us."

"Do as I say."

Ginny swings off the bed and twists the television dial until the sound has disappeared.

She returns to the bed, pouting a little. Behind her, soundless images flutter across the screen.

"This is a very good sign," Chong tells her, "that you would not be too afraid of a man to make love to him."

"You're *not* like Parker. I don't think everybody's like Parker."

"I thank you for that," Chong says. "And I am flattered you might like to sleep with me."

"So why not?"

Chong sighs. "Because there are better ways to show your thanks, I guess. Because people are trusting me to behave."

"I'd never tell anyone. Ever."

"Never is a long time," Chong says, "but that's not the point anyway."

"Well, what *is* the point?" Ginny demands.

"The point is, you are going to be O.K.," Chong says.

"I don't understand."

"And also that you will find someone your own age sometime—I hope not too soon—to risk having babies with. Sex has consequences. We're not free from them." Chong rolls over and finds himself astounded that such a young face is so very close to his, and her eyes taking him in with such ease, an almost marital familiarity. "Look," he says. "You are beautiful. I am very tempted to take advantage of you. You are a desirable girl."

"Why is it taking advantage of me?" Ginny enunciates each word with force. "Why isn't it just doing what we want? What I want, too?"

"Because you run all the risks," Chong says. "Did you ever see an old Chinaman pregnant?"

"No." Ginny does not laugh. She lays her cheek gently on his chest and is quiet awhile. "I wish I was older."

"Don't rush it," Chong says. "You'll be older too damned fast, believe me." The drug makes his mind spin, his spirits sink a notch. "I have to be quiet now." He lays a hand lightly on Ginny's shoulders, and she curls closer to him. "The medicine is making me woozy."

Through Ginny's hair, the garish television colors pour, and the drug and the tender attentions of the girl have laid his heart bare. He is terrified that she will not be satisfied to accept his explanation for their continence, because if she persists now, he will have no resources for resisting her further. Chong knows he could be that kind of criminal at this moment, that his body does yearn for Ginny, and he half regrets his sanity, for letting this rare chance at intimacy and sexual pleasure pass him by—at his age something he swore he would never allow to happen again.

Ginny's hair dances with television color, is alive with dreams, almost like those the shadow of a tree and its leaves, when the wind is blowing, will throw on the side of a building or on the ground. It is a movie! A movie in her hair.

And all the worse for his attempts to subdue his desire, the movie is one of Konarak, holy temple of erotic love. Konarak! A few years before, Wu had introduced Chong to this medieval Indian temple carved and decorated to resemble a great sun chariot, with huge wheels carrying across the sky a pyramid of sculptured figures in attitudes of erotic play and sexual worship. The grainy photographs of the German anthropologists which Wu had shown him come to life now, colored life, in Ginny's hair, and his wonder at the existence of such a religion is rekindled: a whole civilization devoted to the arts of love, which made sexual sensation the focus of their search for God, copulation a form of meditation and discovery. Two women gently lift a third, suspend her over the sex of a male, on a swing of arms, the tenderest union possible, abetted by friends; thin silken ropes drape over the sensuous curves of men and women, jewels spangle; a man's leg tenderly encircles a woman's hip, and her hand carefully cups him, limits his immersion; two men suspend a woman between them as she turns from one lover to the next. . . . The Konarak sun chariot rolls into Chong's dreams and he sleeps finally among the goddesses of the pulsing stream, the wood nymphs whose skirts billow in the wind, the shepherdesses who bathe in the warm pond and know the coolest shade, the choicest beds of river grass, the women who have suspended a bed from the supple branch of a great tree, who kick their legs as the sweet craft pendulums higher and higher, quivers ever more ecstatically, rides into the night . . .

It all goes very simply and smoothly in the morning. Dr. Miranda greets them in the lobby of his office and thanks Chong for his care of the girl and wishes him well.

Chong will not get to meet the foster parents. This comes as a disappointment to him, but he understands the reason for it and is even glad. Not even torture could get the information out of me if I don't have it! He laughs at his naivete about these things.

"Be brave," he says to Ginny.

"Yeah," she says.

As he turns to leave, a little embarrassed, Ginny flings herself upon him, and she kisses him on the face, the cheeks, like a child saying good-bye, then grips his head and kisses him powerfully, all too powerfully, not like a child at all, but like a lover.

He finds himself on the street in bright sunshine, staggering, disoriented. He blames it on the medicine.

He misses Ginny as if his own daughter had been taken from him. Well, he must let go. His dreams of the previous night come back to him, and he reasons them away, to repress the pain of their beauty. Konarak! How had the temple ever survived the repressions and mutilations of more puritanical eras? Survived history's ever-vigilant censors? This ode to love and rapture, the creative force of the world. Chong wants to travel to Konarak and climb among the figures sculptured on the chariot and to become, if possible, imbued with their sense of the eroticized world, to learn this secret knowledge by feel, by direct experience. Sandstone, sun-warmed, cooled by the night sky. A glimpse of Eden.

Chong grumbles now. What fabulous secrets had been destroyed? And why is pleasure, Chong wonders, always taken to be subversive? Why were the secrets of Konarak considered deadly to the current political enterprises, which daily tested the limits of human sanity, and were fundamentally a politics of terror and threat?

Chong stares into the window of the Red Shield store, sees himself staring back. He is such a far cry from the fabulous males of the Konarak sun chariot! And would he want Susan, or even Ginny, in such a world? Perhaps it was after all a mocking cruel fantasy, to demonstrate how free the gods were from the miseries of human life. Was it the promise of a future yet to be realized, an erotic civilization waiting to be constructed from the scraps of human pleasure, creativity, and longing? Was it a model for the congregation, a text on how to live their lives? Was it a yearly ritual only, a Chanukah, a Christmas, a hegira of continuous erotic tumult? The yang sun rolls though the yin heavens. Chong touches the image of himself in the glass on the storefront, shakes his own hand. He laughs, paws the stubble on his chin. If I tried to climb aboard the sun chariot, he thinks, they might kick me off.

At the drugstore on the corner, Chong learns there is a bus that will stop along the road in Lake Ecstasy. It leaves Royalton at one-thirty, and that gives him plenty of time to read last week's New York newspapers, inspect Rubb's New and Used Furniture, and prowl the Army-Navy Surplus Store.

How the day passes he is not sure, his brain has been disengaged, but when he is finally home, has inspected the half-finished painting of his Lake Ecstasy life, and walks out to the pond, he feels more alone, and more afraid of being alone, than he has ever been in his entire life.

13
Careless Love

J im twisted awake to the sound of machine guns and was at
once bathed in sweat. Couldn't be! He was in Barber's house,
and sunshine was pouring through the windows. Then he recognized the sound as Red's ratchet gun banging bolts from a wheel.

The impact of the bullets had been so powerful, the hail of fire so
intense, that the body would not fall, kept jerking in midair like a
gory puppet. Jim shoved the memory away, or tried to. The hail of
fire had kept the dead body dancing while it disintegrated, whole
chunks of the body blew off. It just disappeared. Jim lurched to the
window. Sunshine. Red was working already. A normal day.

After he dressed and came downstairs, Jim found Nancy Wallace
sitting at the kitchen table with a cup of coffee at her elbow, carefully winding thread onto a hook in Red's fly-tying vise.

"Don't tell me he's got you tying flies for him, too."

Nancy bolted out of her concentration. "Jesus, you scared me.
Hey. I'm not tying these for him. They're for me."

"How come you're not at the Inn this morning?"

"Slow season," Nancy said, biting thread. "I called in sick. Can't
you tell how sick I am?" With fingers she pulled down the corners
of her eyes.

"Should I run you to the hospital?"

"What? And waste a good sick day?"

"Are you and Red going fishing?"

"That's what he said last night." She concentrated again on the vise. "But first thing in the morning, here they come. 'Hey, Red, can you fix this right away. Emergency.' 'Hey, Red, I can't work if my machine is down.' "

"You should've made an early start."

"Yeah, well," Nancy said. "We got sidetracked."

"So who's fault is that?"

"I'm not blaming anybody. Christ! How does he get this goddamn fur to stay on?"

"Is the string waxed? Don't you have to wax the string first if you're dubbing fur?"

"I knew I was forgetting something."

Jim fixed himself some coffee and toast and sat at the table across from Nancy. Her brown eyes gleamed with concentration, and Jim admired the dexterity of her hands, which were not delicate at all, but thick at the knuckles, and with close-cropped fingernails—hands that knew work.

"Tying flies now," Jim said, "you'll probably be up to your ears in engine repairs next, if you keep hanging around the redhead."

"Wouldn't surprise me," Nancy said. "I'll bet he pays lousy, though." She quickly wrapped a bead of fur onto the little hook in the vise and left the bobbin hanging as she searched through the box of small tools and then through a disorderly pile of feather and fur.

Jim closed his eyes and leaned back in the chair.

"Hangover?" Nancy asked.

"Mmm," Jim affirmed. He didn't want to talk about it.

"I didn't see you at the Mountaintop," Nancy said.

"I was at the VFW."

"What the hell were you doing over there?"

"Playing pool and getting drunk," Jim said. "And I left my god-damned jacket there."

"I always thought that was a kind of gruesome place," Nancy said.
"It is."

"So why did you go?"

Jim rubbed the back of his neck. "I talked to my wife on the phone for a while and after that I kind of felt bummed out."

"Is she going through with it?"

"That's what she says," Jim said. "It's out of my hands now, I guess. I guess I just wait for the blow and see if I'm still standing afterwards."

Nancy grunted. "Yeah?"

" 'Yeah'? 'Yeah,' what? What's that supposed to mean?"

"I'm just wondering," Nancy said, "if you're taking that position because you really want the divorce to go ahead, or if you really think you can't do anything about it."

"What's to do?"

"You could go to Boston," Nancy said. "You could talk to her face-to-face."

"She says she doesn't want me to come. That it would upset T'isa."

"You've got a right to see your own daughter," Nancy said. "And she's going to be upset anyway. Your wife—Anna is it?—can't prevent that. Neither can you."

"I don't know," Jim said. "I thought maybe if I got straight first—"

"Yeah?"

"What's the matter? 'Yeah' again."

"I don't know you very well," Nancy said. "I hope you do get straight."

"It's too late anyway. Too late for Anna's sake. So where does that leave me?"

"I don't know," Nancy said. "Unless it's right where you want to be."

"I don't think so."

"You made the choices, right?" Nancy spoke lightly, without a tone of accusation. "If you don't do something else, it must be because you like what you're doing?"

"Oh," Jim said, nodding, raising his eyebrows, "nice to know I have so much choice."

"There!" Nancy unscrewed the vise and held up the fly for Jim's inspection. "How's that look?"

Jim reached over and took it from her. Their fingertips brushed in the exchange, and Nancy looked at him frankly. The fly was well made, and Jim said so, a "Mosquito," mostly hackle, and not the easiest pattern to tie.

"So what are you trying to tell me?" He set the fly delicately in the palm of Nancy's hand.

Nancy looked away. "Nothing. I don't have anything to tell you, Jim."

"Don't chicken out now. Who knows? You might change my life."

Nancy shrugged. "I'm not the greatest expert on running a life, you may have heard. I've made a few mistakes, I've got my own hang-ups."

"You're doing O.K., though," Jim said. "You're tough. You know what you want."

"Do I?"

"It looks like it to me."

"Well, I'll tell you what I see," Nancy said. "You can take it or leave it."

"O.K."

"I see a guy who is trying to get straight, who doesn't really want to get straight."

"Yeah?"

"That's what I see."

"O.K.," Jim said. "That's interesting. I appreciate it."

"Don't get mad."

"I'm not mad at you. I'm really not." What if she's right? he wondered. Why can't I make up my mind? "I hope you're wrong, that's all."

"I hope so, too," Nancy said. She smiled a small, crooked smile. "I probably am, in fact. When it comes to men—"

"Don't give me that," Jim said. "You know men pretty well. You could help a guy. Any guy can see that."

"You think so? Really?"

"You do Red a lot of good, I know that." Jim laughed. "Maybe I shouldn't tell you."

"Why shouldn't you?"

"Might upset the balance of power or something."

Nancy laughed now, spread her arms in a gesture of helplessness. "*What* balance?"

"You keep him guessing, too," Jim said. "He's not sure about you, in any way."

"Does he suffer?" Nancy asked with mock glee.

"You bet he does," Jim said. "I shouldn't tell you all this."

"He really suffers?"

"It's agony," Jim said. "He's crazed with it sometimes."

"Now I know you're messing with me," Nancy said. "Men are always conspiring."

"I'm telling the truth," Jim said. "I'm returning the favor."

"Sometimes," Nancy said, "I really wish I had Wonder Woman's magic lasso, the one that makes you tell the truth. I'd put it around Red, I'd put it around you, I'd put it around myself. Maybe all three at once."

"Christ, you're something," Jim said. "I never in a million years would've had a thought like that."

Nancy spooled some fur onto a waxed line. "You don't know what you might think. You might wake up some morning and surprise yourself."

I'd like to wake up, Jim thought. He said nothing, watching Nancy fashion a little bug out of hair, feather, fur: Nancy's "Deceiver," variation on an old theme.

Later in the morning, Jim volunteered to make a trip to Royalton to pick up some tires for Red so that he and Nancy could spend at least a few hours fishing together. Red had made the telephone calls, and all Jim had to do was make the rounds and return.

"And now look at it," Nancy grumbled. "Getting ready to rain."

"Fish don't know the difference," Red said.

"I made all these dry flies," Nancy said. "How dry are they going to be in the rain?"

In the hills, as Jim drove to Royalton, huge gray clouds billowed up and then sent down a cool drizzle that made the road shine and reflect the green of the overhanging trees. In Royalton itself, the rain crashed down for a while, and Jim's shirt was soaked when he finished loading the tires into the trunk and the back seat of his car. In Viet Nam, he had spent so much time in the rain that the pelting now hardly bothered him. After a Viet Nam downpour, all other rain seemed a little halfhearted, a little phony. Jim remembered the rain there was often so fierce you had to tip your head forward to breathe, and then the little space beneath your face and helmet would fill with mosquitoes. They had had a contest: Who could kill the most mosquitoes with a single swipe of the hand. A guy named McAllister had won. Claimed sixty-three of the bastards at once. The mosquitoes were one of the many small details of Viet Nam that threatened your sanity. Your choice was to breathe rain or breathe bugs. Take your pick.

When he was out of the service, Jim had traveled to see the McAllister family in Ohio, where he had been received with suspicion and despair. McAllister's father worked in a Chevrolet plant and was about to go on strike because so much automation was being put in place; his mother worked in a warehouse-type bargain store, housewares department. They liked their garden, motorcycling, and Lawrence Welk, and they voted for Richard Nixon. The moral deterioration of their son had been precipitous, but Jim didn't tell them that. Joe McAllister had cut out pages of his little Bible to hold prophylactics and joints, and he had carved out the pages with standard issue bayonet, an obsolete weapon.

Now it was raining in Royalton, Massachuetts; Joe McAllister, champion mosquito killer, had been dead for fifteen years; and Jim was killing time so a friend could have a little privacy. It's nuts, he thought, the whole weird system of things. How do you make sense of a system like this?

There would be nothing to do in Lake Ecstasy, and since Red would not need the tires for a few hours—maybe would never need them, but had given Jim an errand to get some privacy with Nancy—Jim drove toward the VFW, where he intended only to inquire after his jacket and sunglasses, which he thought he had left there. But a large white car in front of Rubb's New and Used caught his eye, and he pulled in beside it and inspected it carefully. He was pretty sure he had seen the same car before, on the trail to Lake Ecstasy the morning of the car fire. He couldn't be positive, but he decided to wait awhile, piqued by curiosity and the desire to test his memory. He had nothing better to do, and if Red wanted him out of the house awhile, Jim was more than willing to oblige.

Now a man and a woman came down the street. The woman turned occasionally to shout at the man, and when she turned away again, he pushed her, hard, down the street. She weaved carelessly, as if drunk or drugged. Jim could not hear the content of their quarrel, but it had all the earmarks of a lovers' wrangle. The man was not very tall, bearded, had the weather-beaten face of a laborer; the woman was small, but puffed up by her fury. The rain and the shoves of the man had undone the careful upturn of her brown-red hair, and though she was attractive, she looked tired, like a woman who has worried, or nagged, for years. Jim looked away in embarrassment, half of him wanting to step out and ask the man if he enjoyed beating up girls, the other half wanting only to mind his own business. When he looked back, the man had squeezed himself into the passenger seat of the white car, in spite of the woman's protests, and refused to budge although she clearly demanded it of him. Whoa, Jim thought. That's him. And maybe that's the woman I thought I saw. And I've seen that guy somewhere else. At the Inn, maybe. Playing pool.

The woman paced back and forth in front of the car, lips pulled tight across her teeth in anger and frustration, and then with a savage little hop she threw herself into the driver's seat, slammed the door, and shoved the key into the ignition. As soon as she did this, the man backhanded her harshly across the face, and the woman slumped down, hands over her mouth. Now Jim slid out, walked to the car, and tapped on the window by the woman's face. She looked at him quickly and then slumped forward in embarrassment.

"You all right, miss? Do you want some help?"

The man opened the door, stood up, resting his arms on the roof. He was wearing sunglasses now, and Jim thought: that could be him. He's about the right size. The hair curled like that on the back of his neck.

"Take a walk," the man said calmly. "This don't concern you."

Jim leaned to the window and said to the woman, "If you want me to get the police, just say so."

"Hey, pal. J'you hear me, or what?"

The woman shook her head no, waved Jim away. Jim stood, backed slowly to the curb, smiling at the man, who stared back, then sank into the car. He ordered the woman to drive off, and she backed into the street without even a glance at Jim. The engine ticked in a familiar way—tappets sticking, Red would have said—the tires hissed on the wet pavement, and the unhappy couple was gone.

When he returned to Red's cottage, Jim was greeted by a strange sight. Red, dressed only in a pair of swim trunks and the thick dark fishing glasses he liked to have on when stoned, had constructed a circle of rocks in the center of his yard, knee-high with grass and weeds, and was presiding over a roaring wood fire. About a dozen people including Nancy and Betty and the Wild Women were sprawled on the porch and its steps, drinking wine and beer. Betty stood away from the others at the edge of the porch and she waved shyly to Jim when she saw him. Her teeth flashed in a quick smile.

Red looks like a caveman, Jim thought.

As he crossed the lawn, Red greeted Jim with flashes of semaphore signals, using his barbecue fork and tongs, KMA—military shorthand for "Kiss my ass." Then he wrapped his arms around Jim's shoulders in an embrace so loving that Jim was startled by it. He even thought Red might have had tears in his eyes.

"Hey." He punched Red in the gut. "What's going on?"

"Wicked grass," Red said.

"Man, you're wrecked," Jim said.

"Oh, man." Red shook his head almost sadly. "Good news and bad news, guy."

"Lay it on me," Jim said. "Good news?"

"I'm getting married." Red threw back his head now in a great howl of laughter. "I am! To Nancy!" He stretched an arm toward her, and she rose from the porch step and did a little curtsey, laughing with Red.

Jim hooted his congratulations. He pushed Red back and forth across the yard, pumping his hand, pummeling him on the back, as if he believed in marriage, as if he thought it was the best thing for Red, and for Nancy. Was I happy once? Jim wondered, then berated himself for the self-centeredness of the thought. May it be a happy union! Happier than mine.

"I guess I don't have to ask what the bad news is," he said. "I guess I better think quick about moving on."

"I'm sorry as hell," Red said.

"No sweat," Jim said. "I was going back to Boston anyway. There's nothing for me to do around here, and I want to see my kid."

Red continued his unbelievably affectionate, unforgiving hug. "But don't go tomorrow, man. Stay at least until the wedding. You gotta come to the wedding."

"You happy, Red?" Jim asked. "About the whole deal?"

"Look at her sitting there," Red said.

And indeed, Nancy seemed in full womanly bloom, serene and untroubled, her eyes sparkling.

"I am happy, yeah. I'm so happy I could flippin' die."

Betty was sitting on the porch steps now, seemingly quite alone, looking out over the hills where thunderheads were rolling away, taking the rain with them and leaving just the corner of a rainbow.

Red's bonfire crackled and hissed and sent up a column of pristine white smoke. Who is he signaling? Jim wondered. He looked at Betty and thought, Too bad. We might have had a chance.

After a few more days, Chong reclaims the rhythm of life in Lake Ecstasy. The tape on his chest itches, and he has become impatient with it, but feels, too, it covers a big hole where his heart once was. He picks blueberries on the shores of Lake Ecstasy in the early mornings, before it becomes too hot and buggy, and returns to work on the painting with growing but not perfect enthusiasm.

And meanwhile he has been stricken with another idea, which at first seemed silly, but which now possesses him. The idea came to him when he discovered, in the swamp above the pond on his farm, the shell of an old wooden rowboat. The prow had raised itself from the turgid green water like a turtle periscoping for danger, and Chong latched onto it and struggled with it out of the slime, only to discover that while the sides of it were intact and sturdy, the entire floor of the craft had disappeared. It was a boat of immensely simple construction, the frame of it little more than a large "A" boxed in, the bottom flat, just a little pond pram that must have washed over the dam at the state park upstream and banged its way gradually down to Chong's swamp.

Chong had always wanted to see into his pond in the same way one could see into the nearly invisible waters of Lake Ecstasy, to snorkel around its edges and bottom. But he was no longer a good swimmer, and was uneasy about snorkeling alone. The bottomless boat struck him as the perfect way to explore the pond. The frame presented itself as a gift. All that would be required was a clear bottom, a bottom of glass or Plexiglas, which could be applied with screws and marine caulk, and if it would not last forever, it would at least permit him to make the kind of study he has often dreamed of. Why is he so fascinated with aquatic life? It has something to do, he thinks, with the grace of movement of submarine things, the streamlining of the fish, the nightmarish grotesqueness of the other creatures, crab, frog, salamander. Good water is so abundant with life. It becomes obvious to him that he must have a clear-bottomed boat. He can't live a moment longer without one!

The project stalls momentarily when Chong cannot find a good material to cover the boat's bottom. He has rummaged in his barn, attic, basement, and though he has found some old storm windows they are clearly not strong enough to hold his weight, and in any case would be next to impossible to affix neatly to the frame. This little stymie irritates Chong profoundly. He knows a Plexiglas bottom will be expensive, that it would be a reckless outlay of his limited resources to purchase it. Eighty or ninety dollars? But now he has focused on this idea, it has become a need. A need! he tells himself.

While he dabbles with the Lake Ecstasy painting, he works on the boat project in the back of his mind, and one night when he is about to fall asleep in the chair in his living room the answer comes to him as the most obvious and simple thing in the world: the clear bottom doesn't have to support his weight. He can build a little platform for his body that would be sturdy enough to hold him up, and also to help strengthen the boat, stabilize the structure. Then the second bottom could be anything that was watertight; it could even be as simple as a heavy-gauge plastic sheet! And if he wanted to keep pressure and weight off the clear bottom, he could always supply flotation to the sides—a couple of barrels or a cluster of plastic bottles. Chong swings out of the chair and scribbles notes to himself, makes quick drawings of his bottom-viewing boat. When he finally climbs into bed, his mind whirls with possibilities, adjustments he can make, experiments he can try. And then he dreams of sailing out on the water of his pond—which is black as oil in his dream—and seeing down, down into the water, the most marvelous phantasmagoric creatures, giant diatoms with perfect crystalline design, like living snowflakes, dragons of the deep, and in the darkest depths a great hulking shape, quiet and stealthy, and all Chong's dream alarms go off: This is something you do not want to see, something you had better not disturb. He heads for shore, sweating.

It takes him about ten days to build his bottom-probing boat. August is already becoming a dream. The boat is not perfect, for it floats awkwardly and can't be steered precisely, mainly drifts in the current and the wind. Attached to the basic frame, to lift it in the water, are two outrigger bars—hollow plastic drain pipes, capped, to which have been lashed dozens of plastic gallon bottles. (He first thought of bamboo poles lashed to empty gourds, as attended some of the river craft he had seen in his youth.) The bottom itself consists of a pair of storm windows that have been bolted, glued, and caulked together and set in a sheet of marine plywood (painted blue) cut to the exact dimensions of the frame. Just above this is Chong's most ingenious solution to his dream of and desire for a bottomless boat: The inner supporting platform is a simple canvas sling given added strength by a few ropes. This device is simply nailed to the upper edges of the frame, and when Chong lowers himself onto it, it sags so that his face is just above the clear boat belly, and is also very much more comfortable than planking could ever be.

Esthetically, the boat viewed from outside is pretty monstrous, a floating junkyard. Neither is its aquatic performance a marvel, for it is only with the greatest effort of paddling that the boat can be turned at all. This does not worry Chong, because there is nothing for the boat to flounder on except the shores of the pond. Besides, Chong reasons, if he wants better navigation, he can always cut himself a pole and use that, a thing that would otherwise disturb his observations by stirring up the bottom.

But inside the boat, as Chong lies on his belly in the shallows, the esthetics are everything his heart desires. He floats within a floating instrument, bobbing with the bobbing of the boat, twisting and turning like an astronaut, and his view of the bottom of the pond is gloriously unimpeded by reflections, ripples, surface light. The breeze cools his back, the strange shadow of this strange craft ripples over the contours of the pond floor, startling fish, who jet away and then return slowly to ogle the marvel that flies above them. Chong names the craft *Fu Yu*, an elaborate pun since *fu* means both "boat" and "happiness," and *yu* both "fish" and "fertility." This name gives Chong enormous pleasure. So simple, and so complex in Chinese. He is the happy, potent flying batfish man. Wonderful, he thinks, what a single invention can do for life.

A perfect Saturday morning arrives. One of the maples has already had a piece of its crown seared by a portent of fall and gleams yellow and orange, colors that the pond wears, too, amidst the rest of the predominating, lingering green. Chong has learned that when the sun is directly overhead it reflects in his boat window and makes it impossible to see, so that mornings and evenings are the best times for his pond-watching trips. And he is in a mood to sail and play, because he has finished the Lake Ecstasy painting the night before, or believes he has finished it, and is only waiting for the paint to be dry, and to reconsider it before taking it to Verano and the Village Inn.

Meanwhile, the underwater life of the pond has stirred his imagination powerfully, and he knows in his bones that his next works will be based on the free-flowing, soft-edged, merging, blurred, and shadowy imagery from beneath the surface of his pond. So he goes aboard *Fu Yu* with doubled interest, not only for pleasure but as an embarkation on a new artistic pursuit, a new dream-and-real-world esthetic. Sometimes looking into the pond is so like looking into his own mind it electrifies him. And the colors! And when a leaf, say, drifts down and touches the surface of the pond, and leaf-shaped lines radiate out from the point of contact, each wave creating a little rainbow and a shadow on the bottom of the pond, cause and effect, physics is raised to a glorious power.

The breeze is brisk today. Chong strips completely, sits for a moment on the canvas support as he pushes himself off with a pole, then turns over and begins to drift across the pond. Beneath him, an incredible school of minnows surges. Their sides are green, backs black and silver, their eyes like diamonds. And there is such a surge and coiling of them as they pass beneath his window—thousands!—Chong wonders if this is a breeding ruckus, because he has not seen these little fish before, not in such numbers, wonders also if they have come into the pond from the stream. He fears for them—their numbers, their brilliance, can only be enticing to larger fish—and he worries that he will see an attack. But the boat drifts on into deeper water. Below him now, a branch reaches up from the black leaf-packed bottom like a hand, a claw, and a half-dozen red-eyed rock bass hover amongst the twigs like fat leaves. A quick long shadow darts to the bottom, unidentifiable but large and secretive, an old pickerel or trout.

There are flies accompanying Chong today, and mosquitoes sometimes, and he slaps at them and swears, since they disturb his pleasant contemplation of the bottom. He seems to be moving quite fast suddenly, is stung on the neck, sits up hearing a roar of water, and sees *Fu Yu* is quickly gaining on the dam, and a man in waders, sloshing, moaning, fly rod aloft, making pell-mell for the shore.

Chong quickly heaves his anchor over, watches the bubbles plunge down with the cement lump he has tied to the rope, then feels the craft bump as the rope comes taut.

The man standing beside the dam, jaw dropped, looks familiar to Chong. "Oh, yes," he says. "You're Barber's friend, right?"

"You scared the shit out of me," Jim Williams says.

"I'm really sorry." Chong laughs in spite of himself. "I didn't know you were fishing here, I would have stayed away."

Williams seems to have recovered his wits now, and he grins. "I was kind of low in the water there, you know. I didn't know there was anybody in that thing. Then all of a sudden there's this thrashing around."

"I'll toss you this rope, you can pull me over, O.K.? Then I'll go put some clothes on, make some tea. You come by the house when you finish fishing."

Jim catches the rope that Chong flings him and pulls the boat to shore when Chong hauls up his anchor. Chong climbs out beside him, his chest taped, nude, looking like a shrunken samurai, and it is all Jim can do to keep from laughing.

"I think I'll pass on the tea today," he says. "It's still early enough, and I want to try downstream a ways."

Now he notices the boat has a clear bottom, and Chong watches as Jim leans over, pulls the boat to him to look at it more closely.

"I'll be damned!" Jim says. "So that's what you were doing."

As if, Chong thinks, jogging along the shore toward his clothes, he could possibly know.

After looking at it for two days and making only minor changes, Chong decides the painting is ready for the Village Inn. Since he is already entangled in new ideas and experiments, the painting, while it pleases him, is not as exciting to him as it was in the process of its completion. He also knows that if he starts to change it now two things will happen: It will become a whole new painting, and less joyous by far. So stop fussing with it, he tells himself. Let it be.

It is one of the largest paintings he has ever done and will occupy an entire wall in the Village Inn if Verano really hangs it. Life tumbles through it, and it flashes with bright colors, as if Lake Ecstasy were a huge cartoon, a circus, and at the center of this is Lily Walker's bared breasts, Tank Younger's fierce, concentrated scowl, the crowd at the Village Inn. Red Barber rolls out from under a truck on a creeper, wrench in each hand; The Club motorcycles into town; and even Ginny is there, at a campfire beside the bus, marveling at the flames, the way he would like best to remember her. Turner chases a pig around his barn. Chong can't really see the painting for what it is as a structure, even as a celebration, because each small face on the canvas reverberates with meaning, and their fates resonate in his mind like the window that hums when the fire siren blows, like the lily pads on the pond that rock when *Fu Yu* is launched, like the spiderweb in the barn that trembles when Chong starts his car. Proximity matters, Chong believes, and if how it matters is not apparent at once, one only has to wait for the wave to arrive and rock you and pass on.

This is the painting's secret, Chong thinks, but nobody will notice, and it is just as well that way.

He calls Verano to make sure the Village Inn will be open that evening, then arranges for Red to come by his house after supper and help him cart the painting away. During the afternoon, Chong makes a minimal sort of frame so the painting can be transported without damage, lashed into the trailer. Chong is both reluctant to see the painting go and eager to have it out of his sight. He wonders what Oslip and the New Yorkers would think of it, if they would find it amusing and primitive, or if they would respond to the secret beat of it, the vein of clear cool water that courses through the whole of it. What is it worth? he wonders. Three thousand in New York, or three hundred thousand, three hundred here—five cords of wood, a small pig, an acre of apple orchard, a 1977 Pinto, say, tuned up and ready to roll, including inspection sticker. Oh, Jesus—Chong laughs—he'll be lucky if Verano can scrape up the two hundred he said he'd pay for it!

Barber is late, explaining an emergency repair was required on the pump of the fire department's "bushwhacker," a small reconditioned army truck that they used to attack brush fires. The truck had been out earlier in the day, a gasket had blown, an easy but time-consuming repair.

"It's no problem," Chong insists. "We've got all night. At least we're not hauling it to New York."

"You got the wrapping on it already," Barber laments. "I was hoping to get a sneak preview."

"I had nothing to do all day," Chong says.

"Oh, yeah?" Barber laughs as he takes one side of the frame and lifts it easily. "Jim tells me you're quite a sailor."

"Guess I surprised him, huh?"

"Surprised him, hell. Jim says he almost pissed in his waders."

Chong laughs, picks up his end of the painting.

"He'll be at the Inn," Barber says. "He's playing pool with some guys there. He's kind of curious what kind of painting you do."

"I suppose so." They bank out the kitchen door, swing the painting around, place it gently in the trailer, rope it down.

As they drive, Barber asks, "Hey, am I in it?" He indicates the painting with his thumb.

"You'll see."

"It's huge. What'd you do? Paint the whole damn town?"

"You'll see."

"Goddamn artist," Barber says. "Village Wacko, that's what you are."

"Village Fool, that's right. Aren't they supposed to be lucky or something?"

"Hey. You see any big trout with that boat of yours? I mean, really big ones? Trophies?"

"Sure," Chong says.

"Is that right? Where? If you don't mind saying. Where do they hang out?"

"Deep water, in the brush," Chong reports. "Sometimes they root around in the leaves like pigs."

"Ah ha," Barber says. "You know why?"

"No."

"They're eating nymphs, insect larvae."

"Really?"

"Now I know what to tie on when I come up there."

"You mean flies?"

"Yeah."

"I'd like to see them."

"The flies or the bugs?"

"Both."

"To see the bugs, you just pull up a pile of those wet leaves, separate them, and you'll find them. They look like little black shrimp, tiny black shrimp."

"No kidding?"

"For real," Barber says.

"Are they good bait?"

"If you can find any big enough, or find a hook small enough. They're pretty tender."

"Tender!" Chong laughs.

"What's so funny?"

"Tender bugs!"

"I mean soft," Barber says. "Fragile, you know."

"You mean 'tender,'" Chong says.

Red shakes his head in wonder at Chong's amusement, swings carefully into the Village Inn parking lot, trying to avoid potholes. A number of men and women are gathered on the porch, a passage of blue jeans, brown bottles, and baseball caps. Somehow the gathering strikes Chong as a little ominous, since they are people he does not know well, somewhat intimidating in their cliquishness. They eye the trailer and its odd cargo with open skepticism, but this mood lightens at once when the people on the porch recognize and speak to Red.

"What the hell you haulin' now, Barber? Must be a giant pancake or somethin'."

"Tell Verano we've got his town," Barber calls.

"His what?"

"Town."

"*Town?*"

"You'll see." Barber winks at Chong. "Art lovers," he says. He quickly unstraps the package, climbs into the trailer, and lifts the painting out until Chong can get his hands on it.

Verano bursts out the door, apron flapping. "Be careful with that thing. God damn it, you guys, give 'em a hand. And just be careful." He hobbles to the porch steps. "You gotta be kiddin'. I thought a painting was about the size of a Sears, Roebuck catalogue. Where will I ever hang that?"

"You'd better think quick," Barber says. "We're coming in with it."

"Right there between the windows," Verano says. "O.K.?"

"Sure," Barber says. "Clear the way."

Inside, the small crowd gathers, wisecracking, swilling beers, as Chong and Barber pull the carrying frame apart.

"Wait a minute," Verano says. "Ain't this what you call an 'unveiling'?"

"It's not so formal," Chong says, embarrassed.

"The hell," Verano says. "Everybody's got to have a drink for this. Come on"—he waves, heading for the bar—"you'll never get another freebie out of me your whole life long, so you'd better grab the chance."

"God damn it," Chong says, "can't we just hang this and get it over?"

"No way," Verano calls from the bar. "We get a speech out of you, too. Right, guys?"

A feeble cheer is raised, and Chong swears.

"A damn short speech," he says, and the cheer is redoubled. "Too much bullshit!"

Barber is tapping the wall with a hammer, trying to locate studs that will accept the nails to be used to support the painting. Somebody has put money into the jukebox, too, and country and western music crashes into the room. Chong measures the wall, uses Barber's level to mark the line where the nails should go, and Barber whales them in.

"Christ, not so hard," Verano shouts. "You'll knock the wall down. This ain't the Taj Mahal."

"It ain't?" somebody hollers. "You mean this *ain't* the Taj Mahal?"

Jim Williams is at Chong's shoulder now. "Hey," he says in greeting.

The sweet taint of whiskey emanates from Jim, and Chong observes, "You've been celebrating already."

Jim laughs. "Didn't Red tell you?"

"Tell me what?"

"It's kind of personal, I guess."

"He's getting married."

"That's it." Jim claps Chong on the shoulder, and it stings. "Red's been after this lady for years."

"I think I know her." Chong is suddenly shot through with panic. Does Red know about the paintings? If he did, wouldn't he have said something long ago? A whole attic full of incrimination!

"Nancy Wallace," Jim says. "Ring any bells?"

"My God!" Chong slaps his forehead. "I guess we celebrate tonight." Nancy's face is in the Lake Ecstasy painting, too. She walks in the orchard near her house, surrounded by ripe apples; her laundry flaps like gay flags not far away; and no one else may ever see it, but the slope of one of the hills is Nancy, too. Now someone presses a drink into Chong's hand.

"Come on," Verano says, "let's see this thing and get it hanged. Hey! Pull the cord on that damned jukebox a minute."

Except for the chatter at the bar and on the porch, the noise suddenly falls away. The jukebox groans into silence.

"O.K." Chong raises his glass. "This painting Mr. Verano is paying me for. It's about Lake Ecstasy and the things I like here. I hope you like it, too." He turns to Barber and salutes him with his glass.

Barber pulls the outside cover away, and the sheet of dark plastic underneath, and he and Chong quickly raise the painting to the row of nails prepared for it. There is a prolonged moment of curious silence, and then a wave of laughter breaks out and the comments fly.

"Look at the size of that trout, will ya?"

"Wait'll Lily sees that. He got those tiddies just right, hey?"

"Ain't that Barber under that truck? Sure as hell!"

Red throws an arm over Chong's shoulder and gives him a powerful squeeze. "You sly dog!" he says. "It's a beauty."

"Look at the skinny-dippers there. Hope the sheriff don't see this."

Chong slips away from the little crowd around the painting and pulls himself up on his usual stool. He is not sure he is going to like having to look at one of his old paintings every time he comes into this place.

Verano is shouting something, and the crowd applauds when he finishes. He pushes through the bodies and comes around behind the bar.

"That meet with your approval?" he asks Chong.

"Of what?" Chong says.

"Of what I just said."

"I didn't hear it."

"Well, shit," Verano says. "I said I'm paying you what I can for the painting, but it's not nearly enough, and I'm taking up a collection for you to help make up the difference."

"Oh, Christ," Chong says.

"Let me get a coffee can," Verano says. "Something like that." He hobbles down the bar and into the back room, and in a moment emerges with a yellow and black can with a plastic top. He takes a knife from behind the bar and meticulously carves out a slot for the money.

An older man, somehow familiar to Chong, takes him lightly by the elbow. "Did a nice job on that yellow tanker," he says.

"Oh, yeah. You're on the fire department."

"Right!" the man says. "I'm Sweeney. I been to your place twice, brush and barn. Anyway, I'm glad you got that tanker in there. For my money, it's the best damn fire truck we ever had."

"Sweeney, you're nuts," his partner says.

"Beats the hell out of the new one. Reliable. Anybody can run it. Not like this new one," he tells Chong, "you got to be a computer expert just to get water."

Verano props the can on the bar along with a hand-lettered sign: FOR THE NEW PAINTING. DONATIONS EXCEPTED!!! "There!" he says to Chong. "That ought to help you a little, huh? Let me tell you, it's way beyond anything I thought of. It's beautiful!" He leans close to Chong. "Maybe some day, though, you think you could sneak in here and paint a little more hair on my head?"

Sweeney digs into his pocket, crams a dollar into the can.

"Now we're talkin'," Verano says. "Dig deep, you guys. Artists got to eat, too. Right, Chong?"

"Don't make me beg," Chong says. "Please? Just forget I'm here."

"You need another drink," Verano says. "Then you won't be so shy."

The crowd seems to be growing rapidly, and Chong wonders if telephones are ringing, CB's crackling. Jesus, he thinks, I'd better find Barber and get out of here! He wishes Verano would give him his money so he could go.

Near the painting now there is laughter, shrieking, and when Chong turns to see what is happening, he looks up into the frowning face of Lily Walker. She eyes him angrily, hands on her hips, gives her head an angry shake, and says, "Don't you think you should've gotten my permission or something, mister? I think I just might sue your ass—"

"Oh, Jesus," Chong says. "Really, I—"

But Lily interrupts him with a howl of laughter and a crushing hug. "Just kidding you, Chong. I'm glad to meet you actually. Tell you the truth"—she pats his thigh and whispers conspiratorially—"the reaction I got that night, I didn't think anybody would want to see them twice."

"I don't believe it," Chong says.

"Hey, listen. Maybe I could pose for you sometime?" She mugs, smiles.

"Any time," Chong says. "I'd be delighted."

"So, when's the trial date?" someone calls to Lily.

"Settled out of court!" she roars. She gives Chong a peck on the cheek. "Excuse me, I gotta go pick this bastard's pocket."

"She can pose for me any time, too," Jim says.

"Lily's a pool player," Chong says. "Maybe you ought to get a game going."

"Hey, why not?" Jim laughs.

Chong sees Nancy Wallace come in the door, take Red's arm, and disappear into the turmoil in front of the painting.

But in a moment she is shaking Chong's hand. "Congratulations! It's really special. But did you have to paint my laundry in there?"

Chong pulls her face to his. "Does he know? About the paintings?"

"He knows," Nancy says. "It's ancient history, so don't worry about it."

"You're the most beautiful woman in the village," Chong tells her.

Verano presses another drink upon him. "On the house. Somebody bought it for you. I don't know who. Tank, maybe. He'd like to meet you, but he's a little shy."

Chong has already put away two stingers, and looks at the new drink in dismay. He's going to have to slow down. He slides off the bar stool and heads for the men's room, stumbles into the hallway, glad for a moment to be out of the increasing hubbub. As he comes past the pay telephone, a shadow leans out from the wall, silver buttons glitter on black leather, and Chong is smashed into the wall, Parker's beard brushing his eyes. Chong feels a sharp edge against his side and freezes.

"Just tell me where she is," Parker says. "Tell me who she's with."

Chong senses, even smothered as he is under the leather smelling of oil and exhaust, there are others in the hallway now, dark forms crowding close to Parker, shielding him.

Chong wheezes. "I can't talk."

"I hear you fine." Parker applies pressure to the knife, and it stings. "So where is she?"

"I don't know," Chong says.

"God damn it," Parker says, "I don't have time to play. And don't you understand how bad I want to kill you? I don't need too many more excuses."

"They wouldn't tell me anything." Chong is almost weeping, and his voice betrays this. He knows Parker is going to kill him, and already he has slipped outside of his own body, it seems, and he sees himself in a panorama, small, a stupid little man shoved against a wall in a small-town bar, victim of some primitive lover's brawl, and incapable, utterly, of changing his fate.

"Take him with us," somebody advises, the voice a growl. "We can't do it here."

"I want to cut your fucking heart out," Parker says. "I want to cut your ears off. You fucked up my life so bad, you know?"

"Let's move it out of here, Parker."

Parker withdraws from Chong, and Chong, nearly insensate with fear, swoons, slips down the wall, limp, his father scolding him. Then he is quite vividly conscious of Parker's boots, and scrambles to get away from them.

"Hey?"

It is Jim's voice.

"Get lost, asshole. You're always messing in my business."

"This man's my business. Hey, Red! Somebody!"

Chong crawls on the floor, on his fists to keep his fingers from being smashed by the stamping of the feet around him, and he is slammed into the wall but wriggles free. Jim is dancing with a man in a leather jacket, hands wrapped in each other's clothes, then a tumultuous twisting. Chong leaps on the leather back, grabbing for the man's eyes, feels Jim's blows even through the man's bulk. Red is swimming on the black backs, and the waves of battle spill out into the bar, where it is greeted by shocked groans and screams, a clatter of breaking glass.

"Whoa! Whoa!" Verano shouts.

Chong sees a flash of Taylor's face, grimacing, a fist slices through the air past his ear with a rush of air. He goes down with a pain in his side. In the front door now, more men in black jackets tumble in, and Chong is helped to his feet by Lily Walker, who swings a pool cue, whacks shoulders, then is shoved away, shirt ripped asunder, into the oblivion of the scuffle. A chair sails into the air, a red ball skips on the bar, crashes into bottles.

"Break it up! Break it up!"

Red is rolling across the floor, clutching his stomach, and Chong tumbles toward him, but before he can help, Red is on his feet again, flings himself into the fray.

"Knock it off! Cops!"

Anyone with sense, not involved in the fray, has retreated to the porch. Faces press against the door. Chong hears a sickening pop!

pop! and fears a pistol. Someone is shooting! He grabs a chair, finding it heavier than he would have thought, swings into the melee.

Verano screams at him. "Chong! Get back here!" He waves, ducks behind the bar as a beer bottle sails into the mirror.

Chong, sick with fatigue, swings his chair into the butt of a Club man, is swatted away at once, like a dog flicked off by a bear. His head swims.

A siren wails, the sound rolls through the door. A few final blows are exchanged, a chair lofted, quick kicks, then the door and hallway fill, not with local cops but with state police in helmets and goggles, wielding truncheons, wearing black gloves, and at once they are thrusting men against the wall.

"Up! On the wall! Let's go! On the wall! Move it! Move it! Hands up, feet out! Let's go!"

Chong is glad for the chance to rest, cradles his head in the crook of his arms. Jim is thrown against the wall beside him.

"Crazy-ass town!" Jim says.

A trooper prods him at once with his truncheon. "Shut up! Everybody shut up and line up! You'll be processed out that door. One at a time. Into the van. So spread 'em, and shut up!"

As the troopers come down the line, Chong can hear metal banging on the floor, an arsenal of knives and hidden guns.

"O.K. Who's wounded here? Who's bleeding? You cut? Let's see."

"What's the matter here?" A trooper presses tight behind Jim. "You got a problem, mister?"

"I'm bruised, been kicked in the balls, I'm going to barf, my hand's broken," Jim says. "Everything's fine, officer."

"Save it for the report." The officer taps Chong on the shoulder. "Turn around slowly, please."

Chong obeys. The trooper looks into his eyes. "Mister, you're going to have one hell of a shiner."

Jim sits on the cot across from Chong, head in his hands. Barber is on his feet at the jail door and shouting to other men down the corridor between the cells. He turns and fumes.

"Look at this goddamn cell, Jim. Painted *pink*. Like a motel toilet."

"The color's supposed to calm you down," Chong says.

"But *pink*? It's a whorehouse, man. A Hong Kong whorehouse."

Jim says nothing and Red puts his hand on his head. "You O.K., buddy? Are you hurtin'?"

"Hurtin' for certain," Jim says.

"You cut? What's the matter?"

Jim shakes his head. "Down, that's all. Blue. It'll go away."

"Hey!" Red punches him in the shoulder, not gently. "We've been through worse, right?"

"Who needs this?" Jim says.

Now Red flops on the cot beside Chong. "How about you? I checked the painting before they hauled us out of there. A little beer splashed on it, but it's O.K."

"They weren't after the painting," Chong says.

"I can't believe that son of a bitch came into the bar after you. What *did* he want?"

"It's so complicated," Chong says, weary at heart.

"Was it about that Cahill girl who was staying with you?"

Chong looks at Red, shakes his head. "No secrets in Lake Ecstasy, are there?"

Red says, "I wonder who called the cops. Do you know? Turner never showed up. I thought maybe he saw The Club on the road and alerted somebody."

"Or saw them at my place," Chong says. "I'm afraid to go home. I can't stay there alone."

"Well, hey," Red says. "Jim's looking for a place to stay."

Jim drops his hands from his face and looks up with a sick smile. "He doesn't want me around, man. I'm too much trouble."

"Can you cut wood?" Chong asks.

"Can I cut wood?" Jim laughs. "Man, I can decimate whole forests. I can wipe out acres of trees."

"Maybe we could sell some firewood," Chong says.

"Why not?" Red says to Jim. "You could help him fix that barn, too."

"Me?" Jim laughs. "What I know about carpentry you could put in a walnut shell."

"I'll teach you," Red says. "I'll set up the job, and I'll show you what to do."

"I can't pay much," Chong says.

"Oh, take advantage of him," Red says. "He's got nothing else to do."

Jim is pale. He opens his hands. "Nothing at all." He glances at Chong now with an odd surge of pity. "You don't know the score," he says. "If you knew the score, Chong, you wouldn't be so welcoming."

"What's the problem?" Chong says. "You drink too much. What else?"

Jim settles back into the cot, twisted, uncomfortable. "I'm just having trouble, Chong. Sometimes I'm real tired of it all. You hear?"

"Yeah," Chong says.

"Don't pay attention to that crap," Red says. "Just keep him busy. Buy a cow if you have to."

Chong thinks this is not a bad idea after all, nods approval. A cow!

"I just never featured myself milking cows," Jim says.

"Oh, he doesn't have any job prospects, and he's broke, and his old lady left him, and all like that," Red says. "He's a sorry spectacle. Just listen to him, and he'll tell you what a sorry spectacle he is."

"Hey!" Jim is obviously stung. "Do I deserve that? Now?"

"Deserve?" Red laughs. "Who ever gets what they deserve? Do we deserve to be in this goddamn pink jail? Did you notice Parker in this jail or any but about two of his asshole buddies in here?" Red holds up a fist suddenly, and Chong sinks back against the wall, astounded. "I'll give you what you deserve."

"What the hell is wrong with you?" Jim cries out. "Have you gone nuts?"

"This is what you deserve," Red says, pumping his fist.

"The hell I do!" Jim is quickly on his feet, grappling with Red, struggling and grunting as they slam each other from wall to wall, finally tumble to the floor where, incredibly to Chong, they lie panting and laughing.

Red looks up at Chong with a wild grin. "You just got to know how to handle him," he says mildly. "Whip his ass once in a while and he'll be fine."

"Ah, fuck you," Jim says. He folds his hands on his chest, heaves a disgusted sigh, closes his eyes.

Chong tries not to think of him in that pose as a man prepared for the coffin, and the grave.

PART III

FIRE!

1
White
Tiger
(Fall)

The sun rises later now, more to the south, and the summer haze has disappeared from the sky. Swallows shoulder together along the telephone wires, a mile of them! Chong thinks, their feet wrapped around Lake Ecstasy's communications, their wings sharp as knife points, their twittering like the noise of some Rauschenburgian machine.

And every time he attempts to get outdoors to see how Jim is managing in the woods the goddamned telephone rings. Red has called. He and Jim will have to go to court, along with everyone else arrested at the Lake Ecstasy Village Inn "fracas"—as the Royalton *Standard* termed it—and stand trial for disturbing the peace and what Red said were "other Mickey Mouse charges." But not Chong. On another trip out the door, the telephone rang to inform him that he could soon expect to receive a summons to appear in the trial of Billy Parker. This news came from Joe Turner's wife, who was passing the word from her sister, who worked in the district attorney's office in Royalton. As soon as he was located and arrested, Parker was to be arraigned for child abuse and sexual molestation of a minor. Already the trial was proving to be a big event in Lake Ecstasy history, Chong mused, and it hadn't even happened yet. If and when Parker was found and arrested, Chong could expect a summons at once. The paperwork was ready.

"Joe thought you'd like to know," Ruth had said.

"I do appreciate it," Chong had replied. "That gives me time to leave the country."

Mrs. Turner had laughed, but Chong wasn't sure he didn't really mean what he said. For Chong cannot assess himself as innocent, and he knows Parker can blackmail his conscience with the drawings of Ginny, if not also a jury of Mrs. Turners and Mrs. O'Days. Christ! Chong feels he needs to talk to Ginny before Parker's trial, to make sure she knows what she should and shouldn't say, to reassure himself she would not betray him with a lie. Before a jury! I can't afford a lawyer, Chong thinks. I can't even afford to fix my goddamn car!

Finally Chong escapes, carries a jar of lemonade toward the sound of Jim's chain saw in the woods across the dam. It is really too warm to be cutting wood, but Jim had insisted that morning that he had to do something or he would go "plain crazy." Chong didn't argue. At times, he finds Jim a little intimidating. And he seems so huge in Chong's little house—he ducks his head coming through the bathroom door; dishes rattle when he walks into the kitchen; his feet stick out over the end of the sofa when he naps there. Jim's presence in the house makes Chong feel small. He has watched with a kind of awe how much Jim can eat. At how much beer he can drink.

Chong comes upon Jim in a pool of quiet, carefully filing the points along the cutting chain, brows furrowed in concentration. He looks healthier than he has, and the white pall that settles on him when he is drinking heavily is absent now. Still, Jim strikes Chong as a man who lives too much within his own skin, that you would have to reach deep, deep inside to find his own reality. The woods is dry and aglow with color that the pond mirrors—scarlet, gold, and lavender. The air smells of the sap of the black birches Jim has been clearing to make room for the young oaks and maples there. The downed trees surround Jim with a pyre of yellow leaves.

Chong proffers the lemonade. "Take a break."

Jim nods assent, but continues filing for a while. Then he swallows from the jar, puckers at once. "Wow!"

"Too sour for you?"

Jim shakes his head. "Wasn't expecting that." He laughs, wipes his eyes. His checkered shirt is flecked with curls and chips of wood.

"You took down quite a few," Chong says.

"Just the easy stuff." Jim settles on a fresh stump. "I'll limb this stuff out and split it up when it's cooler."

Chong tells Jim that Red has called and that he will have to appear in court along with everyone arrested at the Inn.

"That figures," Jim says.

"I told them you were protecting me," Chong says. "So I don't know why the trial is necessary."

"It stinks," Jim says.

Chong likes the feeling of the woods that Jim has opened up; light pours in, and he strolls the area, rustling leaves, imagining what the woods will be like again in the spring.

"This looks good," Chong says. "You like this kind of work?"

"I'd like it better without all these damned grapevines." The vines tentacle from tree to tree, webbing them together in a haphazard network, so that, Jim explains, a tree cut from the stump may not fall, or may twist dangerously, fall against a neighboring tree, and need to be cut again—may even cause limbs of the trees he is trying to protect to be damaged or ripped down. They were also unpredictable, sometimes tenacious as cables, sometimes snapping like paper for no apparent reason.

"You can bust your ass trying to bring a tree down from one of those vines," Jim says, "and the minute you turn your back, the thing will come crashing down."

"The woods is beautiful now." Chong says this with a silent question mark, unsure of Jim's response, quelling his true enthusiasm, which makes him want to shout it out: Beautiful!

Jim sips from the lemonade jar and laughs uneasily. "I keep telling myself that. But I'll be damned if I haven't been thinking all day of the ocean. Maybe it's the chain saw. Sounds a bit like an outboard motor. Maybe it's the time of year, because this is the season the fish migrate. I'm in the woods, and I'm thinking of the ocean. You figure it out."

"It's hard to be where you are," Chong says. "Artists know that. You have to learn to see what's right in front of you."

Jim looks around. "I've lost my concentration, you're right. I can remember a time when that might have been fatal." He glances at Chong with a quick smile, then turns away. "The sound of that saw is a real narcotic, too."

"You shouldn't be cutting alone," Chong says.

"That's true." Jim stands, then scoops up the chain saw. "Maybe I'll call it a morning."

As they walk toward the house, Jim tells Chong how he intends to harvest firewood and improve the forest. Jim has a practical eye, but he is not insensitive to Chong's wishes, which might seem odd to some, to Turner for example, surely to anyone with business sense. For Chong wants certain trees preserved simply for their looks. Others he justifies saving because they drop sour apples for the deer, or show a spray of berries for the winter birds. And still others he asks to be cut in unorthodox ways, to preserve a certain curve, or shape, or gnarled growth, for sculpturing. Sometimes half the trees seem like torsos, and Chong imagines the smooth wood stripped of bark to be like skin, and the forms both virile and feminine, usually exaggerated, as in the contours of dreams. Chong wonders if a wood-cutter would go crazy if he saw the forest in this way. There were not just elves in the woods; there were sirens, there were hags in the trees, one log was clearly a wild boar and the flakes of the bark curled on it in exactly the way the bristles would fall on such an animal's shoulders and rump.

In his mail this morning, Chong finds a letter from Evelyn Crane, which he devours at once. The collector she had written about earlier, Todd Oslip, is traveling to Boston soon and will "make an effort" to come Chong's way. Mrs. Crane would call when she knew the details, and Chong could expect it to be soon. Yes, yes, fine, Chong thinks, but what about you? You say nothing about yourself. She is so vivid in his memory now, and he wants to touch her, re-members with a stirring of his sex how she would frankly stride up to and unbuckle him, kiss him with her eyes open, as if looking into the back of his head. But now she keeps herself secret from him. Has she nothing more to say? Sometimes she had simply stayed in bed until he arrived and watched him undress, and then lifted the covers for him, permitting just a flash of her body, which he could see aging now in just those flashes, like frames from a time-lapse movie, and they would lie quietly face to face, talking of the day's ephemera, and Chong would become drowsy in the warmth and the smell of her perfume, and with only the slightest adjustments, dreamily, they would be joined, still talking, until the pleasure grew too intense and overwhelmed at last their tangled double conscious-ness. The letter in his hand seems empty, and it angers him. Am I jealous? Chong wonders in astonishment.

He crams the letter in the pocket of his jeans, pulls some toma-toes, lettuce, carrots from his garden, and begins to prepare a lunch. Just as he starts to scrub the vegetables in the sink, the telephone rings—again!—and since Jim is still in the barn, Chong quickly dries his hands and answers it.

The caller does not speak, not even when Chong asks again, "Who is it, please?" A wave of annoyance and dread passes into anger as the silence continues, and Chong jams the telephone down. And then the questions comes at him like gnats: Was it Ginny? Or Parker? Or only some mistake, a classic New York telephone snafu? Maybe Susan was trying to get through. Or Wu?

Turner had promised to call, too, to arrange for Luan's slaughter, and Chong wants to talk to him anyway, to thank him for notifying the police after he saw The Club on the highway headed for the Inn on the day of the unveiling. But wasn't the weather too warm to slaughter a pig? Not Turner, then, Chong thinks, surprised at the relief he feels. Luan butchered in the blaze of autumn, when the trees were on fire with light. Chong isn't sure he can stand the idea and blames himself for naming the pig when Turner had so plainly advised against doing so. Scarlet and scarlet and scarlet. But he's just a pig! Chong reminds himself. He's supposed to die for me. If I feel sad about that, Chong thinks, I will have to feel sad about everything in this life, about killing to live, the whole system of mouth and anus, the endless transformation of one life into another, capitulating in something called intelligence, which makes the process known to itself. And the knowledge hurts. A bad joke! Should I become a vegetarian? Chong wonders. My teeth are tired.

The telephone rings again. Chong allows it to ring awhile, then answers cautiously. Once more he is confronted with a long silence, the deliberate breathing of the caller. This is not a mistake, Chong realizes. He means to frighten me. You fucking coward, he wants to say. I need this telephone. I am expecting calls. You are trying to steal my telephone, too. Again he cradles the receiver.

Minutes later, the ringing begins again, but Chong will not answer it, scrubs his vegetables fiercely, counting . . . fifteen . . . twenty . . . thirty . . . torture! He grabs the phone up, slams it down, and then removes it from the hook altogether.

He utters a stream of imprecations. Every time they pass a telephone, they will slip in some change and give him a call. Day or night. Chong doesn't know what they expect to gain by it, because he will not be able to avoid going to trial. Maybe they just want him to know they are . . . here. Around. All right, I know it. I smell you.

A few minutes later Jim comes into the house, takes a beer from the refrigerator, and drinks it down quickly. Chong offers to fix him some lunch, but Jim says he is not hungry and wanders out of the kitchen. In a moment, Chong hears the hiss of the shower, and shakes off a flash of worry. He's not that unhappy, Chong decides.

Still, Chong cannot resist stealing to the bathroom door and listening, and is gratified when he hears the water shut off and Jim stepping out of the tub. He returns to his cooking, some chunks of chicken brown in the wok, then a handful of vegetables. The food crackles and sizzles, sends up a little ghost of steam. Steam sculpture, Chong thinks. Why not? You could put it in a plastic box, like frost on the windowpane. Congratulations, he tells himself. You have just invented the world's most ephemeral art.

Jim returns to the kitchen in a while and has another beer while Chong eats his lunch. Idly, he replaces the telephone on the hook, and Chong allows it without speaking. Maybe the harassment has ended for now.

"You ought to eat better," Chong says. "It might improve your spirits."

"I'm feeling O.K.," Jim says.

Chong says nothing for a minute, scrapes the sauce from his plate. "Maybe you don't know if you're feeling O.K. or not."

Jim settles his eyes on Chong as he considers the remark. "How could I *not* know?"

"Some people never feel good enough to know the difference," Chong says. "That happened to me."

"*What* happened, exactly?"

"It took me a long time to realize I didn't have to always be afraid."

"When you came here from China?"

"Long after that," Chong says. "After I was married."

"People keep telling me I'm afraid, and I'm not," Jim says.

"I didn't say you were afraid," Chong says. "I just think maybe you can't quite imagine what it's like to feel good. To be happy. Of course, it takes practice."

"Yeah?" Jim sips his beer. "Maybe what made me happy has disappeared from the earth."

"I know about that, too," Chong says. "Some good things got away from me, too, some chances that I missed. What can I do? It's like dirt in the water. You let it settle, then you can drink. You keep stirring it up, you will die of thirst."

The telephone rings, and Chong groans aloud. He asks Jim to answer it, saying that he has been receiving crank calls all morning.
Jim raises the telephone and says, "Hello," but after a moment he
drops the receiver down in disgust. "What's going on?"

Chong explains to Jim that he will be summoned to appear for
Billy Parker's trial and that he suspects The Club is trying to intimi-
date him. "Red probably told you why Parker came after me in the
Inn—because he wanted to know where Ginny was."

"That hardly seems worth a murder," Jim says.

"Well, there's more to it. He's under the impression I'm guilty of
what he's being charged with."

"Nobody will believe it. How could they?"

"That's the problem." Chong looks away in embarrassment. "He
has some drawings I made of her in the nude."

"Is that a crime?"

"No. But you must agree it is suggestive."

"And how did he come by these pictures anyway?"

"He stole them. After the fire in my barn."

"And later he attacked you and Turner. Is he going up for that,
too?"

"I guess so," Chong says. "Turner filed the papers. But they have
to catch him first."

Jim pushes the beer botttle out of the way and settles his elbows
on the table. "I wonder if I could find this guy. I wonder if I could
find those pictures, too."

"Don't mess with him," Chong says.

"Why not? I've got my own beefs with Parker. And I don't believe
he's all that slick anyway. It wouldn't take three days to check out
every house in this town. I might talk to some of his pals, too. Man,
if we could find VC down in rat holes out in the jungle, we sure as
hell can find Parker in Lake Ecstasy."

"Forget it," Chong says emphatically. "I don't want you to get in
any more trouble because of me."

"I'll just check it out," Jim says.

"He's not even in Lake Ecstasy," Chong says. "He's probably in
Mexico by now."

"There's something you learn," Jim says. "I don't know where I
came by this, but it is street wisdom, and I believe it. The rule is
this: If you know somebody is after you, you find him first. You don't
want to be surprised."

"Parker's too dangerous," Chong insists.

"He's a punk," Jim says. "And when he gets to prison, the inmates will make his life hell. They all hate short eyes."

"Short eyes?"

"A grown man who bothers little girls." Jim rubs his forehead as if weary. "For some reason, prisoners make a special effort to make sure such a guy is miserable. Maybe it's because they don't like to think of their sisters out there unprotected."

"I see." Chong feels a twinge of fear suddenly, feels weak. Short eyes. Suppose Parker turns that on me.

"He deserves it, messing with jailbait."

"Jailbait," Chong says. English is such a wonderful language. Jailbait. Short eyes. The world is laid with traps. Suddenly he feels a little ill.

"I think I ate too much," he says.

In the evening, Chong and Jim sit on the back steps and watch the pond turn black in the blue shadows from the nearby hills, watch the crests of the trees ignite with golden halos. Their talk is sparse but pleasant; then, because Jim has just endured a frustrating telephone conversation with Anna, it drifts to the subject of divorce. Chong and Jim are comparing wounds when Joe Turner swings his blue pickup into the driveway and crunches to a stop beside the barn.

"Give me a hand with these boards, hey?" Turner says to Jim as he comes around the truck.

"What boards?" Chong rises to see what is in the truck. "What are you doing?"

Turner reaches into the pickup and throws Jim a pair of gloves. "I just tore down a chicken coop I'm not using any more. The wood is good enough that Red and I figured we could fix your barn with it, maybe before the snow flies."

"You're going to fix my barn?" Chong is more than a little astonished.

"It's all in the talk stage now." Turner slides planks out of the bed, slaps them onto the ground. "All we have to do is find the time."

"I've got lots of time," Jim says. "Somebody just needs to tell me what to do."

"Advice we got," Turner says. "Though it's not the hottest commodity. Right, Chong?"

"Listen," Chong says. "I can't pay for this right now. I've got to hire a lawyer."

"Just so you're willing to negotiate," Turner says. "You got plenty of firewood up there still. Or, I could use some of those extra acres over there for feed corn. We'll work it out."

Chong shakes his head in doubt.

"You want that barn fixed, don't you?"

"Sure I do."

"Well, then." Turner laughs.

Jim follows Turner's lead in stacking the boards, falls into an easy rhythm of work, and the truck is soon emptied.

"Got another load if you want to give me a hand," Turner says to Jim.

"Let's go," Jim says. "It's getting dark."

Chong protests that tomorrow would be soon enough for more wood to be delivered, but Turner rejects his complaint.

"I got time now, and I'm in gear, so you'd better just let me get it done."

"O.K.," Chong says. "You know I'm grateful."

"Don't worry about it." Turner and Jim climb into the truck, and the slamming of the doors echoes from the pond.

Look at this! Chong thinks. Poof! A load of wood. The gift makes him happy, but also uneasy, because he knows he should pay for it somehow. Money is such a bitch. But Turner is not asking for money. Just acres, to plant corn for his pigs. Chong admits that the repair of his barn will repair something in his heart, too. Perhaps it is foolishness, but he feels associated with the things in his life, and he is always agitated when they are broken down—his stuttering car, a leaking roof, the tortured barn, all fill him with agitation. Is this because, as an artist, he tends to see things symbolically? Or simply because he is so dependent on them for safety, survival, happiness? Maybe he only notices the broken things when his life—as it almost always is—is in disarray, threatened with changes he doesn't understand.

As the lights from Turner's truck swing across the field behind his barns, Jim can see Red shielding his eyes against the glare, standing atop a pile of boards and holding a crowbar, a nail puller in his other hand. Turner douses the headlights and leaves only his parking lights on, bathing the area in an amber glow, peaceful as candlelight.

"Why didn't you call me?" Jim asks. "Christ, you guys have done a lot of work here."

"Well, we kinda got into it," Red says. "Nancy was here awhile, too, and we only had so many crowbars, so what the hey."

"He's volunteering for some carpentry work too," Turner says.

"Great," Red says. "You'll get the hang of it. You might even learn something."

Jim nods, wondering for a moment if he has heard a distant peal of thunder, prolonged, like stones being rolled in a box.

"Tell you what," Red says. "Let's take another load of wood over and then have a look at the barn."

"Now don't start getting big ideas," Turner says.

"We'll keep it simple," Red says.

"Oh, sure." Turner bends to a long board and swings it into the pickup. The shadows leap away, gigantic, collide with the night.

"What is that noise?" Jim asks. "That rumbling I keep hearing?"

Turner laughs. "That's my pigs in the barn. They're climbing all over each other to see what's going on out here."

"Didn't realize they would be so curious." Jim lifts the end of a beam that Red has raised and together they carry it to the truck.

"Well, it's an anxious time of year, if you're a pig or a turkey," Turner says. "A real anxious time of year."

"He's going to start slaughtering as soon as it's cold enough," Red says. "That's why it'd be nice if we could get this barn project started now. Once he starts slaughtering, we won't see old Joe for a while."

"That's a fact," Turner says. "And I'll be so sick of chops and sausages when I get done, I just may take a little vacation."

Red scoffs. "That's what he always says. Ruth has been after him for years, but I haven't seen the time yet that he actually did it."

"Some damned thing is always coming up," Turner says. "It's not like it's my fault. One year it's the damned water pump that goes out, and I can't leave my pigs in a drought now, can I? One other time, Ruth's mother took to the hospital, right after I had the car all packed. Not *before* the car is packed, but after. Seemed like she knew just when to get sick."

"Maybe if you kept your plans a secret," Red suggests.

"Like hell," Joe says. "There's no secrets in my family. Not with the wife I got. And the relatives. There's an ear at every window, I believe."

As they work, Turner weaves a litany of farm woes and disasters that always seem to occur the minute he believes he is ready to take a long-deserved vacation at last. He has plumbed the history of these events back to 1964 (the year the oil truck ran into the utility poles out front and knocked out all the farm's motors and pumps so that everything had to be done by hand) when the truck is finally loaded with boards, and groaning under the weight.

"You got any idea how many gallons of water pigs drink in a day?" Turner asks in a tone of outraged indignation.

"Couldn't guess," Red says.

"Well, you find out quick when your pumps are down and you have to haul it all by hand, I'll tell you."

"I'm happy to say that's one I missed." Red gestures toward the pickup. "You guys head on over and I'll follow in the jeep."

A few minutes later, the three men survey Chong's barn with flashlights inside and out and concoct a plan for renovating it.

"You know," Red says, "if we really wanted to do this right, we could make a kind of loft up top there, and in the back section here, something like an office. He needs space to frame canvas, space to store paintings."

"But now you're talking a roofing job, too," Turner says. "And we'd have to get building permits. You're going a little far there, Red."

"I'm just saying," Red goes on, "this place has possibilities."

"I see that," Turner says, "but Chong ought to have some say about it, too. You're talking a major operation here."

"I guess so." Face illuminated by flashlight glow, Red grimaces in the darkness.

"You got a little work to do on your own place, too," Turner reminds him.

"Yeah, you're right," Red says. "We'd better keep it simple."

"Whew," Turner says to Jim. "Glad I talked him outa that."

Turner departs a few moments later, and Jim and Red join Chong at the kitchen table to discuss the plans for renovating the barn.

"I'm just going to write down a few things so Jim can get us started," Red says.

"You're going to try some carpentry, Jim?" Chong asks.

"Nothing else to do," Jim says. "Besides, I like to think I can earn my keep."

"I know Turner's worried we might be taking on too much, but I really think a loft and an office is the way to go," Red says. "We can get some extra help if we need it. Nancy's willing to pitch in, and I can always call up some of the volunteers."

The plans Red has sketched out excite Chong, but he is also afraid to expect too much. A loft, an office would be wonderful. He says only, "My pockets are not too deep. Remember that, please."

"Right," Red says. "But around here we do a lot of scrounging and trading. If we need something, we just need to ask around, and look around a little."

"That'll give me a good excuse," Jim says.

"Now wait," Chong says. "I told you to forget it."

"What are you talking about?" Red asks.

"Looking for Parker," Jim says.

Red's pencil digs into the paper as he makes a series of X's across the bottom of the page. "Parker's probably around, yeah. I've seen too many of his pals lately to think otherwise. I believe I even saw the lady he's keeping company with at the liquor store. But let's build this barn and not worry about him too much. Let's not go off cockeyed about Parker."

"What's cockeyed about it?" Jim asks.

"We need to know more," Red says.

"So? We do some research."

"The way I see it," Red says, "is that it's better to leave him alone. He'll show himself if he doesn't get scared off or sense any pressure. He's too cocky and too impatient to sit still for long."

"I think Red's right," Chong says.

Jim sips his beer and stares at Chong. "Look, you're the one Parker's after. What do you think he's going to do if he's not sitting still?"

"I don't really know," Chong says, subdued.

"I don't think we should allow this guy the luxury of making plans," Jim says. "I think we ought to find him and flush him out."

"Who's 'we'?" Red says.

"I figured you'd want to help," Jim says.

"You figured wrong," Red says. "All I want to do is fix this barn."

"Oh, bullshit," Jim says. "I know you'd love to get Parker. I've heard you say it many times."

"Sure I would," Red says. "And I think the way to get him is to wait and watch."

"Do nothing, in other words."

"You can call it that if you want to," Red says. "But you can also 'do nothing' creatively, too. That's what I'm talking about."

"You been in Lake Ecstasy too long," Jim says. "You're beginning to believe in magic."

"Not magic," Red says.

"What do you call it, then?"

"Connections," Red says. He looks at Chong. "Am I right?"

Chong closes his eyes and smiles.

Jim has received a telephone call from Anna, and it has astounded him. He is up late pacing the house, trying to piece together what it means. She had begun so formally, telling him the name and telephone number of her lawyer, reporting on T'isa's health and activities, and there had been a terrible tension in her voice. Jim had been loose enough, just mildly drunk enough, to sense the struggle behind the information she was delivering, and he asked *What's the matter? What's wrong, babe?* And the sound of love and concern in his voice must have stirred something in her, because she opened up to him, said she worried about him, said she had been through something painful, and had learned from it. Jim wanted to ask, but he was afraid to know. Surely she was telling him she had had a lover, that it went sour. He had faced this possibility already, and he knew it must have been happening, since it would have been unnatural for Anna, in the city and so surrounded by men, to deny herself a sexual attachment. To fall in love. Of course men would take an interest in her. He laughs. No doubt Anna supposed there were some women in his life, too, supposed that the term of their separation had stretched to impossible limits, that he had reconnected. But for a change he had not talked about himself and listened to her, and though what she said was painful, it heartened him that she would talk to him and tell him the truth of her feelings. Exactly this had disappeared from their marriage. They had grown to live separate, secretive lives, and the secretive realm expanded until it made little sense to continue the pretense of a union. But it could be rediscovered! Jim fought off the impulse to call her back—it would be unfair calling so late, 3 A.M. He'd call tomorrow, as soon as she was out of work. Now he turns out the lights and stands on the screened-in porch looking out at the fingernail-slim slice of moon. Except for that light, the Lake Ecstasy night is almost as dark as a night on the ocean. He and his father had fished often at night, anchoring the boat in one of the Kennebec cutbacks, bobbing on the incoming tidewater, in a darkness so complete Jim could sometimes not even see the rod in his hands. Sometimes his father smoked a cigar to keep the bugs away from his face, and the orange pulse would spark with a brightness that seemed to illuminate everything inside the boat. In Viet Nam they had fired flares into the night sky, burst them over the jungle, and the world was suddenly illuminated by an intense spectral, sputtering whiteness. As the flare drifted down, the shadows would move, and if you were really spooked, you would see things and fire, and sometimes the whole watch would rattle the darkness with hysterical shooting, imagining the enemy presence. But sometimes they were there, and you knew it, and the flare would expose your worst nightmares coming true, a field of dark shapes crawling, running toward the bunker, and the firing was not in vain but desperate, loading the darkness with a wall of lead. Was there anything worse in the world than the howl of a mortar round coming out of a black sky and a black jungle?

Incoming.

He and his father would wait for the fish.

Motorcycles growl past the house now, in two bursts, and are quickly gone. At this time of night? Jim wonders. He bursts out the front door and into his car, and is on the road at once. The car, still cold, is sluggish, and Jim despairs of reaching the speed he will need to close the gap. Still, he presses on into the night, cracks over the road. Atop a hill, he thinks he sees in the distance the glow of a brake light, but it quickly disappears as the car drops downslope. Jim tries to imagine where the glow has come from on the map in his mind. Northeast, he reasons. Three clicks. Maybe closer. The Royalton Road. Where he can risk it, Jim buries the pedal, and the car thunders through the dark town, then past Barber's, causing Jim a quick smile as he thinks of Red and Nancy entangled in sleep. But once on the Royalton Road, he feels foolish driving in the darkness of the woods without a prayer of seeing anything because of the trees. He slows the car, feeling weary at last, decides he will turn around when he finds a reasonable place to do so. He cruises past a little settlement of house trailers, then a farmhouse close to the road, and in the rearview mirror catches the arc of a cigarette flipped from the porch, a burst of sparks on the lawn. Jim rocks with the sight of it.

Ah!

An event so small, and yet any sniper would have seen it and chased the glow with a few hot rounds.

O.K., Jim says, I think that's what I want to know. He begins to sweat. Should he make another pass? It might be some farmer cooling off, some kid sneaking a smoke, somebody with the mid-sleep dreads, up for a smoke to cool the fear. Screw it, he decides. He'll cut across Deer Lane and over the hill and head back on Lake Ecstasy Road. Tomorrow he'll check the place out. He hasn't seen any bikes, but maybe in daylight. He hasn't seen anything, just a cigarette flipped in the darkness, 3:30 A.M.

When Jim returns, the telephone is ringing, and Chong is stumbling around in the darkness trying to find it. Jim picks it up, knowing already that he will hear only the dry hiss of silence interrupted by heavy breathing.

"Enjoy your ride?" Jim says, but there is no reply. Stubbornly, he holds on to the phone, hoping to hear something that would give him a clue, but then comes only a violent wet sound, as if the caller spat into the mouthpiece, a jarring click, and silence.

"Nobody?" Chong is trying to hold a blanket around his body, but it keeps on slipping from his shoulders. In the darkness, he looks almost hunchbacked to Jim, aboriginal somehow.

"Somebody," Jim says.

"Leave it off the hook," Chong says. "We need our sleep."

Jim flops in an armchair, more awake than ever now, feels almost angry, but satisfied, too, a new feeling for him, a surprising one that he enjoys. "I think I know where they are," he tells Chong.

"Parker?"

"Maybe not Parker. But the others."

Chong pulls the blanket around his neck as if cold. "So?"

"So maybe I'll check it out."

"Don't," Chong says. "It's going to be light out soon."

"It won't take long just to have a look."

"There's too many of them," Chong insists.

"Maybe, maybe not," Jim says. "I just want to look around."

"I should come with you."

"No way," Jim says. "I know how to do this stuff. Your being there would only make it harder."

"I see."

"No offense."

"No," Chong says. "But I'll worry here. Might as well be there and worry."

"No," Jim says again. "There's nothing to worry about."

"Hah!"

"It's just kind of a little night patrol."

"I wish I could stop you."

"You can't," Jim says. "Believe me, I'm not going to do anything to risk my neck."

Before Chong can muster more objections, Jim is out the door and in the car. He feels a chill as he drives, but shakes it off, supposing it to be simply his body claiming its habitual nighttime rest. Night chill. If he turned on the heater, he could be lulled into sleep, into dreams, maybe of Anna, but he opens the window until his face is stinging with the rush of crisp air.

When he reaches the woods, Jim pulls onto the shoulder of the road, slips out at once, stays close within the first line of trees where there is little brush and he can move with comparative ease and silence. The floor of the forest is dry, but cushioned with pine needles. When the woods breaks at the trailer camp, Jim squats, surveys the fields, trying to organize the darkness. The farmhouse is still a distance away, one window yellow with light, and behind it is a large barn and some smaller sheds that he had not noticed when he passed in the car.

Jim decides to make for the barn, move out from there. The sky is already becoming the deep blue of pre-morning when Jim squeezes into the barn. The darkness is profound, and Jim waits a moment for his eyes to adjust, to make sense of an odd phosphorescent glitter before him.

Then Jim can see the silhouettes of motorcycles, like miniature cattle, the handlebars and chrome giving off a ghostly gleam. He drops to one knee and touches the engine of the nearest motorcycle. It is wet and warm and gritty with dirt. Jim feels a rush of satisfaction, then turns to the door of the barn and opens it slightly to improve his vision. He rummages in the darkness until he finds a tin can, which he uses, staying behind the barn door, to scoop gravel. Now he unscrews the caps on the gas tanks and dribbles the dirt in. One by one, he loads the gas tanks with sand and stones, freezing once when he thinks he hears voices, which resolve finally into the distant yelping of a dog.

The light in the side window of the house is still on, and Jim considers a moment forgoing a closer inspection. Maybe there is a dog. Maybe someone is in the lighted room. But if there was a dog, he would have heard it by now, and the darkness is still deep enough that a person in a lighted room would be unable to see out. The deep blue of the sky is intense, stung with bright stars, the crescent of a moon, and Jim hears the plaintive cooing of a mourning dove. He had met a woman once who had not known the sound was made by birds, who had gone through life believing that she woke every day to the crying of children. The woman was in her thirties when Jim explained the origin of the sound to her. It hits him with some force now that this is what Chong has been trying to tell him, that he has been addicted to a way of feeling about the world, that a single powerful fact might change his life. Jim crouches, propels himself from the barn.

He circles, looks quickly into each window, tries to imagine the layout of the house. On the third side, he stands back a little from the lighted window, sees a woman sitting at a table smoking, a telephone before her. He glides away now and is soon behind the barn, then into the woods again. The sky is tainted with orange when he reaches the car. He smells, he thinks, of dust and mushroom spoor.

Only a few hours later, Jim is wakened by Red, who offers him a cup of coffee even before he has thrown the covers off.

"I thought you were going to have those beams measured out," he complains. "This unit is not STRAC. This unit is drunk and disorderly."

Jim accepts the coffee, his mind sluggish still, crying for more sleep. He listens to Red ramble, holding the hot cup in his fingers, realizing with a start he is burning himself, and sets the cup on the floor.

"Chong says you were doing a little prowling last night. What's the story?"

"Yeah," Jim says. "Who's in that house just after the trailer park on Royalton?"

"One of the Archers," Red says. "They brought those trailers in, too, for some of the family. It's a pigsty."

"Could Parker be there?"

Red contemplates this a moment. "Maybe. The family would protect him. He's been the chief moneymaker for them all. But it seems too dumb, even for them."

"Who rides the motorcycles?"

"Who doesn't in that family? One is Taylor Archer. He lives there with his grandmother. He and Parker are pretty tight."

"Who would the young woman be?"

"Could be anybody," Red says. "It's one of the seven wonders of the world, but they always find somebody to wash their dirty shorts."

"O.K.," Jim says, shaking his head to clear the cobwebs. "What would it take for us to get into that house?"

"Us?" Red says. "I told you, I don't want to get messed up in this."

"Why not?"

"It's too easy for something to go wrong. Seriously wrong."

"I just want to turn the tables," Jim says. "I just want to terrorize them a little for a change. I'd also like to get those drawings. I have a hunch they're in that house. I'll do the break-in, if you're worried about that. All I need is a little help on the recon end, maybe a little cover."

"What kind of cover? An alibi?"

"Maybe. But I meant more like letting me know if somebody was coming while I was in the house. CB maybe. All I want to do is look around in there, and maybe later have a talk with Taylor Archer."

"I don't like it a bit," Red says.

"I need you, man."

"Shit."

"You know the rules, Red. You can't wait around for somebody to come after you. I want the drawings. And everybody wants to know where Parker is."

"So run it down for me. Every move you think you're going to make. Archer's a kid, but he's savage and smart, and he can hurt you if you give him half a chance."

"I know the layout of the house," Jim says. "I can go through it fast."

"The old lady's there and whoever that other woman is. When are you going to find the nest empty?"

"I don't know," Jim says. "They must go out sometime."

"Yeah," Red says. "I think maybe we'd just better fix this barn, like I said."

"Think about it," Jim says. "I know you're as tired of Parker's bullshit as anyone else around here. It's a nest of spiders, that whole family, and we're just cleaning it out. How can you argue with that?"

"I'll think about it," Red says.

"You'll never get a better chance."

"I said I'd think about it." Red reaches to the floor, picks up Jim's coffee, and hands it to him. "Right now it's time for your carpentry lesson."

Patiently, Red gives Jim directions for measuring and cutting the boards, then taps his watch with a grimace and hustles off to do "a brake job on an oil truck."

Jim watches Red skim down the stairs, his broad shoulders sink out of sight, and feels oddly remorseful, as if Red were becoming alien to him. Downstairs, Chong is standing before a canvas, brush dangling from one hand, a carrot dangling from his mouth. He does not seem to notice Jim pass through the room into the kitchen, and Jim is a little uneasy still about how he should behave when Chong is at work. Chong has not been especially self-conscious about painting, or even mindful of noise and distraction. But sometimes he talks to himself, and Jim has mistaken such mumbling for attempts at communication. "I just talk to myself," Chong told him with a shrug. "Don't mind it. It's a stupid tic, but if I don't talk, I don't paint. It used to drive my wife bananas." He laughed at this. "Poor Mai Li. She must have liked to suffer. Then she changed." He turned back to the canvas, worked with quick, jabbing strokes, muttering away, sometimes in a childlike singsong that slipped in and out of Chinese and which Jim thought might have rhymed.

For what? Jim had wondered. Why does he paint? And one evening at dinner as they ate together Jim had braved the question.

"Because I can't do anything else," Chong had said. "I mean it. Maybe it's crazy, but it's all I do even when I'm doing something else, at least I'm thinking about it. There's enough stuff in the world without more paintings, you're right."

"I didn't mean it that way."

"It's like a hole I'm trying to fill up," Chong said. "But I haven't hit the bottom yet."

Jim didn't see Chong's work as self-indulgent, though it was sometimes humorous, as if he didn't take himself or his subjects seriously after all. He was trying to see something, just as Jim had tried to do with the camera. Jim was a little surprised at his own curiosity about Chong's work and what he thought of it, and when Chong was not around Jim inspected the paintings and drawings and tried to find a thread. What drove the man? Why, when he was unable to work, did he feel so thunderously bad, become so grotesque in his complaints?

"All I want to do is get all the demons out, before I start painting," Chong had said. "Before! I'd like to be a kid again, knowing what I know now. Ho! You think that's possible? I mean, I want to see like a kid, think like adult. Not possible, maybe. Except once in a while the old habits get a crack in them, and we can see through that. If you don't break habits, you can't see anything, ever."

Jim had thought about this and admitted that the weight of his own habits seemed tremendous, that he even stooped, physically, under their burden. His feet seemed mired in some sort of hell, and the more he struggled the more he sank, as in quicksand. Another grand choice: Die quiet or die struggling.

This morning, as Jim watches Chong immobilized before his canvas, munching a carrot, he almost laughs, the man seems so comical and comically involved in making images, designs, creations. But it strikes him, too, that he is observing Chong's struggle, his attempt to build a ladder out of the mire, to reinvent his life, and to document the process. To fill a void that, as he had said, might not be fillable at all, the earth was surrounded by so profound a supply of it, the heart's cravings seemed so insatiable, and the simple volume of earthly travail, trouble, and suffering appeared to be so immense. What a wearying effort! But Chong makes it daily, Jim believes. He doesn't know why, he just does it.

And does it matter why? Jim asks himself. He slices bread and sees that his hand is shaking, that he is in a body that is out of his control, full of its own stammers. We'll stop this, he says. No sweat. We will stop this.

Nancy has been on hand all afternoon, helping Jim select good boards from the pile Turner has left them and holding the boards steady as he cuts them to lengths they measure out. She has held the ladder for him as he ascended to the roof and sawed out burned timbers, and then together they used crowbars and hammers to tear off the charred siding. By some unwritten law, they seem to rest at common intervals, and then they talk, first about the work they are doing and then more about themselves, though still tentatively.

"Red tells me you've been looking for Parker," Nancy says.

"He doesn't like the idea, I know."

"He just thinks it's dangerous. Which is true."

"I suppose you don't want him mixed up in it."

"He'll be mixed up in it," Nancy says. "I mean, if you are. He won't let you down, you know."

"I didn't think of it like that." Jim drops his crowbar to the floor— it clangs like a bell—then sits, weary, his shoulders aching.

"I don't want anybody to get hurt," she says. "Not even Parker. I just don't. I don't like cowboy justice. I like justice justice."

"So you told him no."

"Well, I don't see what harm it can do to look through an empty house. If I *knew* it was empty, I'd go in there myself. I can't stand the idea that prick is blackmailing Chong. He tried to *rape* that girl. Somewhere along the line somebody has to say no to this guy."

"I agree," Jim says.

"Yeah, well." Nancy uses the crowbar for support as she lowers herself to the floor, leans against a post in a square of sunlight swirling with dust motes that spark above her. "Red and I do have our hesitations."

"Should I know them?"

"Yes." Nancy pulls off her gloves and runs her fingers through her hair quickly. "We don't want to make more trouble for ourselves by hurting anyone. And we're worried about you, Jim. Your motives."

"Meaning?"

"What's it to you, really? This isn't your town. You're going to leave. Why are you taking up this crusade?"

"Maybe because I'm not from this town. Maybe because I am going to leave. Nobody's grudge is going to thrive on a vacuum. Besides, I don't like what Parker has done to people who have been good to me. He's a terrorist, and he pisses me off."

"Yeah?"

"Yeah."

"And you figure you can help us out, and get away clean?"

"I'm not looking to get hurt or land in jail, if that's what you mean."

"That's sort of what we mean."

Jim understands suddenly, and he spits with disgust. "No, God damn it, I'm not looking to get myself killed. I had my chances, and I lucked out. Russian roulette I'm not interested in. But I didn't go through hell, either, so guys like Parker can mess up our lives." He shakes his head violently. "This is not my excuse to become a martyr or something."

"We just wanted to be sure about that." Nancy's voice trembles a little. Briefly she closes her eyes. "You can't blame us for wondering."

"I don't blame you," Jim says. "I'm just embarrassed a little, sorry I gave that impression. I guess I don't talk enough to the right people. I guess I should have let you know, let Red know, I'm feeling better about things. Some things. It's getting better with me, it really is."

Nancy smiles now. "Yeah, I needed to hear that. And so does Red, Jim."

Jim nods, then laughs quietly. "I don't know why I find it so easy to talk to you. You weasel everything out of me."

"Not quite everything, I'm sure."

Jim clasps his knees in his arms and rocks like a child. They thought I was taking this on to hurt myself, to destroy myself, that I'd be reckless. This idea hurts, stings him because he knows it has been true, and he will have to fight to keep his actions clean, to keep them free from cynicism. It is true that I have wanted to die, Jim thinks.

Red's voice booms up from the first floor of the barn now, punctuated by the clatter of his boots. "It's awfully damned quiet up there for a couple of carpenters." The ladder trembles as he mounts. "You'd better have your trousers on, folks, or I'm going to fire you and keep the cash."

Nancy bites a finger and looks at Jim with a big grin, then says, "Anybody who talks like that, don't you think they ought to be mooned?"

"I'll pass," Jim says. "But don't let me stop you."

A few days later, Red pulls into Chong's driveway, trailer bouncing behind the jeep, just as Jim descends the ladder from the roof. Sweat has been dripping into his eyes, and Jim has a rag tied across his brow.

"Yeah, all right." Red stands below the ladder, hands on hips, surveying the work Jim and Nancy have done during the afternoon— nailing boards across the roof beams and covering these with tar paper.

"Nice to see a guy who can climb a ladder, too," Red says. "I'll remember that the next time we're called to a chimney fire."

"I hate it," Jim says. "I'm O.K. once I get up there, but getting on and off the thing drives me nuts."

Red laughs. "You're a natural."

"Tell that to my insurance agent." Once on the ground, Jim feels incredibly tired, his legs weak, and he leans over, hands on knees, to rest for a moment. "I thought I was getting in shape, but I'm finding new muscles on this job. All kinds of them."

"Where's Nancy?"

"She and Chong took off for some beer," Jim says. "I don't know why they aren't back yet. They left an hour ago."

Red launches into a little essay on why Jim should not work on the roof alone, should always have Nancy or someone there to hold the ladder for him, should not drink beer on the roof in the hot sun. . . .

"I didn't have any beer," Jim says. "I haven't had any for two days, in fact. But it's so friggin' hot today, and now that I'm done—"

"Done!" Red scoffs. "I just got here, buddy. I got some rolls of half lap shingling and twenty gallons of roofing tar in that trailer, and I figure it's time to get serious."

"I've been working all day, Red!"

"So have I," Red says. "And don't give me that. You didn't get up until noon."

Nancy swings into the driveway now, skids to a halt, and leaves the door of the car swinging as she comes running forward.

"Where's Chong?" Jim says. "And where's the goddamn beer?"

"I left Chong at Rubb's," Nancy says, "and no time for beer. But I got something else." She pulls a thick black wire from the kangaroo pocket of the sweatshirt she is wearing, tosses it to Red.

"Coil wire?"

"I believe a certain pair of ladies are stranded at the supermarket," Nancy says. "I followed them clear to Royalton."

"Let's go," Jim says.

"Go? Where?" Red grabs Jim by the arm.

"Archer's. Come on."

"Look," Red says, but is interrupted at once by Nancy.

"Red, we don't have that much time."

"Oh, man," Red says with agony. "I don't know why I'm doing this." Reluctantly he jogs to the car behind Jim and Nancy, and objects when they leave him the driver's seat. "Nancy, you drive. I'll go in with Jim."

"Uh uh," she says.

"Nancy!"

"Uh uh."

"God damn it," Red says.

Jim realizes he is grinding his teeth so hard they ache. His mouth is dry.

Jim starts in the attic of the house, Nancy in the small basement, and they have agreed to hit all the obvious targets first, then, if the drawings fail to materialize, to begin turning things over—dressers, beds—and to take things apart—chairs, sofas, mattresses. They had tried to imagine how Parker thought about the drawings, their importance to him, and how careful he would be to preserve and hide them. Anything locked would be their first target. Amazing and saddening, Jim thinks, how easy it really was to penetrate someone's privacy.

The attic is hot, and a jumble of pathetic junk—broken radios, chairs worn to the padding, lamps without shades, or cords. Jim dumps a box of letters, paws through them quickly. Nothing in the attic seems to have been touched recently—no fingermarks disturb the pervasive layer of dust, golden in the late afternoon sunlight that comes through a gable window. He lifts the tops of hat boxes, old potato chip cans, but the attic seems a forgotten place, and he clicks down the narrow steps into the bedroom.

Now he swipes through drawers, pulling out underclothes and heaping them on the bed, pulling blankets and sheets from closet shelves, whipping them open, feeling the sleeves of shirts and jackets, when he hears Nancy yell. The cry lashes Jim into a panic and he charges to the stairwell so recklessly that he almost loses his balance and falls.

Nancy is at the foot of the stairs holding at arm's length two drawings, each the size of a newspaper folded in half, of a girl seated by a window. Jim regards them quickly. In the first, the girl leans on her fist, pouting, legs twisted uncomfortably, in the way of teenagers, pulls her hair with her free hand into the window light; in the other, she is grinning, holding a strange pig under her arm, an obscene live teddy bear, pawing to be freed.

"In the bathroom." Nancy laughs. "I knocked down a shelf full of pill bottles, and found them under the paper liner. Know what else I found?"

"We weren't going to take anything else," Jim says.

"Ah, but Jim." Nancy tucks the two drawings together, reaches into the pocket of her sweatshirt, and draws out for Jim's inspection two stainless steel syringes. "What do you bet they're his and hers?"

Turner's pickup is in the driveway and Barber's jeep; lights are on in the house, and sounds of music drift from open windows.

"It's too cold for open windows," Chong says to Nancy as he

climbs out of the car. He is irritated and cannot understand having been left in Royalton so long, or Nancy's refusal to explain, telling him only to relax and be patient. Seeing his home lit so brightly gives Chong an odd sensation, that he is at the wrong place, his home taken over, or that he is a stranger and viewing this little house in Lake Ecstasy for the first time. Still not quite ready for talk, he walks past the house to his garden, telling Nancy, "I'll be in in a minute."

His garden still produces. Though the cold nights have slowed it down, the frosts have not yet been killing, and he can see he has tons of tomatoes to bring in yet.

"Hey, Chong, for Christ's sake," he hears Red call. "C'mere, buddy."

When Chong turns, he sees Barber in an almost comic way. His front is dark blue from the light of the evening sky, his back is orange from house light.

"What the hell are you doing out there?"

"Checking the garden."

"You'd better check what's in here, too."

"What is all this damned mystery?" Chong comes into the house to find Turner seated at the table with Jim and Nancy. At the kitchen counter Red is pouring champagne into the jelly jars that Chong uses for glasses.

"What the hell?"

Jim unrolls the drawings of Ginny on the kitchen table, and the hairs rise along Chong's neck as if he has seen a ghost.

"How . . . ?"

Red hands him a jar of champagne. "Some day we'll tell you the whole story," he says. "But even Nixon's Plumbers could take a lesson from us."

"Nixon's Plumbers?" Chong runs his hand over the paper, trying to commit the drawings to memory, to imprint them on his body as well as his mind.

"I'm probably the only one here who voted for Nixon," Turner says.

"The only one who'd admit it anyway." Nancy puts her hand on top of Chong's for a moment. "Happy birthday, Chong."

"Matches?" Chong says.

Turner slides a box of matches across the table.

"Now we will see a fire." Chong zips a match along the side of the box, and it sizzles to life. He cradles the flame in the palm of his hand, picks up the drawings, pushes out the kitchen door, and on the dew-flecked lawn behind the house he touches the match to the papers, watches the flame lick and curl around the edges, then leap to consume the images he once made. Chong is glad it is dark, so he cannot see the images the flames are eating away. But even so, as the papers turn into thin crusts of ash, he thinks he can see her after-image, a soft and ghostly glow of lines. Then the wind blows the black flakes away into the darkness.

The next night Red and Jim sit in Jim's car as far down the road as possible and still be able to observe the traffic at the Archer house. Their vigil is rewarded at last when Taylor Archer pulls out of the driveway in the older white Mercury Jim has recognized and cruises past them, headed for Royalton.

"This'd be a lot tougher if he was on that bike of his," Red says.

"Yeah, you can't miss those taillights." Jim waits until the Mercury disappears, then wheels onto the road and shoves the pedal down.

"Hey! No big hurry," Red says. "This road only goes one place. Stay cool."

"I want his ass," Jim says. "We find out where Parker is, and that's the game."

"So? Stay cool and follow that boy right there. If he doesn't lead us to Parker, we'll have a little chat with him, that's all. Just take it easy."

"Jesus, I got the edge tonight," Jim says. "I really want to even the score a little, and I mean now."

"Well, lose the edge until you need it," Red says. "We don't want to kill anybody, including ourselves, so slow the fuck down."

They follow, and Archer continues down Royalton Road at a high rate of speed, and then into Royalton itself. Jim and Red lose the car momentarily but find it just off the main street in front of the Cricket Club and around the corner from the VFW.

Jim parks his car across the street. "So now what? You think he's meeting Parker in there?"

"We could take a look. We could wait. What do you think?"

"I think he's making a telephone call," Jim says. "I think we should wait. If he sees us, it could blow the whole deal."

"I also can't imagine grabbing him in the bar," Red says. "I'm not exactly a stranger in there."

"On the other hand," Jim says. "I could go for a beer."

"It ain't suds time," Red says.

"But suppose Parker's in there meeting Archer right now."

"The bar's going to close in ten minutes. He's not going to see Parker for ten minutes, is he? He's making a call, like you said. Probably calling Chong while he's at it."

"O.K.," Jim says. "I guess he's not going anywhere without his car in any case."

"Unless," Red says. "he's changing cars. Which is what I would do."

"He couldn't be that slick."

"Who knows?" Red says. "Parker's got a lot at stake here. Six years in Walpole, maybe. He might get pretty cagey."

At two-thirty every car on the block is gone but Archer's old Mercury, and Jim's.

"Guess what?" Red says.

He and Jim break into wild laughter.

2
Flame
of
the
Lotus

Jim looks away from the barn roof into the spectacular patch-work of trees surrounding Chong's farm, edging the stream, smearing colors across the surface of the pond. The vantage point is oddly peaceful, though Jim is not truly at ease on the barn roof, grips the peak with his knees as his hammer claps in a nail. The vista is beautiful, yes, but trite for a photographer, and the haze of Jim's withdrawal paints everything with a kind of menacing glare he would have liked to shed, to have fall from his eyes as leaves broke from the branches in a stiff breeze and tumbled down.

Maybe, he thinks, on the other side of this withdrawal, this head-ache, this anger, I will see whatever it is that Chong sees here. The breeze blows across the sweat on Jim's neck, and he feels cold, even in the sun. Funny, in a way, how just being in the man's house, see-ing what Chong's friends would do for him, had given Jim a sense that his own vision of things was incomplete, that here was some-thing important he needed to learn—and could learn. It crosses his mind that he would like to bring Anna to Chong's house—she sounded curious about him—browse among his things, walk her through the camp and up the hill to the gazebo. What would she see in Chong? An eccentric imp, a man too playful for his age, a renegade? Would she find him compulsive only, or admire his com-mitment to his art? But Jim knows what Anna would say about Chong. She would understand that he is driven by love and a desire to make things beautiful, but is also embarrassed about vying with what the world produces so prolifically and casually on its own.

Jim continues nailing. Each hammer blow echoes in the woods like rifle shots. But that's what he doesn't see, Jim thinks. Bang. Bang. Bang. The idea that he is being fired upon from the woods makes him stop. He wipes the sweat from his face, and swallows. It's O.K., he tells himself. You're safe now, buddy. Safe.

Two crisp reports come from below him, and Jim almost loses his hammer. Car doors. A huge cream-white Continental gleams beside the house, and two gray-haired men in blazers are opening the rear doors for two women who emerge slowly, stiffly, as if they have traveled a great distance. Jim thinks they look like refugees from a country club, the men in pastel pants, the women in cocktail dresses and cashmere shawls. Chong bursts from the kitchen door in an absolute dither and it is plain from his paint-smeared jeans and ripped T-shirt that he has not been expecting these guests. He wipes his hands on his pants and greets the tallest gentleman with shy laughter and a prolonged handshake.

Jim enjoys his Olympian view of this drama only a few moments more, because Chong frantically gestures toward him, asks him to descend. Jim makes his way carefully down the slope of the barn roof, fights off the usual panic he has when stepping over the edge onto the ladder rungs, careful not to lean too far forward and lever the base of the ladder into the air. Red has told him to tie the base to the barn or to a stake driven into the ground, but Jim forgot the advice. He knows from the way his heart hammers now he will not forget it again. God! the butterflies that one moment gives him.

"Jesus, I need some help now." Chong explains to Jim that his visitors are Todd Oslip, a gallery owner and art collector, his wife, and some friends. They had driven out from Boston to view the foliage, were in a festive mood, and Todd thought it would be a perfect time to have a look at what Chong was producing. "Can you help, please? I need a table outside, by that tree. Just toss a clean bedsheet on it. And would you go for some wine? White wine and some seltzer. I have to find things to show him, cook . . . everything!"

Chong is pleased to see that Oslip and party have undertaken a little tour, have discovered the glass-bottomed boat and are regaling themselves by trying to figure out its uses. Oslip, after removing his blazer, ventures to lie down in it, and an argument ensues over

THE PROGRESS OF A FIRE

whether the women will take off their shoes and launch him with a push. Chong quickly picks eggplant, tomatoes, lettuce from the garden, hurries inside.

In less than an hour he has prepared omelettes and white wine spritzers, with bread and salad, and amidst protestations that he has gone to too much trouble for them, a meal is had, and Chong's wine supply polished off. Oslip is wild about Chong's boat, makes recommendations for improvements that Chong listens to patiently. One of the women suggests that they might like to swim, if only they had known about the pond and brought suits.

"You don't need clothes here," Chong says. "Just go."

"But there are so many *men*," Mrs. Oslip protests. She is silver-haired, robust, a woman who could drink and dance all night, Chong guesses. "It's the oddest family I've ever seen. A family of men, and cats, and chickens."

"It's a terrible situation, you're right," Chong says. "It evolved by more defaults than I have time to tell you."

"Why don't you go ahead?" Oslip challenges his wife. "What's life without a little adventure?"

The women debate this possibility as Chong and Oslip go into the house, and the terrible ordeal begins. Drawings and prints are spread on his unmade bed, quickly tacked to the kitchen cupboard, paintings are wrestled down from the attic and lined against the walls and then taken outside and leaned against the house.

"It's never-ending!" Oslip says.

"I've a lifetime's supply," Chong groans.

Oslip peruses everything close-up, far away, walks through and around the house. Meanwhile, the women have thrown caution to the winds and plunge into the pond, where they swim discreetly for an hour, return with hair wrapped in towels, bare feet, and rumpled dresses. They are in a most agreeable state of drunkenness and fatigue. And now that "the coast is clear," the other man lopes down to the water and takes his turn alone.

"It's an absolute feast," Oslip says to the women. "Just look at these things! It's like discovering a sunken pirate ship or something." He takes them through the house in a review of the work Chong has just shown him, but Chong sits on the porch steps, his stomach churning. How he hates this part of his art! How he hates money, and his desire to have more of it! He wishes he could learn to be at ease with money, as Oslip is, but he supposes in order to do that you must have lots of it.

Later, when the group has recomposed, and they prepare to leave, Oslip asks Chong to send him several pieces—he points out his preferences—right away. He writes out a check, advance on sales, to help with the costs of crating and shipping. It is quite a substantial check, and Chong hesitates for a moment, then stuffs the check into his shirt pocket.

When the Continental rolls away, Jim volunteers to help Chong return the paintings to the house. "Or some of these could go into the barn now. Under the new roofing."

"Yes, good," Chong says. He is not paying much attention to what Jim says, distracted by the sum of money that had just come to him, and the pleasant dilemma it has put him in of deciding how to divide it up. He can send Mai Li and Susan something now. He can send Evelyn Crane a payment, too. If he needs to, he can hire a lawyer, and maybe get through the winter after all. But as for shelling out good money for crating and shipping his paintings—that was out. He'd hire Red or Jim to take them down.

Red and Jim pull some boards into the upper story of the barn using a pair of long ropes. Red had insisted it would not be a monumental amount of labor merely to erect a wall and create a large window (which would open like a door) so that Chong could have a larger studio space than his living room provided. They pull in rhythm and the boards come swiftly up.

"Did I ever tell you about my bunji ropes?" Red says.

"Bunji ropes." Jim laughs. "Is that something like Viet Namese engine voodoo?"

"This is for real." Red tells a story now of the Trobrian Islanders, and a rite of passage among them. The young men tie ropes measured to precision to branches high in the trees, tie these ropes to their feet, and then hurl themselves down. In the perfect case, the head of the young man will only graze the earth; and in the worst case—death. "So a couple of things came together for me when I read that," Red says. "The first had to do with my own courage—you know, whether I had courage for ordinary life, things in the world, not in a survival situation. I wanted to know if I had the guts for something like that."

"Don't tell me you—"

"Hang on a sec. The other thing I wondered was whether I could make things so well that I would trust them with my own life. O.K., I repaired helicopters, and you couldn't fuck that up without killing somebody. But what about something else? So I made up these bunji ropes—just ropes but lashed to two heavy pieces of bunji cord, one on either end. I made a little harness for my ankles. I was never a sloppy guy, Jim, but doing this, I think I got the idea for the first time ever of really doing something right. I checked every stitch. Then I tied these ropes, one of 'em, on the old railroad bridge up near Royalton, where you caught brown trout last June. And I hooked one up, and I buckled it to my feet, and I went over."

"Went over! Just like that!"

"It was great, Jim! Some people sky-dive, what the hell. What a rush! Man, you jounce up and down, your head just hitting the water, you know."

"How did you get out of it?"

"Pulled myself up. You can unbuckle the ankle harness, drop in the stream."

"The water's cold there."

"You bet your ass," Red says. "You want to try it?"

"Me? You're nuts."

"Actually, you ought to make your own, to get the idea. Then I came up with another use for it."

"Do I want to hear this?"

"Sure. I made another couple of bunji ropes, but the harness I made would go around your chest, see? So you'd just kind of hang and bounce. You put your feet in the water, and the current just kind of jiggles you and swings you, and it's like flying."

"Sounds like kid's stuff. Compared to the other."

"I told you I made two of these?"

"So?"

"So. I hung two from the bridge. Nancy was in one, see, and I was in the other. And she just sort of draped her legs over my hips, and there we were." He laughs.

Jim is a little dumbfounded by the concept. "Bunji love. The stuff you think of!"

"So? You want to try it?" Red pulls his tape measure out of the holster in his belt and snakes it along the boards they have stacked.

"Yeah, sure," Jim says. "All I need is a willing partner."

"When we get to the shop, I'll toss the cords in the car for you."

"Why? You think I'm going to find somebody I can talk into jumping off a bridge with me real soon?"

"You never know," Red says. "I see people in California are walking on coals these days. Can bunji-cording be far behind?"

When Jim comes into the house, dusk has fallen. He finds Chong brooding over a large notebook and it seems to take him a moment to wake from his trance. His greeting to Jim is barely audible. Jim washes his hands in the kitchen sink, and when the water stops, he asks, "Does it bother you to have me around when you're working?"

"No, no," Chong says. "I'm glad for the company."

"Are you getting anxious for me to leave?"

"Not at all," Chong says. "I'm just not used to talking much, I've spent so much time alone. Don't take it personally."

"Suppose I wanted to hang around after the trial is over, though."

"Ha!" Chong says. "When it's over. First, they must find Parker, and maybe he's not around."

"He's around."

"How do you know?"

"There are some things you just know."

Chong, though he agrees with this, challenges Jim. "Suspicion! You really don't know."

"Evidence," Jim says.

"Like what?"

"How certain people behave. They don't disguise their purposes very well. Red and I know he's around. But the main thing is that we just sense him out there. Vibrations. Red says, 'This place is full of Parker vibes.' And he's right. Does that make sense to you?"

"It's like a shadow," Chong says. "A shadow in the darkness."

"Yes!"

"Not much," Chong says. "But I understand."

"In combat," Jim says, "your senses get pretty tuned up. You get some messages you never knew how to receive. You can tell if someone is watching you from behind, a sniper, say. The wind can be blowing in the jungle, and you can hear a footstep. You can tell the difference between rockets going out and rockets coming in. Red calls it 'the edge.' It's just being aware in ways you don't usually practice."

"Why not?" Chong says. "If we have such skills."

"Because it's painful," Jim says. "Because it tires you out."

"Painful?"

"Once you get revved up, it takes forever to cool down. So you can bear things. So you're not listening to every engine that goes down the road and memorizing and identifying it. So you can relax somehow."

"You drink for that?"

"Yeah," Jim says. "I wish I knew another way."

"There are other ways," Chong says evenly.

"Sure."

"One way is to use your pain."

"Oh, great," Jim says. "Use the pain!"

Jim hears the low dull howl of the bottle a second before it smashes into the window and shards flash into the room. He is on his way out the door before Chong even struggles up from his chair, a keening, rattling Chinese curse on his lips, and he makes it quickly enough to the roadside to see the taillights wink on down the Lake Road and to hear the rumble of the car's exhaust.

"Jim?" Chong is silhouetted in the doorway.

Jim slips into the station wagon and in a moment is banging along the highway toward Lake Ecstasy. He hadn't seen anything. There is nothing he can do. But he is also angry, so angry that the steering wheel warps as he bears down on it with his hands. The little whistle of the open bottle before it hit the window: *Incoming*, he had thought, *incoming, incoming*. The damned little shits had brought it back, just when he was getting relaxed. Who the hell did they think they were to inject themselves into his life? He wants to see their faces. Who . . . the hell . . . did they think . . . they *were?* The old station wagon thunders and slaps over the dark road, and the headlights catch the quick green pinpoint blaze of a raccoon's eyes, the animal no doubt hunching in the weeds with a stolen chicken or an ear of corn. There is blood on the 'coon's teeth. *But you couldn't know that,* Jim tells himself. *You don't even know it was a 'coon.*

He eases up on the gas as he crests a hill, then sees below a pair of cars side by side, but facing opposite directions, at the edge of the road, arms and elbows hanging from open windows, the drivers in apparent conversation. Kids. Jim slows down as he comes upon them and looks the crowd over. They chew and smoke and regard him idly as he cruises by. Maybe it was them. The car that was getting away was met by the other, flagged down. They were bragging and laughing about it, blood on the 'coon's teeth. Maybe, maybe not. There is a car ahead, for Jim can see taillights on a distant hill . . . quickly gone. He grinds his teeth. *When I get my hands on you—Jesus!*

Jim continues down the Lake Road for a few minutes, then pulls into the Lake Ecstasy Village Inn. Inside, he calls Chong from the pay phone, and asks if he has had any more trouble.

"No, nothing more." Chong sounds tired.

"Did you call the police?"

"Why bother? They never do anything."

"Call them anyway."

"Screw it."

"I'll call them, then."

"O.K. Do it."

"I wish I could get my hands on them."

"Ah . . ." Chong is too tired to talk.

"I'll be here awhile."

"O.K. Have one for me."

Jim phones the police and tells the officer what has happened. He feels a little foolish. Big deal. Kid smashes window. Yes, he can understand the officer's boredom. He'd heard it before. Kids today. What are you going to do?

Incoming. That's what had done it, had made him want to kill. Jim has a beer and watches the color television for a while. The screen fills up with lips and teeth, then two boxers bob into a ring and begin throwing punches. *Get him. Get him good. Come on, get him. Kill the fucker. Knock his fucking brains out!*

"All right, all right." Red throws his hands down in a gesture of impatience. "You're right, they're going way too far now."

"I don't think it was a coincidence, just some kids. I think it was them, because we got the drawings, and they know it."

"Of course, Jim."

"Suppose there was some gasoline in that bottle?"

"Will you shut the hell up a minute? Everything you say is true." Red opens his wood stove and stuffs in a log. "The first thing I'm going to do is give Chong one of my shotguns, and I want you to teach him how to use it. If we're gone and they come back, he's got to have something. Maybe I ought to give Nancy a lesson, too."

"What did you mean, 'If we're gone'?"

"To the Cricket Club, in Royalton."

"That's cool. How will we know when Archer leaves home? We can't sit out there every night."

"I'll have Nancy stake it out awhile. She can call on the CB, and maybe we can get a jump on him."

"You're a genius, Red."

"I'm an asshole," Red says. "I'm an asshole for ever getting involved in this."

Two nights later, Jim comes quickly up behind Taylor on his way into the bar in Royalton, grips the greasy black jacket that seems of animal stock more ancient than mere leather, doubles Taylor's hand against his wrist, and before he can swing, shoves him into the doorway where Red has been waiting.

"Hi, Taylor," Jim says. "Just relax a little and nothing will break."

"Or get cut," Red says.

Taylor is strong, very hard, and he takes what Jim knows is a lot of convincing to settle down. He is animal enough to try twice to stamp on Jim's feet, and pays the price for this when Red reminds him who is in charge.

"Maybe we'd better take a little ride," Red says.

They shove Taylor into the back of the car where Jim loops a coil of Red's bunji rope around Taylor's neck. Red drives immediately out of town, pulls off into a lane that snakes into the woods, then emerges at a turnaround near a railroad bridge. Jim has fished beneath the bridge a few times, and he knows the water is deep here, where holes have been sunk to contain the bridge pillars.

Archer is scared, but defiant. He seems too young to Jim, his face unflawed but manly, with thick eyebrows and an almost feminine mouth. The simple beauty of the young man almost makes Jim relent. But Jim had been young once, too. He had been handsome like this, and his radiance in Army camps had made little difference to the Viet Cong. Jim's anger thickens dangerously: kid has everything, has choices, freedom, time, and screws it around. He deserves to die.

But he says patiently. "Look, Taylor, we don't want to hurt you."

"Just kill you," Red says.

Jim and Red knew this routine, and had practiced it—hard cop, easy cop—hoping it would help to break Taylor without true violence.

"Listen to me," Jim says, twisting Archer's face to his own, staring into his eyes. "All we want to know is where to find Parker. You tell us, and you're free, we'll let you go. Hear me?"

"Like hell," Red says. "You promised me some of this boy's ass. Didn't he run you off the trail? Didn't he? Torch Chong's barn? Didn't he toss bottles through your windows?"

"Be quiet," Jim says calmly. "I'm willing to forgive and forget. I just want Parker, that's all. So what do you say, Archer?"

"Keep him away from me," Archer growls. He licks his lips quickly, his mouth dry with fear.

"Take it easy," Jim says. "He won't hurt you unless I tell him to."

"Oh, yeah?" Red says. "I'll crack this fucker's skull right now." He brings his arm back as if to strike.

But Jim reaches across Taylor and puts his hand on Red's fist. "We're dealing here. If this guy deals on the level, we'll let him go. I've given my word."

"I didn't give my word," Red says.

"I'm getting a little impatient myself." Jim sighs. "You have something to say, Taylor?"

"What I got to say," Taylor says, head down, "is you can both stick it."

Now Red does strike, hard, and the kid goes down, but rebounds at once, thrashing in Jim's grasp. Oh, oh, Jim thinks. It's going to take something to hurt this guy.

"That felt good," Red says. "Let me do it again."

"Fuckin' bastard," Archer hisses.

Red strikes again, this time with such force that Archer doubles over with a loud grating cough.

"Bunji time," Jim says.

"Already? Shit!"

"You'll kill him, hitting him like that."

"Serve him right."

"O.K., Archer, sit down." Jim forces him down and waits while Red brings the coil of rope and bunji cord from the car. Jim wonders what Archer makes of the device, whether he can even see the thick rubber strips lashed to either end.

"You're not going to hang me," Archer says.

"Why the hell not?" Red says. "Everybody in town has been dyin' for a chance."

Red kneels now and quickly ties Archer's feet, then loops the bunji cord around Archer's ankles and secures the hook, screws in a bolt which causes it to close completely.

"Heave away," Red says, and he and Jim carry Taylor to the bridge, sit him down while Red secures the other end of the bunji rope to a railing on the trestle. Taylor is tense, stiff as the iron railings that run beneath their feet, reflecting moonlight until they disappear into the trees. Anybody could be in there, Jim thinks. Anybody could be watching this craziness.

"I don't know if this is going to work," Red says. "It might break, and then we'll lose him down there, and he's all tied up."

"O.K.," Archer says. "I don't know where Parker is. O.K.? I really don't. So get me out of this, hey? I mean, what the hell is this?"

"Maybe we measured wrong," Red says. "Maybe his head will go under, and he'll drown, just like that."

"I'm telling the truth," Archer shouts, "Parker's in Florida or something. He's way the hell off someplace."

"Maybe there's a rock down there we didn't see," Red continues, "and his head will smash on that, and mash his little pea brain."

"I mean it," Archer says. "Parker said he would be in Boston sometime. He'd call from Boston, but I don't even know where he is right now."

"Up and over," Jim says. Red grabs Archer's feet, and Jim lifts him from beneath the arms.

"Wait!" Archer cries.

They lift him to the rail.

"Don't throw me over there," Archer cries, struggles, tries to kick. His voice rasps. "I never done any of that stuff, and it was his idea. Him and Ginny's mother."

"One," Jim says.

"See? Parker's got dope in that bus. Heroin. They use it, see. They gotta have money. That's why they sent Ginny to Florida, because Carey didn't want her around dope."

"Two . . ."

"And he'll kill me if I tell where he is, so don't, I can't—"

"Three."

With a little heave, Archer slips over the rail, plummets with a scream to the water, head first, since the rope tied to his feet turned him over, splashes, and then the rope jounces with an ominous, metallic grating sound of the hook against the trestle railing. An iron, resonating sound. Taylor is crying now, shouting with terror more complete than any Jim had heard since Hue. He dangles above the water, jounces at the end of the bunji rope, screams.

"Jesus Christ," Red says. "I think we got more than we bargained for. I think he's gone nuts."

Jim is sweating so profusely he thinks for a moment he is bleeding from the eyes.

"What?" he says. "Never mind. Let's haul him up, give him another go."

The pressure of the rope on the railing, as they haul it up, makes the trestle groan and hum.

Upside down, Archer talks. He tells them where Parker is. He screams it so the whole world can hear. Yes, yes, yes, he will agree to anything, to leave town that night.

They reach down and grab Taylor by his clothes, and when they grapple him to the railing again, Jim can see, hear that Taylor is trembling with great spasms, gasping.

"We damn near scared him to death," Jim hisses as they drop Archer to the flooring of the bridge.

"I guess it's easy when you know how," Red says.

"We'd better treat him for shock or we'll lose him."

"Don't you dare die," Red says, his own face close to Archer's. "Think of all those pretty girls you ain't laid yet. Besides," he says to Jim, "that'd be bunches more trouble than we really need."

Chong waits anxiously for Jim and Red to return from Royalton, sits in the house with his lights off, rehearsing what Jim has told him about using the shotgun. This is ridiculous, he thinks, I can't kill anybody. He has put the gun in a closet by the front door, and he knows it will stay there forever. He can't imagine using it. A gun. He never owned a gun in his life. It is an instrument as foreign to him as a Rolls-Royce. Then the night quiet is shattered by the ringing of the telephone, and he is afraid to answer it, to let anyone know he is at home, but also afraid not to answer it, in case Jim is calling. He screws up his courage and picks up the receiver.

The telephone growls horribly for an instant, clatters, and Chong understands someone is putting a coin into a pay telephone, almost hangs up, when he hears, "Chonger?"

His knees weaken with the sound of her voice. "Ginny!"

"You knew my voice right away."

"Did you think I wouldn't?"

"I thought you forgot me."

"I wouldn't forget you. How are you?"

"I'm at the store. O'Day's. Can you come and get me? I'm afraid to hitchhike any more, because someone might see me."

"You're not supposed to be here!"

"Yeah."

"Oh, Jesus. I'll come right away."

"I'll be out back. Just pull around there and I'll get in the car."

Chong's hands tremble as he starts the car, and he drives drunkenly to O'Day's. He cruises behind the store with his lights out and Ginny emerges from the shadows, pops open the door, and is at his side. She takes his head in both hands and kisses him mightily on the mouth.

"What in God's name are you doing here? How did you get here?"

"I hitchhiked," Ginny says. "I walked some of the way."

"That was very dangerous. Parker's friends are all over the town."

"I had to see you."

"Don't you have a telephone?"

"Yeah, I have a telephone, but I wanted to see you. And I wanted you to see me."

"So what do you expect me to do now?"

"Just drive me home. That'd be great. We can talk for a while."

"I'm not even supposed to know where you are!"

"I'll never tell anyone I saw you."

"Ginny, do you know they are trying to find Parker, to take him to trial for attacking you?"

"Yeah," she says. "I know that. I have a lawyer. I also have a counselor. I have to see this guy once a week."

"Do you like him?"

"He's O.K. It's all right."

"Well? Which way do I go?"

"Back toward Royalton. But it's in Jefferson."

"That's a long way! You came so far! When did you leave?"

"About noon."

"You must never do that again, Ginny. You can call me if you want to talk to me. Promise?"

"Yeah. It was just this once. I wanted you to see how I looked."

Chong pulls out onto the highway, and turns on his lights when Ginny reminds him to. Once they are away from the village, he turns on the overhead light, takes Ginny's hand for a moment and looks her over. Then he snaps off the light.

What was he supposed to see? he wonders. "You look wonderful," he says.

"Yeah." She laughs. "I got all these new clothes. And I put on some weight. They really gave me some nice things. And I have my own bed. And I sleep. I thought I forgot how to sleep, but I sleep good now."

"I told you it would be good there."

"It's pretty good, yeah. Thanks, Chong."

"I'm glad you're happy. And safe."

"It's not perfect, don't get that idea."

"But good."

Ginny tells him that she elected to come to see Chong because of the trial, and because living in a family with three other kids made it difficult to have any privacy. One of the other children was another foster child, and not very friendly, an older girl who was sometimes quite difficult. She had terrible fights with the family, but everyone was trying to make her feel at home. She liked her new school so far, especially music class. Ginny liked the parents, who were tough and patient and very generous. Ginny respected them and felt safe, but sometimes it made her angry that she did not have a home of her own and parents like these, simple access to ordinary things of the world, simple order in her life, boundaries. Sometimes the anger had become uncontrollable and she had wanted to bolt, but this was the first time she had left, the first time she had thought that what she wanted to do was worth the risk of being caught.

"Well, you flatter me," Chong says.

"I didn't want you to be worrying about me, or about the trial. I'll tell the truth, that you were especially good to me. You were like my real dad."

"Oh, Jesus," Chong says. "You are going to be so special."

"You mean I'm not?"

"Of course. I just mean when you are older, too." He laughs. "Oh, yes, and I have something to tell you, too. I got the pictures back. The ones I drew of you!"

"Great!" Ginny says. "I thought of those pictures. I wanted to get them, but I couldn't go back there. You'll save them for me, won't you?"

"I can't!" Chong wails. "I destroyed them!"

"But I wanted them, Chonger. You made them for me, didn't you?"

"Yes, I did." Chong feels a momentary pang of regret, lays a hand on her arm for a moment. "I'm sorry, but I will do some others for you."

"With me in them?"

"Yes."

"Soon. Make it soon."

Chong laughs. "Be sensible. It won't be right away."

In about an hour and a half, Chong drives Ginny into her neighborhood, watches her walk to the front of a large brick house of two stories. The porch lights, one on either side of the entrance, burn brilliantly. A black dog greets her with wagging tail, and she hugs it around the neck with the kind of abandon that Chong finds hopeful, an unconscious, loving gesture. She would always have scars, would always be to some extent a wary cat, but she would find love, too, if she could give it so spontaneously. As he drives the unfamiliar road back toward Royalton, taking his time, he thinks, she'll be O.K. As O.K. as anybody can be in this life. Leaves drift down over the road in sudden bursts, like bats or butterflies hell-bent on throwing themselves beneath his wheels.

After Jim and Red release him, Archer sits in his car trembling violently, then spins gravel driving off, as if drunk, toward Lake Ecstasy.

"I just don't know," Red says.

"I think he'll split," Jim says. "I think he's scared enough."

"I'm shaking a little myself," Red says. "I forgot you could scare a guy to death. It just never occurred to me—"

"Shock."

"Yeah. It's real. I guess you don't need a bad heart, either."

"Let's check that bus." Jim swings the car onto the road and accelerates.

"*Why* check the bus?"

"I want to find that heroin."

"Why? It's not going anyplace if it's there. I'm sure it's accounted for. That stuff always is."

"I want to make sure Taylor is leveling," Jim says. "And it's on Chong's property. And it's one more thing to hang on Parker."

"Jesus," Red says. "You figure all the angles, don't you? But you ought to know you can't mess with somebody's heroin stash and not have it come back on you. It's more important to them than food. Than life." He points ahead to a white car that has pulled off the side of the road. "Christ, is that Taylor's car?"

Jim slows, and they glide past the old Mercury. Taylor, black leather jacket gleaming in the headlights, is leaning with both hands against the hood of the car, his head ducked out of the glare.

"The kid is really shook," Red says. "Maybe I ought to talk to him."

"He's just getting straight," Jim says. "He'll be all right if he's walking around. It's not as if he was in a barrage or anything."

Red turns in his seat to keep watch on Taylor as long as he can. "I wouldn't swear to that," he says. "That's exactly what I did the first time, too. Heaved my guts out."

"It'll give him character."

"Sure it will." Red slumps in his seat, pulls his hat to his eyes.

At Chong's farm, Jim and Red jog through the frosted grass to the dam—flow reduced to a trickle at this time of year—and cross to the camp. Jim is almost asleep on his feet from the late hour, the exertion and excitement of the night; and the shadows thrown by Red's flashlight seem alive, to have substance. Red is dragging, too, breathing heavily. They pull wood from beneath the bus and search there, around the frame, then in the engine.

"Maybe it's in the tires," Jim says. "Did you think of that?"

"I should've brought some tools," Red says. "I'll go get some, if I have to."

Jim pushes open the doors to the inside of the bus, and when he steps up a dark wedge fills his vision, and he feels a sharp crunch on his face, wetness, and he collapses, spinning, the darkness flashing and burning above him.

"Ah, shit!" he hears Red say. "What a fuckin' deal!"

Jim is on his feet in a moment, aided by Red, and out of his clear eye in the beam of the flashlight he sees the booby trap in the doorway of the bus—a section of log studded with the ends of broken bottles. When he had opened the door, the log was pulled from a window ledge, and swung by the force of gravity into his head.

Red continues swearing, mops at Jim's forehead with a bandanna.

"Man, you're going to have to get this fixed, I mean right now," Red says. "The fuckers laid one on you, Jim. The fuckers sure enough caught us napping."

Red finds the heroin the next afternoon, wrapped in clear plastic bags and stuffed into the hollow legs of the bus seats, which were capped and rebolted to the floor. He has not disturbed the booby trap, because he wants the police to find it—edges of the glass still tacky with Jim's blood—and he wants them to find the heroin, too. But if he leaves the heroin where it is, someone from The Club might find it—perhaps even Taylor to finance an exodus—and take it away. He takes the packages, four of them weighing an ounce or two each, crawls under the steering column, and weaves the bags into the electrical wires behind the dashboard. He lies there a moment in that awkward position contemplating the drug and considers keeping one of the bags for himself. Nancy wouldn't go for it, he decides, rolls out, brushes himself off, and sits there, arms over his knees, hungry for something he can't quite name, and entranced by the flickering red and yellow of the leaves.

Fire!

cars! Scarlet slashes across Jim's face. Chong is not sure he understands the explanations made, since Jim has been so curt about them, and he has shied away from Chong all afternoon. When Chong walks out to see for himself what must have happened, he finds Red sloshing across the dam with a canvas bag of tools, and Red discourages him from looking further.

"I think we stirred a few things up." Red drapes an arm over Chong's shoulder and turns him back toward the house. "You'd better stay away from the bus, because it's quite likely to have visitors you don't want to meet."

"Have you called the police yet?" Chong demands. "My God! A thing like that. Maybe there's something else out there."

"It's a good bet," Red says. "I'd watch where I walked out there."

"So why haven't you called?"

"Christ, Chong, I haven't had a minute. I had to take Jim to the hospital, I had to calm Nancy down when I got home, and then I came back here, and I've been working in the bus."

"Oh, boy," Chong says. "Let's call them now."

"Go ahead," Red says. "I found the dope. Some of it anyway."

"There may be more?"

"Maybe. But I found enough to put those bastards away for a while." Red pauses a moment as they reach the house. "Tell Jim to call me when he feels up to it. I've got to get back for now."

"You want me to call the police?"

"Would you?" Red says. "The state police."

Jim comes down from the upstairs when Chong enters the house. He has a patch over one eye and his face is dotted with stitches and the brown-red slashes of disinfectant.

"Is your eye all right?" Chong asks. "Why is it bandaged?"

"It's all right," Jim says. "The cut is around the eye."

"You almost lost an eye!"

"If you're going to tell me I'm lucky, I don't want to hear it."

"Well, you were lucky."

"I got what I deserved," Jim says. "Red was right. I took a breather and I paid the penalty."

"That doesn't sound like something Red would say." Suddenly Chong feels a little afraid of Jim. It is not just the coldness that emanates from him but the demonic look his face has decorated with the medicine. "But I'm calling the police now so they can have a look. Red found the dope."

"Wait." Jim places his hand over the telephone. "Let's think this over."

"I don't understand," Chong says. "Red asked me to call."

"Let me talk to him first," Jim says.

"Why?" Chong says. "What have you possibly got to gain by not calling the police?"

"So what are we going to tell the police when they come to find the dope and that fucking trap? That we tortured Archer and we know where Parker is?"

Chong reels in disbelief. "You tortured him?"

"We scared him pretty good," Jim says.

"Jesus."

"And now I think we ought to button it down. I think we ought to make sure Parker is holed up where Archer said he was. After all, he didn't *quite* give us the whole story about the bus."

"You're going too far," Chong says. "You don't need to do this."

"Then we'll really have something to give them, Chong. Not just a rumor. And Archer won't matter so much. If Parker's really there, then Archer's out of the picture. And if he isn't, Red and I are in big trouble."

"I wish I wasn't hearing this," Chong says. "You're in enough trouble because of me."

"It's not because of you," Jim says. "Parker's messed with me, too. But I don't accept it. I won't stand for it."

"But what do you think you can do?"

"It's what I *have* to do," Jim says. "Don't you see? We're boxed in. We have to be sure we can deliver Parker or we're just a couple of thugs who assaulted Archer. And how do you prove the dope is The Club's? It's in your bus."

Chong sits down with his head in his hands. Black hair sprouts through his fingers.

"Chong," Jim says wearily, "the law is not going to make Parker pay enough anyway. The law doesn't even know, and around here doesn't seem to want to know what his crimes are."

"Do you? And what do you know about how much he should pay?"

"He thinks he's God, thinks he can do what he wants, to anybody he chooses, take what he wants."

"You think you're God, to stop him?"

"I don't understand you, Chong." Jim daubs at the stitches on his face with the tips of his fingers. "Even if Parker goes up for child abuse, what do you think he's going to do to you when he gets parole in a couple of years? The reason a guy like Parker is allowed to operate is by default. He needs to be stepped on and held underfoot."

"But then, that becomes your life, keeping your foot on Parker."

"Come on," Jim says. "There are ways to contain him without my physical presence."

"You think about Parker too much," Chong says. "You give him too much credit. You're obsessed with him."

"You don't think about him enough," Jim says. "The man's a killer. You're on his list."

"He's never killed."

"Really? I'll tell you what I know about guys like Parker. They're murder waiting to happen. That's something you don't seem to understand."

"You want to kill him, Jim?"

"I've almost reached that point," Jim says.

"Because you hate him so much?"

Jim did not answer for a moment. "Not really," he says. "Parker kind of interests me, in fact. I don't feel I'm especially superior to him, except in one way. I don't interfere with anybody."

"It's impossible to leave people alone," Chong says. "We're not as separate as that! And if you can find any sympathy for Parker, then why would you risk your own life to see him eliminated from the world? There are lots of Parkers."

"I'm not rolling over for him," Jim says. "No way."

"But if you kill him, you have no future. Right?"

"I have no future anyway," Jim says.

"What nonsense!" Chong says.

"I've lost," Jim says, "and I don't care. Taking Parker out might even help to make sense of things."

"You're lying to yourself," Chong says. "You don't have to be responsible for Parker. You can help, but he's not your charge. You want him for another reason. You want him so you can fail completely, with a good excuse!"

"You don't understand a goddamned thing I said!" Jim slams out the kitchen door.

Chong trembles as with chill and fever. What the hell is he supposed to do? He reaches for the telephone, but does not raise it to his mouth. He is dumb with confusion.

"I want to show you something." Red comes out of the garage as Jim drives up to it, and has a hold on Jim's elbow almost before he is out of the car. He leads Jim around the side of the garage, stops in front of his pickup truck. The windshield is frosted with myriad cracks spreading out like the veins of a spiderweb from two precise large bullet holes.

Jim stands in silence, witnessing the damage.

"Nancy was driving," Red says. He throws open the door to the cab, and waits for Jim to look inside.

Now Jim can see a star-shaped hole in the fabric of the backrest, a little halo of burned foam rubber around it.

"The bullet passed right under Nancy's ear." Red demonstrates with the flat of his hand. "Half an inch." He slams the door shut and stalks toward the house.

Jim looks the truck over again, and then follows Red, at a much slower pace. Red is angry, and Jim is not sure what he should do about it. Why Nancy? he wonders. Why are they gunning for her?

Half an inch.

"I don't see any sense in it," Jim says when he has caught up with Red. "She's not involved in this."

"In somebody's mind she is. Or maybe they couldn't see who was in the truck."

"I don't get it, Red."

"Who knows?" Red throws his arms down in disgust. "Maybe I

gave one of those guys something to remember me by at the Inn that day. Maybe Archer is right back home."

"How'd Nancy take it?"

"She freaked out, what'd you expect? She doesn't even want to come near me right now."

"No wonder you're pissed."

"That I am, buddy."

"I thought you might blame it on me."

Red snorts. "You didn't invent Parker. The Club was here before you showed up. I just hope Chong has called the police by now. They can't get here soon enough for me."

"I told him to wait until I talked to you."

"Yeah?"

"They almost killed Nancy. They tried to burn out Chong." Jim touches his face. "This mess is the result of a little booby trap of theirs. The cops want Parker for assault, for child abuse. How hard do you think they're really going to press the hunt?"

"As long as they get him, who cares? You think Parker has to be dead before you're satisfied."

"I wouldn't cry about it."

"You're nuts. I'm having no part of it." He turns and climbs steps two at a time into his house.

Jim pursues him quickly and bangs through the kitchen door. Red is already at the telephone.

"Call the cops, O.K., but give me ten minutes," Jim says. "Huh? And tell me about that mill."

"Forget it," Red says.

"Red! For Christ's sake. I'm not armed. What do you think I'm going to do?"

"Get yourself killed."

"Think about it, Red. Think about who those guys really are. You must know better than anyone what Nancy felt when that bullet slapped into the glass. You've taken fire like that. And they're going to get away with that, for what they've done to her mind."

"Go to hell, Jim."

"Did she have glass in her hair? Her eyes?"

"You really want to know?" Red obviously strains to keep from shouting. The muscles in his neck stand out like ropes. "I'll tell you. She grabbed her head, and she fell on the floor. Then she started to scream, like a siren, she screamed and she cried. And now she tells me just to stay away. Just to get the hell away from her. She had some grains of sand on her cheek from where she had been tossing on the floor of the truck. I reached out to brush them off, and she flinched as if I was going to punch her. Does that satisfy you?"

"And they'll never prove anything," Jim says. "They'll be lucky to get Parker for assault. It's even possible he'll get Chong in trouble. I don't know how you can stand it."

"What the hell's the alternative?" Red says. "Murder? You want to wreck our lives for a little cowboy revenge?"

"The war taught me one thing," Jim says. "One terrible thing."

"Only one?" Red says with contempt.

"That I can kill without remorse."

"I don't believe it," Red says. "It's not true for me; and for a lot of the guys I know, remorse is exactly what has been the main music of their lives since that goddamned place and time. And Parker's not worth it."

"O.K.," Jim says. "O.K., O.K. All I can say is that you're goddamn sporting with this asshole. First he tries to blow your head off—"

Red lunges for Jim, but Jim slips away.

"Don't, Red."

"You push somebody right to the breaking point," Red says. "I'm busting my ass to live my own life and forget all that shit out there—"

"I didn't invent Parker," Jim protests. "You said it yourself. I didn't invent The Club."

"Now I'm not even sure of that," Red says.

"*You're* talking crazy now." Jim edges away from Red, aware of his fury. "I am not your enemy."

"Yes, you are," Red says. "In some ways you are. Because you know the anger that's packed down in there, and the sorrow, and you stir it up."

"I'm not going after Parker," Jim says mildly. "All I want to do now is check out the mill. All right? If they're there, I'll come back, and we'll call the cops. If Taylor has spooked them, they'll be gone anyway. Will that suit you?"

"It would," Red says, "if I could trust you."

"Give me a chance," Jim says. "Give me a chance to learn from you."

"I don't know what that means," Red says. "I do what I've got to do to keep the lid on, that's all."

"You do it well, Red. When people let you. When people leave you alone."

"I'm not asking anybody's permission to do anything." Red lunges for Jim, and this time catches him, holds him by the biceps and draws him so close that they are face to face. "Turner and I used to hunt from the mill." Red's teeth flash in Jim's eyes. "There are access roads, but you don't want to use them if you don't want to be seen. The best way is through Milliken's orchards, down through the woods to the river. It's swampy above the mill, rocky below. I've got a pair of binoculars you can borrow." He releases Jim with a little push. "If you double-cross me—"

"I'll just check it out," Jim says.

"I'm going to trust you," Red says. He closes his eyes a moment. "Yes, I will."

Jim drives past Milliken's orchards because pickers throng the trees, and a tractor creeps through the grove pulling a trailer full of red and green fruit. Beyond the orchards, Jim moves into the woods and begins his trek up the first of two hills that lead to the North River valley and the old sawmill. The ground is carpeted with fallen leaves that crackle and hiss as Jim hikes through them. The woods glows with reflected light, and a gusting breeze sends showers of foliage down.

In less than fifteen minutes, Jim has crossed the high slope of the first hill and is in a clearing where piles of slab wood and black birch logs ring a sheltered sugarhouse—a landmark, Red had said, which assures him he is on course. The roof of the sugarhouse sags hugely, indicating its age, and overturned tubs lie rusting in the snow of pine needles and leaves. Here slabs of rock jut out from the mossy soil.

Is it possible? Jim crouches behind the piles of slab wood. Is it possible he smells gasoline? A gust of wind sends the leaves in a spiral across the clearing. Jim waits, very awake, listening hard and trying to reassure himself that he had smelled the gas. Some of the logs had been freshly cut. Could be, he thinks, gas from the chain saws. Or maybe the woodcutters stored some gasoline inside the shed. He moves past the sugarhouse quickly and plunges through the leaves down the hill. On some impulse he doesn't understand, but which feels right to him, he quickly changes course, glances back in the direction of the sugarhouse. The woods seem empty of all life, except for a bluejay which coasts with a cry through the trees ahead of him.

At the top of the next rise, and through the sound of the breeze, he can also hear the North River as it rattles its way through a rocky gorge. The mill should be a little upstream, Jim thinks, but he tries in vain to see the gray siding and green roof that Red had described to him.

Red, Jim laughs to himself. He says he's trusting me. He says he wants me to keep the lid on. And he's lying. I know what he wants. He wants somebody else to do it, and he's willing to sacrifice me. Red wants it as badly as I do, Parker's coming apart.

Anna would love these woods, Jim thinks suddenly. The idea stops him and he squats, swinging his gaze up and down the river, letting his mind loose, feeling almost dizzy. It might as well be me, he tells himself. I've lost everything anyway.

At the sound of a sharp *crack!* Jim whips around, sees a branch twist down from a tree. He laughs. Christ. Strung like a banjo string. That's good, he thinks. I'm awake. So awake I'm almost sick.

Jim decides to move upstream by remaining on the ridge of the hill as long as possible, to keep high ground until he has a better idea of the location of the mill. He makes so much noise moving around in the leaves that he wants to keep a good distance between himself and the little factory. Then, he supposes, if he comes up through the river itself, or next to it, the sound of the water will disguise the sound of his approach. He is glad for the wind and the noise it makes in the trees.

What he would do, how far he would risk his intentions, would depend on whether Parker was alone, which was unlikely. He might be forced by circumstance to keep the lid on, to let the police handle it. The other little hitch was whether Taylor had been terrorized into telling the truth after all, or if even under the apparent duress of the bunji-cording he had managed a little disinformation and sent Jim on a harmless hike through the autumn woods. Jim thinks, That would be amusing, but I believe we broke Archer, believe we brought him to that extreme. I believe Parker is out here. I smell him. I smell gasoline again.

The mill lies on the other side of the river, and Jim has to laugh when he sees it, because it is so small—not much larger than a suburban garage. Of course, they did much of their work outside, Jim supposes. Part of the mill has collapsed to the ground; the stone

dam leaks at every other course; the pond behind the dam has silted
up and is littered with fallen leaves; the shingles on the roof are
almost bald of sand. Jim nestles in the rocks and peruses the mill
carefully with the binoculars.

He cannot see the whole area because of the intervening leaves
on the trees, but he can see that the mill had been boarded up some
years ago—the plywood has grayed and mildewed—and there is no
immediate sign of habitation. The access road had been overgrown
with grass and briars, but the trail is still visible, and Jim knows it
leads to a logging road above, then a fire road, and eventually Deer
Lane. Jesus, he thinks, I would love to live here. I would love to
move in and be lost and forget everything. I could sober up here
and sleep in peace and just forget. I could build an ice house and
store potatoes and venison . . .

The glasses cross over a walkway of some kind that once led to
the water wheel, now reduced to a rusty spindle that juts from the
building site. A rope dangles from the water at that platform, and
yet it is taut, as if tied to something, and then Jim knows that someone is in the mill. He can see, where the rope ends, a gold flash in
the water that here began its fall through the sluiceway. Beer cans,
Jim realizes. Kept cool in the stream. Oh yes, The Club must have
its beer, Jim thinks. I could go for one myself. I might drop in and
drink a couple of Parker's beers.

He keeps the glasses trained on the building awhile, but there is
nothing to indicate how many people may be inside. There is not
even any evidence of car or motorcycle, and Jim reasons they have
left their transportation elsewhere, perhaps closer to the drivable
roads. Another vantage point might be more helpful, Jim decides,
drops behind the crest of the hill, and works his way through the
woods in the upstream direction. He comes to a gully that swings
in close to the stream and follows it. When he can see the mill again,
he is just below it, about fifty yards away. All he needed was a
grenade launcher and he could stir things up. Red handled one of
those with unbelievable expertise.

Then Jim hears a sound he would not have anticipated or imagined: a man laughing, a man howling with laughter.

Yes, a man laughing. When the laughter ceases, Jim nestles into
the rocks a little in shock, and he considers, Well, why not? They are
feeling so safe. They believe they have nothing to fear. And of course
it is "they," for a man doesn't laugh by himself. Not like that. Jim

scans this side of the building and he can see now that the structure has a lower story that is open, overgrown with shrubbery, a place where boards have probably been stored, then hauled up a long ramp to the road. Two motorcycles rest in the shadows, only the windshields and the headlights visible, reflecting sunlight in a way that makes the headlights seem to be turned on.

Jim sits down in the rocks now. He has the information he needs, all that he needs to honor his spoken agreements with Red and Chong. He could slip out now, and the police could come in from two directions and trap Parker in the old mill. He could read about it in the papers tomorrow. But Jim is not satisfied with this solution. He wants to know more. And his excuse is that he doesn't know for sure that it is Parker after all. Yes, and he could cut the fuel lines on the bikes so they couldn't escape. That would be essential. He could creep in under the mill and listen to what was going on in the boarded-up room above, and he could screw up the bikes. If he could do only that, he would be satisfied, and then let Red call in the authorities.

O.K., Jim tells himself. *Go!*

He moves swiftly up through the rocks and the shrubbery, picks his way tree to tree, snake-crawls the last ten yards to the shadowed room under the main floor of the mill. He settles in beside a rusty pile of scrap metal and listens, trying to sort through the steady clatter of water over the old millrace. To his consternation, he can see that a ragged stairway leads to an opening in the floor above, that access between the two sections is immediate. He can hear the voices of a man and a woman now, too, and sees a little haze of sand and dust drift down between the floorboards from where the people walked above him.

The man's voice is harsh and demanding, low, punctuated with a brutal laugh. The woman protests in a weary voice, but the tumbling of the water makes it impossible to pick out the content of their argument. Jim moves closer to the opening, squats momentarily beneath the stairs, and hears "I don't want to, Billy. It's dirty here. I'm tired."

"What'd you come out here for? Come on, Carey, don't make me mad. They'll be back soon."

Now Jim edges to the motorcycles and tugs at spark plug cables, scrapes a flat piece of rusty metal out of the dirt floor and begins sawing at the hard plastic fuel lines. The effort makes the cuts on his face throb with pain, and then he hears, through the veil of water noise, motorcycles purring and growling, close, closer than Jim wants to believe. He leaps to the opening and can see chrome glint of motorcycles through the trees, easing down the incline to the mill, and behind that a pickup with a cap on it decaled with pheasants and leaping deer. And where'd he steal that one? Jim wonders. He waits a moment until the vehicles pass from sight to the front of the building, then breaks downhill, scrambling recklessly. At the shallows, he stumbles across, feet twisting on the mossy stones, and sees the bark of a tree before him open in a white wedge, like an eye opening, then hears the report of the rifle. He zigzags without looking back until he can sprawl in the cover of stones and brush.

Parker is on the narrow platform above the sluiceway, shouting and pointing with the rifle. Jim charges up the slope, stays close to trees, and bullets whine past him, followed by the *chok* of the report. The top of the hill, a few dozen yards away, will save him, because Jim knows he can outrun anyone beyond that point, if he escapes a wound, unless they can get a motorcycle across the stream. It is all too familiar. Then just ahead of him comes a terrible crashing report. A ball of blue smoke rolls up, and the sound of the gunshot echoes down the valley and back from the walls of the mill. The gunshot stuns Jim with a terror he can feel in his teeth, until he hears Red command him, "Get your ass inside the zone, buddy."

Another crashing report sounds. Jim can hear the slug slap the building side below, and then he is over the crest of the hill, and he flops on his back, panting.

"As soon as you're up to it, move on out," Red says. He breaks open his shotgun, ejects shells, reloads. "Turner's at the sugarhouse. Rendezvous there."

Jim rests briefly, regains his bearings, takes off through the woods. Red is not far behind, and Jim would have waited for him except that he knows it would be reckless to get too close, to allow The Club, if it came on shooting, to concentrate its fire, narrow the target.

At the sugarhouse clearing, Turner is seated on a stump with a portable radio in his hands. "You found 'em," he says simply.

"Yeah."

"They don't sound too happy about it." He speaks into the radio, asking the regional dispatcher to contact the state police at once. He is still talking when Red comes out of the woods carrying the shotgun over his arm as casually as if he had been out hunting ducks. He regards Jim icily.

"Thanks," Jim says.

Red shrugs. "Let's beat it. This place could get hot."

"I didn't think you were coming along."

"Fuck you," Red says.

They move out of the woods, through the orchards, and Jim climbs into the back of Turner's truck for the short ride to his own car, then follows Turner to the village fire station. Inside, they open folding chairs and Red pulls beers from the little refrigerator. Jim's mouth is dry and he rubs the cold can across his forehead.

"We figured we could pick up the police band on the radio," Turner says, "and see what comes down out there." The radio crackles with static.

"They're running," Barber says. "They won't stay there now. At least we know they've got guns and will use them."

"That ain't all," Turner says.

"What ain't all?" Red asks.

"Dynamite," Turner says. "They got that, too. Parker stole it from the town. Gary told me."

"Gary's a relative," Red explains to Jim. "He worked with Parker on the road." To Turner he says, "Did you tell the staties that Parker's got dynamite?"

"I haven't had time to tell them any goddamned thing. Believe it or not, I had other plans for today."

"You'd better let 'em know," Red says.

"Here." Turner hands Red the microphone. "You know how this thing works."

The red telephone at Turner's elbow clamors. "Now what the hell?" Joe answers, speaks perfunctorily, calmly, but grabs Jim by the elbow and shoves him toward the equipment rack, indicating with his hands that Jim should gear up. When Joe drops the phone, he touches off the alarm, a deafening howl on the station roof. In the lulls between blasts, while Jim and then Red struggle into jackets and boots, Joe tells them that someone from Milliken orchards had called to tell them that the old sawmill is on fire.

"Why would they do that?" Red shouts. He scribbles on the black-board: OLD MILL OFF DEER LANE. "That was a great camp. We were going to fix it up." He looks at Jim fiercely. "God damn you. Did you start that?"

"No!" Jim shouts. "No! No! No!"

Jim and Turner clamber into the cab, and Red straps himself onto the platform on the back of the pumper. Joe hits the siren as they roar out, then grabs the microphone off the dash and hands it to Jim.

"You might as well call Mutual Aid," he says. "That old mill will burn hot as hell and the woods is dry. There's no question we'll need help."

Jim radios Mutual Aid for support, then speaks to Chief Suski, who is on his way to the fire scene.

"You don't suppose," Jim thinks aloud, "maybe they're setting us up? They wouldn't fire on us in there?"

"They'd do anything," Turner shouts. "Hope the cops are in there first."

The old pumper howls and groans up the hills of Royalton Road. The pumper is faster than the department's tanker, because it's a shade less antique, but still carries a heavy load of 600 gallons of water, enough to start an attack on the fire, although not enough to sustain it.

"I don't know if we'll be able to draft from the mill pond or not," Turner shouts. "Isn't it close to the building?"

"And silted up," Jim says. "We'd suck up mud."

"We'll need bunches of tankers, then."

"Mutual Aid figured that out."

In the side mirror, Jim can see pickups with their lights flashing catching up on the fire truck. One breezes past, horn blaring.

"There goes Sweeney," Turner says. "He's got extra hose in the truck. That's good! That's good thinking."

"I can smell leaves burning already," Jim says.

When they achieve the fire lane into the woods, white smoke curls over the ground like fog. Suski is ahead on the trail signaling frantically, his white shirt open in a V to tan skin, a hearty belly. Red-faced, he jumps onto the truck fender and says,

"Forget the fuckin' mill. It's gone. But see if you can get in ahead there and knock the fire down before it gets in the treetops. It's just blowing right up that gully. I'll send you a tanker as soon as one comes."

A little farther down the road, the men can see a writhing wall of orange behind the stark silhouette of the trees. The wind blows and leaves incandesce at once, a snowstorm of sparks, and the smoke is thick and choking.

"Put your tank on," Turner shouts.

Red is already hauling hose around the truck when Jim jumps down and struggles into his air pack. He lets Red go past and down the trail and then hefts another section of hose over his shoulder and begins the grueling labor. Behind him, he can hear Turner cranking up the pump, readying to send water into the lines. Ahead, Red has disappeared down a slope and into the smoke. Inside the air pack, Jim can hear his heart hammering, his breathing, and he is already tired. Already! When he reaches the end of his coil, he cups his hand under the hose and hurries ahead to find Red—who has no air pack on. The heat is growing in intensity, too, and then Red looms in shadow and they collide. Jim pulls the air hose out of his mask and gives it to Red, who gulps down air for a moment, then replaces the hose in Jim's mask.

"Take it." Red hands Jim the nozzle. "I'll get you water and be back as soon as I have some air."

Jim nods and kneels in the coiling smoke, breathing too heavily, trying to rest and not panic, to wait for the water to come through. A wedge of flame has cut completely through the woods and the point of it is climbing the slope toward the crest. If it reaches that point—now an entire pine tree simply explodes with a single *crack*— it will leap across the gullies, sparks could blow ahead of the main blaze and set off patches of fire.

Where is the goddamn water? Already pine needles and leaves at Jim's feet are curling in a line of bright orange coals. Then he hears the hose hiss behind him and the nozzle cough, and then a thick stream pours forth, reaching farther and farther out as the pressure increases.

Jim slashes the ground in front of him, to give himself some respite from the heat, then directs a hissing stream into the woods, up the hill, trying to smother all the forward edge of the blaze that he can see. Below, the woods is still orange with flame, crackling, intensely hot. When the breeze crescendos—and the fire now is creating its own wind—Jim feels a blast of heat that staggers him. He hopes a tanker will arrive soon, because he does not want to be where he is without water. He needs help to move the hose, too, because there is too much of it stretched out behind him, and it is as heavy as iron. He turns his head and sees that a tongue of flame has licked up to the trail behind him and is burning itself out on the bare road. Still, he thinks, this goddamn fire could go anyplace. Sheets of sparks are blowing straight up into the sky, swirling away in the hot draft.

In a moment he hears sirens, then voices shouting. Then Red is at his shoulder, air pack on and accompanied by another fireman, taking the nozzle from him and ordering him back up the hill to the pumper.

Jim lets the two men take the hose, then staggers up the trail.

"Take a breather," Suski tells him. "There's a van back there, sodas and sandwiches. Be sure to drink something. And get another air tank."

Jim tears the hot mask off his face, sweat stinging into his cuts, but there is no respite here, for the heat is general. At the van he drinks two sodas in quick succession, then finds a pickup with fresh air tanks loaded on it and replaces the one he has been using with a fresh one. He swings back to the pumper now and sits on the running board near Turner.

"They set another one," Turner says.

"Yeah?"

"Down closer to the village. In fact, it's not far from Red's place."

"Jesus. Anybody on it?"

"Royalton's been called in."

"Why, for Christ's sake?"

"Stop asking me that." Turner concentrates a moment on his gauges, adjusts pressure on the outgoing lines. "Parker's revenge? He doesn't know why, so don't ask me. It's not hard to believe he could hate us so much. Hate this place."

Jim rests a while longer, watching Turner work, overhearing Suski's conversations and orders over the radio. The Lake Ecstasy woods is burning all the way from the old mill to the village. Suski is frantic, calling for more apparatus and men.

"You see what they're doing," Turner says. "They're burning their way out. They'll be up at my place pretty soon, then by Chong's. Shit. They're going to level this town."

Jim rises, dizzy with fury. He pulls off his helmet and staggers aimlessly away from the fire truck, listens to the woods crackle, whistle, and ping. Below, the old mill is an inferno with its own wild music; black smoke bubbles up from beneath the old shingles; a wall sags inward. Jim finds Sweeney's truck angled into some shrubs, passenger door hanging open. He is only going to close the door, but the keys are in the ignition, and Jim tosses his helmet on the seat, pulls off his coat, and climbs in. He starts the truck, backs down the trail until he can swing around, flicks on the signal light, and creeps out of the woods through a diminishing haze of smoke. Turner had it figured, he thinks. The Club is moving out in a big semicircle around the village and are on their way to the state park, where they would surely split up and head in different directions— if they hadn't already. And Parker is obviously settling scores; Turner is right about that, too. I smell like I used to smell, Jim thinks as he pushes the pedal to the floor. Like smoke. Like I just walked out of hell.

Chong has been alarmed by the constant wail of sirens, and after a futile call to Barber's house he learns from Mrs. Turner that the firemen are out on a forest fire. Yes, it seems quite serious to her. It is something the town had always feared, since twice in its history, in 1903 and 1957, fires had ravaged the hillsides, claimed lives, destroyed landmark buildings—her parents' farm, a famous hotel, a railroad depot. After his talk, Chong walks across the field and the dam, then up the hill to the gazebo, where indeed he can see blooms of smoke above the treetops, closer than he would have liked to believe, and hear, too, with startling clarity, the blare of the fire engine horns. He thinks he can smell the smoke, hear the crackle of radios, and is seized for a moment with panic. Above, the sky is blue; but toward the village, it is dark, almost brown, oily, like the prelude to a dust storm. Could it be so serious after all? Could it be so near?

His feet crunch in the leaves as he descends the hill, and the sound is curiously like the sound of fire, like the sound made when you crumpled paper, and the dust he raises kicking the leaves seems also like smoke, as if the leaves were prophesying their own fate— even their colors announced it: the end by fire, fire and blood. Chong laughs: I'm scaring myself.

At the clearing where the bus sits, speckled with fallen leaves, is a hunter's pickup truck, pheasants and ducks adorning the cap. Maybe, Chong thinks, one of the firemen has come down the trail to look things over, plans to take water from the pond. From inside the bus comes a violent banging, clattering. He can hear men shouting, and the violence of their language drives Chong to cover. He watches and listens from above, appalled, for the men seem furious and crazed, hurl the bus seats against the walls, and then windows smash, and the legs of the torn-up seats dangle crazily through the jagged glass. The men storm out of the bus shouting at each other, and Chong recognizes Parker now, though his face seems red and shriveled with fury, his eyes explosive. Mad! Parker is barking in a high-pitched voice, his voice torn with the violent volume of his outburst.

They slam into the back of the truck, and Parker's companion comes forward with a green jerry can, slops gasoline around the clearing.

"In the bus! In the bus, too, asshole!" Parker shouts.

The man re-enters the bus, hunched over, pouring gasoline on the floor, and Chong's gorge rises now in terror, for he sees two things at once, as in a nightmare, and stands shrieking uncontrollably as Jim comes running across the dam in strange huge boots, splashing the shallow water into silver crowns, and Parker wrenches closed the bus doors, holds some sparkling thing in hand that he now lobs through the broken window into the horrified hoarse *"no!"* of the man inside. Parker dives for the truck, not seeing Jim but eyeing Chong now with startled sneer as the bus blooms orange inside and the man shrieks, dances wildly in his clothes of flame, and is consumed then in unholy deafening percussion that spews fire and glass, metal and gore.

Parker is laughing, pointing at Chong from the other side now of a wall of flame, and Chong goes down to his knees, dizzy, a rock in his throat as Parker pulls a weapon from the cab and raises it toward Chong—and crashes down under Jim, gun firing skyward.

And Chong thrashes into a tangle of shrubbery, trying to raise himself from the nightmare, to wake himself, to see through the thick hot blanket of smoke that covers him.

The rifle slides off into the flames around the bus, and Jim tumbles with Parker in the hot dust, full of the leather and smoke stink of him, and aware of Parker's crazed and desperate energy as they kick into each other and elbows crash into cheekbones, fingers gouge, and Parker's teeth bury themselves in the base of Jim's neck. They grapple, roll in flame, and then are apart and upright, each hauling down huge breaths of hot air, sweating in streams, and come again at each other with wild cries. Jim can feel the sweat stinging the wound Parker's teeth made at his throat, and Parker's own fierce will pulling at him, at his fatigue, the pounding of blood in his ears. He could lie down and let Parker kill him, and it would be the supreme relief. He is tired to fainting. But when Parker surges at him again,

Jim kicks for the genitals, gouges for the eyes, and Parker slips by, sprawls in the flaming leaves, is up immediately, this time with a smoldering branch in his hand. He charges, forcing Jim back into the heat, and Jim stumbles, plunges into a wave of flame, feeling Parker's lance inside his thigh, but kicked away, pushes himself up on burning hands.

Parker is down in the wave of flames, but the heat is too intense now and Jim staggers away. Parker rises once, gasping like a drowning man, and his hair incandesces, his beard flames red, and Jim staggers away as Parker goes under again, his jacket smoldering and bubbling.

The whole camp swirls with flame now, and the bus turns white, paint flakes off in gray gobs, shimmers behind the liquid veil of heat waves, and Jim plunges into the pond. He comes out of the murky wash of bubbles in terror and confusion, for hands grab at his shoulders, and he has nothing left to fight with, every ounce of energy drained, and he only turns face up to answer for himself which among them it would be to drown him at last.

"Whole goddamn mountain's burning," Chong cries, cradling Jim's head in the crook of his arm. "It's insane!"

The next morning, the woods still steams and smolders. A gray ash covers the ground wherever the fire had chosen to wander, but Chong, sickened as he was by the devastation, is glad to see that, somehow, patches of the forest have survived. A wedge of greenery stands intact from just below the dam to the swamp above Chong's pond, where the fire had not penetrated at all.

But this is not Chong's first concern. He walks cautiously through the area in what had been the snowmobile club camp and finds the bus a black shell that folds in upon itself, narrowing the windows to mere slits, and it is still hot to the touch and ticks as it cools. He steels himself for what he will see inside, but there is really no obvious evidence of a body, and it will take more than casual observation to prove that Parker has murdered there. Chong presumes a chemical analysis will be possible if it proves necessary. Wu would know. The man who died was someone's son, perhaps husband and father. Surely an accounting was due to someone. Chong trembles with the memory of the man's horrible dance of pain, a puppet gone mad. To have seen that!

And now he looks for the remains of Billy Parker. Jim has said that he simply disappeared in a wave of flame near the bus. But surely the fire was not so intense to boil away the flesh and vaporize the bones? Here and there roots still smolder in the ground and send up little geysers of smoke. Chong pokes into the ash halfheartedly, sick at heart, but he feels nothing that would suggest . . . He can't find words for it. Remains, Chong thinks. The flesh transformed by fire. Cooked! He turns and heads back to the house, unable to bear the devastated landscape, or the purpose of his search.

Jim has been sick all morning, and he is sick again when Chong comes into the house. When he emerges from the bathroom, Chong says to him, "You have serious burns, and you've got to see a doctor."

"I feel like I'm on fire," Jim says. "I wish I could sleep."

"So go to the doctor. Let me take you."

"Isn't it hot in here? Can't we cool it down somehow?"

"You need medicine, Jim."

"Leave me alone," Jim says, and turns away.

Chong calls Barber, but receives no answer. The fire sirens have wailed all night, and Chong is sure that the firemen are still out, or that Red is sleeping in total exhaustion from the day's and the night's efforts. He wishes he had a radio.

Jim is very red, with patches of unnatural white on his skin.

"You have to go to a doctor," Chong insists.

"Excuse me." Jim stumbles into the bathroom and Chong is left to endure the sound of his retching and coughing. Jim still smells like smoke, and he complains of pain in his chest—probably in the lungs, Chong thinks. So much smoke breathed down.

When Jim comes out of the bathroom, Chong says, "You want to die, you gotta do it somewhere else, Jim. I mean it. If I don't take you to the doctor, you gotta get out of here."

"O.K.," Jim says. "I'll get out." He lowers himself gently onto the sofa.

"You could have infection in your lungs," Chong says.

"Well, good." Jim coughs, clutching himself. He curls into a ball.

"Good!" Chong says. "What do you mean 'good'?"

Jim shakes his head. "I don't want to talk now."

Chong fumes in frustration. He really wants to talk to Barber, to get his help in getting Jim to a hospital. Or maybe he knows a doctor to call. Jim's burning with pain and doesn't want help. Chong calls Turner's house now and Ruth explains that Red and Joe are still at the fire station, reorganizing hose and equipment, filling tankers, putting the trucks and the station in order after yesterday's chaos.

"Then I know they'll want to sleep," she says.

Chong tells Ruth to ask Red to call him at once, and that Jim is in need of medical help.

"I'll call a man," Ruth says. "He's retired, but he does some emergency things."

Chong thanks her profusely. In the living room, he finds Jim pacing, complaining that his skin itched, that he is hot.

"Fucking *hot*," he shouts. "Don't you have a fan or something?"

"A doctor's coming. Try to relax until then."

"Why did you call a doctor?"

"Lie down. You're very sick, Jim."

"I can't lie down. It hurts."

"What hurts?"

"Everything. Inside, out. My brain hurts."

He's raving, Chong thinks. "Help is coming."

"I told you I don't want help."

"You like to suffer?"

"No."

"Then why not help?"

"Because I want to die."

"Ho!" Chong says. "You think that surprises me?"

"I don't care if it does or not."

"You think you've got it so bad?"

"No," Jim says. "I'm a super lucky guy."

"Feel sorry for yourself, do you?"

"You're amusing, Chong, but you're wrong. You'd have made a good medic. You keep a guy awake, keep him talking."

"Drink something."

"I can't. It makes me sick."

"Then you should be in the hospital a few days."

"Just leave me alone, will you? I can't stand your mothering."

"And I can't stand your stupidity."

"Yes, I'm stupid," Jim says.

He writhes on the sofa, and Chong steps outside, unable to bear the sight of Jim's torment. In half an hour the doctor arrives, a thin gray man in a tattered felt hat, who carries also a black leather bag.

"Dr. Milton," the man says, shaking Chong's hand. "What's the trouble here?"

"Burns," Chong says. "Body and soul."

"The body's more my line." Dr. Milton makes his way to the sofa and stands looking down at Jim. "But sometimes the soul follows along after."

"Not this time," Jim says.

Dr. Milton raises his eyebrows and eyes Chong. "Tough customer?"

"He says he wants to die."

Dr. Milton winces, pulls a chair beside the sofa. "In that case, all he has to do is wait."

Red's fatigue is apparent to Chong as soon as he comes into the kitchen, for he is practically incoherent with lack of sleep. He slumps at the table, listens with difficulty at first to what Chong is telling him. Chong wonders if Red knows he smelled of sulphur and ash, if he is aware that his face and arms are blackened, the rims of his eyes vividly pink.

But he comes to life when Chong tells him what he has seen in the fire, the man dancing in flame, and what Jim has told him has happened to Parker.

Red is staggered. He has Chong repeat the story, and falls back in his chair, sweat running in black beads of grime down his face.

"You didn't call the police?"

"No."

"Jesus," Red says. "That gives us a chance."

"Chance for what?"

"To find Parker's body."

"I looked."

"You did?" Red chews his lip.

"I couldn't find anything."

"You don't know what to look for."

"What difference does it make if we find it or not?" Chong says. "Let someone else do it."

"It's just a way of making sure," Red says. "Mistakes get made. Isn't that what Jim is worried about, that they'll nail him for murder?"

"He never mentioned that to me. He's not worried. He's despondent."

"I'm going to take a look anyway," Red says. "Have you got a shovel?"

"It's out in the barn." Chong watches Red force himself up from the table. He wonders if he should ask to go along, but decides against it. No, he has seen enough. He doesn't want to know what Red will find.

Red finds the smoldering lump by its sour smell, and he brushes the ashes away from it, and some of it is solid, but mostly there is just the perfect pattern of bones in a bed of still hot coals. He stands in the presence of the thing, confused, trying to fight through his fatigue for guidance on what to do now, but he is not rational, and so begins to chop with the blade of the shovel, and chops into the solid and the brittle; and the cap of the skull breaks like an egg and disappears into the ash. And Red carries the detritus, a shovelful at a time, and throws it out, salting the water with the slivers of white, and the dark matter, taking some up the rocky slope and burying it deep, working beyond his fatigue to a place where there is no feeling at all, and the objects of the world glare out with unbelievable discreetness, then lock their beings in terrible, harsh emanation. Parker is buried. Destroyed. Parker does not exist.

"I know you are dying to sleep," Chong says to Red. "But can you stay one hour while I run to Royalton and fill these prescriptions? I'm afraid to leave him alone."

Red gazes past Chong as if stoned. He nods. "Yes."

"When I get back, I'll fix you a good supper."

"Yeah, fine." Red stretches and grimaces. "Get me some ale, too, will you?"

Chong hurries, pushes his car recklessly along the Royalton Road, leaves swirling in his wake. There are still fire trucks on the road, and now and then Chong can see patches of the blackened earth where the fire has zigzagged and leapfrogged through the forest. In Royalton he buys a paper to read about what has happened, and on the way back from Nakasomo's pharmacy (people sometimes ask Chong if he is related to the Japanese proprietor, and Chong always tells them yes), the headlines blare up from the seat next to him: OUT OF CONTROL. It is one of those headlines, Chong thinks, you can use for just about anything. It will make a fine title for a painting.

Back in the house, trying not to rattle packages, Chong arranges the bottles on the table in the order the pills should be taken, according to the doctor's instructions. There are ointments to apply, bandages to change, pills to administer. He looks into the living

room and finds Red with his mouth agape, sprawled in the chair in
a profound sleep. Jim is not on the sofa and the bathroom door is
open.

He sees Jim at the edge of the pond, in his undershorts, walking
into the water. Chong charges through the grass to the pond,
watches as Jim carefully, deliberately wades into the pond, deeper
and deeper, until submerged to his neck.

"That water's not clean enough, Jim." Chong pauses to catch his
breath. "You will get infected doing that."

"It feels so good," Jim says. "I was going crazy."

"I've got medicine for you now."

"I'm not coming out," Jim says. "I burn if I come out."

"I have lotions. They'll keep you cool."

"I don't care," Jim says. "I think I just want to live underwater for
a while. Where it's cool. Where it's beautiful and nothing can burn."
He dips his head under for a long moment, so long Chong begins
pulling off his shoes, readying to dive in. Then Jim flicks his head
up, scattering water from his hair.

"You can always use the boat," Chong says. "You can see everything from the boat."

"You don't understand," Jim says.

"Oh, but I do," Chong says. "Sometimes I paint, you know, because I want another life, too."

Jim nods. "Oh, yeah?"

"Yeah." Chong drops to his knees in the brown earth. "But sometimes this one isn't bad."

"Look at the woods now," Jim says. "And tell me that again."

"I can wait till spring. I have a little patience."

"Good for you," Jim says. "I wish I had some, too."

Chong picks up a pebble and lobs it at Jim's head, comes close
enough that Jim must dodge it.

"Hey!" The water glimmers with little half-moons of reflected blue
sky.

"You going to let Parker take you down, too, is that it?"

Jim does not answer.

"You're going to let him win now?"

Jim pulls his hair back from his eyes, and swims out into the center of the pond. He rolls on his back, contemplates the sky.

"Nobody's judging you," Chong says. He lobs another stone at
Jim. "Nobody else. You did what nobody else would do, and they're
not going to take you to trial. You hear me?"

"I hear you." Jim rolls over, plunges, then re-emerges with a kick that resonates across the pond with the sound of someone striking a melon.

"Listen! I saw him murder. He was trying to destroy the town!"

Jim's voice rises to Chong now like mist from the lake. "What do you care, really, if I live or die?"

Chong does not answer this for a moment, then pulls off his shirt and kicks off his trousers. He wades into the water, surprised at how cold it is, and especially to one his age, with his slowed circulation. But he betrays nothing, watching Jim, watching him even until his eyes are beneath the water and Jim is nothing now but a white wobble which sometimes splits into indistinct amoebic gobs of color. Chong walks and feels the water close over his head; his nostrils close, and he has a moment of panic because his feet will not quite touch the floor of the pond, but it is only a short while until Jim's arms are pulling cascades of silver and blue bubbles as he makes his way toward Chong.

And how gently Jim lifts him up, his hands high on Chong's sides, throws him with a gasp into the air.

"You little son of a bitch!" Jim cries.

Chong howls with laughter as he thrashes away from Jim. "You see?" he calls. "You see?"

"I see!" Jim shouts with vehemence. He lies back in the water with eyes closed and kicks, and kicks, and kicks his way toward the shore.

4
When
Birds
Fly
into
the
Lake

T he October days are bright, fluorescent, and the nights come
down early through a purple evening. The wood stove rum-
bles, and Chong paints, one after another, a series he cannot
seem to purge himself of—"Burning Man," and then "Burning
Woman," too. Jim and Red spend a lot of time together in the evenings now, and except for brief intervals Chong has the house to
himself again.

During the days since the fire, Jim has recovered enough from his
burns to help Chong prepare his woodpile for the winter, pulling
the dry wood to the front of the barn, stacking the green wood behind it. And in the evenings, Jim, who has not been drinking, works
with Red in the old railroad inn, renovating it a little at a time. Red
has bought it, and he and Nancy are thinking of opening a restaurant there when the Veranos retire and close their own village inn,
which seems imminent. Red is anxious to have at least one room of
the inn refurbished in time for his wedding. Chong and Jim suspect
that he and Nancy intend to spend their honeymoon there.

And Jim has been communicating with Anna, by telephone and
by letter, and once, for an afternoon, Anna and T'isa have visited,
and to Chong the reunion seemed promising, if not completely successful.

Chong had talked to Anna alone, and she was not happy that T'isa
was fatherless, but she was too busy and little inclined otherwise to

grapple with the realities of meeting men. Oh, Boston was full of men. The world was full of men. She could have a man if she wanted one, more than one, if she wanted to juggle affairs. But it was Jim she thought about, even when she had experimented with others, and she thought she would be less afraid of him now and was interested in trying again. He was T'isa's father, and the two of them did have a special bond and a special need for each other. But the main thing was the time Jim and Anna had invested in their marriage, in getting to know each other. Would it be possible, Anna wondered, to collect the interest now? She was far from certain that she and Jim could cement things. But she was curious. She was willing to talk. She had touched the scars on his face, and they did not frighten her. She thought he had earned them, that they simply manifested something about his heart, and his life so far. They were the medals he never got.

Jim's mood swings pretty wildly, from a day of bitter anger to one of almost mirthful calm, but this is something Chong regards as a new dimension in Jim, and notes, and encourages. Red is so good for Jim, too, Chong believes. Because Red pays attention to detail and he finds so much to love in people and the world, his curiosity propels him, and he is not out to change everything, but to clarify his own life.

Burning man. Burning woman. Sometimes Chong will open the door to the wood stove and sit entranced by the flame. The cats crawl close and sleep, stretch, luxuriate in desert heat. Chong keeps his teakettle on the stove, and it exudes continuously a wisp of steam, a little genie of white. And Chong looks into the flame and the coals and sees civilizations there, glowing in splendor, writhing in disaster.

One night Chong opens his front door to Carey Cahill. She stands in silence on the stoop and Chong is not sure she will accept his invitation to come in, and because she keeps her arms folded inside her coat sleeves begins to dread she has planned some terrible surprise. Agitated as she is, she takes a long time to talk. Had Chong seen Parker die in the fire, as was reported? The question terrorizes Chong momentarily, and he is glad Jim is not at home. No, he says, I did not see it, but I am almost sure of it.

"I wanted to be sure he was gone," she says. "I want to do some things, and I don't want to wait for him."

"Don't wait," Chong says.

Yes, Carey has seen Ginny recently. She likes her foster parents enough to agree to stay with them, and Carey thinks it best for now, for her own world has been so shattered, and she must reclaim her health. Ginny is healthy and has taken a surprising interest in the piano. She played some very simple things for Carey. Carey tells Chong it made her cry, because she didn't have a piano, didn't have anything her daughter could want. "They've taken everything from me," she says. "My husband. My man. My girl. I'm selling my house. I'm going away to my family."

"You can start over," Chong says, but Carey only curls her lip when he says this, and soon leaves, with little more to say.

The first week of November, it rains and snows simultaneously— a shock of early snow that melts almost at once but thrusts a chill into everything, every room, and not even an extra sweater will dispel it. Since it is too cold to work in the unheated inn, Jim is home, and he is happy because he is preparing to leave for Boston, where he is going to stay for the winter, in an apartment not far from where Anna and T'isa live, working for a friend of Red's who runs a boating supply company and promises to train Jim in marine engine repair. Jim is excited about working again, he says, and especially about the prospect of having access to boats, which he loves, of possibly running some charter fishing trips in the spring for extra money, and the simple adventure of it.

"You should be near the ocean," Chong agrees. "You have saltwater in your veins."

"Better saltwater than booze, I guess."

"You don't need booze," Chong says. "You need something to do, something you love. You got something good set up now and you'll like it better. It has a daughter in it."

By the middle of November, Chong has several new pieces ready for Oslip, and for shows Oslip has arranged for him in Switzerland and Hiroshima. Chong is anxious about how Oslip and others will regard his latest work, such painful, tortured material, when everything else he had done was so fantastical, sometimes comic, a world of playful dreams. Red has agreed to help Chong take the paintings to New York. When he arrives with his trailer to load up, he says, "Jim told me about them, and I guess I think he's right. They're frightening."

"But beautiful?"

"Not a beauty I like to admit," Red says. "Like a grenade burst. Or battleships firing at night."

"This is a state of mind," Chong says. "This is not politics."

"You could've fooled me," Red says.

"This is not the attacker. This is the victim."

"I'm not a critic," Red says. "But I'm not sure everybody else can tell the difference."

They drive together to New York City, deliver Chong's paintings to Oslip, and then head downtown to Mott Street to pick up Susan, who has packed a vast amount of luggage.

"You can't travel with all this," Chong says. "You will have to reduce this by three-fourths, at least."

"I couldn't decide what to take," Susan says. "I still have time, don't I, before we leave?"

"About a month," Chong says.

Mai Li is very agitated "I told her she couldn't take all that, but she never listens to me."

"You should listen to your mother in this case," Chong says. "She was always a very efficient traveler."

"But I never got a chance to show her," Mai Li says.

"You can change your mind," Chong says. "You can come. You have a few weeks to decide, too."

"I would be away from work too long," Mai Li says. "Mr. Soo would fire me."

Chong laughs. "Then why don't you retire? Whenever again will you get a chance to visit Hawaii, Hiroshima, and Peking, paid for by Mr. Oslip?"

"I don't have enough money to retire." Mai Li smiles, shrugs.

"Retire to Lake Ecstasy," Chong says. "You could be my wife again. Why not? I think I am a better catch than I ever was."

"You would think that," Mai Li says, but her eyes light up. She hesitates. "Well, I will let you know."

Susan rides in the back of the jeep, a little quiet at first, but eventually begins to ask questions about Lake Ecstasy, about what it looks like after the terrible fire Chong has described to her.

"All in due time," Chong says. "It's not the prettiest time of year anyway. The woods is rusty, the leaves are soaked and blown down by the November winds. But I think the forest will recover fast. And if it is not glorious again by next fall, then in two years it will be for sure."

When Chong takes Susan to the pond late the next morning, a flock of great geese comes warbling down from the sky, and they splash into water made black by the dense clouds scudding above them. And when the flock has settled, the stately geese glide on mirror images of themselves, on water so still the turbulent clouds above seem to be also inside the earth.

"Jesus Christ!" Chong says to his daughter. "I got so much work to do!"

Robert Abel is the author of two previous books, *Freedom Dues,
Or, A Gentleman's Progress in the New World* (1980), a comic
historical novel; and *Skin and Bones* (1978), a collection of
stories. A graduate of the University of Massachusetts Writing Program, he was awarded a National Endowment for the Arts Creative
Writing Fellowship in 1978. Now living and writing full-time in
north central Massachusetts, he was born and raised in the Midwest,
where he also spent several years as college instructor and journalist.